LAKE SPARK

The Complete Collection Volume One

EVEY LYON

THE LAKE SPARK WORLD

CONTENTS

WORTH THE RISK

WORTH THE CHANCE

WORTH THE WAIT

WORTH THE RISK

HUDSON

The glass of whiskey, neat, slides my way against the bar, and I'm quick to accept the amber-colored liquid. I examine the contents for a second or two, but I don't need to debate it long. I know anything I drink here in this chic, industrial-styled restaurant and bar will be good, and I've had a long day.

After hours of meetings with team management, my brain feels like it may be fried.

"Anything else, Hudson? I'm going to close up early." Wes is the owner of Jupiter, the bar I frequent because the hospitality is excellent, the food is star-worthy, and this place is crawling with Chicago's sports elite even on a slow day—well, except tonight. Right now, it's just me.

I shake my head. "It's all good. I'll drink up then head out."

"No rush. I need to do some paperwork upstairs anyway, plus the weather is that horrible cold rain, so I'm trying to avoid it." Wes is in his early thirties and has a personality that welcomes conversation.

"Why are you even behind the bar?" I wonder aloud, as he is normally up in his office and only circles the restaurant a few times when high-profile guests are here.

He grins. "Because I'm a good boss and sent my staff home early since it wasn't busy. Plus, when I saw you come in, then I figured I might try to get some intel for a few football bets that I have going on with friends."

His humor causes me to tip my head up, with a smirk forming. "I won't be divulging any secrets, but The Winds will have a good year."

Our draft was just announced, and it's May, which means we still have training season ahead before deciding our final roster, and I'm prepared to work those boys into the ground, as I have a record to uphold.

"You are the team's coach, so you may be biased," he counters.

I sigh at the reminder. I love my job, but damn, the pressure some days is a lot. Being a star quarterback back in my heyday was tough, but being a coach in a city driven by sports? Fucking insanity. I question my decision to take this job daily, especially if we lose a game and half the city is cursing my name, but then I get to the field or watch a player excel and I'm hooked all over again.

The sound of the revolving door swooshing open catches our attention. The umbrella, with a pattern that looks like dancing lobsters on it, is obstructing our view of the person beneath, but the sound of heels pattering is enough to tell me that it's a woman.

"Sorry, we're closed," Wes calls out just as the umbrella collapses.

Now I have a full view, and I'm not sure where to start.

The woman has deep-pink heels, and her skirt falls just below her knee, but damn, it is tight. Working my way up her body, I intend to give her the full once-over. Her black jacket is open, and I get a glimpse of a blouse that matches her shoes. Then her lips have a similar color, and they part open, and I just want to do a double take because she is easy on the eyes.

"Oh." She nearly frowns. "That's a shame. I was hoping for an escape from this weather. It's been quite a day."

Wes seems to study her for a second, possibly because my eyes haven't drifted off her for more than a millisecond.

"You know what… one drink," he offers.

A smile stretches on her lips, and she walks in our direction with a sway that seems to be restricted, probably by the fact that her skirt is the type of fabric that must rip easily, and no, I'm not proud that my brain made that connection. She slides her jacket off and places it on the back of the stool, then sits next to me as she swipes a strand of her long, light brown hair behind her ear.

"Let me guess, gin and tonic?" I ask her to make conversation.

She shyly smiles at me. "No. I'm a martini, classic, with three olives kind of gal."

"Coming right up." Wes begins to gather the ingredients.

She holds her hand up to stop. "Wait, can I just have a Shirley Temple?" She nearly groans as she says it.

I scoff a sound. "I wouldn't have expected that choice." I set my glass to the side and then angle my stool in her direction.

"Believe me, I wish it was the martini, but I just remembered that I promised a friend to join her on the no-alcohol-for-a-week train. She wants her mind clear for when her boyfriend proposes, because she feels like it's going to happen any day now," she explains.

"Wow, friendship. But you look like you could use the martini," I highlight the obvious.

Her head lolls to the side ever so slightly. "True." She taps her fingers on the counter. "Ugh, I guess my day trumps maybe-proposals. Martini, please." Wes nods then gets busy with making her drink. Her eyes brighten, and God, I love the curve of her cheeks. "Martinis are my grandmother's favorite. Every day at three after her soaps, for as long as I can remember, it's been her routine. It's traditional, I like that."

"You don't seem like a traditional girl."

The sound of the martini shaker stops just as this woman's brow raises. I realize my tone may have been… playful. But it doesn't matter, because for a moment, we look at one another, our blue eyes connecting, and recognize that we're both taken off guard by this unusual vibration in the air.

Admittedly, it normally takes a lot for someone to make me pause. I'm not easily affected—well, except tonight, it seems.

A smirk plays on her lips, and it feels like it's her slow ease into my presence. "Something like that." She examines me for a second then rests her chin in her hand, her elbow propped on the counter. "What brings you here on a Tuesday evening?"

"Long workday."

"So I gathered. You're wearing a suit yet no tie, which means you took it off at the end of the day. What do you do?"

Wes places a martini on a napkin in front of this woman. "Not a sports fan?" He seems surprised that she doesn't seem to know who I am.

She thanks him with a nod before she entwines her fingers, with perfectly polished pink nails, around the stem of the glass. "No. I know zero about any sport. Why?"

I fucking love that answer. Mostly because during my history as a star player turned one of the youngest coaches with the highest paycheck, I got a title in the press as bona fide bachelor. There have been a lot of women who wanted to hang off my arm for the cameras too.

But to this woman, I'm an unknown.

Nor could she probably figure it out just by looking at me. I'm tall but not overly so, and I'm not bulky, as my career was based on speed and escaping tackles. I keep myself fit, unlike many former players turned coach.

Clearing my throat, I offer my hand. "I'm Hudson, by the way. And let's just say I work with numbers and physics." Partially true. Today's management meeting was all numbers, and we make plays based on aerodynamics.

After a sip from her drink, she frees her hand from her glass and offers me a few fingers to shake. "Piper. I know, it's such a ridiculous name."

Letting her soft, delicate digits go, I give her a confused look. "Why? I like it. It's cute."

Piper rolls her eyes. "Exactly. Cute. I don't know, I feel like people associate it with, like, a little gingerbread person or something."

I laugh at her thought. "Okay, I could see that connection but only because you point it out." Leaning against the back of my stool, I grab my drink once more and get comfortable for a conversation that I feel like I'm going to have with Piper.

"Anyways, thanks for letting me crash your moment of solitude. It was a day from hell."

"How so?" Another sip of whiskey hits my mouth.

Her head bobs slightly to the side, as if she's debating how much information to share, then she seems to shake off the thought. "I was battling it out with a shipping company for something I ordered, fabric that I've been waiting on, and they said someone would drop it off between nine and five, but no one did. I decided to take it into my own hands and marched right down to their office in hopes of getting my package. Nothing. Then Chicago spring decided to laugh at me and pour down freezing rain. It isn't even a full moon, and my aura is really fucked up right now."

She's slightly quirky, and I like that.

"You were running in heels around town in this weather?" I'm impressed.

Her mouth is closed, but it just makes her wry smile sexier. "You never know when you need to be rescued and hopefully by a hot fireman." She winks at me.

I tip my glass in her direction. "Points for surviving in this weather."

"I'm going to head upstairs to look at some paperwork," Wes says in my direction. "Just let yourself out when you're done?"

"Sure."

"Oh, I owe you for the martini." Piper moves to grab her bag.

I touch her arm to stop her from digging into her purse. "Nah, it's fine. It's on me, and Wes will add it to my tab."

Piper flashes me an appreciative look.

Wes clears his throat and gives me an awkward yet entertained smile. He seems to know that either Piper or I are in trouble, the kind that I haven't had in a while. Life has been a little crazy for me, to say the least.

I give a nod to Wes before returning my fully invested attention to Piper. "Fabric. You work with clothing?"

She nods and plays with her last olive on a skewer, and Christ, she sucks that fruit with perfection. "Yes, I'm a designer, actually."

"Yeah? Dresses?" My lips land on the rim of my glass, then the moment liquid hits my throat, I nearly choke because I swear I just heard her say *lingerie*. Swallowing with great effort, my eyes don't blink. "Did you just say lingerie?"

"Yep," Piper proudly replies. "Well, more pajamas, with a special soft cotton fabric and lace trim, but now I'm venturing into evening attire. That is, well… I'll leave it to your imagination."

Fuck me, I only heard lace, and she said it with such simple confidence.

"So, you mentioned numbers, what exactly do you do?" she asks.

"You know, let us stay vague on details. We've both had a tough day, and I'm enjoying our conversation too much to bring work into the mix," I suggest.

She chuckles and throws her olive skewer to the side. "Enjoying our conversation?" She contemplates my answer and taps her fingers on the napkin. "Do you think I'm flirting with you?"

Now I have to laugh. "No. Should I be offended? I mean, am I not flirtable?"

Her cheeks raise and turn a shade of pink. "It's not that. I just don't want you to think I walk into bars and try to pick up random older men. Not that you're old or ancient, I mean, you must be, what, ten years older than me? I'm rambling. That happens sometimes. Sorry." She seems flustered.

I love this woman's honesty and ability to speak her mind. It's refreshing and much like myself. I kind of thrive from speaking openly and making others feel uncomfortable to push their limits toward what I know they are capable of. Except in this moment, while Piper thinks I must be offended, I'm the opposite.

I instantly reach out and touch her elbow. "Relax. Breathe." She responds to my request and seems to calm. "I don't think you're a high-class hooker if that's what you were implying, and I'm happy to hear that I'm not ancient."

Her face turns red in embarrassment. "You're in good shape. How old are you, can I ask?"

"Forty-two. You?"

"Twenty-five and ordering children's cocktails, really demonstrating my maturity here."

"It's okay, you got to the martini in the end, and I won't highlight that I'm old enough to be your dad," I inform her. Consciously, I leave out the fact that I do have a son her age, but for now, I don't want the age factor to be a deterrent for her to walk away sooner than later tonight.

"As long as you don't ask me to call you daddy." She says it so casually as she takes a sip of her drink, but the moment she realizes what she said, her face turns cherry red. "Oh my God, I did not just say that. I need to stop jabbering." She seems mortified.

Her sense of humor makes me grin. I like that her mind may be unintentionally dirty.

Leaning in closer to her, I tease her. "It's okay, I prefer *sir* anyhow." I run my tongue along the inside of my mouth because I'm trying to restrain my enjoyment in this unexpected evening.

She looks at me, impressed with my counter remark, and her smirk grows comfortable again before she nibbles her bottom lip.

Something inside of me is eager to push her buttons. "Do I make you nervous, Piper?" I hear the hint of determination in my voice. A need to explore the curiosity that this woman sparks inside me.

I notice her throat bob with a swallow, but then she sits up straight with confidence. "No, Hudson, you don't." Her tone is sinfully delicious and firm. I bet she could be a little vixen because her tone was pure challenge.

She doesn't blink, and I'm drawn into the deep blue of her eyes that has me thanking the fact that this place is lit just right so I can figure out the exact color of her eyes as they seem now more green.

"Do your eyes magically change color with the light?" I ask her, as we seem to be locked in a stare.

"Not that I know of." Her eyes sideline to her martini, and she is quick to pick it up.

"I take it there's no man to tell you on a daily basis if your eyes are casting a spell on him."

She tries to suppress a smile. "That is a ridiculous line, and you know it."

I chuckle under my breath. "You're right. But for some reason tonight, cheesy lines are rolling off my tongue."

Actually, a sort of light ignites inside of me. I've been so focused on everyone else that I forgot that I'm allowed to have a connection with someone on a physical level. Piper is the perfect reminder, and I think that I'm enamored with her.

"If that cheesy line was your subtle way of asking if I have a boyfriend, you are a little late in the conversation to be requesting that information." The remainder of her drink disappears as she knocks back the glass then slides it back onto the bar.

"Why is that?"

"I doubt you would smirk the way you do if you thought I was off the market."

We study one another, and I feel my pulse quicken. Call me a savage, but I think I want to throw her onto the countertop and lick her like she did her olives. This woman has the ability to steal my breath and make me laugh, and for that reason, I want to make her scream.

But instead, we chat for the next fifteen minutes about the city and food. My cheeks may hurt from laughing at every retort we bounce off one another in conversation.

I look at my watch. I know we need to get out of here soon. Piper seems to notice too that our night may be wrapping up—well, not if I have anything to say about it.

"You're intriguing, but I don't know why. I only just met you," she says.

The corner of my mouth curves up. "Ah, so you are attracted to me."

Piper doesn't answer but looks away with a sheepish grin. "Do you do this with all the women you meet?"

"I'm not doing anything, darling, except talking to a beautiful woman who seems to be enjoying my company… and no, I don't make it a habit of taking a woman to the hotel across the street." Geez, even I recognize the swagger in my voice.

Her eyes widen from my statement. "Wow, how did a hotel come into this conversation?"

"We wouldn't last the extra twenty minutes it would take to get to my place. Plus, it's fucking raining." I look at her with a piercing gaze because I can't look away from this creature who sauntered into my life on a mundane Tuesday.

"Why am I not walking away from this?" she asks herself with a fixed smile because we are being two ridiculous souls acting in a way that I know neither one of us is accustomed to. Because despite the many offers I get, I don't pick up women in bars. I mean, I'm not completely a saint, but I would say I have a 75% moral conscience when it comes to pursuing women. Yet right now, I'm feeling on edge because I want her, and I'm pulling out my cocky card which could be a risky move.

"Why am I acting like a man already addicted?" I softly ponder the truth. She is like something I've never had a taste of, and I recognize a warning in my head that Piper may just pull me in a direction that I'm not used to.

I glance down as I begin to draw circles with my fingertip on her hand that's resting on the bar. Her skin is silky, and I feel her body tense, but not in a bad way. She's surprised maybe by the magnetic attraction that we seem to have.

My eyes draw a line up to her face when she blows out a deep breath. "You have some smooth lines, Hudson. I'm really wondering why the red flag isn't flashing in my head yet." She looks down at my fingers, intrigued. "I'm normally a 'trip to the candy store when I'm stressed' kind of person. I've never tried sleeping with a stranger to let out some bad-day vibes."

"Do you believe in trying everything once?"

"I do… yes."

I move farther into her space and closer to her ear, now letting my hand travel up her arm to touch her hair. "Listen, we need to get out of here. I'm not a serial killer, Wes has seen you with me, you can text a friend, and we can go across the street. Drink, talk, I don't care, but you're curious about something and so am I."

She glances to me, her head angling in a way that brings her mouth near my own. Mint, she smells of peppermint. Her warm breath hits my skin. "Tempting."

Our lips dance on their own accord. She's drawing me in, and I really am questioning why I feel like a man who would get on his knees to beg for this woman. Something in the air feels unique, and it started the moment she walked through the door.

"Do you always make men crazy?" I whisper.

"Do you always make women do things they wouldn't normally do?"

I scoff. "Make? No. Wanting something out of their comfort zone? Completely."

She points a finger at me. "I'm taking a chance that you aren't a murderer." A grin spreads on her mouth before she hops off her chair and offers me her hand.

————

IT WAS A QUICK CHECK-IN, no questions asked because they know me, as I stay here sometimes during the season instead of my place in the city. In no time, we find ourselves walking down the hall to the room.

I spin her until her back hits the wall near the door. I cradle her face between my hands and hold her firmly in place so her mouth is on offer.

This isn't what I was expecting today. And by the fact that Piper is breathing heavy, then I would say this is a surprise for her too.

My eyes are fixed on her gorgeous mouth, the one I'm about to devour.

"Do we need a safe word or something?" She tries to contain her laugh. Her ability to keep the mood light is a trait that I adore.

"Fuck me," I murmur. "I really want to know where your imagination just went."

She wraps her hands around my waist under my open suit jacket. "I'm not sure. You're kind of consuming my thoughts, and then I realize you're standing right in front of me."

"And I'm going to kiss you."

I lean down and capture her mouth, an instant hit of lust and martini creating the only taste I want on my lips. My tongue swipes along the seam of her mouth, and she willingly opens her lips to offer me more. Our spark creates a wildfire that will burn down the entire earth… okay, crazy talk hitting me.

I pull her tight to my body, our lips never parting, then lift her slightly up as I stretch my arm out with the keycard. We find our way inside the luxurious suite, and the moment we finally create space between us, Piper takes in her surroundings, her lips swollen.

She notices the chilled champagne in a bucket. "Who are you? We literally checked in only five minutes ago and already this is here. Not to mention, I noticed security give you a nod." Her question is more amused than curious.

I walk to the bottle as she continues toward the floor-to-ceiling window overlooking the city. Damn, she is a scene. She takes no notice of me as she looks out and tosses her jacket to the side. Even when I pop the cork on the champagne, she doesn't flinch. Instead, she seems mesmerized by the view, at peace even.

"No champagne for me. I want to do this before I lose my nerve." She glances over her shoulder in my direction.

I pause my work on the bottle. "You know, we can just talk." I feel a need to reassure her, touch base, and to be honest, just sharing the same air in this room with her is enough to put me at ease and make my night.

We don't need to do more. But her in my arms, preferably naked, would be even better.

She turns around and begins to stroll slowly in my direction.

"Talk?" She tilts her head with an adorable laugh. "After that kiss? Not a fucking chance." Then she springs into my arms.

My cock rises to the occasion, happy with her choice. Our lips are all over one another, and I debate fast or slow.

Slow.

Fast.

This is like an aggravating play in the scrimmage zone, but at least I know that I'm going to get the touchdown.

Her sounds are lost in our mixed breaths, and I have my answer.

"Slow," I say.

Setting her down, taking her wrists gently in my hands to hold them up, I look down at her thinking she is way too beautiful to be alone for a Tuesday night. Whoever let her go is a moron, but I should send him box seats because it means I get to have her now.

"Let me take something off," she whispers with a seductive grin.

I bring my finger to glide along her cheek. "You do that, then look out at the view that you were admiring."

"Yes, *sir*," she teases me, and I have to shake my head again. "Sit down," she demands.

I love her confident effort to add to our dynamic, and I move to sit on the chaise lounge in the corner. I get comfortable, untuck my shirt from my pants, and begin to unbutton my shirt, with my eyes glued on the show.

She swipes her hair to one side, lifts her blouse off, then shimmies off her skirt. Her mint-green lace lingerie set is a sight for sore eyes, with the bra cups full, the color of lace a perfect contrast to her pink shoes. I could come just looking at her right now.

"An original?" I wonder as I squint my eyes as if it will magically magnify the view.

Her fingers cascade down her skin from her neck to between her cleavage. "Uh-huh, private collection in fact," she rasps.

"Lucky me. Do you have any idea how sexy you are?" I ask.

"I do." Piper has confidence, that's for sure. She flashes me a coy look before walking to the window. "So, about that safe word…" She trails off.

Shaking my head ruefully, I grin, but I also can't control the urge inside me to consume her until she melts into the mattress.

I pounce off the seat and grab ice from the bucket on my way to Piper. I throw away a few cubes until I have one trapped between my fingers. Noticing the way her body shivers, her nipples pebble, and every inch of her is screaming to be discovered, I don't delay.

"Hands against the window, Piper," I order.

The moment her hands hit the glass, the piece of ice between my fingers lands on the side of her stomach, causing her to flinch as the ice begins to melt against the heat of her body.

I smirk to myself, wondering if she will ever figure out my connection to football. "Your safe word can be 'foul.'"

In response, she moans as I slide the ice lower.

2

PIPER

My grandmother hands me the television remote control to set on the coffee table. We just spent an hour watching her favorite soap and sipping our martinis in her living room.

"You know, I haven't watched this in years and yet the same actors are still on there," I remark as I hold my near-empty glass out to the side.

My grandmother plays with her pearl necklace. "It's strangely comforting that I age with some of those characters. Anyways, what else is this old bat going to do?"

I chuckle at her thought. "What don't you do? Symphony, tea with the ladies from your book club, giving the doorman an earful. And you're not old. You haven't hit eighty yet, you have a few more years, and besides, eighty is the new seventy. You're hardly a dinosaur," I assure her.

"Piper, I would prefer you tell me that I'm a frail old lady who needs to see her only granddaughter married one day soon." She gives me a stern eye that only makes me smile more.

"I came here to spend quality time with you, my favorite senior citizen, and this is what I get?" I pretend to be offended.

She drinks every last drop of her drink before placing the glass on the side table which probably cost half my rent.

I can't help but glance into my near-empty glass. The last time I had one of these was a few weeks ago on that night that will go down in my life's history book as unforgettable and one of a kind.

Wild, magnetic, and I felt free.

I've never just hooked up with someone. For the first time in a long time, I felt an opportunity where I felt comfortable and grabbed it before I lost the chance.

I have zero regrets… okay, maybe one. But I don't think too long about that.

"At least tell me that you're having fun. A woman with your looks who is as successful as you shouldn't be spending nights alone." My face must look astonished that she's prying into my sex life, but dear old grandmama has always been bold. "Oh please, you think your grandfather—God rest his soul—was my first? Besides, I've seen your designs, and you must get your inspiration from somewhere."

"This conversation is not happening," I lament.

"Oh, dear, don't even try to hide the facts. You look like a woman who has seen more action than a Vegas showgirl."

There must be a giddy look on my face. It's because of Hudson and the moments from that night that have raced in and out of my head for the last few weeks. He had a command on me that I desire, and experience that I crave. Most of all, he could make me smile with our weird brand of humor.

Now I tip the glass to my lips and make it as dry as the Arizona desert. "It doesn't matter. There is nobody to bring to Friday-night dinner. I'm too busy for a relationship anyway."

"Piper, you're never too busy to find a husband or wife, whatever you fancy. And I mean someone who is a *real* contender and worthy of you." Her pointed look is the reminder of why I am perhaps hesitant, but she won't let me dwell over her reference for long, and I too move past it.

I sigh and put down my glass. "I literally thought 'oh, I could surprise my grandmother on this cloudy day with some cake and watch some soaps with her since I've worked hard all morning.' I'm very much regretting my choice."

She folds her hands together and places them on her lap, straightening her posture with a smirk on her face. "You're right, dear. Tell me, how are your designs? Did you try the new supplier yet?"

I purse my lips, because as much as everything is going well business-wise, it's a lot of to-do lists. "I think it's going to work. I need to see how the fabric stretches over the wiring of the bra of the new bodysuits, but the short loungewear jumpsuits with lace are selling like hot cakes."

My grandmother looks at me fondly. "I always knew you would carry on the tradition."

Now that is praise I can appreciate. Going back generations, my family came to the US from Europe. My great-grandfather was a tailor, my grandmother a seamstress turned corporate dressmaker, and she made a lot of money too. My mother skipped the tradition altogether, and well, me? I'm making my own path. I don't even use my grandmother's name, even though it would have given me an extra boost. Instead, I'm stuck with my father's last name. I'm Piper Dapper—it has a melody and makes me crazy at the same time.

I admire my grandmother; I grew up watching her pick beautiful fabrics while someone with a notebook would follow her around taking instruction. It rubbed off on me, and somewhere in college, I started designing comfortable pajamas with cute prints and the epitome of loungewear, but then… I started a special line of lingerie. My parents nearly spit out their wine at that family dinner when I told everyone, while my grandmother just clapped her hands together in celebration.

"I might need your help. I promised April I would design her wedding dress. She wants simple but elegant."

April is my best friend whom I met two years ago. April works in accounting, hates it, and is way too bubbly to be sitting behind a desk. We met in a jewelry-making workshop, and both realized we had no talent for bracelets, so instead, skipped the class and went for coffee instead. Over cupcakes and lattes, our friendship was solidified.

"She's engaged?"

I nod. "Yes. It happened a few weeks ago." While I was being fucked senseless. "They've been dating for a year, he's a lawyer."

"That's wonderful. Send her my congratulations and ask her where I should send the money to ensure she throws you the bouquet at the wedding." She's teasing me again.

I stand up, knowing I need to get going if I have any chance of meeting April for smoothies later. Then again, I probably shouldn't have had a martini at this time of day either. But everything is about balance.

My grandmother follows me as I make my way through her penthouse, past statues and art, until we reach her front door.

"You know I still have contacts at the big department stores if you want an in," she casually mentions.

"My answer is still no. The future is online stores, and plus, I would be much happier with a boutique anyhow," I remind her as I throw my purse strap over my shoulder.

We hug goodbye, and I'm on my merry way after I promise to visit again next week.

When I'm in the elevator going down, I smile to myself. Partly because a flashback hits me of being wrapped in a tangled mess of arms and limbs.

Then my mind remembers the way Hudson took me from behind while I held onto the bed for dear life. And fuck me, that man has a mouth that would make a hooker blush.

It was a good night.

A great night.

Excellent.

All the more reason why I hate myself for leaving before he even woke.

———

I FIND myself watching my friend approach the table.

"Has something happened, Ginger?" Only April can get away with calling me Ginger, a nickname that she insists on. My friend slides onto the seat in front of me. She has two smoothies in to-go cups and offers me the peanut-butter-banana one.

Quickly I sip from the straw before I burst with a reply that's been running in my head for weeks. "What do you mean?" I pretend that life is completely normal.

April slams her hand on the table, the strength of her amusement causing her blonde hair to fall around her grinning face. "Lately, you've been… daydreaming."

I play with my straw and avoid looking at my best friend until I realize I will never be able to keep this from her. Originally, I said nothing because I wanted her to bask in her engagement and not steal the spotlight from her during our coffee chats.

"I kind of did something out of character a few weeks ago. On one night in particular." I bite my inner lip and then glance up at her.

April just stares at me, and I wait to see if she connects the dots.

"With someone," I clarify.

The moment she figures it out, her mouth gapes open. "No way!" I nod slowly. "Like, with a complete stranger?" She's grinning, clearly invested in this conversation.

"Yes, total. It just kind of happened. It was a long day, and then I went for a drink, which I ended up needing for the liquid courage because that man was something. And let me tell you, he lives up to the cliché of an older man being demanding in the bedroom."

Her eyes widen. "Older?"

I bob my head from side to side. "Yeah. I mean, he looks younger than he is, but I guess he is old enough to be my father."

April nearly spits out her smoothie. "What in the world happened to you? I mean, this is like that thirst trap from the Sound of Music because we all know Christopher Plummer as the Captain is probably what's fueling your need to sleep with an older man."

My face squinches together. "Although a classic, I assure you that was not my motivation."

She waves off my notion. "What else do you know about this guy?"

I debate telling her everything, but I know she would play detective in a heartbeat. "Not much. It's the way it should be when it's a one-night stand. Anyways, I doubt I'll be seeing him again."

"Why?"

I awkwardly look away. "Because… I left before he woke up."

She slaps her hand onto her mouth in shock. "Who are you?"

Blowing out a breath, I wonder too. "I don't really know why I did it. I guess I was scared to face him in the morning. It was a great night and maybe I didn't want to deal with the disappointment that it was only that. We both went into the evening knowing it was a one-time thing, and I'm not accustomed to that protocol, so I guess I freaked out."

"So, it wasn't because of his skill set?" She flashes her eyes at me.

I can't hide my smile. "I mean…" I look around to make sure nobody is watching and lean into the table. "Against the window, on the bed in three different positions, and he went down on me twice. It was unreal."

April turns giddy. "You're still able to walk?"

"It happened a few weeks ago, and I didn't plan on ever telling you. Plus, you were in your engagement bliss," I explain.

"Does he have a name?"

My voice begins to form the syllables, but I'm interrupted by April's phone vibrating.

"Sorry, I need to take this. It's the restaurant for the party."

"It's okay. I need to head out anyway."

She answers her phone and touches my shoulder as she leaves the table because there is better reception out on the street. "I'll see you tomorrow at 7pm, sharp," she quickly whispers on the way out.

I salute her in response, relieved I didn't need to say Hudson's name, because then it would just remind me that the only thing I regret is not staying in the morning.

3

PIPER

Arriving at the restaurant on the seventeenth floor, I know why April would have picked this place for her engagement party. She is a complete foodie, and the chef at this new restaurant is all the rage.

I enter the private room where a large group is busy drinking, grabbing appetizers off of floating plates, and there's jazz playing in the background.

It doesn't take but a second before someone pulls my arm, and I turn to see April smiling brightly at me with her new blue dress. She looks ecstatic.

"There you are, Ginger!"

I adjust my small clutch purse in my hand that matches my pale peach wrap dress. "Sorry, took forever to get a taxi." I smile at her before we embrace for a hug. "You know I wouldn't miss this for the world."

We part and look at one another in an excited mood.

"Did you bring your mystery guy?" She flashes her eyes at me. "I didn't forget about that conversation."

I scoff. "You know I'm here alone because it was a one-time thing. We went over this."

"I still don't understand why you left. Maybe it would have been the most romantic breakfast of your life."

I touch her shoulders to refocus her attention. "Or maybe we should just talk about you marrying the man who gave you that rock on your finger."

She holds up her hand to admire the ring, and her smile grows wider still. "Jeff is around here somewhere. Half of his law firm I think are here. Anyways, I wanted to ask you something."

"Oh?"

She takes my hand and quickly guides me to a quiet spot away from the crowd, grabbing a present off a side table amongst all the gifts in the process. We keep moving until she stops us in a corner, with windows all around, which makes me feel like I'm half in the sky.

April hands me the small pink bag with a lot of ribbon. "I know you promised to design my dress."

I look up at her as I try to untie the bow. "I would much prefer you get a dress from a real wedding dress designer, and I can focus on what you wear on the honeymoon."

"Nothing. I'll wear nothing," she informs me one-toned.

"Fair point." I get the bow off and peek inside the tissue paper to see a small statue. A glass figurine of a lobster, dancing or in an odd pose. "What's this?" I'm puzzled.

"Thought my maid of honor would need something ridiculous for her design table, and I saw it at the market last weekend and thought of your umbrella."

"I'm maid of honor now?" I ask, half-surprised. She nods. "I guess if someone has to do it." I pretend like she's twisting my arm to help her out.

April shakes her head ruefully. "Funny. Okay, so I can check that off the list."

"You can. I accept my responsibility and will place this freaky statue somewhere," I confidently inform her.

"Great. We definitely should insist on weekly coffee meetings to go over all the wedding stuff and for me to hear if there is any chance of mystery guy making an appearance."

I roll my eyes. "Go. Go harass your other guests."

"I will." She grins. "I need to find my uncle anyway; I asked him to walk me down the aisle at the wedding."

"Oh yeah?" I was wondering who would do the job. April doesn't know who her father is because her mom did insemination with an anonymous donor.

"You've never met my Uncle Bay."

"Nope. You talked about him a few times."

April grabs my hand. "Well, then you should meet. It's only fitting since he's walking me down the aisle and you are walking ahead of me down the aisle. He's my godfather too."

"Sounds like he's the perfect man for the job then." I smile, happy for her.

She guides me through the crowd to a pair of men in dark jeans and blazers, with one visible to us and the other who has his back to us. They seem to be laughing about something, but when one man sees us approaching, he touches the other man's shoulder and leaves.

"Uncle Bay, I want you to meet my maid of honor," April announces as we circle around the man.

The moment my eyes draw a line up and land on the man in front of me, my entire body stills.

Those familiar strong hands are currently gripping a fine scotch. His jaw is cut sharp, yet experience makes me know that his nuzzling skills are excellent. I know there is a simple tattoo of an arrow on his shoulder underneath his shirt. Those blue eyes pierce me with surprise, plus something so tense… recognition. That mouth of his twitches barely, but I notice.

"Hudson?" I nearly squeak.

April immediately looks at me, confused.

"This is Ginger?" Hudson asks April, clearly also baffled by what's happening, yet I can't help but notice that he seems unnervingly calm, while internally my stomach just did a flip, and I may be pressing my thighs together in reaction to being in his presence, but whatever.

Looking between us, April smiles like we're crazy. "I mean, yes, this is Ginger. I call her that because her name is Piper, well, Piper Dapper, and she says her name reminds her of gingerbread people."

Now I see the corner of Hudson's mouth begin to hitch up because he knows that reference far too well.

April looks at me again, then touches her forehead like she forgot something. "I guess you recognize my uncle."

"Your Uncle Bay?" I look wide-eyed at April.

She nods her head. "I mean, well, his name is Hudson, but when I was seven, we were learning about the Hudson Bay in school, and since then I've called him that."

Oh my God, no wonder I never knew she had an Uncle Hudson.

"She's one for nicknames, this one," Hudson mentions. He doesn't take his eyes off of me, and I'm still not sure if my mouth is closed because my jaw dropped open somewhere in the last twenty seconds.

"I guess I only ever talk about my uncle who works in sports, never mentioned he was Hudson Arrows. That's how you recognize him, right?" April touches my arm as she enquires.

"Huh?" I glance to April and then straight back to the man who seems entertained by this situation.

"My uncle? He's the Winds football head coach. That's how you recognize him," she states.

My grandmother would most definitely be clutching her pearls if she knew I slept with my best friend's uncle/godfather who is walking her down the aisle, and apparently, he is also the famous football coach that every person who has a sliver of interest in Chicago sports has talked about at some point—except me. Because, apparently, I live under a rock, so I never realized who this man who made me see stars actually is.

Heat spreads through my body as I'm either blushing or getting swallowed by the predicament that I just found myself in.

Because this man is supposed to be walking my best friend down the aisle as a fill-in father, and she has no idea that he's my mystery man.

"Leave her alone, April. Something tells me your friend prefers sporting activities that involve ice." He tips his head slightly to the side before bringing the glass to his lips, and he sips his whiskey while trying to hide that damn sexy smirk.

Because his look tells me that tonight, he may just want me to squirm again.

HUDSON

Piper is standing before me, and yeah, I get my kicks out of her face turning slightly crimson. What are the chances that she and I were connected all along? Damn my niece and her love for nicknames, but this is a fucking fantastic twist.

Or at least, I'm enjoying this ride.

Piper, on the other hand, looks like she may combust. And I don't mind one bit.

"I'm going to check in on Jeff. Do you mind?" April asks us both.

Piper is quick to shake her head. "Of course not."

"Oh, don't you worry. I'm sure I can find something to talk to Piper about to keep her occupied." I throw on a cunning grin.

April smiles in appreciation before walking off, but my eyes remain on the woman who has been haunting my thoughts for weeks.

The breath of fresh air that I had for one night before she disappeared.

"This is not happening." Piper seems to be speaking to herself. Her chest is moving visibly up and down.

Stepping closer, I ensure that I'm close enough for the next few minutes of our conversation to be only between us.

"You know this coincidence is, well…" I can't pinpoint it, but a sound escapes me.

Her eyes dart up to my own. "April can't know about us."

"What? The part that we already met or the part that you love to sit on my face." I offer her a tight smile. I've never had qualms about taking people out of their comfort zone, that's what being a coach is all about.

Piper seems to grow a little agitated by my comment, proven by her sexy-as-hell death stare, but I don't care. After all, she left before dawn.

"You may find this humorous, but… damn it, I told her a few details about that night, not realizing who the hell you were. Oh no." She touches her mouth in a panic. "Exactly why she can't *ever* know."

Admittedly, it's going to be an awkward-as-fuck conversation with April one day if she does ever find out, but I can't help but point out the obvious.

My smirk stretches. "Ah, so you do remember that night in great detail and felt it was worthy of discussion."

Her eyes survey the room before she steps a smidgen closer to me. "That night wasn't… I mean, I don't normally do what I did."

I feel like she is trying to justify her actions, and I won't be having that. "You don't need an excuse, just own it. You are allowed to ride cock the way you do."

"Jesus," she curses. "Do you not have a filter?"

I chuckle under my breath. "Around you? No." That I'm honest about. "Besides, I don't exactly owe you manners after you left a cold spot on your side of the bed."

She sighs and looks away then back to me. "It was supposed to be one night. I thought it was easier that way. Sorry if I didn't follow procedure, but fucking a man old enough to be my father who turns out to be the godfather of my best friend doesn't exactly have a play-book…" Her last word drags for a second, and she seems to be considering something, then she laughs softly, and I'm adoring her all over again. "Now I get it. Foul. You chose the safe word."

I tip my glass to her. "Ding, ding."

She shakes her head but can't suppress a smile. "Clever."

"Is it?" There's doubt in my tone. "You didn't find me after. Could have easily done a quick search on the internet. Handsome guy, Hudson, killer tongue, Chicago, and I'm sure I would have been the first name to come up."

"And you could have done the same. Gorgeous, Piper, lingerie, Chicago, and I'm sure your world would have been blown," she chides but in a playful way.

This back-and-forth on my level is what has me drawn to her like a moth to a flame.

Taking a sip of my drink, I highlight a point. "You made the message clear that you wanted to forget that night."

Right? That's what it means when someone leaves without saying goodbye, or is it just how kids these days are playing the game?

"It's not that, it's just..." She chokes on her words. "I'd never done something like that. I thought it would be easier, and trust me when I say it wasn't something to forget."

That is exactly what I wanted to hear, because it means her departure has nothing to do with our connection.

Stepping dangerously closer to her, I lean in which causes the scent of peppermint to hit me. I know it's her shampoo because I had a fistful of her hair at one point that evening.

"It's okay. I didn't look for you, but that doesn't mean I forgot. On the contrary, you're on repeat in my head far more than I would like to admit." I hear the heat in my tone, and as I step back, I see her slightly trembling as her lips part open.

But this conversation is going to have to take a pause because I see my sister waving at me from the other side of the room and motioning for me to come to her.

"Go grab yourself a drink, a very *dirty* martini, Piper. It may be a long night," I suggest before I walk away.

———

I ARRIVE at the corner where my sister—well, technically half-sister, but family is family—Catherine, watches the room. I can tell she's not herself tonight. That makes two of us.

I pass her a glass of wine that I picked up on my way over and hand it to her. Catherine is thirteen years my senior and works as a lawyer. Her mother was married to our father before they divorced, and he then married my mother. Despite our age difference, we're close enough, as proven by the fact she asked me to be April's godfather. My guess is that since Catherine and April have a different last name than me, theirs is Morris. These missing pieces of the puzzle made it possible for Piper and me to remain a mystery to one another. Especially as I've rarely seen April in the last few years.

"You think there are enough bruschetta plates?" my sister asks as she tugs on her earring. Ah, she's nervous that everything is right for the party.

"Trust me, I think people are more occupied with drinking tonight."

My sister snaps her eyes into my direction. "What's that supposed to mean?"

I shake off my comment and scan the room to find Piper, with no luck. "Nothing. Everyone is having a grand ole time."

"Should your publicist be worried?" She has a closed-mouth smile at her reference. "Use those NDA forms I gave you."

I shake my head. "Absolutely not." If I make a woman sign some form, then I'll never have a chance to find someone. "I'll take my chances, and besides, it just means that I need to be on good behavior at all times."

"Oh joy, you're thinking wisely." She mocks me the way siblings do. "You've done a damn good job at maintaining a positive image in the press on a personal level. That article on you giving kids a tour of the stadium was golden. In fact, you have been in the good books… which causes me to worry, because I know you, and you're my brother. Something must be up. You seem different." She waves a finger at me.

Looking to my sister, I can see she is hinting to something. "As in?"

She shrugs a shoulder before drinking her white wine. "All this wedding stuff getting to you? I mean April, and also Drew."

Now I proudly smile. My son is getting married. The son I didn't even know I had until a year ago, yet we've been trying to bond to make up for lost time. "I guess that's what happens when kids grow up."

"Except you never got to see him as a kid, you haven't experienced the childhood years. All of his firsts. Nor have you found a woman to tame you." She tips her head at me and flashes me knowing eyes.

Fair points on all counts.

Even though Catherine went into motherhood of her own will, she later found a man to call husband, but he only entered April's life when she was already an adult and they're not so close. Me? I've never been married, and as fun as the glorified bachelor title has been, I would like to shake it off at some point.

"Is this a therapy session? Anyways, Drew is sorry he isn't here, but it was just too much with his own wedding coming up next week."

Catherine places a hand on my shoulder. "It's okay, I understand, especially as it is a bit of a drive from Bluetop."

We both stand there in a moment of silence as we watch the room and people enjoying themselves. I don't see Piper, which has me slightly concerned she took off, but she must be here somewhere.

"How is Lake Spark?" Catherine asks.

My lake house is where I hide when the training schedule allows or in the off-season. I much prefer small-town life. In the city, I have no peace, and although I'm appreciative of the fans, it's nice to get away.

"I'm going to head there after Drew's wedding and stay up there through summer training." Quickly my eyes dart to the flash of peach fabric on a fine body. I spot Piper, and she sets an empty martini glass down on the bar before she walks in the direction of the ladies' rooms. "April explained my responsibilities at the wedding then introduced me to some of the bridal party, including Ginger who she sometimes mentioned, yet her actual name is Piper." I play it completely casual in hopes my sister doesn't question it.

"Oh yeah." She smiles. "Piper is such a good friend to her. She's a fashion designer, and they met a few years ago at some workshop. A bright girl. I'm not quite sure why she doesn't have a boyfriend, except she seems to be a bit of a workaholic. That reminds me, I need to talk to her about arranging a bridal shower."

"Right." I swipe a hand over my chin. Can't exactly ask more without Catherine becoming suspicious.

It also registers in my head that I'll be seeing more of Piper, whether she likes it or not. I've seen it with Drew, that weddings involve a lot of small events prior to the big day.

Lucky me.

"Sorry, I need to go chat with Jeff's parents," my sister mentions.

"Not a problem in the slightest."

It gives me an opportunity to find Piper.

———

I FEEL like a hunter as I walk out of the room. An almost animalistic sense hits me in relation to Piper, and I feel like I may know where to find her.

The moment that I reach the hall, my eyes scan for the ladies' room, and I head straight there. There is a joint lounge area between the men's and women's rooms, and I open the door. As I walk in, another man is leaving.

"Arrows!" he calls out. My guess is he's a friend of my niece's fiancé. "That was some playoff series. Maybe next year we'll use a little more offense." The young man smiles in good jest, but still, my return smile is tight.

"Thanks for the tip," I say, hiding my annoyance, and don't look over my shoulder as he leaves.

I take in my surroundings, and I'm thankful that it's quiet except for a member of staff in her forties standing by, ready to offer fresh towels or mints.

Clearing my throat, I throw on a look that is persuasive as much as it is charming as I catch the woman's glance.

Her face turns to surprise. "I know nothing about defense or offense, but my husband is a fan."

"Is that so?" Perfect. I reach out to grab a pack of matches sitting in a bowl on the counter. "By any chance is there a woman in there wearing a peach-colored dress with her hair soft around her face?"

"There is," she answers, intrigued.

I reach into my blazer, and I'm thankful that I have a pen. Pulling it out, I sign my name on the pack of matches then flip the box between my fingers to offer it to the lady. "For your husband."

Her mouth stretches into a wide grin as she slowly takes them. "Thank you."

"No problem." I hold my smile a little longer. "What would be the chances I could go in there?" I motion behind her to the women's room. "And let's say… nobody interrupts while I talk to that woman?" Her eyes bug out, and I realize what that must have sounded like. I'm quick to hold up my hand to calm her. "Relax. She's the maid of honor, and we need to plan a surprise for the future bride, and I wanted to hash out those details real quick."

The woman looks at me still skeptical, but after a few moments, she tips her nose up. "Okay. You have five minutes max, otherwise my boss may kill me."

I bring my hands together. "You are an angel. Thank you."

Without delay, I beeline it to the women's room, and as soon as I open the door, I close it and lock it.

In the mirror our eyes meet, and Piper's breath hitches, as she's startled. She must have been fixing her lipstick which may be useless if I have anything to say about it.

I walk a few strides in her direction, very well determined.

"Hudson, what in the wor—"

I grab her arm and spin her around until her ass rests against the edge of the sink vanity. Her eyes slowly skim up my body until our gaze is locked which only builds the connection between us. I slowly let her arm go, but only because I already know her body and feel like she's comfortable enough to stay. Then I notice the hint of a smile on her lips, and I'm even more certain that this was the right move.

"Was your plan to hide away in here?" I grin.

She scoffs and looks away, only to return her line of sight to me with a warm smile breaking out on her lips. "If only that could work. But no, I just needed a few minutes to escape and come to grips with the fact that you're April's uncle and you are standing right in front of me."

"How did that go for you?"

Piper smirks at me and folds her arms up over her chest, almost as if she's settling in for a long conversation. "Admittedly… I may have searched your name on the internet for a good five minutes."

I tip my head to the side, and I step closer. "Honesty, I would be concerned if you didn't."

She taps her matching peach-colored nails on her crossed arms. "So, Hudson Arrows." She states my name in a tone that I recognize from her as thick with heat.

One step closer.

I'm already drowning in her presence.

"That would be me, Piper Dapper." I return the tone.

Piper's eyes survey me in curiosity to what I might do, and truthfully, all I want to do is run my hands all over her and play with that little bow tied under her breasts.

For a moment we both stand there, almost daring each other to make a move, until her lips part open again to speak. "We have ourselves a predicament."

A sound of doubt escapes me. "Depends on if you grabbed that martini or not?"

She scoffs a laugh, but sadly breaks away from our little bubble and walks to the middle of the room. "Made it a double, to be honest. I can't seem to wrap my head around this, except that April really can't know, especially not now, as it's her moment to shine."

I purse my lips before cutting to the chase. "Listen, we don't have time. My bribe with the lady outside only got us five minutes, and I think I've already used two to drink in the sight of you."

"So, what will you do with the other three minutes?" I see the smile she is trying to control.

"Convince you to see me again, away from here." I get to the point of the only thing that makes sense.

She smirks amusingly. "What makes you think I haven't started seeing someone else since our night?" I give her wide knowing eyes, and her smirk falters. "There hasn't been anyone."

My lips twitch from pride that I was her last. "Likewise. Now, about getting away from here…"

Piper's palm flies up to stop me. "The last thing we need is April seeing us leave together."

My hands go into my pockets as the corner of my lips curve up into a grin. "Love that you're thinking of what we could do tonight, but I meant something else."

Her eyes narrow, and her attention perks up. "You barely know me, Hudson."

"Debatable, as I know some aspects of you very well, but I want to talk to you some more."

Her throat cracks a sound, but no words come out. I take this as my opportunity to lead, and I take a few steps closer to touch the sides of her arms. Our touch ignites a feeling inside of me that I've rarely felt in my life. An inconsolable need to possess something, an infatuation that feels like it's leading me down a winding path.

"My son is getting married next week—"

"Son? The internet didn't tell me that."

I admire the view of my fingertips gliding along her bare arms as I say, "That's because I only found out about him last year, and I'm doing my damnedest to keep him out of the press."

"But you're telling me."

"Sometimes trust is instant with someone." That truth seems to hit both of us, as our eyes lock in recognition. "He's your age, in case you're wondering." That point I add because I know it riles her. Proven by the fact she swallows down a slight shock.

"Right." She looks away. "You're old enough to be my dad, yet I won't call you daddy in the bedroom." Her mouth gapes open when she realizes her mumble was loud and clear. Her eyes snap in my direction, and I can only laugh.

"We may need to circle back to that point one day. But anyway, as much as I would love for you to be my plus-one for his wedding, I doubt it's the time."

Piper tips her head to the side slightly in agreement.

"I have a house up on Lake Spark and tend to stay there when I don't need to be in the city. After the wedding next weekend, I plan on being there for a while. Come stay with me?"

Her eyes grow big. "What?"

I wrap an arm around her middle to pull her tight to me in an abrupt move. "You heard me."

Her hands land on my shoulders. "Like just escape the city with you?"

Arrogant, cocky, I don't care, but I'm not letting this go. "Call it a rendezvous, secret liaison, or my personal favorite heaven. Your choice of title but come stay with me and we can address a few things."

"Such as?" She raises her brows.

I squeeze her body against mine. I can't get enough of her. I want to go home tonight and debate showering because I want to keep her scent on me. That peppermint shampoo is a fucking aphrodisiac that has me desperate for more of her.

"Get to know one another, revisit what we already know." My eyes dip down to her body then back up.

"You're crazy." But her tone is only entertained.

"Tell me you're not curious," I challenge.

She licks her lips, trying not to let her smile break out, but I see her cheeks raise. "I think your five minutes are up."

I laugh at her avoidance of an answer. Instead, I run my hand along her back, sliding down until I land on the curve of her ass before sweeping my hand away. Stepping back, I grab a paper towel from the pile in the basket and pull out my pen from before. After jotting down my number, I hand it to her. I could easily input my number in her phone but writing it down with a pen from my suit is classic.

"Here. Call me when you make a decision."

Piper looks down at the contents in her hand with intrigue, which is promising, but I want to seal this deal. I glide my knuckles along her cheek to give her assurance. "If you remember what our night was like, then only imagine what the mornings could be."

With that, I walk away, leaving her to blush and stand in contemplation.

"Hudson," she calls out, and only when I look back at her does she continue. "Whatever my actions that morning may have implied, I don't regret it."

I simply nod, even more certain that this isn't our ending.

5

HUDSON

I knock a few times gently on the suite door before I check my tie, and when I hear Drew give the signal to come in, I open the door, already knowing I'm wearing my heart on my sleeve today.

The first thing I see is my son struggling with his tie as he looks in the mirror.

"I made it through the trenches and wanted to check in," I announce as I close the door behind me.

Drew is similar to me in so many ways. Those sharp blue eyes, I know they will drive his soon-to-be wife crazy, and I've been told by women that my eyes stand out. His shade of brown hair is much my own, minus the few sprinkles of gray that you can only see if you look closely. And that smile? A fucking Arrows hereditary trait that we can thank a distant ancestor for.

"How bad is it?" he wonders aloud as he grows frustrated with the fabric around his neck.

"I don't know about your fiancée because her sister-in-laws are keeping a tight ship on the area of the farm where they're getting her dressed. And Lucy's brothers? They look serious, double-checking everything is okay, and probably dying for a drink to calm the nerves."

My son is marrying the love of his life who happens to be his friends'—yes, plural—younger sister; she has three older brothers who all welcomed Drew into their family long before Lucy and Drew became a thing. They own a winery and farm called Olive Owl, so there was no escaping a wedding on site. It is convenient, as it is also an inn with a few rooms, such as the one we're in now.

"Let me help with that." I walk to Drew and take hold of his tie, and I can tell he is visibly nervous. Willingly he lets me take over, which is a surprise since he's more stubborn and independent normally. "Thanks for inviting the Arrows clan. My sister picked up my parents, and April will be here soon, she texted me from the car."

"You don't need to thank me. They're…"

We both raise a brow at one another and move past words. It's hard to say family when Drew has only met them a few times. Drew only came into my life a year ago when by chance I discovered an old high school fling had a baby. She's no longer in either of our lives, but it doesn't matter, as I ended up with the winning ticket. My son is the best, and we've grown close.

"And also, my neighbor and a few of the football guys," I add.

Drew shrugs a shoulder like it's nothing.

This tie is a pain in the ass; even I am struggling, but I won't relent, I have to get this right for his big day. "This will probably be one of the biggest days in your life, until one day you have a kid."

"Geez, no pressure or anything."

I snort a laugh. "That was a bad intro for my father-of-the-groom talk, wasn't it?"

"I mean… it was average." He smirks.

I take a deep breath. "Okay, let me try again. The moment I met you, I was lucky, not only that you are my son but that you have people in your life who care, and one of those people is Lucy. I've never known you without her in your life, and I feel like she is a part of you, and you do too. So today, you become her husband, and you'll probably make me a grandfather when I'm far too young and handsome to be one, but I wouldn't trade that for anything."

"Not even for a first-draft pick?"

I laugh. "No football talk here."

Holding the tie up, I assure him, "Come on, let's be honest. A tie isn't you, and Lucy won't mind if we ditch this thing. Your shirt under the blazer is fancy enough."

Drew contemplates and tips his head to the side. "Damn it, you're right."

I throw the tie to the side. "Points for effort, as I know you want to give her the perfect wedding."

We both walk to the room's small sitting area. Drew sits down, but I grab two bottles of water from the side and hand him one.

"You're going to be someone's husband," I point out the obvious.

He twists the cap off and looks at me. "I thought our sentimental talk was done."

I kick my feet up and land them on the coffee table. "Let the father of the groom go all in on this conversation, okay?" I smile to myself.

"Go on then."

"As much as I hate it, since I only just found you, but your wife is now number one. You love her like crazy and can't explain why you can't get enough of her. Every day you want to discover something little that is new and enjoy the things that remind you of why you love her. You are never ever to forget when she asks you to pick up something from the grocery store, and you gotta keep it exciting, I'll let your imagination run wild there."

Drew shakes his head. "And that's the cue to wrap up this conversation."

Probably for the best because my speech is running on instinct and what I assume it would be like.

I feel my phone vibrating in my inner breast pocket. Pulling it out, I check to see if it's Catherine, as she was driving my parents here. An unknown number.

"You can take that. We still have time to kill before I head downstairs."

I bring the phone to my ear. "I'll be quick. It could be my sister since sometimes her number comes up as unknown when she calls from the car." Drew nods, and I hit accept. "Hello."

"Hudson. Hi."

Her voice immediately causes me to straighten up to full attention, with my feet sliding off the table because I need the ground to stabilize me during this surprise. "Piper." My tone is steady, thank God.

Drew gives me a peculiar look with a hint of curiosity.

"Yeah… sorry, is this a bad time?" She continues.

I motion to Drew that I'll be right back in a minute or two and quickly head in the direction of the hall.

"No, it's okay. My son is getting married today, and we're just waiting for the big event."

"Oh, not a good time then—"

I cut in. "It's perfect timing, actually." I lean against the wall and focus on the sound of her voice and breath. A long exhale escapes me. "In truth, I could use a calming voice or more specifically the sound of *your* voice right about now."

"Why is that?" I can hear her smile.

"Being the father of the groom is a bit more daunting than I thought."

"I can only imagine."

"The bride's family I think have already used all the tissues in a five-mile radius, and I think I may be looking for one too," I admit.

She laughs. "Aw, you're a big softy."

"Whoa, I'm not saying that. It just seems like the bachelor party I arranged was a piece of cake compared to today." I adjust the phone against my ear.

She chortles a laugh. "I've never heard of the dad arranging a bachelor party."

I shrug a shoulder. "We have a different dynamic, Drew and me. I wanted to. His friends are the bride's brothers, so whoever arranged the party, it was going to be awkward. Besides, get your dirty mind out of the gutter, Piper. I kept it completely innocent with only one stripper instead of two." I'm joking about the last part, and I know by the sound of her laugh that she gets my sense of humor.

"You are something, Hudson Arrows." My name dances off her tongue, and it will keep me smiling for the next few minutes.

"Something good or something bad?"

It sounds like she is walking slowly. I can envision her playing with a plant or the pencils that she uses to design that lingerie of hers that I loved touching and peeling off with my teeth.

"As we now know, I know nothing about sports other than your coaching outfit from this one article I read looks kind of cozy, and the photos I've seen of you with models were not exactly encouraging, but you seem to have been flying solo for the last year, and I kind of have a problem…"

"Oh?" Something about her tone doesn't have me worried.

A sound escapes her lips. "The thing is, there is this guy who made this crazy offer, and it hasn't really left my mind. I can't even focus on work. But other than the lines of his body or the arrow tattooed on his skin, I think I should know more about him. He wants me to go up to his lake house, and he could be a crazy murderer for all I know."

Now I have to grin. "Something tells me that you had that theory once, then had an amazing night and still came out alive."

"I did, and as much as it was fun, I'm not sure sliding directly back into bed with you is smart. Besides the obvious complication, which is also a saving grace, because if April trusts you then I do, but I need to know more about you."

I think for a moment. "I still need to unravel all your secrets, Piper Dapper. I took a page from your book and looked online. You hide behind a cartoon vector as your profile pic and only post about fabrics and coffee on social media. I'm way too curious about you. You're different, and you have me laying my cards on the table. And as much as I would say my bed is your bed, I have guest rooms. It would be your choice if you use one or not."

She giggles. She actually giggles at what I thought was a gentlemanly offer.

"You're not giving me many reasons to run away, and I need to focus again. Your offer of visiting your lake house..." She's keeping me in suspense. "Will you send me the address?" It's her confirmation.

I'm thankful she can't see my confident smirk of satisfaction because I've been hoping for this.

"Yeah. I'll be there from tomorrow morning."

"Then I will see you sometime in the afternoon and maybe stay for a few days if, well... if it feels right."

I scoff a sound. *If it feels right.* She knows that answer. "Good... this was already going to be a great day, but it just got better."

We both hold on for a moment, just listening to our silence.

"I'm going to run so you can get back to your special day."

"Thanks. And Piper... why did you wait a week to call?" I propel myself off the wall to head back into Drew's groom suite.

She laughs. "Truthfully, I've dialed your number about ten times this week, but something inside me told me I should hit call today."

"Guess it's a sign then."

A sign for what, I'm not sure.

———

My son gives me a stern eye as I walk back into the room, admittedly more elated than before.

"Piper?" he enquires as he tosses his bottle of water to the side.

I scratch the back of my neck, debating what to say. Then again, the fun thing about our narrow age difference is that Drew and I hang out like we're buddies. Proven by our countless lunches, texts, and conversations.

"I've maybe met someone. I'm seeing where it goes," I say as casually as possible.

He looks at me, impressed. "Oh yeah?" A grin stretches on his mouth. "You didn't want to bring her as your plus-one?" He's entertained, I can tell by his tone and look.

"I want to focus on you today, and there may also be one minor detail…" My face must have an awkward expression.

His eyes encourage me to continue.

"She's slightly younger."

Drew laughs. "And? I wouldn't expect anything less. I mean, like what, five or ten years?"

"She's your age."

Now his grin is wide. "Why am I not surprised."

My hands go out as I shrug my shoulders. "Should I be offended?"

"No. Okay, well, that isn't a gamechanger."

I swipe a hand across my chin. "One more thing."

"Go on." Drew crosses his arms as he waits.

"I need you not to mention this… it's April's best friend."

Drew laughs deeply as he scratches his cheek in pure amusement. "Oh man, I needed this today. So, you're secretly seeing your niece's best friend? This is classic."

"Thanks. I'm happy my romantic endeavors can lighten your nerves," I say, sarcastic.

Drew fixes his collar and begins to walk in the direction of the door, indicating that it's time for the big event. "I hope it works out for you. You deserve someone."

"Oh yeah?"

Drew stops with his hand on the handle. "Yeah. I may have beaten you to the altar, but I think you were meant to be someone's other half for a long time now, you just haven't found that person. You're kind of one of those annoying people who loves with all their whole hearts."

"Again… is this a compliment?"

Or is it an unintentional flaunt, because yes, my son is getting everything I know I've always wanted but never had. The whole wife-and-family thing.

"It is. Lucy came back into my life when I found you. Maybe

Piper is coming into your life when your dear son is starting his own family. Timing is just a coincidence, huh, *Dad*."

Hit me in the heart.

There aren't many times that Drew has said dad to me, but now I think I may just need the rest of the tissues in a *ten*-mile radius.

But I will remain strong and fight back the tears stinging to break free. Nope. Will not cry, I'm going to fight those little droplets like the final play in the Superbowl.

I slap a hand on his shoulder. "Let's get you married, kid."

Blinking back a tear, I remind myself that today is about my son. Tomorrow is about Piper who finally agreed to join me on a much-needed escape.

6

PIPER

y heart is pattering at the speed of light, and I nervously tap my fingers on the steering wheel as I drive. I do my best to keep my eyes on the road, but it's hard not to look at the nature surrounding me. As I get closer to Lake Spark, the woods build up and the trees bring a tunnel of green over the road.

In normal circumstances, the scene may be calming, but I'm in an unusual situation.

"Come on, Piper, you agreed to this," I speak aloud to myself. A sort of pep talk for the twentieth time.

The only thing that can explain my decision is that sometimes in life you have a feeling so strong that it can't be ignored. Taking a chance on Hudson's offer is that very instance.

He hasn't left my mind, and that's a problem.

Then again, there was no chance of me forgetting Hudson Arrows from the moment he kissed me, and then the thought was only cemented when April introduced us. Which gives me a twinge of guilt. I texted her that I was going out of town for a few days for a fashion expo, because I have a sneaking suspicion she wouldn't be thrilled if she knew the truth.

I glance at my weekend bag on the backseat, and I feel my nerves building, with butterflies in my stomach running rampant as I approach the turn, according to the GPS.

This is crazy. So spontaneous, and damn, it could go so wrong.

What if we have nothing in common? Or it's only sex? Why am I even questioning this all, as if Hudson is a contender to become more?

I approach the security gate and stop. I reach my finger out to the intercom, and someone must have been watching for me on the other end because the gate opens before I get a chance to press the button.

It doesn't take long after entering for me to arrive at the end of the road, as it is a sort of cul-de-sac of three houses. Beautiful and big houses that are any architect's dream of modernity—well, two seem to be under construction, and the third I'll assume is Hudson's, and when I search for the number over the garage then I know I'm correct.

Parking on the driveway, I take one last big breath. "Here we go, Piper."

My heart rate is picking up, I feel it, but I open my door anyway, ready for this. Just as I slide out, Hudson emerges from the front door and walks down the path. He's in jeans with a white t-shirt, his chin has a little stubble, and his eyes catch the sunlight just right. But it's his widening grin as he approaches that has me weak in the knees.

"Welcome," he greets me. Yet he slows as he gets closer, perhaps waiting for my cue.

I tuck a strand of hair behind my ear. I'm in jeans and a light pink button-up shirt; it's cute, yet comfortable.

"Hi." I give him a half-smile because seeing him again is as exciting as it is daunting.

"I'm happy you made it here." One step closer.

My shoulder slants up toward my ears. "Afraid I would change my mind?"

He tips his head to the side. "Nah, you seem smart and know a good thing when you feel it. My question was more about how there have been a lot of foxes on the road. Even though it's afternoon, they still appear every now and then."

Is he for real? Or is he trying to lighten the mood? "Right, those killer foxes."

Next thing I know, I feel something hit my forehead, as if it dropped from the sky. I whimper in response and see a pinecone fall to the ground.

"Shit. Are you okay?" Hudson steps closer to me and touches my arm in concern.

I rub my forehead and try to smile through my embarrassment. "Wow, nature is trying to knock some sense into me."

Hudson's face floods with relief when he confirms that I'm okay. "I don't even know what to say because what are the odds? I mean, there is a pine tree above the driveway, but still… did it work? The knock-sense-into-you part?"

"Despite the foxes and dangerous pinecones, I still seem to be staying here." I rub the sap residue from my forehead.

Hudson chuckles under his breath. "Good. Do you have a bag that I can carry inside?"

Because I'm staying the night, multiple nights maybe.

"Yeah… let me grab it. It's not that heavy, I've got it."

I quickly open the backdoor of the car, take my bag, then close and lock my car. But I run into Hudson as I turn away from the door, and I feel like he may have done that on purpose.

Either way, the damage is done, and I inhale his cologne, a subtle spicy scent. It takes me back to that night, reminding me that this man has seen me naked and has been inside of me.

Hudson hooks his finger and glides it along my cheek. "I'm happy you're here."

Warmth hits me in a wave and my adrenaline goes up a notch. I feel the tremble inside, but I'm not sure he notices. "I think me too, but I'm so out of my depth right now." I laugh nervously, and it causes him to smirk.

For a moment, our eyes catch, and I wish the power of his gaze would tell me to get back into that car, but it only encourages me to stay.

"Allow me, I'm a gentleman." He clucks the inside of his mouth as he takes my bag from my hand.

Now I have to grin. "Only some of the time." I raise my brows at him, and he appreciates my retort.

He studies my bag for a second. "Dancing lobsters. It's like your umbrella."

"It's a set. You remember my umbrella?" I'm surprised.

"I remember every second, Piper."

Swoon.

The one little ounce inside of me that might have thought Hudson was after a few nights of fun with a younger woman seem to be gone. He seems more invested than that.

Hudson steps aside and then leads the way. "You've come at a good time. The neighbor next door, Spencer, isn't around since he's remodeling. He's a baseball player, and it's game season anyhow. The other house just sold to a hockey player who is originally from around here. Last I checked, being in the sports industry wasn't a necessity to buy property here, but it makes for a good story, I guess."

"Sounds like you have quite the neighbors. Any of them single?" I can't help but tease him.

Hudson pauses as he opens the door to give me a flirty look. "You're already testing my restraint, huh?" His smile is strained.

"Nah, just being here is testing your restraint. It's when you show me the guest room that we may need to shackle you down."

Gone is the nervous woman from the car because something about this man makes me feel what I've always felt deep down but could never fully embrace. I am a confident person. I know I'm beautiful, and I know I have the ability to make someone like Hudson weak. In return, he is the type of thrill that may just challenge me.

"I don't regret my invitation, that's for sure. Shall we head to the kitchen for a drink?" he suggests, and I nod.

Taking in my surroundings, I'm impressed by the clean design and openness of the living and dining area. High ceilings with big windows wrap around the house, with a view out onto the lake. The deep blue water is surrounded by pine trees, and the long dock looks like a dream for the summer.

Hudson sets my bag on a chair before walking to the big fridge. "Maybe a soft drink? We can open a bottle of wine later, or if you want to explore the town, we could do that. I didn't make any dinner plans but thought I could cook."

"You cook?" I ask, impressed.

"Mostly grilling, but yes, I'm pretty decent in the kitchen. You?" He holds up two bottles, indicating for me to choose. Sparkling water or iced tea.

I point to the water. "I'm horrible in the kitchen except for breakfast food. I could eat breakfast for every meal."

He slides a glass with ice and the small bottle across the counter to me. "That's funny. You seemed to run when it involved breakfast with me."

"Fair point." I hold my glass up to him before I take a sip. "I don't think I need to explain myself again."

"You're right."

Setting my glass down, I realize that I haven't asked about yesterday yet. "How was the wedding?"

Hudson smiles with pride. "Perfect in every way. I didn't really get a chance to chat with April and subtly investigate you, I was too busy with father of the groom duties and talking with guests."

I love how he gushes over his responsibilities. "Tell me about your son."

"Drew is the best."

Hudson grabs his phone that was lying on the counter, and he comes to stand next to me, which causes our arms to graze and a spark to sizzle inside of me. Looking at the screen, I see a man who looks similar to Hudson with a woman who is clearly a bride in an embrace beside a haystack. He swipes his screen, then I see a photo of Hudson with Drew, and it melts my heart, as they are clearly happy and, by their looks, related.

"It seems like a lovely wedding. Very rustic, yet chic."

"The wine was top-notch too since Lucy, my daughter-in-law, her brothers own the Olive Owl label. Anyways, they're heading off on their honeymoon tomorrow. It was my gift to them, a trip around Europe." Hudson locks his phone screen and slides the device back into his pocket.

"I'm jealous. Italy is my favorite place, just sitting in a café drinking cappuccino, watching the world go by," I comment.

Hudson nudges my arm. "For coffee, we have a good spot in town."

"Wonderful." My smile fades, and I hesitate. "Can I ask, well, you mentioned that Drew is new to your life?"

His lips quirk then press together. "Yes. I found out a little over a year ago. An old friend of Drew's mother was dying and had a list of things she wanted to do before she died. One of those things was to tell me that Drew is mine. I had no idea. I was a teenager at the time, not from her area. We met at a party, and I never knew. After a little digging, it seemed that Drew was indeed mine. His mother didn't stay long in his life. He was raised by his stepdad who didn't stick around once he turned eighteen. Drew didn't get the life that I would have wanted for him."

I can sense a lot of feelings stir inside of Hudson about that. Instinct causes me to reach out and touch his arm to comfort him. "And now?"

"Couldn't be happier to have my son in my life. Just missed all the young years when he was growing up. He is the opposite of me in some ways, maybe a bit more introverted and not much for sports. He plays guitar and is good at carpentry, even made some of the shelves in my living room."

I squeeze his arm. "Makes his father proud too, I can see it with every word you say."

Hudson smiles to himself. "True. Now how about a tour?" he suggests.

"Sounds good."

For the next few minutes, he shows me around downstairs, the at-home gym, and outside where there is a giant patio and an in-ground hot tub in the corner. It will be nice to sit out there in the morning with coffee and my design book. Color-wise, everything in the house screams bachelor, with neutral colors, except for a beautiful Native American rug hanging on the wall in Hudson's office—oh, and his hallway is decorated with a few of his old jerseys. We kept conversation to the point, Hudson mostly explaining where things were.

But as we walk up each step leading upstairs, that feeling in my stomach returns. A swirl of anticipation and nerves. Maybe he picks up on it or perhaps he just doesn't want to make a big deal about it, but he doesn't show me his room. I thought for sure he would make a joke about it at least. Instead, he points out two guestrooms, and at the third room, he opens the door.

"This can be you." I follow him in, and he sets my bag on the bed. "Towels are in the bathroom over there behind the door in the corner. I guess maybe you want a few moments to freshen up before we head into town or go for a walk, whatever you want."

I notice he's avoiding eye contact. "Thanks. It's a beautiful room." I look around, and I do love the look of the white blankets with deep blue pillows. "I noticed you have a few rooms, so why this one?"

A droll smirk forms on his mouth, and his head lolls to the side as his eyes meet mine. "It's the farthest from my bedroom."

I feel my cheeks heat, and I try to hide my grin but fail, before I swallow and breathe in some composure. "You know, how about we just stay here tonight and open some wine and cook—or I watch you cook so I don't burn the house down."

"Sure. I'll meet you downstairs." Hudson turns to leave and makes it to the door where he stops, with his hand on the pane of the door, then turns back to me. "You know this is crazy for me too."

"So I make you do things you normally wouldn't do too?" I wonder, and I'm relieved that he also seems unsure about what's going to transpire.

He doesn't answer but instead scoffs, a hint of a smirk on his lips, before leaving me there to catch my breath.

————

AFTER CHECKING myself in the mirror, I return downstairs to find Hudson arranging cheese and crackers on a plate.

He glances up, and gosh, I don't think I will ever tire of his smile when he's happy to see me.

"White or red?"

I find a spot on the kitchen island. "Anything is okay, you decide."

Investigating the snack plate, and wow, the man knows how to prepare a charcuterie board.

"I was thinking maybe just steak and vegetables for dinner, but then I realized I don't know what you like." Hudson gets to work on uncorking a bottle of white.

"I'm pretty easy, I don't eat much pork, though." He gives me peculiar eyes, and I explain further. "My mom is Jewish and my dad Catholic, best of both worlds, but my mom won on what we ate in the house growing up."

He pours me a glass. "Ah, well, a wise man knows that the woman leads the way."

"Is that so?" I feel a coy smile stretch on my mouth, as I feel that he is insinuating me and where our day may lead.

Hudson offers me the glass, and he holds his own out to suggest a toast. "I'll cheers to that. You lead the way."

"I like the sound of that." I smile before clinking our glasses together, and I notice our eye contact is intense but in an electric way, which makes me thankful for the wine.

He indicates his head in the direction of the patio. "Some fresh air?"

"With that view, I don't think I'd ever say no."

I take the wine glasses and he takes the board of snacks, then we walk outside, taking a minute to get comfortable in the outdoor seating area, comfy lounge furniture with cloth pillows. He doesn't sit too far from me, but just enough to put my body on high alert. We angle our bodies toward one another as we hold onto the wine.

"So, you're Jewish?" he asks curiously.

"I guess. I was never raised in the religion. My grandmother, on the other hand, is a staunch follower, but more for the gossip from the temple than anything. Her family came from Hungary before the war, and my father's side is Dutch, but again, came long ago to the US. Dapper means brave in Dutch, actually."

"I like that. You are a brave person."

"How so?"

He has a sheepish look before he takes a quick sip of wine. "You took a chance on me."

I can't answer, only let our eyes hold. Maybe I will explain my reasoning when I've got more wine in me. Changing the subject quickly is my diversion.

"Actually, I got into design because of my grandmother. She comes from a family of seamstresses, and she became quite a big designer, back when department stores were king, and now, she's retired, with enough money to live a very good life. My parents were kind of the opposite, met during college, now work as doctors and volunteer time abroad, my brother too." I study Hudson for a second and watch how he listens intently. "If I can be honest, I think because of my grandmother, money and fame don't really faze me. Even though I could use my grandmother's name to get my foot through so many doors, I don't. So, I guess I'm not the typical woman you may have dated."

He looks at me oddly, and I realize what I suggested.

"Oh no, what I mean is, well… it's not right for me to make assumptions, but based on what I've seen online then… sorry." And I do it again, nervously ramble.

To my relief, Hudson chuckles and pops a cube of cheese into his mouth. "You're honest, I'll give you that. And for the sake of honesty, you're probably mostly right, but not as of late."

"Was there ever someone serious?" I wonder.

"Before coaching, I was on a vigorous schedule of training and games as a player. There were a few girlfriends here and there. But eventually, the schedule irritated them, or I could clearly see they were more interested in my fame. Then I turned coach, and my schedule became even more grueling, and life got chaotic. However, since my son came into my life, I've felt a need to slow down where I can. You?"

It's fair enough that he would ask me about my romantic life. I slide off the seat and walk a few steps with my wine to admire the view because I'm not ready to talk about that aspect of my life, not when Hudson could be the very opposite of what I've experienced.

"Such a great view. Why did you pick a house on Lake Spark?"

I feel him now standing and walking closer to me. "We train not far from here during the summer and for spring camps. During game season, I'm mostly living in hotels, and even though I have a place in the city, it isn't home. I even commute back here when schedule allows. I much prefer a small town on a lake, more solitude and calm. People just let me be, maybe because there are several people in the industry that live here, so the townsfolk are immune. My parents live in the western suburbs and will never move, even when I paid off their mortgage. It was the first thing I did when I got my contract money as an athlete. They're retired now. My mom was a teacher and my dad a plant manager. When I retire, I hope it is to here—and by the way, retirement for an athlete, even turned coach, is still young, in case you're concerned about my talk of retirement."

I turn to him with a fond look. "Sounds like a wonderful plan. I'm slightly jealous. I'm not much of a city person, although that's all I know."

"Well, then it's good that you're here. You'll get to enjoy the things that you like and experience something new." I notice a subtle tic of his jaw which means he is insinuating himself; it only causes me to smirk.

Again, we stand there, getting lost in each other's eyes. There's a pull we're both trying to fight, but we have our head in the game.

It takes a few beats before Hudson speaks. "Can I ask you a question?" His tone is almost serious.

I nervously drink from my wine. "Of course. I think questions will be our theme for the next few days," I attempt to joke.

He steps closer, and I gulp, anticipation rising. His fingertips land on my shoulder, and the best kind of tingle runs through my body. "What's the real reason you're here?"

I take a deep breath and remind myself that I'm a confident person who might as well be straightforward. "I guess I'll be blunt."

"Please. Your candor struck me from the very beginning," he presses.

"I want to figure out if you're the man who is the perfect fuck or the man who has the potential to be more."

If a man ever had a winning grin, then Hudson Arrows just displayed it.

He leans in, his lips brushing along my cheek up toward my ear where I feel the tingle of his stubbled chin.

"Baby, I know I can be both, and I have every intention of showing you."

HUDSON

The sound of the knife chopping zucchini against the cutting board fills the room, and I should be paying a little more attention to what I'm doing, but I enjoy looking at Piper watch me. Her eyes almost twinkle from where she's sitting at the kitchen island, sipping from her glass of wine.

"How's the view?" I ask then push the vegetables to the side.

She looks into her wine as she twists the base of the glass. "Can't complain. The apron was a nice surprise." The corners of her mouth hitch up as she says that.

Looking down, I admire my choice of apron too. *This butt deserves a good rub* is displayed on the apron, along with an outline of a cow.

"Thanks. I have a collection, and I'm not even sure how that happened. Matches some of your pajama lines, I guess, or at least your quirky lobster umbrella."

"Your aprons say a lot about you. You have an uplifting personality, you enjoy humor, and life for that matter. At least from what I can tell. You're laid back is my impression, considering the life you live."

"A fair assessment. Speaking of which, I will probably be up early in the morning. I like to work out, then I have a video meeting with team management first thing." I check on the meat that I seasoned earlier and will throw it on the grill for a few minutes.

"You stay in shape, that I can tell, and no, don't take it as an ego boost, I'm just stating the obvious."

"It's the Arrows gene. We reach adulthood then time freezes for about forty years." Amusement floods her face. "But seriously, I don't want to be like other coaches who bulk up in a bad way, I want to stay in shape. I'll be right back, just going to grill the steaks."

"I can set the table," she mentions, as if she knows where everything can be found.

"Okay. The remote for the fireplace is by the coffee table."

A few minutes later, we have food on the dining table and there is an orange ember across the sky to the west. I'm lucky my house sits on the south side of the lake, which means I get both sunsets and sunrises. But in this moment, the sunset with a crackling fire to the side sets the mood perfectly.

We both sit down, and she seems pleased with the steak that I place in front of her.

"Looks delicious," she compliments.

I top up her wine glass, then it dawns on me that I haven't had dinner here with a woman since I bought the place a few years ago. There is a first and last time for everything, and I can't shake the idea that Piper could be both.

She holds out her glass of now red wine to me. "A toast to your meat-marinating skills."

"Cheers."

We clink and then drink before both attacking our plates of food.

Piper clears her throat. "You know, my grandmother would point out the obvious about what I'm doing. I'm basically going back to what my ancestors did, which was to get acquainted with one another to see if they were a match before their parents would barter out the details of how many donkeys to exchange." She's only half serious.

"I'm sure you're worth at least three donkeys," I joke. "I'm positive she would be proud that you got to know my body first, to see if my cock is up to standard. Get to the important stuff first, you know."

She nearly sputters her drink out, then waves a finger at me. "Your humor somehow, unbeknownst to me, I get it."

"Hey, I'm doing my damnedest to be a gentleman here and not have you laid on the dining table so I can make you the entrée," I mention before taking in a decent sip of wine.

Piper purposely takes a big bite of her steak, with her mouth wrapping around the fork. "You have exquisite taste." Her reply is sultry, and I like the way she narrows her eyes at me.

I take hold of my wine glass only to realize that this may not be enough to keep me from leaning over and pulling her face into my hands to kiss her senseless. I'm attracted to this woman and so very curious about what I can unravel to get to know her more.

Thinking of a safe topic to discuss, my mind turns to work, only to remember that this temptress in front of me designs lingerie, and I'm envisioning it on her right now.

"Does your work also entail bikinis? We can go into the hot tub after dinner if you want." There's no point trying to avoid the million ways she could take that offer, so I sit comfortably in my seat, owning my question.

A smile plays on her lips. "Actually no, I don't design swimwear, and truthfully my focus is on pajamas that you wear around the house on a practical level. My lingerie line is not my main business, but admittedly, since our encounter that one night, I may have had a little… inspiration." She quickly takes her wine glass and downs a sip.

"I'm inspiration?" I must have a cheeky look.

"Maybe," she says, playing coy. "But seriously, I got into lingerie because feeling beautiful when you go to bed is important, it's your me time."

I stand up from the table, grabbing my wine glass in the process. "You're killing me, Piper." My grin doesn't fade. "We're going to need more wine."

She waves her hand and laughs. "Oh God, no, I'm already feeling tipsy, and I need to be sharp around you."

It's almost becoming insufferable, the light feeling dancing between us. Obvious flirtation and enjoyment.

I nearly growl to myself because I'm about to snap. Setting the empty bottle back down, I let my urge overcome me, and in a flash, I grab her wrists and pull her up and out of her chair, bringing her close, tight to my body.

My move startles her, yet her eyes are ablaze with excitement. Piper glances down to see my hands wrapped around her delicate wrists before her gaze returns to lock with my own.

"I'm going crazy not touching you," I say huskily. I'm dying to slam my mouth onto hers, but I won't. "Your smile every time you talk, I could stare at it all night. I'm completely fucked if you don't feel this attraction between us."

An almost sly grin forms on her mouth. "I would say so, considering I'm staying here for a few days."

"So you're not going to leave first thing?" I double check like it was even on the cards.

She gently shakes her head. "All indications are no. Depending if that pinecone incident turns out to be a concussion, but ya know." Her playing it cool is killing me as much as it calms me.

I loosen my grip and set her free, our tense embrace now dispersing into the air, but our eyes never break contact.

"Come on, Hudson, we have steak to finish and a hot tub to get into." She tilts her head in the direction of the table, even gently taking my hand and leading me back to my spot at a safe distance from her.

As we sit down and she grabs the bowl of salad, she highlights the obvious. "Hmm, I wonder if I packed a bathing suit, actually," she says doubtfully, bringing a finger to her chin. "I might have to go naked."

Damn, we lasted two seconds before she taunts me again, but that's what I enjoy about her, the banter, or the fact she isn't overwhelmed by me.

————

THE REST OF DINNER, we talked about food, and travel, and just kept the conversation easy. She helped clear the table, but I told her not to bother too much, as my cleaning lady will come tomorrow morning. Piper disappeared upstairs to get ready for the hot tub, and I quickly threw on my swim shorts, started the tub, and got in to keep warm.

Luck is on my side, as the stars are out, and a half moon hangs above us. My head perks in the direction of the house when I hear the door slide open, and every step that Piper makes in the thick bathrobe that I left in her room just ups the ante of whatever in the world will transpire tonight.

"You're curious about what I have on underneath, aren't you?" She grins almost shyly, yet she has no problem being direct.

I stand in the water to offer her my hand, even though the tub is built into the ground and there is a sturdy railing to my side. Piper flashes her eyes at me and slowly unties the robe while I bite my bottom lip, trying not to be extremely turned on. She keeps the robe closed as the tie hangs loose at her sides, and she pauses to draw the thrill out.

"The options are all in my favor, you know." Bikini, bra, naked… all possibilities I approve of.

"I'm well aware, Hudson Arrows." The way she's toying with me or the sound of my name on her lips is enough to make me want to get on my knees to beg her to let me worship her body all night.

Then she lets the robe slide off her shoulders and fall to a pool at her feet, leaving her standing before me in a dark bikini that does a half-ass job of keeping her large tits covered, but that's beside the point—this woman is a goddess.

She throws me an appreciative look and takes my hand as she steps into the water. I lean in to mumble against her hair.

"You're making the stars jealous."

She chortles a laugh. "Wow, you have some lines." Finding a seat across from me, we both sink into the water, submerging our bodies as much as we can. "I love this. Did the architect design this area?"

I lean back in the water to get comfortable. "Yeah, and we made sure that at night I can see between the two tall pines over there." I point behind her. "I thought about a pool. Maybe I will do it, but it's just that the lake is right here, and a pool in Illinois is only usable from May if we're lucky until early September. There's an old guy across the lake who swims every morning, even when it's cold. The only time he doesn't swim is when there's ice."

"Oh yeah? Swimming in cold water is all the rage these days. They say it stops the aging process and is great for your circulation. I can't handle cold, so I'll take a pass," Piper explains before she too exhales a relaxing breath and admires the sky.

"Me too. I prefer to stay warm."

After a moment, she turns away and rests her head against her crossed arms on the edge of the tub. "I could look at this all night."

Me too, but not the sky.

"There is something about the silence here. If you listen closely you might hear an owl somewhere."

She hums a sound as she finds her peaceful moment in my presence and looking at the stars.

"We have kind of avoided talking about April," she mentions but remains in her trance.

I run a hand through my hair and continue to watch Piper. "The good thing about being here is that we're in our own world, and we don't need to address it quite yet." Because truthfully, I know April, and she will not take this lightly, and my sister will never let me hear the end of it, but I think this whole dynamic is more complicated for Piper than it is for me.

"True. I can just get lost here." She half turns her body to look over her shoulder to study me, and the light in the water warms her face. "I spent five minutes upstairs debating what I'm going to do."

"Hopefully to me," I quip.

The corner of her mouth curves before her gentle eyes peer up at me. "This attraction between us scares me." She swims the small distance to sit next to me, allowing our arms to graze. "For the sake of transparency, because you were open with me earlier about your son and everything really… I'm used to being cautious, and I'm not a risk-taker in terms of guys, I play it safe."

I assume there is more to it than that, and I won't press until she is ready to talk about the reason why, but her words only confirm that I need to let her lead.

Her voice grows soft. "You are a lot of things that could make my life implode, but this trust I feel around you was instant, and I just want you to kiss me."

"Say no more."

I don't waste a second, and I slide my hand into her hair to bring her closer. My lips meet hers before I take more, and her lips are at my mercy.

Piper murmurs a sweet sound, and I dip my tongue into her mouth to get more. My mind becomes lust-filled, and I am captivated by the taste of her lips and the feeling of her arms looping around my neck. The water shifts around us as I slide her closer to me, inviting her to sit on my lap, and I love that she obliges.

Reangling my mouth, I cover her lips because I want to devour her. She has the ability to take over the atmosphere, and the overpowering desire to be inside of Piper has my mind stuck on the crossroads of lost and where to kiss her next.

We need to part for air, but I think I'm only able to breathe if I know I get to plant my lips back onto hers after.

Our foreheads touch as we take a moment to inhale, but it only takes a second for me to realize she's sitting on my lap, and I'm going to lose my composure any second.

Before I can warn her, her lips are back on mine and she's kissing me like I'm the prize she's been waiting for.

Her murmurs get lost as she deepens our kiss, and my hands move to cradle her face between my palms. Admittedly, I like to lead and control, yet I've been patient all day, and I'll continue to be until she gives the sign. Just in this minute, I need her to know that I enjoy her… a lot.

"No understatement, I can't get enough of you and only you."

My breath is heavy as I speak against her mouth before pressing my lips back to hers.

"I noticed," she mumbles as she softens our kiss and glances down.

My guy didn't get the memo to wait for Piper's cues, but it doesn't seem to bother Piper, proven by the fact she licks her lips and grins.

"He knows a good thing when he sees it," I remark.

But the moment our kiss breaks, she returns to sitting next to me and rests her head against my shoulder.

I have no idea what I'm doing except acting like a man besotted, which goes slightly against my persona of calm and assured. I have no qualms for this change, and I take the opportunity to interlace our fingers under the water as we both look up at the sky again.

"As damaging as your kissing skills are, I'm still sleeping in the guest room," Piper declares. I glance to my side with wide eyes, and she scoffs with a smile. "We get a touchdown for being attracted to each other, but I need to have a clear mind when it comes to you. Plus, that bed in the guest room looks ridiculously comfy."

I kiss the top of her head. "I'm too much of a gentleman to try and persuade you otherwise."

"Good. Now tell me about your views on pets…"

———

WE TALKED until our skin began to wrinkle from too much time in the water, but now I feel the night is about to come to a close as we walk up the stairs wrapped in towels.

Damn, I would love to offer Piper a shower in my room, but I'm okay waiting because I know it will be worth it.

Arriving at the top of the stairs, she pauses. "I believe I'm this way and you are that way." She points to my room.

I sigh and keep my disappointment buried. "That is sadly the layout of my house."

Her smile hasn't faded in the last hour. "I'll see you in the morning. Thank you for a lovely evening."

"No need to thank me. I wanted you here because you stir something inside of me that I can't seem to shake, nor would I want to."

Her doe eyes pierce me with fondness. "Night, Hudson."

I lean in to kiss her cheek when all I want to do is throw her over my shoulder and spank her ass, but she's the one play where I have to follow the rule book she set.

It doesn't mean I can't throw in a few words. My lips brush along her jawline. "Think of me when you touch yourself tonight, and I'll do the same."

"You're confident that's what I'll be doing?" She gently pushes me back with her fingertips so I can see her challenging and entertained look.

"Baby, I'll be imagining such wild things that you'll feel it from your room, and I remember your body, and the way you look right now tells me you are already hanging on tight when all you want is to let go."

Her mouth parts open and her face turns pink before her confident smirk comes back. "The question is if I'll be doing it with or without lingerie on. Goodnight." She stands up on the balls of her feet to give me a quick peck on the cheek.

I already wish that tomorrow would come faster.

8

PIPER

Walking into the kitchen, I feel like Hudson must have already been up for hours, as there is a half-filled pot of coffee. When I came down the stairs, I heard him talking in his office which was expected as he told me he would be up early.

It's nine in the morning, but it feels like I slept in. When I woke, I laid in bed recapping the last 24 hours and realizing how much I want this feeling that is moving inside of me. Maybe I shouldn't, but it's for my taking if I'm willing to take the chance.

I grab a mug that Hudson left out near the pot to pour myself a cup, then I breathe in the smell as I look out across the room to the windows and the lake. It looks like it will be a beautiful day.

"Morning," I hear in Hudson's deep timbre voice.

I look over my shoulder to see him walking into the kitchen wearing jeans and a dark t-shirt. Damn it, it only brings out his eyes more, and with the charcoal color, his skin looks a little tan.

"Good morning." I smile as he walks to me with determined eyes, and I know what he's going to do, what I want him to do.

He hums a sound as his fingers slide into my hair and our lips fuse together. It's the kind of smooth and sweet kiss that is by far better than coffee to wake me up.

"We're making progress… you're joining me for *morning* coffee," he teases as our mouths part.

I smile shyly at his reference. "I said I would be here in the morning, and I keep my word." I notice our hands have linked of their own accord as we stand here in the middle of the kitchen. "How was your morning?"

"I didn't wake you, did I? Had a bit of a tense meeting. One of my guys that we just drafted has an injury, and it could be a toss-up if he'll be better for summer training or not."

"Not a great way to start the day, no."

He tilts his head to the dining area. "Breakfast or want to head straight into Lake Spark to explore a little?"

"You haven't eaten yet?"

"No. I normally just have a shake and then I don't eat until around now."

"In that case, a little breakfast would be great."

He begins to move in the direction of the stove, but I yank his arm back so he doesn't get far. "Bran flakes and raisins are fine."

Hudson looks at me like I'm crazy. "So, no omelet? I need to make sure you have your Hudson protein intake this morning." He winks at me, and I playfully slap his arm.

I give him serious eyes, but my smile doesn't fade. "Let's keep it simple, we have enough complications as it is."

He taps his finger on my nose before he breaks free and grabs supplies. By the time we're sitting at the dining table and pouring cereal into our bowls, I realize that I'm perfectly relaxed around Hudson, almost as if I walked into his house like I've been here before. I blame it on our connection, the bond that I wasn't expecting when I walked into a bar all those weeks ago.

"You'll love Lake Spark. There is a surprise for you." He plays with the spoon in the bowl.

"Really?"

He flashes his eyes at me, clearly not willing to elaborate.

An obvious issue dawns on me. "Uhm, I need to ask…" I nervously pull my hair to the side over one shoulder. "I mean, won't people notice that we're walking around town together? Do we have to worry about, well… April finding out? The world for that matter, but I am more concerned about April."

Hudson leans back in the chair and presses his lips together before he blows out a breath. "No. Or at least not the locals. I guess I'll just scratch the whole kissing you senseless on Main Street idea, and I'm probably going to have to ditch holding your hand as we stock up on condoms at the store too." I hear the humor in his tone, which I do appreciate, but I give him a look and he turns serious. "I'll make sure we get a private table for lunch, but I can't make promises about privacy unless we decide that we will never leave this house while you're here, which I mean, could be a great option, but I would like to show you around."

"That sounds reasonable."

"Good. And don't worry about April, she's a big girl."

I look at him, astonished that he's so laid back about this. "You slept with her best friend; I'm sure she'll look at you completely the same come Arrows family Thanksgiving," I say sarcastically.

The corners of his mouth twist. "Lucky us, I'm not at Thanksgiving, as it's one of the most important game weeks of the year for me. Besides, we happened, Piper, and considering we don't regret it, then we might as well own it." He tilts his head slightly to the side. "Now, if you decide that you want to trade down to some other guy, then yeah, it may be awkward as fuck, but we know that won't happen."

His cocky confidence is oddly not a deterrent.

I cross my arms over my chest. "Why are you so certain?"

Hudson stands to head back to the kitchen like he forgot something, and on his journey he stops and leans down to whisper near my ear. "Because we haven't even started yet and already it's promising."

———

WALKING along the main street of Lake Spark, it isn't busy. It's clear the flowerpots are filled with newly planted flowers, the flag flying above the hardware store is well taken care of, and there is a café that smells delicious, plus a few little stores and a barbershop. It all reminds me of a scene from a classic movie.

"This is adorable, I love this." I admire the town as I let Hudson lead us to wherever our destination is. "It would be a perfect spot for a boutique over there." I point to an empty shop.

"That place used to have some great tailored suits, but the owner was pushing eighty-five and wanted to retire. Haven't heard any of the latest gossip if he's willing to sell yet, as rumor has it that his kids are arguing over the place. Is that something you want? A boutique?"

"Eventually. For now, I have my online store and rent some space to put the orders together, but the landlord already let me know that he is most likely selling soon. My grandmother always pushes for me to go bigger, but a boutique is more my scale and pace," I explain as we continue to walk.

"Your instinct will lead you in the best direction."

Huh, that phrase hits me right. So simple, and I'm not sure why I haven't heard it before.

I notice we're stopping, and I assess the location, a candy store called Jolly Joe's. "What's this?" I have to laugh.

Hudson's hand is firm on the handle of the door he is about to open. "Your surprise."

"Really?" I'm beaming like a child because I'm curious.

We walk through the door and a little bell chimes. The store is a classic candy store, with jars and jars of different types of candy. It's open-plan, and it seems two stores broke down the wall to become one.

"You told me once you are a stand-in-the-candy-store type of woman."

Ah, yes, I did. The night we met.

"True." I touch his arm to insist he stay close, and I lean in to speak low. "But you know I'm not that young, right? I'm very legal and can't be bribed with candy."

Hudson roars a laugh and continues to grin wide as he guides me by the hand farther into the store which has an ice cream parlor set up as a 1950s diner. Then my eyes catch a display, and I know that it is the reason why he brought me here.

"Gingerbread," I gasp. There are entire families of gingerbread cookies and different gingerbread men in different themes… doctors, firemen…

Hudson moves to stand behind me, and he rests his hands on my shoulders. "Look to the left."

My eyes dart to the end and a wide smile takes over my face. "My goodness, you are a local hero." There is a gingerbread man with an iced jersey that says coach, and I realize it's Hudson.

"I've always loved gingerbread." I hear his sinister undertone.

Ignoring him, I'm too much in my element and walk closer to the cookies behind a glass display case. "You've been hiding this up your sleeve this whole time?"

This is quite a coincidence, considering my nickname and references. Mostly, I love that he brought me here. He put thought into it.

"Wait." He holds up his hand. "Is this our gamechanger?"

I can't help it, and I walk into his arms that naturally wrap around my middle. "No, but this is quite a surprise and may just be the highlight of our day."

His look warns me before he pulls me closer and runs his hand down to my behind since nobody is around. "Highlight of the day? Not a fucking chance."

———

I STOCKED up on a bag of cola gummies. Hudson wasn't impressed with my choice, as he went for licorice. In the end, we didn't buy any gingerbread. Turns out the owner is not actually called Joe but Pete, an older man who clearly runs the place for fun. He is also the swimmer in the lake every morning. Hudson spoke to him for a few minutes while I stayed to the side, not quite sure how to interact. What does one do in my position? My awkwardness didn't last long, as Hudson kept glancing at me with a wink or soft smile.

After that visit, we moved to the restaurant on the lake called Catch 22. As soon as we entered, the staff looked at Hudson like he's royalty, yet Hudson didn't seem to notice. Instead, he asked one of the waitresses how her daughter was and asked the bus boy who brought us water how college was going.

Despite the lunchtime hour, it wasn't too busy, but still we nabbed a table away from everyone outside on the deck.

"Is there anyone in this town whose name you don't know?" I ask, quite taken by the man in front of me.

Hudson places his menu to the side. "I'm nobody special. I may have money and name, but I eat and sleep just like everyone. If I'm treated differently, then I have no hope of trying to live a somewhat laid-back life. I only use my fortune when I need to."

"Such as?"

He takes a sip of his iced tea. "A nice house, and when I found out I might have a son, I made sure I had the best investigator and lawyer around. And you better believe that I made sure Drew has a top-notch honeymoon too. I wasn't allowed to contribute to the wedding, as my daughter-in-law's family went traditional."

"Good for you, Hudson, and you have excellent taste in location when it comes to real estate. I don't know why I haven't been out here before. April mentioned Lake Spark a few times."

"A lot of people from the city head up to Wisconsin or Lake Galena. I'm not complaining, though, it keeps this little corner of the state a secret paradise." He untucks his sunglasses from his shirt and throws them on over his eyes. "Have an idea of what you want to eat?"

I examine the menu. "Probably the chicken club sandwich with fries. I'll do an extra Pilates class when I'm back in the city."

"There is actually a Pilates and yoga studio in the hotel, Dizzy Duck, that's the name. In case you want to join a class for future reference, in case you ever decide you want to return." His voice dances, and I know he's testing the waters to see what I'm feeling.

"I will remember that." I close my menu and sit tall just as the waitress arrives to take our order.

By the time food arrives, I realize I've lost track of time because I'm enjoying every word that Hudson speaks. It's a calm feeling that I felt the moment I woke up, but now it's just more… confirming. I'm where I should be.

"I had a bad relationship," I admit out loud, and I'm not sure why it rolled off my tongue without thought.

Hudson immediately darts his gaze to me and takes his sunglasses off. "Don't we all at some point in our lives?"

I shrug and stare at the fork in my hand. "It's a little more than that. We were living together very briefly. Not many people know. I was young, foolish, and it wasn't meant to be. My grandmother refusing to have him come to Friday dinners should have been a sign. She didn't approve, and she's a good judge of character."

Hudson moves up and out of his chair to sit next to me, and he scooches the chair closer to me. He's quick to take my hand and weave our fingers together. "What happened?"

A disruption, that's what happened. Or at least it felt like it.

I feel a numb hole in my stomach from the thought. "Can we just leave it at that for now? But let's just say that because of it, I'm even more cautious of what people may think. Besides, I buried myself in my career afterward, so I've moved on."

"I won't press, but it doesn't matter what people think. For years, I was called a lot of things, when I played ball and now when I coach. Too good for some and not good enough for others, you can't make everyone happy." His thumb glides along my hand as we remain linked.

"I know, but I still struggle to believe that. Anyways, I thought I would mention it because for some reason it made sense to tell you. I wanted to tell you. But now I just want to enjoy the afternoon together."

He smiles softly before kissing the curve of my shoulder gently, not caring that my skin is covered by my summer dress. "I'm getting to know you piece by piece. Normally I'm an all-at-once kind of guy, but for you, I think I could wait until I find every piece of your puzzle."

That's what I needed to hear, and it only makes me nuzzle my nose with his, eager to get back to his house.

———

OVER LUNCH, we laughed and enjoyed our meal before we ordered another few rounds of soft drinks because the early summer afternoon is just too perfect. But after a few drinks, I desperately needed the ladies' room, so I went to freshen up while Hudson settled the bill.

Returning to the table, I see that Hudson is talking to a little boy who looks to be about twelve.

"Next year, I'm in seventh grade, and I'm going to join the team as a linebacker," the kid explains.

I set my sunglasses on my head as I watch Hudson sign a napkin. "You are going to love it, but just remember to have fun. It's more important to play as a team than score. If you're too focused on scoring, then you'll never become a better player."

"Okay. What about the Winds? Will they reach the championship this year?"

Hudson laughs as he hands over the napkin to the boy who is clearly a fan. "Maybe. Either way, we'll play better than Wisconsin…" It earns him a laugh. I don't know much about football, but I do know that the Riders are the bitter rivals.

Hudson's eyes catch my own, and he quickly turns his attention back to the boy. "I think you're going to do great with football if that's something you enjoy. I'll be too busy with football season, but I'll tell Coach Goodwin over at the middle school which day to bring the team to watch practice." He touches the boy's shoulder and stands.

The boy's smile is from ear to ear before he runs off.

I slowly step closer, feeling my heart melt a little. "A fan?"

"Yeah. I can't say no to a kid. He was having lunch with his grandparents inside." Hudson grabs his phone and wallet from the table to slide them into his back pocket. "Shall we head back?"

I nod slowly, and I know what question is about to burst out, but I couldn't control it if I tried. "You want more children one day?"

"Oh, we're onto this conversation already?" he teases me.

I poke a finger at him. "Funny."

"Yeah. I do. I never got to do the baby/raising-a-little-human thing. I missed out. But I also know that a baby wouldn't be a replacement for Drew. However, I'm very aware that at this rate I'll be a grandfather before I'm a dad to a baby."

"Okay," is all I manage to say and grab his arm to drag him toward the exit.

But I know why I asked it. We have an age difference and that can sometimes mean we want different things in life, and while I am in no rush for kids now, or at least I don't think I am, I want the option one day.

The drive back is quiet, but more so because the weather and scenery just make it the type of drive that is better when nothing is said. It's peaceful and in truth lets me clear my thoughts.

Because later when Hudson is opening a bottle of wine in the kitchen while I change upstairs, I decide exactly what I want this evening.

As I walk into the living room, Hudson nearly drops the full glass of expensive champagne in his hand as he sits on the sofa. His eyes grow hungry as he watches me, surveys me, drinks in the view of my maroon satin nightie that barely covers my ass, and the thin straps fall off my shoulders when I move in a certain way.

I'm straddling him before he can speak. I plant a finger against his lips so he doesn't let a word escape, and I take the glass from his hands, drink a quick sip, then set it on the side table next to the ice bucket that holds the bottle of champagne.

His eyes survey me up and down as he hisses a breath. "About time."

I don't get to speak because his mouth covers my own before I get the chance.

Which is kind of what I was expecting when I strolled into the living room, because I want Hudson Arrows to take me the way he did the night we met.

9

PIPER

"I packed for all occasions." I give him a sultry look and rest my hands against his firm shoulders.

"You are such a good girl, Piper," Hudson says huskily, and I hear desire laced in his tone. He pulls my body closer and ensures that I'm positioned over his now-hard member, which causes me to let a moan of approval escape my lips.

He runs his hands up my body, and the material of my nighty drags with them to reveal that I have on a matching thong. He tips his head to get a better view, and after his inspection, he whistles in approval.

"A *very* good girl."

Our mouths meet and the kiss is warm and slow, a confirmation that this is what we want. He presses his firm lips to mine, and his tongue delves inside of my mouth. This man has the ability to kiss my breath away; I'm not immune to that fact floating in my head.

I break the kiss and reach over to the bucket of ice on the side table, and my body position gives Hudson ample opportunity to slide the strap down my shoulder and brush his lips along my skin and collarbone. The movement causing a sensation to spread across my breasts and my nipples to peak.

Grabbing a piece of ice, I hold it up to show him. "I want that night again," I whisper and press the cold cube against my neck, gliding it down slowly in the direction of my breasts.

Hudson's chuckle is a devilish rumble, and he acts quickly, because next thing I know, he grips my hips and tosses me off his lap where I land on my back along the couch cushion. Before I can even settle, he's hovering over me with confident eyes.

He coaxes my thighs wider, and he settles his body between them.

"As much as I want to watch you touch yourself with an ice cube, I think you'll remember that you won't get a chance to lead, but points for effort, baby." He pins my wrists above my head and leans over me, taking the ice from between my fingers in his teeth.

I remember. How could I forget? There's a reason this man is a coach. He likes to demand and be in control, and he has a winning mindset which works in my favor.

His eyes meet my own for one last check, and I can only nibble my bottom lip because my entire body is on fire, and my back lifts off the sofa to give into the feeling of the cube against me.

The burn of the cold ice isn't going to be enough to unwind me. Instead, Hudson is causing me to writhe from a desire that makes my pussy clench and ache. With the ice visible between his teeth, he uses his hand to pull the fabric down to reveal my nipple, and he squeezes and pinches, but it's more a quick caress or warning.

Using his mouth, he begins at the base of my neck and glides the ice to my nipple and circles, leaving a wet trail. He gives attention to each hard bud then pulls back slightly, showing me the ice is still trapped between his teeth. He does this while he pulls my legs up toward the ceiling, resting my ankles against his shoulder and he slides my thong up and off my body.

The moment my underwear flies through the air, he is already bringing my feet back to the couch. Keeping my legs wide, he dives in eagerly, the ice hitting my clit in one swift move, and I whimper before my breathing grows labored.

I let out a gasp and comb my fingers through his hair, then

tighten my grip to hold on. Looking down at him, I watch as he uses the ice with such skill, creating a pattern up and down on my pussy, only to land on my clit. He circles and circles, causing me to teeter toward an edge already arriving.

Hudson peers up at me because I know he likes to watch me, especially when he's holding my thighs to keep them parted.

"I'm almost there already," I warn him with a strained breath and my vision is hazy.

My statement grabs his attention because he abandons his efforts, brings his head up, but still holds me wide then spits out the cube onto the floor.

"I want you to come, but it has to be on my tongue. I love your taste; it lingers in my mouth for days." He nearly jumps off the couch before he picks me up and slings me over his shoulder.

"What are you doing?" I can hear the smile in my voice.

He walks in the direction of the stairs, spanking my ass in a playful manner, as my lingerie is in a mess around my waist. "No fucking way you're coming on my sofa. The first time in this house is going to be on my bed."

This man is in far too good of shape, as he's carrying me up the stairs like I'm a doll, and it's so fucking hot.

"But my first time coming in this house was last night," I correct him with a coy voice, reminding him I was alone in the guest room, knowing damn well that it's a tease and the truth.

He growls at my words as he walks into his room and sets me down in front of the bed. I take a second to take in my surroundings of a large room with windows wrapped around the corner to overlook the lake. The bed is big enough for four, and I'm taken back by the white linens with a soft green throw blanket and matching pillows.

But I'm snapped back into what is happening when I see Hudson eagerly getting his shirt off.

"As much as I want you against the window, we're going to deviate a little on the replay. On all fours, Piper. Middle of the bed," he orders as he swings his shirt to the side onto the floor, and he begins to work his jeans.

Doing as I'm told, I get onto the bed and glance over my shoulder. Hudson is now down to his boxer briefs, and when those come off, he touches his ready cock and inspects his view of me.

The sight of him makes me want to touch him, but he's pulling me to the edge of the bed on all fours and caresses my ass before sliding a finger between my folds.

"Soaking wet for me," he comments right before his mouth lands on my pussy.

"Oh fuck," I moan.

He's licking me from behind. "So good, so damn good," Hudson murmurs before he switches to a new pattern against my bundle of nerves, and he brings another finger inside of me.

My hands clench the sheets, and I'm already too wired from downstairs that it only takes a few more strokes and I'm at my cusp, shaking against his tongue and crying out in pure satisfaction.

But he doesn't let me rest, because he flips me like a pancake so I'm on my back, then he's over me in full command.

It's his eyes, however, that have me trapped at this moment. A momentary stillness as we both get a little lost in our reflection of lust and want.

He balances his weight on one arm, which enables the fingers on his other hand to sweep away some of my loose hair.

"You're beautiful but about ten times more so when you're naked on my bed about to let me take you deep." Hudson kisses my lips, at first a peck, then he takes his time kissing me like it matters.

And I think it does. Or maybe I hope it does.

I sink into the mattress and let his kiss carry me into another world. I wrap my legs around him which causes his cock to rub against my pussy and instantly twitch against my clit. It only makes me pull him closer against my body.

"Careful, I may just slide right into you because you're so ready," he warns as his lips brush along my cheek.

The idea causes my walls to pulse, eager for his words to be true.

I should be wiser right now, considering I'm not on birth control.

Reaching between us, I take hold of his cock and work from the base up in long smooth strokes. His eyes hood closed for a second before he rolls us so we're lying on our sides facing one another, offering him the opportunity to touch me again, which must have been his goal, as his fingers play with me.

"I can't control myself around you. You cast a magic spell or something. I'm going to take you the way you should be punished for making us wait a day, then I'm going to make you come the way you should when you're with me," he warns in a whisper.

"I don't even know what that means, but I need you inside of me." I roll my hips in waves, trying to get friction against his skin.

He scoffs a sexy-as-hell laugh before rolling off the bed. I peel off the scrap of satin dangling down my middle as Hudson grabs a condom.

But everything is happening so fast because before I get a chance to take a moment to breathe, he is back at the bed and guiding my body back to all fours, and his hand pushes my upper back down so my ass is in the air.

"Tell me if I get too rough," he reminds me.

I nod but say nothing, as the feeling of his fingers testing my entrance is a distraction, and the moment his tip enters me, I feel full again.

He hisses with pleasure as he works his way fully inside of me. "So tight."

Hudson goes deep and finds a rhythm, and when he's comfortable with his speed and pace, he grabs my arms and brings them behind my back to hold them down in a fold, and now I know what he means about fucking me for punishment.

My body surrenders to him, and I'm relying on Hudson to hang on. I have no use of my arms as they're held tight, and he drives in and out of me relentlessly. My breasts jiggle with every movement, and I couldn't stop my feral sounds if I tried.

"Deep and hard," he states.

I feel my lips curve into a smirk. That night when we met, he did the same, except I was pinned to a window during round one, rode him on top during round two, and the man had a thing for discovering my flexibility during round three.

And here we are now and he's fucking me as though I'm familiar, his, and he knows my limits. The funny thing is, he knows my body. There is a natural current between us where we are attuned to one another's needs and wants.

"Hudson," I nearly scream as he grunts when he's fully inside of me before he pulls out then goes back in.

"You're going to drive me insane." His breathing is heavy.

Hudson lets my arms go, but they don't move as he had held them in a bind and they need a moment to loosen. He spanks my ass then encourages me to lie on my back, but his eyes inform me that he's switching to his softer side.

He guides my body to scoot back until my head lands on a pillow, and he's over me, re-entering and bringing my knees up to my shoulders to take me deep. My hands come out to cradle his face and our eyes meet in a gaze.

Inside of me, he moves slower, allowing us time to soak up the moment.

"You make me want it all at once." His tone is missing his confident edge. I wonder if he means position or maybe… us.

This is the most insane notion of my life. It must take more than a night and a few good days to feel like the world turns differently.

I shake the notion from my head and plant my mouth on his, kissing him as he moves inside of me.

We nuzzle our noses and let our mouths explore down our necks as we move together with every thrust.

"I remember the way you took me. I want you in my mouth again, I want to be on top of you and for you to fuck me, guiding me just the way you like it," I explain in a daze of lust.

It causes Hudson to half-grin, and he slides his hand to the back of my neck. "Next round. Right now, I need to do what I've wanted to do since you showed up at my house."

I feel my impending orgasm and reach between us, only to have my hand pushed away. Hudson's knowing grin reminds me that he will handle it, and I feel the imprint of his long finger pressing against my clit.

He moves slightly and brings my legs to one side as he reangles to take me in a spooning position, but I'm able to stare straight up into his eyes that haven't broken contact.

"It's okay, baby, let go," he murmurs as he continues to draw a line along my collarbone with his lips.

I can't take this anymore, and my hand touches my forehead as I pant and moan.

"That's it. All over my cock, show me how much you enjoy me inside of you. How good you take my cock. Come on, baby, I won't come until you're trembling."

His praise takes me over the edge, and I begin to shake and tighten around his length as I coo his name. He brings his hand to softly cradle my jaw. "That's it, just like that." He speaks against my skin, his warm breath adding to my sensory overload.

I cry out as my orgasm draws to a finish, panting, my entire body heavy. I feel dizzy and almost as if I might black out, and my body is his as Hudson moves of his own accord to get himself to the other side.

He joins our hands together against the mattress, and a slew of curses comes out of his mouth as his hips buck and still, reaching his freefall.

Hudson is careful not to crush me, but he collapses next to me, keeping our bodies close and staying inside of me. He kisses the curve of my shoulder as we both lie in bliss.

We look at one another and chuckle in the backs of our throats before kissing really quick.

"There is more to come," he confirms.

● 10

HUDSON

Walking into my room, I see a beautiful angel sleeping in my bed. Naked, thoroughly fucked, and showered in the morning sunlight.

Sliding off my boxers and then crawling back into bed, I wrap Piper into my arms and tuck her head underneath my chin. I've already noticed on several occasions how she molds perfectly into my arms. She sleeps way too peacefully.

I slept deep, and admittedly, that isn't normally the case when there is someone else between the sheets. They either move too much, breathe too hard, or I just let them stay because it was routine.

Not with Piper.

I still woke early because that's just my internal clock, but Tuesdays are my quieter days, and I don't have anything on the training or meeting schedule today. Still, I went downstairs to make sure the coffee machine had enough beans for when we have breakfast later, then returned upstairs and stood on the balcony to catch the sunrise. I thought of waking Piper, but she needs her rest after last night, as we were at it until the early hours, and we will be doing a repeat later too if I have any influence on the matter.

She hums a sound, and I feel her shuffle in my hold. "Mmm, good morning." Her drowsy murmur is weakening me, I feel it.

My eyes dip down to see the line of her lips stretch, and she has an elated look, with her eyes fluttering open.

"Morning."

I should let us lie like this, but she's wiggling against me, pressing her body into mine, and her heated look informs me that her version of waking up isn't the sweet scene I attempted to create in my head.

"Piper." I chuckle softly before I roll us slightly until I'm on my back and her body is splayed on top of me.

She presses her finger against my lips. "Shh."

I don't protest, nor would I ever. The feeling of her hand wrapping around my cock, gripping and pumping to see if I'm ready to go, has me slipping into another world, one where I am equally relaxed yet have no patience.

I quickly slide my fingers between us, and I feel how she woke up ready. I attempt to reach to the side table, but it's hopeless, and Piper completes the task of grabbing the little square package.

I get my guy secure in record time, and when I feel her pussy wrap around my cock, we both moan in harmony.

She places popcorn kisses along my face as her forearms rest by my ears. Her body is flush on top of me, and my hands hold her hips in place as I thrust up into her.

We simmer in this position for a few minutes, using kisses instead of words until that turns into panting breaths.

By the time she is completely spent on top of me, I'm not sure leaving this bed is even in our cards for today.

I stroke her hair and kiss her forehead, mumbling against her skin. "This is how every morning with you should be."

"I agree."

Energy must overcome her, as she rolls off me with the sheet tangled around her body. The color on her cheeks is my doing and a sense of pride roars inside of me.

"Shower then breakfast?" She seems wide awake now.

"Lead the way." I grin.

She yanks my arm and leads us to my bathroom. The shower is quick, but she takes the opportunity to caress my body, and I do the same to her. In no time, I'm out on the patio in cotton shorts and t-shirt, sitting on one of the lounge chairs, looking at the lake with mugs of coffee in my hands. I see Piper walking toward me in yoga pants and a tank top, and I realize this woman has me wrapped around her finger, and I'm not complaining.

Handing her the coffee, she comes to sit between my legs with her back to my stomach. Nice. I like this position too.

"I'll bring my sketch pad out here later if you don't mind."

"Not at all. I'll do some reading and we can call it a domesticated morning."

A lazy morning of breakfast, coffee, reading, and Piper sounds idyllic. We can do laid back, and I appreciate that she seems to enjoy the little things in life.

"This is perfect. The air is so clear and crisp. Not too cold or warm, and just looking at the lake and trees makes me feel so relaxed," she mentions before taking a sip of her coffee.

"Here I thought it was what transpired last night that did it," I retort.

She glances over her shoulder with a smirk then kisses me quickly on the mouth before resettling into our embrace. "You don't have coaching stuff this morning?"

"Nah, you somehow have impeccable timing and had your way with me on the perfect night of the week. Tuesdays are the league's down day. For now, I'm free, but when the season starts then Tuesdays are my days to go over videos with the other coaches."

"When does game season start?"

"Well, we have summer training starting in a few weeks, then September to February is football season, and February depends on how good we are. Wow, you really know nothing about football, and you live in Chicago." I'm still astonished by this fact.

She shrugs. "I'm the exception."

"That you are." I purse my lips against the rim of the mug for a second. "Anyway, when it's season time, my schedule is crazy. Trainings, games, management meetings. We travel half the time. It kind of takes time to adjust if you're not used to it." I hear it in my voice that I'm throwing out testers to see if she can handle it.

"Sounds grueling." She sounds unenthused.

Oh, not what I was hoping to hear.

She continues, "I guess it just means you need someone waiting for you when you get home. And if I get to look at this view every day, then I may just volunteer for the job." Her tone is peppier.

I wrap my arms tighter around her, as her answer is good enough for now. "Listen, with summer training coming up, I won't be in the city, as the training facility isn't far from here. Will you come back?"

Piper moves to angle her body to look at me. There's a look that I can only describe as vulnerability on her face. "You want me to come back?"

"Have I done anything to you in the last 48 hours that says differently?"

She licks her lips. "You have been a perfect host. But coming back… I have no clue what we're doing," she states.

"Getting to know one another. Not trying to run away from this chemistry between us Enjoying the view. The list goes on," I assure her.

The corner of her mouth tugs into a soft smile. Clearly, she likes my answer.

"Can we talk about the topic you kind of brushed under the rug?" she asks.

"Which is?" I take another sip of my coffee then set it to the side table.

"April."

I tip my nose up in recognition then sigh. "You know, I always tell my son that it's only complicated if you make it complicated. As I said, she's a big girl, but I think you're closer with my niece than I am with her. I love the kid, and I'm happy she asked me to walk her down the aisle, but I don't see her as much as I used to. I would like to think she would find the coincidence of our meeting charming."

Piper subtly shakes her head. "That's not April. Besides, I'm not sure what we would even tell her because I have no idea what we're doing, but not telling her seems like a lie too. There is no win, but I know she will be mortified when she learns you're the mystery guy, considering what I told her. I just don't want to take away from her moment of happiness with her engagement. Actually, I just don't want to lose a friend, and this could be a one-way ticket to that."

I lean back on the chair and take Piper with me. "Okay." I hear defeat in my tone.

"Okay?"

"You said it yourself that you're not sure what we're doing." There is a tinge of annoyance in my tone and not because of Piper, but at myself, because I don't have a clear answer either, other than I'm completely infatuated.

"This may implode one day, Hudson, but I don't want that to happen right now," she adds.

I blow out a breath. "I *maybe* see your point. By the way, my son kind of knows."

Piper immediately comes up to sitting and presses her hand against my chest. "What?!"

I laugh at her facial expression. "Drew isn't April. We have an unusual relationship, we talk about things, and when you decided to call me, he was there, so I explained."

"Which details?" She seems concerned.

"Who you are. But don't worry, he'll only tell his wife."

"You're crazy, Hudson." Now she seems entertained.

I take the mug of coffee from her hand so we have nothing blocking our ability to touch. "Listen, you're right, and we'll keep our secret… for now." I slide my fingers through her hair until I'm holding her head firmly in place. "As much as I love the idea of this place being our hideaway from the world, eventually, if this thing between us is something more, then it will come out."

And I hope she can handle that because I see something unrecognizable in her eyes.

"Tell me you'll come back next week?" I feel almost desperation inside of me. I need more of her.

She nuzzles her cheek against my wrist. "I think… I can make that happen."

"Can and want are two different things," I inform her.

The corner of her mouth curves. "I maybe shouldn't, but I can't seem to say no… I want it to happen."

That was the answer I needed, and I cover her lips with my own in a demanding kiss.

"I have a week then to decide what I'm going to do with you next time," I confirm just as I slide my hand up under the fabric of her shirt.

PIPER

ooking into my cup of tea, I dip the bag as I sit waiting at a table. I feel a smile threatening to stretch on my mouth as I recall in my head the last few days.

Gosh, Hudson does something to make me feel alive.

Every conversation is light, every joke a laugh, and he is one of those people who lives life without a care in the world. And he's asking me to come along for the ride.

That's what it is, right? Fun. That's what it should be, but I can't shake the feeling that Hudson Arrows is a lightning strike that hits deep inside of me.

The pure thought spreads warmth inside of me, and I smile to myself.

"Hey, Ginger," April greets me as she slides her purse onto the high-top table.

I gently shake my head to bring me back to the present. "Hey there, stranger."

"I ordered a gin and tonic when I came in. Why are you drinking tea?" She smiles in bewilderment as she adjusts her hair and sits on the stool.

Looking at my drink and then April, my mouth parts open but

stalls. In truth, I'm drinking tea to ensure alcohol doesn't influence what I say to April. Already, I feel slightly sour in my stomach from my lies, and a few nerves float inside of me.

"Saving myself for my grandmother's dinner tomorrow. You know how she gets with serving wine," I explain half-heartedly.

April seems to accept that answer, and she thanks the waiter for bringing her drink. "How was Austin?" She sips from her lemon-slice-rimmed glass.

"Austin?"

"Yeah, you had that fashion expo thing. You went to Texas, no?"

Right, I did say that. "It was normal. Nothing exciting, just good to network. So, tell me about wedding planning." I'm quick to divert our topic.

April frowns. "Okay, I guess."

"What do you mean? Haven't you started to talk about venues or something?"

She shrugs and takes another drink. "Not really. Jeff has been busy this week."

I reach out to touch her hand. "That kind of conversation needs a lot of attention, so if he has been busy, then it's probably not the best time," I do my best to assure her. Squeezing her hand, I tell her something to make her smile. "I began to play around with a design for your dress. I forgot the sketches at my office, which by the way I'll need to move out of next month. The landlord confirmed it today."

"Yay for dress designs. Boo for office. What are you going to do?"

I bob my head side to side as I sink my shoulders and lean back. "I don't know. Something inside me says to wait it out and have my living room become a chaotic nightmare of boxes until I figure out a more concrete option. My grandmother has a storage unit in her building that she said I could borrow. I'm trying not to think about it."

"Did my lobster statue curse you?" She attempts to smile.

"Nah. He may still bring me good luck, but I don't see it yet."

April's eyes scan around the room and then she scoffs a laugh.

"What's so funny?"

"My uncle is on the TV."

My eyes snap in the direction of the flatscreen over the bar. When I arrived it was playing the sports channel… which now in retrospect shouldn't be surprising.

I can't look away. I can't hear what he's saying, but Hudson is sitting in an interview, with that winning grin that makes me want to melt. The screen bounces back and forth between him speaking and a replay of a football game.

"He always knows how to schmooze for the camera. I remember this documentary, a sort of history of Hudson Arrows becoming one of the best coaches of our time. They really missed out on interviewing me." I can hear her joke in the last sentence.

I study the screen more intently and realize the replay is of a younger Hudson playing football, before the blonde-haired interviewer asks another one of her questions, which causes Hudson to smile in this suave manner that makes me internally shake my head, amused. He's charming everyone.

But that just makes it even better because something I've learned about Hudson is that he is genuinely the kind of guy who wears his heart on his sleeve. It isn't for show.

"How come you never mentioned what he does?" I wonder aloud but can't tear my eyes away from the screen. Partly because I don't think I will ever get bored of looking at Hudson.

"He's just my uncle, no different than me. Besides, you already know he's down to earth."

My eyes whip back into April's direction, with fear running to my heart. "I do?"

"Yeah. I mean, you spoke with him at my engagement party, right? What did you two talk about?" she innocently asks before playing with the lemon from her drink.

"You mean when you left to go speak with someone?" I hope that's what she means, and I'm relieved when she nods her head. "Oh, um, you know, nothing crazy. He asked about work and how I know you." I take another sip of tea to hide any unease that may show on my face.

Only a few minutes in and I realize that I'm a horrible liar.

"Well, I'm sure he didn't flash around the fact that he is the highest-paid coach in the league or that everyone is waiting for him to show up with a Mrs. Arrows any day now," she casually mentions.

I cough a little from unease. "Really?"

"I think so. He hasn't really dated in a while or at least since his son entered the picture. Plus, the rumor is my uncle Bay will get traded next season."

"Why is that?"

"Another team may sweep in with a better offer, that's what the public notion is. But I think he may actually trade in pro-ball for college ball because he wants a bit of a quieter life. He isn't a recluse by any means, but he likes to retreat to his lake house." April raises a finger. "I should totally ask if we can borrow his house one weekend for a bachelorette party. You would love his house. Well, I mean, his neighbor is a pain in the ass, but we can just go during baseball season to avoid him."

I try to evade her eyes and only awkwardly nod.

This is unbearable. I just want to scream that I've already seen his amazing house, and yes, I know that Hudson enjoys his own little world on Lake Spark.

"Hey, so while I was waiting, the table behind us had a bit of a bombshell conversation happening. Crazy, really. The one friend told her other friend that she hooked up with her dad. What does a person do in that situation?" A total made-up story, but I need to test the waters somehow.

April flashes me wide eyes. "Wow, I missed that? Damn. Could you imagine? I mean, total end of a friendship there. What a betrayal, right?"

My throat feels tighter. "Right." That was weak-sounding, I'm sure of it.

"What a way to start an evening. Wild. Speaking of dating, any news on mystery guy?"

"Oh, uhm. Yeah, total bust. I reached out and it's just not meant to be," I lie yet again, securing more points for the award of bad friend.

"Other fish in the sea, right?" She gives me a consoling look.

"Absolutely."

"Want to head to the flea market next weekend?"

I pull on my earring and think up an excuse. But half the truth is okay, or at least a start. "I can't. I'm going to be out of town."

"Again?"

"Yeah, heading out for a family weekend. My grandmother mentioned something about some fancy hotel in Wisconsin with cheese and wine. Nobody says no to my grandmother."

"Sounds fun."

I feel like a horrible friend right now. April is sitting in front of me, oblivious, and I'm selfishly lying to her because I'm giving in to desire.

I look up at the television again and see a scoreboard comparing game wins between Hudson coaching the team and the former coach. The numbers don't interest me, but the picture of the man does.

In that moment, it's what I need to remind myself that I had a plan for good reason. I don't know yet how to explain this to April, and for the first time in years I want to enjoy being with a man before addressing the consequences, or maybe I'm hoping that the end result isn't a consequence at all but rather a choice.

And I can't seem to figure out why I'm ignoring the risks so blatantly. Probably, because I'm counting down the days until I see him again.

12

HUDSON

With a solid soundtrack from Live on full blast from the speaker in my car, I drive along the road back to my house. I'm in a good mood because Piper is visiting again. I texted her this morning to ask for any requests for our menu this weekend, as I was heading to the grocery store, and she said she wanted me to surprise her. It made my trip to the store a little harder but by no means impossible.

What has been impossible is controlling the excitement that's been filling my lungs since the last time I saw her. This is what's supposed to happen when you want to be with someone, right?

Well, I mean, I know something is different because every time I think of Piper and me escaping the world together, my mind runs to the idea that maybe one day she will be waiting in the second row to watch me coach a game, there to support me as the woman in my life. I would be lying if I said that spending more than a few weekends with Piper hasn't come up in my mind.

I'm thinking of a longer timeline.

Arriving back to my street and crossing through the security gate, I notice that my neighbor, Spencer, is here talking to his contractor. I haven't seen him since my son's wedding.

He nods his head at me in greeting.

Rolling down my window, I quickly call out, "I need to drop some stuff in the fridge but want to grab a drink in five minutes?"

Spencer grins and lifts his sunglasses off his eyes to rest on his short brown hair that has been lightened by the sun. "Deal. Plus, my house is a mess, so your place it is." A cheeky look spreads on his face before stern lines return on his face when he glances at his contractor.

I laugh to myself as I drive away because clearly construction on his place isn't going to plan. Spencer is an athlete, focused and strong-willed. The pressure of the team is on his shoulders, as he has the winning arm that the media focuses on at every game. So yeah, he can be a bit... stiff to some.

After I get my car in the garage and unpack the groceries, I grab two bottles of Matchbox beer because that stuff is perfect for a warm summer day. When I head out to the patio, it's just in time, as Spencer is rounding the corner.

"Lucky me, I get laid-back Spencer. I would hate to be your contractor right now." I offer him the bottle.

Spencer scoffs a laugh. "I'm going crazy. They are behind schedule yet again and telling me the indoor pool is the issue, and I told them to sort it out, as it's not negotiable."

We both sit on a few chairs in the mid-afternoon sun.

"What are you even doing back? It's baseball season."

"I have a mini-break between home games and figured I would check on my place since I'm eager to move back in. You know? Avoid the city, humans in particular."

I chuckle at his humor. "Well, I can understand that and hope the house is ready soon because the noise some days makes me want to egg your house."

Spencer grins as he takes a sip. "I'm perfect neighbor quality."

I tip my bottle to him. "That you are."

"What's been happening? Heard from Drew?"

I shake my head. "No, he's on his honeymoon but should be back next week. Thanks again for coming out to his wedding, considering it's baseball season."

"No need to thank me, happy to have been there. Any plans this weekend? I can get you seats for my game. Our team PR loves that stuff."

"Can't. Have plans."

He raises his brows. "Plans? You say it with a ridiculous smile. What's going on?"

"Nothing."

"You're such a bad liar."

True. Lying isn't for me, which is exactly what I'm doing to my niece. However, I feel it is more delaying the truth and allowing the opportunity for this thing between Piper and me to be explored and built. To me, that isn't lying.

Looking at my watch, I know Piper will be here any moment.

"No fucking way." Spencer seems entertained.

My eyes snap up to see him grinning.

"Hudson Arrows has a woman in his life."

"What makes you say that?" I can't deny the look of contentment forming on my face.

Spencer sets his bottle to the side. "You're expecting someone, that I can tell."

"There is someone," I confirm.

His eyes widen. "Do tell."

"No, because there is nothing to confirm or deny."

He eyes me skeptically. "Really bad liar," he reiterates. "What, did you meet in a bar or something?"

I don't answer.

Spencer chuckles and takes my lack of response as an answer. He crosses his arms over his chest. "Wow. That sounds unlike you. I mean, you know a good bar or two, but I've never seen you pick up someone at a bar. She must be something if you took a play from my book."

I lean back in my chair. "Sometimes, someone comes along who makes you do things."

"Shit. I haven't really seen you like this. You look rejuvenated, and I mean you looked pretty fucking happy at the wedding but what father wouldn't at his son's wedding? How long has this been going on?"

I sigh because I could use an ear. "Not long. We kind of met, then didn't reconnect until a few weeks later. She somewhat runs her own timeline." I leave out the detail she is the one who left before I woke. As much as I don't love that minor detail, I'm at peace with it now, as the world conspired with us to ensure we met again.

"Does she? Or are you just completely smitten that you let her run the show?" Spencer challenges me.

I lick my lips before biting the corner of my mouth. "I know patience isn't your strong suit, but sometimes it pays off. Besides, so far it's working, I mean, she isn't running away."

"I just kind of assumed that you would be so persistent that the poor woman wouldn't know what hit her, or are you just waiting for the right moment to throw in that aspect?"

"Hey, I'm being persistent, just adding a gentle touch," I justify.

"Hope it works. Of all the people I know, you are the guy who should have a woman locked down because you're just meant for that stuff. You've been waiting for years to find someone and always put other people first. I mean, damn, since Drew entered your life, it's like..." He brings his hands up to an uneven level with one another to indicate priority. "Football, Drew."

"Move that football hand down a notch. My kid goes first," I correct him proudly.

Spencer does as I say before bringing one hand even lower. "Then Hudson putting himself first is here."

I sigh because maybe he's right. Except only until recently, because now I am completely putting myself higher on the scale. I want to be selfish, and Piper is the reason that feeling resonates inside of me.

"That may be changing," I tell him.

His hands fall down. "Fucking hope so."

"Why in the world are you talking like you are the authority on this?" Spencer is me maybe ten years ago. He has no interest in settling down with someone, and he has reasons for that too.

Spencer shrugs. "No clue, except I envision you with a woman who dotes on you and preferably bakes so I get a neighbor who brings me cookies."

"She isn't much of a baker or cook."

"Huh, what good is she to you then?" he jokes.

"She is a lot of things. Good things. My blood flows differently lately, that kind of good."

"Does mystery woman have a name?" He takes a sip from his bottle.

The sound of the sliding door to my patio opening draws our attention to Piper who hesitantly steps out, as she must have just arrived.

I'm quick to get up and walk to her. "Hey. I didn't hear my security app ping me."

As soon as I reach her and touch her shoulder, I notice she seems out of sorts.

"Yeah, there was a construction worker keeping the gate open so they could get a truck of cement through, and your front door was unlocked, so I just kind of rolled right in… Security fail," she quips as her eyes stay fixed on Spencer.

Ah, I realize we have an audience, and she is slightly uncomfortable.

"This is my neighbor, Spencer."

Spencer stands and walks to her with his hand out to greet her. "Hi there. Spencer Crews. You must be..." He's waiting for me to make an introduction.

"This… is Piper." I think for a second. "She's a friend of April's and…" I have no idea why I'm trying to hide this. I have no desire to, but I'm following Piper's cues.

"I came here to discuss…" Piper seems to be coming up with a story. "A bridal shower that I need to throw for April… here." She bites her bottom lip.

I rub a hand across my jaw while Spencer looks between us and snorts a laugh.

"Well, aren't you two obvious. You may want to come up with a better cover story." I notice Spencer is looking between Piper and me, studying us. A droll smile forms when his brain seems to connect the age difference, and he clearly approves.

I clear my throat before Spencer makes a joke because I know he will. "Spencer here plays baseball."

Piper looks between us, bewildered. "Okay."

I love that she is completely unaffected that a star athlete is in front of her.

"Piper isn't into sports. Your name means nothing to her," I explain to Spencer.

Spencer looks at her, impressed. "She's a keeper."

Piper politely smiles in response.

Spencer points a thumb at me. "Hope this one has enough stamina for you?" There it is. The age reference.

Piper chuckles under her breath but also blushes at the same time. "Perfectly in shape."

My neighbor flashes an overdone smile at her answer. "I'll leave you two alone. I need to head back to the city anyhow. Nice meeting you." He tips his head slightly with a little wave.

"Likewise."

"Good luck with your game this weekend," I call out as Spencer disappears.

I then turn my attention to Piper who I'm beyond happy is in front of me.

"I wasn't expecting anyone else but you," she mentions.

I wrap an arm around her middle and walk her over to my chair. "Relax. He's my neighbor, friend, and a pain in my ass sometimes. He won't tell anyone that you've come here to get your Hudson fix."

She gives me a tight smile, but all worries get thrown out the window when I sit down and pull her onto my lap, with her arms looping around my neck.

"Hudson fix? Is that what I'm calling it?" She has a cute-as-fuck curious look on her face.

"I don't care what you call it, just kiss me, because I've been starving for you for days." I lean in to capture her willing mouth.

Kissing her again brings back the feeling of being with her. Instinct has me believing that her in my arms is where she is supposed to be, because despite every angle that I've tried to look at it, with her I feel grounded.

She murmurs a sound of satisfaction before dragging her lips along mine. "The entire drive here I couldn't stop smiling," she admits.

I retreat a little to allow myself to look at her face, and I run my fingers through her silky hair. "That's promising. I was worried we might need a pinecone to hit you on the head again to knock sense into you."

She nearly snorts out a laugh. "That was such a ridiculous moment."

"You're in luck that it didn't happen when I met you. Otherwise, I would have to include that detail in the how-we-met story."

She nuzzles into my neck, and I pick up on the fact she inhales deeply, as if she's taking in my scent. I don't call her out on it, instead relishing the thought that she is taking in this minute.

"Was there traffic?"

"A little. I mean, this weather is fantastic, so people seem to be escaping the city. It'll be nice to just sit out here all weekend, preferably while I watch you cook."

"You're just using me for my view," I joke and tickle her side.

She begins to wiggle, and in retrospect this move was a bad call because it's causing friction against my dick, and I wanted to romance her a little before I have my way with her.

Piper giggles until I stop, wrapping her tighter in my arms before we kiss to calm us down. A soothing kiss that feels as natural as the air I breathe.

She dips her tongue into my mouth, and I welcome her. I'll give her anything she asks for.

I cradle her cheek and swipe my thumb across her skin. "What am I going to do with you?"

"I don't know. I gave you a week to think about it, remember?" she reminds me with knowing eyes.

"Oh, don't you worry, that part I know. I mean, should I wine and dine you first or throw you over my shoulder and take you upstairs?" I ask her seriously.

Piper hops off my lap to stand and holds out her hand. "That's an easy decision."

I join her in standing, with the corners of my mouth twisting, as I want to smirk. "Oh yeah?"

"Uh-huh." Her voice turns sultry, and she grabs the fabric of my shirt to pull me to her. She steps closer and her lips come back to my ear to whisper, "To the kitchen, I'm starving."

Looking at her, I realize that she is dead serious, and as much as I hate that answer, I equally love it because I want to hear about her week and talk. Besides, when we go to my room today, then we sure as hell aren't leaving it until breakfast.

————

FOR DINNER, I kept it simple, with Halloumi with grilled red onion, asparagus, and a vinaigrette pasta, for which Piper fawned over me in amazement that I cook. We ate casually at the counter before grabbing a bottle of wine and headed out to the dock to catch the last of the evening sun before it sets. I even turned on the decorative lightbulbs that hang along the dock.

We sit opposite each other on a blanket with wine glasses. There is a very gentle breeze on this warm June evening. I hope we survive, as the mosquitos may get us, but the sound of the water lapping gently is a soothing backdrop.

"I know I need a boat here but maybe next season," I explain.

"I guess it would be nice." Piper's lips tilt into a smirk. "So, the other day I was with April at a bar…"

I'm not sure why I'm scared. It isn't because she mentions April, but I'm fairly confident that it's the thought of some guy Piper's age probably trying to pick her up that has me on edge.

I adjust my neck in discomfort but patiently wait for her to finish her sentence.

"You were on the TV in some documentary."

I chuckle in relief before taking a sip of my wine. "Oh yeah?"

"About your football career."

I recall a documentary I did two years ago when I signed with the Winds. "They still show that thing?" I look into my glass, but I feel Piper's eyes on me.

"Yep. Can't lie, I was intrigued. Anyway, April mentioned that there is a rumor that you might get traded or something."

I peer up, wondering if it's concern that is laced in her tone. I swear that I sense it. "Only rumor. My contract with the team is for two more seasons, and they're already negotiating with my agent for a renewal, but I said I won't give an answer until mid-season. Otherwise, the option of another team somewhere else is on the table."

"Oh." She quickly occupies herself with her wine.

I set my glass to the side and take her free hand in mine, interlinking our fingers and staring at our dancing hands. "You can't get rid of me that easily. I'm staying around. If it's another team, I'm thinking of leaving pro-ball and moving to college ball in Hollows which isn't far from here."

Her lips twitch, and I have my answer; somewhere inside her, she was worried.

"Wouldn't that be a step down?"

"Don't particularly care," I say honestly and let her hand go to lean back on my propped elbows. "In the coming years, I expect a change in rhythm. It's been a grind since I was eighteen. First in college ball, then pro, then coaching. A break or slower pace is just what I'm after. Fuck, my son will probably make me a grandfather soon."

"I hope you get what you want."

"I always do, Piper."

"I could use your confidence in career direction. With my lease ending on my office space, I need to hurry to outsource a few things and really make operations run smooth for my online store." All week we sent little messages to ask how each other was, and she mentioned her talk with the landlord. "I began to look into a few options, and now I know why my grandmother always recommends that I sign a contract with department stores, as they do the hard work. But I still think this is right for me, keeping it small-scale."

"It's only complicated if you make it that way."

She smiles at me. "Your philosophy, how can I forget."

"Take time and assess your risks, and maybe they're not risks at all." I'm referring to her business, but I think it's a front for really meaning me.

Piper contemplates for a few seconds. "You're right. I'm sure fresh lake air will give me some perspective, and possibly a trip to Jolly Joe's if we can swing it. I mean, town seems pretty packed which doesn't equate to staying under the radar."

I tilt my head and study her which only entertains me. "You mean for you and me? Are you worried someone might plaster us online? The good-looking coach and the hot-as-fuck lingerie designer?"

She looks away from me. "Something like that."

"Piper, if that happens, then I would be honored to be linked to you, if that's what the millennials are calling it these days." I take another sip of my wine.

She points a finger at me. "That's because you, Hudson, don't care what people think."

"Nope. I don't." I survey her facial expression, and then it dawns on me that something about this runs deeper. "But you do care."

"I don't know what I think about people's opinions, to be honest."

I invite her to come into my arms. "Why is that?"

She crawls on her hands and knees before nestling into my chest. So innocent, but I'm already imagining what she's got on underneath her skirt. Piper is about to speak but hesitates. "The sun is about to set."

Clearly, she doesn't want to talk about the root of her thoughts, and I don't push. But I can't say that I'll do the same tomorrow.

Instead, I bring her with me as my back rests against the blanket.

"For someone who may or may not care what people think, you know you're in my arms on a lake, and anyone could sail on by while I make you come."

Her eyes shoot up to look at my face. "What?"

"All afternoon and evening you've kept me waiting to touch your soaking panties, but that ends right now."

13

PIPER

He kisses me, and it's as warm as the summer air. Hudson's hand roams down my body and then slides up my thigh, dragging the fabric of my skirt with it on the journey.

"You know how much damn control it's taken to be this fucking patient since you arrived?" He speaks against my lips before nipping the corner of my mouth.

I bite my bottom lip as I smile to myself and press my fingertips against his chest to allow me to see his face. He adjusts to lying on his side, but his hand doesn't leave my thigh.

"Want to take this back inside?" I ask.

"No, I don't." Hudson's tone is so matter-of-fact, and his eyes pierce me as the sunset casts an orange hue over his face. "The thing is, it'll be dark the moment that sun disappears over the pines, but I'm not going to wait. You were a good girl and came prepared by wearing a skirt to cover where I put my fingers, and I have every intention of making you come because I've smelled your arousal all afternoon."

His fingers inch closer to the line of my panties and I feel my breath catch. My nipples turn rock hard, and my clit swells from a desperate need for him to touch me.

"That's some statement there, Coach."

He growls into my neck and uses his teeth to grab hold of some skin in a playful manner. "I haven't heard you call me that yet, but I'm in favor of it."

I instantly reach my hand down to touch the bulge in his pants. "Let's go inside so I can taste you."

He tsks me just as his fingers curl around the fabric of my panties and pull them to the side. "I said here, Piper. Trust me, nobody will know, and later you can ride me, with your beautiful tits bouncing… Nah, scratch that, I want to see your latest creation."

My laugh turns to a hitched surprised whimper, and my head falls back because he's running his long finger along my pussy then circling my clit.

"Soaking wet." His finger enters me, and he pumps his hand. "I have every intention to lick you later, preferably while you sit on my face, lean over, and suck my cock, but we don't need to get into logistics now."

There it is. Hudson's ability to sound serious but always bring humor to the moment makes me smile.

"Whatever you say, Coach." My voice is breathy because another finger is inside of me, and his thumb gives attention to my little bud.

My body moves with his fingers, finding a rhythm, and I look down to see his hand moving under my skirt, and I part my thighs wider.

I moan as he picks up the pace, and I'm not sure if it's Hudson or the thrill of anyone being able to see this, but I feel that I'm on a cusp of an orgasm already.

"You are so fucking beautiful when you let go."

Our eyes are fixed as his hand and fingers work their magic.

"Take me," I insist, and it surprises even me. But I'm about to burst because I feel my inhibitions letting go and my trust is literally in Hudson's hands. "Slide into me from behind." It'll look like we're cuddling.

He chuckles softly under his breath. "Impatient."

"I'm serious," I wail a plea, and I reach for the button of his pants. "I've been waiting for you all week too."

Hudson ignores my request and focuses on making me come. "You are something magnificent, and don't you worry, I plan on living inside of you tonight. But right now, come so we can enjoy this sunset."

I can't answer as I begin to unravel around his fingers, my entire body's senses heightened.

And when I finally succumb from my orgasm and his fingers leave me, he lifts my skirt slightly and tilts his head down to inspect. That smirk forms with pride before he covers me again and straightens my skirt.

While I recover my breath, I watch him taste his fingers, and I nearly pant again. Then when he gives me a bruising kiss, concern hits me that maybe we are more passionate than anything.

That thought scares me, because you can't build a relationship on passion alone.

But then he tenderly kisses me, with his palm cupping my face.

"See? Your name suits you. What I like about you Piper is that even if you hesitate, you are brave enough to try things. You just need the reminder that you are willing to try, and I mean with every-thing in life. Me, your work, me again, and if you want to attempt to cook dinner then I wouldn't say no."

I laugh, so ridiculously happy. "I think I'm only more willing to try things when I'm around you."

"That's called trust, and I'll be damned, but you also bring out a trusting side of me too. Now before you overthink it, lie with me and let's look at that damn sky."

The feeling of his arms wrapping around me erases any doubts.

"Did they seriously put a jellybean in your coffee instead of sugar?" I ask in awe as Hudson and I walk out of Jolly Joe's.

"Yep." Hudson proudly takes a sip of coffee.

Last night after staying a little longer out on the dock, we went upstairs. He was very pleased with my choice of a cotton-and-lace black nightie. It was one of my simple designs, but the material feels like heaven on your skin, and it easily falls off too. Rolling around in bed with Hudson was a wonderful way to spend a Friday night, even if I'm slightly sore today.

We slept in—well, to us, nine is sleeping in—got dressed and headed into town to beat the crowds.

I reach into the paper bag and take out a cinnamon roll from the bakery next door and bite into the sticky dough. "Yum! Wow, this is… what? I mean, is this magic?"

It's a damn good cinnamon roll, which people forget is not an easy thing to make. Any sign of dry dough and it's game over.

"Probably. Sometimes they have orange rolls and those things… Christ, I'm gone."

Hudson offers me his arm, and I accept without thought. Well, not entirely true, but I throw caution to the wind.

"We can hit up the farmers' market and pick out some stuff for dinner, then maybe go for a walk up in the state park," he suggests.

"Sounds perfect."

I look around and see that nobody is taking much notice of us. The occasional passerby says *good morning*, but people seem to do that for everyone here.

"I kind of hate myself for living in the city and not trying to live in a small town. But my friends and grandmother are there, and I'm not sure delivery logistics would be as good as same-day delivery in the city."

"Surely, I'm not that old and need to explain that modern advancement means they don't rely on a horse-drawn carriage to deliver mail here, right?"

I swat his arm with my hand. "Funny."

"I need to enjoy this peace before my schedule gets crazy," he mentions. "Coaching staff have meetings all next week since summer training starts in two weeks."

"And then you have to travel for football season," I add on. The thought has crossed my mind that the luxury of our time and place has a running clock.

"Give me your phone later and I'll add the security system app for my house so I don't need to be home when you visit," Hudson states as if it's nothing, and we continue to stroll down the sidewalk.

"What do you mean?" I feel my chest tightening.

"You can come and go as you please. My house is your house, right? That's the saying."

I stop and tug him back when he tries to continue to walk. "That's kind of… for you not crazy, but for me…"

His eyes squint and lines form on his forehead. "It isn't a big deal."

"It's…" I can't get the words out, but I want to tell him. "A step."

"It's practical," he counters and touches my arm like I'm being ridiculous.

I nod quickly. "You're right. I'm being silly." I begin to walk, but this time it's Hudson who reels me back in like a yo-yo.

"What's going on in that pretty little head of yours?"

I glance away then back to him. I feel my leg twitch because I'm debating telling him something I've barely told anyone, but damn, honesty with Hudson comes so easily.

"Remember how I said that I lived with an ex?"

"Yeah."

"It was only for two months, and it just isn't a great memory."

Maybe he hears sadness in my voice, but concern spreads across Hudson's face and his eyes scan the scene. The coffee that is only half-empty in his hand is quickly thrown into the nearby trash can so fast that I can't comprehend time, but all I know is Hudson's hands are on my face, with the pads of his thumbs rubbing my cheeks, every circle filled with care.

"What happened?"

"It's not a big deal. I mean, it's not tiny either. Let's just say that one day when I decided to explore other types of nightwear, Vince wasn't thrilled. As in he ripped up my entire book of sketches not thrilled."

Hudson steps closer. "Go on." He sounds like he may kill some-one, and I haven't even finished the story.

"He threw the remainder of the book at me, missed, but still. I don't even remember all he said, but I decided that seeing my papers crumpled on the floor was enough. I wasn't going to stick around to find out if his temper could get worse."

"Shit." He pulls me into a hug.

I place my hand against his chest to push him back because I want to finish my story.

"It was a few years ago, and we had been dating for a year, taking things slow, then suddenly when I lived with him, I saw a different side. I know my worth and moved out that night, and I decided that my focus would be on my career."

"Dapper, right? Brave you are," he whispers, and he doesn't blink, instead staring at me almost… in admiration.

I scoff a laugh. "Maybe. But Vince's parents, friends, our mutual friends, and everyone including the mailman didn't see it that way. He'd been deployed in the military before we met and maybe even blamed his experiences overseas for his outburst. Everyone felt I abandoned him in his hour of need. I was the one destroying his happiness after his military tour, they all said, and I was called plenty of things."

"Is that maybe why you're afraid of people's opinions?"

"Probably. And for whatever reason, your simple suggestion reminded me of living with someone, and then my mind went from one dot to the next, and here I am before you like a nutcase."

"Not at all. The exact opposite. You are fucking amazing, and I get it. I understand what you're saying."

I smile softly in appreciation.

"But I'm not him. You're safe, and I love your career choice, as long as nobody ever sees your late-night creations on you except me." His tone is assuring, yet he brings a comforting lightness to the topic. But his eyes grow dark with a protectiveness. "I'm not going to back away from my offer." His hands grip my shoulders to ensure I stay perfectly in front of him, and I can't escape. "Because in football we sometimes run with the ball. We go for it, run and run, don't toss it or pass it, we don't even blink an eye, we just see an opportunity and race to get the touchdown. You, Piper Dapper, are my rush. I couldn't stop this play even if I tried."

———

WE WALKED QUIETLY DOWN to the lake at the end of Main Street. There's a gazebo and a small park. There was a little food truck with coffee, and we got another one, which was more than half-decent brew. For the most part, we didn't say much, just enjoyed each other's presence and the summer air. By the time we were driving back to the house, my thoughts were running rapidly as we rode on the winding road, with the beautiful green trees blocking the sun.

The same journey that I've taken a few times now.

Several occasions.

And I know that indicates the obvious.

Which is exactly why I feel like a smile wants to break through. My daze is interrupted by the feeling of the car parking, and I see that we're back at Hudson's.

Getting out of the car, I circle around until I'm staring at Hudson, and we both stand in front of the path to the front door, looking at one another.

Hudson is quick to jump to the side and wave his arm when a pinecone falls near him. "That damn tree has got to go."

"You should call a tree person and see about cutting it down to use it for firewood."

"Good point. So, hot tub or bottle of wine?"

I take hold of his arm and pull him to me. "I was kind of thinking you could set up that app on my phone so I can walk into your house whenever I please." A confident look floods my face since I'm satisfied with my decision.

And I need that app too, as I have every intention of surprising him.

HUDSON

"This is so great that you stopped by," I say, slapping a hand on my son's shoulder as he walks beside me up the path to my front door.

Drew and Lucy were in the area to pick up an order for Drew's work, and Drew wanted to deliver a new creation for my house. Even though I had a hell of a day at summer training, I will always make time for him, especially since I haven't seen him since his wedding. When he called this afternoon, there was zero hesitation. We'll just order pizza and throw back a beer.

"Truthfully, I knew I would get a free meal out of this," he jokes. Lucy is in the car quickly finishing up a call.

Drew and I walk through the front door, and maybe I'm so buzzed by the happiness that Drew is here, but I miss the fact that someone is already present in my house.

And as we walk into the kitchen, my entire world shifts.

Piper turns around where she's standing in the middle of my kitchen. "I thought I would surprise y—"

"Piper, you're here."

And fucking rocking it in my old training jersey and heels.

Those pink shoes from the first night we met are on her feet, which contrasts with her legs covered in deep blue stockings because she is clearly matching with my jersey, which she tied just above her belly button, and it's paired with gorgeous deep blue lace panties.

It takes a few seconds of me admiring this view, because I've never seen such a perfect image knowing it belongs to me, before I realize what's happening.

Piper squeals.

Drew curses, "Oh shit."

And only then do I understand that my son just walked in on my girlfriend trying to surprise me in a sexy manner that absolutely will be rewarded later.

"Okay, so that whole 'come and go as you please' idea kind of took an unexpected turn. This is *not* how this was supposed to go." Piper explains, absolutely mortified, I can tell by the shade of red on her face, but she seems to be holding it together.

"Why are you two just standing here?" I hear my daughter-in-law call out from behind me as she arrives, oblivious. "What the..." Her tone changes when she registers the scene.

From the corner of my eye, I already see Drew awkwardly looking away, but I'm quick to storm forward and grab any cloth that is in sight that may help before standing before Piper as her human shield.

But I feel the grin on my face not fading. Is that bad?

"Oh my God. This. Is. Not. Happening." Piper is embarrassed as hell.

This scene is moving so fast that I'm praying my son and daughter-in-law may erase it from their minds.

"Points for effort," I mutter into Piper's ear as I hand her what I grabbed.

"What in the world am I going to do with a tea towel?" she gasps.

I look down at my hand and tilt my head slightly to the side. "Okay, won't cover much."

Looking over my shoulder, I see my son has turned around, but Lucy looks like she struck gold and stands there, elated, with her hand across her face doing a half-ass job of covering her view. "I mean, I can't even tell you how this just fed my inspiration with writing ideas."

"I mentioned she writes romance books, right?" I quickly clarify to Piper.

Piper gawks her eyes at me. "Maybe we can do the introductions when I have a little more on the coverage front?"

"Oh yeah, sure. Why don't we give you a few minutes and you can meet us out back?" I suggest, and I know I'm being far too calm about this.

Piper quickly nods and scoots sideways out of the kitchen.

I can't help myself and I watch her head in the direction of the stairs.

Wow, she is a beauty. But it is way more than that because she wanted to surprise me.

With summer training now in full swing, our ability to chat via text all day is limited, and unless I have a meeting in the city or she can drive out to Lake Spark, then our availability to be with one another is sparse. But she came out from the city during my busy week to be here waiting for me, and I love the idea of a woman waiting for me at home, even more, if it's Piper.

The clearing of a throat draws my attention back to my other guests.

"Coast is clear," I declare then turn my attention to Lucy and Drew.

"That's Piper?" Lucy asks with a wide grin.

"Yep. The one and only." I smile awkwardly. "What are the chances we can erase the last two minutes?"

"Zero. Fucking zero," Drew answers, one-toned. "It's stuck in my brain, and I think I may need therapy."

I comb my hand through my hair and blow out a breath. "Let's just order pizza."

———

WHILE LUCY and Drew get comfortable outside with drinks, I head back inside to find Piper. I make it to the stairs just as her feet hit the bottom step. She's in jeans and a tank top now, but it doesn't deter any attraction in the slightest. My hands land on each side of the banister to form a human gate because I don't want her to step any farther until we have a check-in.

"Piper," I begin.

"Can I just go hide?" Her facial expression is slightly deflated

I run my fingers along the skin of her cheek. "Nah. I wouldn't be able to focus knowing you're here. Besides, I want you to meet Drew."

"I'm sure with clothes on," she quips.

She tries to avoid my eyes, but I hook my finger under her chin to draw her sight back to my own. "I love the surprise. I mean, I feel so lucky that it will live rent-free in my head."

"I've probably traumatized everyone else."

I grin, because of all the things in the world, this is the least of our worries. I must be giving my carefree attitude away, as I feel that I'm smiling to myself.

"Oh my God, you get a complete rise out of this," Piper accuses me, with her eyes ablaze.

I bob my head side to side in contemplation, knowing she isn't wrong. I wrap my arms around her middle and pull her flush to me. "A little. You will find the humor in this one day."

She slaps my shoulder playfully. "How? I am so embarrassed, and I literally made the worst first impression."

"Only in your mind is it that way. Trust me, they're laid-back people, and besides, you're brave, so you can handle this."

"Hudson, I'm… sorry."

My face turns puzzled. "For what? Looking like a complete goddess in my favorite old jersey? Don't apologize." I glide my hands through her hair to cradle her head. "Now let me finally kiss you."

I plant my lips on hers and kiss her with what I hope is reassurance, and if I'm being true to myself, then this kiss is selfishness because I've missed her. I don't like the nights when she isn't here. And I just love kissing her soft lips that often taste of some vanilla lip balm, and any stolen moments that I can get with her are appreciated.

She murmurs a sound of delight as she pulls away from my kiss, clearly a tad calmer. "I needed that." An exhale accompanies her shoulders sinking down.

I kiss her forehead. "Come on, we have pizza and proper introductions to make. It shouldn't be a long night, as they plan to drive back tonight. They were in the area, and Drew made a wood shelf for me and wanted to drop it off. I also need to be at the training facility bright and early, so we won't be late."

"Okay." She takes the hand I offer because I won't let her go. "Wait!" Piper pauses us for a second. "I'm meeting your son."

"And?"

Her eyes grow big and indicate that I need to catch up. "Kind of a big step, Hudson."

"Wasn't exactly planned, but I'm not complaining." I cluck the inside of my cheek because I don't see this as a big event.

Our train is moving, and I hope she gets on it.

I see the subtle hint of a smile form on her mouth, and it's my sign to yank her hand lightly to follow me. I feel her hand tighten in my own with every step closer to outside.

"Babe, you may need to loosen the grip. I need this hand for later," I mutter and smile at the same time as I see Drew and Lucy in our view.

Piper obeys, and I decide my hand is better on her lower back to ensure she doesn't run away.

The moment we step outside, all eyes are on us. Looking between everyone, I ruefully shake my head, as this doesn't need to be awkward.

"This is Piper. Piper, this is my son Drew and his wife Lucy."

Drew gives his signature fingers in the air for a little wave. "Hi." He uncomfortably half smiles.

"Hi." Piper's smile is tight.

"Nice to meet you." Lucy offers a warm smile.

"I'm sure this will go down as memorable," Piper says as she flops on an empty chair.

I have to grin to myself as I pick up the bottle of wine on the table to pour Piper a drink. "I think this is turning out to be a great evening."

"Ignore him. He takes joy from uncomfortable situations," Drew mentions before taking a sip from his beer bottle.

Lucy is quick to clarify. "I mean, there is nothing to feel uncomfortable about. I think it's awesome that we got to witness this, slightly out of the box on the introductions, but if you and Hudson are a long-term thing, then I can totally bug my husband that he walked in on his future stepmom who is his age half-naked." She grins, completely at ease.

What I love about my daughter-in-law is that her words are 100% genuine and not malicious in any way. I have to laugh, while Piper's face stays blank, and her eyes don't blink.

I walk to Piper and hand her the wine while looking over my shoulder to my daughter-in-law. "You know, Lucy, I always knew you would be a good addition to the family."

"Okay, I'm putting my foot down on both of you dragging this out," Drew states.

I sit next to Piper and intertwine our fingers. "Message received. Does the shelf fit on the wall?" He went to check when I ordered pizza.

"A perfect fit, the wood is the right shade too."

"Hand-carved by the greatest," I add. "By the way, did you have a look at the schedule of which games you want to come to?" I ask him.

He shrugs a shoulder. "Not yet. I'll get back to you later in the week"

Lucy turns to Piper. "My husband doesn't provide much data, but I love him anyway. He mentioned that you make pajamas, and well, what you were modeling earlier."

Piper seems to relax. "I do. I own Piper Ginger—"

"What!" Lucy's excitement is in full swing again. "I love those pajamas. So soft and cute. I got a pair with frogs with crowns on it."

Piper smiles brightly. "Oh yeah? I actually have a box of new designs in my car if you want another pair."

Lucy looks at me and winks. "I approve of this match."

"I'm positive I don't need your approval, but fine, I'll take it," I tell her. I can't help but look at Piper affectionately.

"Hudson mentioned you write romance." Piper attempts to keep the conversation flowing.

Lucy nods. "I do. So, apologies if I look at you two like you're a case study. How did you two meet?"

Piper nervously giggles. "Uhm, well, fun story really."

"She walked into a bar, and I bought her a drink. Kept it classic."

Piper glances at me, and I see a keenness to my answer.

"I had no idea who he was. A sort of mystery." Piper squeezes my fingers once.

"Well, mystery solved." Drew surprises me with his straight-forward reply, as normally he's one to stay neutral, but I sense something is on his mind.

Piper just continues on. "Hudson talks about you all the time. He showed me the pictures from your wedding, and they were lovely. Also, the pieces of furniture you made are beautiful." She touches my shoulder. "Hudson doesn't brag much, except when it comes to you. He is a proud dad for sure."

"Yeah, I'm getting used to it. Sometimes he can be a real pain in the ass, but he always means well," my son responds with a bit of humor. "Do you like Lake Spark?"

"Love it. I wish I had visited this place sooner; the town is so ridiculously over-the-top quaint, but it's perfect."

It's the last thing I hear Piper say as I get a notification that the pizza guy is at the security gate. I'm quick to excuse myself and go to collect the pizza. Returning a few minutes later, I see that the three of them managed to get on with the conversation without me. They're talking about how I need to get a boat for my dock when I arrive with the pizzas.

The rest of dinner is simple yet feels right. We talk about Drew and Lucy's honeymoon and their favorite stops in Europe. They gush about Italy, and Piper shares about her visit there. We discuss Bluetop where they live and Piper's grandmother. Conversation flows, and I didn't doubt that it would.

By the time it seems to be getting late, Lucy goes to freshen up, and I head to the kitchen with Drew while we carry plates inside, and Piper gathers things from outside.

Drew places the dishes in the sink. "She's… nice."

My head perks up, as I sense this is Drew wanting to have a conversation in private. It's his opening line. He leans against the sink, and I cross my arms as I rest against the opposite counter.

"Oh boy, I feel something coming."

"April still hasn't figured it out?" Drew asks, and it surprises me, as he's one to normally keep the peace.

Since Piper is here then I plan on talking to her about it. "No."

"And you know what you're doing? I mean, this is going somewhere, isn't it?"

My eyes grow wide. "Are you giving me a relationship talk? Have we actually reversed the roles?"

He shrugs a shoulder. "So what if I am?"

I smirk to myself that I find myself in this situation. "Just say it."

"You always wear your heart on your sleeve. I can see you like her a lot. Piper would be lucky, but is this all the same for her as it is you? Is she as invested?"

"Wow, you are going deep here. Do you have red flags or something that I'm not aware of?" I adjust my stance, and I do listen to him intently, because if my son has something to say then I will always listen.

"I don't know. I do like her, I just… don't want you to get hurt. You deserve… a lot."

My heart grows heavy, because in front of me is my son who every time I see, it feels like our relationship is getting stronger, and a twinge of sadness hits me, that I didn't get all the years until now with him.

"I hear you. I promise, I know what I'm doing."

Drew slowly nods. "Okay. Well, we should head out."

I grab the kitchen towel because I need to keep myself busy from the fact that I feel so lucky that he cares. "It's getting late. Are you sure you don't want to stay?"

He chuckles. "After what I witnessed earlier? Hell no. I'm not staying in this house tonight." He propels off the sink to walk out of the kitchen. "By the way, old guy, you do realize if you wait too long then the chance your future grandkid is older than your baby is quite high."

"First off, not old. Second, are you trying to make it a competition for who has a kid first? And thank you, by the way, for highlighting that fact." I shake my head at him before I pull him into a side hug.

Just then Piper comes into the kitchen. She exchanges goodbyes with Drew as she walks in and he walks out. I quickly stop her in her tracks by touching her arm.

"I'm going to walk them to their car then head upstairs for a shower. It's been a long day." My end-of-day shower is a sort of ritual to clear my mind.

"Sure. I'll finish up in here."

I squint an eye at her as she seems to be acting funny. "You were eavesdropping, weren't you?"

"Maybe," she admits.

"All parts or just the last part."

Her face turns cartoonish. "Maybe all parts."

I run my knuckle along her cheek as I smile. "That's okay. I'll see you upstairs."

The discussion will have to wait.

———

I STAND in the corner of my bedroom with a towel wrapped around my waist. Piper won't be able to see me unless she turns around, which is exactly what I want, and the moment Piper walks through the door, I initiate my plan.

"Don't turn around, Piper." My voice is firm.

She freezes in place, and I slowly walk to her from behind, a tie hanging from my hand.

I notice her body trembles when I stand at a breath's distance.

"Allow me," I say and bring the cloth over her head to blindfold her.

"This…" She gasps. "Is…"

I tie a knot. "A surprise. I know. The theme of the night clearly."

"Hudson," she softly purrs.

"Shh, baby. Good girls should be rewarded."

15

HUDSON

I circle around Piper, observing her like prey. I love how her mouth is partly open in curiosity. I hook my finger under her chin to tip her mouth up for easy access before I kiss her with warm intent, drawing in her breath, humming satisfaction.

Pulling away, I brush my thumb along her bottom lip. "You trust me, don't you?"

She swallows. "Fully. It's unexplainable."

I move my fingers to the edge of her tank top to slowly pull up the fabric. "What you did earlier could easily bring a man to his knees."

A smirk forms on her lips as I urge her arms up over her head to get the tank off. "Is that what you're going to do?"

I scoff a laugh. "No. But it is what *you* are going to do. As much as I loved your surprise, you are a bit of a naughty girl, so get on your knees, Piper."

Her lips part open and her tongue darts to the corner of her mouth. She is about to obey, but I tsk.

"Uh-uh, take those jeans off first." I tap the button above her zipper with my long finger.

Her breath is audible, and she moves to take action. I have to bite my lip when I see her in only a bra and the panties from earlier. The stockings she had on will have to make an appearance another day.

I toss my towel to the side and I'm naked, but she has no idea until I grab her hands and place them on my hips before she drops to her knees.

"The blindfold will be good for you. You'll be more sensitive to touch," I tell her.

"I like the sound of that." Her tone grows sultry.

I look down to see that her tongue is out of her mouth, ready to lap the head of my cock, and I tangle my hands into her hair to help guide her when the time comes.

Heat coils below my navel the moment her wet tongue begins to lick my length.

"Mmm, dessert," she whispers before licking droplets off my tip. "I want so much more." She takes me into her mouth, starting with a slow long stroke before working herself into a rhythm.

I want so much more too.

This woman knows how to make me feel good. She alternates between using her hand and mouth. It's a talent she has, and I feel like my eyes may already be rolling to the back of my head, but I want to enjoy a little more of her watery mouth taking me in until I hit the back of her throat.

I'm a barbarian maybe because I like her lips swollen and the way she sounds when she moans as she pulls my hips closer to her. Piper is a determined woman in the bedroom; her confidence comes into full swing when sex is involved.

We're having a moment, and I'm not going to let us go too fast.

I grab hold of her shoulders. "Come here, baby."

She returns to standing and wipes the back of her hand along her mouth. "Hudson, give me more." She's nearly pouting.

I walk us back to the edge of my bed, and I sit down, yanking her down until she's over my knee with her lace-covered ass in full view.

Piper glances over her shoulder even though she can't see. "I've had this fantasy going in my head for a long time now." Her grin brings a light-heartedness to our intimate moment that I appreciate.

"Like this? You deserve it." My palm lands on the flesh of her ass and the sound of the spank fills the room.

She whimpers in delight, and her behind goes pert and up, as if she's offering me more. I run my hand along her spine in a soothing line. I love wandering all over her body.

"I like this set. Another original?"

Piper glances over her shoulder again, and even though I can't see her eyes, her face tells me I'm crazy for asking the question when I clearly know the answer. "Always. You're my inspiration, Coach Arrows."

I unsnap the clasp of the bra. "I love when you talk dirty," I tease because she knows what hearing her say that does to me.

In a swift move, I wrap my arms around her and toss her onto the bed. "On your back and your legs wide." My hands coax her thighs open, and she plants her feet onto the mattress. Her body is already writhing in anticipation. "Forgive me, but these panties have to go, and I may rip them in the process." I don't think twice, and I slide them up and off her legs in a gruff movement.

"I may accept the apology."

I chuckle as I eye her glistening pussy. "Oh, you will. I see you've been waiting for me."

"For days," she gasps.

I use my tongue to explore her pussy, my instant addiction kicking in.

"Mmhmm, right there." Her hand touches the top of my head.

I'm not going to go gently. I want to drive her to insanity and leave her begging. In fact, I will only let her come once tonight, because I'm selfish and it can only be while I'm buried deep inside of her.

But she doesn't need to know that plan quite yet.

I work at her with my fingers and tongue. Her thighs part wider from instinct, and I hold one down while my other hand reaches along her body and settles between her breasts and next to her heart. I want to keep her firm to the mattress and under my spell.

Peering up, I see Piper licking her lips, and her nipples are pebbled, ready for attention too.

"Definitely more sensitive." Her breath is ragged. "Everything is more sensitive." She takes hold of my hand to hold it securely against the one place of her body that I'm not sure I have any control over – her heart.

I suck and lick until I feel her getting close. I know her cues by now, and just as she begins to hit the peak of the mountain, I stop and kiss up her body.

"Not yet." I tug on her nipple with my teeth and love the feeling of her legs wrapping around my waist, the tip of my cock sliding along her slickness. "I'm going to bury myself so deep inside of you." I drag my lips along her collarbone before taking the other nipple.

"Take this blindfold off me. I need to see you."

"Why? Because you missed me and came all the way here to surprise me?" I look at her face and wonder what she's thinking.

Her expression is serious. "Exactly that."

The air in the room nearly evaporates because the sincerity in her tone stops us in our tracks. It's no longer fun and games, she feels something too.

I lean on my side and untie the blindfold, and it falls low. Her beautiful blue eyes slowly flick open and blink several times before a smile grows on her mouth.

Looking down at her, our eyes lock, and I don't dare look anywhere else. "Hey there, beautiful."

She drapes her leg over my hip and pushes me back until she's on top of me and I'm lying on my back. "Hi there." She leans down to plant a kiss on my lips.

But I like her under me, and I roll us over which causes Piper to giggle. "Tell me I get a raincheck on that whole outfit from earlier?" I ask.

"Sure. I'll remember to pack it next time."

"Fuck that. You can have a damn drawer here." I reach my fingers between us to toy with her again.

Her eyes hood closed then open. "Why do you say things that don't make me run away when they should?"

"Because it feels right to you. I leave that to fate." I speak against the skin of her neck because my lips need to be on her, anywhere, just her.

The feeling of her fingernails gliding along my back is subtle, but I enjoy when she does it. There isn't an inch of our bodies getting ignored.

She squirms underneath me and the tip of my cock is dangerously close to her opening, and I should take this opportunity to grab a condom, but her eyes have me kind of lost and we are simmering in a moment together.

Our relationship has been evolving throughout the last few weeks and months, and this is our moment of confirmation.

"It does feel right. I'm a little scared, but even when temporarily blind, I see you," Piper whispers.

I give her a quick kiss. My entire body wants to mold into her as I slide my lips down the curve of her shoulder. "You were waiting for me."

She hums in response as she rubs her pussy along my cock.

"Wait."

"It's okay," she whispers. "Please, just…"

I cover her mouth with my own, and I'm diving in even deeper both literally and figuratively with what I feel for her.

My eyes close as I feel her warm pussy envelope around my cock, and her body curves into me as we both moan together.

It's in that moment of entwined bodies that I realize what it is that has me completely at the grace of this woman when my plan was to have her at my mercy.

But I'll show her now and explain later.

———

PIPER RESTS her head against my chest, and I pull the blanket over us.

"Your hair smells like peppermint."

She giggles under her breath. "Probably because my shampoo has mint in it."

"It's damn distracting. It's a scent that keeps me alert."

"My apologies, I'll be sure to find a shampoo that puts you to sleep," she says, sarcastically.

I squeeze her close against me. "It wouldn't matter, I have my guard down around you anyways. It's just that the mint reminds me to think clearer."

Piper looks up at me with a brow raised, resting her chin against my pecs. "Penny for your thoughts, Hudson?"

"I couldn't have asked for a better night. I'm happy you met Drew and Lucy, and you only reaffirmed my thought that you are capable of surprising me."

Piper kisses quickly against my chest before moving to straddle me, her hair a wild mess. She clasps our hands together and rests them on each side of our joined bodies.

"He is right, you know. You should be careful." She's insinuating what she overheard earlier.

"Should I?" I challenge her. "Here's the thing, Piper. I've never been against the idea of relationships or love or walking into the sunset forever. I know I want it. I just didn't find someone who came anywhere close to being my other half. Until you walked into my life with a fucking dancing-lobster umbrella."

Her breath hitches slightly. "What are you saying?"

I don't like her being over me in this moment. I let go of her hands, grip her hips, and use my weight to flip us, tangling the sheet in the process.

"We're happening. I think you feel it too. You put in the effort tonight, showing up, getting to know my kid, and hell, you didn't run away. You may have looked like a deer in headlights once or twice, but you stayed."

"I do feel it. It's just…"

"April. But you will tell her next time you see her, or I swear to

God that I will do it for us. Do you understand?" There is an edge in my tone that I think surprises her.

She slowly nods. "Okay. You're right, it's time."

"Good." I kiss her brow. "But not tomorrow. Tomorrow, you stay here and wait for me to come home."

Piper reaches her hand up to touch my cheek as she smiles warmly. "I'm not sure I'm any good at wearing an apron and cooking dinner, but I can pretend."

I growl low because the thought will keep me going tomorrow when I'm yelling at the new recruits on the field.

"I can have a chef come," I offer.

She chortles and rolls her eyes. "I love how you say it like it's nothing. But it's okay, I'll swing by Jolly Joe's for coffee, work on my laptop, and pick something up from the grocery store."

"Sounds good." I lie next to her and let out a long breath. "Sleep. We probably need a few hours of that. I'll try not to wake you when my alarm goes off."

"Don't worry. I'm not going anywhere."

I can't help but taunt her. "You have really developed since that first night." I smirk to myself.

She playfully slaps me then cuddles into my arms. "Funny, old man."

"Ouch. You're getting vicious."

"Nah, just getting comfortable."

And that's exactly how I want her.

———

I RUB my eyes and walk into the kitchen. The house is dark except for the small light next to the coffee machine that is on a timer.

Looking up from straightening my hoodie, I stop in my tracks when I see Piper leaning against the counter in only my shirt with my coffee thermos in hand.

"You really are trying to shock me in the kitchen these days, huh?" I say, and I'm completely adoring her even more. Walking slowly to her, I take the thermos she offers.

"Snuck down here when you were in the shower. Thought I could wish you a good day."

I kiss her good morning and wrap an arm around her middle. "Next time join me in the shower."

"Uh-uh. I think you have a schedule to keep, Coach." She flashes her eyes at me.

"I'll break every damn rule if it's worth it."

Our eyes meet and a brief silence overtakes us.

"I think it might just be."

And I hear it in her floaty voice that her words mean us.

16

PIPER

I look over the design on my tablet and nervously await my grandmother to give me feedback. The other day, I spent the whole afternoon sitting outside Hudson's house, overlooking the lake and drawing away. Creativity just flowed out

"You think April will like it?" I ask as we stand over the table with my tablet.

My grandmother with her small frame looks up at me, her glasses perched on her nose. "It's beautiful. The lines along the back really bring the wow factor." She takes her glasses off and walks to her sofa.

I smile proudly to myself as I close the cover on the tablet. "I'll show her later today. I've been tossing ideas at her for the last few weeks, but now I feel like I can show her the final blueprint, you know?" I say and sit down on the opposite sofa. My cheeks hurt from the smile that doesn't want to fade. Not only for the boho chic design on my tablet but life lately.

"Have some tea, dear. You look like you could use something to calm yourself down." There is amusement in her voice.

Quickly, I whip my eyes in her direction, and I see that she is assessing me with a self-assured smirk.

I tuck a few strands of hair behind my ear. "I'm…"

"There's a man." She waves a finger at me. "I'm disappointed you haven't told me sooner."

The gushing smile spreads, and my heart feels full. "There is, and I haven't told you because, well… I wasn't sure where to begin."

She brings her cup to her lips for a sip before placing it back on her saucer. "You invite him to Friday dinner, that's how you begin. You can make up for all the ones you've missed nearly every week the past month or two. That was the first giveaway that you met someone, and the second…"

"There's a second?" I sit up straight.

"Yes. It's your face and the way you just explained the dress you drew, a dress that I'm not entirely sure was inspired by April."

I shake my head. "What? What are you insinuating?"

"You poured your own emotion into it."

My smile fades, and I have to think about her train of thought. It leads me to internally admit that maybe she's right.

"Tell me everything I need to know."

"Hudson is… different."

She touches her pearl earring. "They always are, dear. Now, will you get more specific or do I need to head onto the socials and stalk you for clues?"

"Socials? You're going to show up on my feed again, aren't you?" I grin to myself because this woman has no qualms about modern technology.

"When it comes to you? Yes. Which way will it be? Give your dear old grandmother the facts or I log in to my fake account."

I laugh at her antics and lean back on the sofa. "Why am I not surprised? And sorry to disappoint but you won't find anything online. We have been a little off the radar, and besides, I don't really post personal things online."

"Fine. But I'm waiting… Details, please. Does April approve?"

Just like that my elated look fades as guilt hits me. "She doesn't know. Not yet, anyway."

"I'm truly touched that you're sharing the news with me first." My grandmother touches her heart for theatrics.

I sigh and look away then back. "It's a little complicated."

"How so?"

"Hudson is April's uncle. I didn't know who he was until after we'd already met."

"Uncle, hmm, he's older then?"

"Yes."

A warm reassuring smile graces her lips. "Your grandfather was older than me. It's better that way. You need someone who will lead you and support you, who knows what he's doing in both life and the bedroom—"

My palm flies up. "Do *not* finish that sentence. Geez, have we not established boundaries?"

"There is no harm in talking about sex, dear. You design lingerie, for crying out loud. I don't live under a rock. I'm sure you model your collection for him, as you should with those legs."

I haven't blinked in the last thirty seconds as I sit here with a blank face.

"So April doesn't know. You think she will not be pleased?"

"I don't know what to think other than the dynamics make it an awkward situation."

She waves a finger at me with a tsk, and I feel like I'm eight again and stole candy from her jar. "Be bold."

"I'm going to be. Hudson thinks like you, says things are only complicated if I make it that way."

"What does this wise man do?"

"He coaches football."

My grandmother's eyes grow full of interest, and she grabs her phone from the arm of the sofa. I roll my eyes because I know exactly what she's doing.

"Want me to save you the trouble? He coaches the Winds."

Her finger scrolls the screen with vigor. "My goodness, Hudson Arrows is a looker. Certainly has quite a few articles that I shall read later. I've heard about him, I mean who hasn't in this city, right?"

I hold my hand up. "Me. I didn't," I answer blandly.

"I could see you on his arm. He must be good to you if you've cancelled on me more than once lately." She looks up with a contrite smile before resuming her research. "I expect to meet him as soon as possible."

"May be hard, as it's training season and they train up by his lake house on Lake Spark."

Her mouth falls open. "That's where you've been hiding away? It's beautiful there. Your grandfather used to take me there for romantic weekends. Is there still that old inn by the water?"

I nod. "Yes, and there is an old-fashioned candy store. Everyone seems nice up there. A refreshing change from the busy city."

"Sounds like a perfect match then."

"You know, it feels good to share this with someone. At first, I wasn't sure if we were just… well, anyways, something inside me keeps telling me to take little steps."

My grandmother leans back and taps her fingertips on the sofa. "A good strategy considering your history, but don't let one bad apple make you hesitate for life. Don't be afraid to take risks, Piper."

"I think I'm slowly realizing that."

"Good. Now that I know your secret and plan on finding out every detail about your prince, then you have no reason to come up with ridiculous excuses for not visiting me."

I smile nervously. "The conference on organic fabric in Wichita was a giveaway, huh?"

She pulls at her earring. "I mean, it was creative, dear."

"I just hope April sees all of this as a positive too."

"Go. Go talk to her. Falling in love is better when you can share the news with a friend."

I stand up. "I think so too."

And I'm not sure, but I think both parts of her statement ring true; sharing with a friend and falling in love.

———

APRIL and I wait for the bagels that we ordered from the deli counter.

"I have the final design," I tell her as someone hands me my plate.

"Oh." April doesn't sound enthusiastic. "I hope they didn't toast the bagel, they always do that even when I ask them not to."

Huh, she's diverting the conversation to bagels.

We walk to a table and sit down to inspect our sandwiches.

"It looks not toasted today. You're in luck," I add and know that I can only stall for so long.

"I guess," she replies, slightly deflated.

It seems that now is as good a time as any.

I take a deep breath. "There is something I kind of wanted to talk to you about," I begin.

April looks up from her basket plate and the potato chip she's playing with. "You met someone."

I'm surprised she guessed it; she's making it easy for me. "Yeah. How did you know?"

"You're never around anymore, as you always have some work trip." She shrugs her shoulder. "Is it mystery guy?"

I swallow. "It is. I lied and it wasn't a bust at all. I just wasn't sure where it was going."

"I get it, maybe." April seems unusually calm, somber even.

"I really wanted to tell you, but I needed to wrap my head around it."

She nods slowly in understanding.

"And the thing is, I need to tell you something else." Nerves fill me, seeping through my veins, and I feel like I may throw up, but I need to do this. Hudson and I have become the worst-kept secret since so many people know. I hope April will be understanding and maybe we can even laugh about the coincidence that Hudson is the guy I met.

"Jeff and I ended our engagement last night," April blurts out, and tears pool in her eyes.

Oh, shit.

"What?"

This wasn't what I had planned for today, and concern for April overpowers anything I thought of saying.

I'm quick to slide off my chair and come to sit next to her. I touch her shoulder as she wipes away a tear. "What happened?"

"I'm just not good enough to be someone's wife," she cries.

"That's not true," I say, quick to assure her. "It's his loss."

She wipes her cheek with the back of her hand. "Oh, come on, Piper, you never really liked Jeff."

I tip my head to the side in doubt of how honest I should be, because yes, I didn't quite see them as forever, but when your friend seems happy then what are you to do? "It doesn't mean that I would want you to feel like this."

"I feel so numb," she wails.

I hug her and rub circles on her back. "It'll get better, I promise."

"Easy for you to say when you're in the lovey-dovey stage with some hot older man."

There's a twist in my gut, knowing that she may hate that she just said that when she discovers the truth. Maybe we should just lay everything on the table now. Yet when I look at April and she appears so sad, I feel like it isn't the right moment. I was so in my element that I didn't press her when we came into the bagel shop, even when I noticed she seemed off.

My friend is in pain, and I don't want to take the chance that I add to her temporary misery. Today is not the right time to tell her who the mystery man really is.

So I hug her and don't say a word.

HUDSON

I throw my water bottle to the side in a fit of anger. The assistant coaches around me take a step back as we walk along the field in the late-morning sun.

"I want to see Lewis in my office this afternoon. Is he not following workouts in his own time? He's out of shape and doesn't seem to have studied any plays at all. This isn't the standard I expect."

"I'll set up a meeting," Arnold our team manager pipes up.

"Good. I want him off the field for the rest of practice. He's a distraction and needs a rest." I rub the back of my neck in pure aggravation.

Lewis, my second season linebacker is pissing me off, and unlucky for him it's on the wrong day. Ever since Piper told me the other day about April, I've been conflicted.

I wanted to reach out to April, but from my understanding, only Piper knows, which means April would know Piper and I are in contact. As much as I don't care that April knows that fact, I am sensitive to April's moment of despair. But this means we're stuck in a holding pattern until April finds out.

Yep, unlucky Lewis for pissing me off on the wrong day.

"Kimberly is here," one of the assistant coaches announces.

Ugh, just what I need now, the team's new PR coordinator who focuses on social media. She just graduated from college, and her idea of building buzz is creating little videos every day and posting them online. When she asked if she could take a video of what my lunch was, that was the day I almost lost faith in humanity.

I roll my eyes before I rub my face when I witness her clearly flashing an overly sweet smile at one of my players as she walks my way.

"Hudson!" she calls out with a little wave. "We need to go over the calendar."

"Can't this wait? I want to do one more drill with my guys."

She looks down at her tablet. "The schedule says they should have a break now."

I hear Arnold chuckle under his breath, and I give him side-eye. "You handle the team; I'll get this over with."

He slaps a hand on my shoulder. "Just remember that sponsors love the shit she spews out."

"Don't I know it." I turn my attention to Kimberly, cross my arms, and smile politely. "What's on the agenda today?"

She flings her hair behind her shoulder. "Well, we need to finalize details for the pre-season team dinner, the charity BBQ, and the press conference coming up. I think you have the press conference under control, but I need you to confirm how many guest seats you want for the dinner and BBQ."

"You know I do those things solo."

"I know, but someone from the events team mentioned sometimes a Drew and Lucy come?" She studies her screen, clearly having no idea who they are.

"It's okay, Kimberly, they're my son and daughter-in-law. We don't actively advertise that fact."

She smiles genuinely. "Oh, okay. Well, let me know if they'll be coming. Which brings me to the other question." She attempts to hold in her smile. "Do we need to plan for a plus-one for your upcoming functions? Otherwise... damn it, why do they make me do this," she mutters to herself, and I appreciate that we've established enough trust that she can curse in front of me.

"Spit it out."

"Marketing wants to know if they can agree to a feature on you that may emphasize that you're a bachelor. They think it draws in the female demographic." I can tell she doesn't enjoy being the messenger.

I'm quick to answer. "Plan for a plus-one."

"Really?"

I glance over at the guys setting up for a scrimmage. "Yes."

"So… there is someone?"

My attention turns back to her. "Yes."

"Care to elaborate? Because they will only send me back here tomorrow." Her face is pleading.

"There is someone in my life, so yes, Piper will be with me."

The thing about aggravation is it shoots determination through me and sends me on a direct path to what I want. I know April will figure everything out soon, and that means that Piper and I can continue to take steps, and I want nothing more than to have Piper by my side.

"That is such an adorable name. Can I have a last name, social handles, and any dietary restrictions?" Kimberly returns to business mode.

"Nope. How about we keep it easy."

Kimberly stomps her foot in slight frustration. "You know Smith's wife started posting several times a day about a day in the life of a football wife, often taking pictures and videos when she visits him at practice, videos of what she cooks him for breakfast before training, those kinds of things. She gained a hundred thousand followers in one week. Fans love that stuff."

I hold my hand up. "No disrespect to Smith's wife, but Piper is not that kind of woman." Piper carries herself with a sort of demeanor that my parents would call classy, yet behind closed doors, she's the best kind of dirty.

Kimberly holds up a finger. "One post. One picture when she visits you at training. Give us something."

"Can we focus on my guys again, please? What's happening to that whole football-players-with-puppies charity event? I mean, sign me up for that. It's puppies," I tell her half-heartedly.

"Fine. I get the hint."

"Good. Now I need to get back to coaching." I throw a thumb over my shoulder and walk back to centerfield.

I shake my head. As much as Kimberly's suggestions are ridiculous, I can't help but smile at the idea of everyone knowing who my girl is, making it clear Piper is off-limits and I take complete claim for her. And hot damn, I'm sure we would blow up the marketing department's social media quota.

———

MY SISTER CATHERINE walks into my office at the training facility that is my home for most hours of the day as we prepare for the new season. It's a mess at this moment due to having extra screens up so I can compare plays and footage. She was in the area to collect intel for one of her depositions and called if she could stop by, and I have an afternoon break that I don't normally take.

But this is perfect timing, as I was going to call her anyway to share the latest news in my life.

"Hey, big sis," I greet her with a hug.

She hugs me back. "Hey, trouble." She sits on a chair in front of my desk while I head in the direction of my small fridge

She admires the new photo from Drew's wedding, a photo of me and the happy couple. "Good photo. He's settling into married life? Or have you not seen him yet since the wedding?"

"I saw him the other week when he delivered a shelf he made."

I bring her a sparkling water then slide my phone off the desk, unlock my screen, and show her the photo of Drew's latest creation.

Catherine examines the screen. "It's beautiful. I wonder if he could make me one."

I admire the woodwork in the photo and smile at the fact that Piper left a creepy lobster statue on top of a book. She said it brings luck, and she had it in her car as she was moving things from her office to storage.

"You know he will."

She taps the screen with her nail. "Send me this photo so I have an idea of the measurements." Catherine makes herself at home and opens her bottle of water. "I won't stay long, just wanted to quickly chat in person," she calls out.

I head behind my desk and let out a sigh of relaxation because it's the first moment of the day that I don't need to discuss football.

"April and Jeff broke off their engagement," she explains.

I ditch my seat and head to my coffee machine on the side table and hit the button for a cup of caffeine that now seems like nirvana since we are heading straight into a serious conversation. "I know."

"How? She only just told me last night."

Grabbing my cup, I have no intention to lie to my sister. "Piper told me."

My sister tilts her head in curiosity as she studies me. "I didn't realize you two had contact."

Sitting down, I lean back, throw my feet on my desk, and take a sip of my coffee. "Want to make this about your daughter or me?" I counter.

"I'm concerned about April. She must be heartbroken, but I hate myself for not giving in to the red flags and telling April she could do better."

"Fate stepped in then." I hold my coffee up to her in a toast. "I'll reach out to April if you want. Maybe she could use a weekend here at Lake Spark."

"That would be a good idea." Catherine brushes a piece of lint off her slacks. A silence overtakes us, and she examines me before giving me a pointed look. "You're sleeping with my daughter's best friend?"

I grin because of her bluntness. "I would like the think we are more than that, but yes. Piper and I met before we realized how we're connected. Funny, huh?" I stay calm and collected, in fact unaffected by my sister's facial expression of intrigue.

"Yet April has no clue," she highlights the fact.

"Piper was going to tell her the other day, but April wasn't in a great place. I'd do it myself, however they should figure it out between them. I don't want to get in the way of their friendship."

"How noble of you." I sense sarcastic undertones in her words. Catherine gives me a stern look before she throws her hand in the air. "You're right, though, it's for them to work it out." She studies me for another hot second. "Piper? Really? I mean, she is a lovely girl, don't get me wrong. But your niece's best friend? Like, really? Is this a mid-life crisis thing?"

I give her a pointed unimpressed look and swing my feet off my desk to sit up straight. "It's not. She's good for me."

"April may be crushed."

"Why? Wouldn't she want her best friend and favorite uncle together?" I place my coffee to the side.

My sister gives a short laugh. "Listen to that statement you just said. And I don't know, maybe she'll be thrilled. She has a lot going on right now, so I can't predict it."

"Well, I'm not going to hide my relationship with Piper anymore."

"Uh-oh. Bullheaded Hudson is coming out. You were this way when you discovered you have a son. Determined as hell and nobody could get in your way. Just be sensitive, please, it involves my daughter," she reminds me.

I nod in understanding. "Is it so wrong to grab hold of what you want when you discover what you have?"

Catherine chortles. "Well, I'll be damned. You are under a spell, and let's just all hope it doesn't wear off when you're out in the open, no longer sneaking around, or that Piper is just as ready as you seem about a future."

Her statement takes me off guard because she's right. Piper needs to be on the same wavelength, or we have no chance.

"Is that concern I hear?" My brows lift.

She folds her arms over her chest and taps her fingers along her forearms. "It's logic. She's young, maybe doesn't want to jump into all the things you do, well, at least not on your timeline. But heaven help us if you actually listen to me."

I smile to myself because I hear the caring undertones but admire her ability to still lecture me as an adult. "I'll take it into consideration."

My phone in my pocket vibrates, and I pull it out to see that Piper sent a message.

PIPER

> Hey, I know you're supposed to be in focus mode during training, but I'm going to try and head up to Lake Spark later this week. I'll drive up, avoid foxes and killer pinecones. Hopefully won't have terrible timing again too. I want to see you.

A hint of a smile tilts on my lips, and my sister's advice now only hangs by a thread in the back of my head.

Because I've got everything under control. Even the slither of doubt within can't shake my standpoint that I'll get exactly what I want.

18

HUDSON

With my hands in my jean pockets, I lean against the door pane to stare at the woman in my bed. It's the kind of view a guy could get used to. Piper is wearing one of my old hoodies, legs bare, and her knees are up which means the glimpse of bare skin confirms she only has a thong on.

She tosses her tablet to the side as she looks up to greet me with warm eyes and a welcoming smile. "There you are."

"Making yourself at home?" I smirk and head into my bedroom while I take off my t-shirt and jeans. My body is drained, but I have a woman who is beckoning me to fall into her arms between the sheets.

Piper doesn't move, instead lying there waiting, watching, and looking confident that she is supposed to be the queen of my bed, and pats the spot next to her to invite me to join her. "I knew you would be late, and I just wanted a cozy night to catch up on emails."

I set my knee on the bed and crawl to her to steal a kiss. "I was waiting for this." I speak against her lips before the tips of our tongues touch for a little tease.

Her hands come up to frame my face. "You seem tired."

A short laugh escapes me. "I've been up since five and it's now almost eleven. This is usual as we prepare for pre-season games."

"You drove?"

"I have a driver for the next few weeks. There is no way I'm driving this late after a long day, plus I can use the drive to go over notes for tomorrow's training."

"Come to bed. I'll massage your shoulders." Her thumb swirls on my cheek.

I would love to collapse on the mattress, but I'm a man who survived a day of sun, running up and down a field, and standing around with sweaty guys needing a lecture. I give her a peck on the lips real quick. "A two-minute shower then I'm back."

Piper pretends to pout and grabs my arm as I leave. "I can be of assistance."

"Oh, I know you can, but I'll be fast," I promise.

She nods in agreement.

The moment, I get the shower on, dim the lights, and throw some music on the Bluetooth, I'm regretting not dragging Piper in here. But I need a few minutes to myself after this day, and even the drive back wasn't peaceful, as one of my assistant coaches had sent a long email that I needed to process.

My evening shower is a sort of ritual to turn off my football brain and refocus on other aspects of my life.

Warm water cascades down my body as soon as I step in. A deep breath and I can already feel the thoughts float into my head about the fact that Piper is here and finding a routine at my house with ease. But a few hours every night are not enough. I'm asking a lot that she always comes here to Lake Spark, but I get the impression she prefers it here to the city anyhow. Then again, once the season starts, then my time here will also be minimal.

Turning the water off, I grab a towel, and two minutes later I'm back to my bed. Piper is now only in my t-shirt. In fact, I think she has been wearing my clothes at night more than her own line of pajamas that she designed.

Piper pulls open the duvet to offer me a spot while I grab a pair of boxer briefs, never breaking our gaze.

"Kept the bed warm," she proudly states.

It's only a second after my ass hits the mattress that Piper is on top of me, straddling me, with her hands resting on my shoulders as I sit against the headboard. Despite her warm heat on top of my dick, she isn't even being sexual. She's caring.

Her fingers begin to knead into my shoulders. "Is it always like this? You're a little tense."

"This is normal. It's long days now, and when games start, it's a little less long but more pressure. Welcome to my life for the next six months." I rub my hands along her forearms and take in how good it feels to have someone massaging me with purpose.

"I have to say that it sounds awful, but you seem to enjoy your job. It's just… maybe I'm beginning to really understand why you haven't had time for… other things." She's acting sheepish, but I know what she means.

I stop her from massaging me further and have to smirk at her thought. "As in a relationship?"

A knowing grin is faint on her lips. "Maybe that is what I was getting at."

I comb my fingers through her hair because her lush brown locks frame her face and it's slightly distracting, as I just want to wrap her hair around my hand and pull her mouth to mine. "Partly, yes. But if you put in the effort then it can work. I never wanted to put in the effort… until now."

Piper shimmies closer to my body, causing my cock to twitch, but I stay on point and pull her closer to me to wrap her tightly in my arms.

"Summer training is over in a week," she says, "then it's pre-season games and then game season where you stay in a hotel the night before home games too." She's showing off her knowledge that is a mix of what I've told her and exploring the internet.

"I hate that time isn't on our side, we only have small windows.

Speaking of which, stop by the stadium tomorrow for lunch," I suggest.

Her face freezes for a brief second. "Oh, I kind of planned to do my usual coffee in town, walk around, and some old lady mentioned they have a drawing class by the gazebo every day during the summer."

My eyes raise to her, and I'm kind of taken aback that she's pushing back. "Piper."

"Hudson," she returns my authoritarian tone.

"I don't like this avoidance. I've been patient, but now is the time to rip the band-aid off and tell April. Besides, I want to see you more outside of our bubble. Soon, I won't be at Lake Spark as much."

Her lips quirk out, and she seems sad by that thought. "I'll miss it here."

"Using me for my house," I joke.

She playfully pushes my shoulder. "I like it here. The home you built, the man who lives here. When I'm here with you, it's our own little world."

"We get to have the whole world as ours if you speed up the avoidance of truth with my niece issue. And my house is your house, so use it even if I'm away."

Her eyes turn appreciative. "Thank you, and I hear what you're saying about April. I just wanted to give her time, nor did I want to flaunt my romantic life to her when her own combusted."

Another reason that I can't seem to be angry, only annoyed. Piper has a heart of gold and doesn't want to hurt her best friend. But in the process, I'm drowning in limbo and it's no fun.

"Soon, Piper," I nearly chide.

"I hear you. I promise."

"Good, because I told the team publicist to expect you at some of our events and games," I inform her confidently.

"W-what?" she nearly shrieks.

A cocky smirk tilts on the corner of my mouth. "You heard me."

Her face lightens gently, and she glances at her fingers drawing circles against my chest. "It's a big deal, Hudson. It puts me in the public eye, and I'm not used to that." There's more to it, I hear it in her voice, but I don't press.

"I respect that, but that is kind of what you sign up for when you're with me." I lean down to kiss her fingers.

"You keep your son out of the press," she is quick to remind me.

"True. But it's easier. The press is a little too eager to know my romantic life. Hell, if I have to stand through another photo shoot for a bachelor coach article then I may have to punish you for that," I say in an attempt to lighten the mood.

Piper rolls her eyes. "How about we save this talk for tomorrow when we're not as tired?"

I study her for a second, and she has a valid point because my eyes desperately want to close. "Sure."

"You can slide into me whenever you want," she offers with a mischievous sly grin.

We both begin to shuffle around to get comfortable for the night. "That is some offer. You know I may just take you up on it at 4:55 in the morning before my alarm goes off."

"Sounds like a perfect way to wake up."

We both lie on our sides and face one another, her leg hooking over my hip and our hands resting on one another.

"Everything is perfect when I'm with you," I faintly whisper.

Her lips twitch which informs me that the statement affected her. "Can't argue with that."

For tonight, that's enough.

———

WALKING OUT ONTO THE FIELD, I notice the group congregating near the twenty-yard line, a mix of football players in practice uniforms and women all cooing in a circle. I glance up at the stands, as we now have open practices which means fans can watch, and in this very moment, they're all standing and taking photos.

"What in the world is going on?" I ask Arnold who is by my side.

It was lunch break for an hour, but we just ate in my office to discuss the team.

Arnold smiles and tips his head in the direction of the group. "Jefferson's wife had a baby the other week, remember? Even scheduled the induction on our day off." My eyes go wide, as that is some commitment, although not the first time that I heard of a player's wife doing that if the stork decides to deliver a baby during season. "His wife must have brought the baby to visit."

That explains why everyone seems to be in a good mood. Often, players have their partners or family watching practice or stopping by. Jesus, Smith's wife drives me crazy when she stops by without fail to kiss her husband, take a selfie, and post it online. Mostly because I seriously doubt her intentions of real love and wonder if she is more interested in the fame.

But truthfully, I know there is a twinge of jealousy inside of me that a twenty-four-year-old linebacker gets something that I don't—a romantic relationship. I glance toward the parking lot, and disappointment flickers inside my stomach because Piper didn't stop by. In reality, it's probably for the best because it was a tight window of time and I needed to work anyhow. But even a kiss would have given me a little extra energy and pep.

Arnold and I walk toward the group. I hear someone call out *Coach Arrows is here*. For some reason my name causes everyone to step back to create a path and grow quiet, as if I'm the boogeyman. My path lands me in the middle of the circle with everyone's eyes on me, or at least I feel them, but I'm staring only at one player in uniform and light pads holding a tiny squishy baby.

Jefferson looks up at me nervously. "Oh hey, Coach."

I smile with ease and hope it reassures him that I'm not the devil. "Your son?"

"Yeah. Getting him into the game early."

I turn my attention to his side, to his wife who's wearing one of those carrier things. "Congratulations."

The petite blonde woman who looks slightly tired smiles. "Thank you. We'll get out of everyone's hair now."

I look down at my watch and see that we should be starting, as we have a strict schedule and a long afternoon ahead of us, but I can't bring myself to be a hard-ass. "It's okay, we'll start in five minutes."

Jefferson's smile grows wide.

Leaving everyone to it, I head away from the group to the table on the sidelines. That short walk is enough time for me to question my soft demeanor that just happened. I normally reserve it for my private life. I'm changing, probably because I feel like these same moments that my players, my son, hell, most of the world get are now within my reach.

Doesn't mean I will go easy on them during practice, though. I'm going to make these guys work damn hard, with a completely selfish motive to let us off a little early tonight so I can finish my discussion with Piper.

———

PIPER LOOKS up from the glass of water she just poured from the fridge dispenser. I'm home early, although I will need to watch footage of the practice later in my office. I texted Piper when I was in the car.

"Want me to attempt to cook? I started to make snacks." She walks to me, oblivious that I'm agitated. It's only when she attempts to kiss me and I don't put in the effort to kiss back that she senses my mood. "Everything okay?"

I shake my head gently as our eyes meet in a tense stare. "No. We need to talk."

She tips her head back, with her smile now faltering, but keeps her arms looped around my neck. "What's wrong?"

"I'm done waiting. I need to know that you're ready to move forward, no more stalling. I know you want to, but I can't figure out why exactly you're hesitating." I unhook her arms from around my neck and hold her wrists gently up to keep her in my hold.

"What do you mean?"

I snicker. "I'm done running around like we're a secret. If you can't make the jump, then what are we doing?"

"Hudson," she sighs.

"Don't do that. Don't come up with excuses. We both know that what we have is more than what either of us thought would happen the night we met." I yank her closer, drop her wrists, then weave my hands into her hair. There is passion in my movement, and Piper draws in a breath as a response. "I'm not going to wait; my patience is wearing thin. I want you by my side no matter where we are. You're driving me crazy, you're always on my mind, and when you're here, I just want more and more. I think I've warned you that I'm a man who jumps right in, but I only jump in when it's right."

Her eyes are almost pleading. "I'm going to tell April, okay."

"Great. But there's more for us, I need more commitment. I want you cheering for me on the sidelines, visiting me on breaks so I can fuck you in my office or car. Let me meet your grandmother and tell me what you see in our future when you're lying in my arms." I hear the vulnerability in my voice.

I continue my explanation of what's going on in my head. "You feel it inside of yourself that you want us, but you can't say the words that you're all in." I walk her backward until her back hits the edge of the wall. I let her wrists go and kiss her hard until she murmurs while she fists the fabric of my shirt at my chest. I kiss the corner of her mouth then speak against her lips. "I'm going to give you an ultimatum, but I don't believe I need to. You know how I know you want us?"

"Enlighten me," she rasps with her eyes drawing a line up and down my body.

I step between her knees to part her legs open while our foreheads touch, and I sneak my fingers up her thighs and under her skirt. "You let me come inside of you and I know you're not on birth control." My fingers dive into her panties to touch her soft heat, already wet. Her face looks panicked as if she has been caught out. "I'm not mad, baby, I could have stopped us, and I didn't." I don't break our connection and the tips of our noses touch.

"I haven't done it intentionally, I just... I can't explain it. Sorry, I should be more care-"

"Shh." I kiss her lips and continue to stroke her pussy. "Your body already knows what you want before your thoughts catch up. It takes two, and I'm a selfish man who wants to fill you up, and I don't care if you get pregnant, so I'm not going to say *we* should be careful. Hell, I'm not getting any younger, and the thought of you pregnant with my child is something I envision. But the point is that you wouldn't take the risk unless you have the trust and felt it was worth it. Tell me I'm wrong."

Piper frantically shakes her head as her fingers fumble with my jeans. "I can't. You're right. I trust whatever is happening between us." Her head falls forward and rests against my shoulder.

"It's our future, that's what is happening." I guide her arms over her head against the wall.

"You want to know what makes me hesitate, what scares me?" I hear so much vulnerability in her voice.

I press my forehead against hers. "Tell me," I whisper. My eyes lock with hers to encourage her to speak.

"We're moving fast, but if I blink, I know I could have it all with you because I see it. I've never experienced this before."

Her answer is exactly what I needed to hear.

We press our bodies against one another, and we kiss, hungry, before I drop to my knees and bring her foot to my shoulder, giving me ample opportunity to travel up her smooth thigh with my mouth, brushing my lips delicately before inhaling her scent and licking over the fabric of her drenched panties.

I feel her losing her balance, and her hands land on my head to brace herself. "What are you doing to me?"

A devilish chuckle escapes my throat. "Making you mine."

"I'm already yours." She breathes out as her hips curve in my direction.

I needed to hear that, which causes me to change our course. Standing, I hoist her up onto the counter beside us, and immediately I hook my arms under her knees to splay her out. Our mouths fuse together, and I feel the urgency to take her. I bend down and dive between her legs, yank her panties to the side, and get a taste.

"You're soaking, Piper," I mutter as I keep busy.

"And you're eager," she counters. Her breath is thick with an equal desire to get lost in one another.

"For us? You have no idea." My tongue lashes out against her pussy.

Her hands wind into my hair. "Hudson," she cries out.

I run my mouth back up to her lips and cover her mouth with my own. I feel like a man possessed. A man who wants to be consumed by her.

She begins to drag her shirt up and off, and of course, I assist her. When her shirt goes flying in the air, I'm already tugging her bra cup down her breast and suckling on her nipple. Her head falls back, and a soft moan escapes her lips. I move to her other little bud and twirl my tongue and nip her skin.

"Ah, so good," she hums.

I pull back slightly, with her legs still hooked around my arms. "Good," I chuckle under my breath. "It only gets better from here, baby."

I unzip my jeans and pull them down just enough. In a rapid movement, I slide her to the edge of the counter. Tonight, I'm lacking a bit of finesse, but we have confirmations to make.

My mouth trails up her neck, causing her to lie back on the counter. I drag her arms up over her head and pin them down. Her entire body arches up against me, a sort of surrender. Our kisses are messy, and her breath is heavy.

"I want all of you. Don't you realize you're mine? Your pussy will only ever feel my cock from this moment forward. So when you go to sleep tonight in my bed, next to me where you belong, lying against my chest, remember what you choose, because I want all in."

I don't wait for her to answer. I plunge into her, and we both moan at the sudden movement. Her hands walk her upper body up to sitting, one arm encircling around my neck. I can feel her breath against my skin.

"I understand," she gasps.

I continue to pump in and out of her without an ounce of grace. Reaching between us, I grab the edge of my shirt, and she helps me pull it up over my head, and soon it lands on the floor. Our bodies are inseparable, our hands glued to one another, wandering and exploring. But every kiss feels more intense. The emotional element is underlying which only makes our senses work in overload.

Every time Piper breathes my name, it only encourages me to fuck her a little harder. She isn't complaining either, because her legs wrap tighter around my waist with our bodies moving together in a rhythm.

A sheen of sweat breaks out on my skin and her hair is a mess. She looks like a woman at my mercy, but the fact she clenches around my length reminds me she's an equal partner in our journey to bring each other to the edge.

Piper tightens her arms around me and buries her head into the crook of my neck before kissing the base of my throat.

I pause in movement but remain inside of her as I cradle her head in my hands. "Do you understand?"

"Yes."

I kiss her eyelids that hood closed. "I'm crazy about you." I kiss her jawline. "It isn't just infatuation; the damn future is with you because I'm in love with you."

Her eyes shoot open, and her body is near panting, but the corners of her mouth twist into a subtle smile. "I was sensing that, but I like hearing it." Ah, she's being a smartass. "I'm in love with you too, and I'm not just saying that because your hard cock is inside of me."

I laugh because that's Piper, surprising me with her mouth at random moments. Our lips seal together as I move again, this time a bit more frantic.

Finally, when she's trembling in my arms, I'm chasing right behind her with a few more thrusts, and then I'm doing exactly what I plan on doing every chance I get, filling her up because she is mine.

19

PIPER

"Can't keep up, old man?" I holler over my shoulder to Hudson as we walk up the path in the woods behind Hudson's house.

He quickly runs to catch up and grabs me by the waist, pulling me against his body causing me to squeal. "Watch it there or I may need to teach you a lesson." Playfully, he swats my ass.

It's Sunday which means he kind of has a day off. Or at least the morning off; Hudson and his coaching staff are meeting later at Catch 22 to discuss the team. We decided to do an early-morning walk to get some fresh air.

I look up to meet his lips for a kiss.

"I was admiring the view, you should too."

"I guess I get into my power-walking a little too much."

He pulls back and laughs. "I know. It's like take off the heels and throw on some sneakers and you're a bionic bunny."

I stretch my arms into the air. "It's a beautiful day, fresh air, and I'm wide awake."

"You're obviously not sore enough from last night, I'm not doing my job right." He says that without breaking, but I can only grin.

We begin to walk again, hand in hand. "You also seem very happy." His voice turns sincere.

"I think you know why," I remind him and give him a sly look.

He brings his arm around my shoulders. "Oh, I do. I think we went over it several times last night in bed."

We approach a lookout point at the edge of the tree line that overlooks Lake Spark just as a man in his fifties walks away, with his golden retriever on a leash, and we greet them in passing.

This is such a great view. It's different to Hudson's backyard because we're higher up and looking down. I can see the town square on one side, someone fishing in the middle of the lake, and I spot someone swimming.

"Pete's at it again. No rest for the wicked and old," Hudson comments.

"He has to burn off all those jellybeans."

"He's a good guy. We have a team fundraiser for this children's charity, and he donated like half his candy store. Speaking of which, want to come to practice this week? I mean, I am assuming you can just stay here for a while since you seem to work from my house."

"True. I can work from anywhere, although my grandmother does like to see me in physical form to make sure I'm still alive. But I haven't really thought about the next week, I only packed for a few days."

He chortles a sinister laugh and releases his arm to lean against the railing of the lookout and face me. "Not a factor. You already left a few things last time you were here, you know where the laundry room is, my shirts look good on you, and my favorite solution is how you can just walk around my house naked."

I loll my head to the side slightly with a closed smile. "Valid points, Coach Arrows."

"You're stalling again." Lines form between his brows. "Speak to me."

I roll my lips into my mouth. This man can see through me. "It's…"

He steps into me and is quick to bring his hand to my cheek affectionately. "Go on."

"I'm mentally preparing for people's opinions of me personally." That was a lot easier to admit than I thought.

Hudson nods once, with his eyes filled with understanding before placing a gentle kiss against my temple. "I kind of assumed it had something to do with that."

I rub my cheek into his hand. "It's silly. I'm an adult woman, and I'm not ashamed of anything. I just stay away from public stuff; it's why I never model my lingerie and have someone else handle the marketing stuff. Piper Ginger isn't really me, you know? But Piper Dapper? Well, she didn't enjoy the last round of people's opinions or critique. They made me feel like I was a horrible person."

"Baby, you are not. Anything but. You put others before yourself, and so what, you put yourself first this time. You're allowed to and thank goodness you did."

I shrug. "I keep telling myself that. And I know you do your best to keep a low profile, and I said I didn't care who you are, but I know that you are, well… popular. It will be hard to keep a low profile. Besides, geez, have you seen Smith's wife? If that's the standard I need to follow, then I'm not sure my photos of avocado toast and coffee will suffice." There is a little humor in my tone because I don't want to drag this morning down.

He rolls his eyes. "First off, you don't need to be her. Instead, you are a beautiful woman who has a successful business and knows the meaning of making people happy. All I can say is that I will promise to do my best to protect you."

"I believe you."

"One step, okay? Just come to a practice."

I swallow because a sexy smile wants to form on my mouth. "I *may* be intrigued to see you in action."

"I bet you are. Now, want to power-walk it back to the house, hop in the car, and grab some brunch in town?"

My head perks up. "You mean coffee and cinnamon rolls? I could never say no. I heard a rumor the other day at the general store that they changed the recipe for the cinnamon filling and the knitting club decided to write a letter demanding the old recipe comes back."

"Eavesdropping next to the butcher's counter again?" He flashes me a humorous look.

I scoff a sound. "You know it."

We begin to walk back, but I'm quick to grab his wrist. "Hey… I love you."

His suave grin appears. "Love you too. Now let's go get caffeinated."

I yank his arm again. "Maybe we can take a photo of our coffees next to one another to make it official and send it to your publicist for kicks. You're right, I'm ready to go all in."

An almost vulnerable look appears in his eyes as the corner of his mouth curves up. "I don't know what I love more. The fact that you love me or the fact that you make every conversation enjoyable."

"You get both, Coach Arrows."

He growls and tugs me along. "Fuck me, when you say my name like that I'm a goner."

―――――

It's a thirty-minute walk back, and as we emerge from the tree line, we stop still at the end of the driveway.

My heart nearly skips a beat because April is leaning against her car with her arms crossed.

"Fucking knew it," she grits out, and she doesn't seem impressed.

I glance to my side at Hudson who has an awkward wry smile on.

"April," I say. I had planned on telling her when I was back in the city, but I guess she beat me to it.

"Morning, April, how did you get in?" Hudson asks completely in a normal tone and scratches the back of his neck.

"Your asshole neighbor, the baseball player, sped out of the gate nearly running into me, not even caring, so I drove right in while the gate was open," she explains, with her eyes never leaving me as she has an intense stare.

"Right." Hudson accentuates the T.

There is silence for a beat until April begins to shake her head.

"Funny thing. My mom was showing me a photo of a shelf that Drew made for my uncle, then I noticed the unique statue on it. A lobster. I thought, 'wow, that seems oddly like the one I gave Piper.' Then I remembered that Piper is seeing an older guy." April holds a finger up into the air. "Lucky guess."

I step forward. "I tried telling you last time, but it didn't seem like the right moment."

"It's no big deal," Hudson says. "Now you know, and we can all go for brunch." Hudson is still far too relaxed. "Great." He claps his hands together.

April looks at him like he's crazy. "Fuck that. I need to erase a hell of a lot of information that Piper shared with me about you that is just plain… traumatizing."

My face squinches together. "I swear, I had no idea who he was the night I met him."

"But you both figured it out the night of my enga— that stupid party." I can tell her engagement is understandably a sensitive matter.

Hudson and I glance at one another, then back to April.

I breathe out because I want to be honest. "Yes."

April throws her hands up in the air. "So you have just been coming here to be with my uncle and play housewife? Unbelievable."

I rub the back of my neck. "We had to figure out what we were doing."

"And did you?" She gives me a pointed look.

"I think so."

Hudson pipes up. "You know, I think you two need a moment. I'll be inside. April, don't be mad. Even if you are, unlucky for you, I'm your uncle, so I'm sticking around. As for Piper, she's part of my life now."

"Touching." April isn't amused.

Hudson just shakes his head and walks away, grazing my arm in reassurance as he passes.

I step closer in April's direction. "I promise, I was going to tell you next time I saw you."

"Don't blame this on the current state of my mess of a life. You are my friend, we are supposed to say anything."

"Without judgment?" I wonder and fold my arms over my chest.

She scoffs a laugh. "That's not fair. You're sleeping with my uncle who is old enough to be your father. The rules get a little blurred."

I stand tall. "I know. I've been trying to figure them out."

"Oh my God, Piper. Like, despite my relation to him, how do you live in a city so focused on sports and not know the guy you bang is like sports royalty?"

My hands land on my hips. "I don't follow sports," I justify, and my voice squeaks.

"So, what now? You two are like really *together* together? This isn't some weird passionate tryst?"

"No, it's not. It's the real thing," I confirm.

April pauses in thought for a second, her thoughts clearly in turmoil. She says nothing but returns to the driver's-side door.

"Where are you going?"

She opens the door and looks at me with a sharp stare. "I came to solve the mystery, and I did."

"Okay. Then stay and let's have brunch together. Can't you be happy for us?"

April laughs bitterly. "The thing is, when I think about it, the problem isn't you and my Uncle Bay. I want him happy, and I want you happy. Maybe I even can see you two together. But what *is* the problem is that you both lied to me, for months. It also seems like everyone knew but me. That feels like a betrayal. And right now, when life kind of sucks, it's like a knife. So, congratulations, it's your ability to keep a secret and lie to me that has me questioning our friendship, and until I figure that out, I don't want to speak to you."

"April…" My heart hurts, and I want to stop her, but she is quick to get into her car and turn the engine on.

I throw my arms up in the air because there is nothing I can do now. With remorse, I head back into the house to the living room where I find Hudson pulling on a fresh t-shirt. He must pick up on my look because his neutral expression turns to a frown.

"Where's April?"

"She left. She's angry that I never told her."

Hudson walks to me and rubs my arm for comfort. "April will settle down, you'll see."

"It isn't great. I feel really bad now."

He points a finger at me. "Don't." He's firm. "Give it time. Least she knows now, the hard part is over. We can go public without having to worry if she's aware or not."

"Maybe we should wait on that."

An aggravated breath escapes his mouth. "I'm not going to go in a circle. Piper, I'm losing a little patience. I love that you care about my niece, but I'm in the picture now and need the same thought."

It hits me in that moment. I watched my friend leave, and now I'm staring at the man who I think I've been waiting my whole life for. I may be losing a friend, but I've gained a man who loves me, and I don't want to lose him too.

20

HUDSON

---

y arms stay firmly folded over my chest, and I know that my serious coach look is plastered across my face. But it's almost time for a mini-break, and it's the third time we have run this play, and in this moment, I'm calling bullshit on the third-time's-the-charm theory.

"In the lines," I call out, reminding my guys to focus instead of ending up a jumbled mess.

"We're getting near the end of training camp; they're a little exhausted, I guess," Arnold pipes up.

I give him a stern look. "All the more reason they need to get it together, as we have a pre-season game next week."

He gives me a look that informs me I should probably calm down.

I grumble loudly and roll my eyes. "Blow the whistle. Break time." My tone is sharp, and I point my finger at him to make my stance clear. "Doesn't mean I'm going to go easy in the afternoon practice. I want to speak to the offense coordinators tonight, and I want to add more names that will be off the roster."

He throws his hands up. "I know, I know."

While he blows the whistle, I look at my tablet to go over the morning's playbook and the list of players that I will soon need to cut. This season it seems to be the rookies that have it more together, or who are at least more focused.

I don't take much notice of the guys grabbing water and walking to the bleachers. This is normally when they quickly catch up with their respective others and confirm their lunch plans. It's only when I hear two of my players mentioning the fresh blood on the sidelines with a whistle that I look up.

I'm ready to swipe those smirks off their faces because I don't need them distracted, and someone has these two mid-twenty-year-olds looking all googly eyed. My head turns to get a glimpse of who has their attention.

The moment my eyes land on Piper in a pink summer dress, high-heeled strappy wedges, and sunglasses on her head, I'm torn inside. I'm completely elated that she's here because I've invited her more times than I can count. But the other half of me feels feral, and I'm quick to head in her direction.

"You both may want to study those drills some more," I mention to the boys in passing, taking slight pleasure in the fact that my role can make their life miserable if needed.

My grin spreads as Piper leans over the railing from the seats with a soft smile, as if she isn't quite sure how she should behave.

"Hi." She nibbles her bottom lip.

"You've finally come… here. I mean, we know you come often."

Her mouth drops open. "Hudson, anyone can you hear you say that." She looks around to check that we're in the clear.

I chuckle as I hop on the step and lean up and over the railing to kiss her. My hand touches her upper arm, and to the bystanders, I'm giving a respectable kiss, but if only they knew my tongue inside her mouth is giving Piper a preview of later when I plan on re-enacting some dirty-as-fuck positions.

Pulling away gently, my eyes connect with her own and they sparkle in a way.

Piper attempts to give me a smile, but it's weak. For the most part, I know she's happy. We laugh and have good evenings together, but I know my niece giving her the silent treatment weighs on Piper's mind. Still, she made the effort to come and see me at practice, which I know is out of her comfort zone.

"I had to check you're still alive after this morning's smoothie attempt. I just thought that if I added apple this time and nixed the cabbage." She shrugs her shoulder.

A stunted laugh escapes me because yesterday she attempted to make me a green protein shake, and it was a little brutal on the taste-buds. This morning she changed the recipe, and the apple did fuck all.

"It tasted fine," I lie. "Thank you for waking up early this morning, every morning really."

I want that every day until the day I die. This woman in my kitchen with the lights dimmed, five in the morning, and her eagerness to see me off so I have a good day.

"Hazards of dating a hot coach, his schedule kind of sucks." She smirks at me, and her fingers play with the neckline of my t-shirt. "And I kind of owe him since I kept him up past his bedtime."

Have mercy on me, because I love her sultry voice and would do anything to stop the clock and take her right now on the goddamn bench on the sidelines.

She must notice that my mind is thinking impure thoughts. Piper playfully nudges my other arm with her fist. "It's okay that I'm here, right? I'm not a distraction?" Piper seems to wonder if she is approaching her attempt to surprise me all wrong.

It draws my attention back.

I offer my hand so she can climb over the railing. "Of course, you can be here. Besides, you are the right kind of distraction," I admit.

She lands in front of me, and we look directly into one another's eyes.

"Okay. I mean, I guess the cheerleading outfit can stay in the closet." Now she is testing me, and I throw an arm around her shoulders to walk with her side by side.

"You'll be here for a quick lunch? Or did I bore you already? How long have you been here?" I wonder.

"Maybe twenty minutes, and yes, I will keep watching until lunchtime, but then I'm heading back to the city."

I sigh at the thought, as I hate that she isn't a permanent feature at my home. I make a mental note that we need to streamline our timeline. I haven't discussed it with her, but I don't see why living together can't be an item on our agenda. "I guess I'll see you at a game soon?"

"I'll do my best. My mind is kind of occupied as I need to go back to see my grandmother and hopefully try again with April, or at least see if she will speak to me." I hear her disappointment.

"She'll come around."

Piper doesn't answer, instead surveying the area. "I guess we have an audience."

I tip my head to the side. "We are very much in public. But don't worry about it, only people on the list are here, and the wives of players in a way follow a code, which is keep other people's lives private." I scan the area and indeed we have a few eyes on us.

She leans in and speaks low. "Coach Arrows is kind of hot. He seems demanding and bossy, wouldn't want to get in his bad books." Piper's attempt to hide her giggle falls short. I give her raised brows, as I'm not sure where she is leading her thoughts. She is quick to clarify. "You're more serious when you're on the field. The opposite of laid-back Hudson in ridiculous aprons."

"It's been a rough day. I would like to think I'm more approachable to the guys, but today is brutal, they're tiring quickly."

Piper nods in understanding. Our gaze with one another is, however, broken when Kimberly waves and walks to us.

"Hey, Coach!" She widely smiles, clearly thrilled that I'm not alone.

I give her a short wave. "Hi there." I notice Kimberly keeps her eyes set on Piper. "This is Piper who I mentioned. Piper, this is Kimberly who works on the events-and-marketing team."

"Oh." I hear a lack of enthusiasm, but Piper is a sport and offers a genuine smile. "Nice to meet you."

Kimberly looks between us. "Wonderful to see you here, Piper. We were all a little bummed that we had to cancel the bachelor article on Hudson, then celebrated that Hudson under the love spell would also be a great spin. Someone finally tying him down, you know?" She rambles as she normally does around me.

"Whoa. I'm here. Filter it, Kimberly."

Kimberly shakes her head. "Oh shit. I said that all out loud, didn't I?"

Piper's face doesn't flinch as she waits to see where this conversation is going.

It takes a beat. "...But if you two are going social media official, could you maybe add a Chicago Winds theme somewhere in the photo?"

"For sure. We will absolutely take a photo of two Winds mugs with a comment that breakfast is better together." Piper is completely sarcastic which makes me chortle under my breath.

"That would be wonderful." Kimberly continues without picking up Piper's undertone.

"Oh, I was joking." Piper now looks amused.

Kimberly doesn't stop as she looks at her tablet. "Wait... you're the owner of Piper Ginger?" Piper nods proudly. "I love your stuff. Those pajama bottoms with moon prints are my favorite. I could live in those."

"Thank you. Those are my bestsellers."

"Anything else?" I ask. "I kind of need to get back to what I'm paid for." I do my best to swerve Kimberly away.

Her sight lands on me. "I've sent you an updated schedule for the coming weeks. You have a few morning news slots coming up after you announce the season roster."

"Usual business then. Can we catch up later?" I suggest.

"Sure. Maybe I can go over a few things with Piper and the team engagements coordinator during the next hour of practice?"

I look at Piper who seems lost. "It's just protocol. The dos and don'ts of what can be discussed. Not a big deal since you didn't even know who I was when we met."

"What?!" Kimberly looks at Piper.

She shrugs her shoulders. "I know zero about sports."

"Well, that will change soon."

I grin again. "You okay?" I check with Piper.

"Sure, no problem." Piper seems at ease.

"Great. I will give you two a minute then." Kimberly walks off.

Piper looks at me, clearly entertained. "Have I just walked into a cult and this is my initiation?"

I rub both of her shoulders and hold her gaze. "Nah. It's just a different world, a little closed-off sometimes. People kind of keep their distance unless you're married or engaged to a player."

"Oh." Her eyes flutter.

A smirk spreads on my lips. "We can make that happen if you want."

She scoffs a laugh. "Hudson Arrows, always on the fast track."

"I'm not sure slow is for us." I'm serious, and by the way her face stills for a second, I think she understands my sentiment.

"You haven't even met my grandmother yet." It sounds like a challenge.

"I'll rectify that."

Piper glances away then back at me. "I don't doubt that."

"Don't worry, you're the coach's girl, so by association they may be a little scared of you."

"Duly noted."

I glance at my watch and know that I've already let break carry on for a minute longer, and it may have people thinking I'm going soft.

"I'm happy you're here. Also, that you're not running for the hills after the last five minutes."

She steps closer to me, her hands sliding up my arms to land on my shoulders. "Nah, running for the hills would mean that you would only chase after me, and I like when you lead the way."

There is something about her words that lingers inside me the rest of the day. Piper seemed at ease after chatting with the team coordinators, and a quick lunch was a refreshing change to my schedule. When I bid her goodbye, I could tell she was at peace yet still missing a piece of her life to make her feel fully calm.

And I have every intention to rectify that.

21

HUDSON

I give my best grin, with my swagger out in full force, as I sit on the sofa across from Piper's grandmother who is examining the gift I brought her, completely welcoming the fact that I showed up unannounced and without Piper's knowledge.

"Don't worry, I made sure it was top quality," I assure her as she sets the bottle of vodka, ideal for martinis, to the side. Adjusting my suit jacket, I didn't put it on for her, but I know this outfit gives me an extra edge.

"You get points for the initiative. My granddaughter has no idea you're here, and I think I like that. Although she will be here soon." The woman's red polished nails tap the sofa arm.

"Well, my schedule is a bit tight these days, and I'm in the city, as our season is about to start. I had an hour to spare and figured that I should cross some essential meetings off my list," I explain and insinuate meeting her.

She understands and a smirk spreads on her face. "My granddaughter talks about you, and don't take it personal that she hasn't dragged you to meet me. I can be… opinionated."

"You have good judgment."

A sound escapes her as she stands and walks to a tray of crystal glasses and alcohol choices in well-designed bottles that hold expensive alcohol along the side of the living room. She goes straight for a scotch, stopping mid-pour to look at me and question with her eyes.

"I never let a good-looking woman drink alone and my driver is downstairs."

I may be laying it on thick, but I can tell she likes to play along, and a minute later when she hands me a glass of amber-colored liquid, she pauses to study me once more before returning to her seat.

This place screams old money or at least decorative tastes that take you back to another era.

"So, what really brings you here, Hudson Arrows?" she asks before taking a sip.

I lean back, confident. "Truthfully, I'm being a selfish man. I'm crazy about your granddaughter, and I figured that I would throw in some tradition. It might make Piper blush like a rose, but I'm used to that."

Ruth snorts a laugh. "I'm sure you keep her satisfied."

My eyes bug out slightly, as this lady's humor is on par with my own. "If I wait for Piper to invite me, then I may be waiting a while, and I know you're important to her."

"Piper has reason to hesitate, as I'm sure you know about her past relationship. But she also hesitates to accept anything good that enters her life. It's in her nature. When she had her bat mitzvah, she questioned me for six weeks if the necklace I gave her wasn't too much. She has a kind heart, but make no mistake, she has a backbone and can be stubborn and confident when needed."

"Couldn't agree more. I'm just a little stuck, as my niece wasn't thrilled with the news about Piper and myself, and I know it's keeping Piper down."

She waves off my notion. "April and Piper will find their way back to one another. Something will bring them together again."

I hum at the thought. "I think so too. Maybe I should do more, I've kind of stayed on the sidelines."

Her eyes stay fixed on me and don't blink. "As much as I'm sure my granddaughter's friendship suffering from her choice of gentleman suiter is a topic of discussion, I'm more interested in your mention of being a traditional guy."

I laugh, as she sees right through me. "Fair enough. I'm sure you've done your research on me, so I don't need to go over my backstory."

"Certainty have, and the media loves you, as do the women at my Tuesday-night book club."

"Fun." I move quickly on. "I just need you to know that my intentions are honorable, and I hope when the schedule allows, that we can have dinner together. Until then, I promise that I'll take care of Piper, always."

She lifts her nose and folds her hands over her skirt. "Sounds like some long-term plans."

"They are. I've made it clear to Piper what I want in life, and she's still around which tells me she thinks I'm a keeper." I tone down my cockiness for a second.

"You've kept her busy the last few months, that's for sure. I have a talent, they say. I can judge someone's character within ten seconds, and my thought about them will never change. Unlucky for many, but exceptionally lucky for Piper, as I'm never wrong."

The corners of my mouth twist while I wait for her to continue.

"I have a good feeling about you."

"Only good?" I joke.

"You would get an extra point if you tell me you have a Jewish grandfather or something, but meh."

I chuckle because her face is dead serious. "If I say I have every intention of making her my wife, would you still have a very good feeling about me?"

She wiggles her long finger in the air. "I don't change my opin-ions of people."

Ah, she agrees with me.

"You may think I'm moving fast, but I'm not getting any younger, and I live a life where my days revolve around a game that you always want to win. No room for error, nor opportunity to slow things down. So the moment that I put in the effort for something, then everything goes out the window. That's it, I want it until I have it. For the first time, I put in the effort with a woman, and it's because I can't imagine my life without her. I wouldn't even know how to let go if I tried, nor do I plan on stumbling either."

"You sound like Piper's grandfather. He had the same demeanor. Also, older than me and a smooth talker. I understand where you are coming from. It may scare Piper like crazy, but sometimes we need someone to take us out of our comfort zones, albeit in a positive way."

"Couldn't agree more."

In that moment, we hear the front door to the apartment open, and our attention turns to the entrance.

"They only had roast beef. Simon swears you didn't have an order in for this week," Piper announces as she juggles a bag and her purse. When she drops the bags and looks up, she stops in her tracks, and her mouth parts open in surprise. "Hudson?"

I stand to greet her. "In the flesh."

She slowly walks to me and looks between her grandmother and me, a nervous smile appearing on her face. "What are you doing here?" I hear the disbelief in her voice that she walked in on this surprise.

I'm quick to give her a kiss hello, far too chaste for my liking. "I had a little free time and thought I would introduce myself."

Piper's eyes have a hint of shock. "Oh, uhm, and you thought to take matters into your own hands?" I can't quite figure out if she's mad or entertained.

"See, Ruth, she is a smart woman this one." I play into the amused side.

Her grandmother focuses on Piper. "Relax, dear, we were having a good discussion. About you, of course, and we covered the essentials. I mean, I'm just going to assume his *package* is up to my standards."

Piper's face turns near white. "Oh my." She shakes her head and walks to the tray of alcohol. "This is why I was petrified of this scenario." She pours herself a decent drink.

"I didn't even do an inspection and my special sense told me that he's a keeper within ten seconds."

"What in the world is the inspection?" Piper looks petrified, but I can only laugh.

Her grandmother stands. "Well, I haven't asked, and I was kind of hoping, but you know what? I think I've given up that particular criteria, and being circumcised is more for your enjoyment than tradition, but it's fine. Besides, I have a feeling this guy would be the type of guy to ask for my input on wedding rings and maybe name my first grandchild after me, so we are good to go."

Piper takes a long gulp.

I walk to her and bring my hand to her upper arm. "Are you okay?"

"Of course she is, she has you in her life to take off those lacy pieces she designs."

Piper's mouth falls open again when she looks at her grandmother. "Tone it down." She looks at me. "It's not that I didn't want you to meet, I just know she has zero filter, and it requires like a few hours of mental preparation for dealing with you two in the same room."

I rub her shoulders. "And now you've had no mental preparation. I like the element of surprise."

"She's fine. She loves my candid honesty. It's more likely she was afraid that I might not like you and now she can relax because you have my seal of approval," her grandmother announces.

Her head perks up. "You like him?" Piper's voice turns soft, and her eyes fill with that familiar glimmer of hope and admiration that I've seen a few times now.

Her grandmother nods, and that's what it takes for Piper to relax and smile an honest smile.

"I'll give you two a minute while I do some things in the kitchen. And if you need *a moment,* just use the guest room at the end."

"Well, that's a special offer," I retort.

When Ruth is out of the room, Piper's head falls against my shoulder. "Are we not allowed any normal family meetings?"

"That wouldn't be fun."

Piper looks up at me, and I'm quick to cradle her face in the palms of my hands and kiss her soft and long until she's murmuring into my breath. I haven't seen her since the other week, and while she knew I was in the city, we didn't set a time in stone for when we would see one another.

"It's a busy time, and I wish I could stop the clock," I admit.

"Me too. I hate city life now, and I hate sleeping alone or at least not knowing the pillow next to me smells of you."

I kiss her forehead. "You can always stay in Lake Spark, even if I'm not there."

"I know. Maybe I will head there sometime in the coming weeks. I can focus on work, hang with the knitting ladies since April is still MIA from my life, and survive on coffee with jellybeans."

"Could be a solid plan."

Piper stares at me and her eyes flutter, and I know her soft playful voice is about to come on. "You should be in trouble for this move."

I pull her flush against my body and wrap my arms around her. "Sometimes you need a little push, and I wanted to be a little traditional."

"Should have done this before you spanked me in the bedroom then." That fucking sexy voice.

My brows raise from her boldness, and I pull her tighter against my body. "I'm a little late on that, but I can spank you harder next time."

She purrs into my neck and loops her arms around my neck, then she tilts her body against my dick. This woman is being a little vixen.

"Stay for dinner then we can leave together?" she offers.

"I wish, but I have a dinner with sponsors and won't finish until late. Football season isn't going to be on our side."

She sighs and nods in understanding. "I get it."

I crook my finger under her chin to tip her face up. "There are 168 hours in the week, of which about 115 of those hours are coaching and 35 for sleeping. I hope every sleeping hour you are next to me, and any hours left in the week are for you, but even so, it depends on where a game might be. But it doesn't matter, as you are always on my mind."

"I know. I'm getting used to it."

Piper's grandmother interrupts us. "You know if you marry, the coaches' wives have an association."

We both look at her, and she shrugs her shoulders.

"How much have you heard?" Piper wonders.

"Enough."

I scoff a laugh again. "You're something special, Ruth."

"I know." She doesn't hold in any modesty.

Looking back at Piper, I'm happy that we can strike another milestone off the list.

———

HOLDING my phone to my ear, I wait for my sister to pick up. My driver is getting me to my next location for the day, so I have some time to kill.

"Oh dear, what have you done now?" Catherine greets me on the other end.

"Love you too. Can't a guy call his sister?"

"You can, but you've been occupied lately. Speaking of which, I hear April is still giving you and Piper the silent treatment."

I look out the window where we are stuck at a traffic light during rush-hour traffic on the north side of Chicago.

"She is, but I'm hoping to rectify that, as Piper and I are not going to fade away. I was hoping they could sort it all out, but that doesn't seem to be happening, so I'm tapping in. I need your help."

Catherine hums. "You understand where April is coming from, right?"

"Partly, but not enough that it's an issue. Look, I know she hasn't had the best of romantic endeavors lately, but even more reason why she could use her friend, and I need Piper happy too, especially now that she's losing me to the football season schedule. I'd feel better knowing she has her best friend back."

"For selfish reasons, you call, but luckily I love you, and you did promise that I could have a spa day at the Dizzy Duck Inn on your account—"

My body sits up in reaction. "That's it. You're a genius. See, I knew phoning you would be a good idea. Thanks!"

"Wait, what? What just happened? I'm confused."

"Gotta go, need to call April." I hang up and quickly dial April's number, even adding video.

I wait and wait, but eventually April answers.

"Yes?" I hear attitude which only makes me smile.

"You can't stay mad at me. We're family, and my son is connected to the best winery around and I coach your favorite team, so you need me."

She holds her hand up. "Oh, don't worry. Drew isn't getting my silent treatment since he didn't sleep with my best friend. Why did you, my cool uncle, have to become a cliché?"

"I'm not a cliché. I found a beautiful woman who I want to spend my life with, and she just so happens to be your age and your friend. I can't apologize—"

"I know. You have no problem staying firm on your stances. It's why you're a coach."

I smile at her thought. "I know somewhere in your smart head that if you look at it more, then you would understand. Anyways, it happened and here we are, and I just wanted to invite you to Lake Spark sometime soon for a spa day. I promised your mom it would be on me and thought I would extend the invitation."

April looks at me, intrigued yet doubtful.

"Will Piper be there?"

"No. Would it matter, though? I know you miss her. I mean, she misses you. Just the other day she was in a mood because she saw a dog and said it reminded her of you."

"Was it a beagle?" April nearly smiles.

I nod and see we are approaching our destination on all counts.

"Listen, I've got to run, but will you make it happen? Visiting Lake Spark?"

"I mean, I guess I can cram it into my busy schedule of ice cream, ripping up photos of my ex, and wondering where I went wrong in life."

I cringe at that thought. "How are you doing with that?"

"Swell," she says, sarcastic.

"You deserve so much better, and you will find someone."

"If I had a penny every time someone told me that, then, well, I would be swimming in coins."

I unbuckle my belt as the car comes to a standstill. "All the more reason to have a nice escape. Just send me your available dates."

"Fine."

"We'll be in touch," I say as the car door opens.

"Bye."

"Bye, kiddo."

Satisfaction spreads on my face because I have every intention of trapping April and Piper together, and I know they will thank me later. After that, we can just all move forward, because surely we've crossed every possible blip off the list.

Hudson fixes his collar. We're sitting in the back of the car with his driver up front. Admittedly, I got a little handsy when we had a two-hour window. Between his meetings with team administration and the schedule of getting on a plane for an away game, this is what we get.

But it's okay because Hudson picked me up from my apartment. We drove around with the full intention of grabbing something to eat but got side-tracked.

Since the other week when he showed up at my grandmother's, something has swelled inside of me. To some, his move may have been a step too far, yet it felt perfectly right. Typical Hudson, too, as the man has zero patience except when it involves football. And he completely has my grandmother wrapped around his little finger. He had dressed to impress and spoke with honesty; it was enough to slay any woman's heart.

"You may want to straighten your blouse. I'm not a fan of other people gawking at your beautiful tits." He gives me a stern eye with a subtle smirk on his mouth.

I glance down to see my buttons are undone. "You've left me disheveled yet again."

Hudson angles his body toward me and slides his hand along my cheek. "Don't kill me for saying it but you seem different."

I work my buttons closed. "Oh? Well, work is a little crazy, I guess. I'm lucky that I outsource so many things and I rely on internet orders, but I really need to find a new spot to kind of set up base. I also had a hell of a week. I wasn't too thrilled with the model who showed up for a photoshoot for the spring collection, and I mean, April is still, well…"

"You're stressed."

I tip my head to the side in contemplation. "Maybe… a little." I'm missing a confidante in my life, in the shape of a best friend.

"I can tell. But I have just the thing to help. How about you drive up to Lake Spark for the weekend and have a spa day, your boyfriend's treat."

Curiosity floods my face. "That's quite an offer."

"When you go to Lake Spark, you're always occupied with me, which is a perfect way to enjoy Lake Spark, but the spa is one of the best."

I rub the back of his hand with my thumb and hold his wrist. "I mean, I guess a few days of calm would be good for me. I've worked at your house before, and I wouldn't complain about nabbing a coffee with jellybeans every day."

"It's settled then."

I lean in to kiss him on his lips. "Thank you." Because it's a sweet gesture, and I think he's noticed that I've been down since April made it clear she wasn't happy with how I handled my relationship with her uncle.

"I'm being selfish. I need to know that you're okay while I'm thousands of miles away."

The corner of my mouth tugs, and I move to straddle him and hook my arms around his neck, ensuring our eyes are locked. "Don't worry. I'm fine and as prepared as I can be for your mind to be in the game many hours of the day and the fact you need to focus. I promise to only send any inappropriate selfies after 10pm."

He playfully pinches my sides. "You'll be at one of the upcoming home games?"

I nod my head, but inside I feel my breath get caught because that means more eyes and cameras. "How about I send you a pre-game photo of what I'm wearing underneath my Winds t-shirt to keep you motivated?" I throw him a sexy look.

He growls before he kisses the base of my throat. "If you do that then I'll absolutely devour you later, take you to the edge, and leave you hanging. There will be consequences," he taunts me back.

"That's not a deterrent."

Hudson quickly looks out the window and sees that my drop-off is approaching. "Here we are. I hate this."

"You be safe. Get sleep and eat well. It'll be a good season," I assure him.

He smiles gently. "I like hearing you say that. It's refreshing to hear it from someone not trying to kiss my ass." His fingertips brush a loose strand of my hair behind my ear. "Actually, I like having someone to share this world with who isn't a sports person."

I kiss him again and pull my body tighter against him to hug with everything I have.

"Easy there," he warns me.

I giggle as the car stops, and I hop off his lap. My hand is on the door handle, even though I know the driver will open it. Hudson stops me. "Piper, what I was saying earlier about how you seem different…"

"Yes?" I look at him, puzzled.

The gentlest of closed-mouth smiles stretches on his mouth. "Still no birth control, right?"

I shake my head no.

He looks at me, waiting for me to catch on.

But it takes a little longer for my brain to connect. It's only when his eyes gawk at me that I understand.

"Oh."

Hudson reaches out with the back of his finger once more to rub my cheek. "Yeah, oh." He flashes his eyes. "It's the way I want it."

I know he hopes that I'm pregnant, but truthfully, it hasn't crossed my mind, as we're not actively trying, nor actively being safe either. We don't say anything else about the topic as we bid one another goodbye.

———

ARRIVING at the front desk of the spa, I'm occupied with tying my hair up into a messy bun. Nonetheless, the calming music does bring me down a smidgen on the stress scale, and the candles, green plants, and swinging chairs all set the tone that I've entered tranquil territory.

When Hudson suggested this the other week, I just kind of agreed to be polite. Well, staying at his house wasn't, I was honest that I focus well at his place, so I have no qualms about coming to Lake Spark while he's away, but a spa day is kind of special, and I figured it was something he was just suggesting to be nice. But Hudson doesn't suggest, he acts. So, a few days later, he told me that he'd booked me in at the Dizzy Duck Inn.

"Good morning, you must be Piper." The woman my age with impeccable skin greets me from behind the desk.

"Yeah, that's me. I have, or my boyfriend, he made a reservation for me." I'm still getting used to calling him that, but it makes a small smile break out.

The woman studies the screen with a welcoming look. "Indeed, he booked you quite a day. Full-body massage, facial, nails, and you also have a lovely lunch later on the terrace, and you can use the sauna and jacuzzi, of course. Can I get you some mint water to start? You are having a massage first."

My brows raise, as I'm impressed that Hudson arranged all of that, and wow, I am a lucky girl. "Water would be good."

"Sure. I will show you the changing room so you can throw on a robe, and I'll get you that water." She grabs a few folded towels from behind her on the shelf and indicates with her hand that I should follow her. "Your friend is here already."

"Friend?"

She glances over her shoulder. "Yes. The day is for two people… or did you not know that?" An awkward smile forms on her mouth.

I laugh under my breath before my lips roll in then quirk out because I should have seen this coming. Hudson isn't shy to do things. "Let me guess…"

She opens the door and in my full view is April tying her fluffy white robe. "Piper." April's voice fills with disdain, but even that feels more for theatrics.

The lady from the spa looks between us and manages to hold her smile. "I'll give you two a few minutes and get some water. When you're both ready, you have a partner massage in room three."

April and I don't take notice of the woman leaving, instead we stare at one another.

"I guess my mother isn't meeting me for a spa day… Sounds like typical Hudson." April crosses her arms.

I step into the changing room and walk to the hanging robe, not bothering to look at April. "Maybe I knew deep down that he would conspire to get us into a room together." I grab the robe.

"Right. Because you two are soul mates now." April's sentence is dripping with sarcasm, which causes me to throw a glare in her direction. Immediately, April seems to look remorseful. "Sorry," she clips. "But I'm not leaving."

"You don't need to," I say as I begin to undress.

"Good. Because I could use a spa day."

"Me too."

"Fine."

Silence takes over the room, and when I tie my robe, we seem to be in a stare-off. "We should probably head to our massage."

April lifts her head. "Okay, but if we get a hot masseuse, then obviously he's mine."

I shake my head. "No argument there."

I turn to put my phone in the locker, and I see Hudson is calling me on the screen, as my phone is on silent. I quickly answer and bring the phone to my ear. "Can't talk long, as the massage is about to start." I speak in a near-hushed tone.

"You're not going to kill me?" I can hear him grinning through the phone.

Looking at April, I smile tightly. "No. I… appreciate the deception."

"You're getting a spa day *and* your friend out of this, baby. I'm sure you will show your appreciation later." There is sinfulness in his tone, and it causes me to grow bashful.

"Now isn't the time for this discussion. I'm sure April won't kill me, I mean, as long as her masseuse is hot and single."

Hudson snorts a laugh. "Not a fucking chance. I made sure you have two women. I'm not having some guy stare at your fine body. I'd rip his head off, even if he is being professional. Nobody sees you naked but me."

Whoa, there is some possessiveness in his tone, the good kind. Well, bad, because I feel an effect between my legs and I'm now going for a massage.

"Okay, okay, we need to go. I'll phone you later. Good luck with your team meetings today." I quickly end the call.

April gives me a pointed look before pivoting to walk down the hall. I follow her and roll my eyes. I know it may take a little for her to warm up to me.

And during the massage, we made one step when I noticed a hint of entertainment when she realized she wouldn't be getting any good-looking spa men today, and she seemed relaxed like me when the massage was finished, even asked if I enjoyed mine.

Now we're sitting on rocking chairs with masks on our faces and overlooking the indoor water feature while sipping on cucumber water. As much as I have a bunch of questions so we can catch up, I'm waiting for her cues.

But then when I see her watching a small group of women leaving the changing room with pink satchels that indicates it's a bachelorette weekend, then I know what's occupying April's thoughts.

"I bet lunch will be delicious," I attempt to divert her attention.

April looks at me. "Ginger, it's okay, I'm not going to burst into tears."

Is this a step? She called me my nickname for the first time in a long time. I give her a sympathetic look. "You don't need to get married to have a nice spa weekend."

"No. I just need a best friend who is sleeping with my rich uncle." Her tone and look are actually a relief because I know she was attempting to make a joke.

I try to hide my smile. "So, I'm still your best friend?"

April sighs and places her glass on the side table. "I have a right to be mad. You lied to me for months."

Setting my own glass down, I angle my body toward her. "I could have handled it differently, I know."

"And I'm a horrible person," she states.

"That should probably be my line in this situation."

April blows out another breath. "I think I was also mad because… you get to fall in love when my heart has been stepped on. What kind of friend doesn't want their friend to be happy?"

I reach out to touch her arm in comfort. "The kind of friend who is human and just had an engagement ripped away from them because the guy is an absolute tool, and even though it's for the best, it still stings."

"He is a tool. We were supposed to go to Italy on our honeymoon, and now I have to ditch those plans."

"You can still go. Maybe now you can do that cooking course instead of what he wanted to do."

April attempts to smile. "I guess I can get a dog now too since he was allergic."

I give her a knowing look. "But was he?" My voice raises to a near squeak. "Or was he just saying that because he doesn't like dogs?"

April laughs and tries to keep her tears back. "Fuck, the signs were there all along, weren't they? We weren't a match."

I shrug. "I don't know, I mean, opposites attract, so don't beat yourself up about that."

"Are you and Hudson opposites?" she wonders.

I take hold of my drink again to occupy myself, as I'm not sure how to talk to her about my boyfriend who happens to be her uncle and godfather. There are some topics that may be a little too uncomfortable to discuss, I'm aware of that.

"In some ways, sure. He's all or nothing, determined, focused yet laid back. I'm… laid back, focused, and hesitant with many things in life. So maybe we meet in the middle."

"Are you hesitant about him?" April asks point blank.

A warm smile comes naturally. "I feel different when I'm with him. From the moment that I met him, actually. I've always done slow, and he does… fast. But it's okay, as I feel safe and free. That was something I didn't think I would ever feel again in a relationship."

This time April reaches out to touch my shoulder. "He is by far the furthest thing from your douchebag of an ex."

"I know. I don't think that really comes into play, it's more the feelings in general. But I'm not sure I'm coach's-wife material, I mean the whole in-the-spotlight thing."

"First-world problems, I guess. But just be yourself. It isn't about you in those moments. I don't see my uncle often because he's married to his career, maybe not even by choice. Being head coach just takes a lot of hours, but for the first time he wants to attempt to be tied to something outside of football. It just so happens to be my friend."

Our eyes meet, and perhaps this is our turning point. "It really sucked not being able to share things with you."

"I know the feeling."

"Can we move forward?" My voice is hopeful.

April seems to contemplate. "I've wallowed for weeks. Maybe I needed the time to digest the news about you and my uncle too. I think we can move forward… but if you and my uncle don't work out, then it might be awkward, so I guess that means… you need to work out." There's a humorous undertone. "And I know lingerie is your career, but maybe let's put a pin in those discussions, or at least don't add my uncle's name into the same sentence."

"I can live with that." I nod.

"I guess it only took a massage and facial to get us to talk. I was kind of expecting we would at least need the pedicure too before we really talked," she quips.

"I'm happy we're ahead of schedule then because I've really missed having a best friend in my life," I admit. "I have so much to share, and I was so worried about you."

"I could use my friend back too."

The corners of our mouths curve up and tears form in our eyes before we lean in to hug one another, then tears actually burst out. "I'm so sorry."

"Me too."

We squeeze tighter in our hug, careful not to make a mess of our face masks.

The spa attendant comes to interrupt us to take our masks off, and just in time, as I feel my face cracking.

"Oh God, are we going to get weird lines on our faces because we cried with this magical mud on?" April wonders.

The attendant smiles. "Believe it or not, you two are not the first to cry while in the mask. You should be fine. Some even say the tears enhance the experience."

April and I look at each other and burst out laughing.

———

Now back in normal clothes, I arrive at our table overlooking Lake Spark. It's clear blue skies today.

April looks up from her phone. "They offered us a high tea with little sandwiches and cakes, but I changed it to burgers and fries."

"Oh, thank God." I'm relieved that she knows me so well. "I feel like that massage was like running a marathon. Or maybe it was the sauna, but I'm starving."

"I guess you are all up-to-date on Lake Spark, so did you go to Jolly Joe's or Catch 22?"

I nod as I sip from my iced tea. "It feels like a second home almost. Just kind of sucks that Hudson is now in football season so won't be here much."

"It sounds like you will, though. Moving in?" she asks simply.

I laugh. "No. Well, it's more like my apartment in the city is a place where I sleep and here it feels like… a home."

She raises a brow at me. "That's promising."

"Actually… there is this little boutique on Main Street. Apparently, it's been empty for a while, but the family didn't want to sell. I saw a sign go up today that it's for sale." Excitement comes out in my words because it would be great spot for Piper Ginger.

April studies me for a second then grins. "Exactly what Lake Spark needs, a classy lingerie company."

I wave my hand. "It's just a silly thought."

"No, it's not." She looks over my shoulder. "Ooh, I see our food arriving."

A few moments later, with food in front of us, April checks her phone for a moment. "That dress is stunning by the way," she mentions.

"What dress?"

"The one you were wearing when you were packing on the PDA with Coach Arrows."

My face turns bewildered, as I don't understand, and April notices, so she shows me her phone. "You're online. One of the players' wives posted a video from practice and someone pointed out what they saw in the background… you and my uncle."

I look at the screen, and my stomach sinks because there I am in Hudson's arms. It looks innocent enough, but very much makes the message clear that I'm his significant other. "Oh, I didn't know about this. We were going to announce when we were ready with a photo of coffee mugs or a view of a sunset or something like that."

April snorts a laugh and takes her phone back, scrolling frantically. "Well, a little late for that. You are an entire hashtag. Oh, 'arrow to his heart,' that's a cute comment. Actually… you and my uncle are kind of blowing up the internet." She tilts her head to the side. "Ooh, I see we have a few new articles. 'Coach Arrows is no longer a bachelor!' There is also 'This is the year for Coach Arrows on and off the field.'"

"What?" I feel a sense of panic come over me. A waiter walks by, and I quickly signal for him to stop. "Can I have martini?" My head is spinning, but just as quickly as I requested the drink, I backtrack. "Wait! Can I just have… a Shirley Temple maybe."

April's eyes blaze open and her mouth drops. "Holy shit. You just turned down alcohol."

I breathe out a long calming exhale and hold my palm up. "It's not what you think."

23

PIPER

I throw another bar of chocolate into our shopping basket while April appears with two bottles of wine in hand. I give her a skeptical look.

"You know what I love about the Lake Spark general store? It's like a grocery store from the city, with an abundance of quality wine choices. I don't think there is one single bottle of crap wine on the shelf here. And I can't decide if it's a rosé or straight-up white wine kind of night. Are you sure you don't want any vino right now?" she double-checks.

I shake my head and confidently offer her the basket. "I need a clear mind."

At the spa it took a solid few minutes to convince April that I'm not pregnant, even when I explained that I really just want to be able to think clearly this weekend and was feeling the effects of the massage. I convinced April to ditch her night at the inn and stay at Hudson's since he's away anyways.

He texted that he would call when he was done with team meetings because he saw the video of us online, to which his response was, *"Damn it, should have had my hand on your ass for the extra wow factor."*

We turn down the next aisle and nearly run into Spencer, Hudson's neighbor. "Oh, hey there, ladies," he greets us, and I notice immediately how his eyes land on a glaring April.

"Hey!" I look between them then brush past it. "I was hoping to run into you, as I think you've been collecting the packages of materials I had delivered, and you left them by the back door. I wanted to thank you."

"Yep. That's me."

"He's a real saint, I'm sure." April's tone is pure snark.

This is one weird vibe happening. "So, uhm, I guess you're around more now that baseball season is over?" I attempt to make conversation.

Spencer turns his attention to me. "I am. Just give me a shout if you need something. Hudson texted to let me know you would be around more and then mentioned something about the pine tree or some shit like that."

"Yeah, he has this annoying tree." Silence fills our bubble, and I'm not entirely sure April or Spencer realize I'm still here, but they both look like they may kill one another. "Right. So April and I should probably head back to the house. Beat the weekend fox rush on the road, you know."

Silence.

I grab April's arm. "Okay, bye."

"Bye, ladies!" Spencer calls out.

April and I approach the register, and I let her arm go and look straight at her. "Explain."

"He's an asshole. I met him once when my uncle had a BBQ, and he was at my cousin Drew's wedding. Every time he talks, I want to bang my head against a wall. He just constantly brags about his success." She pretends to gag.

"Well, he's nice enough to me."

"Lucky you."

I shake my head and focus on our turn at the register.

A few minutes later, we're back outside and ready to load my car, but I stop when I notice the for sale sign on the empty store for the second time today, a reminder of my crazy thought.

April looks in the direction of my sight. "You're really considering it, aren't you?"

I smile and shrug it off shyly. "Nah, it's crazy."

"Is it, though? Your living room became your warehouse, so I guess if you were looking to move away from the city then this is a sign."

"Real estate isn't that cheap here."

April's eyes grow big. "You have some money saved, a growing business, a rich grandmother, and an even richer boyfriend. You're good."

I laugh at her absurdity and get into the car. Yet the image of the for sale sign doesn't leave my mind on the way to the house.

———

SITTING on the edge of the bed, I hold my phone up as Hudson graces the screen.

"You're lying in bed, aren't you?" I flash my eyes at him.

"I am. I'm a little beat."

My lips quirk. "You'll get a good night of sleep and annihilate those Cougars tomorrow."

"Would be a better night of sleep if you were here."

"Ah, don't go soft on me, Coach." I lean back on the bed, and to tease him, move my shirt slightly off my shoulder. "Besides, I need to behave because your plan worked and now April and I are having a night in with snacks and movies."

Hudson smiles proudly. "I'm a smart man."

"You're annoying," I joke. "You make things happen."

"I do have talents," he quips. "So, about that video. Smith's wife apologized and also asked the engagements coordinator for your number to send an apology. She didn't realize her error. But really, it's no big deal, right? I mean, now we don't have to spend ten minutes trying to figure out if our coffee mugs have the right light for a photo."

I laugh. "True that. It's not a big deal. I mean, we knew it was coming, she just put us a little ahead of schedule." We were going to post something after the next home game.

"I got questioned during press rounds this afternoon, so you may want to watch that."

"Ooh, now I'm curious."

He throws an arm behind his head. "You'll be at the next home game, right?"

"Oh." I bite my bottom lip because I feel a pool of doubt in my belly. Fears resurface of people's opinions and uncertainty over whether I'm moving too fast. "I'm not completely sure," I admit. The comments I saw on the latest article seemed to emphasize that I'm a trophy. Never mind the fact that I run a successful business, I'm now a glorified doll.

"What do you mean?" I hear disappointment in his voice.

"It's a lot of press, and I'm not entirely sure I feel up to it energy-wise."

Now he looks at me, confused. "What does that mean?"

"My mind is a little overloaded right now, and I haven't slept so great. Can I see how I feel at the end of the week?" I say it before even thinking it over.

But Hudson's disapproval is apparent on his face. "Piper... I'm going a little crazy on the merry-go-round of hot-cold-hot. I need to know that you're on board with this life. I can't make it disappear. So yes, being with me means you are probably going to have to get out of your comfort zone more than you are accustomed, because I want to be with someone who *wants* to be at my games and there for me, not dragged along."

I hold my hand up. "I don't think we should talk about this now. You're tired, and April is downstairs."

"No, we're not going to talk about this now. In fact, I don't want to talk about it until you've thought this all through and have made a decision that you're comfortable with. As much as I love you, you're bringing out an uneasiness that I haven't felt in years."

Shit. I'm ruining this, but he's right, and I need to clarify my standpoint and thoughts before we discuss it further.

"You're right," is all I can say.

And just like that, we have our first fight.

———

I THROW the remote for the fireplace to the side and look at April who is studying me intently while she pours herself a glass of wine at the coffee table in Hudson's living room.

"It's kind of weird seeing you in this habitat. It's like you are the lady of the house."

I snort a laugh. "What in the world does that mean?"

She takes a sip of her wine. "You know where everything is, walk around like it's your home, and seem calm here. I'm going to assume most of your romantic rendezvous with my uncle took place here, so that explains it, I guess."

My jaw flexes side to side. "Your thought process might be on point. And yes, I feel at home here, whether Hudson's here or not."

"That's a big deal."

I shrug it off and instead glance at the television that is mounted on the wall and that we put on pause. "Is it bad if I watch it again?"

April smiles at me. "Kind of sickly cute."

I press the rewind button, with guilt plaguing me. Pressing play, Hudson appears on the screen in the clip that he mentioned from earlier. It's the sports channel that I've gotten used to watching in recent months. I know they always have media following the team around while in season and today one of the reporters stopped Hudson after practice.

On the screen, Hudson is in jeans and a long-sleeved shirt with the team logo. He folds his arms as he listens to the man with the mic ask a question. "Everyone is counting on a win this week, but the

Cougars have a strong defense from what we've seen this season. How are you feeling about tomorrow's away game?"

Hudson's face remains stoic, with a hint of cocky confidence twisting on the corner of his mouth. "My guys have been practicing hard and continue to study the plays, whether we need to have a strong offense or defense tomorrow. We also have a lot of new blood on the team this year, and I'm confident that they will bring some fresh energy to the game to support some of the best returning players in the industry that have come back this year."

"Would you say you're not going to lose sleep tonight about tomorrow's game?" The man with the mic returns the device to Hudson so he can speak.

"Nah. Only coaches who don't have confidence in their guys lose sleep."

The commentator laughs. "Fair enough. There is also a rumor, thanks to a recent video, that you're now sharing your life with someone off the field. Care to comment?"

Hudson's grin is now uncontrollable, yet it's so incredibly suave. "My personal life has no effect on tomorrow's game, but it's true that I can now say life is better when you know there's someone waiting for you after a winning game, and I'm lucky that it's Piper."

"Will she be at your home game next week?"

"Whether Piper is there or not, I'm sure she'll be wearing a Winds shirt wherever she is." Hudson looks at the camera, and I swear every woman in America may just melt from that glint in his eye that feels like a secret message only for me, yet the female population's minds may be running wild.

I turn the television off, and I know I have a silly look on my face.

"Geez, no pressure or anything. My uncle really knows how to lay it on thick, right?"

Rolling my eyes, I sigh. "A tad. He likes to get what he wants, I guess. It's kind of endearing, and I'm maybe an idiot for thinking that."

"Nah, he takes care of you. Maybe now I can go to games with you and we can find me a hot sports guy. Before Hudson would never introduce me to anyone, but maybe you can soften his stance for me. I mean, you did draw me a wedding dress that I'll need to use one day." April crosses her legs, with her feet resting on the sofa.

I'm kind of surprised she brought up the dress. "I'll keep the design for you."

"Can I look at it?"

My eyes narrow. "Is that a good idea?" I ask, doubtful.

She sighs. "It's fine."

It takes a second before I search on my phone for the folder with the design. I debate if I'm only fueling April's misery, but she seems content with her request. Handing her my phone, I watch her study the screen.

"Boho chic, fitted yet comfortable, even has hidden pockets," I list. "I went for floor length, and the elements of lace are more traditional."

"It's beautiful." She sounds wistful.

"Thanks. It's not my forte, but the inspiration was there."

April hands me my phone and a knowing smirk forms. "I would have loved to have this dress, but you know… this is more your dress than mine."

"What?"

April nods her head. "That's right. You designed your own wedding dress."

I scoff at her thought. "No, I didn't."

Her facial expression turns goofy. "Uhm, yes, you did. Where did you get the inspiration for traditional lace?"

"My grandmother's dress." The S slurs. "Oh."

April laughs. "I remember you once told me when we were at your grandmother's for dinner that you would want to use some of the lace from her dress on your own wedding dress one day."

"And?"

April sets her wine glass back on the coffee table. "The dress. Your housewife skills. The boutique that caught your eye in Lake Spark for your future shop. Sounds to me like you've been setting all the puzzle pieces in place to make a life with someone. You did that because you found the right someone, and your heart knew it before your head."

"That's some theory." But the realization hits me like a ton of bricks, and I feel emotions running through me but in a way that is pure elation. "He is kind of angry at me right now because I keep taking a step forward, then step back. He wants me at his game, and I said maybe."

Her expression turns pained. "Yeah… probably not a smooth move on your part. He's never had a woman at a game, and now he's asked you. It's a big deal because he's laser-focused during a game."

"Even more reason for me to be slightly scared. People will have their eyes on me because it's unusual for Hudson."

"It's not about you. No offence, but as your newly reunited friend then I'm going to highlight that you're being a fool. The only opinion you should care about is the one you and my uncle have of each other. You know that too."

I run through my history in my head and know she has a solid point. The hesitation I have is unlike me because I've grown into a confident woman over the years.

"I know it's crazy, but I love him, and even though we are newish, I feel it in my bones that we are right. Maybe I thought it was lust and it would fade, but it's like we've been slowly building something profound together. It's just happening *already*."

"You two happened faster than some, but that's all the more reason why you maybe didn't realize it until now, when your extremely smart friend highlighted her brilliant ideas." She brings her hand to her heart with pride.

A smile tugs on my lips. "I probably should get it together, huh?"

April tips her wine glass to my direction. "Yep." She pops the P.

———

THE NEXT MORNING, I'm sitting outside and watching the sunrise with a mug of coffee in hand. I pull my knees up on the chair and one hand wraps my sweater tighter around my body.

There are exactly two things that I need to figure out before I talk to Hudson. It was during the night that I realized what those two things are. It may take a few days, but maybe the space will be good for us. We've been on a rollercoaster the last few months anyhow.

24

HUDSON

I grin when I see my son standing at my office door. One of the coordinators is standing at a distance to give us a bit of privacy, but not venturing far because I only get a few moments with Drew. In principle, players and staff don't see family or friends before a game, as I want the team focused. But it's still two hours until game time and my son is the exception. He is a calming necessity.

Holding out an arm, I give him a side hug. He has never been one for hugs, but I can tell it's growing on him, as his smile can't be hidden.

"I'm happy you're here."

Drew seems to brush it off. "A free ticket is a free ticket," he jokes.

"Yeah, yeah, yeah." I wave him off. "Sorry Lucy couldn't come." She wanted to help one of her brothers with the kids while her sister-in-law visits her parents.

"It's fine. Plus, I kind of assumed Piper would be here, so I won't be alone." He takes a seat on one the chairs while I perch at the edge of my desk.

Piper. The woman who drives me crazy and makes me constantly wonder if my love for her is infatuation in overdrive. But the truth is, I get the best of both—lust mixed with love. There is no doubt that I want her in my future because she is all I see when I think about it. Which makes her proclamation that she might not come to an important part of my career a bigger blow. It's a letdown to say the least.

I scratch my chin and wonder what to say without painting Piper in a bad light. "I'm not sure she'll be here."

"It's a big home game." He looks at me oddly.

I can only nod, roll my lips in, and say nothing.

"I don't particularly want to get into my dad's romantic life, but since it seems to be weighing on your mind, all okay with you two kids?"

My eyes give him a warning, because I think he may still have doubts about Piper. "She isn't feeling so great," I lie. Now my son returns the look that I gave him less than ten seconds ago. "Okay, I don't think she's coming."

Drew's eyes grow big, and he slides his thumb along his jaw. "So, there is a little trouble in paradise," he states more than asks.

"I wouldn't say that. I think Piper just needs to wrap her head around a few things. What, I'm not entirely sure, but she'll figure it out."

"It may not bode well for you." He highlights that fact.

I sigh and play with a pen that's lying on the desk. "Can't think about that now, it's game day."

"Ah yes, your brain compartmentalizes, an Arrows gene. Sometimes you forget that not everyone thinks the same way."

"Oh boy, my son showed up a wiseass today." A cheeky grin forms on my mouth.

"What?" He seems offended yet smirks. "Some people think in boxes, others don't. But that's not even the problem. You have zero patience. It's all or nothing, and because you have no patience, you try and get what you want at record speed."

I hold a finger up. "Wait a second. Are you trying to make an excuse for Piper? Are you on her team?"

He tilts his head to the side. "Anybody who sits through a dinner after what went down in your kitchen when I walked in gets a point from me. If she hesitates now with your relationship but figures out that you're for her, then I get where she might be coming from because we both know that you already have it in your head what kind of ring you might buy her. But if she can't figure it out or hesitates too much, then yeah, I think you should walk away."

I stand when I see one of the coordinators hold up his wrist to indicate time, but a hint of a smile doesn't fade from my lips. Not because of Piper, hell no, her not coming to the game would be a letdown and the mere thought has me wanting to throw a tantrum. My smile is for my son who just turned the table on me because a year ago I was dishing out romantic advice to him and now he's returning the favor… because he cares.

Drew stands, and I pat his shoulder. "I hear you, okay? You're going to stay at my place in the city tonight or drive back?"

"Not sure, depends if you guys lose or not."

"There is only one option for my guys." I'm a little cocky. "Go steal some food from the press box before you head to your seat," I remind him.

"Ah, you remember the only reason why I came," he jokes.

I shake my head and guide him to the hall by the shoulder. "Get out of here, kid."

Pausing for a second as I watch him walk off, I think about Piper and what Drew said. A twinge of understanding hits me, but not for long, as I need to focus on the upcoming game.

———

I'M ready to kill my quarterback, as his concentration seems to be lost. But we have enough time on the clock to get us the last point which would take us over the edge. It rained earlier, which will only make this messier.

"He seems in better position," I hear my assistant coach say in my headphones, as he's up in the press box overlooking the field.

Nodding to myself, I keep my focus on the field in front of me and stand firm in my spot. To many, I may appear calm and collected, but inside, I know I have a lot on the line if the last-minute play change is a miss. I would feel better knowing Piper was here, or rather if the agitation that she didn't want to come didn't have a firm spot inside of me, but I have to ignore it right now because I'm in coach mode.

I don't even look at the clock, just keep my attention on my quarterback who is calling out a play for the scrimmage line. We have twenty yards to go, and we can do it.

It's always the same, the last minute of a game. A blur. At the speed of light, someone may kick or run a pass, anything is possible to get the final point.

There isn't much more I can do, and I know I already have to mentally prepare for a post-game talk with the team and a press conference.

Relief hits me when I hear a ref say touchdown, and a whistle is blown to end the game. Immediately, I have assistant coaches slapping my back and players running to congratulate one another. I rub my face with my hand, suddenly relaxed. Post-game after a win is by far ten times better than a loss.

It's a round of handshakes with the opposing team's coaches and players, and a few of my team's guys too before I notice.

My smile changes to pure love.

Piper is standing on the sidelines, a perfect image. Fitted jeans, one of my team sweatshirts, and pink high heels. I make no mistake that they are the ones from the night we first met. A badge hangs around her neck that allows her to be here on the field. She wiggles her fingers in a cute little wave, and her closed-mouth smile tells me that she is unsure what to do yet satisfied that she caught me by surprise.

I pick up my pace and walk to her, quick to loop an arm around her middle and pull her to me.

"You're here." I speak loud enough for her to hear as the noise from the stadium fills our ears.

Now she smiles brightly. "I wouldn't miss it."

"But you said you—"

She shakes her head. "Now isn't the time to get into that. You just won, and I have no idea who can hear into that headset around your neck," she amusingly points out.

I chuckle. "God, you're here."

She glances away. "Kind of a perk of being your girlfriend. I get a free ticket." Her eyes turn back to me, this time with seriousness.

I look over her shoulder and see Drew giving us space and pretending not to watch us.

"He didn't give you a hard time, did he?"

Piper snickers. "It was a rough few minutes of convincing him I was here with good intentions. He thawed when I offered to get a round of beers, and when I admitted to him that I made a mistake, then I think he finally gave me your signature smile."

I want to press her on the fact she just said that she admitted to making a mistake, but this just isn't the place. Instead, I rub her back.

Her mouth parts open to speak. "I shouldn't have let you doubt if I would be here or not. I know how much this means to you, so I *wanted* to be here. Actually, there is a lot I want, and I can't wait to tell you."

Her answer slays me, and I slide my hand through her hair to bring her face to me so I can cover her mouth with my own for a quick kiss that won't raise too many eyebrows.

I step closer to her, casting a protective touch to her elbow, aware that there are cameras everywhere. I lean in to speak so only she can hear. "I wish I could kiss you like crazy right now, but I have to talk to my guys and then face the press. Plus, I should probably review the video of the game while it's fresh in my head since that's what they pay me millions for."

She nods her head in understanding. "I figured. But I happen to know it's bye week, so you get a little break soon. Can we hold out until then?"

"Shit. I hate to say it, but we have no choice. By the time I'm out of here, I'll only get a few hours of sleep, then I'm back with my coaching staff."

The back of her hand runs along my jawline. "What's forty-eight hours more then, right?"

I scoff a laugh, look away, and then back to Piper. "Knowing there seems to be a promising conversation at the end of the wait, then yeah, we can do a grueling forty-eight hours." I take her hands in mine to give her fingers a quick squeeze with my own.

"It's *very* promising." Her eyes grow bold, and her closed-mouth smile insinuates that my patience may just pay off.

25

HUDSON

Truthfully, while players get to head home and be with their loved ones for a few days, I know I don't get to enjoy bye week the same way. Sure, my schedule is a little lighter than normal, but I will still need to strategize the season so far.

At least I get to head to Lake Spark, and I know Piper is already there, as she headed up first thing in the morning since she was already on the north side of the city to see her grandmother.

Arriving at my house, I open my car door and take a deep breath of lake air. The leaves are falling, and it's been a few weeks since I've been here. I'm happy Piper is keeping the house alive in my absence.

When I arrive inside the house, it's quiet. I know Piper is here, though, because she sent me a text, and I can tell she had a coffee in the kitchen.

"Piper?" I call out her name.

I drop my small bag on the ground and throw my keys onto the side table before I nearly jog up the stairs to my room.

Arriving at my bedroom door, I stop in my tracks when I see that Piper is sleeping peacefully on top of the blankets with one leg hooked over a pillow and her arms splayed over her head. Her heels are on the floor next to the bed. The light from the windows makes it clear that it's the middle of the day, which makes it all the more amusing that she fell asleep, because she doesn't nap.

Slowly, I approach my bed and the corners of my mouth tug just as my hand lands on her back to give her a soothing stroke. The mattress dips when I sit next to her. As much as I don't want to wake her… I need to. Our conversation can't exactly wait.

She must sense my presence, as she begins to slither in her spot, a groggy noise escaping her mouth.

"Hey there, sleepyhead."

Her eyes flutter open, then she adjusts to the fact I'm in front of her. The moment she registers that I'm here, she sits up.

"I must have dozed off." She yawns and stretches her arms over her head, causing her shirt to rise and her belly button to be on show. "Crap." Her hand comes to her forehead. "I was planning on surprising you with something new."

My brows knit together. "New collection new?" I'm hopeful.

"Something like that. I think we've established I'm not really good at timing surprises."

I swoop her hand into my own. "It's okay."

Her eyes connect with mine, and after a beat, she begins to speak. "Hudson, I'm sorry if I've been out of sorts, or rather cautious of a lot of things."

"I don't want you to feel like you have doubts."

She squeezes my hand. "The thing is, I don't have doubts. I know that because it seems my life has been slowly interweaving with your own. I've been setting up the steppingstones this whole time. I just needed to think clearly and realize that."

Her words are confident and everything to me. I kiss her hand like a gentleman would, but make no mistake, my plan to show her my satisfaction with her words is aligned with the brain of a dirty sailor.

"How did you realize it?"

She smiles shyly at me because she knows I like when she says it. "I'm insanely in love with you."

"What a coincidence, because I feel the same."

"That's good because I've kind of decided that I'm going all in on a future with you. I know I want to be waiting for you at every opportunity, and by chance, the old suit shop went on sale, so I decided to phone a realtor and make an offer. I don't know if I'll get it, but I gave it my best shot."

I can't control the approval flooding my face. "That's… great." It's commitment that she wants her life here with me.

"I think so. I could really make it a boutique and base for all my online orders. Plus, an endless supply of coffee from Jolly Joe's across the street. And an easy commute home, because that's what it feels like. Here, I mean, with you. Home." I love her words. They thrill me, and it unlocks the chains that have me trying to sit here politely and listen.

I pat her arm with my hand, an indication that she needs to scoot over. But side by side is not going to happen, I need to be between her legs with her eyes on me as I drive myself inside of her.

I coax her thighs open and walk my arms forward and swing my legs up onto the bed until I'm between her legs, with my head resting on her stomach.

"It's not easy. I know that. But I wouldn't have let us continue if I didn't think you had it in you to be by my side," I admit.

She rakes her fingers through my hair. "You take care of people, guide people, but right now, let me do that for you."

"I'm not used to that, believe it or not. Leading the way is more my style."

"Oh, gee, I hadn't noticed."

I grab hold of her shirt with my teeth and pull it up for a tease before releasing the fabric.

She laughs. "What in the world is in your hair?" Her fingers seem to grab something from a few strands, and we both inspect it when she holds it up into the air.

Pine needles.

"It's that fucking tree by the driveway," I groan.

"Ah yes, killer pinecones and needles." She tosses the needle to the side.

I lift my body onto my forearms because we both have a task to do.

"Take it off, Piper." I hear the desire in my voice.

We both take everything from the waist down off. Slow and sweet will be for later.

I get a glimpse of her lace panties that were just flung to the floor and then give Piper a curious look. "I have full intention to check if you're wearing a matching bra later, but right now…" I touch her clit with my finger and feel that she is already soaking onto my fingers. "My focus is on being inside of you." I align myself and cradle her head in my hand, with my thumb planted on her bottom lip.

Her body tilts up when I slide into her, the sensation of me going deeper causing us both to moan and our lips to collide. For some reason, this feeling is more intense than usual.

I look at her mouth when I pull away and a sultry smirk begins to form on her swollen lips. "Keep going. Ruin me. Ruin me for other men." God, her playful tone slays me.

"Baby, I did that the first night I laid eyes on you."

Our eyes hold as I slam into her again and again, her legs tightly wrapping around my waist, offering herself to me, and I take every piece she'll give.

And lucky for me, she gives it all.

———

I LOOK DOWN at the eggs in the pan, going for over easy today. The autumn sun is illuminating the kitchen, a solid track is playing on the Bluetooth, and the smell of coffee is strong. I told Piper to let me sleep in, as it will be my only chance as we head into the rest of the season, but I'm not made for long mornings in bed and still woke before her.

Glancing up from the sizzling of the skillet, I notice Piper straightening her hoodie and searching for her car keys

"What are you doing?"

She ignores me as she grabs her sunglasses. "Going into town for something."

"You look like you're trying to go undercover or something."

She freezes, her hand on the keys, and she peers up to stare directly at me. "Because… I don't want to be noticed."

"It's Lake Spark, nobody cares." I grab my coffee mug and indicate that there's a spot next to me. Taking a sip with one hand, I hold out my other arm to invite her to join me.

"Maybe I need to get something without anyone catching wind, and I was going to go first thing, but I slept in, Coach."

I chuckle under my breath. Every time she calls me that I know she is going to say something to surprise me.

"I know I haven't lost my touch if you're worn out after a night like last night."

We didn't really leave the bed, except for some dinner downstairs when I whipped up some pasta and pesto with chicken. We talked about what she'll do if she gets the shop on Main Street, what my schedule looks like in the coming weeks, which games she will be at, which dinner with sponsors, and what she can expect. All the things that we talked about before but this time she is committed. She'll even meet me at some away games, which is an effort since she can't travel with me due to team rules but can stay in my room at away games.

Slowly she walks to me. "Uh-oh. You have John Mayer on and you're wearing an apron to cook eggs?"

"I know you like it." I look down at my *This coach has a foul mouth and a big heart* apron. "Don't divert the topic. Again, what's with the outfit?"

She ignores my comment and approaches me tactfully. "So, I'm going to come at you from the blindside here."

"Ooh, she's talkin' football," I tease her.

Her wry smile stays stoic.

I turn the element off and move the pan to a cooler spot on the stovetop. "So, what's the deal? Why do you need to head to town?"

"The thing is, I wanted to do the whole buying property, moving into your home without asking, showing up to games thing for the right reasons, and even though they are risks, it's okay because I want it all and knew it would be okay. And since I'm confident with all the possibilities that could happen, then I think I need to address another elephant in the room…"

I'm not catching on. "As in?" I rest my hands on her shoulders, soothing her.

Her unusual look doesn't change. "We haven't been careful." I don't respond until her eyes bug out.

"No complaints," I answer.

The remnants of a smirk on her lips inform me she thought I would say that. "I thought I wasn't pregnant, even took a test the other week. For some reason I don't know, I was kind of disappointed but also thought it was for the better, so I could make all these decisions without a baby being part of the equation. Last night I went to sleep knowing that I had confirmed my future with you, and we talked about it yesterday. Everything feels right."

"What are you saying?"

"My body kind of did this weird thing where it felt the need to gag at the thought of toothpaste, and then I realized I lost the box with the second test, so now I need to sneak around and buy another…" she rambles.

I feel my heart pounding. "Wait… hold up."

Piper takes a deep breath. "I'm not sure that test was correct, because it was maybe too early, so I need to take another one," she clarifies.

I blink a few times then something clicks me into action mode. "I'll go."

She doesn't get a chance to protest and two minutes later I'm back in the kitchen grabbing my car key. Piper never left her spot.

"Hudson!" she scolds me.

"What?"

Her eyes assess me up and down. "Did you not get the memo about being on the down-low for this outing?"

I give myself the once-over and realize my error. I'm literally wearing a hoodie that says Coach Arrows, not exactly subtle.

"Solid point." I guess I'm a little nervous. "I'll go change."

Piper shrugs. "Just, I don't know, buy a few things, then maybe nobody will notice. Like literally walk down the aisle and grab a box like a football pass, you don't even need to stop."

"I've totally got it covered," I assure her. "How about you just eat some breakfast and I'll be back before you know it."

She nods nervously, and I kiss her forehead.

Fifty-three minutes, a cinnamon roll pick-up, and a diversion of one morning fox later, I find myself staring out my bedroom door to the balcony and turning my head when I hear the bathroom door click open. I'm calm, though definitely excited at the prospect too.

Piper's face is unreadable. She takes one step closer.

"And?"

Piper's face erupts into a wide grin. "Looks like you're going to be a dad again."

My heart swells right before the reminder sinks in that I missed the young years with Drew, so this is just as new for me as it is Piper. I reach out and grab her wrists to pull her into my arms.

"The baby has good timing too, as he or she should arrive just on time in the middle of off-season." Tears form in her eyes, the good kind, because her mouth is stretched into a ridiculous grin.

I cup her cheek with the palm of my hand. "You really know how to make me happy, huh?" She nuzzles into my hand, the lids of her eyes closing. "We're getting married tomorrow."

Her head perks up. "W-what?"

"I'm not wasting time. You're having my baby, and there is only one way that I want this to go."

She scoffs at me, but her face says she's entertained. "We can't get married tomorrow. You can't even legally arrange it that quick unless we go to Vegas, and no, I'm not going to Vegas." She gives me a warning glare.

"We can get a license at the county clerk's office in the morning and then Pete can marry us."

"The owner of Jolly Joe's?"

"Yeah, he's a retired judge… the candy shop is a retirement hobby."

Piper blinks her eyes several times. "Oh… you're serious about everything you said in the last minute?"

I pull her tight then lift her up onto the dresser, setting a hand on each side of her body. "Of course I am."

Her fingers play with the tie of my hoodie that does not say coach. "I know you are." She kisses the corner of my mouth. "And lucky for me, I don't want to take the risk of you losing your patience, otherwise a wedding cake will magically appear anyway."

I kiss her forehead and interlace our hands. "Is that a yes you will marry me then?"

"Is this the proposal?" She cocks an eyebrow at me.

"Not even the beginning," I promise.

EPILOGUE: PIPER

ONE YEAR LATER

I feel a tickle on my chest, and my eyes flutter open before my body jerks awake.

"Hey, relax." Hudson speaks in a hushed tone.

It takes a second for my eyes to adjust to our dim bedroom, and then panic sets in when I look down to see my daughter in my arms.

"It's okay, you fell asleep," my husband assures me with his hand resting on my shoulder from where he's standing next to our bed.

Grogginess fogs my brain, but I register that during feeding the baby I must have dozed off. Meanwhile, Grace Ruth seems to be at peace in my arms, alas awake, with her little eyes wide open. We call her Gracie for short.

"What time is it?"

Hudson brushes his finger along my bare breast to Gracie's cheek. "It doesn't matter. You go to bed and get some sleep. I'll take this one and burp her."

I blink my eyes a few times. "Hudson, you have to travel later for the game. I am positive you need more sleep than I do."

"Me going away is the very reason that you need a break now. Don't argue with me." His voice is soft yet firm as he coos at our daughter. "Mommy just needs to obey a little more."

A short laugh escapes me. "She may have you wrapped around her finger, but Mommy runs a tighter ship." I smile because Hudson and I have a tendency to speak in a saccharine tone around Gracie. It happened as soon as she was born, as if we were possessed.

Hudson begins to take our daughter out of my arms. "Go on. I'll see you at breakfast."

I yawn and reality hits me that I probably need an hour of shut-eye if I'll have any chance to survive the day. "Fine, Coach."

He is already patting her back as she rests her head against his shoulder, and he stares intently at Gracie. "Good girl, Piper."

Daddy Hudson is my undoing. He has an uncanny ability to sound so incredibly sexy, even when he is in full-on father-duty mode.

I begin to shuffle down and back under the covers of our bed. The moment that my head hits the pillow, I already feel sleep hitting me. Since Gracie is so young, and Hudson is in football season, I keep her in our room in one of those co-sleepers to avoid going back and forth, but we are evicting her as soon as she wakes less at night, and truthfully, she is growing so fast that she could use her crib too.

My eyes close, and I vaguely hear Hudson leave the room.

The next time I wake, I know the sun is up and it's morning. I have no idea how long I slept, but I take advantage of the fact that Hudson is downstairs with our daughter and decide to take a shower and throw on some makeup to accompany my yoga pants, t-shirt, and the mom-who-needs-sleep look. At least I know my bra is always sexy, even if I look a jumbled mess. I started a line of nursing bras, especially for my current state of life.

Heading down the stairs, I hear little noises from Gracie, and there's music on too. We have her on Bruce Springsteen in lullaby tones. I sigh when I see Hudson's suitcase by the front door as I walk to the kitchen. For the most part, we have found a routine, and we do our best to accommodate his schedule, but a lot of the away games are just too far for such a short period of time with the little one.

I smile at the view of Hudson leaning against the counter, drinking a smoothie, and making faces at our little girl in her bouncy chair. His eyes instantly turn to my direction when he notices me.

"Morning, beautiful."

I wave a hand in the air. "Get real with me. What time was it when you woke me earlier?"

He chuckles under his breath. "It was five, but just pretend it was eleven."

I groan as I grab a glass from the cupboard. If it was five, then it means I only got two more hours of sleep.

Hudson is quick to wrap his arms around me, take the glass from my hand, and pour me some smoothie. "Drew and Lucy said they could come up this weekend, even if I'm not here."

"When did they say that?"

"Check the family chat." He pulls his phone out of his pocket and slides his thumb along the screen, then he shows me.

I smile brightly because Gracie is in her onesie that says Coach's Daughter and she seems at peace. He must have taken the photo earlier this morning, as it's the outfit she is wearing now, accompanied by Hudson's mug of coffee next to her that is one of those "world's greatest dad" mugs.

Drew wrote a message back.

DREW

> She's growing so quickly. Lucy and I want
> to come to babysit. This weekend? We can
> watch the game on the big screen.

Our daughter is a spoiled little girl. By everyone—her dad, brother, my grandmother, April, and I know I will be stopping by the baby aisle in the grocery store later when we don't need anything at all.

"I guess... well..." I'm reluctant, then Hudson gives me the pointed look. "Yes! Please send reinforcements my way," I admit with such relief.

I love motherhood, our routine, and our days together. But damn, this lack of sleep is a whole new world of crazy, and I welcome any opportunity for extra help.

Hudson smiles with reassurance. "Thought so. What's the plan for today?" He hands me a glass of green smoothie that I hate, but I know all the vitamins are exactly what I need, especially while breastfeeding.

The corners of my mouth stretch, and my face must look elated with happiness as I answer, "The usual. Pack up the stroller, stop in town to check on my boutique, then grab some lunch because I'm always starving these days, then naps, do laundry, afternoon walk, and sleep… hopefully."

"I will be back in two days," he reminds me.

"We'll be watching in the living room, I promise."

Hudson's fingers crawl up my arm, and he has a look that is the devil's good work. "We have a Sunday-afternoon game down in Kansas City. I'll be back late, but maybe Drew and Lucy can stick around Sunday night so I can take you to breakfast on Monday? Just you and me."

"I'd like that."

He leans his head down, and I stand on my toes to kiss him. "I'll miss you," he murmurs.

"Me too. But next week is a home game. We'll be there, and we are making this work. I promise to send you videos later today."

"Good." His phone gets a notification that his driver is here. He kisses me again, this time with more force and longer for good measure.

"I love you."

"I love you too, Mrs. Arrows."

We both look at our daughter who coos. Hudson is quick to go to Gracie and kiss her chubby cheek. "Of course, we love you too. Remember our talk earlier."

"Talk?" I wonder.

"The usual reminder that she is never to date athletes." He smiles at our daughter. "I'll be back soon. Be good for your mommy and protect her from pinecones."

"It was one time!" I protest.

"Yeah, and it knocked sense into you," he teases before ruffling our daughter's hair.

I wave a hand at him to get out of here, and exhale loudly, because even chaotic, life feels perfect lately.

————

AFTER HEADING TO TOWN, checking on my boutique where my staff was packing a bunch of orders, I went to the general store to pick up a salad at the deli counter and chatted with the old ladies from the knitting club who reminded me that there is a Lake Spark festival coming up. By the time I got home, I was ready for a long walk, so I put Gracie in a baby carrier and did my usual round up to the view-point and back.

But to my surprise, as I approach the house, I notice that April is parked on Spencer's driveway next door, and she is opening the trunk of her car.

"April?"

She looks at me as she swings a suitcase out of the back and her new beagle dog jumps out too.

"Oh, hey."

"Uhm. Think you parked at the wrong house. I wasn't expecting you. I mean, it's great, I just need to change the sheets in the guest room." I look down at my daughter, fast asleep.

April brings her hand to her hip and looks at me awkwardly. "I'm not here to stay with you."

"Right… then what are you here for?" Now I'm just confused.

April smiles tightly then bites her lip. "I'm… going to *temporarily* live with Spencer." Her hand comes to cover her face, as if she doesn't want to see me and would rather hide.

Which makes sense because I'm puzzled and don't understand.

"As in my neighbor? The guy you hate? Wait, the guy who you actually call the asshole baseball player?"

"Yep." She pops the P with her lips.

"Why?" I ask blankly.

She nervously laughs. "Fun story. Or not. Remember your baby shower?"

"Of course." I smile because it was amazing. It was more a party for Hudson and me. We did a gender reveal, had lunch at the Dizzy Duck Inn, ate cake, and Drew even made Hudson play ridiculous little games. It was a bigger event than our own wedding, which was a handful of people on the dock at the back of the house, a few weeks after Hudson proposed. "But what about the baby shower?"

She motions with her fingers to indicate size. "I might have made a teensy-weensy mistake with Spencer, and the man forgot to use the delete button. So, I need to hide out here in case the press figures it out." She speaks at the speed of light, but I heard a few keywords there.

When my jaw that went slack returns to normal position, I speak. "Oh my God!" I'm shocked but totally in a good way, well, minus the leaked-video part.

Her dog Pickles makes a whimpering sound, as if he agrees with me.

April waves at me. "Howdy, neighbor." She smiles weakly.

"We are *not* telling Hudson the specifics of this," I state.

"Please don't," she agrees.

I shake my head, but as I register everything, then a smile grows because I could kind of… see her and Spencer together.

"Oh, hey there, roomie," I hear Spencer call out as he appears to walk slowly with a swagger down his driveway.

April's face turns stiff, and she holds up her middle finger to him, but her eyes stay fixed on me. Her nostrils flare before smiling sweetly at me. "You'll be my alibi if a hot baseball player turns up at the bottom of Lake Spark?"

My grin doesn't fade. "I shouldn't highlight the fact that you just called him hot, should I?"

She grumbles as she starts her march in the direction of her new temporary home, but I have a feeling it might not be temporary at all.

My phone vibrates in the pocket of the carrier, and I'm quick to pull it out to see a message from Hudson that he landed and already misses us. Glancing between my phone and a disgruntled April walking away, I chortle a laugh. They're the reminder that the best risks may just turn into something well worth it.

WORTH THE CHANCE

APRIL

Plié, arabesque, jeté. *And* champagne spills over the edge of my glass.

Oh well. Another sip.

I gaze at the half-eaten tier of strawberry shortcake that is calling my name over there on the table. I would have done the icing a little differently, but who am I to criticize the award-winning inn in this little town of Lake Spark, Illinois?

I'm just the friend who had her fiancé leave her, and now I'm the twenty-six-year-old woman who left her job in accounting because, well, it wasn't for me. With that consideration, I grab hold of the near-empty bottle of champagne in my left hand and pour another glass.

Looking around me as I move, I reflect on the fact that I am alone in an empty private dining room at the Dizzy Duck Inn. A pool of pink confetti crunches between my bare toes, as my new heels were killing me, so I took them off after all the guests left. We may have gone a little overboard with the baby shower decorations, but it isn't often that your best friend is having a baby with your uncle/godfather.

To add to the pressure, everyone wanted an invite since he is the one and only Hudson Arrows, football coach extraordinaire. But we kept it low-key and classy. My mom, my cousin Drew, and I arranged the baby shower—well, more party because it was a team dad and team mom event. I'm happy I could do this for Piper. After all, we had a bit of a falling out when I discovered she was sneaking around with my uncle, but we're all good now. Because even a fool could see they are perfect for each other.

Fifth position, assemblé, back to fifth.

It's been years since I've done ballet. I let my feet gravitate into their own dance, the knee-length teal dress swaying out perfectly and making me want to watch the fabric flow. I'm not sure why in this moment dance is calling to me, but someone, literally, *is* calling out to me.

"April." That tone fills me with dread.

My body tightens as that voice satisfies my disdain quota for the year. Exactly what I needed tonight; baseball royalty rolling in. "Spencer."

Ugh, he chuckles under his breath. It's irritating because of how it is enticing, *if* I were the kind of woman who finds arrogant baseball players attractive. And I. Am. Not.

Spencer appears in my peripheral vision as he walks right past me to grab another bottle of champagne from the bucket of nearly melted ice. Damn it, I missed that bottle. He gets to work on breaking the foil.

He's wearing dark blue jeans, dress shoes, and a shirt that only accentuates those upper arm muscles that earn him millions. God, his cologne is a little strong today, and his new haircut of short summer length just seems a little overboard for his sandy-brown hair.

"Where's the tutu?" he asks, which means he must have spied on me in my little dance escape.

That's it. I feel my face forming a sneer as I slowly turn to face him. "Do you not have to go home? I mean, thank you for gracing us with your presence at the baby shower, but I feel the ground turning cold which must mean your stellar personality is freezing the earth."

He scoffs a laugh as he perches against the table, and with his brown eyes set on me, I notice how the shade of green of his shirt complements his eyes, which is beside the point. "I love that you dislike me so much. It's not often I share mutual feelings with a woman."

"Gag. Don't put me on a list with your gazillion skanks."

"Wouldn't dream of it. Plus, gaggers don't get a place on my list. I'm more a swallow-and-smile kind of guy." I would literally throw up if it wasn't for the fact there is a hint of sarcasm in his voice, the saving grace from this horrendous conversation.

I roll my eyes. "I knew there was a reason I avoided you all day."

"Nah, you did that because I bring out the worst in you and you wanted to be on good behavior for Piper and Hudson."

I really want to throttle him. Good behavior my ass. I'm not Ms. Prim and Proper.

Pop. The cork goes flying, but neither one of us seems to notice.

He continues to speak. "I wanted to drink today, avoid the last of the construction on my house, and maybe have a spa day tomorrow with a hot masseuse before I head deep into baseball season, so I'm staying here tonight. Hudson texted that he thought he forgot some gift in here, some silver duck or something, so that's why I am submitting myself to your presence again."

My eyes bug out. "You live literally four miles from here." He's my uncle's and Piper's next-door neighbor. I met him through my uncle Hudson at a BBQ, and I always saw him at other events. It was an instant dislike, mostly because Spencer possesses a smug smirk that I just want to…

He pours himself a glass. "And? Foxes on the road this time of a day can be a killer."

I snort a laugh, because as ridiculous as it sounds, it's true because Lake Spark is surrounded by woods.

Offering him my glass, he cocks a brow before filling my glass up too. "What's your excuse?"

"I don't live in Lake Spark, and I didn't want to drive back to

Chicago today. So, alcohol and a soft hotel bed it is." I struggle to give a tight, closed-mouth smile.

He pauses before finishing his task of filling my glass to the brim. "Hopefully they put us on opposite ends of the hotel then."

"Oh, wow, we agree on something," I counter. I take another sip and realize I should pace myself around this man.

In a bizarre twist, I trust the man in a "he would keep me safe" kind of way, but I don't trust… myself around Spencer Crews, star pitcher of the Bluelights.

"You know there was a stop sign," he mentions.

Aggravation seeps through me that he wants to go down memory lane, starting with the time I was arriving at Spencer and my uncle's street once and nearly had a car accident.

"Yes, there was. You probably didn't see it because of the bush by the sign. So I was right with my traffic skills, and I had the right of way."

"No, you didn't," he insists.

"You nearly hit my car in the process!"

He tilts his head to the side. "A little dramatic."

"Really? And what about my uncle's BBQ a while back? What is your explanation for your asshole tendency there?" I slam the glass onto a table.

"Oh, that's easy. You walked around all holier than thou, and your boyfriend at the time is the kind of jackass that will cheat on his future wife and only look out for himself."

The air in the room evaporates, and he instantly seems to regret his words, as his cocky demeanor fades into almost remorse. He's close with Hudson and Piper, which means they must update him on my life.

A twinge below my heart ignites as my eyes fall to the floor. "Well… joke is on me then, right?" I say softly.

Spencer steps closer. "I'm sorry. That was… out of line."

I peer up. "It's the truth, isn't it? If only I had known then what you so wisely figured out. I mean, I could have saved myself an entire engagement." I fake a laugh.

I walk past him and straight to the window overlooking Lake Spark; the sun is setting which casts an orange and purple hue across the sky.

Time seems to still as I try to forget the fact that I would've had a wedding coming up if it weren't for Jeff deciding that I'm not what he needs.

A tap on my shoulder causes me to look down, and I see a glass of champagne held out in a firm hand. "Here."

"Did you add poison?" I wonder.

"Nah, to have me in your company is probably agonizing enough."

I straighten my posture and take the glass. "Right. We irritate each other."

The corner of his mouth curves, and I seem to notice the five-o'clock shadow around his lips more than I care to admit.

"So, what's with the dancing earlier?" He looks into his glass.

"Old habit."

A long breath escapes his mouth before he leans against the window and seems to be casting his gaze on me. "You were a ballerina?"

"Somewhat."

His eyes go wide, as if he's waiting for more. "Care to elaborate?"

"No," I answer bluntly. In truth, it's nothing special. I only danced until I was fifteen, then turned in my point shoes for the swim team. I wasn't very good at that either.

Spencer bites his inner cheek before his jaw slides side to side. "Do you always act like a child, or do I just bring out the best in you?"

My hand finds my hip. "Forgive me for having a zero-tolerance policy for jerks who play baseball."

"Come on, give me some credit. I'm an MVP jerk who plays baseball with any team willing to pay for my arm."

I set my glass down, and my hands fly into the air. "See? Your arrogance is something else."

"Confidence is a good thing to have, April."

"I have confidence," I say, quick to defend myself.

He doesn't answer but instead shakes his head subtly, as if he's amused. "You stopped dancing the moment I came into the room."

"Because you dampen the mood with your pure existence."

The corners of his mouth twist as everything I say only seems to entertain him. "Well, on that note, I'll let you be." He propels his body off the window that he was leaning against and glides his way across the room with the champagne bottle hanging from one hand and his lips sipping from the glass in his other hand.

I don't say anything, just watch him leave with derision written all over my face. When the door closes behind him, relief fills me, but I can't seem to look away from the exit, as if he may just walk back in, and my eyes linger longer than needed on the door.

————

I'M SLIGHTLY dizzy yet way too sober to be knocking on Spencer's hotel room door. I don't bang with elegance. I thought when he left an hour ago that I wouldn't have to see him again until he shows up on a TV screen because of a baseball game.

"Spencer, open up."

It takes only a few seconds before he complies. "Fuck, what in the world? I was recording a video of my arm flexes for my trainer."

Gah, sounds like the perfect recipe for his egotistical ways. But never mind, I have bigger problems.

I barge in his direction, brushing past him into the room. "You have something that's mine." I pivot sharply to give him a death stare.

He walks slowly back into the room with the door clicking shut, while he drags the back of his fingers along his chin before a sinister smirk forms. "Is that so?" he rasps.

My hands land on my hips. "The hotel staff accidentally delivered the leftover cake to your room. Please, can I have the cake?"

His eyes squint at me, like I've said something crazy. "You came here for cake?"

"Yes! I wanted a piece. They said they would bring it up to my room."

"Fine. But I keep the champagne." He tips his nose in the direction behind me, indicating where the cake is sitting on a table.

I march on over and grab the fork to dig right in. Okay, maybe I am a little tipsy, and food is my refuge.

"God, this is so good." I admit that I moan as I suck on the fork.

"You know my mouth may have been on that fork, but I'm sure that's just your fantasy, right?"

I glance over my shoulder to find him sitting on the edge of his bed with arms crossed and a cunning grin.

"The only way I like your mouth is when it is taped shut."

His eyes grow bold. "Kinky. I like that."

I growl at his way of taunting. "Stop trying to piss me off more than normal."

"What am I possibly doing now?"

"Y-you… you're trying to egg me on by thinking I have some crush on you or some bullshit like that. I'm not other women, I don't care who you are, and I certainly do not find you attractive. Besides, I'm not even your type."

Why, April? Why did I even say that?

He only hums a sound, followed by a long pause. I feel like he is studying me. "You're right. My type is overconfident chicks who don't stop dancing on my account."

"Fuck you. I didn't stop because I'm not confident."

Oh no, we're bickering again. Feels like a flashback to the time Piper and Hudson had us over for dinner and they had to change the seating arrangements between salad and steak courses to ensure Spencer and I had distance between us.

Spencer smiles to himself and stands up to grab his glass of champagne.

Damn. Looks like he nearly finished the bottle.

He takes a drink then offers me the glass that I stupidly accept, as if I need to replenish my liquid intake.

"You seem a little edgy. Is it me?" he pretends to be concerned.

I swear I snarl at him. "Like, I totally understand why you are single and ready to mingle. It's impossible to enjoy even a millisecond with you."

"Mmm, I care to disagree. I'm just currently stuck in the proximity of an uptight woman."

I instantly act and splash the glass of champagne in his face. "I'm anything but."

When his face stills and his tongue darts out to taste the alcohol on the corner of his mouth, I realize my error. My jaw drops open, and I can't believe I just did that.

He uses the back of his hand to wipe away a few drops from his cheek as his eyes darken before he gives me a pointed look. "What the hell."

My shock fades into a smile that wants to spread.

He steps closer, and I don't move.

"Unpredictable. I'm unpredictable," I declare because inside I'm acting this way for reasons that have nothing to do with Spencer, but I don't want him to know what's going on in my mind.

But before I can process the elation I feel that I may just be everything my former fiancé thought I wasn't, I feel something gooey hit my cheek.

I blink and realize that Spencer reached over and grabbed cake with two fingers before he smothered it on my face.

He's standing far too close to me with a satisfied look. "Oops."

I touch the sticky icing with my palm, only to quickly shove his hand away, but he is quick to circle his fingers around my wrists. "Don't start something you can't finish," he warns.

"I'm very capable of finishing, thank you very much," I snipe back.

His look turns to a mix of warning and interest. "I bet," he rasps.

"Please do."

I break my wrists free from his impressive grip that is equal parts gentle yet proof of his career as a pitcher.

But the moment I'm free, his arm circles around my middle, and my response is to grip his shirt with my fingers. I feel like something is combusting inside of me, a form of hysteria that has me drawn to his eyes, then darting my vision down to his mouth before snapping my attention back to his piercing gaze.

And I'm not sure who in this moment is more eager to take a chance on a wager.

2

SPENCER

A FEW MONTHS LATER

I peer up from my phone as I approach the restaurant. I've heard teammates rave about it, but that's not why I'm here. It's the end of the baseball season, or rather our batter struck out at a key moment running up to the World Series, so our team is out early, and hopefully, the batter is getting traded for next season.

I was finishing up some meetings with my agent and publicist when I got the message that added another complication to my life.

I should be in my car with music on full blast while I drive back to Lake Spark. Instead, I'm walking down a sidewalk in downtown Chicago with a few people noticing me, but I have no intention to smile and sign autographs. It's not because I'm an ass, it's because I'm on a mission. Okay, I'm not a fan of people either.

Opening the restaurant's door, I glance at the screen on my phone and see my mother sent me a message with a picture. It causes my lips to tug, but my mouth doesn't commit to a full smile as the message is a reminder of another life that I keep under wraps.

Arriving at the hostess station, a brunette smiles at me and flicks her hair behind her shoulder. Her eyes fill with recognition. "Hi.

Welcome, can I get you a seat?" I can tell she is a supporter of my career—or wallet—by the eagerness of her voice and overdone smile.

I swipe my sunglasses off my face and tuck them into the pocket of my black button-down. "No, thanks. I'm here to meet someone."

"Oh. Nobody mentioned you would be joining us tonight, but we are happy to have you here." Her smile doesn't falter. She seems keen.

I scan the busy room. It's 7pm which means those who worked all day are now carrying on their evening with business dinners. That was never my scene. I'm more of a "throw back beer with the guys" type of man.

"It's kind of a surprise," I mention, as I now search the room, determined.

Ah, bingo. I spot her.

Wearing a black dress and hoop earrings, it kind of suits her, but I don't think about it for long. She is next to the window and sitting across from a guy, wasn't planning on that, but this day is already hell enough, so what's one more obstacle?

"Found her. If you don't mind, could you send over a scotch on the rocks and make it a double? Thanks, you're a doll." Before the hostess can answer, I'm walking at a fast pace to the table by the window.

I'm not in baseball season which means I don't need to think twice about drinking alcohol. In season, I stay off the hard stuff and only have a beer if it's a few days before a game. I haven't committed years to the sport to throw it away to a bad practice or game because I'm hungover.

Assessing the scene, I sense that I'm witnessing a date, clearly.

Grabbing a chair from a nearby table before I reach my destination, I pull it up just in time to hear the mystery guy talking about anesthesia, and April is politely listening until she does a double take when I appear in her vision.

"Spencer!" April shrieks when her eyes land on me, obviously surprised by my presence. Her brown eyes grow big, almost in wonder that I'm in front of her. And hell, I could think of many other people who I would rather be sitting in front of right now. This woman detests me.

And in a moment where logic left me, I found her bratty ways attractive enough.

"Oh, hey there! Am I interrupting? Surely, I'm not interrupting." My cocky smirk is out in full force.

The man who could use a steak or two looks at me peculiarly. "Aren't you Spencer Crews?"

"I am. And you must be…?"

He answers me in awe, "Ted."

"Ted's a doctor, a cardiologist actually," April pipes in, and I'm instantly amused that she feels the need to try and level the guy up.

Now I have to grin. "You know, I think I read once that cardiologists have like, I don't know, the highest rate of heart attacks or burnout due to stress, plus long work weeks. Must be grueling for your future wife." No clue why I decided to highlight this stranger's faults to April.

April's face is fuming, and I can tell that I've hit a nerve. "As opposed to baseball players who retire by thirty?"

"Are you retiring? Shit, now the Bluelights are going to suck," Ted adds his commentary.

"Spencer lives next door to my uncle," she explains.

I turn my attention back to the guy. "So, you are April's new boyfriend?" I internally question why I'm curious.

He grabs a piece of bread from the basket. "It's actually our first date."

"Oh, wonderful. And here I am interrupting." I lean back just as the hostess hands me my drink. Perfect timing, as I could use the liquid encouragement right now for what's about to go down. But my confident look doesn't fade.

"How the hell did you know I was here?" April asks, clearly agitated.

I tilt my head gently to the side. "Your love of cameras."

Her eyes fill with recognition as they don't blink, and since her dress is hanging low at her tits, then I notice her breath pick up.

I'm quick to clarify. "You posted on your social media story a photo of your cocktail, and the logo of the place was on the napkin. You really should work on safety first."

Her hands nearly claw the tablecloth. "And why the hell would you be looking at my social media?"

"Do you two need a moment? I feel like I'm missing something," Ted says, but neither April nor I look at him, as we are too busy in a standoff.

"How about I just steal this pocketful of sunshine away for a moment?" I suggest to Ted.

April's body stiffens, but she gives the doctor a tight smile. "Just a minute, I'll be right back, and then we can order dinner."

Ted gives us an odd look. "Oh, uhm, sure."

Clearly, their date wasn't going so great anyways.

April grabs my arm. "Two minutes," she grinds out.

She pulls me out of my seat, and I follow, only I don't like being towed along. I step forward and place my hand on her lower back to take the lead, for a second, I appreciate the fact that her dress is a little snug around her hips.

I lean in and nearly murmur, "Don't you have a sweater or something?"

She flashes me a death stare. "Why?"

"I just think Hudson would appreciate that I'm watching out for his niece and ensuring Dr. Stress keeps his gaze appropriate," I attempt to justify.

But fuck me, Hudson may kill me for what is transpiring and what I did with his niece who is his goddaughter and wife's best friend. I should have probably thought about the rules of our friendship a little more, but then again, Hudson is laid back and even attempted to push me in April's direction once or twice, like at the baby shower a few months back. I'm not blind.

The moment we are at an empty spot near the bar, she shakes me away and turns her full attention to me.

"No sweater." Her tone is clipped. "Which, by the way, it's a little late to be concerned with manners that my uncle would approve of." Her brows arch; she's in a feisty mood. "Our first contact in months, and I already feel like knowing you is a regret. Now explain why the hell I am being graced by your presence this evening?"

My lips quirk out as we both take a beat to look at each other. I haven't seen April since that night a few months ago. Her blonde locks are in waves around her face; it looks natural, but I get the feeling she put in the extra effort with her hair tonight. I guess her skin is tanner too. I heard she went to Italy for a little while in place of the honeymoon that she had hoped to go on. Piper told me when I ran into her on my driveway, which makes me wonder if Piper knows…

"Does anyone know about—"

"Hush your mouth!" She is quick to interrupt and steps closer, a sort of warning as she nervously searches the room. "And what? Admit my mistake? God no."

I debate my words for a second, but I can only chuckle nervously. "Okay, well, we have a tiny problem."

Her brows raise in curiosity, and I see concern spread across her face. "What do you mean?"

I look over her shoulder to ensure nobody can hear and lean closer to whisper, "The video."

Her entire body tenses, and concern is replaced with fear. I notice because she peers her eyes up, causing our breaths to mingle, as we are close in proximity. "The video?"

I scratch my cheek. "You know, the one we accidentally made while we were—"

Her palm lands against my chest to stop me from continuing, and it creates space between us. God, this woman touches me like she knows exactly which spot awakens a feral need inside me. It's downright infuriating.

"Do *not* say the words," she nearly barks then throws on a small fake smile when the barman walks by our spot to collect a glass.

The moment he passes, our eyes lock, and I see the fear, but it's laced with… heat. I know it's there.

"You deleted the video. I saw you delete the video." Her voice has panic in it.

Licking my lips, I'm about to bite the bullet. "I did… but I kind of…" It's dragging out.

Her nails sharply dig into my arm. "Kind of what?"

"I forgot that it autosaved to my cloud."

"Of course, it saved to your cloud. What kind of person doesn't know that you need to delete it from your phone *and* the cloud. Fuck." Disbelief is strong in her tone. She steps back, and her hand fans her face as she is clearly trying to calm down. "I knew you were trouble. Holy hell, this is…"

I lean against the bar to watch her, but admittedly, guilt does ping inside of me. "I'm sorry."

Her eyes draw a line up to my own again. "Wait, why are you telling me this?"

I'm quick to straighten my posture and land my hands on her arms to have her full attention. "I was hacked, and I'm not quite sure what will come of it."

"Oh my God!" She is about to melt down. "This isn't happening. No. Nope. This. Is. Not. Happening."

Closing our distance, I pull her to me, as if I'm her protector, but in truth, I'll be damned if anyone leaks the video. I have my own personal reasons why it can't happen, but April is still the major factor. "My publicist and lawyer are on it. I don't think it will ever see the light of day. This kind of thing happens to my teammates all the time. We just need to stay on the down-low until it's solved."

"What the fuck is with my life? Exactly what I need now. I mean, my lawyer mother will be so proud that her daughter made a hate-sex tape with her favorite baseball player," she bites out.

"I'm her favorite player?" I can't help but smirk proudly.

Her eyes bug out at me. "Not the time for your stupid arrogance. Holy shit, this is bad. Like, *really* bad." Her hand finds her forehead. "I mean, we didn't even intentionally mean to make it."

True. We were kind of at each other's throats before ripping our clothes off happened, and then we went at it like two wild animals. By the time I realized that my phone video was on while it sat on the docking station, it only seemed to encourage us more.

"They can tell it's more me than you. Besides, I won't let the leak happen." I hear the sincerity in my voice, a sort of possessiveness that I feel, like I want to owe it to her.

"How are you going to do that, Spencer?" She attempts to breathe out a calming breath.

My head lolls slightly at an angle, and I feel my face strain because if I didn't know she enjoyed my dick, I'd be worried she may just hit me in the balls in a second. "It's best if we're off the radar for a bit. I was heading back to Lake Spark, but I think you should also stay there for a while."

"What?"

"It's better to tackle this when we are away from the city. We need to be near each other to stay updated, plus if shit really hits the fan, then it's easier to spin that you are a long-term…"

Her finger flies up to stop me. "Don't say that either."

"Girlfriend? I mean, we don't need to fake a relationship, just if the press somehow finds us, then it looks slightly better, and they'll be more sympathetic."

April cocks a brow. "Finds us?"

I swipe a hand across my jaw. "I mean, I hate suggesting it, because I can only imagine that hell resembles something similar to living with you, but you should stay at my place until the dust settles."

She throws her hands up in the air to demonstrate that she has given up on this conversation. "Roommates. Just fantastic." This woman seethes cynicism flawlessly. "How long do you think this will take?"

"Two weeks maybe. Look, I'm sorry, truly I am, but I think it's for the best that you tell Dr. McLoser to take a hike since there was no way you were enjoying it anyhow, then go home and pack your bags."

"Hey, Ted could be a real contender if you didn't interrupt." She sounds almost offended.

I look at her skeptically. "You looked bored until I showed up."

Right on cue, Dr.McLoser taps on Piper's arm. "Hey, the hospital called, and I'm needed."

"Really?" I throw out my doubt.

"Hey, man, could I get your autograph before I go? I'm such a fan." Ted looks at me, excited.

April shakes her head, as if she has nothing left to lose.

I shoot him a fuck-off grin. "You know, I don't do autographs after dinner time. Work-life balance, am I right?"

"Oh, yeah, sure, I totally get that." He tries to save himself and then turns his attention to April. "I guess I'll…"

She rolls her eyes. "It's fine. We don't need to pretend we'll call one another. Have a good night."

"You too."

Jesus, that was painful to watch.

I wait for the doctor to disappear and for April, who now looks defeated, to say something, but she doesn't. Instead, her shoulders fall before she plops herself on a free bar stool. She raises her finger to grab the barman's attention.

Stepping closer to her, I lean against the bar as she asks for two shots of vodka. Yikes, this is bad, as that's a bold order.

"April," I say her name with firmness, but I need her attention again.

An audible breath escapes as she twirls on the stool to focus on me.

"Are you okay with the plan?" God, I wish I had another option.

"I have no choice. So, shacking up with you it is."

Huh, I thought this would require a little more debate.

My jaw flexes as I ponder that thought before it registers that by letting April stay at my house, I'm letting her into the parts of my personal life that not many people know. I require a lot of trust when it comes to my life outside of baseball, but April staying at my place is the only way. I need to chance it, and a part of me doesn't seem to be second-guessing about letting April in.

The shots of vodka show up, and we each take one. She doesn't hesitate and downs it.

I tap my drink on her now-empty glass that she set on the bar. "Cheers."

Her head makes a sharp turn in my direction, and she narrows her eyes in on me. "How do you know they can tell it's more you than me?"

I scoff a sound instead of giving her words.

"Did you watch the video?" she wonders.

It isn't anger, nerves, or fear that is in her voice. It's almost an acknowledgment that there is something underlying if I did.

I've been caught out because I may have watched a scene or two. "How could I not? Hate sex brings out the best performance, which means we were award-worthy, since we might've actually looked like two people who passionately want each other."

I stand and decide this is my moment to leave her.

We'll have enough time to soak in our situation when she is under my roof.

3

APRIL

I want to see the video. That can't be a bad idea, right? I should demand to see the proof of our little escapade. It's my right.

I swing my legs out of my small SUV, and I groan at the fact that I just pulled up to Spencer's house. He lives on a cul-de-sac with two other houses, one of which is Piper and Hudson's, and the other belongs to a hockey player. All the houses deserve a spot in an architecture magazine, plus they all back onto the lake.

Rage fills me as I walk to the back of my car to grab my suitcases because I'm here for God knows how long.

As I'm opening the trunk, I hear a familiar voice that may just be my saving grace in this situation.

"April?" Piper asks as she approaches with baby Gracie in one of those wrap things. Despite being sleep-deprived, Piper always looks put-together, and her brown hair is up in a bun that looks messy in an on-purpose fashionable way.

I look at her as I swing my suitcase out, and my new beagle Pickles jumps out onto the driveway too.

"Oh, hey."

"Uhm. Think you parked at the wrong house. I wasn't expecting you. I mean, it's great, I just need to change the sheets in the guest room." She looks affectionately at her daughter who is also my cousin. I know my uncle isn't around because there is an away game this week.

It dawns on me that this situation took such a fast spin that I haven't updated Piper on the latest.

I bite the bullet and bring my hand to my hip, knowing there is an awkward look plastered on my face. "I'm not here to stay with you."

"Right… then what are you here for?" She seems confused.

I smile tightly then bite my lip. "I'm… going to *temporarily* live with Spencer." That was painful to say, and I cover my face in near shame.

"As in my neighbor? The guy you hate? Wait, the guy who you actually call the asshole baseball player?"

"Yep." I pop the P with my lips.

"Why?" she asks blankly.

I laugh nervously. "Fun story. Or *not*. Remember your baby shower?" God, I'm going to admit this, but it's better she if knows the details, because the only plus of this situation is that I get to hang with my bestie more due to her close proximity.

"Of course." Piper smiles because I'm sure it is a great memory for her. "But what about the baby shower?"

I use my fingers to indicate size. "I might have made a teensy-weensy mistake with Spencer, and the man forgot to use the delete button. So, I need to hide out here in case the press figures it out." I'm speaking at the speed of light.

Piper's blank look fades to shock. "Oh my God!"

Pickles makes a whimpering sound, as if he is agreeing with Piper. Thank goodness I adopted him when I got back from my Italy vacation; I could use a therapy dog right about now.

I give a weak wave and smile to Piper. "Howdy, neighbor."

"We are not telling Hudson the specifics of this," Piper states, still in shock.

"Please don't." I couldn't agree more.

"Oh, hey there, roomie," I hear Spencer call out as he appears to walk slowly with a swagger down his driveway.

My face turns stiff, and I hold up my middle finger in his direction, but my eyes stay fixed on Piper. I feel my nostrils flare before smiling sweetly at my friend. "You'll be my alibi if a hot baseball player turns up at the bottom of Lake Spark?"

Piper seems to be grinning. "I shouldn't highlight the fact that you just called him hot, should I?"

I grumble and wave her off as I start my march in the direction of the house, with my hound in tow. I vaguely hear Piper say, "See you soon." I am sure she flashes Spencer a smile because that man has everyone wrapped around his finger.

Spencer slows as we come face to face. "What's with the dog?"

"My ex hated dogs, so I lost the ex and gained a dog. Clearly a win. We are a package deal. You need me to stay here, then Pickles stays too." I shoot him a glare.

He responds by smirking. "Fine. Shall I get your suitcase?"

"It won't move itself." My eyes flick down to get a glance at his white t-shirt that hugs his muscles, and I see half of his tattoo on his chest by the v-neck. An anchor with tiny numbers along the outline of the shape; I know that because I've seen his entire body.

"Great, I get to live with children," I hear him mumble. Creases form on my forehead that he said that plural, but I don't think too long.

Mostly because I'm mesmerized as I enter his home. He was working on this house for a long time. Everything is state-of-the-art and modern. An open staircase greets me, as does the one-room level with floor-to-ceiling windows. It's huge, and I don't know where to look. The living area, a dining area, then my eyes land on the kitchen.

I'm a little eager as I continue my journey to inspect the kitchen. This fridge is a dream, and is that a pizza oven? I think I've entered heaven. In Italy, I partook in cooking workshops every day, but my apartment in the city just doesn't suffice for some of the recipes, but this? I can literally stare at this all day.

This will be great.

I mean, don't, April, don't get a warm fuzzy feeling about this arrangement.

I turn to face Spencer, who has left the luggage by the stairs and followed me in my exploration. "Since I'm here, I might as well stay occupied and use the kitchen for my own enjoyment." I hear my attempt to cover my excitement.

"Sure." He scratches the back of his neck. "We may need to stock up on supplies. We can head to the general store if you want?"

My voice turns sickly sweet. "I would say I don't need your company, but I do need your credit card since this shall be an unexpected all-expenses-paid trip, because the reason I am here..." My voice turns full of venom. "Is because you forgot to use the damn delete button on your cloud!"

His satisfied smirk is unaffected. "Fair point, but it did take two to make it."

Ugh, he's right. I soften a smidgen and blow out a confirming breath.

"Do you need me to show you where you can work or something during the day?"

"No. I'm currently unemployed, on a sabbatical, trying to figure out life, yadda yadda, whatever you want to call it. I made a deal with my old company when I left, so I can weigh out my options for a little. I'm about to finish a nutrition course, but that's online, and I'm practicing recipes."

"Hmm, I could see you as a nutritionist." He walks past me to the fridge to grab a soda. "Want a drink?"

"No, it's okay. But I should get some water for Pickles." We both look at my dog who is standing in the middle of the kitchen panting.

Spencer angles his head to study my pet. "Does his eye always twitch?"

"Yes. I adopted him from the shelter. He's older, so nobody wanted him, but he is a big softie and a good dog."

To my surprise, Spencer grabs a bowl and fills it with water. He is already confusing me with his effort. I thought he would tell me to get it myself.

He sets the dish down. "You can have any of the guest rooms."

I stare at him with a neutral face. I thought for sure he would take the opportunity to reference that night, but he doesn't, and I'm not sure why that disappoints me. Shaking off the thought, I get us back on track.

"I'll take the room farthest from you. It will be less enticing to strangle you in your sleep."

He rubs his face in aggravation. "Your maturity level needs work."

"Well, you do bring out the best in me." I plaster on a fake smile before walking past him. When I reach my suitcase at the bottom of the stairs, I clear my throat, indicating for him to carry my bag. I'm going to make the man work because we are in this mess because of him.

Spencer scoffs and reluctantly follows me until he purposely leans over to grab the handle and grazes my body in the process. He is doing that on purpose, right? I mean, his shoulder touches my arm, and the smell of his freshly shampooed hair hits my nose. Something inside of me feels heightened.

"Remind me to find my handcuffs in case you get out of line," he mentions before heading up the steps.

Leaving me to picture the thought in my head.

———

OF COURSE, Spencer speeds along the road to the general store. I guess what man wouldn't when you have a Jaguar like this?

"When is your lawyer updating you on the situation?" I ask as I look out the window.

"I have a call with Celeste tomorrow. I think she works with your mother, as they are in the same firm." He focuses on the road with his hand on the wheel.

My lips roll in from the thought of my mother finding out about the video. "Yeah, she does. Since I know she has client confidentiality then I won't worry about her telling my mother. But make no mistake, this goes down as the worst one-night stand in history, hands down."

"Let's maybe not get into it while we approach the sharp turns around the lake."

"Fair point."

He glances to his side real quick, I see it in the corner of my eye. "I forget that Lake Spark is your family spot."

I smile to myself because it's true. "Well, I've been coming here for years. My mom and uncle always visited, and then Hudson bought his house, so Lake Spark became a frequent visit. Then my best friend decided to become his wife. I don't need a map for this area, as I'm here often enough."

"Good. I can just let you be and not worry about you getting lost in the woods or something."

I shoot him a glare. "Touching."

Arriving at the general store, I know it's anything but a basic stop. This place is a gourmet supermarket for all the people of Lake Spark who enjoy paying an arm and a leg for almond milk.

Spencer and I get out of the car, and I grab a cart that I pass on to Spencer.

"I need to get a few things," he says as we enter the store and land right in the produce area.

"I would assume so, as assholes do need to eat."

He stops the cart, causing me to stumble against it. Spencer's eyes turn stormy, and he steps closer, leaning in to mutter so only I can hear.

"Considering your fingers loved to dig into the shape of my ass, then I would really start coming up with better retorts. Speaking of coming, what was it…" He pretends to contemplate. "Oh yeah, three times, of which two of those times were around my big cock."

His fingers tuck a strand of my hair behind my ear as he pulls away, and just like a bubble popping, he grabs a bunch of bananas, as if the last five seconds didn't happen. "Oh, look at that." He inspects the fruit. "Just a little too small to compare, but hey, we need our potassium, right?" He throws them into the baby seat of the cart and starts to push again.

I bite my tongue and swallow any words that are fighting to come out.

"Should we split up? You know, divide and conquer?" I suggest in a normal tone.

"Sure, I need to find the jars of apple sauce."

What the hell? I don't see this guy eating apple sauce, but I don't want to carry on this conversation.

"Fine."

He leaves the cart with me, and I begin my moments of solitude, throwing in items that look good, with no thought process. I figure I will just scrape something together when I'm in the kitchen.

Avocados for sure because that is essential. The unrefrigerated oat milk also goes into the cart. Throw in some boxes of granola. Hitting up the international food aisle and going crazy on sauces, I get an idea to make tortellini from scratch. Since they have a pasta maker on sale, I don't think twice. Realizing I need fresh cheese, I head to the deli counter, lost in my own world.

But when I grab my little paper number from the machine for my turn, I freeze when I hear a familiar voice talking to two other guys, and not in the "oh joy, an acquaintance" way. This is "dread and throw me under a bus" kind of way.

Turning to face my demise, I see Jett, my ex-fiancé's brother. Shit, I forgot his brother comes to Lake Spark often for "corporate retreats." It's how I met Jeff, on the Lake Spark beach one weekend. And yes, their parents should be questioned for naming their kids Jett and Jeff.

"April?" He looks at me.

I wiggle a few fingers. "Hi." There is no excitement in my tone, but I attempt to offer a friendly look.

"I-I… well, uhm, it's good to see you." He is trying to be polite as he looks awkwardly at the two guys next to him. They all look like preppy accountants who cheat on their girlfriends. "This is April."

"*The* April?" one of the guys asks, then his face turns cartoonish.

"Yep. Jeff's ex," I confirm. "What a coincidence. What brings you three here? A weekend getaway?" I raise my brows.

Jett awkwardly scratches the back of his neck as his jaw flexes. "We are kind of checking out the area for a bachelor party later in the year. Surprising the groom."

"Bet you are."

"It's Jeff," one of the guys mentions.

I try to hold it together, but I want to throw up, as this is news to me. Rage fills me, and pure outright hurt. I was ditched, and clearly, someone moved on, ready for marriage in record time. I have no clue what my face gives away or what to say. It's been a year since Jeff broke off our engagement, and even though I now know he would have made a horrible husband, I wanted him to have a miserable year or two.

But the problem wasn't us, or him, it was me. I'm the reason that we had no future.

I feel my throat burn, as if I want to scream or cry. Humiliation is what's crossing my mind while everyone waits for me to react. I can't hear or blink, I'm lost in how to respond.

An arm wraps around my middle, breaking my trance.

"There you are, baby." Spencer pulls me flush against his body, and his hot breath brushes along my jawline before he nuzzles his nose against my cheek. "Did you get everything we need for our dinner tonight?"

My mind now focuses on him and the fact my body seems to remember his touch. I think I might even relax slightly.

"Holy shit, it's Spencer Crews," one of the guys calls out.

Spencer keeps me in his hold and gives a hard look to the guy. "Yeah, but I kind of want to finish up our grocery store trip soon. Got a busy night planned with my girl."

My eyes draw a line to Spencer's face, and I swear I see a flicker of empathy that I both equally appreciate and hate.

He takes it up a notch and moves in, with his mouth landing near my neck. The feeling of his breath spreads against my skin. A flicker of a flashback of him doing this once before hits me, and my body curves into him in response. Then he places a kiss to the side of my neck with a little teeth action for good measure.

I softly gasp from the bite, but I play along. "Babe, I just needed to grab the cheese, then we can head home."

"You're living with him?" Jett asks, confused.

"Jett is the brother of my… ex," I mutter in explanation with a tight smile.

Spencer entwines his fingers with mine to hold my hand before looking to Jett. "Well, only unwise men give up another man's treasure." He tugs my hand. "Come on, I'm sure Sean behind the counter will toss us the…" Spencer flashes a persuasive grin to the college-aged guy in an apron behind the counter before turning to me to answer.

I'm in a daze from the last minute. "Oh, right, fresh parmesan and pecorino."

"Sounds delicious. Hope we actually make it to the main course this time."

My eyes blaze open, as he is laying it on a little thick.

Jett looks between us. "I… it was good seeing you."

"Yeah, same," I call out as he waves, and his minions follow as he walks away.

When the group of guys are out of our sight, my attention reverts back to Spencer who is biting his inner cheek.

"Isn't pecorino the same as parmesan?" He is attempting to ignore the fact of what he just did.

"I'm not a damsel in distress," I rasp because his poisonous spell is clearly affecting me.

His eyes look at my mouth and then back to my eyes. "Of course not."

Realizing we are still in an embrace, I push against his chest with my palms. "We should probably go."

"Good idea."

APRIL

That man is a curse.

In the last forty-eight hours, Spencer has brought nothing but bad luck to me.

I was silent on our way back to his house. In truth, my thoughts couldn't muster any words, as I was lost in what just happened over the last hour. If I'm honest with myself, I know it's because I feel I wasn't good enough for my ex, which only infuriates me.

Following Spencer into his kitchen, we both carry groceries. He stalls when he sets the bags on the counter.

He tilts his head at different angles. "Your dog is lazy."

My eyes follow his line of sight to see Pickles in the same spot that we left him in before we went into town.

"He isn't lazy. He is just enjoying the finer things in life which is called relaxation. Don't be a hater on his life balance," I chide.

"As long as he doesn't destroy anything in the house, then he can enjoy his life of Zen."

I blow out a breath because I feel uneasy. I'm not quite sure what to do with this nervous energy.

"I'm sure you can handle this." I indicate to the groceries. "I'm going to go swim in the lake."

"It's early October?" Spencer questions.

"Cold water is good for the skin."

"Or you can just use the indoor swimming pool like a normal person."

Something ticks inside of me. It's his words, and Spencer has no idea.

Crossing my arms, I state the obvious. "Well, I'm not a normal person, am I? Remember, I'm the idiot who decided thirty minutes with you was something worth trying."

Spencer tosses an avocado into the fruit bowl. "Is this the cue to establish ground rules for you living here?"

"No. Because I will absolutely not walk around as if you are the commander of the house and I shall obey."

His brow raises, and I feel like a dirty thought just slipped into his brain.

"And here comes your stellar snark," he says, sarcastic.

I feel anger boiling. "You, likewise, have nothing nice to say about me. Can we just agree that we will stay out of one another's way? Which means when I am cooking, then leave me the hell alone."

"I believe you just set a rule which you were adamant we don't do." Smartass is really going all in on the irritation front.

My hands finds my hips, and I'm now just agitated. "We will only go in circles in every conversation. Shall we end this now before I throw something?"

"I'm a good catcher." He offers me a contrite grin.

I step closer to him. "You know, for someone who is a pitcher and throws curveballs, you sure as hell don't anticipate them. So, thank you, Spencer, thank you for ensuring we both end up in a situation like this where I have to be stuck under your roof because of your mistake."

He scoffs a sound. "Because your life was going so well." He walks past me, his shoulder hitting my own.

As he leaves the kitchen, I know his words hurt because insecurity is a bitch.

———

IT'S A LITTLE BRISK, I'll admit that. The water in the lake, however, is doable for a quick swim. A fast swim is what it will need to be, as the sun is setting.

Every stroke is filled with my emotional state which could be a little calmer, I confess.

I hear Pickles' low bark. My faithful canine has been sitting on the dock watching me. I'm not quite sure he even knows how to swim or at least the water is probably too deep for him.

But I hear a splash, and I stop mid-stroke to assess the scene. Even treading water, I manage to roll my eyes when I see Spencer's sporty physique swimming in my direction.

I swim a few feet until I know my toes can touch the bottom, and Spencer meets me there.

After he walked out of the kitchen, I whipped up some cookie dough to set in the fridge and pulled together a chickpea salad. Keeping my hands busy in the kitchen was my distraction, just like Spencer going for a run or workout, whatever the hell star pitchers do in the off-season to keep themselves busy.

"You know this water is as cold as your heart," he informs me as he swims in place.

"Then why are you here? I would assume you have other cool-off methods as part of your training." I move my arms to keep me afloat.

He shakes his head. "Because it's barely light out and you are swimming in a dark lake." His tone feels like he is scolding me.

"Not your problem."

"Really? Tell that to Hudson and Piper when we find your body in the morning." He takes me by surprise and grabs hold of me, bringing my body to his.

My breath catches in response. "Let go of me."

"No, we're getting out of the water, even if I have to carry you back."

I set my hands on his shoulders and that move catches him off guard. For a moment, we both stare at one another with the glow of the evening sky tracing our faces.

"I was almost done," I breathe out.

He doesn't respond instantly; instead, his eyes peer down and up. I know the temperature is causing two pebbles to appear through my suit. It's only when I study him that I realize that he jumped into the water still in his workout shirt and shorts.

"Don't you have strength training to do after your cardio? Clearly you are not following your schedule," I quip.

His hands swiftly move to my waist and in one go he lifts me into the air. "There. Strength training is done. Now can we get out of the fucking water, after you promise to keep your swims to the pool?"

He doesn't bring me back down, and I realize he is waiting for me to answer.

It is freezing, I can't deny it. I need to move as soon as possible. "Fine. I promise."

As if I am a delicate piece of glass, Spencer slowly brings me back down into the water. Our eyes never part, especially when my body slithers against his.

"Good girl, now let's get the fuck out of here."

We both swim to the ladder on the dock and get out. I grab the towel that I had left earlier by Pickles and wrap it around my body.

Spencer is already walking away in a stormy mood. He jumped into the water unplanned, so he has no towel and his workout clothes are wet.

He seems angry, and I follow at a distance behind him. When he abruptly stops, I do too.

Spencer glances over his shoulder. "Do me one damn favor. You may hate being here, nor am I celebrating, but while you're here, try not to do anything that I wouldn't want a child to do. Lead by example."

My mouth gapes open. "Are you comparing me to a child again?"

His face looks pained, and he rubs his temples with his fingers.

"That's not what I meant. I didn't mean…" He bites his lip and seems to be debating what to say. "All I'm saying is stick to the kitchen for getting out your stress, it's safer."

"I doubt that. Kitchen injuries have a lot higher statistic for emergency rooms than dark lakes."

Spencer rolls his eyes to the side, and I see a hint of a smirk because the outside lights in his backyard are on. A long breath escapes him. "Just get inside."

"I'll go inside because I want to go inside, not because you told me to," I say as I walk by him.

"So cooperative," he retorts.

I don't look at him, but I can only imagine he follows me inside with annoyance.

————

SITTING AT THE KITCHEN COUNTER, I tear a piece off a warm, gooey chocolate chip cookie and take a bite before I inspect the rest of the cookie. These are damn good.

I'm tired and should probably head to bed. I'm certainly not doing myself any favors by eating before bed, but I'm still taking in my surroundings and the fact that I am in this situation.

The man of the house enters the room, but I don't bother looking up from the plate of cookies. Nor do I care that I am in tiny shorts and an off-the-shoulder t-shirt. Might as well make myself at home.

"Vampires don't sleep, guess that explains why you're here."

I give him the death stare as he grabs a glass from the cupboard. "Nor does the devil, so I guess we know why you're not asleep."

Spencer leans against the counter. "That was some damn excellent salad. The chickpeas are exactly what I need for my protein intake."

My body straightens from the compliment; not many people have tried my new flare for cooking.

"Not too much lemon?" I narrow my eyes. He shakes his head.

"Garlic balanced out?" He nods. "More feta next time?" His head bobs side to side.

Jesus, he is agreeing with me on all fronts.

"The poison should kick in soon."

He toasts his empty glass at me. "Wouldn't expect anything else."

I watch him pour a bottle of water into his glass before he swipes a cookie from the plate in front of me. A sound escapes his mouth that causes my eyes to widen slightly, a throwback to a time that shouldn't have been.

He enjoys cookies the same way he enjoys my pussy.

A long silence graces us, and I wiggle my fingers against the countertop.

"Do you have any hard liquor?" I shoot out.

"Are you sure that's a good idea?"

"After the way this week is going, yes, I'm sure. It's after 8pm, so I'm leading by example." I give him a cocky look.

He shakes his head ruefully. "All right."

Spencer walks to a high cupboard near the pantry and pulls out a bottle of tequila. I kind of assumed a guy like him would have a whole bar for entertaining, but alas, no.

A minute later, he has two shot glasses on the counter, and before he has a chance to find lime or salt, I pour a glass and quickly down it.

"Whoa, slow down, horsey." He takes the bottle from me.

"It's been one of those days," I lament and hold my glass out again.

"No shit. Want to talk about how you've been in a mood since the grocery store?"

Great, the reminder. I had nearly put the grocery store fiasco to the back of my head. Now that emotional boil begins to resurface… again.

"You have shitty timing," I inform him.

Spencer also takes a shot without the essential lime and salt. "I beg to differ. When it comes to baseball and sex, then my timing is right on par."

"Of course, you would say that. I just need no more surprises for a while.'

He pauses for a second and his jaw flexes side to side. "April, about the child comment—"

My hand flies up to stop him. "Don't remind me. You are as bad as Jeff. It's not true, you know?" I hop off the stool and hold onto the shot glass for dear life. "I'm a fun person."

"Riveting," he deadpans.

But my rant continues. "I would have been a good wife. You know, sometimes two people just are not sexually compatible or maybe he is the one who's no good in bed. So good luck to his *new* fiancée. Besides, how wrong is he, I mean, I made a sex tape because I can be wild, so fuck him and his opinions," I ramble, take a shot, then realize to my horror what I just admitted.

My eyes shoot up to Spencer who is studying me intently. "Is that why he ended your engagement, because he thought you weren't good in bed?"

I avoid his eyes because this is beyond embarrassing. "Can we just ignore the last minute?"

"No, because it isn't true."

My gaze snaps in his direction, and I can't read his face. "You don't need to lie on my account."

The corner of his mouth hitches up. "When you talk, sometimes I want to ram a soap bar into your mouth, but damn, you have a talented mouth."

I feel my jaw drop because he has such strong conviction in his voice, and his words are probably the sweetest thing someone has said to me in a while, which has me questioning my sanity.

Spencer steps in my direction, and I feel like anticipation moves in a wave through me. I'm not sure what he's going to do, especially when his glass clinks against the counter when he sets it down in passing.

When he reaches me, his fingers grab my glass. "You may want to go easy with this." He sets it behind him on the counter.

"Show me the video."

He clucks the inside of his cheek. "Not a good idea."

"If you get to watch it then so do I."

"Why, because I was the point you needed to prove? The proof that you are not terrible in bed?" his voice rasps as he steps closer to me, invading my air. The heat of his body enters my realm. One step closer and we'll touch.

"Show me the video," I bite out.

"Admit my theory is correct," he counters.

I don't blink or move. My face feels tight but so do the internal walls between my legs. "Fine. You know my secret. What the hell was your excuse for that night?"

His lips stretch in a closed-mouth leer as the pad of his thumb finds my bottom lip. "Let it be known that I don't think this is the smartest of ideas. But okay, you are a player in our little show. If you want to watch the video, then we will do it right now."

I bite his thumb gently. "We?"

"My condition. I'll show you the video, but I get to watch you beg that night. So, would you like to keep it low-key and watch on my phone or should I connect it to the big screen?"

"Oh, now you know how to use technology," I snipe.

He chuckles, a sinful velvet sound, almost a warning.

"I need another shot for this," I admit because his conditions be damned. I'm going to watch that night on replay.

5

SPENCER

April sways her way to the sofa in the living room and sits on the edge of the cushions. Her facial expression is tight, but she splays her arm out to indicate the television.

Bold choice for screening options, but I like the enthusiasm.

"Again, I need to ask, as the mature one here. Are you sure you want to do this?" I ask and sit on the other end of the sofa. My thumb is already busy connecting my phone to the screen.

"Stop questioning it and just do it." April is a little on edge, but that only makes me grin because I am curious for her reaction.

I lean back against the back of the sofa and get comfortable. I hold the remote out in front of me ceremoniously.

"Here we go," I announce.

Glancing to my side, I see that April is playing with a strand of hair at the back of her neck, nervously twisting the gold lock around her finger.

Hitting play, I bite my bottom teeth into my upper lip because it's not every day that this situation arises. And truthfully, I only watched thirty seconds, I haven't actually watched this in full.

My eyes focus on the screen. Conveniently my phone was on the desk dock which meant we got a frontal view of the bed where April and I stood in an argument.

I'm holding April by the waist as her hands grip my shirt. Admittedly, we are in an intense stare-off. Leaning in, I tangle my fingers into her hair. She doesn't flinch.

"You're despicable," she whispers.

"Good thing you hate me then," I murmur against her cheek as I pull her hair gently to bring her neck into a perfect angle for me.

"Insufferable."

"Feeling is mutual," I hum near her skin, a scent of sugar hitting me.

But then time stops, and I'm not sure who made the move, but our lips slammed together in a kiss. A hard, messy kiss that was equally energizing and addictive.

Different angles. Short gasps of breath. We seemed to be on a determined road to a destination that we were not quite sure of.

I watch the screen where April is tugging my shirt.

"See, I'm going to call that as you made the first move," I comment.

"Fuck off, Spencer, can we just watch this in silence?"

Looking at April, I see that she's pulled a cushion tightly into her lap, and she's looking intensely at the screen.

My eyes track a journey to the screen, back to April, and return to the movie where I'm pulling her dress down with no politeness.

"You have no respect for expensive clothing," she one-tone quips.

"Oh yeah? You have no idea how to work a buckle."

"This thing. It's a pain. Why won't it come off?" April says in a breathy tone as she looks down at her hands that are fumbling with my belt.

"April. It's a belt." I slow us down and give her knowing eyes as I show her how to unbuckle the basic accessory.

Her response is to push me back on the bed. "Asshole."

She's in a black bra and panties and is now straddling me, her pussy right on top of my cock. Using my arms, I walk myself up to sit, her breasts tight against my chest, and I reach my hands up to unclasp her bra, and when I kiss the curve of her shoulder, I notice my phone on the docking station on the desk.

"April," I say softly.

"Shh. Don't speak." She continues to attack my neck with her mouth.

I bring my hands to her shoulders to pause her. "Wait."

It gets her attention, and she looks at me as I peel myself away from under her, depositing her body to the side in the process like a toss of a ball into a glove.

"What the hell."

I walk to my phone. "Fuuuck."

"What now?"

"The video is on." I reach my thumb out to stop it.

"Don't!"

Creases form on my forehead as I look at her, my hand frozen in mid-air, and I feel an entertained smirk forming. "Don't? As in, let it keep recording?"

April is sitting on her knees, and I'd be lying if I said she didn't look cute as fuck with her tits pushed together between her arms at her sides.

"Now you're shy?" Her sass never fades.

"No. Just surprised you would want the proof for later that I've made you come more than once."

She snarls a sound. "Don't set yourself up for failure, sailor."

With that I give up on my phone and return to the bed in a flash, pin her down by her wrists above her head against the mattress, and urge her thighs open with my knee because I have a point to prove.

In the present, I feel April looking at me. It causes me to glance from the movie to April who immediately turns away when I catch her. She appears warm, or rather hot, and definitely bothered. Her legs are crossed rather tightly, and I have no qualms about admitting the fact that my cock is twitching against the fabric of my jeans.

"Want me to pause? Take in the fact that you were the adventurous one?" I haven't forgotten what she let slip earlier. It makes a little sense where her logic was that night and what a tool her ex was.

My guess is he couldn't deliver and placed the blame on April who is by no means a bore in the sack.

"No."

I slide along to couch closer to her, well aware that she is watching pre-season me licking her senseless with her body writhing under me while I had to use my hands to hold her hips down.

"Not an inch closer," she grits out.

"Why? I already notice that your hand is under the cushion. It's okay. Now isn't the time to be shy," I encourage her.

Her eyes dart in my direction. "Don't even suggest it." The movement of her chest bounces up and down, and the nipples under her shirt are hard. I don't see the outline of a bra which means there isn't one.

I unbutton my jeans and unzip. "Do what you want, but I'm not going to stay constrained. Luckily, I'm king of this house and can do as I please."

April's jaw drops, but her eyes don't tear away from my hand that dips into my jeans.

"You really just want to watch? Your body isn't aching to be touched? Don't have a toy you packed?" I cast my doubt.

"Oh, trust me, it's more adequate than you."

I cluck my tongue. "I think the screen proves that theory wrong."

Quickly, she looks to the television where her fingers are threading in my hair as I lick her clit and bring two fingers inside of her. The volume is on low, but her moan is apparent.

Her eyes dart back to me, and she nibbles her bottom lip in contemplation before tossing the cushion to the side to make a point.

"You do your thing and I do mine, okay?" she breathes out.

She sinks her body into the sofa and her fingers disappear under her waistband, but her face is turned forward to watch.

On the screen she is about to come. I remember it well because she tasted like fucking strawberry shortcake, and as the sound in my living room confirms, she screamed my name and a flurry of F-bombs.

Making her come for some bizarre reason felt like a win, better than striking the batter out. I was determined to fuck her hard, and that meant making her come because I'm a team player.

I had only given her a few seconds to recover before I was pulling her by the arms up to sitting, and my ass is now in full view since she wrapped her mouth around my cock, as if she was eager.

Present me has my palm stroking my length, and April's knee gently drapes near my own as she spreads her legs to get a better angle.

The camera position meant we only get to see the outline of April's hands holding my hips and her head bobbing. But I remember the way she took me as deep as she could go, and her tongue glided along my cock.

"That's a good girl," I praised her.

"You're right, if they only have this part of the video then it is all you, well, your ass, but mostly you," she comments, her voice breathy.

Looking to my side, I see that the loose fabric of her top has sunk low enough that I get a peek at her hard nipple. She is assessing me, and she knows what I want, which is why a sly smile curls on her mouth, and the fingers on her free hand find her nipple to play with.

"Your tits are always pert."

"Tsk-tsk, you should be watching the video."

"I think we both know that you took me to my edge before I slammed into your pussy with my cock where I made you come twice."

Her lips part open, and her arm with her hand in her shorts picks up speed, as does my own efforts on my cock.

We both glance to the screen where I had positioned myself over her, wrapped her legs around my waist, and worked my way inside her wet and tight walls until we both moaned in sync.

The next few minutes are a blur. A mixture of watching our present selves get off and our video selves move in different positions during sex. Video us were not delicate. April bounced on top of my cock as I thrusted up, I pumped inside of her with her leg over my shoulder as I kept her under me, and finally, we are on to the pièce de résistance, doggy style.

But I only watch snippets, as does she. Instead, our eyes are trapped in a locked gaze that our current selves somehow find sensual.

I want to slide my hand up her thigh to feel her, to soak my fingers in her readiness then bring her fingers to my mouth for a taste before she touches my cock.

But that's not our game right now.

Tonight is about watching.

The sounds from the television are only upping the ante.

In both timelines, we are almost there.

"You're going to come while watching me inside of you?" I husk.

"Uh-huh." She's in a daze of desire. Humans always act differently when an orgasm is at play.

The lids of her eyes hood closed, and my own pace runs hard.

An explosion of screen us and present us happens as we all come within seconds of one another, my heart rate fast as we come down, only for us to look at one another, and reality hits us like a ton of bricks.

———

WE SIT THERE in silence as the video comes to a stop. That night, she quickly dressed and told me to delete the video; in fact, she watched me delete the video and left.

Now we both try to straighten our clothes after watching our replay because I forgot my phone auto syncs to my cloud, or maybe deep down, I just ignored that piece of knowledge.

"See, we had good angles," I attempt to joke.

April's lips quirk out. "I mean, as far as performances go, then I think we hit it out of the park."

"I guess. I've never made a video, so can't compare."

Surprise fills her face. "Bullshit."

"No, really."

"Oh."

My shirt that I used to clean my stomach, I form it into a ball and throw it across the room in the direction of the laundry room.

The mood in my house has shifted, as you would assume happens when you decide to watch a sex tape that you made with a woman who costs a lot of energy, yet for some reason, I feel a slither of sympathy for her within me.

April abruptly stands. "We will never speak of this again."

Before I can even say, *"Here we go,"* she storms out.

There goes any prospect of having a discussion with her tonight.

Which is a shame because if she is going to stay here, then I need to share something else.

I blow out a breath because sometimes I still wonder how in the world I became a dad.

6

SPENCER

Leaning against my closed garage door with my hands in my pockets, I take a deep breath of the autumn morning air. I'm staring at the situation in front of me, the one that I should have had a few more days to prepare for.

My mother gets out of her car. Dana Crews is a force to be reckoned with. She may be pushing sixty, but make no mistake, she is in shape and is probably changing our schedule because she has a hair appointment to color the blonde hair that she's had for years.

"This isn't what we agreed." My voice is stern.

"Spence, this shouldn't even be up for discussion. The baseball season is over, and you know the deal," she chides as she circles around her car.

"The deal was until next week," I remind her. A deal is such an odd way to state our situation; there was never a negotiation, therefore it's more of a request.

She gives me a sympathetic look. "You are already missing so much; you should be relishing these moments."

She has a point, and it's what I want to feel, but this is a complicated situation.

"Besides, your father and I booked a last-minute weekend away and there is no school today for Teacher Institute Day." That's good, they deserve it.

My mom opens the back door of the car and immediately puts on a silly face for the passenger in the car. "Guess where we are?"

I walk a few steps so that I'm in view, and I do have a curiosity, even excitement somewhere within, however mostly I feel fear.

Maybe I soften an ounce when I see my six-year-old daughter give me a little half-smile. Her blondish-brown hair is up in a bun, and she is in a black leotard with pink tights and a tutu.

"Hey, Hadley." I give her a tiny wave.

Hadley's mom is no longer—or rather never was—in the picture, and my mom pretty much raises Hadley when it's baseball season. My parents have a house here in Lake Spark that I bought for them a few years ago so that there is no disruption to Hadley's school schedule. I've always been in Hadley's life in some way, but it feels like we are strangers to one another sometimes due to my schedule. It's a confusing time for her, I'm sure.

My mom helps my daughter out of the booster seat, and Hadley walks to me before she pokes my leg with her finger. "I'm staying with you now."

Awkwardly, I scratch the back of my head and lean down to her eye level. Her brown eyes are filled with curiosity. "Yeah, kiddo, you are. Remember what we talked about?"

"Yes. Sometimes I stay with Grammie and other times with you."

"Very good. You're going to stay with me for a while now, until spring."

"Right. Baseball." She seems deflated. I wish she was more excited about my career. Isn't it the dream? Saying your dad is a professional athlete?

I touch her shoulder. "But that's exciting, right? I mean, I have the pool, your playroom is all set up."

She nods her head and begins to walk in the direction of the door, dragging her feet.

I quickly go grab her bag from the trunk and grab my mom's attention in the process. "She doesn't want to be here."

"It's difficult for her too, but give it a day or two and she won't want to leave," my mom assures me.

Closing the trunk, I sigh. "I'm not here alone." I just get it out.

My mother's eyes grow wide and she looks elated. "You have a new girlfriend?"

"No. Just a…" I pause for a second, as I have to swallow around this lie. "Friend. Hudson's niece, actually."

Her brow raises. "Just? Hmm."

No, Mother, we made a sex tape, and the world may soon know.

"Really. She would rather see me on a BBQ skewer, but for a, uh, project it was easier if she stays here." I plaster on a fake smile. "I thought that I had a little more time before Hadley would be here."

We begin to walk side by side back to my house.

"She doesn't know about Hadley, I assume?"

"Not many people do, Mom, you know that. Besides, it's better that way because I enjoy my privacy. Anyways, April wasn't awake when I woke for my workout, and by the time you called to let me know you were two minutes away, unplanned, then I haven't had a chance to prepare her."

Holding the door open for my mother and balancing a bag in one arm, I lead us inside.

A pitched squeal fills the house, which fills my blood with a compelling need to run straight in the direction of Hadley's sound. Dropping the bag by the stairs, I run to the kitchen and into a scene that instantly makes my lips curl into a smile when I stand in my tracks.

April is wearing pineapple-print pajama pants and a tight tank top, and she's standing in the middle of the kitchen with a spatula in the air, a dusting of flour on her cheek, with her eyes glued on the little pink tutu in the air because Hadley is leaning over to pet Pickles, who is in the exact same spot as when I woke up and tried to convince him to go for a walk with me.

"You got me a puppy!" Hadley's excitement hits a new level that I didn't know was achievable.

And now I'm about to pop her dream. "Pickles belongs to April. He's staying here for a little bit."

"Oh." Hadley is disappointed but now sits on the floor and hugs the dog.

My eyes draw a line from my daughter to April who still hasn't moved, including the spatula in mid-air. "I have no idea what is happening," April admits one-toned in a daze.

I look at my mom, and my face must show that I'm struggling to come up with words. She affectionately touches my shoulder. "Maybe I should give you two a minute before I head out?"

Blowing out a long breath, I turn my focus to April.

"Who's April?" Hadley asks as she somehow managed to get Pickles to lie on his back with his paws in the air.

"A friend," I say.

"What's going on? In no world am I your friend," April mumbles, as she can't seem to tear her eyes away from Hadley.

My mother chuckles softly. "I like her."

"I'm Hadley. My daddy lives here," Hadley announces, and I'm not sure if it's from pride or because even for her age she isn't afraid to be bold.

April nearly chokes before her jaw drops, and her head makes a sharp turn in my direction.

"Can I see you for a minute?" I request nervously.

April quickly turns the stove off where she was making something that resembles pancakes and follows me down the hall to the laundry room.

The moment we step through the open doorway, her eyes bug out at me. "What the hell? Daughter? You don't have a daughter. There is nothing in this house to suggest that you, Spencer Crews, are a father, let alone to a little girl in a pink tutu."

I grab her arm. "Well, *April*. I *am* a father."

"This doesn't make sense. She just like, *poof,* magically appeared." April's hands make gestures to accompany her words. "Not one single clue in this house screams that you are rocking the dad bod," she reminds me again.

My eyes squinch together, and I nearly groan because I'm already tired of this conversation. Pulling her by the arm, I walk us across the hall to the other door.

"Why are you taking me to a closet?" April protests.

"It isn't a closet."

"Yes, it is—" I open the door for her, holding it open with purpose while she peeks her head in. "Oh." Her voice drops.

April takes in her surroundings, a room filled with toys. A playhouse in one corner, a wall with different levels of shelves filled with books and puzzles, a pink rug in the middle, and a dreamcatcher stenciled on the wall.

"Yeah, *oh*. Not my fault if you don't take in your surroundings."

April shoots me a glare. "Snooping around was going to happen today. I've not even been here 24 hours, and I got side-tracked yesterday for many reasons… as you know." Her tone is sharp, and her hip is tipped out. "Besides, it looks like a closet door."

"Doesn't matter. Hadley is here now and will be staying. I thought she was going to arrive next week."

"When were you going to tell me this important information?"

I rest my hands behind my head as I stretch. "When the moment was right."

April seems at a loss of words. "H-how come you never talk about her?"

"I'm protective."

"Still, at some point in the last few years of knowing you, then surely she would have come up in conversation." April seems to be in disbelief, and I get it. Hadley is my best-kept secret.

"Can I get into the details another time? Preferably when alcohol is involved?" Because the story isn't easy, nor what she probably assumes.

April nods her head in agreement. "Fine." She points her finger at me. "Any more surprises you have in store for me? Or are we done on that front?" She doesn't seem impressed, which is understandable since I keep throwing grenades at her lately.

"I'm not making any promises, because I don't know what I may need to do to keep you in line."

She scoffs a sound. "Cute."

She moves to walk away, but I instantly grab her arm to stop her. "Where are you going?"

"I'm going to meet up with Piper for coffee. I think it's better that I get out of the house for a little bit. You know what, maybe it's not such a great idea that I'm here. The whole sex tape thing will blow over, right? I mean, surely we're overreacting."

I give her a peculiar look as she rambles nervously. "Even more reason for you to stay. If it does leak, which it won't, but if it does, then the last thing I need is any more reason for it to turn negative. I have an image I need to maintain for my contract, and also for Hadley, who may look back one day at articles."

I swear a flare of empathy warms April's brown eyes before she swallows. "Okay."

She doesn't move, nor do I, and our eyes are locked in a moment that feels like we are even on the vulnerability front. I know the reason her fiancé left her, and she knows about Hadley.

And for some reason, even though I don't need to, I even the playing field even more. "That night," I begin.

April glances away then back to me.

I continue, "I needed an escape for one night."

A hint of a smirk tilts the corner of her mouth. "Must be something in the Lake Spark water then, because you chose to spend it with me," she attempts to make a joke.

We both acknowledge the realization of why that night happened. Our own personal reasons led to finding refuge in one another's arms, of someone we love to hate.

April makes a sound with her tongue, debating how to leave. "Uhm, I'll be back later. I think a breather for a second or two and coffee is a good idea."

"Sure." I step back with my hands in the air to give her space before leaning against the wall with my arms folded over my chest.

She slowly walks away and then stops to look over her shoulder.

"I kind of have a lot of questions about the whole you're-a-dad thing, like, *a lot*."

"Understandable."

She returns on her journey to the stairs but pauses again and turns to me with her finger in the air. "The apple sauce. It's for Hadley, isn't it?"

I nod in agreement.

"That's a relief. I've never known a grown man to eat from an apple sauce jar with a cartoon on it."

I scratch my cheek, trying to suppress my laugh.

"Super confused," she whispers, and I can tell she is still taking in the situation, but she continues to make her way upstairs.

I give myself a moment to consider the predicament that I find myself in. I have two girls living in my house. One a woman who speaks her mind, often at my expense, yet she just gave me a temporary truce for the last ten minutes. The other is a little girl who I wish would tell me the thoughts in her head. Now I have to balance them both in one house.

APRIL

I scoop out the jellybean from my coffee. I'm sitting in Jolly Joe's, the soda shop-styled candy store, ice cream parlor, and bakery that decided that putting jellybeans in coffee was a good idea, but it's truly revolting.

"Surely the bean melts in my coffee, so essentially my no-sugar latte is now a sugar latte." I highlight this fact to Piper who's sitting across from me bouncing her baby daughter in one arm and stirring her latte in the other, sporting her big shiny wedding ring on her finger.

Piper glances around the store, which is decorated like an old soda shop, including a jukebox in one corner. "It's fun. You never know what color you'll get," she points out.

Taking a sip of my, okay, admittedly delicious coffee, I hum an answer that maybe she is right. Setting my coffee down, though, I must point out the obvious. "I'm kind of done with the surprise train for a little bit."

"Why?" She scouts the room then leans in to whisper, "Sex tape wasn't enough for you?" Her humor causes me to roll my eyes because only she can get away with it since she's my best friend. "Is that freaking you out?"

"Nah. His lawyer is only the best, she works in my mother's firm. I mean, she hasn't lost a case in like forever. The sex tape is looking tame compared to other events. Apparently, Mr. Pain in my Ass—"

"But is he, though?" Her voice is full of doubt. "Sounds like you enjoyed the view of his ass at least once in your life." Now she's just teasing me.

However, the image of the video plays in my head. The part when he pinned my arms above my head against the mattress, and then a flicker of the scene from last night when his eyes landed on me as I watched. Heat runs through my body, but I shake it off.

My signature unimpressed look appears, which only makes Piper chuckle more. "Must we remind me of the error of my ways?"

Piper smiles. "I'm sorry. You're right. What else has Spencer done?"

"So, after imprisoning me in his house due to his lack of understanding for how his damn phone works, I get another surprise this morning."

"Ooh, mysterious. What could it be?" Piper looks at Gracie with a funny face.

I slide my coffee cup to the side. "Spencer is a father, apparently. A little girl just magically ran into the kitchen when I was attempting to make my crepes as a form of stress relief."

Piper's face turns serious, with her eyes darting in my direction, and clearly, she is studying me. Her lack of words makes it obvious.

"You knew?!"

Piper slowly nods.

"Why didn't you tell me?" I wonder.

Piper pulls Gracie close to soothe her by stroking her cute little baby hair with her hand. "It's not my story to share. Besides, up until yesterday, I thought you and Spencer couldn't be within a foot of one another, so I assumed you would be the last person he would want to know."

I open my mouth but struggle to get words out until they fall off my tongue. "Now that explains why he looks like a pro at holding Gracie in the photo you sent in the family chat group."

Piper's brow raises, and I can see a smirk that wants to spread on her lips. "Oh, so you noticed that."

Sighing, I blow out a breath. "The man doesn't have many positives going for him, so the very minimal pluses are noticeable. I'm slightly confused, where is Hadley's mother in all of this?"

Piper's face turns saddened. "Not my story to tell," she reminds me.

My little cousin reaches her chubby little hand out for me. Piper offers Gracie to me, and I'm quick to shake my head no.

"You know I'm not great with kids."

"You are fine with kids," she corrects me.

My lips quirk out, and I lean into my hand on my propped elbow. "I guess I have no option, as my new roommate comes with a pint-sized girl in a tutu. Oh, crap!" I throw my hands into the air and quickly grab my phone from my jacket pocket.

"What now?"

I find Spencer's name in a chat conversation. "I was in such a shocked state that I quickly changed and left. I forgot Pickles. See? I can't even take care of my own dog!" I'm horrified, I never forget him.

ME

Uhm, I think Pickles may need to go outside. Sorry, I forgot to bring him with me.

I drop my head into both my hands. I feel like a hot mess.

"Did something else happen? You seem a bit flustered or out of sorts."

I may have watched your neighbor come last night.

I look at Piper like she's crazy. "The last twenty-four hours have been a whirlwind. Oh my God, I didn't even mention about the general store yesterday. I was there stocking up on supplies when I ran into Jett."

"Jeff's brother?"

"Yeah, and he made sure to let me know that Jeff is now engaged, because clearly, he found someone suitable," I say, sarcastic.

Piper gives me a pained look. "Ouch. What did you say?"

I pause for a moment when I recall what happened. I slowly take a sip of coffee and set it back on the table. "Well, uh, Spencer might have, kind of… you know." I brush it off.

"I don't know," she states plainly.

"He made it look like we were there together. I guess so I don't look like a pathetic loser, you know."

A satisfied smirk appears on Piper's face again. "Really?" Oh gosh, it's one of those incredibly interested *reallys*.

"Can we stop talking about him?"

"You know, Hudson thinks you two would be kind of good together," Piper points out as she grabs a toy from her bag.

"Hudson is kind of positive about most things."

My phone pings a sound.

SPENCER

Figured. It's fine. He finally moved when Hadley went outside to play. He doesn't seem to run far, so I didn't bother with the leash.

The photo he attached unnerves me for some reason. Pickles is lying on the driveway with his head perked up. Thick chalk crayons are scattered around him, as he is next to Hadley who is drawing.

Oh. Thanks.

I tap my long fingernail on the screen, as I'm just not used to this interaction with Spencer. It takes some getting used to.

"So, what's the plan for while you're hiding out in Lake Spark? Babysit your favorite baby?" She sounds hopeful.

"No. But I will accompany her if her mother is present." I smile sweetly.

Piper shuffles in her seat. "But seriously, what are you going to do?"

"Actually, the only bonus of this situation is that Spencer has an amazing kitchen, so I can practice all my recipes. Maybe I'll start that blog I keep talking about."

"That's a great idea!"

"Yeah, figured that I should probably start a new career chapter soon. My mother's daily texts are starting to sound concerned." I lean back in my chair.

Piper is now shaking a little rattle. "When I talked to Catherine last night, I played dumb and said the last I heard from you was that you had a date with some doctor, which got her a little excited."

"It really sucks my mom is your sister-in-law. I sometimes wonder if your loyalty has changed," I say, entertained.

"Nah, you have my full loyalty. I haven't even mentioned this situation to Hudson yet, but that is pure luck. I would never break news before a game. But after the game…" She rolls her eyes.

I wave her notion off. "He is the least of my worries."

"So, are you ready to head back *home*?" Piper flashes her eyes at me.

Looking into my empty cup of coffee, I growl a sound. "Guess I can't hide forever. Besides, I wanted to make pasta from scratch, and that's time consuming."

"I won't hear you screaming at Spencer from across the street?"

"No."

"Good. You never know what will happen."

"Nothing." I stand and grab my jacket from the back of the chair. I can tell Piper doesn't believe me, but we don't talk about it, as we are too busy getting Gracie bundled up and into her stroller. Piper is going to check on her boutique where she sells pajamas and lingerie.

Coincidentally, I was wearing her pajama design this morning when a little girl ran into my life and her father stood by, visibly ready to share another insight into his life with me.

————

Returning to Spencer's house, I immediately hear Spencer and Hadley when I walk through the door from the garage to the hall near the kitchen.

"I don't eat that!" Hadley sounds frustrated.

"Well, you have to, otherwise no apple sauce." He has an authoritarian tone.

"Grrr." Hadley actually just growled at Spencer like an animal, and it causes me to smile to myself.

I pass Pickles who is sleeping on a bed of blankets that I don't remember putting there. I lean down real quick to pat his head. Walking slowly into the kitchen, I see Hadley sitting at the kitchen counter and Spencer attempting to put a sandwich on her plate. All eyes turn to me.

"Hi," I hesitantly greet them and wave my fingers in the air for a little greeting.

Spencer sighs, and for the first time ever, I don't think I am the cause. He looks like he is exhausted.

"Hi." Spencer rubs his temples. "I guess you are owed a proper introduction. April, this is Hadley. Hadley, you remember April from this morning."

"Dog lady," Hadley announces.

Spencer chuckles. "I think you mean Pickles' owner?"

"Well, if Pickles likes me more, then maybe I can keep him."

I lean over on the other end of the counter, a good distance from everyone. "Let me guess. You made a bed for him?"

She nods her head.

My eyes slide to Spencer. "I guess I have competition." There is a moment's pause. "So, what's shaking?"

What's shaking? Yikes, I'm clueless how to communicate.

"Hadley isn't really a fan of food. She only eats apple sauce, donuts, and fries."

"Solid food groups," I comment.

He throws a kitchen towel to the side. "Yeah, I'm sure the pedia-trician would agree." There is a lack of assurance in his voice.

I crawl my fingers on the counter as I debate what to say or do. "Well, if you don't mind, I'm going to get to work on my pasta."

"Is that what I bought yesterday?" He indicates his head to the cardboard near the sink.

I walk straight to the box. "Yep. A pasta maker." I begin to work on the box.

"What's a pasta maker?" Hadley asks.

I focus on my task as I speak. "It helps me roll out the dough that I'm going to make."

"Is it messy?" she continues her line of questioning.

"Can be. I need to use a lot of flour."

"Can I help?"

My eyes immediately find Spencer who is avoiding my gaze. I look between them both, and I'm not sure no is really an option right now.

"Sure. But you might need to change. I would hate to ruin your ballet outfit."

"Getting her to change hasn't been a winning point today," he mutters.

Hadley bounces up in her chair. "Can I throw the flour?"

I laugh as I set up the machine. "Maybe not throw, but you can help me roll."

"Okay." She jumps off the stool and runs in the direction of the stairs. I make a mental note that I need to figure out which bedroom is hers. I'm going to assume it's the one near Spencer's that I thought was a door to a linen closet, because I seem to think Spencer has a gazillion closets.

A clearing throat draws my attention to Spencer.

"She isn't great with listening or eating," he states. "You also don't need to be afraid to say no."

"Duly noted."

Awkward silence floats between us, and I hate it. "Any news on the situation?"

He shakes his head. "No. An injunction was issued, and I have confidence in my lawyer. If she says not to worry, then I won't worry."

For some reason, I trust his words, and I should question that more. "Who hacked you?"

"Probably the same guy who hacked a teammate and wants money. He might not even have the video and is waiting to see if we'll call his bluff. He sent us each a message, but I didn't answer, only had my team check it out. I'm not the first famous person to have this happen. I don't know more, but since it isn't just me then the lawyers actually have a better chance."

"Right." Why am I too calm about this? I should want to know every detail. Instead, I begin my quest around the kitchen for items that we got at the grocery store yesterday.

"Aren't you going to ask?" Apparently, Spencer notices my focus is on other topics.

I play it cool, but I am bursting at the seams. "Okay. What's the story with Hadley?" I grab a bowl from the shelf.

"She's mine." There is strong conviction in his voice.

"Got that when she announced you were her daddy."

"Our relationship is a struggle sometimes due to my career," he mentions, and it pulls a pin on the grenade inside of me that sometimes surfaces.

I set the bowl down with a bit of force because the bomb inside me just detonated. "Putting your career first? My God, are you one of those guys who just hands the kid off to the nanny? Why am I not surprised." I scoff.

Spencer steps forward and grabs my arm, pulling me to him and taking my other arm too. "No. I'm. Not." He seems offended. "What the hell. You just want to think the worst of me."

I close my eyes, and I recognize my own insecurity and how I'm out of line. Opening my lids, I own up to my error. "I'm sorry. My biological dad isn't in the picture."

He loosens his grip on my arms. "Right. I forgot about that."

It's not a hidden fact that my mom used sperm donation so she could experience motherhood when she had nobody in her life because she was married to her career and felt she didn't have much time left on her clock.

"As much as I think it's great that I am the product of sperm donation and my mom was able to have me, because she is a great mom, I can't help but be slightly mad at Mr. Anonymous because he doesn't want to know who I am." It's the sore point of my life. Part of me is thankful that he gave the gift to my mom, otherwise I wouldn't exist. The other part of me simply can't comprehend why he wouldn't want to know who his child or children are.

"I get that. But it's not the same situation." Letting go of me, we don't take a step apart.

"What *is* the situation?"

"I've always been in her life," he states, and it feels like he has a point he wants to prove.

"Okay."

He walks to the fridge and grabs a beer. "Just trust me, I love her like a father should."

My breath catches because his words strike me in an unusual way. But before I can speak, the sound of feet running down the stairs draws our attention to Hadley in leggings and a t-shirt, closing the opportunity for more questions.

"Can I have an apron?" she requests as she runs to the counter. It seems more of a demand that she throws at Spencer.

"You mean please?" he corrects her with eyes that feel like a warning.

I shake my head, accepting that the conversation Spencer and I just had needs to be replaced by focus on Hadley's entertainment.

Spencer looks to me as he begins his journey to where I would assume he hides aprons.

I try to take in the information that Spencer just told me, but questions are still popping up, and I don't have time to think because a little girl claps her hands together to get my attention.

"Why are you staying here?" she asks curiously as she investigates the items I set on the counter.

I debate how to answer because I'm beginning to wonder if the original reason is the most important factor anymore.

"Because…" I draw the word out, as I'm not sure how to answer. "Sometimes baseball players do something that requires their acquaintances to live in their house temporarily."

"What's an aquit, akee—"

"Acquaintance. Someone you know but who isn't close enough to be a friend."

"So, you're not our friend?" The little girl seems very confused.

I sigh, as explaining this to a child, I need to take the easy way out and lie. "I am a friend. And friends use friends' expensive kitchens to cook."

"How long are you staying?" she asks as I hand her a measuring cup.

"As long as it takes," Spencer announces as he holds out aprons for Hadley and me.

Grabbing my dark apron, I notice his eyes are piercing with a sort of stormy command that irritates me.

Because my treacherous body has excitement swirling somewhere within me.

Hadley looks at me with her head cocked to the side and a puzzled look. My eyes dart from her curiosity to the dining room table where April has set up a formal dining setting around one plate and a fancy decorated dish with the tortellini that she and Hadley made from scratch. There is even a fresh basil leaf thrown on for good measure.

"Is this how every meal is going to go?" I ask as I watch April standing on a chair to get a better photo of the plate of food.

"Yes. But you are assuming I'm cooking for you." She takes a shot then turns her head to me. "I'm trying to do something with my life, and while in prison, I might as well make opportunities arise."

"Highly doubt my state-of-the-art kitchen, indoor swimming pool, and lake views are considered a prison."

April smiles sweetly at my daughter and then a hint of venom joins her smile when her eyes meet mine. The problem is, every time she attempts to show her dislike for me, it only comes across as a playful game that I have no problem participating in.

"Silly me and my choice of words. This is, of course, a completely wonderful five-star unplanned vacation." I roll my eyes, as now she is just overdoing it. "Okay, enough photos, methinks. Shall we eat dinner?"

"Eww. I'm not eating that," Hadley protests.

April seems ready to stand off against my daughter. She hops off the chair and brings her hand to her hip before leaning down to Hadley's height. "Strange. You helped make it, and when you weren't looking, I even put in magic."

"Magic?" Hadley seems interested.

April nods her head. "Yep. It makes little girls grow and makes their fathers be compliant."

"Compli—" Hadley attempts to say.

My hand lands on my daughter's shoulder. "I'm curious about this magic. I thought April was only capable of witchcraft," I mumble through my teeth.

April walks to the kitchen counter and grabs Hadley's plate to show her a different version of the pasta than on the table. Hadley's version is simpler with no fancy stuff. Just tomato sauce and cheese.

"What's that?" Hadley investigates the plate.

"Magic pasta for girls who want to wake up tomorrow with special powers."

"She won't eat that," I tell April, because Hadley is a picky eater, and sometimes, I feel to defy me, she avoids eating what I suggest on purpose.

April takes a slow step, as if she is about to walk away. "Fine." She sighs. "I guess Pickles and I will enjoy our superpowers tomorrow morning alone. I think the magic I added was for making donuts tomorrow, or was it to get your daddy to take you wherever you want to go within a ten-mile radius, I don't quite remember." She taps her finger on her chin in contemplation, and I feel an odd sensation as I watch April make an effort with my daughter.

"Anywhere?" Hadley is suddenly invested in the situation again.

April pivots to look back at Hadley. "I mean, I guess if you have like six bites then that will be enough for the magic to kick in."

"I'm six!"

"Exactly. So…" She offers the plate.

Hadley takes a step forward and then another step. "Three bites."

"Five bites."

Damn, these two are in negotiations with one another like it's habit.

"Fine." Hadley doesn't sound thrilled but hops up on a kitchen counter stool, and April smiles proudly as she places the plate in front of Hadley before handing her a fork.

We both watch as Hadley slowly takes a bite, and relief hits me that I don't need to battle it out for her to eat again today, April did it for me.

April's gaze and enlightenment from her win shifts to me and her smile fades slightly, possibly because I have a new look on my face of appreciation for how April is putting her distaste for me to the side to put my daughter first.

———

AFTER GETTING HADLEY TO BED, I walk into the kitchen to find April setting the last of the dishes in the dishwasher. To my surprise, she left me a full plate of food. We didn't get a chance to eat. After Hadley ate her token bites, I brought her upstairs to get ready for bed. Bedtime is the one thing where things seem to gel between Hadley and me. It just runs smoothly.

"Is this really safe to eat?" I have to ask, as I'm not sure why she is being kind to me.

She gives me a death stare. "Not that you deserve it, but yes."

I make a point of grabbing a fork and take a bite, fully expecting to spit it out, as I don't take April for a cook, but the moment the stuffed pasta hits my tastebuds, I'm taken to another world. Garlic, mushroom, and thyme hit my tongue in an explosion.

"Damn," I nearly moan.

April flashes her eyes in agreement as she throws the kitchen towel to the side.

"Good?" She seems proud.

"No way Hadley would eat this," I note.

"She didn't. I made a different version for her. Cheese, and I pureed carrot into the tomato sauce so she will never know she ate a carrot."

I slowly swallow as I study her and wonder why she put in the effort for my daughter, but all I come up with is, "Thank you."

She nods once, and we don't speak any more about it.

"I guess pasta goes against your protein shake regime, but I was never agreeable to your needs."

"Not exactly true," I quip, and the air nearly leaves the room when we both take in that I'm referencing our one night together.

Clearing her throat, April walks to the fridge to grab two bottles of beer. "Shall we finish your explanation of your life situation?"

I take another bite of food to give me an extra second or two, but she's right. It's time to finish our conversation from earlier.

Taking the bottle of beer she offers, I grab the opener lying on the counter to pop the cap. "Where shall I start?" And what do I want to share with her?

"I'm not sure."

I wrap my lips around the bottle to take a decent sip of the beer, a specialty brew called Matchbox. "My mom has always helped raise Hadley, because Hadley's mom never wanted to be a mother."

April leans over the counter onto her arms and holds her bottle between her hands. "Who is she?"

"Just a hookup who signed away her parental rights the same week Hadley was born."

She offers me a sympathetic nod. "I would say I could never understand how someone could do that, but I get it. Not everyone wants to be a parent. Her loss, Hadley is a cute kid."

"I would say so," I breathe out. "And Hadley doesn't come to my baseball games, so she has never been around the media. That's more because she's too young to sit through a long game."

"Baseball games do drag," April confirms, and I flash her an unimpressed glare. "But people in Lake Spark know?"

"One of the joys of this small town is that everyone keeps what happens here in our bubble. I mean, your best friend and uncle literally walked around for months in Lake Spark together with not a word coming back to you."

"True." She rolls her eyes.

"And I've never brought Hadley to any of Hudson's parties since she's a young kid."

April straightens her posture. "That explains a lot. But I don't understand you."

"What do you mean?"

"Your effort is…"

I get defensive and stand up from the stool, my hands landing on the counter that I tower over. "What the hell does that mean?"

She shrugs her shoulders. "I just mean that, well, hell, I don't need to protect your cherished emotions, but damn, Spencer, try harder!"

"What the fuck?" I feel steam brewing between my ears. She has some damn nerve.

"Okay, hear me out." She holds her hands up to try and calm me down. "You keep her a big secret. I mean, you literally compartmentalize her life here into two rooms in this house. I don't even see any photos of you both anywhere around. And outside? I mean, get her a swing or something that says, 'this is your yard too.' Instead, you have a netted area to practice your pitching."

"She can play outside," I'm quick to justify.

"When she asks to bring toys outside. Why did she mention during pasta-making that a babysitter is coming next week?" She gives me a stern look.

I bite my inner cheek trying to suppress my rage. "Because I need the help."

"It's off-season," she counters.

I circle around the kitchen island to get closer to April, because this chick makes something inside of me want to throttle her, as I don't need her parenting views.

"I need someone to help around the house, and last time I checked, I'm missing the housewife."

April raises a finger. "Ah, so you need someone to help clean and do laundry. Not play with Hadley while you try to avoid her?"

"I'm not avoiding her. I'm doing my damn best, and I don't appreciate you criticizing me after only a day here of seeing us together. Don't take your daddy issues out on me."

April's mouth drops open then slowly closes before she abruptly turns and leans against the counter to take a sip of her beer. "You're right. I just hate to see anyone miss opportunities with their parents."

Her statement is like a knife to the chest because I couldn't agree more, but I'm not going to highlight that.

"No. You just want to make me the bad guy," I correct her.

"It's easier that way," she says before pushing herself away from the counter and walking away, calling to Pickles in the process.

————

THE NEXT MORNING, I wake early, as I normally do, and work out in my at-home gym before making a protein shake. By the time it's eight, I find it unusual that Hadley hasn't woken up yet.

Heading up the stairs, I slow my steps when I hear murmurs of voices.

"You smell like candy," my daughter states.

"Why, thank you." April doesn't seem to mind that Hadley must have made her way to the guest room.

"Your skin is more beautiful than Grammie's, hers has lines."

April chortles. "That's because age plays a factor."

"You're the same age as my daddy?"

"A few years younger."

I approach the room to see the door is open, and as I take a step into the doorway, I can't seem to tear my eyes away from the sight of April with a white towel wrapped around her body and a towel on her head, while her hands are busy using a makeup brush. Damn, the towel is barely past her ass, and I'm far too curious if she is still completely naked under it.

Hadley is leaning against the dresser in her pajamas, watching April.

Clearing my throat, I knock on the door pane. "Morning." I find my voice despite the image in front of me doing a number on my brain.

April doesn't take notice of me and focuses on the mirror. "Someone found me this morning."

"Sorry. I guess working on manners when a guest is here is new."

"Hey! It's more fun to watch April get pretty than go downstairs."

"Why is that?"

Hadley shrugs. "I don't know. She has sparkly powder."

"Sparkly powder? I think you are still stuck in your dreams, kiddo." I cross my arms over my chest.

April smiles. "Nah, she's right. I have this sparkly body powder that I was putting on when she came in."

My fist finds my mouth as I look away, and I'm now imagining where the hell that powder goes.

"Daddy, I don't think it's polite for you to be here. This is girls only."

I tip my head in the direction of Pickles who is lying lazily at the edge of the bed. "Pickles is here."

"He doesn't count," Hadley justifies.

"She's right, you know," April pipes up. "Your eyes should be somewhere else other than the room where I slept all night, only to wake, shower, and am now wearing a towel that could fall at any moment." I hear her taunting me as she applies mascara.

"See? You need to leave," Hadley declares, completely unaware of April's innuendo.

I shake my head ruefully. "Fine. But you are coming with me, Hadley, you need to get ready for the day."

Hadley's finger finds the air. "Did the magic work? Since I ate my bites of food last night. Do we get to go anywhere I want?"

I open my mouth, but then hesitate, remembering what April said last night about making an effort with Hadley. "Sure. Jolly Joe's?"

"Uhm, I want to go to Pioneer Park."

"That's still around?" April wonders. "I used to go there as a kid."

Fuck. It's Saturday, which means Pioneer Park will be packed with little heathens that I can't stand. I only like select children who tend to have parents whom I know.

"Can we?" Hadley brings her hands together as she pleads and bounces in her spot.

"Oh, sounds fun," April says, taking pleasure in this. "Merry-go-rounds, weekend parking, kids, people, autographs, farm animals, more people, all the things your daddy loves."

A sly smile spreads on my mouth. "Sure. Pioneer Park it is, *and* a special guest of honor will join us."

"Really? Who?" Hadley's face lights up.

"Princess Sparkly Powder herself," I declare.

It grabs April's attention, and she turns to face me with a tight smile. "I'm joining in?"

"For crowds, candied apples, more kids, and people in costumes? Not to mention proof that I'm an attentive parent. *Absolutely*." I don't blink, as April and I are in a locked gaze.

April takes a deep breath. "Fine. But we are stopping at Jolly Joe's for my coffee, so sign me up for this adventure."

Hadley is already running off, listing what she will wear, leaving me in her wake to look at the woman who wants to challenge me on everything.

"Might want to wear a sweater. It might get nippy out, and we know how your nipples get," I suggest with a satisfied smirk.

She begins to untie the knot of her towel above her perky tits. "Sure. I'll just get naked first. Are you going to turn around or pull out your phone that you don't know how to use?"

April turns around, dropping the towel to reveal a very naked back and a black thong. She takes pleasure in teasing me because that's what it is. There is nothing about the last five seconds that I hate.

She is a willing participant in the image that will now haunt me all day for our impromptu group outing.

SPENCER

My head lolls to the side against the driver's seat headrest. I blow out an exhausted breath as April gives me a knowing look.

"What? Your beast of a car could totally fit in that spot back there."

I look at her like she's crazy. "No way, I can't risk scratches, and this isn't a beast. This is the latest model of the best SUV on the market because I have precious goods to drive around."

We've been circling the parking lot of Pioneer Park for only a few minutes, and April wants to comment on my driving at every chance.

"Fine. Looks like we just have to get in line after that birthday party group that just arrived in a big van." She tips her head forward slightly to the car up ahead.

Ugh, more people, just thrilling. I steer the wheel to an upcoming spot that is far too small for my liking. I don't even need to look at April while I park to know she has an accomplished smirk on her face.

"Yay, we're here." Hadley is already reaching for her seatbelt.

"Just easy when getting out. Let April help you," I call out over my shoulder.

The next minute, we're working our way out of the car, meticulously holding doors and squeezing through tight spaces before we commence our short walk to the ticket counter—or the gates of hell as I like to call it.

Pioneer Park isn't quite a major theme park, but it's a step up from the typical park-district petting zoo. There is a little train you can ride on, a classic merry-go-round, a mini old-fashioned town, animals, and people dressed as pioneers.

Standing in line for the entry tickets, I hear tiny voices chattering, and before I can investigate, April is nudging my arm. I swipe my sunglasses off my face to get a view.

"Aren't you going to wave hello to your little fans?" April gives me a scolding look.

Looking over my shoulder, I see a few boys maybe a year or two older than Hadley staring at me with amazement.

Giving April a serious look, I tell her point blank, "No."

"Grumpy," she mumbles.

"I'm not grumpy. I'm trying to have a weekend with Hadley." We step forward as the line moves.

"And they are kids. Isn't gratitude one of Hadley's theme words at school this week?" She is completely making that up, but it's effective.

Hissing out my breath, I turn back to the boys and offer a short yet effective wave. The boys instantly grin with excitement before their parents usher them along in the line.

A slow clapping sound hits my ears, and I turn to see April clearly congratulating my efforts. She's exasperating, but at least her efforts to annoy me are amusing sometimes.

"Daddy, I want to go straight to the log cabin," Hadley says, pulling my arm.

"You're the boss."

After getting our tickets, we enter the fictitious prairie town, a sort of tribute to the area from years far back.

Hadley is already walking in the direction of where we need to go, and I can't help but notice someone else in our group moving with gusto.

"Someone is excited about the log cabin. When was the last time you were here?"

April glances to her side as we walk. "Years ago, but something tells me it hasn't changed. I wanted to go a while back for fun, but Je—, I mean, someone thought it was childish, so didn't want to play along. Besides, can't you smell the wood burning? I love it."

Taking a sniff of the air, I do smell the fire.

"I wonder if I can make a candle like last time," Hadley mentions before interlinking her arm with April's.

Watching them skip a few steps ahead of me, I don't like it. Hadley is taking to April, and maybe I wanted Hadley and me to be a team on our tolerance level of April. But now I'm truly two against one, and I can't help but feel an odd spark inside me that maybe all along I wanted April and Hadley to instantly click.

I do my best to ignore my mind meandering into unknown territory, but I seem to zone out slightly as Hadley and April approach the log cabin with excitement. A woman who looks maybe twenty is dressed up and is stirring a caldron over a fire.

"Something about 1800s-inspired fires just hit the spot." April takes in a deep inhale, stretching her arms into the sky as she stands next to me and watches Hadley disappear inside the cabin.

"Oh yeah, calms me completely," I say, sarcastic, as I scan the scene to see that everyone seems to be in their own world.

Hadley waves through an open window, and I return the gesture.

"You know she is completely checking you out," April points out.

"Who?"

"Witch lady."

"I don't think she's a witch; did you not get the memo that pioneer times is the theme?"

April snickers and gives me a knowing grin. "Fine. The twenty-year-old who likes to dress up is checking you out while she stirs the pretend soup."

I glance at the woman by the fire, and she is shooting me some serious flirty eyes before her hands adjust her costume in a not-so-subtle way to boost her cleavage up. Crossing my arms over my chest, a wide grin spreads on my face when I turn to look at April who almost has a soft pout.

"Unlucky for her, I don't pick up women when I'm in Hadley's presence."

"Sounds more like her lucky day then." April tries to avoid her eyes, meeting my own. "Oh, look at that, the sheriff arrived on a horse, probably to arrest the soup-making pioneer for her scandalous ways." April is quick to power-walk to the scene to meet Hadley who is curious about the arrival of the character.

I can't help but smile at the fact that, if I do say, Miss April is a little jealous.

———

ENDING the call on my cell phone, I jog to meet up with April and Hadley up ahead. April hands me back my drink without ever losing focus on the brochure she and Hadley are looking at.

We're walking along the overdone Main Street of Pioneer Village, taking sips from our soft drinks.

April points to the upcoming old-fashioned post office on the right. "There. That's where I think bonnet-making is at one." She continues to look at the little brochure to double-check something. "After that, we can do the train."

"I think then we have pretty much seen everything," I affirm to our little crowd.

"Don't be such a spoil," April throws me some shade.

"That's one of our words," Hadley proudly reminds us.

Hadley and April have been going over the pioneer dictionary in the back of the brochure.

"It is. Now go *mosey* along so you get a good spot for bonnet-making." She scoots my daughter in the direction of the post office door.

April and I both slow our pace as we watch Hadley join all the other little girls sitting around a table.

"Huh. This word is fitting. 'Dander; a strong emotion or anger.' That's going to be my word of the day," April comments as she reads the paper.

Grabbing the brochure from her pink-polished nails, I skim the list. "Funny. I thought you would pick *hankering* as your word."

"Hankering?" Her eyes grow wide with intrigue.

"Yeah. In modern times, we call it desire."

Her mouth parts open and an undescribed sound escapes her mouth. "Trust me, that's not what I'm feeling today. I'm kind of wishing a plague or something was part of the theme here to wipe me out."

I click the inside of my cheek. "You're having a blast here. I can see it."

She studies me for a second before a smile erupts. "Okay, smartass, you may be right just this once." She playfully hits my arm.

"Was it the merry-go-round or riding the covered wagon that took you over the edge to happiness?"

"Both. I don't know, it's kind of nice being a kid again. What about you, grumpy? You don't seem miserable."

I debate if I should let a comeback fly off my tongue or be honest, and when I look at April's deep eyes as she wipes a strand of hair away from her face, I have my answer. "Hadley's happy, so I'm happy… and thank you."

"For what?"

"You're making this a nice day for her."

Her shoulders come up toward her ears, and she seems to brush off my compliment.

"She's a sweet kid; must have gotten that from her grandparents."

We both look at Hadley who is busy with crafts.

"She is. Just an unusual situation," I admit.

April taps my arm with hers. "Nah, many kids have only one

parent and turn out amazing. Just look at me. And an unusual situa-tion would be dragging your video partner along after making her stay at your house—oh, wait." She brings her hand to her mouth in pretend shock. "That's us."

The corner of my mouth tugs up from her humor.

I step into her space with my hand finding a spot on her lower back. "Watch it, April, I might have to throw you over my shoulder when we get back to the homestead." There is far too much swelter in my voice than I would care to admit.

Yet April just chuckles a sensual sound under her breath.

"Careful. I might actually tolerate you today," she warns.

And hot damn, I hate that I'm enjoying this flirtation between us.

SPENCER

By the time I'm driving up to my house, Hadley is out like a light. My neighbor Ford is busy unpacking his car. I wave at him as we pass. We're good friends too, and when we're both in the city for our teams, then we often meet up.

"Ford Spears is looking mighty fine." April looks on with wide eyes, but I get a sense that she is trying to rile me.

I sit a little taller in my seat. "Doubt it."

"Huh, I knew that his house was finally ready to live in, and he apparently now lives there, but he looks a lot hotter in person than what you see online."

Ford plays hockey and spent a lot of his childhood in Lake Spark too. Being in his late twenties and with his short haircut and trim physique, it gets a lot of attention from girls, apparently April included.

"Down, girl, I'm confident he is waiting for someone."

"Jealous?" She looks at me, amused.

"No… Hey, doesn't Pickles need a walk?" I change topics as I pull us up in the driveway.

"Yeah, he does. Should I wake Hadley?"

Parking the car in the garage, I turn the engine off. "Nah, it's okay, I'll do it. She needs to wake up or she won't sleep later."

A minute later, I'm peeling Hadley slowly off the backseat and into my arms, resting her head against my shoulder. I'll wake her once we're inside and I set her on the couch.

I notice that April is staring at me, her eyes fixed on the scene.

"You okay?" I whisper. "You look like your cold heart might actually be thawing."

Her lips quirk out. "Just noticing that… it doesn't matter." She twirls around and heads out of the garage before I can figure out what is crossing her mind.

I don't spend time trying to figure out where April's head is at, because I have my little girl wrapped in my arms. I have no illusions, I know that this won't last forever; Hadley is growing at record speed.

When I lay Hadley on the sofa in the living room and she begins to grumble as I slowly wake her, I feel like she is at a stage of life when I'm enemy number one. The teenage years already spook me, and we're not even halfway there yet.

"Come on, sweet pea, time to wake up." I tuck her hair behind her ear, but her little hand swats me away.

"Grr."

Her sounds only make me smile to myself because she is adorable.

"It's not even dinner time yet."

She slowly pulls herself up to sitting and rubs her eyes. "Can I watch a movie?"

"That's all you want to do," I note.

"Because you're not good at playing with dolls or drawing."

Hadley isn't afraid to speak her mind, sometimes ruthless, but I can't even be mad. She has a point, I'm not great with playing, and I feel relief every time a babysitter comes to help out and play with Hadley.

"We can go outside to play. Want to throw the ball around?" I suggest.

"No. It's always me watching you practice throws."

"I can go gentle, grab the tee-ball set." I hear the eagerness in my voice.

She shakes her head in disagreement. "I don't like baseball, I like ballet."

I really struggle to find a mutual interest to bring us together. I'm the hard-ass who keeps my head in the game, and I don't have it in me to play dress-up or dolls.

"You had fun today, right?" I hear that I'm concerned on all fronts today. "I thought you wanted to go to Pioneer Park."

"I did have fun. April helped me find all the good places and pull you along." Hadley shuffles on the sofa to dangle her feet off the edge.

I scratch the back of my head. "Right. April."

"She's a fun friend."

"That she is." Damn it, she's outshining me. Maybe April staying here is a bad idea. I should be focusing on my relationship with Hadley, not adding extra roadblocks.

Hadley surprises me when she cuddles against my arm. "Don't worry. You're still really good at reading me stories, and you have connections to the tooth fairy, you promised you did."

A warm smile hits me as I loop an arm around her little body to bring her closer to me.

"I do have connections," I promise, because I know that phase is coming soon. Grabbing the remote from the side, I put on the screen to the streaming service. "Let me guess, Encanto?"

"Uh-huh."

Pressing play, I soak up this moment with Hadley, reminding myself that I'm trying.

The sound of dishes moving in the kitchen causes me to glance behind me to see that April must have been listening or watching, although she's pretending to focus on whatever she is creating.

A while later, with Hadley well into the movie and my tolerance for songs at a peak, I leave her with a blanket and head to the kitchen that is now empty.

Grabbing a water, I station myself at the kitchen counter and begin to skim my tablet, heading to the online toy store.

I tap my finger on the screen as I debate what in the world I could buy that maybe Hadley and I could both enjoy.

The smell of sugar hits me, and the feeling of another person walking behind me fills my body with a full feeling.

April walks straight to the oven to open the door and check on something, not saying anything to me in the process. When she seems to approve of whatever is cooking in the oven, she looks up at me and throws an oven glove to the side.

"Everything okay?" She rolls her lips in.

"Yeah, just looking at toys."

"I meant you escaped Encanto. Is it because you got to the scene about the abuela?"

"No," I say, defensive.

Her eyes narrow in on me "Really? Because I heard a rumor that you get emotional during that scene."

"Absolutely not." Or yes.

"Alright, I'll let it go, but I know your secret." She laughs. "And toys? You don't need more toys, you have plenty of those."

"I know, but something I could do with Hadley." I look into the other room then back at my tablet. "What about Princess Legos?"

April offers me a soft smile. "I really think she has enough toys in her special room."

I begin my search in the bar of the website, but then excitement takes over me. "Maybe I should have someone install a ballet barre in her playroom."

"Now that is a perfect idea. She will go crazy," April assures me.

Something else dawns on me, a memory. "Aren't you the ballet pro?"

Our eyes catch because she knows I'm referencing that night.

"You twirl and bend like one, anyhow," I add.

She raises her brow but says nothing. I notice her cheeks blush a shade of pink. I pause for a beat and look at April who is watching me intently. "What's cooking?"

She blinks a few times. "Oh, that. Uhm, just a macaroni cheese bake, and truffle potatoes with chicken for the adults. Didn't have it in me to make stew or anything pioneer themed."

"It sounds good. What time is dinner?"

"Should be in twenty minutes, but I'm going to leave you two at it. I'm going to work on some things on my laptop." She seems to want to avoid us, and for some reason, that disappoints me.

April ignores us for the rest of the night, and it causes me to toss and turn when I should be sleeping.

————

WHEN I WAKE, I seem to run harder for my morning workout, as if something is bothering me, which makes sense considering my current life predicament. Standing on my dock on the lake after my brutal run, I pick up a baseball from the basket of many and throw it out across into the lake. I do this on repeat to relieve stress.

"Whoa, isn't this a waste of baseballs?" I hear Ford approach me, as he must have been on a morning run.

He jogs in place once he reaches my spot.

"Sorry. It's been a hell of a week." I stretch my arms over my head then throw another ball. "This is no different from golfers and their golf balls."

"Fair point. Nothing to do with the woman who was in your car yesterday? She looked familiar."

"April?"

"As in Hudson's niece?" He brings his foot up behind him to stretch his quad.

"Yeah, she's staying with me for a little bit."

He makes a winding gesture with his hand. "Hold up. You clearly haven't told your best friend what the hell is going on."

"She's the one." He looks at me, as if I need to offer up another clue. "As in the one from the wild night I had after Hudson's and Piper's baby shower."

Ford laughs deep. "Oh man, does Hudson know?"

I shake my head. "Trust me, it was one night only."

"Then why the fuck is she living in your house?"

"A complication arose."

His eyes grow big. "Like a nine-month-later complication?"

"No. As in 'we kind of did something and need to ensure nobody sees it' complication."

Ford now laughs hysterically.

"It's not funny."

"Yes, it is. Everyone knows that with a good lawyer you'll be fine. I mean, how many guys on my team have done something stupid and nobody ever found out? It is way too many to count."

Raking a hand through my hair, I know he's right. "Anyhow, it's a temporary stay, and we argue most of the time."

"I do remember you mentioning you're not a fan. But why did you invite her to stay? You never let women near Hadley."

"I didn't have much choice. Besides, I can get away with saying she is a friend to Hadley since she's always around Piper and Hudson."

Ford bobs his head from side to side. "Maybe."

"Maybe what?"

He touches my upper arm. "You'll figure it out. I need to run, get my shake, and head back to the city." He begins to run in place.

"Don't forget about the charity dinner later this week," he says as he runs backwards. "You are expected not to come alone," he calls out.

I wave him off in the air with a little two-finger salute.

I take my time with a cool-off walk back to the house, making a mental note that I only left the house because I knew April was there in case Handley woke, which clearly happened as I hear them in the playroom as I walk past the hall. I backtrack a step but stay hidden as I listen.

"So, what should a princess expect?" Hadley wonders. They're sitting in her little tent with books scattered around on the floor. My daughter is still in her pajamas, whereas April is ready for the day in jeans and an off-the-shoulder sweater while she strokes Pickles' head.

"That her prince decorates the room with candles and makes it a special evening when he asks her for her hand in marriage. Most definitely not in their apartment while they wait for a taxi to pick them up and he suggests they get married." I can hear the truth in her voice. Honestly, it kind of sounds like Jeff's proposal, well… sucked.

"Hmm. Should there be cake?"

"Maybe. The prince should go all out on grand gestures."

"Can the princess be happy without both parents at her wedding?"

April's shock at the question is apparent in her pause. "Why, of course. What makes you ask that?"

"Because I only have a daddy."

"And? I only have a mommy; well, she found her prince recently, but he isn't my dad. Anyways, I still have every plan to be happy on my wedding day."

"Why don't you have a dad?"

"I was specially chosen by my mom. Sometimes we only have one parent, and that just means they have more love to share. I'll let you in on a little secret." I can hear her pretending to whisper. "They normally give us extra cookies because they want us to be happy."

I laugh softly, before I clear my throat and make my presence known.

They both look up at me.

"There you two are."

"He's up." Hadley doesn't sound thrilled.

April swipes Hadley's ponytail to the side. "Yes, because your daddy works extra hard to stay in shape to make millions of dollars off of throwing balls so he can buy you all the cookies in the world to show his love."

Why do I feel like a melting puddle of goo? And why does it not filter through my brain when I tell April, "Throwing a curveball at April makes my day complete, which is why you're coming with me to this charity dinner later this week… as my plus-one."

APRIL

What nerve that man has. I chop my peppers with extra vigor, slight aggression escaping me on every knife cut.

He actually thinks he can just order me to attend some charity event with him. He didn't even ask, just demanded. I don't even have anything to wear. I mean, I didn't exactly add black-tie attire to my suitcase for this last-minute trip. I stuck to a wardrobe appropriate for sweater weather, jeans and layers of shirts.

My phone vibrates on the counter, and I see my mother is calling. Blowing out a relaxing breath, I prepare myself for this and tap the green button.

"April, finally! I feel like you've been avoiding me the last few days." My mom seems to be sitting behind her at-home desk, with her blondish-brown hair tied in a low shoulder-length ponytail.

"Sorry." I lean against my propped elbow. "I've been busy with a project."

"Clearly. Where are you? That doesn't look like your place."

"It's not. I'm at Spencer's house."

"Spencer? As in Spencer Crews? Your uncle's neighbor? Star baseball player?"

I nod my head with dread for the upcoming minutes ahead of me. "Why on earth would you be there?"

As much as I would say my mother and I are close, I'm not about to spill the beans on the true reasoning of how I ended up in the amazing kitchen with an asshole fastballer, who is currently playing outside with an adorable child.

"Uhm, he needed… a sitter." I doubt my lie that just came out then realize I shared a fact. "Can we throw in your lawyer confidentiality card for the last part? He doesn't really want people to know about his daughter."

My mother purses her lips together, and her expression is unreadable. "Sure," she simply replies. "But I didn't realize being a nanny was what you wanted career-wise."

"Oh, it's not. This is temporary. However, I do get to use this kitchen, and I've been nailing a few recipes."

A warm smile spreads on her face. "I saw. Your social media has some lovely photos and recipes."

"Anyway, when are you coming to Lake Spark?"

"To see my precious little niece Gracie?" she nearly coos.

I give her a fake unimpressed look. "I get it, the baby wins. Kind of hoped your badass adult daughter would get a higher ranking."

My mother chortles a laugh. "You're right. I'm happy to see you're okay. I had an odd feeling that something was up. Mother's instinct."

The corner of my mouth curves up. "And father's instinct. You have it all."

"I have no other choice."

"Do you think it goes the same way for fathers who raise their kids alone? I mean, do they also have a mother's instinct?"

She shrugs her shoulders. "I don't know. Everyone parents differently, and families come in different shapes."

"That I know. It's just kind of weird seeing Spencer do the single-dad thing; it's so different to when you did the single-parent thing with me."

My mother folds her arms over her chest. "Well, I think it must be hard when he travels so much for baseball, but all that matters is that the effort is there. Sometimes as parents we put in a lot of effort, but things still don't happen the way we want it to. What's important is that we can never doubt we tried."

I'm not sure what to say, or why I asked. But then I recall the last few days and how my view of Spencer has been thrown for a loop.

The man watches braiding videos while he tries to twist Hadley's hair, he attempts to feed her vegetables when he knows no kid that age will agree, and he still takes her to places that make her happy, even when she gives him the cold shoulder.

"I think I might have been a bitch," I admit out loud.

My mom gives me a stern eye. "Elaborate."

"I might have been a little hard on Spencer."

Disapproval spreads across my mother's face. "April."

Geez, still she has the power to say my name to shake me into fear of a timeout.

My palm flies up. "Okay, I will be a little nicer… when it comes to Hadley."

"Good. You are full of kindness."

"He brings out the evil in me."

Her grin is a knowing one. "Hmm."

"Anyway, I need to get these stuffed peppers in the oven." I begin to move, bringing my phone with me. "Wait. You knew about Spencer's daughter?" It dawns on me that Spencer is using her colleague to deal with our little situation, probably because he already uses their firm for all his legal woes. "Let me guess, he has used your services for family law?"

"I'm not at liberty to say."

That's a yes. I groan softly. "You don't talk about cases with Celeste by any chance, do you?"

"No. Not unless she needs my advice but won't mention names. Why? She asked how you were doing the other day, by the way."

"I'm just splendid," I deadpan.

"I'm sure you are." My mother sounds amused. "Bye, sweetie."

"Bye."

Kneeling down to look at the oven, I see the light is off to indicate it's warm and ready to insert my tray bake. My mind repeats my new rule that I will be nice to Spencer when it relates to Hadley, but for everything else, all bets are off.

———

I FOUND HIM.

After avoiding him all day, I arrive at the last destination where I can think to look for Spencer, and coincidentally, it's where I was going to head for the evening anyhow.

He's swimming his laps in the warm indoor pool, and the lighting is dim yet perfectly outlines his chiseled form. The light in the water causes a blue glow in the center of the room, and a wall of glass overlooks the lake.

Since this morning's demand, I've stayed out of Spencer and Hadley's way. I didn't want my anger to boil over in front of the little one, and I also thought maybe they needed some alone time since it's the weekend and tomorrow she is back to school. I went to the grocery store, walked Pickles, cooked, and left food for both of them while I went to check on Piper next door. As soon as I knew Hadley would be asleep, I began my quest to find the man.

Now I'm staring at Spencer, oblivious to me, as he creates waves in the pool from his long, deep strokes.

I whip my robe off and walk down the steps into the pool, wearing my deep purple triangle bikini that barely covers my globes, but cleavage is a girl's best friend.

Spencer must notice that he is no longer alone, as he suddenly stops and stands in the pool, shaking his head and wiping the water from his face.

"Ah, the mermaid appears, actually swimming in a pool this time."

"Well, I mean, this will do," I say as I submerge myself into the warm as bath water.

"I could have sworn you've been keeping to yourself all day on purpose, yet here you are in my pool." He walks closer to me, and now I have a full view of his bare chest and the tattoo.

"The number. It's her birthday, isn't it?" I comment. The anchor I know is a logo from the first team he played baseball on, but the number…

He looks down at his chest. "Could be. Days and months do have numbers."

Fuck, something just tugged on my heartstrings.

"I'm sorry," I blurt out.

"For what?" He looks at me, intrigued, and slowly moves closer.

"I was maybe a little judgmental of you in regard to Hadley."

His eyes nearly bug out. "No shit. Is this an apology, April?"

"Yes." I do my best to avoid looking into his eyes. "I know you try with her. And it can't be easy."

He takes in a breath, his nostrils flaring slightly. "Apology accepted."

I do a double take. Why is he being so agreeable? I thought he would make me grovel. We look at one another in amazement that we both just made it easy for each other. But then I remember that it was only part of the reason that I wanted to find him.

Immediately, I push against his hard pecs, causing water to swoosh around us. "You're unbelievable."

"Way to ruin a moment of peace. What the hell now?"

"You can't just order me around and tell me that I'm going with you to some charity event as your plus-one." I splash water at him.

He instantly pulls me close and turns us so I'm trapped between the edge of the pool and his body, his hands landing on each side of me, creating a wall.

"Oh, I can. While you're staying here, I need you to be on my team. We both have a lot at stake, and the more clues we leave, then the better it looks just in case the world sees how you scream my name." His tone has a sort of dominance that is irritatingly sexy.

I give him a pointed look. "And where are we with that? Any updates? I feel like this should be progressing so my ticket out of here is sooner rather than later."

He growls in annoyance. "No news, and I said I would tell you when there is something to tell."

"Why can't you just be a gentleman? You know, actually ask a woman if she would like to accompany your big ego to an evening for charity? I mean, wouldn't you want Hadley to only ever be *asked* by a man, so she knows she has a choice?"

Spencer hums a sound of disapproval. "Don't bring her into this, and fine, I'm sure I'll make it up to you."

"How the hell do you plan on doing that?"

His eyes linger down to my tits and then back up to my mouth. "Not tonight."

Disappointment floods inside of me, because for a second, I felt a need for what my imagination was playing in my head.

"Since this is my pool, I guess you should follow my swimming rules."

I scoff a sound. "Oh geez, what rule did I forget this time?"

His fingers are quick to land on the knot of my bikini top on my back where he tugs slightly and then stops. "Women whom I fuck only swim naked in this pool."

He pulls a little more.

I lean in to let our breaths mingle, an ache forming between my legs, but I want to have the upper hand. My lips barely trace his jawline.

"A shame that you only *fucked* me, past tense. Loophole of your rule," I whisper.

A devilish smirk forms on his mouth.

Tug.

My top falls loose and my nipples appear.

He hisses a sound. "Oh no," he says, feigning regret. "Accidents do happen."

I own this moment, and with purpose grab hold of the bikini top that is about to float away and throw it behind me onto the deck of the pool.

He moves closer, my clit beating against the movement of water for any relief that I can get.

"Do you know what I hate to admit?" He tips his head to the side, his breath hitting my neck.

"That you're a headache to the female population?" I breathe out, but it's shaky.

His fingertips trace the curve of my breast, and I feel my body shudder from his touch.

"I like when you're feisty, completely unreasonable, and a pain to have a normal conversation with."

"Who the hell enjoys that?" I wonder as my body molds into him.

He pinches my nipple. "The guy who has every intention of fucking you into compliance."

Spencer grips my hips and hoists my body up, my legs naturally floating to wrap around his waist where I feel his hard cock.

I bite my bottom lip because my hand weaves through his hair to guide his head down where he takes a nipple into his mouth, and I moan in approval.

All logic is slipping away, and I'm giving into this need that my body has, a void that only he can fill, caution thrown to the wind.

His lips pull away, but he traps my little bud between his teeth, and he playfully teases me. Looking down and I see him peering up at me.

The sound of his popping lips fills the room. "Get out of the pool, April," he demands.

I'm taken aback. "Excuse me?"

"Unfortunately for us, the friction of pool water is not in our favor. So, get the fuck out and walk slowly to the shower over there." He tips his head to the stone wall with a shower behind it, the kind of shower you see at a spa after the sauna.

"What makes you think I will comply?"

He's quick to loosen the ties on both sides of my bikini bottom in one go.

"I don't, but either way, you're pretty much as good as naked, so I already win. Now be a smart girl and get out of the pool."

His commanding voice is hard to resist, I admit.

He swims away and exits the pool, and I don't feel any resistance inside of me, so I slowly swim a few strokes to the steps and, with a cautious sway, get out and walk to the shower where he is already under the spray of water.

"The friction of water isn't in our favor, remember?" I retort.

He snags my wrists, yanks me forward, and turns us so my back is against the stone wall, with the shower over us. The whole move is kind of exhilarating.

"Pool water isn't. The shower is different."

He steps back, finishes the job of tugging my bikini bottom ties free, and throws the fabric to the side, leaving me naked. I should feel vulnerable, but he gives me the once-over, and I feel extremely turned on that he is assessing me like a prize. He reaches between us, and he hooks his finger to trace my pubic bone with a satisfied smirk.

"You always wax or just when you know that you want to fuck the guy whose house you're staying in?"

My eyes blaze with slight fury at his words. He never needs to know that I *may* have gone for a quick wax before I drove up here a few days ago.

"Here is how this is going to go, April. You will be by my side at that charity event."

"Oh gee, I don't have anything to wear," I counter with an excuse.

"I'll arrange that."

I roll my eyes. "Controlling."

"Nah, controlling would be telling you that you're not going to wear an ounce of fabric underneath the dress because we need you ready for every moment that I plan on punishing you for that mouth of yours that just runs wild with words."

"I feel like this is a one-sided dislike. You keep making it sound as though I'm the only one in our dynamic who hates when we're together," I say huskily as my mouth spars with his, trying to get a taste, but he denies me because taunting me is his game.

His fingertips travel up the side of my body as he presses his body into me. "Hate is a strong word, but damn, you are irritating. So irritating that I want to fuck you as a consequence."

"Spencer." My voice sounds more desperate than the warning that I intended.

He plants his long finger on my mouth to shush me. "The next time you open your mouth it better be to moan."

Dropping to his knees, he brings my leg over his shoulder and his mouth covers my center. His tongue instantly hits my clit, causing my body to bolt from the momentary relief.

I voluntarily rest my arms by my head against the wall, a sort of surrender.

Spencer is relentless in his pursuit of my pussy. Jesus, that tongue is a weapon.

I feel like I'm nearly unable to breathe, only made worse when I look down to see Spencer on his knees and on a mission. And despite the water cascading down our bodies, I'm not sure the warmth is helping, as my entire body is peaked with arousal. Little goosebumps appear on my skin, and I feel like my balance is about to be lost.

Especially when he adds a finger to the equation and works his way inside of me.

"Fuck, fuck, fuck," I mutter to myself.

His tongue finds a rhythm, and my lungs want to burst out of my chest because I can't breathe.

"Spencer," I attempt to say his name, but it comes out a long slew of letters. My hand lands on his shoulder so I don't fall.

Then he throws me off when he interlaces our hands against the wall, but he doesn't stop with his tongue. He keeps stroking me and making sounds like he's enjoying every millisecond.

I close my eyes as I melt into the feeling of being ravished. And they stay closed until I'm unraveling against his mouth, convulsing from the effect.

He stays on me until I seem to have calmed down before he slowly rises to stand, with the water the only sound between us, our eyes intense as we both visibly breathe out of pace.

I move to touch him, return the favor, but he stops me by grabbing my arm.

"Trust me, the stone wall won't be comfortable for the way I plan to fuck you. Good night, April." He runs his knuckles along my cheek before he is quick to step away, grab a towel, and disappear.

What in the world just happened?

I'm totally lost.

Because the next day, after avoidance, he surprises me when he returns home from picking Hadley up at school.

When I look at the kitchen counter, my blood boils yet again…

12

SPENCER

April looks like she is going to kill me.

I look between the bouquet of autumn orange roses that I left on the counter and April who is standing by the fridge, dumbfounded, her mouth parted open and her throat visibly gulping.

"What in the world?" Her eyes could drill a hole into the flowers.

My cheeky smirk comes out in full swing. "I'm doing what we call *listening*." I walk around the kitchen island and look over my shoulder at Hadley who I picked up from school and who is now eating a snack of donut bites. They have hidden zucchini and apples in it, and April conveniently left them out on a plate with a juice box, ready for Hadley's arrival.

April is thoughtful that way. It irks me, and not in a bad way either, but I can't focus on that feeling when a scowl sweeps across her face.

"Listening?" April approaches the flowers as if they might destruct.

I turn to Hadley. "You see, a guy should always *ask* if you would like to go somewhere, and sometimes they bring flowers to soften the deal. Then you should think about their offer, probably discuss it with your dad, and then give an answer."

"Huh?" My daughter just looks at me, uninterested, before popping another ball into her mouth.

"Yeah, what she said." April looks at me with hesitation.

Taking a few steps with confidence, I glue my sight on April, ensuring her bewildered eyes stay fixed on me. "Well, April, will you accompany me for this charity event?"

She straightens her neck and looks around the room. I have her trapped because Hadley is watching us, which is why her sight pauses on my daughter for a second before focusing on me.

"I think I'm missing a please." She cocks her head to the side.

Difficult, this one. My grin turns tight. "Will you *please* do me the honor of accompanying me to the charity event."

Now she smiles with accomplishment, one hand finding her hip and the other touching the roses. "Sure. Nice touch with the roses, by the way."

"Does this mean you get to dress up like a princess?" Hadley asks April.

April awkwardly hums a sound. "Depends on what your daddy has in mind, but I'm sure a potato sack wouldn't suffice."

"I don't know, gives good leg action," I mumble so only April can hear.

"Can I go watch TV?" Hadley is already swinging her legs off the stool.

"Sure. Take your snack with you," I suggest.

The moment Hadley turns her back to us, April's smile fades, and she points at me.

"You. Laundry room. Now." Her words sound seething.

Yet I follow her willingly, watching her feisty march and sway. When we get to the laundry room, she closes the door behind me, and she jabs her finger into my chest, sending a bolt of electricity down my spine.

"You're mocking me," she begins.

"What? Me?" I play coy.

"Yeah, you. You're taking my words from yesterday and mocking me. You didn't really want to get me flowers, you just wanted to prove a point," she loudly whispers, because she doesn't want Hadley to hear.

I swipe a hand across my jaw. "And? So what if I did? You get roses out of it."

"I now want to pull every petal off its stem to work out my absolute exasperation with you." Her hands come up in the air, as if she wants to throttle something.

"Exasperating?"

How am I the issue?

I step closer. "Heaven forbid you actually say thank you for the roses."

"No. To you? Absolutely not." She stares at me blankly before stepping closer. "You are the most confusing human on the planet."

"How so?" I'm slightly offended.

"You have no manners," she declares, with her hands gesturing with her words.

"Do explain."

She hisses, "Mocking me with flowers, going down on me last night. I mean, who does that? You didn't even kiss me."

And here I am in yet another predicament with this woman. Because around her she makes my control come undone. She makes my head spin when she opens her mouth, that I instantly find so incredibly sexy.

That mouth.

That fucking gorgeous mouth. It taunts me when she speaks and makes me go feral when it's shut.

She weakens me in a way that no man enjoys because it means she potentially has the power to wrap me around her little finger that is currently jabbing my shoulder.

"You're pissed that I didn't kiss your mouth?" I'm in awe that making her come on my tongue wasn't enough. I'm slightly offended too, as I thought my skills were way above exceptional. "That's what has you in a tantrum?"

"No." I swear a sound dings. It's a horrible lie.

Does this woman ever drop her defense? Wait, she has. A lot. And around me. First that night with the video, again when we watched it, and last night by the pool.

April just needs to be prodded like a bear and fucked like she could be everything.

In a snap decision, I grab her face, cradling her head with her chin in the palm of my hand.

"God damn it, April," I husk. I hear thick want in my voice, and I wonder if she notices. I feel a throbbing sensation in my chest, and her eyes have me lost in a daze similar to last night.

This keeps happening.

A need to touch her, tease her like no man has, challenge her the way she challenges me. All logic goes out the window when it comes to her. It's the attraction that's messing with me because nobody wants to sign up for her daily rants and raves.

And I normally do better by Hadley. I don't invite women into our lives, yet that's all I seem to do with April.

Her eyes penetrate my own with want.

A sound escapes from the back of my throat because there will be no more suspense in this moment.

I slam my mouth onto hers, and her sound of surprise vanishes when I draw in her breath. She gives in by kissing me back. I haven't kissed her since those months ago, yet still she tastes like cake, a distinct taste that I remember because I had spread it on her cheek.

Her murmur rumbles into my mouth as we struggle to pull our lips apart for a breath. But this isn't going to stop. We manage to take a quick inhale before our mouths seal together again. A rush takes over, and no thoughts come into my mind. I just give in to this moment.

April's arms loop around my neck, and I lift her up onto the washing machine that is conveniently on.

A laugh escapes, and she untangles our mouths, but her lips brush along mine. "Everything is vibrating," she whispers.

I grin to myself because she means the sensations from the machine, and hopefully what my lips do to her.

We go at it again, making out like two teenagers. Hands roaming, tongues dueling, and our mouths and necks getting thoroughly explored.

"Does this make up for yesterday?" I pant.

"Shh. I enjoy this more when you don't remind me of the reasons I don't like you." She doesn't elaborate because she kisses me again.

The height of the machine makes it perfect for her center to meet mine, and tilting my bulge into her, my hard cock must take her by surprise as she yelps and smiles against my jaw.

"I am trying to contain myself from ripping this sweater off of you," I warn. It's knitted, off-the-shoulder, and distracting.

She hums in approval.

This is a version of myself I don't quite recognize. Everything I do lately is the opposite of my structured rules and routine.

"April," my daughter calls out and seems to be walking down the hall.

Shit, Hadley.

April and I instantly freeze mid-kiss before I back away, swiping a hand through my hair.

"Yeah, kiddo?" April calls out and hops off the washing machine, quickly adjusting her shirt and glancing over her shoulder at me with a semi-panicked look, then her eyes dart down to my impressive member, and I turn away, my fist clenched in the air.

Hadley opens the door. "What are you doing in here?"

"Oh." April gulps. "Your dad was showing me how to turn on the washing machine."

With her hand clasping the handle, Hadley looks between us, skeptical.

"What did you need, sweet pea?" I ask, avoiding turning my full body to her.

"Can I walk Pickles?" she inquires with excitement.

Relief seems to flood April's face. "Sure. How about I come with you. Your dad mentioned he needs a cold shower or swim now anyhow." April begins ushering Hadley out, not even looking back.

When they're both out of sight, my hands land on the washing machine in frustration. I curse and growl because I let that moment happen.

I'm not even sure what has me in a mood more. The fact I kissed April while my daughter was in the other room so close, or the fact that Hadley interrupted us.

And both options are a problem.

———

WALKING along the sidewalk in downtown Lake Spark, I take in the fact that it's getting colder outside. The cool air is needed, maybe it will snap me out of my mood. Since the laundry room entanglement the other day, April and I have done our best to avoid one another, only keeping to small talk when Hadley is around, as my daughter is, unbeknownst to her, a peacekeeper.

I only have half an hour before I need to pick up Hadley, but it would have been a wasted drive home only to turn around. Plus, I can imagine April is in the kitchen making something ridiculously delectable yet again. A quick stop at the drug store to pick up razors that I don't really need is clearly a more thrilling option.

Looking ahead, I notice a familiar tail and slow wobble. My eyes draw a line from Pickles up his leash to the blonde walking in my direction, her glare strong.

Clearly no escape or avoidance options on the table today.

"April." My short greeting is all I can manage. I'm not sure what to do.

"I wasn't expecting to see you here."

"I thought you would be back at the house. I'm running an errand while Hadley has tap class."

Pickles sniffs my leg and wags his tail, clearly happy to see me, and at least someone here is in a good mood.

April pulls him back slightly. "We don't like him, remember?" She's speaking to the dog.

Rolling my eyes, I'm reminded of why I never before placed April in the contender category. "Real adult."

Her eyes bug out at me, and her sound of disapproval flies off her lips that have a fresh coat of Chapstick, because, yeah, I fucking notice.

"Wow. You have some nerve. I mean, you are the king of mixed signals." She stalks forward with her shoulders puffing out and that damn finger pointing at me again. "Not that I would want any signal from you, other than that our video situation is solved and I can finally go on my return journey out of here."

I'm calling bullshit on this.

"Babe, that is the lie of the century. You have no problem following my signals, that's all you do."

"Don't call me babe," she growls.

Blowing out a breath, I prepare myself for this merry-go-round. "That's what you took away from that sentence?" Now I have to smirk. "Oh, right, you enjoy it when I'm in control, so you can only agree with everything I say."

"Spencer, your holier-than-thou baseball-player mindset is a real piece of work. You're the one initiating everything."

Now I chuckle under my breath, leaning into her space, close enough for our air to evaporate. "Nah, it's your mouth that gets us into these predicaments. Remind me to pick up a bar of soap when I hit the drug store."

"I much prefer tape when you want to get kinky," she jokes but in such a serious tone that she freezes when she realizes her error.

Chuckling to myself, I find this way too entertaining. I grab Pickles' leash from her hand, and she doesn't fight me as she just stews in her confession. And I don't mean the tape part; she admitted in non-plain terms that there will be another time.

I tug on Pickles' leash, and April peers down to watch him quite energetically walk closer to me.

"What are you doing with my dog?"

"He's coming with me."

"No, he's not," she volleys.

"Pickles is just living his life of Zen, remember? He suddenly has energy when he sees me."

"And squirrels. So congratulations, you are in the same category as squirrels," she states flatly.

Stepping dangerously close to April, I scan the scene to ensure nobody notices us before I speak in a low voice. "I'll take him back to the house. Hadley will love seeing him when I pick her up from dance. Besides, his owner needs to take a walk and cool down because she has to think about the fact that she still has to be my plus-one this week, and you best believe I'm going to make sure you look like the woman every guy wants to fuck but won't because they'll know you're there with me."

And I wouldn't need to do much because she already looks the part.

"What woman in their right mind falls for this shit you spew?"

I don't know, but you have me unable to think clearly.

I reach my finger out to tap the tip of her nose. "The one who is sleeping in my guest room because for one night she took a chance and decided I'm the guy she could have an adventure with."

"A nightmare. That's what this is." The line of her lips twists.

"Then why is a smile curling on your lips, and ten seconds ago, your hands found their way to my arms to hold, as if I'm the guy every woman wants to fuck but they won't because you're making a public claim."

Her eyes drop down to see that she is holding my wrists in an affectionate manner. She instantly drops my arms, and I hate that something feels absent.

"You will be a gentleman, a perfect gentleman tomorrow," she calls out a warning before turning to march away in a mood, leaving me to smile internally to myself.

She only marches a few steps before she makes a sharp turn to look at me. "We're acting insane."

"Completely." I can only agree, with my grin pulling on the corners of my mouth.

The hard line on her mouth disappears and a gentle smile begins to spread. "We always bicker."

"Isn't it fun?"

Her cheeks tighten because her smile only grows.

"Pizza tonight? I think Hadley will love to make her own pizza, and I can do a cauliflower crust so she has no clue she's eating a vegetable," she rambles as her temper from a minute ago fades into oblivion.

Hell, I'm no longer in the mood to spar. Not after she just made that offer for dinner.

"She will love that." And I do too.

One nod and then April begins to turn slowly, her smile not fading.

"You still better be a gentleman tomorrow," she reminds me with a little wave goodbye in the air.

"Still debating," I tell her, purely to keep the banter up.

But looking down at Pickles who wails a sound when he looks up at me, I know that every living creature can analyze this situation and see a fire.

A fire that I hate to admit, but I don't think I want to escape the flames.

13

APRIL

W ell, this is ridiculous.

I look over my shoulder at my reflection in the long mirror.

"I'm not sure I should be wearing this," I mention as I take in the fact this long black dress is near backless which means no bra for me, especially as it ties around my neck.

"Spencer picked this out?" Piper asks for the tenth time as she sits at the edge of the guest bed, focusing between her baby girl lying on the mattress playing with a toy and staring at me in my predicament.

I can't tear my eyes away from the mirror. "This is not what I had in mind."

Piper smiles like a cat who found their prey. "The slit between your cleavage is a bold choice."

My eyes grow into saucers. "I know, right? But…"

Her smile grows wide. "You look smoking."

My own excitement comes out, especially because my updo is perfection. "I *do* look smoking."

This dress hugs me in all the right places, and it's a beautiful and very expensive dress. I'm not sure I want to know how Spencer managed to pick this out, he had to have enlisted someone's help. I feel like a million bucks.

I walk to the dresser to search for earrings. I hold up the long one and the stud for Piper's approval.

"Go simple," she suggests.

Studs it is.

I'm not quite sure why I have butterflies in my stomach, but this has been an unusual week, and I would be surprised if I didn't have nerves. The last few days have been unexpected.

It feels like a game with Spencer, yet I volunteer myself as tribute every round. Since our laundry room make-out the other day, we have basically ignored each other except when Hadley is around.

She is such a sweet little girl. Funny too. She gives Spencer a hard time, but at random moments does something to catch him by surprise in a way that I hope brings them closer.

"At least you will have fun at the charity dinner. It's for a good cause, to add a further addition to the new sports center where they'll hold summer camps for kids. If Hudson didn't have an away game this week then I'm sure we would be there too."

"It's kind of you to watch Hadley and Pickles. I guess we won't be that late."

"Don't sweat it. Unlike you, I have no problem with Spencer. I owed him a favor for the number of times he has signed for packages for me while I'm taking an impromptu nap."

I nod in understanding as I take a long breath to look at myself once more.

"You know…" I can tell Piper wants to point out the obvious. "You're Spencer's plus-one, people will see you together…"

"I'm just his plus-one," I reiterate.

"I doubt any cameras there will agree with that. But you don't seem to mind. Something you want to share?"

I focus on blending with my highlighter brush on my cheeks. "No." Because I don't know how to explain it.

"Just remember that you will one day find the guy who will erase all past mistakes. He'll be the magic you've been waiting for.

So be it, he might not appear that way at first." She splays her hands out.

Before I can protest, I see Hadley in the corner of my eye arriving at my open door and walking straight to the dresser.

"Did you already put on the sparkly powder?" Hadley rummages through my makeup.

Of course, that's what she would be after.

"I did, but I can always use more." I take the case and brush, dab it in the powder, then offer it to Hadley and give her my arm to spread the stuff.

"Can you tell Daddy to let me have powder? When you're not here, I won't get to use this." She focuses on spreading the brush along my arm.

When I'm not here. Sometimes I forget that this is all temporary. I'm getting comfortable here, which should be a warning.

She hands me the brush in accomplishment, and I dab the brush on the cleavage line of my breasts without thought until Piper chortles a laugh.

"Interesting choice," she mutters.

Like a hot potato, I drop the brush back on the dresser because clearly, my subconscious is up to tricks.

"You look like a princess." Hadley smiles, and I can tell one of her front teeth is loose. I remember the conversation that I heard the other day between her and Spencer about the tooth fairy.

I stroke her hair with my hand. "Why, thank you." I pick up my clutch purse from the bed. "Now I just need to find my ogre," I mutter.

———

WALKING OUT THE FRONT DOOR, I feel my body fill with anticipation, but then I internally growl in irritation when I see Spencer leaning against the dark SUV, as he hired a driver for the night.

And I'm fuming inside because he is incredibly handsome.

He's in a tux, his hair slicked back, hands in his pockets, with a smirk on his mouth. Then he propels his body off the hood of the car, and he approaches me with swagger.

But the worst part?

His breath catches, and then he hisses a whistle of approval when he's a short distance away.

"You're late."

Ah, we are going to play this game.

"By two minutes because some baseball player apparently picked out a dress that involves a tie that acts as a lifeline for my cleavage."

"I approve." It feels like he is drinking me in.

I clear my throat. "You look..." How do I explain that I may drool?

"Everyone will be looking at you, and I might be regretting my choice now. Should have gone for the turtleneck option."

A wry smile doesn't leave my face. "Well, you did want me to look fuckable, as you put it in your ever charming terms."

"Nah, you look way classier than that. Come on, we should go." He offers me his arm. I'm slightly taken aback by his manners, but I interlink our arms anyway.

A whiff of his spicy cologne hits me, but it's enough to make my senses melt. His arm feels strong, and I need to get used to it because I think I'll be glued to him for most of the night.

By the time we're in the car and on our way, I recognize that the air between us has shifted; we're easy around one another.

I decide to break the ice. "Looks like the tooth fairy will be in business soon. Hadley's front tooth looks loose."

"I noticed that." An elated look spreads on his face. Spencer taps his fingers on his thighs as he looks out the window until he turns back at me. "How's the food blog?"

"I'm stockpiling recipes and photos, thanks to your kitchen. A total opposite to my life as an accountant."

"Good. That's good."

We don't seem to know how to handle this new dynamic between us, probably because we can't define it.

"New sports camp, huh?" I attempt to keep the conversation flowing.

"Yeah, it would be good for Lake Spark. Once I retire, then I'll have something to do."

"But you don't like kids except your own," I point out the obvious.

He rolls a shoulder back. "Doesn't mean I don't recognize that it's good for the community, or maybe I want to work with teenagers."

Oh my, I was not expecting that response.

"You'll retire soon?"

"I probably have one or two more good years, then I'll need to do something. I don't think coaching is for me."

"It does generally require interacting with people," I state.

He gives me side-eye. "Funny." His jaw eases. "I would like to spend more time with Hadley."

"Of course." I lean against the window, taking in the fact that I'm dressed to the nines and sitting with Spencer whose hardened exterior feels softened. I try to remember the last time I was at a black-tie event with a man. My soured feeling must be apparent because I feel like Spencer has a sneer forming.

"You okay?"

"The last time I went to an event like this, I was with my ex. It was his firm's Christmas gala." I puff out a breath. "Truthfully, I didn't have the best of times. He was all work and forgot about me most of the night."

"Nothing I've heard about this dude has been positive."

"Now, no. Sometimes we get stuck in the idea of something and ignore that we might not be with the right person to make it happen," I explain. Because I don't think my ex was the one; I'm mostly bitter because I felt humiliated.

Spencer adjusts in his seat, even slides closer to me. "You mean, your dream wedding?"

I narrow my eyes at him because I'm not sure if he's mocking me. "Enough about me. Am I going to run into any of your exes tonight?"

"None of my exes are from around here."

"Oh? But I do believe you have the 'women who you screw in your pool are only naked' rule."

He grins a pretty damn swoony grin. "April, sweetheart, you're the first in my pool."

I'm not sure why it hasn't crossed my mind, the idea of other women in his house, maybe because I assumed he has had special guests since he has so many options when it comes to women, or perhaps I've been too focused on the moment. That's a change, as I'm always thinking about the dream ahead or something that happened in the past; it's never in that moment, except when Spencer is around.

A tickle at my hip bone breaks my thought, and I peer down to find a talented finger tracing a line. Spencer is touching me of his own accord.

"A problem?" I raise my brows.

A smug accomplished smirk slowly appears. "You're wearing fabric underneath."

"Wow, he observes."

"You know in baseball when I pitch, I'm restricted to certain types of throws. It's actually rigid and doesn't leave me much choice, I have to stick to the program. Don't get me wrong, it's still exciting, or rather there are other ways to make a game interesting. For example, I could try to pitch an entire game to get a shutout, ensuring the other team doesn't score at all, and by end of game, my team wins. Want to know what I think?"

His lips brush along my bare shoulder like a feather, and a tingle runs through me. I pray my nipples don't give me away.

"That I need a sweater," I quip.

He chuckles, and I love how it's a sound that pulls me in and feels like an enticing offer.

"I think tonight will be like a shutout. I have no intention of letting anyone else score."

"Ah, but one problem." I rest my hand on his thigh, playing the part of a doting other half. "You won't get your homerun or whatever baseball term I should be using, because I may look the part, but I'm not in the mood to be fucked like you hate me."

His face is unreadable, but his jaw ticks, and I'm surprised he doesn't have a jab in return.

The car slows down, and glancing outside, I see we have apparently reached our destination, the sports center, with an outside marquee with heaters, thankfully.

When the car stops, Spencer gets out, buttons his tux, and leans back in to take my hand and help me out.

But as I stand and straighten my dress, the man leans in to whisper in my ear as he wraps a protective arm around my middle to bring my body to his, my upper half molding into his shape.

"Listen, beautiful, think what you want, but I'm not going to let anyone else score, so get used to being by my fucking side."

14

SPENCER

Why can't I stop watching her?

All night, I've kept my word, and April hasn't left my side. Instead, I've played a part that I'm not exactly used to… Prince Charming.

I fill her glass with wine when it needs a refresh, I keep my arm permanently on the back of her chair as we watch the auction, and I listen with a keen ear when she talks to the table about her trip to Italy and adopting a dog.

April wanted gentlemanly and I'm giving it, but I'm not sure why I care so much. Probably because this woman is possessing my thoughts.

"I'll be back." April breaks my moment of being lost in my head.

"Huh?"

"Ladies' room. I'll be back. Am I allowed, dear master?" she taunts me, clearly entertained. I stand up to help her pull her chair back, and her eyes turn strange. "Who are you when you wear a tux?" She seems astonished, and quite frankly, so am I.

"Cute. Real cute. I just believe I'm obeying your request that I be a gentleman tonight."

She hums a response before swaying away, just as Ford is walking back to our table and holding out a glass of scotch for me.

"You are completely enamored." Ford smirks to himself before taking a sip of his own glass.

We both sit down.

"She may be getting under my skin a little," I admit. Assessing the area, everyone is busy eating desserts and sipping wine. There are a few sports stars here, but in true Lake Spark fashion, it's the town mayor who takes center stage.

"I would be worried if she wasn't. Besides, she looks completely into you. It's funny watching you two together, like two teenagers with a crush."

"Come on, Ford, it's not that bad. Besides we're just comfortable around each other since she is staying at my place." I lean back in my seat and stare into my filled tumbler.

"And why is she staying with you? Oh yeah, because she already took a ride with you, consequences be damned."

I flash him an unamused look. "Enough about me. Why are you here solo? Wasn't the memo to bring a plus-one?"

His brows raise, as if he's surprised I asked, as I should realize the answer. "You know I don't bring dates to my home turf. It wouldn't feel right."

Biting the corner of my mouth, a wave of empathy hits me. I'm an ass for asking, because he treats Lake Spark like holy ground, as it's where he had his first real love and heartbreak, and if he had his way, then Brielle Dawson would also be his only love.

"How are you going with that?" I wonder.

He sighs a breath. "I see her every few weeks for ten minutes to discuss our boy and that's it."

I slap a hand on his back. "It'll work its way out. Besides, hockey season is about to start and will keep you busy."

"Thank fuck for that." He tips his head in the direction of the exit. "April is back. You're good if I ask her to dance?"

Shooting him a warning glare, it causes him to chuckle.

I slide out of my chair and quickly charge a few steps to meet April halfway, and in a flash, I loop an arm around her middle.

She startles from surprise. "What in the world?"

"Let's dance."

"Really?" She seems skeptical. "You dance?" But she doesn't protest and follows me to the dance floor where a slow song is playing.

A faint smile graces her lips when our eyes meet as we face one another, her arms finding a home around my neck as we move our bodies to the music.

"How was your temporary escape?" I joke.

"Not bad. Listening to the old ladies debate if the hockey player or baseball player is better suited for their granddaughter was absolutely amusing, especially when they realized I was standing there in line."

I relax into this moment. "You're the threat, clearly." I feel my phone vibrate in the front pocket of my suit. "Sorry, let me quickly check that in case it's Hadley related."

April's eyes have a sort of admiration hinted in them; they sparkle, but that's probably the light. "Absolutely."

Reaching into my tux jacket, I slide out my phone and see that Piper texted. I swipe my thumb across the screen, and I can only internally celebrate the development.

"Everything okay?"

"Yeah." I tuck the phone back into my tux. "Piper took Hadley and Pickles back to her house, as the baby needed an extra change of clothes. Hadley is going to sleep there tonight since it's easier."

"Lies, I tell you. There is no way that baby needed an extra change. Piper never leaves her house without at least three outfits for the kid." April laughs.

Sounds about right. Piper did insert a winking emoji that I didn't tell April about.

"Ah well, we are now in no rush or anything." I pull April flush since I feel like I can let go tonight without restrictions.

"Or anything," April barely echoes in a whisper.

It makes me scoff, as I like where her mind goes. "Having a good time despite being stuck with me?"

"Actually, this is kind of fun. Thank you for insisting I be your plus-one against my will." She clicks the inside of her cheek with her tongue.

"I brought you flowers," I remind her.

"You did, and you paid an exorbitant amount for the private chef at the Dizzy Duck for one night in the auction. I may soften my stance on you if you let me be your plus-one for that so I can assess if it's a good menu."

I twirl her around. "I think you've already softened your stance on me."

"Maybe true," she replies point blank, and her honesty catches me off guard.

I bring her hand to rest against my chest, near my heart that has been prodding me lately. "You would want to go back to the Dizzy Duck with me?"

"It is a dangerous location, but I do what I must for good food and conversation."

"So now I'm good at conversation too?" I tease her.

She playfully swats my chest. "Sometimes. Outside of Hadley and baseball, you're still kind of a mystery to me."

"Really? What do you want to know?"

"Hmm, what would you do if you didn't play baseball?"

I try to suppress my grin. "I only know baseball, but I'm not blind that at any moment it could all end, so I guess in the back of my mind, I would want to invest in a hotel or something. I studied business in college."

"Okay, I guess that's straightforward. Can I ask something else?" She focuses on her finger playing with the button on my white shirt. I nod. "Why are you so… unapproachable to most?"

I chortle a laugh. "Wow. Are you asking why I'm grouchy? I'm not always. I just worked hard to get to where I am, I need to be focused. My parents didn't have much, I wasn't handed a silver spoon, but now I can have it all. And besides, what went down with

Hadley… I have every reason to keep people at bay." A ping deep within my heart aches.

"I get it, and I'm not going to say sometimes we need to move on to new chapters and try again. I've seen people at their worst too."

"Their loss."

"I think so," she agrees.

We dance in place, swaying, our eyes piercing in a locked gaze. Inside, I feel an internal battle; the fact I kept the video, yet I'm thankful I did, otherwise we wouldn't be here.

"You don't hate me, do you? Like really hate me because I kept the video?"

Her chin tips up as she breathes a long breath. "Detest isn't hate. And… I don't know. Is it strange that I'm not mad? Fine. I admit it. I'm not that mad. A little nervous the whole world may see it, but at least I can say it led me on an adventure, with an added bonus of benefitting from your kitchen."

I debate what to say next but settle on simple. "I can live with that." In the corner of my eye, I notice the floor clearing, and then it dawns on me that the music is fading. "We should probably head back."

"Yeah, a good idea."

I strip off my jacket to drape on her shoulders, and she gives me a peculiar look. "You gave me the standard of being on good behavior, remember? Plus, you must be freezing."

"I think you wanted it that way."

We begin to walk side by side, our arms grazing. "Why would that be, April?"

"Because you like when I suffer, despite whatever is going on in that head of yours, and I'm fairly confident that your mind is going wild." She is sure of herself, and she isn't far off.

The only clear point in my brain right now is that I feel lucky tonight.

———

LOOKING out the floor-to-ceiling living room window, I glance at the stars while I drink a nightcap. My tie hangs loose around my neck.

We had a silent ride back, and the moment we stepped inside the house April disappeared. Fair enough. I haven't touched her to prove a point. I could have slipped my fingers between the slit of her dress to feel her wet and ready, but I refrained because I knew that was what she was expecting.

Now, I'm taking a moment to relish the fact that Hadley isn't here, because off-season, I don't have many breaks from being a dad, and during baseball season, I have no breaks from being a star pitcher. It's all one continuous grind.

"Hey, can you help with this?" I hear April approaching behind me.

Turning halfway, I see she is indicating to the zipper that conveniently rests on her lower back, causing the dress to become a second skin to the curve of her ass.

Smirking to myself, I know what she is trying to do, but I'll play along.

"Come here," I say and set my drink on the side table.

April slowly turns in front of me, offering her back, and my fingers willingly find the zipper to tug, but I pause. Instead, I inhale her flowery perfume and feel bold.

"I'll help you, but you have to do something for me."

"What?"

"Take off your panties."

I'm far too curious if my theory is correct.

She throws me a coy look over her shoulder, hesitating at first, but quickly skims the bottom of her dress up her silky legs and reaches under to pull down the black thong. It slides down her legs, and she steps out of them, holding them up for presentation.

I grab my prize, and my smirk of accomplishment is immediate. "My, my, someone has been soaking." The fabric feels damp, and I bring it to my nose, her distinct smell as sweet as I know she tastes. Her lips part open as she watches me.

"Will you help me now?" Her brows arch.

I step closer to her, and I'm quick to shove the ball of panties into her mouth. She mumbles something from surprise but doesn't spit them out. "Now I will." My smirk is now cocky.

My fingers return to her zipper, and I pull slowly down, feeling the softness of her sparkly powdered skin and the firmness of the curve of her body. The fingers of my other hand entwine in her hair to find any form of a clip, then I slide it out, which is followed by her hair falling loose around her shoulders.

"If you're going to play the game then go all in with your efforts," I suggest.

She glances over her shoulder with a wicked look and spits out the fabric. "Wishful thinking." With purpose, she brings her arm to the bow at the back of her neck, tugging, before her arms come forward to shield her breasts as the fabric hangs loose around her body.

"Night, night. I need to go hang this up, as this dress is prone to wrinkles."

She walks away, clearly satisfied with her performance, and I watch every step as she fades out of the room.

Blowing out a deep breath, I take one last sip of my drink to calm me then scoop up the destroyed thong.

I want the upper hand, and I will not go after her. Challenging April is the highlight of my day lately, and that means not doing what she would expect. I'll just take a shower and go to bed.

Simple as that.

FIVE MINUTES LATER, I'm in my bathroom unbuttoning my shirt, waiting for the water in the shower to warm up, yet I can't seem to commit. Physically, I don't want to step under the stream to find relief.

Not when the best release is a few doors down.

What the fuck am I doing?

Everything inside me is going crazy for this woman. All week,

I've wanted to lead, but the truth is, she has the ability to make me follow. To make me not use rational thought. Hell, I've invited her into my home and interwoven April into Hadley's life. I'm not the type of guy who thinks of a future with someone, but if I think of tomorrow then April is in every second of it.

This is frustratingly new. I should be mad at her just for that.

Fuck it.

I turn the water off, and in a full-speed walk, I head straight to April's room. Opening the door without a knock, I stand in the doorway to find her sitting in the middle of the bed, leaning against the headboard in sexy little pajama shorts and my old team t-shirt that she must have cut because it's hanging off her shoulder and doesn't go an inch below her belly button. The smirk on her face is like she won the World Series.

She was waiting for me.

"There you are." She plays coy, pretending to examine her nails. "A minute longer than I predicted."

I shake my head, and my genuine smile from this situation spreads. I storm to her bed, take hold of her ankles, and pull her to the edge of the mattress. She squeals in approval.

"No fucking way we are doing this here. We're heading to my bedroom," I tell her before throwing her over my shoulder.

15

SPENCER

Throwing April on my bed, I don't question why I had a primal urge to take her to my room, but the guest room just wouldn't do.

April leans back on her elbows to assess me as I stand at the edge of the bed.

"I guess you've never been in here," I note as I slowly bring one knee to the mattress and then the other.

A sly grin appears on her lips as she comes up to sitting, her hands splaying against my searing skin, pressing my chest for a feel. "Silly boy, I snooped around here days ago. Even stole a shirt, in case you didn't notice." She yanks my unbuttoned dress shirt down my arms before returning to lying on my bed.

"Oh, I noticed." One arm lands on the side of her and our eyes cling to one another. I glare a warning before my other arm finds a spot near her shoulder to cage her underneath me.

"No pressure or anything, but you did say the other day that you would fuck me so hard that a stone wall just wouldn't do, and lucky me, there seems to be a mattress this time." Her sultry tone is toying with me.

I growl from her playfulness, a refreshing change to our fiery exchanges during all our previous rounds. Slamming my lips down onto hers, I make it clear that I have every intention to take her the way I've been wanting to for days.

I dip my tongue into her mouth, and she purrs a sweet sound that makes me eager to kiss her harder.

Her pointed foot travels up my leg until it lands on my ass, opening her up wide to me, and I'm ready to lose my mind.

"I have no intention of going slow with you."

"Good, we are to the point," she jokes against my lips.

My hand roams her body, wanting to touch her everywhere yet unsure where to focus. April seems to be in the same predicament, as her hands mimic my own.

"I should spank you for looking so ridiculously beautiful tonight, then fucking blowing my mind by wearing my shirt."

"What if I jinx your team?" she one-tones.

I chuckle as I drag my lips down the soft skin of her neck. "I'll take the chance." She tugs at my belt. "Don't tell me you've practiced," I warn her before taking over to finish the job.

There is a glint in her eye. Her breathing is different, like maybe she wants to say something but doesn't. Instead, the moment I'm over her again after removing my pants, she sneaks into the waistband of my boxer briefs, and her fingers wrap around my length. I close my eyes and let out a sound of agreement.

April isn't afraid to lead, but that's not how I roll. But damn, her hand feels good on me.

"We need to get there faster," she coos.

I begin to yank down her little shorts as she does mine, and we both pause in our fast chaotic movements to finish the task of removing layers. I'm quicker, and it gives me the opportunity to pin her wrists against the mattress as my other hand heads straight to the only place I want to be this evening.

Feeling between her folds, the warmth of her juices causes me to hiss, as she is ready. Finding her little bead, I rub her arousal in a circular motion against her clit. Another finger drives into her center, and I feel her tightness. It made me near delirious the other day when I went down on her.

Maybe I've essentially been gearing her up all week, yet I can't help but wonder. "Why are you so tight, April?" I study her face as her breath catches and my finger continues to work her. I can't lie, I love having control over her.

"You know that answer," April whispers, and I could swear I hear vulnerability.

She doesn't give me a clear response, so I stop my effort to bring her to her edge. I walk my fingers up her flat stomach and underneath the flimsy shirt, and I find a nipple to pluck. "You haven't been with anyone since our video escapade," I point out the fact.

Her tongue darts out to lick her lips. "Have you?"

I smirk to myself; I have no problem admitting the obvious. "Don't read into it. I don't fuck random people during baseball season." If she can do the math then she knows that she was my last.

She figures it out, because she leans up, wraps her arms around my neck, and pulls me into a kiss. A passionate kiss that shows she enjoys our truths, and hell, I kind of agree with her.

We draw our kiss out until the need for air hits us.

It's intoxicating how lost I am in this moment. We both want me to plunge right into her, and we can't get there quick enough because our mouths and hands run wild.

Proven by the fact that she rolls me to my back and straddles me with a confident look before she ensures I'm watching her peel the shirt up and off her body, revealing her beautiful tits. I smile as I reach to my nightstand table for a foil package before I flip her right onto her back again and coax her to shimmy up the mattress until her head rests on a pillow.

I part her legs wide, diving in to place my mouth on her heat, kissing her inner thighs, blazing a trail of determination in the process. I lick her once, twice, but that's all she will get because we have one goal right now.

Crawling up the mattress to cage her in, I breathe near her ear, her hair extra flowery, and I hate her for the fact that it will linger on my pillows.

"Wrap those pretty little legs of yours around my waist," I urge.

"I'm always, what was it you said…" She pretends to search for a word. "Compliant." April tilts her hips up against me to highlight her efforts.

I sheathe the condom on. "The thing about this scenario is that I've worked you up all week so this round we don't need to be gentle."

A lazy smile appears on her lips as I tease the tip of my cock around her opening, gliding between her slick heat, taunting her clit, entering her without warning then backing out.

My finger does one more test round, exploring her, and she yelps in surprise when I touch her intimate back opening. A sinister hum escapes me. "Relax. We'll explore that another round."

Her eyes grow wide before her delicate long finger circles my shoulder while I align myself with her opening. "You keep referring to rounds, plural?" She cocks a brow.

Driving myself in until I reach her hilt, we both gasp from the force. "Okay, multiple rounds," she breathes out in agreement and gets lost in the feeling of me filling her up.

I pull out only to push back in, doing it a few times until I feel April ease underneath me.

Our eyes hold as I move inside of her, until a few pumps later, when our foreheads touch and we slow the pace.

Slowing it down makes this far worse. I'm sinking into her, wanting to drag out every second of this because she feels like the best thing that could ever happen between the sheets. I was never meant to play any sport but baseball, and now I think I may not be meant to fuck anyone but April.

That frustrating point causes me to fuck her with a bit more force, hooking my arms under her knees to draw them up toward my shoulders, her body willingly offering itself to me.

Her warm wet pussy that is as good as her snide remarks.

The sound of skin slapping and our heavy breathing fills the room. I feel heat spread throughout my body, and I notice the blissful look on April's face.

I peer down to get a glimpse of my cock sliding into her, and it's a magnificent view. But not quite as good as April's mouth in an O shape, with her breath trapped because she is lost in the feeling of having me inside of her.

"Breathe," I remind her.

"Fuck," she bluntly replies.

A laugh escapes me as I continue her request.

My finger lands on her clit to bring her to the next level, but truthfully, the next few minutes are a blur because our mouths continue to fuse, and we keep turning the tide with slow, fast, slow, fast until her teeth are clenching into the corner of my mouth as I bring her to her edge.

"Spencer." My name on her lips sounds like a plea, one that I ignore because I want her undone.

Her shaking and trembling while I'm inside of her is the only way that I'll accept this, and it's what happens as she quivers and her breath turns ragged.

I slow my strokes and look down at her face, softening as she comes down from her orgasm, and when I know she's ready, I continue to pump into her to bring me to my own release. It doesn't take long.

Short and fast was how this was going to go. It's the only way when you've been torturing one another for days.

I feel the sensation travel from below my navel and to my cock before I unload into the condom. April's heat wraps tightly around my length.

"Shit," I say as I fall forward, holding my weight so I don't crush April, but I rest my head against hers for a moment.

She rakes her nails along my back as we both lie on my bed in a stew of our own bizarre attraction.

And I have enough experience to know that when you enjoy the seconds after the climax just as much as the main event, then you have a situation.

Because right now, I don't want to leave this bed.

APRIL

I want to strangle him as much as I want to kiss him.

It's unfair because the all-night stamina of an athlete is something that I'm unable to compete with.

He has me on my side, back to him, and my arms stretched out over my head as he pumps into me, and he doesn't go easy or sweet. Yet, I'm completely relaxed, and I sink into another round of ecstasy because Spencer somehow knows how to take care of my body.

Sounds escape my mouth, creating my own original tune, my body jolts on every deep thrust, and his lips placing a kiss on my shoulder blade is probably the real cause of my undoing that hits me in a wave.

"Good girl," he grits out as he holds my hip down and continues his quest.

"Spencer," I purr because I hate that he teases me with that phrase.

He follows me shortly after, and I don't look over my shoulder when I feel him slide out of the bed. Instead, I lie in *his* bed, completely spent.

When he emerges from his bathroom, I can't help but take in the scene of him naked. A freaking sculpture of perfection, right down to his endowment size. Such a shame these qualities didn't spill over into his personality. I smile to myself because that's not true either; I'm peeling away his layers.

"What's on your mind?" he asks as he works his way back into bed.

"Nothing. My brain can't function because I've been fucked all night." I pull the covers up a little higher, and I'm not sure why.

Spencer yanks the sheet back down slightly before he lies on his side and props his head against an elbow. "It's going to be a little rough this morning. We barely slept, and Piper will bring Hadley home soon."

I wince from the thought. Now I can relate to Piper and her lack of sleep and need to still parent.

"Some days are pretty brutal. Kids aren't afraid to speak without a filter and will point out your faults whether you are well-slept or not."

"At least you only have to deal with it for half of the year." The moment it slips off my lips, I feel horrible, especially when I see the hurt in his eyes. Instantly I reach out to touch his arm. "I'm sorry. I didn't mean for it to come out like that."

"Yeah, you did." He sounds somber.

"Okay, maybe in the literal sense, but not in the 'you're a douchebag' sense," I try to assure him.

He blows out a breath. "It's fine. Let it go."

"Is it? I mean, here, I'm giving you a free pass. Take a dig at me." I pat his arm with the suggestion. "Remind me that I only date boring doctors and lawyers who never make it past the first date."

Spencer smirks to himself before getting more comfortable in his position. "That's only a plus for me, April. It means your pussy is molded to my cock."

I ruefully shake my head, because of course he will take us back to vulgar talk. Flopping back to rest my head on the pillow, I blow out an exhausting breath.

A few beats of silence grace the room, and I take the moment to recall the night. I feel the smile on my lips then pause when the obvious hits me.

"*So*, this, well…"

Spencer looks at me, patiently waiting for me to finish the sentence, and he seems entertained. "Go on," he insists.

I swallow. "Piper will be here soon; I should probably go shower and make breakfast."

"Why would you need a shower?" he says, playing dumb.

I toss a spare pillow at him. "You know why."

He blocks the pillow and manages to take hold of my arms to bring me into his embrace as he rests against the headboard. "You're sore?"

"I don't know. I'm debating if my center of gravity has changed."

Spencer chuckles and wraps me tighter. "If it hasn't then let me know and I'll fuck you in the pantry later for good measure."

I slap his arm and then decide to test the boundaries by inter-twining our fingers. "So last night," I return to my earlier attempt to bring some clarity to the situation.

"It is what it is," he comments with no hint of where his mind is at.

"Right." That's my cue to slip out of bed and find some clothes.

I begin to do just that, and as my ass is about to slide off the bed, I hear him sigh and grab my arm.

My eyes dart to his hand on my elbow, then my sight pivots up to meet his steely gaze.

"I'm not the guy to be more than this," he says.

"Just a little hate sex, we've been here before," I brush it off.

His cheeks raise and his mouth quirks. "Last night wasn't hate sex. If it was then I would have pulled your hair a little more and bit you somewhere visible just to annoy you that you wouldn't be able to forget me until the mark fades."

That's actually quite a turn-on. "Rain check then."

"To my utter dismay, you're getting under my skin in a way that I'm not used to."

Fear that he may have regretted last night fades, and my body softens into his words. "Likewise."

"Something is shifting."

"I agree." I can't blink, and nerves now hit me, the kind you get when someone catches your eye and takes an interest, except this time it's a heavier feeling, more intense.

"I have nothing else to offer right now except that you're staying here in this house, Hadley adores you—"

"Don't sweat that. If I didn't have Pickles then I would be completely boring to her." I do my best to downplay the situation.

He smiles gently at my attempt to reassure him. "Can we just leave it as we had a good night together?"

"Sure." I avoid his gaze.

"And I'll confess that there may be a tiny little hope that you sneak your cute ass right back in here tonight." Ah, there is his cocky look.

That grin of his stretches, and I feel my own subtle hint of a smile returning, especially when I look down to see that he hasn't let my fingers go.

And for now, that's good enough.

———

"You know, this screams that you are trying to cover something up." Spencer grabs a piece of fruit from my bowl.

Scanning all the dishes I just prepared, I guess he has a point. A simple breakfast somehow turned into waffles, fruit salad, eggs, bacon, and I even have donuts in the oven that I'll roll in cinnamon sugar later.

In truth, I'm a little nervous. Mostly because I know it's obvious to Piper what must have happened last night, and I don't want Hadley to think something is different.

"I guess I should have stuck to coffee and your protein shake laced with superpowers, but I got distracted," I admit.

Spencer runs his hand up my spine, and my body shivers in delight.

I enjoy a few seconds before I shake him off. "Down, boy, I need to recover, and besides, I think daylight may be highlighting my wrong life choices." I give him a stern eye.

"Your body says something else." His eyes dip down to my nipples that are peaked under my t-shirt. I'm quick to fold my arms over my chest for cover.

The sound of the door opening catches our attention. A mixture of paws on wood, a baby cooing, and Hadley running in.

"Yoo-hoo, I come bearing gifts," Piper announces as she walks into the kitchen holding up a box from Jolly Joe's in one hand, and she's balancing Gracie on her other hip. Pickles pads along beside Hadley. Piper's smile drops to confusion when she sees the buffet laid out on the kitchen island. "Oh. Clearly someone needed to be occupied this morning." She flashes me an overdone smile.

Spencer gives me knowing eyes as he walks to his daughter who just hopped up on a stool. "I'm not hungry," Hadley declares.

"There are donuts in the oven," Spencer informs her.

"Still not hungry."

He grabs her a plate and dishes up some fruit anyways. "Well, I'm sure you'll change your mind." He turns to Piper. "Thanks for watching her, I owe you one."

"It's all good. I let her play dress-up and she helped me with the bambino. You two look absolutely tired," Piper points out, sneaking in a smirk as she sips from her to-go cup.

"It was a late night. I mean, the charity thing." My fingers fumble in the air.

Her chortle causes Spencer and me to glance at one another, as Piper is onto us.

Snapping, I bite the bullet. "Piper, a word in the other room, please." I smile tightly.

She looks giddy. Without even asking, she hands her baby over to Spencer.

He is quick to protest. "I don't do babies."

"Sure, you do. You're a pro. Thanks, you're a doll." She ignores him and nearly skips to the end of the hall.

When I arrive at the door near the garage, she has a golden smile, with her arms crossed over her chest.

"Just tell me you didn't make another video," she requests.

I shake my head.

"The 'I had a good time last night' look does great things for your complexion," she comments.

I roll my eyes, and as much as I pretend to be annoyed, I erupt in a joyful sound and grin. "Can we forget this?"

"No, because I want you to wake up and accept that your shitty dating life lately might be solved with a guy who knows how to throw a fastball."

Quickly I interject, "It's nothing more than physical."

"Sure, it is." She's certain. "Listen, just don't get hurt, and also be open. I honestly don't know what to make of this situation other than wow, you look like you're enjoying life for the first time in a long time. He's a good distraction." She affectionately touches my arm. Quickly, she gives me a hug. "Okay, we're not going to overstay our welcome."

She begins to walk away, and I call out her name. "Have you not seen the kitchen counter? Please stay."

Piper waves me off. "Nah, I'm sure Spencer worked up a big enough appetite." She winks before continuing her path.

She leaves me there in reflection that indeed for the first time in a long time, I'm having fun and smiling, and it isn't forced.

———

THE REST OF THE DAY, Spencer played with Hadley. He took her to the playground in town, while I stayed at the house because I needed to work on a paper for my nutritional course. I'm so close to being finished, and then I can start applying for jobs because a successful blog may be wishful thinking, but at the very least, it takes time to grow.

A knock on my door disrupts my focus on the screen. Looking up, I find Spencer casually leaning against the doorframe, t-shirt hugging his muscles, and my eyes enjoy the view.

"Checking to see if I threw out my vibrator?" I wisecrack.

He slowly steps into my room. "I already destroyed that a few days ago since you won't be needing it."

I tilt my head to the side before I lean on the side table and pull open the drawer. I bite my inner cheek because the devil actually did it, and I didn't notice because he has been fulfilling my needs in that department, from that night in the pool to last night.

"You owe me a new one when I return to the city." I set my laptop to the side and scooch forward and off the bed to meet him in the middle of the room.

"About that." He swipes a hand across his jaw, struggling to bring his thoughts together.

Immediately, my fear surfaces. "Oh God. The video, it's leaked?! Shit, I need to text my mother." I begin to pace the room. "My uncle may kill you. Let's say goodbye to my future job prospects too. Then there is my spiteful ex who will not let me forget this, I'm sure," I ramble, but a strong arm stops me.

"April." Spencer's voice is calm, and he cradles my head between the palms of his hands, the print of his thumb dragging along my bottom lip. "It's fine. We're fine. No longer an issue."

"Oh."

"Lawyer did wonders, and the file is deleted, all traces gone."

Well, that's… great. It should be fantastic. But why do I feel deflated? Oh, right, because that means…

"I guess I'm no longer a prisoner here." I sound disappointed.

His jaw flexes side to side. "True."

Neither one of us seem to know what to say. I glance over my shoulder. "I guess I'll pack up and head back—"

"Stay," he blurts out.

"Stay?"

Tone down the hope, April. Geez.

Spencer shrugs a shoulder as he runs the back of his knuckles along my cheek. "Yeah, I mean, you need my kitchen, right?"

His kitchen?

"It is a great kitchen."

The subtle hint of a grin tells me that it's code language for finding a reason that isn't obvious he wants me to stay.

Stepping closer to him, I roll my lips in, confident with my theory. "I do have a lot I still need to do, recipes, of course."

He stands taller and inches closer. "Settled then."

"Uh-huh."

Our mouths of their own accord move to trace one another's lips, but neither one of us dares to commit. A simple brush of our lips is enough for this moment, the hint that something bigger is underlying. Neither one of us could be that blind to ignore it.

"A few extra days wouldn't hurt. I mean, I'm sure you can tolerate me for that long," I whisper.

A soft rumble leaves his mouth. "Something like that." He bops his finger on the tip of my nose before giving me a subtle smirk as he turns to leave.

I watch him go as a swirling feeling of excitement and fear travels through me, because Spencer Crews is turning out to be everything I never imagined him to be.

SPENCER

She shakes her booty in my kitchen. That's what April does when she thinks nobody is watching, and she's focused on her latest creation. She keeps her ear pods in and dances around. I even caught her in full-on down-to-the-floor moves while she sang "It's Tricky" by Run DMC. She had no idea I caught her until she turned around.

But today, I return from dropping Hadley off at school to find April rocking her hips as she swirls a wire whisk in a bowl, unaware that I'm back.

The moment my hand rests on her lower back where I'm standing behind her, she's startled at first, until she melts into my touch.

"Hmm, I thought you had a meeting with a sponsor." She wiggles against me.

"Canceled," I whisper into her ear.

April slowly turns to look at me. "Oh, so you thought you would pencil me into your calendar for a workout?" She gives me a warning glare.

It's been a few days since I asked her to stay, but she wanted to help Piper with the baby, and I don't have many opportunities to get April alone, as I'm busy taking care of Hadley.

"We'll see about that." I tip her chin up with my finger, drawing her sight to me, and I'm tempted to press a warm kiss against her lips.

She seems to be onto me and tickles me away. "Down, boy. Go throw some balls or something. I need to get this frittata in the oven."

I still don't know how she manages to come up with a new recipe to cook every day.

"How about a swim before lunch?" I ask.

April gawks at me. "Do you literally fuck like a rabbit in the off-season to make up for baseball season when you keep it all in?"

I interlace our fingers, well, only with one of her hands, as the other is busy whisking. My need to keep her close unnerves me slightly, but I'm past the point of caring, this is what I want in this moment.

I'm already scolding her with my eyes as a grin tilts on the corner of my mouth. "It's not that I don't have sex during baseball season, I just don't do random hookups. If I'm in a relationship, then we work it out."

April bursts out laughing. "What in the world does that mean? Oh my God, you literally have a sex schedule around your games, huh?"

"That's maybe a stretch." Slightly. Barely.

"Good luck to her then." She returns to her experiment, and it causes me to pause that she doesn't see herself as a contender. It shouldn't bother me. A relationship is not what we are doing, but it feels close.

The sound of the door opening makes my head perk with attention to my mother walking in, carrying a laundry basket. She has the security code so she can come in when she wants, but she normally doesn't unless it's important.

"Oh, hey, sorry, I didn't realize you have company." My mother assesses the scene with intrigue as she slowly sets the basket on a chair at the kitchen island.

"It's fine."

I notice in the corner of my eye that April is straightening her apron as she watches my mother enter the picture.

"I guess you two only met briefly. Mom, this is April. April, my mom."

A genuine welcoming smile spreads on my mother's face. "Wonderful to meet you. Sorry, where are my manners." She stretches out her hand. "I'm looking at you so strangely, but I just thought you were staying for a few days."

April quickly wipes her hand on the apron before giving my mother a handshake hello. "Uhm, the plan kind of changed."

My mother's face immediately whips to my direction. "Fun."

I roll my eyes and clap my hands together. "What brings you by? How was the getaway?"

"Can't go wrong with Arizona. We're planning our next trip already. Your father wants to take me to Yellowstone so I can fulfill my Kevin Costner fantasy."

I shudder from the thought while April chortles a laugh and returns to her oven pan.

"I forgot I had all this laundry for Hadley. I was going to just leave it here and hoped to check if you lined up a babysitter for the coming period?"

My head drops slightly, and I rub my cheek while I groan. "The babysitter we had lined up dropped out due to a sick relative. I have my team reaching out to another agency to find someone."

My mom begins to look in her purse, probably for a Tic Tac if I know her well enough. "Spencer, it needs to get sorted out. Your father and I can't watch her forever. I love my grandbaby, and we will help when we can, but you know that it isn't what..." She pauses when she realizes she's struggling to finish the sentence.

I save her and jump in. "It's fine. I mean, I really just need someone to cook and clean, and I can take care of Hadley."

April offers me a soft reassuring smile before she turns to put her food in the oven.

"I'm happy to hear it, but you still need someone as a backup.

Even in the off-season, you have all those fancy meetings, and you train a lot," my mother explains.

I sigh, as she makes valid points. "I'll find a way, okay." I'm getting slightly frustrated with this conversation; I don't enjoy being reminded of what I can improve on.

My mother turns her attention to April who doesn't notice, then returns her gaze to me. My mom's eyes grow big, as it is her way of asking for an explanation. I mouth back, *"Friend."* She subtly shakes her head that she doesn't believe me.

"I hope my son and his daughter aren't wearing you out," my mother says, attempting conversation.

"Not at all. Hadley is adorable," April comments.

"April has gotten Hadley to experiment with food," I add.

"Maybe you should be her next nanny then," my mother jokes.

April smiles. "I think you need a professional for that role, and I'm heading back to the city soon anyway."

Right, because April doesn't live here in Lake Spark unless I have a sex tape about to be leaked.

"Well, I'm going to leave you two alone. I have errands to run. By the way, you remember Hadley has her check-up with the pediatrician next week, right?"

I salute my mother. "Yeah, it's in the shared calendar."

My mom waves to April and she says goodbye. A minute later, we are free from my mother's watch.

But still, I heave a sigh at the reminder of my responsibility. It makes me feel like everyone is waiting for me to fail when all I want to do is prove them wrong.

Leaning against the fridge, I wonder if this feeling of missing a piece will ever go away.

April nudges my arm with her own and comes to my side, and we both look forward at the ground. "She seems nice."

"Can't complain."

"Hadley will love having more time with you and less with a babysitter," she points out.

I'm not entirely convinced, and my face stiffens as I feel my lack of assurance set in.

April gives me a soft look, almost empathetic, as if she wants to say something more, but instead she smiles shyly and looks away before walking to the other side of the kitchen to grab Pickles' leash.

"Don't be in a grumpy mood today," she calls out. I'm bewildered as to how she understands my brain because I'm not exactly on the express train to happy right now. The last few minutes put a damper on my day.

Before I can argue, she is out of sight but not out of my mind.

––––––

Tiptoeing to Hadley's bed, I'm careful to lift the pillow under her head while she sleeps. Thankfully her night light is on, which gives me enough coverage to ensure my task is successful. Pickles perks his head up from where he is lying at the end of her bed.

Slipping the hundred-dollar bill under Hadley's pillow, I grab her little plastic treasure chest that holds a tooth.

I stroke her hair and take in the view of her lying there like a little angel holding a stuffed butterfly.

My journey out of her room is a slow walk, and I stop at her door to get one more image of her in my head, because every moment is another one gone, right? When I'm gently closing her door behind me, I'm startled.

"Tooth fairy duty?" April whispers as she leans against the wall in the hall, wearing her little shorts and tank. She must have been watching me this whole time, and I'm not sure how I feel about that.

I step to her, holding up the little treasure chest as proof. "First time."

"Oh yeah?" She arches a brow, and her fingers claw my shirt. "What's the going rate these days?"

"One hundred."

Her jaw drops, and she shrieks softly. "What? Are you crazy? Five would have sufficed."

I shrug. "Anything else you care to critique in relation to my tooth fairy skills?"

"Nah, but the tooth fairy is kind of hot." She pulls me closer.

Finally. We've been simmering in flirtation since we slept together. This is our moment to sizzle and pop.

An approving hum draws out of my throat. "No shit, the tooth fairy does it for you?"

"Uh-huh." This look on April is familiar. It's hungry, sultry, and playful.

Which is why I follow her as she tows me along to my room and walks me straight to the edge of my bed. Before I can process, I'm sitting and she's swinging a leg on either side of my waist to straddle me.

"This is not the role-playing scenario I had in mind," I joke.

"Nah, me neither. But watching you do the dad thing back there was… it does things to a woman." She drags her lips along my neck, and my dick is already hard.

I plant my hands on the sides of her body underneath the flimsy shirt. "What kind of things?"

"Dirty things. I would definitely go on the tooth fairy's bad list."

I snort a laugh, as this is slightly ridiculous, but I'm always a team player. "What in the world could you do to get on the bad list?"

"Use my tongue in inappropriate ways." She flashes her eyes at me.

I pull her flush against my body, and we fall back against the mattress. "I'm all game for a demo." Yet I wrap my arms around her and rub soothing circles on her back, keeping us in an embrace.

She peers up at me and studies me before she sighs a breath, but in a relaxing manner, not an annoyed way. April must pick up that I need a minute. I guess I'm having a delayed reaction to the fact that my little girl is having milestones.

"I… was wrong." She pops her lips.

"About what?"

"You are a great dad."

Looking down at her, I appreciate her words and the fact she genuinely means it.

"That's not what you said a week ago," I remind her.

"I was wrong."

My eyes grow wide. "Say that again."

"I… was wrong," she declares again.

I didn't realize that I needed this confidence boost, but it feels good. Sometimes, I feel like people around me are just waiting for me to fail. None of this was planned, after all.

The corner of my lip tugs, because I want to smile but don't want to appear that my ego is getting a boost.

Ah, what the hell.

"I think this tooth fairy deserves a reward," I mention.

April giggles as she adjusts her body and sits on top of me, wiggling her hips and creating friction against my cock before she slips down my body. She playfully brushes her lips along the waist of my jeans, tugging the button free, and her tongue hits the corner of her mouth in the process.

She peeks down into my boxer briefs before pulling them lower. The moment her lips wrap around my tip, my eyes instantly close from the feeling of her tongue gliding along my length.

I groan from the sensation. "You should go on every bad list of every fictitious character there is."

April pulls off for one second with swollen lips, her breathing labored. "I bet Santa has a whip." Then she's back on me.

I cradle her head between my hands, gently guiding her and holding her when she decides to take me deep.

Her eagerness only ups the ante, but it's watching her that is the true bonus of this moment.

"Right there," I breathe out as she finds the perfect movement.

This is going to be short-lived if I don't do something, but I want to be selfish. I'm allowed to be, I remind myself. Especially when I know I'll make it up to her another time.

And fuck me, because I'm already anticipating another time. I don't think this is how we planned this whole situation to go.

She moans, and any logic exits my brain because she brings me back to the moment where there isn't a care in the world, just us having fun.

"April," I warn. "Be a good girl."

She understands and wraps her lips tighter around me. I swear I see colors in the air when I unload into her mouth, stroking her head as she works harder, and her eyes seek approval because that's who April is, a pleaser.

"You like that? Hmm? Taking every last drop?" I grit out as my climax overpowers me, especially when I feel her swallow.

With purpose, she slowly licks up my length until she circles my tip for good measure, creating space with a satisfied look. She walks her long fingers up my torso as I lie there, completely relaxed.

"There is no other way to do it," she rasps.

"You could leave me hanging."

She waves her finger in front of my face. "Ah-ah, I wouldn't dream of that since I have every intention of being repaid."

April begins to shift her way up my body with her knees on either side of me, straddling me.

"Why, whatever can I do to such a wicked girl?" I play along.

"You tell me. You are the one with magical powers tonight."

I feel my energy kickstart again, or it's the fact that I can feel she is ready for me where her pussy rests against my ribs.

A smirk possesses my lips. "Sit on my face, let me taste how much you're turned on from fucking me with your mouth."

She blushes but willingly moves until my head is trapped between her thighs, her pussy within a breath's distance, and I smell her sweet honey arousal. She glances down at me, maybe unsure or maybe to taunt me.

I kiss her inner thigh, tugging aside her skimpy sleep shorts to expose her core.

"Don't set yourself up for failure, sailor," she taunts, a phrase she said to me once on that very first night.

"Wouldn't dream of it," I promise. "Bite into your arm if you need to, we can't have you noisy, and I intend to eat you like a meal before my dick is buried deep inside of you."

Her eyes enlarge slightly and look impressed. "Don't go too crazy, I need to walk back to my room after this."

Her wet sweetness hits my lips before I can protest. Something inside me wants to say that she can stay the night and sneak out early.

Then again, fun is all we're doing. No?

I watch through the window in the dance school between the waiting room and the studio. A little group of girls in leotards are dancing in a circle together. I can't help but smile at the little ballerinas who seem to be enjoying their class.

Spencer asked if I wanted to hang with him and Hadley, and it was an easy yes. He's in the car on the phone while I came in to pick up Hadley. He explained he doesn't enjoy listening to the dance moms who always have drama, so I would be doing him a favor; plus, his agent called in the car. Parents are only allowed to watch the kids dance during select weeks, but I can't help but be a rule-breaker.

"Sorry, are you here for Hadley?" the receptionist asks. She's sitting behind a little desk with a laptop. The woman herself looks like a dance teacher, my age too, and completely stunning, with light brown hair and a great complexion.

"Oh." I tuck a strand of hair behind my ear. "I am, actually."

"The new nanny?" She smiles politely.

"No, I'm…" Why can't I say a friend of Spencer's? "Uhm, a friend of the family. Spencer asked me to help Hadley grab her jacket after class. He's out in the car."

She gives me the once-over, but her smile doesn't falter. "I get it." She tightens her ponytail. "I'm Romy, I own the studio."

"Oh right, well, this is a lovely little place. Hadley talks about dance class all the time." I do my best to be friendly.

"She is a sweet little girl." Romy holds a finger up. "Before I forget, her new ballet shoes came in." She leans down to a delivery box on the floor, filled with new shoe boxes, picks one up, examines the side to check the size, and then hands it to me.

"Thanks. I guess little feet grow fast," I comment.

Romy crosses her arms and looks at me, almost entertained. "I'm sorry. I must be staring, I just… I've never seen anyone here other than Spencer, his mom, or a babysitter that changes in rotation. I kind of thought Spencer doesn't really do relationships, you know?"

My brows arch, as I am trying to figure out if she is talking from experience or genuinely attempting to make conversation. "Really, it's nothing. We're good… friends."

"Good. Really good, perfect." Her lips roll in and then quirk out as she pulls her sweater tighter around her body, and I think I have my answer of why she is asking, but then she surprises me. "He doesn't let many people into his inner circle, but it's nice that he has, is what I mean."

"Sure." I nod.

The sound of the class wrapping up and a door opening from the studio breaks this awkward conversation.

"Well, maybe I will see you around. I've gotta run, I'm teaching the advanced pointe class next," she mentions and begins to move.

Advanced, of course.

Romy touches my arm in passing. "Please thank Spencer."

"For what?"

"I know it was him who paid for the extra shoes and costumes for one of my students whose family could use the extra help now." She offers me one more smile before heading off.

I don't have time to digest this fact that I've learned, as Hadley is skipping in my direction.

"April, did you watch me?" She hops in place with excitement.

"You bet I did. Those were some amazing sautés, mademoiselle." I place my hand on her shoulder and guide her to the wall of coats hanging on hooks to encourage her to gather her things.

Her bun nearly knocks me over when she leaps in front of me to grab her coat. "Where's my daddy?"

"In the car, but if we play our cards right then we can convince him to go to Jolly Joe's."

"Yes! I'm hungry."

"Well, then hot chocolate here we come." I tuck the box with her new shoes under my arm and follow Hadley to the front door. She waves to all her friends.

It's turning cold out, which means we race to the warm car. The moment we get in, I declare our plan. "The ballerina has spoken and to Jolly Joe's we shall go."

"Oh, has she?" Spencer gives me a knowing look.

"Please, oh please," Hadley pleads from the back with her hands together before petting Pickles who's sitting on the seat next to her.

Spencer rolls his eyes at me. "I'm outnumbered, aren't I?"

"You are." I toss the box to Spencer. "Here, her new ballet shoes arrived. She should probably wear them around the house a little before she uses them, to avoid blisters."

"You're the pro, so I may actually listen to your advice." He begins to pull out of the parking spot, his forearms on display as he rests his arm on the back of my chair as he shoulder checks out the back window.

It's a few beats before I realize that Hadley is occupied with Pickles and this SUV is big enough that I can ask Spencer something I have no business knowing.

"You know who is a pro?" I begin. "I met the studio owner back there, a real delight, very interested in your private life."

Spencer gives me a humorous side glance before focusing on the road. "And?"

"I'm sure she is more than advanced at her techniques."

"Not having this conversation here," he rebukes.

I cross my arms and nearly huff, instead opting for silence for the next three minutes until we get to Main Street, and say nothing until we are inside Jolly Joe's and we order at the counter.

"Can I pick out a dog treat for Pickles?" Hadley asks before we sit down at a fifties-style booth. Jolly Joe's makes little peanut butter treats to give to dogs, as they are welcome here.

"Go wild," I say.

She skips off, and I check to make sure my loyal beagle is lying at my feet.

Spencer looks at me with a wry smile, and his eyes possess a curious glint.

"You were saying?"

He isn't going to let me forget.

I play with a napkin. "Nothing. Just all the dancers and pioneers in this town over the age of twenty seem to be drawn to you, or is it you already went there with good old Romy?"

God, I hate the way I sound. Why do I care?

Spencer takes a sip from his water, calmy, almost as if he is calculating what to say. "I wouldn't hook up with someone who is responsible for Hadley's favorite hobby."

My nose tips up.

"I mean, that was the rule I made *after,* but you know," he adds. My mouth opens but no words come out until he starts to laugh. "Relax, I'm messing with you. Romy has a husband. She's high school sweethearts with the contractor for my house renovations, actually." My jaw relaxes, and I feel silly. Spencer reaches across the table to touch my arm. "Jealousy is kind of hot on you."

"I'm not jealous," I lie.

"A little jealous."

"Not at all."

"It's okay. I think I might strangle a guy who looks at you like he has a chance too."

My eyes dart to his, and I can't read him, but I sense that he is letting a chip off his steely exterior, and it causes a line to creep up on my mouth.

For a moment, I forget where we are, and it feels like it's only me and him, and I like that we are at peace with one another, relaxed enough to be ourselves with no walls, otherwise we will just tear them down. We aren't capable of hiding, not around each other.

"You know, many athletes perform good deeds and make a big thing about it for attention or publicity, but not you, Spencer Crews."

"What makes you say that?"

"Romy wanted me to thank you for the extra cash for supplies," I mention.

"Hmm. She must be confused." He avoids my penetrating gaze.

Admittedly, his lack of wanting praise is a surprise. This is the guy who loves to hear that he has a winning arm, but when it comes to a noble act he plays mute.

And that makes me add another point to the scoreboard when it comes to Spencer.

The waitress disrupts us when she brings us a giant kitchen sink of ice cream covered in whip cream, sprinkles, and a few cherries. Hadley is not far behind.

"This is dinner?" Spencer pretends to be unamused.

"No. This is what Hadley and I are eating for dinner. You were Mr. I Don't Eat Ice Cream So I Will Have a Water." I grab a spoon and scoot over so Hadley can sit next to me. "Don't forget our deal." I hand Hadley a spoon.

"I know. I have to eat some of the banana from the ice cream." She frowns.

"Banana splits are not banana splits unless you have a banana," I inform her again.

We both assess where to dig in first.

"Are you sure we can't convince you to have a bite? If you ask nicely, I'm sure we will share. Oh look, peanut butter, that's protein." I point out the section of the sink bowl with peanut butter and chocolate.

"Daddy doesn't eat many sweets. He's boring like that." Hadley speaks with a full mouth.

Spencer immediately looks taken aback. "Boring?"

"I'm sure he will prove us wrong." I hand him a spoon.

"He never eats ice cream," Hadley reminds me.

Spencer holds up his spoon for show before taking a spoonful of whipped cream and ice cream.

Hadley and I look on with interest and watch him eat his first bite. We both gasp at his move.

"I'm completely cool." He now speaks with his mouth full.

Hadley giggles before she takes another bite.

"See? I bet you want another bite too." I'm confident with my appraisal.

He tips his head in doubt, catching my eyes for a brief second, before ceremoniously dipping into the pile of ice cream again.

Hadley giggles, and this time a big smile erupts on Spencer's mouth. And the next twenty minutes is an abundance of ice cream tasting, smiles, and listening to Hadley talk ballet. I sense that it's their way of bonding, and I feel special that I get to witness it.

By the time we make it home, Hadley is out like a light, and Spencer carries her up the stairs. I follow because I just want to change into my pajamas, as the ice cream was heavy.

"April," Spencer loudly whispers.

"Yeah?" I yawn as we reach the top of the stairs.

Spencer turns to me, and it's quite a sight to see him holding a child this way. Another drop of my melting heart hits the ground.

"Want to sneak into my room in like an hour?" His voice does sound tempting.

"Hmm, maybe," I coyly reply and never confirm.

Instead, I walk straight to my room.

BUT, of course, I have no spine anymore around the man, so exactly sixty-two minutes later, I creep through the door to his bedroom to find him waiting in bed.

"You're late." He grins.

I stand before him and elongate my neck. "Ooh, were you counting down the seconds?"

He laughs and moves the duvet to invite me in. "Seconds is maybe a stretch, but I'll give you a minute or two."

I don't hesitate and slowly glide a few steps in the direction of the bed he has kept warm. "We keep meeting here."

Sliding between the sheets feels like a prize. It's all the things I enjoy; warmth, sex, and apparently, Spencer.

He lies on his side, quick to trace the lines of my body with his finger while he watches me sink against his mattress. "Why do I see a glimpse of something as pink as a Barbie?"

I laugh under my breath, as he must see my bra strap. I like my choice today; it's hot-pink and has strings across my cleavage. "Might have dressed for the occasion."

His mouth nips my shoulder as he sounds his endorsement. "I like the effort."

I reach up to stroke his face, my thumb rubbing a circle along his stubbled jaw. "Did you have a good day?"

"I did."

This is us having our moment. Where we check in with one another like two people who care and are attentive to one another before we go back to fulfilling each other's needs.

He combs his fingers into my hair. "I feel like I keep repeating myself and saying thank you a lot lately."

"It's called manners," I retort.

"Is it strange we just kind of gel together?"

"It happens when you live together, even if for a few days. But Hadley knows that I'm just a friend, right?" I double-check.

"I think so."

I draw a circle on his bare arm that is holding me. "I'll head back to the city at the end of the week, nonetheless. It's probably better for her."

He doesn't answer, but I feel his fingers entwine tighter around my locks.

"For now, I'll sneak out after you ravish me," I attempt to lighten the mood.

"Stay the night and sneak out in the morning," he states.

I peer up at him, and I see it's what he wants, maybe needs, but most of all, I hear a command, as if I'm his.

I nod in agreement before our lips meet for a kiss that I realize I've been craving since the last one.

Because I may not have figured him out, but he managed to peel away the layered walls that I had around him, and right now, I just want to fall asleep in the comfort of his arms after we do the one thing that we've always been good at; making each other feel free for a moment.

19

SPENCER

Opening my front door, I beam a smile when I find Hudson standing there with Gracie in a baby carrier on his chest, arms and legs stuck out like a starfish. In true Hudson fashion, he has sunglasses over his eyes and swipes them off with style, and a winning grin is permanent on his face.

The man is in his early forties but is the image of every man's hope of aging well, down to his lack of gray, not even a strand in his dark hair.

"I believe we need to discuss something," he announces.

I scratch my cheek and make an awkward attempt at a grin. "Don't you have a football team to coach?" I hold the door open as he walks right in.

My neighbor, friend, and April's uncle. I knew this moment would come, and somehow, I knew he wouldn't want to kill me either.

"I have a few hours off before I need to catch a flight for our next game, and I welcome the opportunity to investigate why I hear rumors around town that my niece is temporarily living with you, and my wife isn't spilling the tea."

"April isn't here, by the way."

"I know, I saw her leave with the dog for a walk. That's fine. I wanted to talk man to man." Hudson leans against the window wall of my living room.

I roll my eyes in entertainment. "April is heading back to the city, probably tomorrow."

"Why is she staying with you to begin with? I thought you two detest one another." It feels like his eyes are trying to catch me out.

I clear my throat. "She's using my kitchen."

His look tells me that he is waiting for more.

"Helping with Hadley."

Still no response.

"Can we leave it at that?" I try my luck.

He studies me for a second, looks down at his daughter, and his face softens. "Fine."

I blow out a breath of relief.

"Was it the baby shower?"

My eyes snap to him and panic sets in. "Baby shower?" My voice is uneasy.

"Yeah. I sent you back for a gift that I might not have really forgotten." He winks at me. "Was that the start of whatever you two young ones are up to?"

I chuckle a laugh. "You could say it's something like that." I kind of figured he was attempting a setup, but I gave him the benefit of the doubt.

"The thing is, I think this is great, you could use someone like her, and April deserves to move on from that little punk who I think we are all happy didn't lock her into marriage. But April is…"

"Feisty?"

"Yes, but I think she is still recovering a little from the last year. So, all I can say, and I know you know this, is that April isn't one of those girls who will wait for you after your games for a good time. She can give a lot if that's what she receives. You'd be lucky."

I stare at him intensely, more because I'm lost in thought of her visiting me at a game.

"I hear what you are saying." Boy, do I hear him. He now has wheels turning in my head because I'm already trying to figure out what's happening.

"It's kind of big… I mean, she is involved with Hadley now."

"We're friends," I reiterate.

Hudson holds up his hand. "So you said." I hear the disbelief. "But I've never seen you bring any woman around Hadley that is just a friend."

I adjust my neck as he points out all the facts that I already know, and I'm well aware that anyone on the outside can see my predicament too.

"Uncle Bay!" April calls out as Pickles walks in before her. I forget she sometimes calls him a nickname, something about studying the Hudson Bay in school.

Hudson is quick to meet her halfway and offers an arm for a side hug. "Hey there. Heard you've been shaking up my neighborhood."

"Something like that." April gives him a hug and touches Gracie's head before walking into the kitchen. "Coffee anyone?"

"Sure. I have time for one quick cup," he calls out.

April is busy looking in a cupboard. "Hey, Spence, where are the extra coffee beans? They're in the pantry, right? Can you show me?"

"Ooh, she's calling you Spence," Hudson mumbles to me and flashes his eyes.

I laugh under my breath at this odd morning. "Be right back."

Following April to the pantry, she's pretending to be searching for something before she closes the door behind us.

"He's here!" she loudly whispers. Her calm persona has faded into curious fear.

"Yeah, and? We knew he would eventually get the memo that you're shacking up in my humble abode."

"Is he being all… I don't know… uncle-y?"

"Is that a word?"

She pokes a finger into my chest. "Now isn't the time to be a smartass. I don't want him to find out what we did, I mean the video."

Now I'm having fun. "But he can know about everything else?"

She growls a sound before plunging forward to kiss me hard on the mouth. It is so fucking good. I like the way she kisses when it's spontaneous.

Pulling away, she smiles as her thumb glides along my jawline. "Thought you might need something to calm you down."

I step closer to her, framing her hips with my hands. "I'm calm. I don't falter under pressure. Babe, I'm a baseball player."

She bursts out laughing. "Well, won't you just save the world." She's mocking me. "Oh, look, I found the coffee!" she announces so Hudson can hear and reaches behind me to grab the coffee. I love that she follows through with her performance because I just filled the coffee machine this morning and I know it doesn't need beans.

Following her back into the kitchen with a bag of coffee beans, I know it's obvious that we look like two souls who just had a G-rated version of a frisky pantry fling. Proven by the fact that Hudson's smile is still just the way we left it.

"Heard you're heading back to the city," Hudson says to April as I lean over the kitchen island.

"Yeah, can't stay in this perfect little town forever." She focuses on pressing buttons on the coffee machine.

"You'll be back soon, I'm sure," he adds and then looks to his side at me.

"I mean, I always come visit Piper."

Why do I want her to say she'll come back for me and Hadley? This is Hudson's way to trigger my mind, I know his tactics.

April hands him a cup of coffee. "You know, I once had an uncle who was very adamant that I'm not allowed to date athletes. In fact, I wasn't even allowed to attend his games for fear a big bad athlete would hit on me. Where did that uncle go?" She feigns curiosity and brings her finger to her chin.

He grins wide at her humor. "Spencer isn't just an athlete, he's on my Hudson Arrows approved list. Besides, I need to focus on indoctrinating my daughter for the next eighteen years that athletes are a no-go, so I'm releasing you from my reins." His voice turns saccharine as he coos with his daughter.

"Don't be a player hater," April quips, and it causes me to laugh.

"Are we done with this topic?" I suggest.

Hudson waves a hand in the air. "Sure. I've made my voice heard." Hudson turns to me with his lips on the coffee cup, taking a sip. "By the way, Ford is going to come to one of my home games, want a seat also? A little neighborhood block party in the stands?"

"Sounds good."

"Swell. You'll be in the city then, and I'm assuming April is in the city too. Okay, great. That's me, gotta go." He strings words together, sets his cup down, and claps his hands.

I just shake my head at his ability to literally set us up for a last-minute play, no different than his football games when he coaches to win.

And maybe April could be the winning play in the home stretch.

———

APRIL STANDS by her car and closes the door, with Pickles in the back.

"That's us, all packed and ready to go," she states.

She made a big breakfast for Hadley before coming with us for school drop-off. But her departure is happening now while Hadley is at school, which is probably easier.

I knock on the hood of her car. "Yep. Back to the city, free from me."

"Hmm, yeah."

She's trapped between the car and my body, and neither one of us seems ready to move. Last night we had dinner with Hadley, and after Hadley went to bed, April snuck into my room like she has been doing every night this week.

"I labeled a bunch of stuff in the freezer, in case you get stuck on dinner, since you don't have a babysitter yet," she mentions, and I love that she's taking care of us as a parting gift.

"We'll eat it, I'm sure," I promise.

Her eyes are searching for a clue.

"You'll let me know when you get back? Those foxes on the road, you know. They come out of nowhere."

Her closed lips move side to side. "Just like pitchers, I guess."

"Why is that plural?" I raise a brow.

She grabs hold of my open jacket. "Pitcher. He was a real piece of work at the start."

I slant a shoulder up to my ear. "Bet you loved it."

She nods once.

We are drawing out this minute. "It's been fun." She looks away, and I can tell she's putting up a defense.

But I want to tear it down.

"April."

Her eyes meet my own, hopeful. "Yeah?"

"Do you think that I can visit you in the city?"

"Sure. You're always welcome." She doesn't seem to get it.

I tilt her chin up with my long finger. "As in, I want to keep seeing you. I can visit you, and you can visit us here."

A smile begins to form. "I mean, I guess that makes sense. Pickles and Hadley kind of have a bond I'm jealous of."

I step closer, bringing her mouth closer to mine, at a distance that has our breaths mingling. "Stop avoiding the obvious. You don't want this to stop, and I don't want it to either."

"Telling me what I feel, now?" She's impossible, yet I grin before I slam my lips onto hers to kiss her and to confirm that I'm absolutely right.

She dips her tongue into my mouth to deepen our kiss. A sound vibrates from the back of her throat into my mouth as her body arches into mine.

I don't dare break this moment, but we can't stay like this all day. But damn, there is a fire inside of me that I didn't know was possible. A want for someone that I can only describe as new, but I'm not ready to let it go.

She reluctantly breaks away; our lips push and pull in a magnetic dance.

"You're right," she rasps between kisses.

"I'm always right."

I cradle her face in my hands and our eyes lock. I even nuzzle our noses together, and I'm beginning to wonder what version of myself this is, softer for sure, and I recognize a sweltering flare inside of me that realizes this woman could bring me to my knees because I want her.

"I guess I'll be seeing you around then?" She attempts to hide her smirk.

"Lucky you." I follow her to the driver's seat and hold the door open as she slides into her seat.

"Yeah, maybe I am," she laments.

I hope she is because that would mean I'm the guy that deserves to share a life with someone like her, and I'm still not sure I believe that.

20

APRIL

Folding laundry is a boring Sunday task, but I light a beeswax candle, clean the apartment, and use the day as a reset for the week. I've also been listening to my mother for the last ten minutes debate if the sweater she bought me is forest green or palm green, whatever the hell the difference is.

"I can return it if you want. But it does look great on you, fits perfectly, and most importantly, will keep you nice and warm for winter." She folds the sweater and slides it to the other side of the counter before grabbing her mug of coffee.

"It's fine." I focus on folding my laundry. Pickles is crashed out on the couch.

My mom and I went for brunch, and after, she came back to my apartment, because I know she likes to check everything is in order because I'm forever her baby. I live in a simple apartment, but it's in a safe building with a condominium board that ensures the elevator always works.

"I guess staying warm is already taken care of for the winter," she mumbles before pretending to take a sip of her coffee.

I stop folding and look at her with a jarring stare. "Something you wish to bring up, dear mother?"

She smiles warmly. "You were looking at your phone all the time when we were at the restaurant."

"And? It's how people these days transfer messages, share updates on their life, send inappropriate GIFS." I find a missing sock and pair it together. I know where she is going with this, and Spencer and I have been messaging all week. Updates about Pickles, Hadley, his questions about reheating food I left, and jokes that I'm sure he heard in the locker room.

"I know, I get your bombardment of Pickles photos, and the Arrows family group chat is a delight during football season," she jokes. "But I have a feeling a particular baseball player is responsible for keeping you distracted. You didn't even steal a bite of my cheese-cake today."

Throwing the sock pair into the laundry basket to put away later, I glance at my mom and debate what to say. "Your point?"

"You haven't really updated me on what's going on with your romantic life, maybe even avoided that topic, and I didn't want to push. *However*, the radiant smile that doesn't leave your face has me interested, and I'm going to assume Spencer is the culprit since you had a little getaway to Lake Spark."

I bite my lip before my defense completely falters. "Can I plead the fifth?"

"Not with me."

"Fine. Yes, he *may* be responsible for my mood." Now I can't help but gush, and I feel my facial expression give me away.

My mom taps her nails on her mug. "Do tell."

"We… are… just going with the flow, you know how it is." I wave a hand at her, and she gives me the warning glare that she needs more data. "Early stages. Just seeing where it goes. No rush. No need for nosy mothers to get involved."

"Good. Enjoy it, and the moment you think your mother who is a smart cookie needs to be involved, then you phone me."

I nod and grab my own mug of tea. "You know, for someone who is excellent at tearing down the opposition in a courtroom… did you not see the signs with Jeff?" It's funny how once a relationship ends, everyone states how they were never in favor of it. Could have used the clue beforehand.

My mother grabs her purse and walks to me, tentatively touching my arm. "When you think you're in love, you choose to see what you want. Would you have listened? Besides, you're my daughter, so I'm blind when it comes to you. I wanted you to be happy, and maybe that's what I tried to see, even if I had doubts. But you are a strong lady who will end up with someone better. All exes lead to the one."

"Let me guess, you're hoping it's a star pitcher?"

She bobs her head side to side. "He isn't half bad." Her smirk tells me enough; she approves.

I offer a half-smile before she hugs me goodbye.

The next hour, I finish up the laundry, unload the dishwasher, and take a long shower to unwind for the rest of the day. A long binge session of *The Bear* is calling my name.

But as I'm about to hit the play button, I hear a knock on my door, which is strange, as the doorman would normally call up. Pickles decides that he needs to act the part and actually jumps off the couch and attempts to run to the door.

Following, I glance down to ensure I'm halfway decent. I'm in Piper's original pajama bottoms and a tank that stops at my midriff. Meh, it will have to do. I wrap my cardigan tighter around my body.

Opening the door, excitement hits me in a wave, but I play it cool because Spencer is standing on the other side of the door, leaning against the frame with a faint grin on his lips. His coat is open to reveal his jeans and dark fitted sweater.

"Surprise," he informs me with a piercing gaze.

My hands find my hips. "Indeed, a shock." My voice remains calm and even.

"Aren't you going to invite me in?"

"For the guy who probably paid off the doorman and then showed up while I'm in my pajamas?"

He takes a step forward through the doorway, ignoring my feigned attempt to prolong our front-door conversation. "I don't think I've ever complained about your pajamas before, so no issue." Spencer walks into my apartment, looking around curiously. He drops a small overnight bag to the ground.

Pickles' tail wags as he remembers Spencer. He sniffs once then returns to the living room.

Closing the door lazily behind me, I scoff a sound of utter amazement as Spencer confidently walks in as if he owns the place. It's not even arrogance, it's a swagger that I've learned is a natural part of his personality.

"You know it's rude to invite yourself in."

He takes hold of my hands, interlaces our fingers, and gives me a tug in his direction. "I'm sure you would have."

"What brings you by?" We didn't have it on the calendar to see one another again until next weekend. I was going to drive up to Lake Spark because it's just easier with Hadley.

"My publicist needed to reschedule a meeting for tomorrow morning, so I thought I would surprise you."

My lips curl into a smile. "Guess I'll have to cancel my Sunday-night date."

"Funny." He pulls me tight to his body. "If you don't mind, I'll be crashing here tonight."

I tip my chin up. "Oh, will you now?"

Spencer growls as he plants his lips on mine to kiss me hello. It's soft but by no means weak. Pulling away, he touches the tips of our noses. He's being… sweet.

"Where's Hadley?" Finding a babysitter hasn't been easy.

"My mom is watching her and taking her to school tomorrow."

I loop my arms around his middle. "I see. We'll have to order in for dinner; I'm not in the mood to cook."

His eyes haven't left me. "Sounds good. We'll order later from that new Italian place. They don't deliver, but they owe me a favor."

"I might kind of like you because of that. Later? We have other plans first?"

Spencer chuckles and slides my cardigan off one shoulder, dragging the strap of the tank top and bra down to reveal bare skin. He kisses me on the curve then trails a line of kisses up to my neck. "It's my first time here, but I think I have an idea of where we need to go."

In one swift move, he lifts me up and throws me over his shoulder, fireman style. I squeak and squeal as he carries me to my bedroom.

Throwing me onto my mattress, he moves over me with a sly grin, and I can't wait. My lips search for his, and I kiss him.

Then I urge him to roll over, taking me with him. Our lips tease, and we smile against one another's skin.

"I think you're happy with my unexpected appearance," he rasps, kissing my jawline.

"Don't put this on me. You're the one who probably missed me because I'm amazing," I counter.

He rolls me back so that I'm under him again. "Don't get cocky now."

"No, that would be your hard dick that's pressing into me."

His head falls forward near the corner of my neck as he laughs.

And for a moment we stop in our frantic moves to stay in an entranced gaze before he places a long deep kiss against my lips, and I wrap my legs around his waist.

Swallowing, I'm scared to blink and to find this could be a dream.

"You're right. I'm not complaining that you're here," I whisper. "Shh. Don't you dare come out with an arrogant remark and ruin the moment," I warn.

A devilish smirk forms on his mouth. "Wouldn't dream of it. Now let me inside before I lose my mind." His hand disappears between us, and my body follows his lead.

And to my surprise, we move slowly, savoring the moments as clothes disappear and our hands explore. The moment he's inside of me, I now know another fact about Spencer Crews; he's trouble for my emotional state.

———

Lying in bed with my head against Spencer's chest, the sheet is tangled around us. His fingers graze my arm in long strokes.

"Can I ask you something?" I break our silence as we've laid quietly for a few minutes.

"Sure."

"I know you use my mom's firm for your legal stuff. Hope you get a neighbor discount since Hudson is her brother, but like, how much have you worked with my mom? She's not allowed to say, yet she seems to be a fan and not in the baseball sense."

He scoffs a laugh and squeezes me tighter. "Enough. She helped with some family law matters. You two have a few similarities, but you are quite different too."

"I would say I get that from my father, but I don't know who that is."

Spencer dips his gaze down. "It's not about biology when it comes to being a parent." His tone is firm, adamant almost.

"I know, but my curiosity runs deep."

"Ever thought of running one of those genealogy test kit things?"

I think for a second. "No. I guess I don't want to rock the boat, you know? I was given a great life, and in the end, it was a choice of whomever it was and a choice for my mom to have me this way. He gave her a gift, so that's enough for me to respect his decision, whomever he may be."

Spencer seems to ponder my words. "I wonder if more people have that theory," he states simply. "Do you think you are at peace with it all because you always knew? Like, what would you have done if you found out when you were older?"

"I think knowing from the start is a big part, but everyone is different. I had a friend who was adopted and only found out when she was eighteen, and it got to her. She wished she never knew, because her parents were her parents, and their lack of shared genes wasn't an important fact that she needed to know. I guess they are all okay now, though."

"Right." He goes quiet for a second. "Can I ask you something now?"

"Of course."

"You want kids one day?"

His question surprises me. "Wow, we are already at this stage of discussion?" I tease him, and he flashes me an unimpressed look. "It's not something I have an overpowering feeling about, but I think one day, yeah. If you are asking if Hadley is an issue, then, well, you know I like her more than you."

Spencer smiles to himself and begins to brush my hair with his fingers.

"She doesn't know that I'm seeing you. I just told her I had a meeting in the city."

"I get it. We don't really know what we're doing. My mom never introduced any dates until they hit the three-month mark, there were only a few."

"I think we know what we're doing."

The tips of my fingers land on his cheek to guide his head in my direction. "Do share."

"If I needed a fuck-buddy then I have options."

My mouth goes slack. "Wow, you better speed up your explanation."

His other hand holds my arm in place because he probably knows I want to swat him with it.

"I'm just saying that you're not that, and you know more about me than most. I would like to think next time you visit Lake Spark I don't need to sneak you in and out of my room. And when baseball season hits, then you'll be there in the stands."

He just did a one-eighty because that's the total opposite to where I thought this conversation was going. "Baseball season is still a few months away," I point out.

"Then tell me what timeline you're working with."

"I don't have one. I just… not getting hurt is more my priority. The last year has been one letdown after another from the men in my life. It takes a little to recover."

"I get that."

I focus on the tattoo on his skin. "Will you get another one?"

"Probably."

"Hey, since we're asking questions, out of curiosity, what would your girlfriend do during baseball season other than fuck on a schedule?"

"Come to my games. I don't know, haven't had one in a while." He kisses along my collarbone.

"Girlfriends are hard to come by, I hear." I pretend to be unaffected that all his words and moves today are making me giddy inside.

"I do have high criteria. Cooking is a plus." He kisses lower. "Sparkly powder on their skin that highlights their curves is a bonus." And lower. "A mouth that I want to kiss sometimes to shut her up is damn near the perfect find."

"Hmm, sounds like you might have found someone." I close my eyes and my breath feels calm.

Spencer kisses the valley between my breasts. "I think I have. She just needs to step up to the home plate when she's ready, because I think I am."

My chest thumps like my heart wants to break free. "Hmm, is that what that white square thing is? I'm there. Just need to see if we are the winning team together."

He moves to my belly button, stationing himself between my legs as he lies on his stomach. "I'll take the challenge."

His tongue hits the perfect spot, but it's the honesty so apparent in his eyes that sends a chill down my spine.

21

SPENCER

I stare at the box that April just tossed onto my sofa. I'm not sure what this stuff is.

The other week, I got overcome with a need to see her, and I surprised her at her apartment. Eating takeout while being forced to watch a new series was kind of a relaxing change. The next morning, April grabbed breakfast when she walked Pickles and brought it back so we could avoid running into people. She didn't let me forget that fact, as she teased me several times, but I prefer staying under the radar when I'm in the city.

I only barely managed to leave her place, because I knew she would be back to Lake Spark, and I had my agent waiting for me.

April drove up and arrived a few minutes ago. I'm still in my workout gear and am kind of sweaty since I hit my gym for an extra session, as Hadley is with a friend at her house after school.

"That's everything," April announces and collapses on the couch next to me and places her feet on the coffee table.

"Explain."

She giggles and rolls her head to the side to look at me. "Relax, I'm not moving in. I just have a few extras for this visit."

"Oh yeah?" I begin to rummage through the box. I pull out a new makeup kit, but it appears to be for a child. "Hell no."

"It's fine. It's not real makeup. It goes on clear against the skin."

"What's the point then?" I toss it back into the box.

April's mouth opens and pretends shock. "Make-believe, silly."

I roll my eyes, even though I know Hadley will be over the moon. "The only make-believe I'm going for is a little role-play between us."

She snickers a laugh. "Oh yeah? What did you have in mind?"

I don't really have anything in particular in my head, I just said it in jest.

"Look in the box," she demands.

Searching the box, I notice a fancy square with a bow. Grabbing it, I hold it up to check this is what she meant, and she nods.

"Know what it is?" she asks and seems like she's trying to contain her excitement.

I study the label. "It's from Piper's boutique."

"Uh-huh." She brings her knees to her chest and bites her lip, patiently waiting for me to get a clue.

But I'm confused. "You got another pair of fruit-print pajamas?"

She nearly scorns me with her look. "Get there faster," she urges. "Piper also has another line of evening attire." She raises her brows and waits for me.

Got it.

"*Really*?" I'm fully invested now and tug the bow.

"Yep."

Lifting the lid off the box, I'm faced with a layer of tissue paper. "Isn't it weird to buy lingerie from your aunt?" I taunt her because I know she hates being reminded that her best friend became her aunt.

"I'm regretting my effort, right now."

Searching through the paper, I feel lace. An approving growl escapes my mouth as I hold up the thin strings of black lace to reveal a one-piece with little triangles that will barely leave much to the imagination around April's breasts, and quite frankly, this see-through lace may be an obstacle to reaching the real treasure.

"Fuck me, I don't regret your effort one bit." I lean across the couch to capture her mouth for a kiss, and she circles her arms around my neck. She pulls me to her, and I fall on top of her which causes her to giggle. "I'm all sweaty," I say, with our lips still attached.

"I like you sweaty," she says huskily.

"I should go shower, and you can meet me upstairs. We have a window of opportunity."

April pulls back and waves her finger in front of my face. "Uh-uh, Mr. Eager, I need to get dinner started."

"It's not even three o'clock." My voice breaks.

She hops off the couch and straightens her shirt. "I know, but I want my soup to simmer, and I need to send my resume to a few job opportunities that I saw online."

"I want to simmer. Inside of you." I hear my lack of enthusiasm, even though she's attempting to put a damn good meal on the table later.

April makes a sound and sends a flirty glare my way before leaving me with a hard-on and impatience.

I rest my head against the back of the couch and close my eyes. I attempt to breathe some calmness into my body, but no luck.

"Spencer!" She sounds kind of pissed now. It causes me to get up off the couch and look to the kitchen where she has her hand over her mouth and seems like she might combust.

"What now?" I walk to her.

"Are you kidding me?" Her eyes narrow in on me as I approach her.

I hesitate, as I'm not sure what's going on. "With what?" Her arm splays out to the direction of the mixer. "Uhm, it's a mixer."

"It's not just a mixer. This wasn't here last time."

"And?"

"It's the one I mentioned once. It has like a gazillion different functions." She walks to the red machine and begins to assess all the little features.

I might have ordered it with her in mind. It's huge so will never fit in her kitchen, which makes me internally question why buying her supplies for my kitchen is coming so naturally. But I wanted to do something for her. We're past flirtation, and we could be something longstanding. I've mentioned my intentions, but that doesn't mean we need to make a big deal out of my gestures, though I'm sure my mother would call it sweet.

"No biggie." I downplay this act because I need to. I can't overthink this.

She slowly walks to me, step by step, ensuring our eyes hold, giving me a chance to stare at her soft lips stretching into a smile. "Now I'm going to have to replan the entire weekend menu," she chides.

"My fault?"

She nods. "You never make it easy for me."

"It's no fun that way." I welcome her into my arms. I miss having her in my kitchen daily. "Plus, I'm not a good guy."

"So I thought," she faintly replies, and it feels sentimental.

Her fingers claw my shirt, and I know her well enough now to know that she wants to ditch her kitchen plan and instead head upstairs, which I'm on board with.

"Going to join me in the shower or wait for me in bed?"

"Join you in the shower, for sure," April purrs.

I lift her up at the same time she climbs me like a tree. We make it to the bottom of the stairs, but my phone goes off, and as much I hate to break the mood, it could be the mom who is letting Hadley play with her daughter.

"Babe, I need to check."

She's already reaching into my pocket with her hand, which causes her to feel my cock through my pants, but I'm sure that's what she wanted. She pulls out my phone and wiggles it in the air with pride.

I read the screen and see the message that Hadley will be dropped off soon, as they're on the way back from the park.

Humorously, I laugh to myself because this is our luck. "We have ten minutes tops."

"Doable," she promises.

"That's my girl." I continue us on our path upstairs, very much aware that April may just be my girl.

————

Looking into Hadley's room, I see she isn't in her bed as promised, to wait for her bedtime story. Somehow April managed to get Hadley to eat tomato soup with grilled cheese that she cut into shapes, then we watched a Christmas movie. But it's way past Hadley's bedtime now.

Walking down the hall to the guest room, I spot the door open and hear Hadley.

"Why are you sleeping in here?" she asks, and I hear April crack a sound.

"Uh, why wouldn't I?" April has doubt in her tone.

"Nova, my friend, said that you are a special friend of daddy's. It's what her daddy has too, because her parents don't live together, so she has two houses."

Clearing my throat, I swoop right into the room to end this conversation. "There you are, sweet pea, I thought I said wait in bed."

"But I wanted to say good night to April," she justifies and looks up at me so innocently.

"That's sweet of you, but it looks like April could use some alone time."

April shoots me a humorous stare. "April can speak for herself, and it's fine."

"I kind of figured you are a special friend of daddy's."

I rub the back of my head and debate what to say. "Is that a problem?"

"No." Hadley seems unfazed and unconcerned. "But Nova said special friends sleep in daddies' rooms, so why is April staying here?"

April sets her brush on the bed and kneels down to Hadley.

"Because I was just a friend of your dad's, and just friends stay in the guest room."

And I'm tapping in.

"But now she is a special friend, so it will change. I'm sure April was just visiting this room for old times' sake." This is our opportunity to smooth the sails and make the transition, plus I want to be a selfish man tonight. Something inside of me wants to dive in, but that's always the case when April is around.

"Or April is in here because we didn't agree on the timeline for this conversation," April mumbles to me.

I touch Hadley's shoulder. "Are you okay with all of this, sweet pea?"

She looks between us. "Am I ever! I get a dog."

"Well, you don't exactly get Pick—" April cracks out an attempt.

I'm quick to intercept with a smile. "Pickles is yours most of the time." We have to keep this convo smooth.

April gives me a comical warning glare because I shouldn't be throwing out false promises.

"Nova also said that there are special friends and there are girlfriends. Which are you?" she asks April.

"Nova's father has been busy," April tells me, and I have to agree. She returns her focus to Hadley. "I'm…"

April looks to me for a clue, and I answer for us. "April is more than a special friend, a lot more." I'm not going to put her any peg lower because she *is* more; she makes me happy and fits into our life.

"Like she will be my new mommy?"

Fuck, an arrow through my heart. I knew this would come up, how can it not when you're a child? It's just a harsh reminder that I need to tread carefully because I have the ability to break both of these ladies' hearts if I don't approach our dynamic with care.

In this moment, I have no words because my head is spinning at the reminder that Hadley doesn't have a mom, and I feel my mood sink. Not for any reason April would guess.

"Wow, aren't we full of questions today," April says. "You know, getting a mommy is a big deal. It requires a lot of time and sparkly powder before you can welcome a mommy into your life. Even if we enjoy being around someone, we have to wait before we can welcome them into our life that way. I had the exact same experience as you when my mommy found someone."

"Okay, I'll ask again later."

"Like a few months later," April suggests before tapping Hadley's nose. "Now I think it's way past your bedtime. Is Pickles already waiting?"

"Yep. Will you help me tuck him in?"

April stands and offers her hand to Hadley. "Always." She gives me a reassuring half-smile.

Lucky for me, April answers with the type of care that makes me wonder if long-run us isn't so crazy.

———

Standing in the middle of my bedroom, I stare at April who is standing in the doorway giving me a curious smile.

"You're not in bed?" she wonders and steps into the room.

Truthfully, I'm too anxious to settle under the covers. I'm a smart man to know that it's because of what just went down half an hour ago with Hadley. Maybe I'm slightly shaken.

"You okay? You were a little quiet during the bedtime routine."

I lunge forward and cup her face in my hands before crashing my mouth onto hers. "Can we not talk?" I plead.

She studies my eyes for a moment and seems to grasp that I need an escape and she nods gently.

Kissing her again, I lead her back to the door and pin her arms up.

"No bed?" she muses in a whisper.

My answer is to lift her up and walk us a few steps and plant her on the dresser, causing something to fall to the floor, but neither one of us cares.

"Okay, no bed," she answers her own question before kissing me again.

I grip both sides of her flimsy t-shirt, and in one pull, I tear the fabric open, and my mouth travels her skin with no ordered pattern. I just want to take what she is offering. She doesn't question it either as her hands help lower my shorts, and it doesn't take long before I'm pounding into her, as she is ready and willing.

Her legs tremble and her pussy squeezes. My mouth seems to be taking my inner wrath out on her. The dresser shakes, and her breathy moan breaks my delirious thought.

I place my hand against her mouth. "Shh, baby, we have to be quiet. You understand?" I whisper, and she nods, with her hair now a disheveled mess. Removing my hand, I can't stop staring at her swollen lips. "Squeeze more," I demand.

Her eyes try to pry an answer out of me as to where my mind is, but I offer no answer because her body follows my cues, and her arms hold me tighter.

"Spencer," she whispers.

"Am I hurting you?" My voice is hoarse.

"No. Deeper."

I groan into her ear, because that's my girl, joining in on this ride.

We stay a tangled mess on top of my dresser until we both come undone sooner than I would have hoped.

She rubs circles on my back, as I stay put inside of her. I appreciate that she doesn't ask what just happened, because the truth is that she has managed to sneak into my life to the point that I don't ever want her to go, but my body and brain have connected that this means I need to share the secrets that I've been holding onto and may just push her away…

22

APRIL

B rushing Hadley's hair, she is wiggly today.

"Two more seconds then we're done, I promise." I touch her shoulders to force her to look straight. She has on her favorite dress, because today is a special occasion.

"What's going on?" Spencer asks as he enters the living room.

I quickly glance over my shoulder, trying not to lose focus on my task. "We're getting ready."

"For what?"

Closing the clip in Hadley's hair, I scoot her away. "All done. Just don't get messy." Turning my full attention to Spencer, I plaster on a big smile. "I have a surprise."

He scratches the back of his neck, unsure. "What would that be?" He peers over my shoulder and notices a woman with dark hair outside. "Who is that?"

Stepping closer to him, I take his hands in mine. "Don't kill me, but I know someone who takes pictures, and I think your walls could use some family photos. You don't really have many."

"Oh." His look is perplexed. "I guess, you did mention once that I keep the house compartmentalized."

Tugging him with me, we walk to the living room wall where

there are photos. It's just Spencer and baseball teams. The only somewhat personal one is of him in which he looks like he is in high school with a friend. They seem to be laughing in the parking lot next to a baseball field, I can tell by the fence in the background.

"Sport photos make sense, but a few photos of you and Hadley will make this wall perfect, don't you think?" I ask, noticing his eyes are stuck on the photo from high school.

He swallows a breath. "Yeah." His voice is supple.

I stand on my toes to kiss his cheek. "I booked a photo session for you and Hadley. You will have a bunch of photos to choose from."

His face softens, and a smile forms. "That's really sweet of you."

"Is it? You look not convinced."

His smile turns sincere. "I just never thought to do something like this. But it's really… special. Thank you."

He leans down to kiss my mouth.

"Just throw on some nice jeans and a sweater. You don't need to match."

"It's not like matching pajamas or some shit like that?"

I shake my head. "No. I promise, you won't even know the photographer is there. Super natural and just be yourselves."

Spencer looks at Hadley who is staring out the window at the photographer while she tests her camera, then his eyes return to me.

"I don't know what to say."

I quirk my lips out. "Nothing. The thing about relationships is we get to surprise one another."

He pulls me tightly to his body to hug me tight, lifting me off the ground slightly. "You're right. Okay, let me go change."

A quick peck on my lips and he sets me down before going upstairs. I touch my heart, knowing this will be a wonderful day for Spencer and Hadley, which is exactly what I wanted for them. It selfishly makes me happy to be able to do something for them; that's what caring for someone and love are, right?

———

STROLLING SLOWLY BEHIND THE PHOTOGRAPHER, I do my best to stay out of the way. My cheeks hurt from smiling so much.

In this moment, Spencer is down on one knee on his dock with Hadley sitting on his bent leg. He's showing her a baseball, and I think because Hadley loves the camera experience, she's taking an interest. I can't hear what he is saying to her, but it makes her giggle.

During the last hour, we've tried different poses in various locations outside. Even though it's chilly, they are dressed warmly enough. This scene, however, seems to be the winning shot.

"April," Spencer calls out.

He indicates for me to join him, but I shake my head. This is their time. He ignores me and still persists.

The photographer glances at me. "Go on."

I'm still reluctant, but now Hadley is waving for me to join them too. Hesitating, I walk over.

Spencer stands, with Hadley by his side, staring at me with a smile. The feeling of Spencer's arm pulling me close causes me to smile.

"You know, there is an unwritten rule that unless you're married or the baby momma or daddy, one should not ruin family photos. You never know if you have to erase someone out," I joke.

"I will gladly take the chance." He pulls me tighter, and my body curves into his shape. "Besides, it's just a few."

I squeal when he kisses my neck, and a tickle races down my spine.

"Thank you," he whispers.

"Having fun?" I ask both of them.

"Yeah," Hadley answers before running off to Pickles who is trailing behind the photographer.

The photographer follows Hadley to grab a few photos with her and Pickles.

"Pickles didn't get the memo about the unwritten rule," I comment as I watch them.

"Relax," Spencer assures me.

My eyes meet his gaze. "You have some great photos. You're

such a natural in front of the camera, Hadley too. She must get that from you."

"It must run in our blood."

His lips twitch for a second, but whatever thought is in his mind, he ignores it as he tips me back for a deep kiss. Clearly, my surprise was a success.

———

SITTING ON THE SOFA, we just put Hadley to bed and are ready to look at a few unedited photos that the photographer sent.

"She is fucking adorable," Spencer proudly states as he sees the first photo where Hadley is hanging off the branch of a tree.

"Boys will go wild for her when she's older."

"Not on my watch," he warns while he slides his thumb across the screen.

"You can pick a few to blow up and frame. The rest we can make into a photo book. You must have a photo book of Hadley somewhere from when she was a baby."

Spencer doesn't look up. "Somewhere. I love this one." He holds the phone up to display the photo of him showing her the baseball while they were on the dock.

"Thought you would."

"My mom will go crazy for this."

"We'll make sure they get a copy."

We both pause when we see a photo of just the two of us. It almost scares me how natural and happy we look.

"Not bad."

He gives me a pointed look. "This is a keeper."

I don't say anything, instead watch him swipe to the last photo and nearly gasp. It's all three of us, and I have butterflies in my stomach. It's confronting, but in a good way. My eyes land on a perfect photo of a family of three. Three people who seem immensely happy. It fills my soul with hope.

"A good memory," he notes as his thumb traces the screen.

"A keeper," I repeat his words from before.

But I don't want us to get too sentimental. Maybe we should slow down, but I don't want to. I should, considering my history, but everything feels so right.

I bounce off the couch because a million thoughts are floating in my head. Walking to the wall of baseball photos again, I cross my arms.

Spencer is fast behind me, his arms wrapping around me from behind.

"You okay?"

"Totally," I lie.

He kisses my cheek as we both look forward, yet neither one of us seems to be looking at anything in particular. "Thank you for today. It was unexpected yet exactly what we needed. Sometimes I forget that a photo can be the proof. I actually look like a good father in the photos."

"You shouldn't have doubts." But he does, I sense it sometimes. He is confident about everything, except slightly shaky when it comes to his daughter.

We stand there in an embrace for a good minute, just holding one another.

"High school you was kind of hot," I say, breaking the ice, my head indicating to the photo.

"Thanks. Some people would say I had it all from the start, but I'm beginning to think I'm only just realizing what that means."

His words strike me, I can't pinpoint why, but when I look over my shoulder, I can see that Spencer seems lost in thought again.

And any worry I have, I do my best to bury.

23

APRIL

I interlace my arm with Piper's as we watch through the window the ice hockey game down below. We are in the box seats, which means we have an abundance of snack options behind us.

"It's nice that you got away for a night," I mention. The baby is nowhere in sight.

"Much needed. The joys of having an adult stepson. It means he can do babysitting duty with his wife. My grandmother is great, but she can't handle overnight visits. Anyways, Hudson and I put Lucy and Drew up in a fancy hotel room with the promise they will watch Gracie for a few hours. Tomorrow I will take her to visit my grand-mother before stopping by the football field to see our favorite coach," she explains while her head angles as she tries to follow the game happening.

"I'm still upset you didn't bring the baby," my mother calls out from where she stands next to the buffet because her law firm supports the team.

I take a sip of my beer bottle and ignore her. "Remind me again why every athlete in Lake Spark decided to use my mother's firm for their legal woes."

Piper smiles and touches my shoulder. "Because they follow Hudson's advice when they need a city lawyer who is a shark in heels. Plus, I am super confident they get a discount."

"Fun." I'm not enthralled.

We both search for our men. Ford invited us all to watch his hockey game since they are now heading into mid-season and, according to him, are now in their prime of excellence. Spencer and Hudson went to sit down by the ice where there is more action, and I think they did it for a media op to show support for Ford.

"I bet Ford's ex is here somewhere," Piper notes.

"She comes to games?"

"Yeah, more for their son than anything is my guess. They are on good terms, just not the terms Ford probably wants. I've met her a few times, and Brielle is super sweet. She's studying law and interns at your mom's firm. Brielle doesn't like coming to Lake Spark, but maybe we should invite her to something here in the city."

"Why not? Is there some secret athlete partner's club that I get initiated into?" I try to keep my smile small.

Piper nudges my shoulder. "It would seem like you and Spencer are on a path forward."

"Surprisingly so." But as much as he has been the kind of boyfriend a girl could dream of the last few weeks, especially since Hadley discovered our secret, not to mention he makes my heart flutter and occupies my thoughts, I can tell something is on his mind. "I just hope he doesn't get cold feet. That tends to happen when men are around me."

"You think that's happening?"

I shrug a shoulder and then my face squinches. "Yikes." I notice two hockey players slam into the boards together.

"Am I allowed to say that this sport is by far more interesting than our guys' sports?" Piper speaks in a hushed tone.

I scan the room to ensure nobody can hear us. "Hockey totally is."

"And what you said about Spencer. I don't think he is losing interest. He just has Hadley, and I'm sure the closer to baseball season we get, the more his focus shifts."

Blowing out a breath, I turn to walk to the buffet. Piper follows me, and we each take a plate to grab snacks. "I mean, in the grand scheme of things, the only thing that is my hard red flag is when someone lies to me, I've had enough of that."

The sound of a throat clearing makes me glance over my shoulder to find Hudson and Spencer arriving in the room, and maybe he heard me. Spencer just continues to have a wry smile.

Piper walks to Hudson to give him a kiss. "How was it down there?"

"Cold, but damn, Ford is fast and ruthless." Hudson wraps an arm around Piper.

"I'm sure he will appreciate that we're here," Spencer adds.

Okay, I think he definitely heard me, as he is avoiding eye contact.

"I think I'm going to run to the ladies' room, I'll be right back," I announce.

Leaving the room, I can't help but feel a familiar pit in my stomach. A feeling of impending doom.

And five minutes later when I return, I see Spencer talking with my mom. It isn't the "charm the girlfriend's mother" type of mood between them either, it seems to be more serious.

"It's your decision." My mother's voice is the last I hear as they both notice me, and their posture changes. They give one another a confirming look and throw on smiles.

"Everything okay?" I ask just as Spencer brings his arm around me for a side hug.

He smiles weakly at me. "It's fine. The game is almost over. We're in the lead, so we can escape now if you want, before it gets busy."

"Yeah, sure."

"Enjoy your evening, you two. Don't forget to nail down those holiday plans, then we can schedule when to meet," my mother reminds us before hugging me.

Searching for Piper and Hudson, I see they are busy talking with someone, probably my uncle's lawyer. They both wave to us, and Piper blows me a kiss before indicating with her fingers to call her.

"Bye, Mom," I say.

Stepping back, Spencer takes my hand in his and leads the way. Security offers us a different way out to avoid the crowd, and the entire walk feels like something has shifted.

The car ride back to my place is no different, and by the time we get into my apartment, I can't take it because he is what I want, and I thought I've been clear, but that also means I will be shattered if he doesn't feel the same way.

I throw the keys onto my kitchen counter and turn to Spencer. "If you want to break up then do it now, this silence is excruciating."

Spencer looks at me like I'm crazy and steps to me, quickly interlinking our fingers. "Why in the world do you think that?"

I don't look into his eyes. "Because you've been acting strange. Especially since Hadley upgraded me in the friend book, you've been… I don't know. Something is on your mind."

I notice his chest rising as he heaves a sigh. "I heard what you said." My eyes shoot up to meet his. "About how lies are your red flag."

"And?"

Nerves seem to flood his face. "I've been trying to find a way to tell you…"

"Tell me what?" I feel that pit in my stomach crawl up inside of me, reaching my chest and causing my throat to strain. I hate fear.

"I want to be honest."

"About what?" I feel like I may throw up.

Spencer glances away then looks down at our hands entwined together. "I lied about the video."

I drop our hands like a hot tamale. "What?"

"I mean partially. My cloud was hacked and the video was on it, it's just that it didn't take as long to be solved." I can tell he is biting his inner cheek.

"But you had me stay with you when we hated each other." I'm trying to grasp what this all means.

"At first it was true, but I might have delayed telling you some important details." He pinches his nose, unsure where to look.

I weave my fingers through my hair as I attempt to put the puzzle pieces together. "What details?"

"It was solved already the day we went to Pioneer Park."

I feel my eyes go bold. "But you only said a week later that the situation was solved."

Finally, he looks up at me with guilt flooding his face. "I know. The call I got at Pioneer Park wasn't my agent, it was Celeste from your mother's law firm to confirm."

"Why didn't you tell me?" My hands come up into the air, and I clench my fists together. "I thought for a week longer than I needed to that someone might leak a video of you and me doing something wildly good but totally for nobody to see."

"I'm so sorry. I just… I don't know, seeing you with Hadley, and you were jealous of the pioneer making soup—"

My palm flies up. "Are you kidding me? Do not bring that twenty-year-old dressed in a bonnet into this discussion. What would possess you? We wanted to kill each other that day." My voice is fuming.

"Something inside me just, I don't know… was curious."

Damn it, his smoldering eyes do something to me, and when he steps closer, I feel my heart quicken.

"Do. Not. Step closer," I seethe out. "I will not let your wicked ways break down my resolve," I admit.

I shake my head before I rub my face into my hands. Spencer is quick to grab my arm, hooks his finger under my chin, and ensures I'm staring into his ridiculously handsome eyes.

"Who knows, maybe if I didn't do that then we would never have happened, and I'm so happy we happened." His face is pleading with me to understand.

But I feel a tear form in my eye. "It's not even about the video. In some fucked-up way, maybe one day I will think your ridiculous scheme is sweet. But you lied to me, and I hate lies. Would you have even told me if you didn't hear me making that comment?"

"Yes. I've been wrestling with it for weeks, and with so many other things I want to tell you," he swears.

"Lies are lies. My ex lied to me when he said he wanted to marry me, Hudson and Piper lied to me when they were seeing one another in secret, now you lied to me. I hate feeling like a fucking fool and like I'm some idiot for not seeing the signs sooner." I'm boiling with anger.

Spencer still kisses my forehead, as if it will make it all okay. "I'm so sorry. I promise you, I didn't do it to hurt you. I want to be honest, put it all on the table."

"I'm so angry."

He bows his head, ashamed. "Tell me what to do to make this better."

That damn salty tear streams down my cheek. "I think you should leave."

"Not until I tell you something else that you should know."

Shaking my head and stepping back, I stand firm because I know I will just crumble into his arms. "No. I need space right now to calm down."

"April, please—"

"No. I'm having complete déjà vu to a time where you drove me nuts in all the wrong ways," I snipe. "Please." I hold my palm up to him and feel defeated. "Just go."

His face stills before he flexes his jaw. It takes a few seconds, but he relents and walks past me and out the door.

24

SPENCER

I swipe my palm across my face in the hope of rubbing off my exhaustion. After April asked for her space, I gave it to her by heading straight to a hotel. It was two glasses of bourbon before I attempted to sleep and that didn't really happen.

Now I'm staring at a plate of bacon and eggs, but all I want to do is throw it against a wall.

A hard knock against my hotel room door is maybe welcome, even though it's not April. "Open up." Ford is on the other side.

I walk to the door to open it and immediately walk back to the sofa in my lounge area. "What are you doing here?"

"I always stay in this hotel after a game, you know that. Plus, you sent a *Ford, I think I fucked up* text at midnight. I was asleep and need to head to a team meeting later this morning, but I thought I would kill two birds with one stone, so pass me the bacon and tell me what's going on." He doesn't even wait, he just takes my plate of food off the cart that room service brought in.

Kicking up my feet, I lie back on the sofa and take a bottle of water with me. "It's kind of a big deal or not. I mean, hopefully, April wakes up and realizes it's a minor thing. I kind of delayed telling her when the video situation was under control, and she's pissed."

"Why on earth would you do that?" Ford is busy chomping on a piece of crispy bacon.

"Okay, I admit that it doesn't go down as one of my finer moments, but I guess something inside of me wanted her to stay before the rest of me caught up. I thought she wouldn't stay otherwise."

It's kind of sweet, surely she must see that.

Ford throws an orange at me, and I'm quick to catch. "Vitamin C, man. You have a kid, and they bring home bugs along with their adorable little smiles. While this is probably something your best man at your wedding may joke about… you literally made her think someone might leak the tape of you two longer than needed. She should strangle you."

"Shit." I growl, as his words are not reassuring. "She also mentioned how she hates lies."

"Kind of goes hand in hand."

"I let her down, I know. But I want to lay everything on the table, and she wouldn't even let me finish."

Ford shakes some pepper onto his eggs. "Do you know what is also interesting about this situation?"

"Tell me, oh wise one, who still pines for his ex from ten years ago." I give him side-eye.

He offers me a stiff fake smile before continuing. "You want to lay everything on the table because you feel a lot for her."

"Fuck, really?" I say, sarcastic. "Because that wasn't obvious."

"Geez, someone woke up on the wrong side of the bed. I'm just saying that maybe you should start by telling her that and then confessing whatever else you have going on in your head." Now he is onto buttering a piece of toast.

For one second, I wonder how his physique is long and trim when he eats like that, then remind myself he burns off a hell of a lot of calories on the ice. My temporary distracting thought, I shake away.

"Well, now I have to find a way to see her again. I texted her this morning, and I'm getting classic April again."

I glance at my phone to give myself another dose of agony when I re-read the messages.

ME

Hey, I really want to talk about last night. Can I come over? Maybe I can grab breakfast from that place you like on my way?

APRIL

No. I didn't sleep well. Had a strange nightmare then woke to realize that it's reality, and now I need to find spells to curse your team next season.

Okay then. I'll wait for our next chat.

Yeah, you do that.

Throwing my phone to the side, I pop my lips and rub my forehead again.

"I don't want to show up out of the blue because she did ask for space, and besides, I need to head back to Lake Spark for Hadley."

"Then I'm sure you will find a way to get her to come to Lake Spark."

"Maybe."

A long silence hits us, and I take the moment to walk to the cart and pour myself a cup of coffee. I inhale the scent to make me more alert, not that it will change anything.

"I've never seen you invested," Ford speaks up.

I grab a croissant from the breadbasket. "What do you mean?"

"In a woman, in creating a family. That's what you're doing, by the way."

My jaw flexes side to side. "Shouldn't that scare me more?"

Ford stands up and confidently smirks. "Nah, as long as you love her because it's her, not because she is a mom substitute to Hadley. When a kid is involved then you need to close your eyes, and as horrible as it sounds, if you can imagine yourself in the future in a scene without a child, then is that woman still with you? And if it's a yes, then she's the one."

I study him for a few ticks. I know he is speaking from experience. "Yet sometimes you have to let them lead the way and let them go if that makes them happy."

Ford licks his lips and thinks for a beat. "No. You may work with their timeline, but you strike when you need to because letting them go isn't an option." He flashes his eyes at me before giving me a wave with his two fingers on his way out the door.

I give him one nod, but mostly just stand there recalling his words, and I couldn't agree more.

———

WALKING INTO MY LIVING ROOM, I find my mother reading a magazine with a country house on the cover. She glances up at me but seems to be more interested in the article. "Hey there, how was the game with April?"

I laugh nervously to myself and fall onto the sofa next to my mother. "We kind of… you know what, never mind."

My mother tosses her magazine to the side and focuses her attention on me. "Disagreement or ending?"

"I hope disagreement," I admit.

She loudly exhales. "Over what?"

"The truth." My words cut the air in the room into two, if that were possible.

My mother doesn't blink as she stares with concern. I'm quick to reassure her. "Not that. Something else, totally unrelated."

She curls her lips in, debating what to say. "Fixable?"

"I think so. I'm just giving her some space." I look around for a sign of Hadley. "She's in her playroom?"

"Yes, enjoying the life you have given her, living like a princess with that ballet barre in her playroom." She touches my arm. "You know… eventually you will meet someone whom you want to share a life with, but to do that you need to be completely open with them… I get that." I hear the sadness in her voice.

Because this situation affects her too, in a way that we rarely discuss. That's not what the Crews family does. We do, we act, and move on.

"I'm going to tell April the truth," I confirm.

My mother's eyes water, and she squeezes my arm. "Then she must be the one." The line of her mouth stretches, and she blinks a few times, as if she is gathering herself.

"To my surprise, yes," I attempt to add humor to this situation.

"Surprises are what make our life path," she reminds me. We both understand and give one another a confirming look. Her head indicates to the wall. "The photos of you and Hadley are beautiful, a wonderful image of father and daughter."

"I think so too."

She stands and resumes her unaffected demeanor. "Hadley only had a snack, so she will be hungry soon. This babysitter situation is taking a little longer than we all anticipated, but I'm sure we'll continue to make it work. And I keep finding dog hair everywhere. Really, ask the cleaner to look into one of those pet-friendly sweeper things."

"Ma." I stand up as I attempt to stop her list. She looks at me with her full attention. "I'm allowed to have someone in my life, right?"

She touches my cheek as if I'm still a boy. "Of course, you are. Now just make sure you don't lose her."

"That's the plan," I promise.

APRIL

SPENCER

I really want us to talk, but I can't leave Hadley. I know you hate me right now, but she will only eat macaroni and cheese, but she says I don't seem to make it the way you do…

That's because you use the box stuff.

It's simple.

It's typical.

Tell me what to do?

You'll actually attempt to make it?

Well… I mean… I'll try.

Great, let's call the Lake Spark fire department while we're at it.

See? This isn't so bad… talking.

It's texting.

So agreeable.

You almost had me sending the secret
recipe. I mean, you love secrets.

I growl at our text conversation from earlier today. He never responded after that, but it doesn't matter, because here I am in Piper's kitchen whisking a cheese sauce. I faltered halfway through the text conversation, got in my car half an hour later, and drove up to Lake Spark.

"Remind me again why you are here instead of the house next door?" Piper throws a thumb over her shoulder as she twirls on the stool at the kitchen island in her home.

"That would mean extra time with his eyes on me, and I'm just going to drop this off and get right back into my car." I whisk with more aggression.

Piper snorts a laugh. "You drove all the way up here to deliver macaroni and cheese, don't tell me you don't want to hear him out."

I grab a casserole dish. "You know what he did." There is scorn in my voice.

She shakes her head in astonishment at me. "I see it more as he tricked you, not exactly lied. He was able to do that because you let him lead the way, and you didn't seem that bothered about the video."

"Because he was taking care of it."

"And you felt safe enough for him to do so, there was trust already there."

"It's not about the video," I acknowledge and pour cooked pasta into the oven dish. "It's the concept of lying."

Piper slams her hands down on the counter. "Yet here you are because I think you want to hear him out and are using macaroni and cheese as an excuse."

"Hadley is probably starving because Spencer is incapable of cooking," I justify and point a wooden spoon at Piper.

"Fine, since you are doing this all in the name of the kiddo, I'll deliver the macaroni and cheese." She's testing me.

I shrug my shoulder and stare at my creation. "I mean, I should do it. I need to explain the re-heating instructions."

"Really? So you *will* see him and talk?"

Growling a sound as I grab the box of crackers, I admit defeat. "I'll give him exactly thirty seconds."

"You can do a lot in thirty seconds," she deadpans.

I throw her a warning glare and begin to crumble crackers over the top.

"Are you actually adding cheesy crackers to the dish?" Piper seems mortified.

"Yes, it adds texture and flavor."

Piper seems to shudder with slight disgust, and she attempts to reach across the counter to grab my hand, but we're too far apart. "April, you've been happy. At least talk, I know you want to, otherwise you wouldn't have gotten in your car at the speed of light."

"I want to be stubborn, thank you very much." Placing the dish into the oven, I set the timer and then wipe my hands together in accomplishment.

"You're both bickering, not fighting. I understand where you are coming from, but it's not about what happened, it's about where you end up."

I sigh because I know she's right, and if I'm being honest with myself, I miss Spencer, even though it's only been two days since I saw him. I'm sure his intentions were somewhat noble, although poorly executed.

"I'm kind of scared." My admission surprises me. "I don't want it to end, but maybe that desire is so strong that I fail to see a sign that we won't work in the long run. It happened before."

Piper rests her chin on her propped arm with a sly smile. "Maybe you will find the puzzle piece to answer that. Sometimes we only find those pieces by *listening.*"

She's right. It's irritating because I feel like marriage and mother-hood turned her into a confident wizard.

And hopefully one day, I can see relationships from her angle.

Nervously, I look at the oven timer, knowing every minute brings me closer to seeing Spencer.

———

EVEN THOUGH I have the security code, I press the doorbell. He doesn't know I'm in Lake Spark since we had radio silence after this morning's text chat.

Glancing down at Pickles under the porch light, I warn him, "Don't look at me like that. You're not right." He woofs a sound.

The moment Spencer opens the door, my throat feels tight, and I'm unable to speak, as my heart wants to burst out of my chest, and I can't tear my eyes away from his that are glimmering with hope, and the white t-shirt he has on only adds to the chiseled-muscle, haven't-slept look. He has clearly had a few days of turmoil.

"April, you're here." A smile tugs on his lips, but he's unsure.

Remembering why I am here, I clear my throat and hold up the casserole dish. "Well, I can't have you burning down your perfect kitchen now, can I?"

"Macaroni and cheese?" He opens the door wide, stepping aside to allow me to come in. Pickles heads straight to his spot on the couch.

"Yeah. It's crackers, by the way… the secret ingredient, I mean," I say as I walk straight to the kitchen, and I feel his presence behind me, a heavy cloud of mixed hurt and desire.

"Odd, but okay."

I set the dish down next to the stove. "I can write down the instructions for re-heating since Hadley is asleep. I'm going to assume Hadley and the macaroni and cheese was a ploy?" I give him a knowing glare.

He smiles awkwardly and rubs a hand across his short-scuffed chin. "Yet here you are, knowing me so well."

Damn it, so true. Deep down I knew the chances of Hadley having a meltdown today of all days were slim, it's the oldest trick in the book, and I willingly played along.

"I'll head back after I write down those instructions."

"Like hell you are." He's direct and sharp. "It's dark out, and you're not driving back."

"Fine. I'll stay in the guest room. I'm familiar with that room." Again, I knew this would probably happen too.

A long silence overcomes us as our eyes lock and don't let go. We're lingering in an inevitable.

"I'm sorry," he whispers. "Can we talk?"

I fold my arms. "Might as well, since I'm here."

My demeanor amuses him, I can tell. He walks to his wine fridge to pull out a bottle of white. I recognize the bottle, as it's from Olive Owl, the winery of my cousin's wife's family.

"Let's go outside, I'll turn on the fire. It's better if we talk there."

I nod, as it doesn't sound like a terrible suggestion, but I stop in my tracks when I see he finally hung the photos from the photo shoot. "See? Perfect décor for the place." I still when I see he added a photo of the three of us along the line of photos. I want to smile but remember why I'm here. I know he's watching me, though.

A few minutes later, we are outside on the patio with the dark lake ahead. The glow of the fire and light from inside the house ensures we can see one another as we sit on the same sofa, but with enough distance between us. With glasses of wine in hand, I notice how beautiful this scene is.

"How come we've never really sat out here?" I wonder.

"Because we run a risk of you swimming in the lake," he jokes.

I take a sip of the wine. "I guess we stick to the swimming pool, the kitchen, and the bedroom."

"Not bad, but here we are now."

"Why do I feel like the video thing is the least of our worries?" A heavy feeling hits me that in the grand scheme of things, it's minor.

"Probably because it is, or maybe because you knew I always did everything in my power to protect you so the video wouldn't be leaked. Okay, I delayed some information, but it was only because you grew on me faster than I could have imagined, and I couldn't think clearly."

The sincerity in his tone pulls near my heart, our eyes holding again.

"Does my mom know? Is that why you two were talking so close the other night?"

A laugh escapes him. "About the sex tape? Nah, she doesn't know."

"Oh, okay. Guess I can go back to being the golden only child again," I attempt to joke and swirl the wine in my glass.

"She knows something else, though, and I want to lay everything on the line because I don't want to lie to you, because we are going somewhere." I sense that he is about to burst.

I don't want to make this hard for us. "You mentioned you wanted to share something else, but I may have been a *little* hasty in my 'get out of my apartment' spiel," I say, admitting defeat.

Spencer takes hold of my wine glass and sets it on the low table, along with his own glass, before scooting closer to me on the sofa.

"You're right. Honesty is important, and I don't want to lose you, so I…" He interlaces our fingers and focuses on our connection. "I need to tell you the truth about Hadley."

"What about Hadley?"

His eyes strike up and pierce with so much emotion that it spills into me when he says, "Hadley isn't my daughter."

SPENCER

er eyes flick up to land on me, and I sense the shock in her, especially when her mouth opens yet no words come out.

I wait a few seconds to allow her to grasp what I said. My deepest secret that I've never shared with anyone whom I've also shared a bed with.

"You said you shared the same blood," she mentions with her voice rasping.

"I do."

"I don't understand."

I rub my thumb in a circle on the back of her hand. "I'm her uncle."

April's head tips gently to the side, with her eyes squinting with confusion. "I didn't know you have a brother or sister."

A ping of guilt strikes my heart. "A brother… I had."

Her hand squeezes my own tightly, and she waits patiently for me to continue.

"Cameron. My twin, actually, not identical, and we were different in so many ways. I was sporty, and he was into motorcycles and skipping school. The photo I have on my living room wall from high school… that's him."

Her mouth forms an O shape.

I continue, "He disappeared for a while, working in a bar on the west coast and partying a lot. We kind of grew apart, and it had been a while since we spoke, but one Christmas he told my folks that he'd become a dad. Hadley's mom, she was a fling, took off after a few weeks and signed away her rights to Hadley, but Cameron turned his life around. I saw him once after he became a dad, because baseball kept me on a schedule, and I didn't get many opportunities to see him."

I don't even know if I'm explaining this right, it's odd to say it aloud. My parents and I just live, we make no effort to say the words, we just acknowledge the situation in our own way.

"What happened?" April moves closer to me, her hand landing on my shoulder for comfort.

"One week in the off-season, my parents got a call. Hadley had just turned two, and Cameron was on his way back from work. There was an accident…" I feel my throat tighten and bile swirls in my stomach. My eyes close, and I have no desire to finish that sentence.

"I'm so sorry." The light from the fire makes her sympathetic eyes more intense.

"Apparently, he had made a will when Hadley was a baby and without telling me made me Hadley's guardian. To make it worse, we managed to see him for a few hours before he passed."

"Spencer…"

It was a grueling few hours because nobody wants to see their brother give up.

"If I could have switched spots, I would have. He always told me how much he resented that everyone focused on me and baseball, but for some reason, he chose me to raise Hadley."

"I don't know what to say."

I drift my eyes back to her. "Nothing. Just listen. I'll never know why he chose me, but he had an idea in his head that it should be me. I promised I would raise Hadley and be sure she knows who her father is, but he made me guarantee that Hadley would only ever know one father… me.”

“Spencer.” April’s voice is shaky, and a tear falls.

“He wanted to argue to the very end, but ultimately, I followed through.”

April hugs me and pulls me tighter to her. “He chose you for a reason.”

Taking a deep breath, I note to myself how it feels like a relief to share this. I’ve been holding this in.

“It’s fucked up. I wanted to hate him, but she is the best gift, and now I can’t imagine life without her.”

April creates a little distance from us but still holds me. “You’re a dad, Spencer. A real dad.”

“I try.” I blow out another breath. “She was young enough that she doesn’t remember him.”

“Your parents?”

“They had a rough few years after losing Cameron, but Hadley was the light for all of us. Sometimes I wonder if it can be that she gives them a reason to be happy, yet at moments it becomes too much of a reminder. Anyway, they are in a good place now but want to honor Cameron’s wishes, hence why my mom isn’t here every day. She wants me to be the father that it seems my brother thought I could be.”

“Who else knows?”

“Hudson, but I doubt he told Piper, and if he did then she seems to be keeping it to herself. And your mom knows.” April’s eyes flood with recognition as the dots connect. “She helped arrange the legalities.”

April nods in understanding. “That’s what you were talking about.”

“Yeah. I told her that I was going to speak with you.”

She nibbles her bottom lip before it begins to tremble. “Why did you tell me?”

I move my body to get a better view of her, squaring us off, because I need her to have a clear view of how confident I am that I should share everything with her.

"No secrets. Only honesty." She reaches out to rest her hand on my cheek. "That day at Pioneer Park, for a reason I still can't explain, I saw a glimmer of a possibility of being with someone, not just for Hadley but myself. I didn't… want to let that go."

"But you hated me."

"We bickered, not exactly hate when we both reluctantly agreed to spend a Saturday in a park… together." I raise a brow because I know I'm right.

The corner of her mouth curves. "I guess I didn't put up a fight."

"I don't want to lose you, so here I am, leaving no stone unturned, because you and me? We're worth the chance."

A tear falls down her cheek, and I'm quick to wipe away the warm drop from her skin with my thumb. "Thank you for sharing this with me. It fills in a few puzzle pieces… puzzle…" April stops mid-sentence and seems to be registering what she is saying. "Missing puzzle piece." Her smile tilts a little more.

"What's going on?"

"Piper mentioned that I'll find the puzzle piece to answer my question if we are meant to be together in the long run," she explains.

I'm scared, but I've got to ask. "What's the answer?"

April stares at me for a second, lost in thought, drawing this moment out. "That I'm not going anywhere," she promises.

The last few minutes of a painful reality are replaced with my heart feeling full, and it's because of this woman.

I cradle her face in my hands and draw her to me. "April, I'm sorry. I could have handled everything better, but I didn't want to lose the chance."

"You have a lot to deal with, it makes sense. I was kind of adamant that you were a cocky baseball player who was bad news, until I got to know you, and now you're the guy that I hope doesn't break my heart, which means you kind of have my heart." She's rambling slightly but smiles softly when she speaks her last words.

"Having your heart is good because I kind of need it since I love you." And I have no problem saying that; it's not a big deal because it's as natural as the air I breathe.

April plunges forward to crawl into my arms and begins to shower my jawline with kisses. "I love you too."

I don't hesitate to kiss her, cementing this moment, taking her breath only to repeat and repeat.

———

KISSING APRIL'S NOSE, I move inside of her. We're facing one another in bed, lying on my side with her leg propped over my hip.

Our eyes lock as our bodies move in ripples together.

The first time was frantic, a mess of kisses and confirmations. Afterwards, we stayed naked in bed and talked about how we will lock away the secret that I shared. It doesn't change anything in terms of Hadley. I keep a picture of Cameron in the house so she's unknowingly surrounded by him, and I will explain one day she had an uncle. I will honor my brother's wishes, and maybe when Hadley is older, I will re-evaluate, or if there is ever a medical reason that she would need to know, but that's not what Cameron wanted, and now she's my daughter, and I don't want to lose that connection to her.

Last night was a lot of talk and decisions. We ditched condoms and are relying on April's birth control, because we just want everything to be more intimate and committed. All through the night, we've been in different positions, and in sleep, we remained in a tight embrace, and when we woke, we said nothing and let our bodies find their way.

I slipped right into her warm wet pussy, and her soft moan into my ear was the first sound I heard this morning, up to now when a string of sounds escapes from April's lips.

Kissing her to ground myself, I remind myself we are going slow for this round. But her heat envelops my cock as I drag my length in and out, and I just want to get lost in her.

Her eyes close, right before I drag my lips along her neck, tickling her with my morning scruff.

"Oh." Her moan is louder, and I feel her tightening around me.

I hoist her body closer to me, our bodies flush as I pump harder into her, reaching as deep as I can.

"I've got you, baby," I whisper.

"Spencer," April coos, linking our fingers resting on her hip.

"Don't worry, I'll fill you up. To the rim," I warn her.

It earns me a long hum, and her breath hitches from my speed picking up. We're reaching the final stretch, and watching her unravel in my arms while I'm inside of her is the way I hope many days and years ahead go. There is something satisfying about both of us already being fulfilled with an orgasm before eight in the morning.

I'll like it even more if she doesn't shower and walks around with my mark still inside of her.

I hold the back of her neck and our foreheads touch as we both move together. "You're mine, April."

"I'm yours." Her eyes sink closed, and her body begins to quake.

And it's not far behind that my orgasm chases hers.

A few minutes later, I'm lying there, still inside of her, as April combs my hair with her fingers. She places a soft kiss on my forehead before she lies on her side against her propped elbow.

"Can I ask what you say when Hadley asks what she was like as a baby? Or if she wants to see photos?"

I trail her arm with my fingers. "She's only asked a few times. I do have photos of her that Cameron had, but yeah, I hate lying when she asks about her first step or what her first word was. Instead, I tell her that she was so tiny and didn't do much, but when she turned two, then the magic happened."

She gives me an affectionate look. "You know what I think?" she laments.

"That my dick should wake you up every day like this?" I attempt to divert us.

She playfully spanks my ass, with her foot wrapped around my middle. "No. Although, I feel like we will be going through a lot of sheets. But really…" Her tone centers us again into normal conversation. "I woke in the middle of the night, and I couldn't stop thinking about the fact that some parents give a gift to someone else. You and I are connected in that way. We both got a gift in the end. I was a gift too, as I was born because someone helped my mom out, which means I got to experience this life, and you got a gift because your brother gave you Hadley and you're able to be the great dad that you are."

I tilt my head resting against her breast to peer up to see her beautiful face. "Who knew we would have so much in common then."

"We didn't. We definitely didn't know until now, but here we are. We can guide each other, you as the gift receiver and me with the experience of being a gift. You're not alone." April's lips quirk into a fixed permanent angelic smile.

"You're ready to keep going, you and me?"

"Absolutely." She captures my mouth for a soft quick kiss. "The tattoo is the date you got her, not her birthday. I've figured it out."

"It is. Day and month."

She traces my anchor with her fingers. "It means it's also the day you lost a brother."

"But I became a father." She plants a kiss against the numbers. "Destiny," I whisper.

A silence hangs in the air. "Now, if you'll excuse me, I need to get dressed and get pancakes on the griddle. Protein version for you, secret-hidden-vegetable pancakes for Hadley, and the Pickles-friendly version."

Reluctantly, I peel myself off her and slip out of her heat, feeling a loss. "I still remember you standing in the middle of the kitchen with pancake mix and confusion when Hadley ran in."

April flashes me a fond look. "It was crepe mix and apparently one of the luckiest days of my life, but I had no idea." She quickly kisses me once more. "I'll be down in five minutes, just need a quick shower."

"Like fuck you are. No shower. Two minutes."

"What?" She takes the sheet with her.

"I said no shower." I roll onto my back.

Her eyes grow piqued. "Are you already telling me what to do, and I want to argue?"

"Sounds like us."

She giggles and walks in the direction of the bathroom. "Maybe I'll listen. Maybe." She slants a shoulder up toward her ears. "But since I love you, I may be inclined to follow instructions," she calls out.

And I'm not ever going to get tired of hearing that I'm leading the way or that she loves me.

NEXT BASEBALL SEASON

Tugging Hadley along by the hand, I spot our two reserved seats in a prime location for Spencer's baseball game. I've been a few times now, as a player's girlfriend, but this is a first—bringing Hadley. She's never been to Spencer's games because he thought she was too young and didn't want people outside of Lake Spark to know about Hadley. But when she took interest in tee-ball for exactly eleven minutes a few weeks ago, he decided that she can come to his game and see him in action.

Sitting down, I hand Hadley her hot dog, but she seems too interested in the big screen.

"Do you see your dad?" I point to Spencer warming up with throws to a teammate. He takes no notice of us, as he is deep into focus mode.

Dating an athlete is no joke. He was legit serious about the sex schedule. He can't be too relaxed for a game. And his schedule is at times a challenge, especially when he travels, but I moved into his house a few months after he laid everything out.

Since it's baseball season, Hadley spends most of it with her grandparents, but I'm putting in the effort to see her a few times a week since I got a job as a nutritionist for the school district one county over. Spencer knows his end days of baseball are fast approaching due to his age, which means Hadley can stay with him for every season soon.

"How long is this?" Hadley asks before taking a bite of her hot dog.

"Hmm. Well, it can be kind of… long." Not going to lie, football and hockey have bonus points for shorter games. "But I know where we can sneak into the fancy boxes and get cake."

"I want caramel corn."

"Good choice."

I watch Spencer toss a ball to one of the team managers before he runs a few strides to our area of the field, and he hops up on the fence to wave to us.

I touch Hadley's shoulder. "Look, someone came to say hi."

Hadley waves her hand furiously at Spencer. A few teenage fans are skipping down the steps of the stadium to get to the net fence and speak to Spencer, but his attention remains on us.

I blow him a kiss before the mob of fans blocks our view. It doesn't matter, Spencer has to get back to his team, as the game is about to start.

"These people came here to watch my daddy?"

"Yep. I mean, the whole team, but if you want to know a secret. Psst." I pretend to look around for eavesdroppers and then lean close to Hadley. "I think they came to watch him because he is super good."

"Like better than my tap dance?"

"Nobody is as amazeballs as you during that winter recital dance, but he's close enough."

She smiles with her toothless front on display because she's lost another tooth, which makes me snort a laugh because the fairy sent her a letter explaining that she will now be getting smaller surprises because the fairy is switching to e-pay and it's tax season. It was a ridiculous letter but did the trick because everyone except Spencer agreed one hundred dollars was a bit too much.

"Where do you think my grammie and grandpa are?" Hadley wonders as she focuses on her hot dog.

"They're here. They were waiting for their burgers that seemed to take longer." Spencer's parents are always kind to me. We never talked about it, but I know they're aware of what Spencer told me. Maybe one day they will share more when they're ready.

Spencer and I, according to some, are still in the early stages. It's been over eight months since he showed up on one of my blind dates, and nearly a year since our hotel escapade, but our speed is a winning formula.

Still, I would have no problem if he were to surprise me with the next step because I feel ready, and everyone around me also confirms that I've chosen a keeper.

———

A FEW WEEKS LATER, I'm walking down the hall in the Dizzy Duck Inn. I was told by the receptionist that Spencer was waiting for me in the private dining room, as he is finally cashing in on his private-chef experience that he won at the auction months ago.

I toss my phone into my purse right before I reach the door.

The moment I twist the handle, my eyes are hit with a scene from a fairy tale.

I stop in my tracks, and my entire body stills as I soak in the setting.

The room is illuminated by candles everywhere and white fairy lights hanging from the ceiling. Champagne is on ice in a bucket near the table set with expensive white table linen.

The hue of light creates a glow, which only highlights Spencer's satisfied smirk as he leans casually against the windowpane, yet he is dressed in nice jeans, a crisp white shirt, and a dark blazer.

"What's going on?" I manage to say, but a smile is slowly dragging up my lips. My heart is beating so fast because this doesn't feel like a normal dinner.

He slowly walks my way, his eyes smoldering, and when he reaches me, he collects my hands knowing damn well he has thrown me off.

"This is where it all started," he reminds me.

"You want to make another video?" I deadpan, but deep down I think I know what's happening.

He laughs before walking me a few steps to the middle of the room. "I once heard you like grand gestures."

I tilt my head back slightly. "Perhaps."

"Damn it, I knew I should have gotten the hot air balloon," he jokes.

"Depends. What is this?" I'm not sure that I've blinked in the last minute.

Spencer tucks his hand into his blazer.

I swallow. Oh God. He is really doing this.

He pulls out a little plastic treasure chest and holds it up between his fingers.

I'm slightly confused. "Hadley lost *another* tooth?" I kind of thought we just completed the last wave of missing teeth.

"Nah, but since she isn't here, I had to incorporate her somehow."

Breathe. We are back on track. Breathe.

Spencer is kneeling down.

"Wait." I hold my palm up. "Does Hadley know you are here about to do what I think you're going to do?"

He scoffs a laugh. "Babe, let me do my thing. I have one day off between games, so let me take advantage of that. We can talk logistics after."

I ease into a smile again. "Okay. Do your thing."

"April, to my dismay, you are by far more than I anticipated. The good kind of more. We took a chance, a lot of chances. But it was worth it. I kind of want to make sure that you can't taunt any other man, and I enjoy having you around too much, so I'm hoping you will be my wife. Will you marry me?"

Tears sting my eyes, especially when his face has a slight shade of nerves. Does he really think I wouldn't say yes?

My sight darts to the ring in the little pink plastic treasure chest, then I feel shock. "That's huge, I mean the rock, the ring rock, not your rock."

"Oh, okay, that's where this conversation is going." He still seems to be entertained.

"I'm going to sink when I go swimming!"

"Only if you wear the ring, because you agree to wear the ring, as in you say yes to becoming my wife. Preferably lock in that confirmation in the next few seconds or so, as I'm kneeling before you holding up a ring."

I wipe away happy tears and smile ecstatically before I lean down and throw my arms around his neck. "Yes!"

He slams his lips onto mine. "Good decision," he murmurs against my lips before creating space to slide the ring onto my finger.

Standing up, he pulls me up and loops his arms around my middle, with our eyes locked in a trance.

"You told Hadley once that you wanted a prince who went all out. I figured I would try this."

"Listening to our prince talks again?" I give him a glare. "She's in on this?"

"Not the specifics, but she helped me pick the ring. Something shiny for Queen Sparkly and a promise that she can wear the biggest pink dress there is," he explains and brings my hand to his heart.

"A wedding full of tulle fabric it is," I promise. Then it dawns on me how different this experience will be. I was engaged once, and everything felt like a compromise. This time, I'm with a man who treats me like nothing is an ask, only a wish he wants to make come true, and I want to make him happy.

Our mouths find one another for a kiss.

"Tonight, we can enjoy our dinner, and tomorrow the whole

world can know," he suggests. He slides the back of his knuckle along my cheek, and I love the feathery touch.

I squint my eyes. "Why do I feel like the important ones already know?"

Spencer tilts his head to one side. "Okay, so I had to seek your uncle's approval, Piper needed to give me intel on your ring size, Hadley was bursting to tell you all day, hence why she said she was taking Pickles to practice being a ring bearer, and Ford gave me the advice that I should get down on one knee when I asked. So yeah, if you said no then this would be slightly fucking awkward."

I laugh and walk with Spencer hand in hand to the table. "Good thing I wouldn't dream of saying no."

He pulls my chair out, and I sit down. We both get settled in our seats, and Spencer pops the cork on the champagne.

I chortle a sound because last time we were in this room, we were arguing and drinking before we combusted later that night.

"Times have changed," I say and accept the glass of bubbly he hands to me.

Tipping his glass to mine for a toast, he grins. "It was a good night."

"Is that what we're toasting to? We made a video, and it was a good night?"

"An excellent night. The catalyst for us." He clinks our glasses. "And if that's the way we started, then imagine the ride ahead." He winks at me.

"Cheers to that." Because I couldn't agree more.

WE'RE STANDING outside the front door of our house, and he kisses my forehead. Last night, we enjoyed our dinner and then stayed at the Dizzy Duck Inn, this time waking in the same bed.

But now we are ready to see Hadley and share the news. Piper was watching her for the evening.

"Don't be nervous." He rubs warmth into my arms.

"I'm not. Well, I mean, I'm sure Hadley is excited, it's just that before she and I were friends, and now I'm the stepmom. Stepmoms don't get a great rep in her fairytale books." I exhale a long breath.

"You're more than a stepmom to her. You are the only mother figure she's ever known. And I mean, if all else fails then just use the dog."

I pull his arm from his humor. "Come on, smartass."

When we arrive in the house, even Spencer stops cold. What should have been Hadley and Piper is now… a large group.

"She said yes?" Hudson is quick to start the question train. Piper tsks him.

"Can we see the ring?" Spencer's mom asks.

"You have a glow," my mother comments with her hands together.

I turn my attention to Spencer and quickly pick up that he had not planned this. Nor does he know what to do.

"Clearly people don't have jobs to get to," he mutters under his breath.

I smile awkwardly and hold up my hand to show my ring, which causes the room to erupt in cheers.

But the noise doesn't deter us from searching for Hadley who is walking toward us. We both lean down to her level.

"I want chocolate cake for the wedding, and pink flowers, and pink shoes, and I think Pickles should be mine now since we are a family."

I try to suppress my grin and instead offer her a serious look. "Of course, whatever you suggest."

Spencer musses her hair before Hadley gives me a little hug that is good for the soul every single time. She also said we are a family now, and it's such an amazing bonus to landing the man I want to marry.

She skips off, and I fan a hand in front of my face to ensure no tears fall because, damn, that was a heart-tugger.

Piper brings me a mimosa, and before long, I'm traveling between questions and answers.

It's a good twenty minutes later when I get to steal a moment with my fiancé.

"I want him back," I tell my uncle. "Besides, shouldn't you be at training camp or something?"

Hudson holds his hands up in the air. "Whoa, message received. Just wanted to ensure he treats you well, do my spiel, and I'm expecting I'm still allowed to walk you down the aisle?" He was supposed to last time around, but this time he seems actually excited at the prospect because of whom I'm going to marry.

"I mean, if you have time." I pretend to be unaffected and cross my arms over my chest.

Hudson pulls me into a side hug. "He's a keeper, April," he murmurs. When he pulls back, he points a finger at Spencer. "I'm still going to be watching you."

"Excited for the prospect," Spencer calls out, unenthused, as Hudson walks away.

Walking into Spencer's arms, I inhale the smell of his shirt, a subtle spicy scent. "I guess we'll bask in this another time."

"It's okay. We'll have plenty of moments together."

We both stay in an embrace as I hug him tightly, and my eyes catch something outside the window. I do my best to figure out what I'm seeing. "Hey, Spence, what is Ford doing?"

"I'm not sure, Hudson said Ford was going to stop by."

I jab Spencer's arm. "No. Look outside. Is Ford with a woman?"

We untangle and walk a few steps to get a better view of outside. It's definitely Ford with a woman. He has her thrown over his shoulder.

"Hot damn. I forgot to mention that Brielle is here."

"As in his first love? The ex?" I double-check.

He chuckles under his breath. "Yeah, more like trapped in his house alone with him until further notice. I think he mentioned something about a fake ring, but you know how it goes."

My mouth drops from the news. Maybe Ford is finally getting his second chance…

BONUS SCENE

Shaking my head, I lean against the kitchen island to watch my very pregnant wife attempt to reach the top of the cake with her piping bag. I'm entertained, as April always forgets that her bump gets in the way.

"Come on, babe, I'll help you with this one," I offer as I wrap my arms around her from behind, my hands landing near her navel.

My head rests on her shoulder as we both examine the three-tier birthday cake for Hadley.

"Fine. But, Spencer, don't ruin it. Remember to use a steady hand and gently tease the cake." She hands me the bag of icing.

"I shall treat the cake like a lover," I tell her seriously, but inside, I'm amused.

She glances over her shoulder at me and rolls her eyes before she hands me the icing and carefully supervises my hands as I attempt to decorate the cake.

"It's not every day she turns nine, and we are moving past the princess phase. She's onto more sophisticated things, so a simple cake with a few colors and sprinkles will just have to do."

I give her side-eye. "This is a simple cake?"

"I mean, of course, I made a fresh strawberry filling, and each layer has a different flavor, but I didn't melt any chocolate or anything." She steps away from the counter to rub her big belly and glances around the living room that we decorated last night. "Maybe more balloons?"

I set the icing down and grab April's hands to hold, giving her a quick peck on the back of her hand. "Relax, your mom is bringing more balloons, and my parents are picking up more drinks."

Her eyes hit me, full of love. "I just want it to be extra special for her. It's her birthday, and soon she will be a big sister. I want her to feel like nothing will change."

My lips form an appreciative smile. "We've done our best to include her in everything, and she loves you. You're doing great." Hadley calls April Mom now, and they truly are a team together… against me. But I don't mind, I spoil them rotten.

A dog's yawn breaks our gaze, and we look down to see Pickles looking at us with droopy eyes. How this guy is still hanging on, I'm not quite sure. I'm ninety percent certain that it's the special dog treats April bakes for him. Or maybe it's the occasional walk past the driveway that I convince him to join me on now that I'm retired from baseball. I have a few ideas of how I will occupy my time, but for now, I'm going to enjoy every moment with the new baby.

"He keeps following me around, like everywhere," April says as she examines our dog.

"That's because he knows my baby brother is about to pop out," Hadley announces as she enters the kitchen, with her eyes set on her phone that she's scrolling on.

April is quick to shove me in front of the cake. "Hey there, birthday girl," April says with a funny tone. "You shouldn't see your cake until the big reveal."

"It's fine, most likely this party won't happen."

"Why do you say that, sweet pea?" I'm a little concerned.

Hadley points with her phone to April. "Dad, Mom is overbaking my brother."

"I told him that he can't come out until *after* your party," April says, proud with her promise.

I snort a laugh, because nature may have other ideas. We're already two days overdue, yet I'm kind of relieved, as it delays meeting him. I'm excited, but the baby thing is new for me, and it's scary in an exhilarating way. I didn't get to experience Hadley's baby months, just like sharing a pregnancy with someone was a first for not only April but myself. It's brought us closer too.

"Why don't you go sit down, I'll finish my supreme icing technique," I suggest.

"No way, I need to get to work on my spinach dip." April is now agitated, but I let it go, because we know it's an unusual time.

Hadley smiles at me with reassurance before she walks over to the sofa to flop down.

It's two hours later when we have family filling our living room. My trusted neighbors, April's mom and stepdad, plus my parents and a few of Hadley's friends from dance class.

Hadley blows out her candles, and I hope her wish has nothing to do with her crush on Ford's son, Connor.

Immediately, the grandmas are into helping mode with cutting and dishing out cake.

I don't drink a beer because I'm on call for the moment I need to rush us to the hospital. Speaking of which, I notice Piper and April whispering in the kitchen.

Walking to them, I have to grin. "Up to tricks, you two?"

April laughs tightly. "Always."

My eyes dart to Piper who gives me bold eyes. Instantly, my sight whips back to April and my hand lands on her upper arm. "Honey, are you okay?"

"My contractions started. We may need to leave after everyone goes." April blows out a breath through pursed lips.

"Or now," Piper suggests.

My heart fills with excitement that this moment has arrived.

April looks between us, panicked, and loudly whispers, "No! It's Hadley's day."

"Our boy has decided." I study my wife's face and see that she seems conflicted, as she knows the clock is ticking, but her heart believes Hadley should have her day.

"No kid wants to share their birthday with their sibling. He can't come out today. See, I told you morning sex wasn't a good idea," April scolds me.

Piper holds her hand up. "My cue to leave. I'll take over party duty."

She walks away, and I can only grin at April. "It's okay, it could be a while, and he may not appear until tomorrow."

"You're right. I just…"

I rub her shoulders to soothe her. "We're parents to two now, that means we owe it to both Hadley and our boy to do what is right so they are healthy and happy. Our baby needs a hospital because I'm sure as hell not delivering him in the kitchen next to the jar of your sour dough starter."

"I'm being ridiculous."

"You're nervous."

"Kind of. We skipped all the classes, and all I know is that this may hurt a little."

I swipe her hair behind her ear. "It will be worth it. I'll even throw in an extra push present if you want."

April's lips quirk side to side. "I might take you up on that."

"You should. Now come on, we need to get out of here."

"Why don't we just tell everyone that we need to run to the grocery store."

I snort a laugh. "And come back with a baby? Yeah, not going to fly with this bunch."

She groans as I begin to walk us in the direction of the front door where a bag has been waiting for a few weeks now. I give an indication to my mom that it's showtime, and luckily, she brightly smiles, making no commotion, instead offering me a thumbs-up.

But then April's mom notices and shit hits the fan.

Her hands go over her mouth as she tries to hide her squeal, and Hadley looks up from her plate of cake then to us.

"Were you just going to leave without saying goodbye?" Hadley seems disappointed.

"Of course not. It will take five minutes before we even get shoes on my feet," April states.

Hadley walks to us, and we patiently wait despite the rush we should probably be in.

"Grams will bring you to the hospital when it's time, okay?" I remind her of the plan. Pulling my daughter into a hug, I kiss the top of her head. "You know you're my favorite daughter, right?"

"I'm your only daughter."

"Lucky me. I'm sorry we need to leave your party, but your brother got excited and wants to come out."

Hadley thinks for a moment. "It's okay. You'll just have to name him what I pick."

Glancing to April, she nods in agreement.

"Deal."

Hadley jumps in place. "Yes, I win."

I smile at her excitement. "Save me some cake, okay?"

She gives me one more tight hug before running to April for a hug.

———

Driving around the lake, I'm beginning to freak out because we're not moving. It's early spring which means today of all days the city council decided to clean up the trees that fell during the winter storms that we had.

"Fuck me, I never want to see another deer-crossing sign in my life," April breathes out, clearly in pain.

"Trees are the culprit for our standstill, not deer." I tap my steering wheel with nervous energy.

"I know, but I've been focusing on that stupid deer-crossing sign for the last five minutes. Good God, I'm going to deliver a baby on this road like a wild animal." A wave of pain hits her.

I rub her back as she grips the door handle. My body tightens, as I am afraid her ridiculous statement may come true.

"Relax, I see they're moving up ahead."

She finishes her contraction and looks at me with near possessed eyes. "Don't tell me to relax. You said that nine months ago and now look where I am!"

It must be bad that I want to smirk, but even in this situation, April keeps me on my toes and makes every second an adventure, the kind I want to spend eternity on.

"I love you," I tell her.

"I love you too, but please move this car."

Luckily, it's our turn to pass, and we're driving again. With a new speed and our route time declining as we reach the hospital, I can only reflect on the many drives around the lake that I've taken with this woman.

"Remember the first night that you were here in Lake Spark and we went to the grocery store?"

"Yes, when I was unaware that you had trapped me here, only to make me fall for you, marry you, and now deliver our little bundle of joy. How could I forget that wonderful drive?" A warm smile spreads on her face as she rubs circles on her belly.

"I'm lucky it's you."

"You *are* lucky."

I quickly glance to my side before focusing on the road. "You were stubborn and standoffish. A lot like now, and that's a good thing, because it's exactly what our boy needs. You're going to be amazing at bringing him into the world."

I can tell she's staring at me, sentimental. "I can only do it if you're with me, so lucky me."

Grabbing her hand, I bring it to my mouth for a kiss before holding it tight on the middle console.

Chances and luck can be the same thing.

That's what we are.

And twelve hours later, we are lucky enough to hold our son, with Hadley arriving early in the morning to name him Ashton Crews.

April and I look between our children, well aware that both of them will break and mend hearts one day, but they will also get to experience the love that April and I have in this very moment.

And we'll be there to watch and support them.

WORTH THE WAIT

WORTH THE WAIT PLAYLIST

1. My Sweet Baby by Thieving Birds

2. Don't Give Up On Me by Zach Bryan

3. Name by The Goo Goo Dolls

4. The Freshman by The Verve Pipe

5. Collide by Howie Day

6. Brick by Ben Folds Five

7. Bigger Than The Whole Sky by Taylor Swift

8. Around Again by Hovvdy

9. Anti-Hero (country version) by Josiah & the Bonnevilles

10. High Beams by Zach Bryan

11. Glue Myself Shut by Noah Kahan

12. Thumbs by Zander Hawley

13. Oh My Heart by R.E.M.

FORD

on't look at her fingers. I'll regret it if I do.

First, I will admire the way Brielle swipes a few strands of her silky brown hair away from her cheek, and then I will follow the line of her jaw until I stare at her soft lips that always curve in a soft smile when she talks about Connor, our son. And finally, the pièce de résistance, her hands. And it's why I'm going to regret locking my gaze on her fingers, because there is something missing from her ring finger, and it's all my fault.

Man, I know I'm torturing myself.

I look.

I get lost for a second—okay, maybe two.

"Mr. Spears, wouldn't you agree?" A lady's voice breaks my turmoil.

Blinking my eyes a few times, I look forward and see my son's soon-to-be-retired teacher smiling at me from the other side of the table for our end-of-year parent-teacher meeting. I only glance for a second, as my sight whips back in Brielle's direction, where she's sitting beside me. Brielle Dawson or Elle to me, mother of my child, the most beautiful woman I've ever known, and the only one I've seen a future with.

But the chance was ripped away from us ten years ago because of a promise.

"Ford, are you okay?" Brielle double-checks with me; her blue eyes have a curious glint in them.

I clear my throat, remembering what we were talking about. "Of course, we'll make sure he keeps reading over the summer."

"I know Connor is excited for hockey camp, and I hope he enjoys it, but it's important he arrives to the fifth grade ready. It's his last year before middle school," Mrs. Clark reminds me.

Brielle gently touches my arm. "We will be sure to get the books on the summer reading list," she assures the teacher.

Mrs. Clark brings her hands together. "Wonderful. I just wanted to say that, despite his little outburst recently, he is a sweet boy, and I will miss him."

My jaw tightens about the reminder of a few weeks ago when he had an argument with a classmate. Glancing to Brielle, I see her strained look.

"You two should be proud of him, and if I may say so, be proud of yourselves too," Mrs. Clark adds.

"How so?" I wonder.

"I can't tell you how many times I've had these meetings go south when the parents are separated, and their child has issues in class because of their parents' behavior toward each other."

Brielle taps her nails on the table and throws on a tight smile. "That's not us." She takes a deep breath. "We only want the best for Connor."

Fuck me, how is it years later, and I still hear the sadness drenched in that sentence?

"Thank you for the compliment." I awkwardly attempt to stay calm. "If Connor hasn't said anything at school, then I guess we're doing a good job."

The teacher's smile falters slightly. "If I may be frank…"

"Please." My tone is clipped.

"He's all smiles when he talks about you both. Not many kids can say they have a famous hockey star as their dad. But sometimes he mentions that you both live in two different worlds and only ever come together at set times, and he knows it's because of him."

Brielle's breath cuts short, and she looks off into the distance out the window.

I swipe a hand through my hair that's still short from hockey season. "Kids are intuitive, aren't they?" I say in a flat tone, not so amused.

Mrs. Clark laughs awkwardly. "They are. Well…" She glances between us. "That's everything. I wish you both a great summer."

Brielle offers a polite smile. "You too, and thank you for ensuring Connor had a great school year."

We all stand and say our goodbyes.

Brielle and I take the longest walk in silence out of the school and to our cars that are side by side in the parking lot. I know something is weighing heavy on her mind because my own thoughts feel like a brick too.

We both hit the unlock buttons on our key fobs, yet neither one of us makes a move to climb in the driver's side. Instead, we face one another, with the late-afternoon sun on full blast.

Our eyes lock and so begins our usual lingering gaze.

It happens every damn time.

Every drop-off, pick-up, birthday party, meals we have together as a family for Connor's sake, every time she brought Connor to my games to watch, and I would catch her staring as I glided by on the ice.

It's all a fucking simmer that never boils over.

"That went well," she notes and nibbles her bottom lip.

I throw my sunglasses on because I need protection from staring at her blue floral-print summer dress with an annoying button loose at the top. The dress deserves to be hanging off the edge of my bed because it was thrown off in a moment of clarity.

"It always does. Parenting we're good at."

She snorts a cute little laugh. "I would say we aren't that bad. She had to bring up the other week, didn't she?"

A sound escapes my mouth as I debate if I can tease her about this or not. "It will go down as memorable."

Her hand finds her hip. "Easy for you to say, you were the one who had to deliver the news to me."

I hold my hands up in surrender. "I was put in an awkward position, thanks. Not easy for either one of us."

"Connor asked you to deliver the news that I'm no longer allowed to write notes in his lunch."

"Elle, he's getting a little old for that, and when someone bothered him at school about it, then yeah, he thought it would be better if I talked to you to deliver the message of no more notes. Along with the need to no longer pre-slice his apples. Trust me, I feared that conversation with you all day." I can't control my smile at this.

She throws on a fake pout that is too fucking adorable. "I can't handle him growing so fast." We're still young ourselves.

"Kids tend to grow up. If you're missing having a baby, then I can volunteer my services again," I joke, but the humor hits a little too close to home.

Her smile stills, unsure even, and it's a good few seconds before her tone turns serious. "Should we be worried about what Mrs. Clark mentioned about the set-time-togetherness thing?" She whirls her fingers in the air.

My head lolls to the side. "Maybe."

"I guess we should have a look at the schedule again since you'll no longer have games."

Ouch, that reminder.

The season that just ended was my last as a professional hockey player as the center and captain of the Chicago Spinners, thanks to age and one injury too many. Nothing major, but I don't recover the way I did ten years ago when I was twenty. I feel a shade of pain spread on my face.

And she knows me so well, as she studies me with a knowing wry smile. "Going to miss it, huh?"

I shrug a shoulder. "It was my life for so long, but yeah, I'm good. I have a plan B, been planning it for a few seasons now."

"Right, the new sports training facility near Lake Spark."

I chuckle to myself at the way she says Lake Spark, as if it's a mystical place that she fears in a funny kind of way.

During hockey season, I was on the road and stayed at hotels in the city. In my downtime, I escaped to Lake Spark in upstate Illinois. The place I remember from my childhood, through summers as a teenager with a particular brunette, and now it's the place where I fully intend to make a life post-hockey career.

Brielle lives in Hollows, a perfect middle point between Chicago and Lake Spark. She's always had Connor for most of the year, since I had training and game seasons.

"I enjoy it there. You still need to see my house again now that it's finally finished, and you can see if you approve of Connor's room. The interior designer did a good job, I think."

She waves a hand at me. "When it comes to our son, then you know I trust you."

"Still, you can't avoid Lake Spark." I reach out to touch her shoulder, to both comfort her and grab an opportunity to touch her skin because I know she'll tolerate it.

She tilts her head to the side and allows her cheek to nuzzle into my wrist near her shoulder. It's a throwback to a time when we could have had everything. Through the years she occasionally does this, reminding me of the trust we have with one another, the connection we will always share, and the reminder that a different ending floats in our minds.

"I'm not avoiding Lake Spark. I'm just debating what to remember." Her voice is delicate.

I step closer to her, and I move my hand to her cheek to brush my thumb along the stretch of soft skin on her cheekbone. "Everything," I say huskily.

Something must strike in her mind because she attacks her bottom lip, and she steps back. "So, uhm, I guess you have Connor for the first few weeks of summer vacation, and I know he'll enjoy hockey camp one of those weeks." She is changing the subject.

Her avoidance of topics causes me to smirk. "Yeah, we'll be fine, like always. Are you ready?"

"Studying for the Bar exam is a job in itself. I'm lucky I could give up my part-time paralegal job. Thanks for changing the schedule so I have some alone time to study."

A proud smile takes over me. She's been waiting for this. College took longer because Connor was a surprise, then she had LSATs and law school. It was the plan and dream she always wanted, and now it's within her grasp.

"You'll nail it. And you take all the time you need…" I remember she mentioned Illinois only has the exam twice a year. I want her to succeed, which is probably why it spits out of my mouth. "I've got Connor covered and can bump up child support if you need."

The moment it slips off my lips, she raises a brow at me and gives me a stern look. But she isn't mad. She shakes her head at me, entertained. "We're fine." Her pride is strong, or rather, she will never ask for more because I know she appreciates the generous child support I give; it's to cover her needs too. She reaches out to gently shove my shoulder. "Look at you, Mr. Big Shot Retired Hockey Star with millions."

"If only I had it all," I say it in jest, but the truth is underlying.

I may have the house, the money, the car, and a great kid, but I don't have her.

A car slowly drives by, reminding us that we're in a parking lot.

"I should probably go. Connor's at a friend's having a sleepover, and I promised to meet someone for drinks."

I tense. "Someone," I mutter.

Clearly not quietly enough, as Elle chortles a sound. "Another mom from school. Lena, you know her."

Rolling my eyes, I remind myself that I knew that. Connor makes it a point to tell me which single dads are swimming in close waters to Elle at school pickup, because even my kid tries to light fire under my ass.

I nod once. "Have fun then. I'll text Connor later."

"I know. You always do."

Damn straight. Even when it was hockey season and I was traveling for games, I texted every day.

"My sister will pick him up for camp on Friday since I have a meeting," I remind her.

"Is Violet excited to help out with camp?"

I grin to myself. My sister is in college studying business, so I offered her a summer job to do administration. "Excited may be a stretch, but she is appreciative, I think, and it will be good for her resume."

"I bet. Just warn her that when she picks up Connor, I'll be out back probably bawling my eyes out that he's going to camp. You know how it goes." She grins as she says that.

I scratch my cheek. "Yeah, I do."

"Well, I should go. Text me if I need to pack anything special, I just figured you have the hockey equipment thing sorted out." Her hands make gestures in the air because she seems unsure what to do.

I give her a little salute. "Yes, ma'am."

She playfully swats me in passing, and I pretend to be hurt. But that's us. Incredibly comfortable with each other.

I truly believe it's because I'm her guy, and she won't let anyone else have a slither of the connection that we have. She just doesn't admit it.

I watch her for an extra second as she gets in her car to leave, very much aware that this feeling of wanting her is more apparent now because my life is changing. The rush of hockey is gone, which means that underlying feeling is louder than ever. I have no more distractions.

I also remember every day over the years how I wanted this to be our time.

———

FIVE MINUTES LATER, I'm on the road heading back to Lake Spark, the small town that most people find charming and quaint, but it's been the backdrop to my life for every good and bad memory. Zach Bryan is playing on my stereo while, as per usual, Brielle lingers in my mind.

It's so damn simple.

We haven't been together since before Connor was born.

Then the first years with Connor, we were overwhelmed, or rather Brielle took the brunt of newborn life while I was off playing hockey, and by the time the baby years were gone, and Brielle was on her way with college, then that became the focus. I was at the height of my career, and I barely saw them half of the year. There were also those few years I played in Nashville, only to be traded back to Chicago. It's only in the last year or two that we found a pattern with Connor who's no longer a baby and is fairly easy, but by then, the distance between Brielle and me had been created, except for… those moments.

God, those moments.

Always there but now more frequent.

She would take Connor to a few of my home games and watch me, and the times when we briefly talk after I drop Connor off, and I always swipe her hair behind her ear while her eyes sparkle in a way I swear is only for me.

We have been looming in the inevitable. I knew my days of playing hockey were numbered, and there were no more years of preparing for the Bar for Brielle.

Nothing is in our way except us.

I'm bursting, ready to snap.

Either I find some miracle to keep myself in line or this is where ten years in the making shatters and sends us in a new direction, one where I finally do something about us.

My car speaker informs me I have an incoming call, and I hit the button on my steering wheel.

"Hey, buddy," I say, looking at the caller ID. My neighbor Zand friend Spencer is on the other end. "Shouldn't you be throwing balls or something?" I tease him, as he's a pitcher for the Chicago Bluelights.

"Yeah, yeah, yeah. I just wanted to check in on how it went. We know how you get after seeing Brielle, and I'm not around to offer you a beer since I have a game."

I turn onto the next road. "The usual. Nothing is going to change. We made a promise, and I don't see that changing anytime soon."

Spencer scoffs a sound of disapproval. "You know you can't avoid the obvious forever, right? I mean, hockey is no longer a road-block, that's for sure."

I sigh. "It's complicated." I repeat this mantra on a daily basis, and now I'm telling Spencer.

"Doesn't have to be."

My jaw flexes, as I always tense when I think about the possibilities, partly because it feels so close. "We kind of dug ourselves a hole."

"Then climb on out of it," he urges.

I groan because I've been contemplating what I can do. We have seven and a half more years before Connor is eighteen, which means seven and a half years of limbo with his mother while we are responsible for his life as a minor.

We both see what we want, but we say nothing. What are we waiting for? The cards have changed.

My phone beeps, letting me know that someone else is trying call.

"As thrilling as this conversation is, I have someone else trying to reach me right now. I'll call you later."

He agrees, and I quickly answer the next call. I didn't look at the screen, but as soon I hear the other voice say hello, I know it's Margo.

"Hey, Margo." She's the closest thing to a grandmother I have, a close family friend who may have dated my grandfather before he passed, we're not sure, but they were good friends and he was a widower. She's pushing her early eighties, and although mostly healthy, Illinois winters are too harsh for her arthritis, so she's moving to Florida soon. "To what do I owe the pleasure?" I smile because every conversation with her is upbeat.

"I ran into your neighbor the other day at the general store," she begins.

"Which neighbor?"

"The sporty one."

I laugh. "That doesn't help, I live next to a football coach and a pitcher."

"The one with a kid."

"Again, not narrowing the field. Hudson has a baby and an adult son, and Spencer has a daughter a little younger than Connor." I focus on the road although it's mostly clear up ahead.

"With the young girlfriend or wife."

Blowing out a breath, I chuckle. "Okay, we're going in circles. They both have that, so my guess is that it's Spencer, since April drags him to the grocery store at every chance since she's into cooking."

"Yes! He did mention recipes. Anyhow, he doesn't hold it in, and we chatted about you and how you *maybe* need to rethink your priorities on a few things."

"I'm sure you did." No enthusiasm seeps through my tone.

"The thing is, I have my birthday coming up, and I have a small request."

"I'm not sure what else you would want." She lives a life where money is no issue.

Margo hums a sound. "Are you driving? You may want to pull over…"

And a few minutes later, it clicks how this really is my moment of opportunity.

Because I'm done waiting when it comes to Brielle.

2

BRIELLE

Glancing down at my floral-print dress, I shake my head at myself that I purposely undid one button at the top. Grabbing my glass of Chardonnay, I internally berate myself for the button move, knowing I did it because I was going to see Ford today.

"You seem kind of out of sorts," my friend Lena tells me. "It was a Ford day, wasn't it?"

I notice she smiles to herself as she drags her brown hair to the side. We are sitting at the bar while we wait for our table to be ready. It's a chic enough restaurant, but then again, everything in our small town of Hollows is decorated with perfection, down to the lighting hanging over our heads.

"Yeah, it was. I think it's worse now. I mean, now we don't have another hockey season looming over us." I take a sip.

"And hockey is what kept you two in line? I really don't get you guys." She grabs some nuts from the small bowl.

"It's complicated."

She scoffs a sound at me. "Enlighten me."

"You know the story. I was eighteen, unexpectedly pregnant, and being together wasn't really…" I can't even explain it.

Lena affectionately touches my shoulder. "That was then. You're telling me through the years, the opportunity didn't arise for you and Ford?"

"No." I'm firm on my answer. "For so many reasons. Hockey pretty much ruled the schedule, and I couldn't even imagine being in a relationship around that. I had law school to focus on. Plus, we both tried to move on."

"How did that go for you?" She raises a brow at me with a knowing look.

"Well… I've dated, so has Ford." And it was excruciating on all counts and a big-time failure.

"Yet you are both still alone."

"Doesn't mean we should try being together. We have Connor to think about, it's way too risky." And my heart can't handle another heartbreak with Ford involved.

He already affects me enough; I can't even imagine what it would be like to feel as though our possibilities could become a reality.

"I'm just saying you shouldn't be getting butterflies in your stomach at every parent-teacher meeting and pick-up or drop-off. I see my ex and feel blank, nothing."

I nudge her shoulder with my own. "That's because you now have a hot professor to occupy your life." Her ex-college sweetheart is now her fiancé after reconnecting after her divorce.

She clinks my glass with hers. "That I do. Which also proves the point that second chances are not a fairytale."

I play with the stem of my wine glass, trying to shake Ford out of my head. It's a hard task since summer Ford is an extra dose of handsome. Even all these years later, his skin warms well with the summer light, and he keeps his tall, slim figure in shape, even if he isn't training, and God, his brown eyes complement his matching hair that I know he'll start to grow since it's the summer months.

It's the shape of his shoulders that I like to look at the most. They're broad, but the curves remind me of the way he used to hold me, the nights I would lie in his arms, and the time I leaned against him as I cried for hours.

Lena snaps her fingers in front of me. "Holy cow, you're lost in Ford thoughts again. I can tell by your face; you are dreaming away."

"Ahh, okay, you're right. I guess the meeting today is still fresh in my head. I will be back to normal by the main course, I promise."

She hops off the stool. "I'll hold you to that. Be right back, need a ladies' room stop before dinner."

"Sure. I'll order those mozzarella sticks you promised me." My favorite by far. She offers me a warm smile.

Sighing, I look into my wine glass before taking a drink, thankful that Lena is the designated driver tonight.

"You're too pretty to have a frown on your face." A deep man's voice grabs my attention, and I look up to see a man in a suit at the bar. I didn't notice him before. He looks a few years older than me, and admittedly, he isn't bad on the eyes. I can tell the gel in his hair makes his hair seem darker than it is.

"Oh, just a weekday reflection. Nothing a deep breath and a glass of wine can't fix."

He indicates with his fingers in the air for the barman to come to him. "I know how it goes. Luckily, I use the train rides back from the city to clear my head, but I need a drink before I work on a deposition until the early hours."

"You're a lawyer?"

"I am." He nods to the barman. "A whiskey neat, and the lady will have…"

I shake my head. "Oh, nothing. Thank you. I'm here with a friend."

"Let me know if you change your mind." The corner of his mouth hitches up.

I smile politely. "What kind of law do you practice?"

"Corporate. Does that interest you?" He has a suave grin.

"Actually, I'm sitting the Bar this summer. I finished law school at the university here in Hollows."

"No way." He slides to the free stool next to me. "That's my alma mater. What kind of law do you want to practice?"

"Family law or property, I think."

He thanks the barman for his whiskey. "That area would suit you."

I have a conspicuous grin. "What makes you say that?"

"You have a soft face." He seems proud of his comment. "I'm Brody, by the way."

"Brielle."

"That's a beautiful name." I swear he is investigating my lack of rings on my fingers.

"I hate it sometimes. Nobody knows how to shorten it, Bri or Elle or even Rie."

"All still nice names."

I feel Lena return as she touches my back. "Our table still isn't ready?" She notices that I seem to be in conversation. "Ooh, he's a looker and hopefully single for you. *A distraction,*" she mutters under her breath.

I shoot her a warning glare, but Brody seems to have heard. "I don't want to interrupt your dinner plans, but here…" He reaches into his suit pocket to pull out a card and offers it to me. "Maybe you would like to meet up to discuss law, Brielle?"

Lena nearly chokes, probably because we both know that was not what he means—or maybe he does. My flirting skills are a bit rusty. "Take the card." She utters her suggestion with an overdone smile.

Hesitating for a few seconds, I can't tear my sight off the card, reminding myself that I'm not taken, need a diversion even, and my fingers flex out.

"Or not." Lena yanks my arm out of nowhere. "Ex."

"What?" I look to her and see her eyes are blazing with shock.

"Hockey baby daddy, nine o'clock," Lena whispers.

At the speed of light, my head whips in the direction of the door where I see Ford standing there with a steely look, hands hanging at his sides and forming into fists. His jaw flexes, and judging by the fact he is storming in our direction, then I know he witnessed the last minute.

"Ford?" I'm confused as to why he's here.

He is quick to bring his arm to the back of my chair, as if he needs to make a claim, and his eyes land on Brody who left the card on the bar.

"What are you doing here?" I ask him.

"You know this guy? He's Ford Spears, a hockey legend." Brody seems surprised and looks at me, as if suddenly I'm an alien. "You watch hockey?"

"Oh…" I nervously tuck a strand of hair behind my ear, as that is the connection Brody is making to Ford. "Actually…"

"Elle is the mother of my child which makes me the father of her child, so we *are* connected." Ford flashes a victorious smile, with his eyes seeing red.

Protective Ford is a force not to be messed with, and it's oddly sexy as hell.

Rolling my eyes, I sigh, as I know there is only one way out of this. "Excuse us. It was nice to meet you," I tell Brody who has a neutral look because he seems to recognize that Ford and I have a delicate relationship, to put it mildly.

I grip Ford's shirt sleeve and yank him with me as I head to the door and out onto the sidewalk of Main Street.

Turning to him, I don't know what to think. "What are you doing here, Ford? I thought you were going back to Lake Spark?"

His eyes stay glued to me, not blinking, while his feet stay firmly planted. "I'm clearly saving you from men in suits who are only after one thing."

I scoff in disbelief that this is where our conversation is heading. "Not that it's any of your business but I was waiting for Lena, and he was just making small talk, he's a lawyer."

"A man giving his card to a woman looking like you do in that dress is not making small talk."

"What's wrong with my dress?" I step closer to him and poke his chest with my finger. "You have some nerve."

He is quick to defend. "When it comes to you, yeah, I do."

I could cut the air with a knife. He knows how to break down my defenses because I cherish the idea that he feels he has a claim to me.

I drop my finger and blow out a breath as I gather my thoughts, and I realize that I still don't have my answer. "Why are you here?"

He pinches the bridge of his nose, clearly agitated. "Would you have taken his card?"

I fold my arms over my chest. "What? I don't know. Maybe. To be polite."

It's the truth, maybe he would be the key to forgetting about you.

Ford scrubs his face with his hand. "Don't be polite."

I shake my head because we'll go in a circle. "Answer me as to why you're here."

He tilts his head to the side and licks his lips. "I've been thinking about what Connor's teacher said."

"Oh." My heart pinches.

"I think it's a point we needed to hear, maybe we should be putting in more effort."

"What more can we do?"

"Summer vacation, we should spend time together, the three of us."

My eyes grow big, and my mouth opens but no words come out. I feel my throat go dry, and I swallow. "Like a family trip or something?"

"Something like that. Why don't you come stay at my place after Connor's hockey camp finishes? A little lake time, all three of us." There is so much conviction in his voice that I know he believes his suggestion is a plausible solution.

A gasp escapes me. "You're serious?"

"Very."

I step to the side as I take in the last minute. "I'm not sure it's a good idea."

It's really not.

It would mean more time with Ford, memories of our younger

selves, and the confrontation that Ford is no longer married to hockey.

Ford is quick to grab my arm to draw me back to him, ensuring our eyes meet. "It's an excellent idea. We've had family dinners together, but this is something more and for him. Showing Connor that we are all one team."

"One team." I huff a laugh because this isn't what I imagined calling my dream family.

"He needs this, Elle," he pleads.

"I… I don't know." I'm doubtful. *Very* doubtful.

There is a pause as we both stand there as two former lovers trying to find our road forward.

We both promised to always put Connor first, and that's my inner turmoil at this very second. Do I ignore the warning signs if it means putting Connor first?

"Margo… it's her birthday, and she's asking that you visit." He adds fuel to the fire.

"Ford…" What do I say to that? Margo did so much for us. She stood up for us when nobody else would.

"We owe her."

I blow out a long breath. "I know."

"Is it so bad that we give a little time for Connor and Margo?"

I look at him like he's crazy. "You know it's not just that."

Do I need to spell out all the reasons this is a bad idea? His heated look is reason one, and my jumping heart is reason two.

"Come on, Elle, neither one of us will be able to sleep knowing we could give Connor a week to help ensure he knows all is okay."

"You're right. It's just…"

He catches my gaze and places his hands on my shoulders so I can't escape. "You can have your own room… if you want." Ford's swaggered-mischief ways cause me to smirk, but I still give him wide eyes. "You can study and relax whenever. We can take Connor to places together on your breaks."

I should be more focused when studying, but Ford is presenting an offer to consider.

"I mean, I guess a little family time would be reasonable."

"Then agree."

I puff out a breath. This isn't going to be my smartest move, but it's for Connor. "Okay."

Ford's long finger brushes my cheek. "Good."

My face is blank. "You hunted me down instead of calling?"

He grins. "Of course, you're easier to sway when we're face to face."

It's because I melt a little inside every time I see you.

"Is Lena driving you home or do you need me to drive you?"

My thighs tighten from the thought of being stuck in a car with him. I know he would walk me to my door, and because I hate the idea of him driving back in the dark, then I would offer him the sofa and drive myself crazy.

My voice nearly croaks. "I'm good."

I kick a small pebble on the ground and cross my arms over my chest, shaking my imagination away and focusing on his request for family time. "But Ford, let's just remember that... we had a plan." Agreed on long ago.

He exhales loudly. "Plans can change."

His statement stirs something inside of me, hope mixed with fear.

Gently I tip my head up to acknowledge that I heard him. "Night," I say.

When I walk away, every ounce of me knows he is right. Plans *can* change. But that doesn't mean they should.

By the time I'm back inside, Lena is at our table for dinner, and I join her.

She props her chin up on her hand as she patiently waits for me to explain.

"I just agreed to spend a week of family holiday time at Ford's lake house." I take a long breath.

Lena smirks as she holds up the card from Brody and ceremonially rips it in two. "I don't think we will be needing this then, like *ever.*"

"I'm in way over my head," I say, admitting defeat.

3

BRIELLE

I've been to Ford's house a few times. It's new, or at least he's been working on it for a year or two. For the most part, he handles pick-up and drop-off, so I never have to drive here. When it comes to Connor, Ford does his best to make it easy for me.

Even though Ford gave me the security code for the gate to the cul-de-sac and for his front door, I still hesitate when my hand covers the handle of the front door. Maybe it's better if I press the doorbell.

This large modern lake house is as overbearing as the thought of the week ahead. At least I'll get to stare out onto the lake.

Lake Spark is a small town where people escape the city and enjoy boutiques and cute cafés. It's also the place where teenage Ford and I would escape to his family's lake house and get lost in time. I was seventeen when I first met Ford at a party on the lakeshore, and even though we lived in separate towns and he was in college, we made it work my senior year until the summer that changed our lives.

God, why does he want to live on this lake and be reminded of everything?

It's warm out, so I'm thankful I'm in a black tank top and jean shorts.

The door opens, and Ford greets me with a subtle grin. His white t-shirt and jeans draw me in because it only makes his eyes more intense. "Going to come in or wait for a pinecone or fox to get to you?"

As ridiculous as that sounds, it's completely accurate for Lake Spark. The woods surrounding the lake attract foxes, and apparently, his neighbor has had a few pinecones fall onto her head on a frequent basis.

"Sorry, just taking in my surroundings." He steps back, inviting me in with his arm. "The house looks good with the finishing touches, the outside, I mean." I take in all the changes as I enter his house, and I'm in pure amazement. "Inside too, it seems." Open-plan and everything state of the art.

"Thanks. The designer really picked up the vibe I was going for. Modern yet country, with a bit of local art thrown in. The pool is finished, and Connor loves that."

I keep stepping forward until I reach the floor-to-ceiling windows, and my eyes skip the view of the outside pool and head straight to where I can't tear my eyes away from the deep blue lake with glistening specks from the sunlight. "Beautiful," I say softly.

"Yeah… it is."

The way Ford's tone lingers in the air causes me to glance at him, and I see his eyes are on me, and I wonder if they ever left since I arrived. I don't say anything.

"Uhm, I can get your bags if you want and bring them to the guest room." He scratches his chin which has short stubble because he's a man now; he always was, but now he's older and still we're barely thirty.

"You don't need to do that. I'll get them in a minute."

He tips his head in the direction of the sliding doors. "Come on, the weather is far too great to be inside. Want a drink?"

"No, thank you." I follow him outside and again I'm caught by surprise.

The backyard is a bit more put together than the last time I was here. The pool isn't too big, but there is an inflatable alligator on the water. In the corner of my eye, I see a rope hanging from a willow tree that is an equal distance between the lake and the house. My eyes scan the scene, and I see the dock with a rowboat at the end of it, plus a small speed boat. The patio I'm standing on has new stone tiles and lounge furniture, with a bench swing which causes me to smile. I love bench swings.

"You did a really good job. Connor must love this." It's a lot more than my townhouse, but nothing has been a competition between us. Maybe internally, I've always known that Ford would be the cool dad with over-the-top presents, and I would be the mom with structure, and I'm okay with that. Ford and I don't speak negatively about one another, and I've never had a fear he would outshine me.

"I hope so. I guess we don't need to worry about him sneaking girls into the house or taking off with the boat yet. Give it a few years, though."

I huff a laugh. "If he is anything like his father then we are in serious trouble when he's a teenager."

"Nah, I know every possible hideout in a five-mile radius where he could sneak off to. Good luck to him," Ford proudly states as he tucks his hands into the back pockets of his jeans.

I walk to the bench swing and flop myself down, noticing that Ford follows, sitting beside me. "This is such a difference from a few months ago when you were missing grass. It's now a real home."

He leans over with his elbows on his knees. "Happy you approve."

"You don't need my approval."

"Still, I like it."

Heat spreads through me at the way he says that, and it only intensifies because I can feel the warmth of his body next to me. I swallow some air and resilience.

"What time are we picking up the kiddo from camp?" I do my best to change the topic as I propel us to swing with my foot.

Ford chuckles under his breath, low, deep in his throat, and sinister. "This is where you're going to kill me."

My full attention whips in his direction. "What do you mean?" My foot brakes on the ground to stop the swing's movement.

"We have a slight change of plans." I can tell he is easing me into something.

I stand up and throw my hands to my hips. "Ford, what is going on?"

He looks up at me, with his smirk satisfied and strong. "Technically, when Connor is with me, then I make the parental choices."

"And?" I don't blink, and my tone must tell him that I'm not amused.

Ford slaps his hands on his knees before standing to tower over me. "He enjoyed camp last week, so I signed him up for another week."

"What?" I shriek, fuming.

"It's good for him."

"He's ten!"

"Exactly, which is why he wanted to do another week, and he will stay with Violet."

My jaw drops, and I swear I snarl. "You should have discussed this with me!"

"He is ten miles away. I visited hockey camp several times last week and will go this week to help out. He really wants this." Ford remains calm and collected.

I shake my head. "I can't believe this. How the hell is this supposed to be family time if Connor isn't even here?"

Ford says nothing, and instead crosses his arms and stares at the ground before he peers up at me with his smirk never fading. "Connor not being here is kind of the point."

"For what?" My voice cracks.

"Come on." Ford begins to walk toward the dock, and I trail behind, marching in pure rage, demanding answers.

"Calm down, Elle, we can use the next few days to talk and come up with a new schedule."

"Are you kidding me? I'm not staying here alone with you!"

I continue to follow him in tow as he grabs the rope from the dock post. "I think you are. Margo is expecting us tomorrow."

"You had this planned, didn't you? You could have called me, but you waited until I was here to tell me this change of plan." He is so unbelievable.

"Relax. You can still study for the Bar, enjoy the lake, wear that bikini you probably packed or no bikini at all, and at the end of the week, we can pick up Connor." Ford is completely satisfied with this situation as he calmly brings the rope to the rowboat.

My eyes dance between the boat and his hand holding the rope. "So now I'm going to be here for two weeks?" This week and another week with Connor.

"Oh, so you are staying then?" His smug look causes movement below my navel.

This is very bad.

Everything about this situation is a red flag. Ford and I have never been alone together overnight without Connor around. We always have safety blocks between us—our son, hockey games, and parent meetings. It's never been Ford and me alone in a gorgeous lake house, let alone the lake where we created a child.

I comb my hands through my hair and pull slightly as I pace a few steps back and forth, completely ready to scream.

"Who the hell does this? This is crazy."

He ignores me. "Are you joining me?" Ford holds up the rope in the air, and all he has to do is throw the rope in the boat and row off.

"Is this a joke?"

"No. Although I do hope you put sunblock on, it's a warm one out here." It's like he is oblivious to my rage.

Fuck me, he isn't flinching, he is completely in his winning mindset. I should march right back to my car and leave, but he's right. Margo is expecting us tomorrow, and I don't want to let her down, especially if she asked for me.

My heart races, and I debate what to say or do. My feet shuffle a step forward then back, but ultimately, an inner power beyond my train of thought makes me move to the rowboat.

Call it curiosity, but I'm too seething to drive anywhere anyhow, so I let my hand land in his warm offered palm to help me into the boat.

The moment I sit on the seat, I know this must be the shock kicking in for being tricked. No ounce of my normal intelligence would agree to this.

When Ford steps into the boat, causing it to wobble on the water, I only watch as he sits down, slides his sunglasses on, and his muscled arms flex as he begins to row.

Do. Not. Stare. At his biceps. Just don't do it, Brielle.

I rip my eyes away from facing him and see water around us. How did I manage to get in a boat with him? It's like a curse was cast on me.

"Happy you decided to take a roll on my boat." He fails at suppressing his smile.

I fold my arms over my chest and sulk, refusing to speak.

"This is going to be a quiet ride if you aren't going to talk. But that's okay, I need you to listen anyway." He continues to row.

"I never get angry at you, but I might right now," I declare.

His lips quirk out. "Oh, I'm sure you will."

"And you seem happy about that."

He shrugs a shoulder. "You're cute when you're mad."

I nearly growl in aggravation. "Unbelievable. You have completely crossed a line."

"You have no idea." His cocky smirk doesn't fade.

So frustrating.

Ford slows down his rowing until we're floating. I look around to see we are far enough away from the dock that it would be a bit of a swim back.

"Why are we stopping?" I hear the caution in my voice.

"We're enjoying the view." His eyes don't leave me. "Want a water or something? I packed some drinks in the box over there."

I look over my shoulder and then do a double take when I see a little cooler. Shit, he really planned this.

"How considerate of you to trap me in this situation and provide beverages," I say, sarcastic. But *I am* a little parched, so I might as well enjoy a drink. I lean back and twist my body to reach for a water bottle from the cooler.

"No, considerate would be ensuring you can't escape so you can mull over something."

Turning around to face him, I drop the water bottle instantly as my body freezes.

Because Ford is leaning back against the bow, legs stretched out into the middle of the boat and one arm resting behind his head as he is lying in a relaxed pose, except that a small open velvet box is on display in his hand, with a ring sparkling in the sunlight.

"What is that?" I grind out.

"Your engagement ring, Elle."

Oh no.

This is not happening.

He is seriously doing it.

He's on a mission to break our promise.

FORD

The rain is drowning out the sound of Brielle's sobs as we sit in my car in a parking lot. Not being able to hear her sniffles doesn't offer any relief, though. Just looking at her and my heart breaks, and I already thought it shattered forty minutes ago when I picked her up.

My hand finds her soaked cheek, and I cradle her face, bringing her gaze to meet my eyes.

"I can't," she whispers again. "I can't do it."

I established that the moment I saw her this morning when she got in my car, and when I drove, I didn't push it, but I needed to hear her say it.

Now she has.

I nod once in understanding. "Then we don't. I promised you that the choice is yours."

"But…"

I wipe away a fresh tear with the pad of my thumb. "No buts," I assure her.

"They all think I'm not keeping the baby."

That's what our parents want. They gave us an ultimatum.

"Fuck what they think."

Her hand covers my own against her cheek. "It's not that easy."

Blowing out a breath, I know she's right. In this moment, I hate myself. It's my fault that she's eighteen and pregnant. She should be heading off to college; instead, she is dealing with this.

"I know." I sigh.

"I'm ruining our lives."

I react quickly to her statement. I bring my other hand to frame her face, and I hold her firm.

"Listen to me, you are not. We are in this together. Your decision is my decision. This isn't what we planned, not now, but it doesn't matter. You and I are now connected for life, and that ain't half bad." I'm barely hanging on but do my best to bring a positive.

Her eyes stay locked on me. "We're going to be parents," she laments.

"In around seven months, yes," I remind her, and the corner of my mouth attempts to smile, but I struggle and can't.

This is the girl I love, whose smile melts me more every time. It feels like yesterday I met her at a party on the lakeshore. Our families were in Lake Spark for the weekend, as they often are, since my family has a weekend house here. I met Brielle at a friend's party. She was wearing a light pink sweater that fell off her shoulder, and every time our eyes met, I was drawn to her a little more. Then, there around the bonfire, I made my move and asked her if she liked ice. She laughed in my face because she thought the next thing I would say is that I was a hockey player. She went hysterical and couldn't stop grinning when I, indeed, confirmed that I was in my first year of college playing hockey.

But our talk turned into hours. I gave her my hoodie by the end of the night, and over the weeks and months that followed, she was mine, and most weekends we would see one another. We could never keep our hands off each other, and every chance we had, we would lie on the shore late into the night or take the boat out to the secret lagoon.

I love her.

There isn't anything I wouldn't do for her. I see her in my future, watching my games, and one day, when I'm making millions, I'll give her anything she wants.

Right now, she wants this.

And I do too.

"We'll tell our parents together that we changed our minds," I breathe out.

I see the fear in her eyes.

For weeks, since the moment Brielle told me she thought she was pregnant and we took a test, we've been going back and forth over what to do. We told our parents together that Brielle was pregnant. They all made it clear what they thought the solution was, which is why we are sitting here in a parking lot for an appointment that we promised we would make.

As much as she's eighteen and I'm near twenty, we are barely adults.

I'm in the draft for pro hockey, but I haven't signed a contract yet, and Elle is supposed to start college in a few weeks.

She sits back, causing my hands to drop from her face. She rests her head against the seat but turns to pin her eyes on me.

"Margo convinced them to let us have another option," I repeat the facts.

Margo heard our parents yelling in the living room after a summer BBQ where we thought was the opportunity to tell them. Brielle's parents were angry that I ruined their daughter's future of becoming a lawyer, reminding my parents that their only child is barely eighteen, and my father was worried my future as a pro athlete would be no more and that my girlfriend is ruining my focus on the sport, not to mention the example I'm setting for my little sister. My mother didn't have much opinion since we barely see her after my parents divorced.

Margo calmed everyone down and convinced them to be more supportive, but our parents' version of supportive is meeting us only halfway.

And this is where I try to suppress my own tears.

Because our other option should be easy, but it's not, as it means I don't have Brielle.

"There must be another way." Her voice cracks.

I interlace our fingers on the middle console of my car, and my eyes can't glance away from her fingers. In my world, I would ask her to marry me.

I swallow, knowing if I want to support her right now that I have to be the logical one. "I think we know it's the only way, Elle."

Already, I feel the pain in my throat from saying those words. She continues to cry, but I have to highlight the obvious. "You'll still go to college but will have time if you need it, your parents will help raise the baby."

"You'll go pro in hockey as planned."

"Yeah… and we won't be together."

Because that's the deal.

Her parents will still pay for her college, and my parents will help to financially support the baby until I have high earnings, as long as Brielle and I follow our plans and aren't a distraction to one another. They don't want us in a relationship because they think we are dealing with enough, and our boundaries should be clear.

I wanted to scream that they could all forget it, but I'm not yet a star player who can give us the financial means, and I won't let Brielle give up on her dream of becoming a lawyer. I'll be so busy with hockey training and games for half the year, and I know it's not just financial, she needs help with raising the baby and support that I can't give when I'm on the road, but her parents can.

"It's for the best. We get to make something of ourselves instead of struggling with a newborn. It's a long road to becoming a lawyer, and I won't let you miss the opportunity to follow that path."

She nods in understanding.

The sound of the rain is somewhat calming at this moment.

"You can focus on your career. You're destined to be MVP. I guess you wouldn't be around much anyways for a relationship, plus balancing a child. It's probably for the best that we do this." I only half believe the words she just said.

"You know that's bullshit, although slightly practical." I scoff a sound. "Maybe the plan can change one day."

"Ford," she says my name with pure reverence.

I lean into her, our foreheads touching because I need her close. "A hockey career is only so long. Maybe when you finish college and I—"

She interrupts by slamming her long finger against my lips. "Don't. We'll drive ourselves crazy wondering if or when we might have a chance to be together again. I'll go crazy with that in the back of my head. You will too."

I kiss her finger away. "I want to believe there is more for us."

"Me too. But we have a child to think about, and we can't play around with trying to maybe work somewhere along the road. That's not fair to him or her. It would be confusing for all of us."

I can't even argue with that. "We'll both accomplish everything we wanted before we got pregnant. Even if this feels so wrong, yet I know it's right." I despise this, I'll never forget this moment.

"We're not being selfish, I guess that's what parents are supposed to do. We are putting this baby first. Our focus is trying to balance the baby and the career paths that will ensure they have a good future."

Our foreheads connect again, and I can taste a salty tear from her skin when I nip her nose with my lips. "It may be co-parenting and careers now, but we'll show them, Elle, and one day we can have it all."

"I can't think like that. My heart is already breaking, and I can't do this with the thought that maybe one day you will fix it. I'm protecting my heart. I need to be strong for this baby."

She's right. It's not fair to either of us to always be wondering. It's better to have no blurred lines on our plan forward. We have a kid to think about.

Brielle glances out the window then back to me. Her piercing gaze has me concerned because it strikes me in my heart. "I need you to know that I love you. That I want you involved with this little girl or boy's life. You'll be a great dad. But I think for both of our sanities, we accept that our only option is this, being apart." Her voice cracks. "Waiting for a moment when maybe we have a chance to make this work for the three of us will be painful, and that's not healthy for us."

I sink into the driver's seat. "We'll do this as two people who are putting our child first." I turn my key to start the car. "Let's go for a drive, we need some time before we talk to our parents."

She buckles her belt, and I get us on the road. A cruel twist of fate, the Verve Pipe's "The Freshman" comes on the radio, which is only fitting in this moment.

I'm at a total loss for what to feel right now. We're going to have a baby that I'm thankful for, but I wish the circumstances were more giving for us all.

We drive in silence for what feels like hours, but it's been maybe thirty minutes when I pull off the side of the road before a forest preserve.

Turning the engine off, I know exactly what to do right now at least.

"Come on, let's go to the back of the car."

She doesn't question me. We both get out of the car and get into the back. I bring her to my chest to hold, kissing her forehead. She wraps her arms around my middle, squeezing tight.

"I love you, Elle. Always will," I whisper.

"I do too, which is why this is hard." She glances up at me, and we kiss softly.

This is our last hour together like this, and we know it.

"I need you to promise me that we will put the baby first. Our hearts know the deal, and we accept that. It's the only way we can move forward with this. We eliminate the what-ifs and do exactly what this baby needs. Can we promise that?" she pleads softly.

I'm beginning to feel that her fear of a broken heart runs deeper than I ever imagined, and she has no idea my heart broke already an hour ago. Even if I have no intention of letting her go, right now she needs me to be the strong one. She probably barely slept last night, and her body is changing. Hell, it's her life that is about to be upended more than mine. I get my hockey career, and she will be delivering a baby when she should be at a lecture. I have to do right by her. If she wants me to promise, then I have no other option, it's the best way to support her.

And if I'm being honest with myself, I would go insane waiting for us. Doesn't mean the idea of a different path won't be lingering inside me somewhere.

She looks exhausted, and with her face puffy from her crying, her eyes are so innocent and vulnerable. I kiss her forehead, nose, cheek, jaw, before placing a firm kiss against her mouth.

"I promise," I murmur against her lips, and she sighs with what might be relief, sinking deeper into my arms.

A man can tell a lie if his intentions are pure, right?

5

FORD

I 've never forgotten that day. I'm sure we both think about it at some point between waking up and falling asleep, and here we are ten years later.

I can tell she wants to kill me. But she won't. Brielle is the type of woman who makes you pull over to save a squirrel. Except, right now? Well, she may just flip.

Her eyes don't tear away from the ring in the box that I'm holding in my hand.

This is unconventional, I know, but the opportunity has arisen.

"What the hell, Ford? Why is there a ring in your hand?" She quickly looks around the quiet lake, then her sight lands back on the ring before darting up to meet my eyes which are dead serious. "Unbelievable," she whispers. "You trapped me in the middle of the lake so I can't escape."

"Maybe." I smirk. "Get comfortable, we need to talk."

I've been thinking about how I want this all to play out since I saw her the other week. Hell, this whole situation has been years in the making.

My feelings for her have always been constant, and I've done my best to keep the promise I made to her, but now I've hit my breaking point, and I'm not going to let us keep simmering under the surface.

"The r-ring, why?" she stammers softly.

I sit up and close the box then toss it between my palms, examining it. "Okay, so here's the deal. Tomorrow Margo is expecting us, and she might be under the impression that you and are back together—"

"What?" she nearly spits out.

My shoulder slants up toward my ear. "She hasn't been feeling her best lately, and she's anxious about her move," I remind her.

"I know, that's why I promised to see her, but how does this—" she motions between us "—come into play."

"She mentioned on the phone that she always wished to see us together and hoped it would be soon." It's the plain truth.

Brielle hums a sound before leaning back on the boat to get more comfortable on the slab of a seat. "Sounds like something she would say." A gentle smile of fondness displays on her lips. "She always sends me a Christmas card, not so subtly mentioning how Connor is the perfect image of two parents' love." She looks up at me. "But how does a ring come into it?"

I inhale a deep breath because maybe she will find this humorous… or not. "She told me her birthday wish, and it blurted out of my mouth that she didn't need to wait."

Brielle's beautiful mouth gapes open. "You lied to her?"

"Is it a lie? It will make her happy."

She runs her fingers through her hair. "Ford, you realize by lunchtime everyone else will think we are back together, and that eventually affects Connor."

I have thought every scenario through. How would I not? Through the years, I've created a whole damn playbook of how our situation could go.

"She only really talks to Violet these days, and I'm sure my sister would get behind this to safeguard that Margo has an easy few weeks ahead. Connor wouldn't find out." Because by the time he does, then stage two of my plan will be in effect.

Brielle shakes her head slightly. "And let me guess, you didn't just lie that we are back together, you upped it and said we're engaged?"

Now I have to grin. "You know me so well."

She huffs out a breath and crosses her arms over her chest, and she pretends to be furious, but after a few seconds, the faintest of entertained smiles forms on her mouth that she desperately tries to suppress.

But only for a second, as disapproval returns to her look.

"I don't know, Ford. This is… not wise."

I lean forward to scoop up her hand and hold it between my palms. The sudden contact startles her, mostly because it's an electric shock between us, a current still strong, maybe more intense as time goes on.

"Margo is like a grandmother to me, always on our side, and when she told me on the phone that she really had hoped to see us back together before her time comes, because yeah, she got a little dramatic on the age front, then it just seemed like the right thing to do." It's the truth, although it's only the tip of the iceberg for what I have planned.

Brielle licks her lips, debating. "I know where you're coming from, I just…"

I duck my head down, then I peer up to catch her sight. "Don't trust us faking it for a day?"

Her lips roll in, and she doesn't answer, but her eyes say enough. She doesn't trust us.

"You know what I think?" I prod.

"What?"

"We've been able to avoid the obvious for years because we had things to keep us on a path. My hockey career, your education, Connor… but now hockey is no longer a factor, and you finished college and law school." I notice her chest moving up and down, and I wonder if she knows what's coming. "It's our time to re-evaluate."

She is quick to sit back, her hands falling out of my grasp. "Don't! Don't do this. You promised." She's enraged.

My body stiffens and shoulders straighten because it's time to lay down some hard truths as the sun warms us and the water glistens around us.

"We both are exactly where we started." Wanting each other.

She shakes her head, wishing not to listen, but damn, I know she believes in what I'm saying.

Energy shoots to my heart. I know relief is coming because I'm sharing it all. "We are still waiting. Fuck, we tried over the years to move on. Kept ourselves busy, we tried to find other people, and it always failed because it's not us, and Christ, the number of times I wanted to kiss you. This isn't new, you're thinking this too."

"Ford, it's true, hockey and becoming a lawyer are no longer our blockers, but we still have Connor to think about. I would hate myself if you and I were to try and it didn't work out, he would be crushed."

I stand up in a flash with a bitter laugh. "Do you really think we wouldn't work out? Are you crazy?"

She points a finger at me, rising from her seat. "Are *you*? You are the one who brought me to the middle of a lake to have this talk."

My hands come out to my sides, and I have a cheeky smile. "It's a great play. We're talking."

"On the lake where we probably conceived our son," she shrieks.

I hook my finger and nudge her cheek, purely entertained with her comment. "Ah, so that memory has flashed in your mind while we're out here."

She gives me a death glare and wags her finger at me. "Don't even." Her nostrils flare, and she wraps her arms around her body. Our eyes dance as we watch each other, standing in a rowboat on the lake.

Here is my chance. I'm throwing it all out there. "Stay the week with me and let's be everything we wanted, give us this. One week, and then you can keep the ring or say we fulfilled our curiosity."

Her jaw drops, and she moves to slam her hands against my chest, but she rocks the boat in the process. We both wobble, and I fall back to sitting against my propped hands, with my legs splayed out.

"Whoa!" She loses her balance, and her body lands right on top of me.

I have to smirk at fate giving us a hand. "See? Already in my arms."

Brielle doesn't move; instead, her nose tips up, and our mouths are dangerously close. I feel the magnetic connection between our bodies. It's taking willpower beyond my known ability not to slam my lips onto hers.

I rake my fingers through her hair to cradle the back of her head. "Think about it, but I know you already feel your answer. I see it in your eyes, and I feel your heart racing."

There is a glint in her eyes, they've already given me the answer I want to know. But my ears are waiting for her words.

She digs her fingers into the front of my t-shirt, and lucky me, her leg willingly adjusts so it's hooked over my thigh.

It's so perfectly clear to me. I've never seen her in a different light because she's always been mine.

"Ford," she pleads. "We are playing with fire."

"I'd burn the earth down if it means we get a chance." It comes out simply as my eyes stay fixed on her mouth.

I lean in to nuzzle my nose into her hair that smells of papaya.

"Row us back, Ford."

"You haven't answered."

"I can't think when we're like this," she says honestly.

"Because your body knows what it wants."

She moves to return to sitting on her spot. She's either burning from the sun or blushing, and I choose to go with the second option.

Brielle straightens her hair and avoids looking at me. "Row us back, please. I really need some space right now."

Blowing out a breath, I grab the oars. "Only if you promise not to get in your car and leave."

"I won't. Either way, I promised to see Margo tomorrow."

I begin to row and internally remind myself that I was voted

MVP for four seasons straight because I'm always determined to win. And Brielle Dawson? She's the only goal I've ever wanted.

————

BRIELLE IS quick to march along the dock straight into the house. I let her go because I know when not to press.

Tying the boat up, I notice in the corner of my eye my neighbors Hudson and Spencer. Hudson is in his forties, looks like he drinks age-defying water, and is the head football coach for the Chicago Winds, and Spencer is home for a quick break from his baseball season because he has grand plans for his girlfriend.

I wave to them and meet them halfway at the point where the dock ends. Hudson has his baby girl Grace in a carrier, and she's staring at me, arms and legs out like a starfish.

Spencer is quick to pat my shoulder. "Hey, man, Brielle is here?" he asks.

"Yeah."

"I thought Connor was at camp," Hudson asks.

Spencer chuckles humorously. "He is. But Ford here has a scheme he's playing out."

Hudson looks between us. "Do explain."

I rub a hand across my jaw. "Brielle is staying here… we are working out a few things."

"Really? That's great." Hudson is enthusiastic.

Spencer gives him a blank look. "He tricked her into coming here, letting her think Connor would be here."

Hudson shoots his gaze to me. "Ooh, that's… not good?" It sounds like he doubts what he should think.

In this moment, I think I regret telling Spencer my initial plan the other day. Coincidentally, we went ring shopping together. While I was initially there to help him pick a ring for his girlfriend April, I might have picked one out myself that he doesn't know about.

"Ready for your big night?" I change the subject.

Spencer grins, ridiculously happy. "Completely. I got Hudson's approval."

Hudson throws an arm around Spencer. "He's going to marry my niece. He had to go through the checklist."

"She still needs to say yes," Spencer reminds Hudson.

"I doubt a no is coming your way," I assure Spencer. "Enjoy tonight." He has a big proposal planned.

Spencer tips his sunglasses down his nose to assess me. "Is there something you're not telling us?"

Hudson watches as he bounces the baby against his chest.

"It's fine. I'm just…"

"Nervous your plan is going to fail?" Spencer finishes my sentence.

I tip my head side to side in contemplation. "Nah, we've been waiting for this."

Just then Brielle storms out my back door, breaking all our attention, and she stomps in her fast stride all the way to me, her face slightly fuming.

"Give me the box," she demands, holding out her palm.

I've never seen her so determined and buzzed with frustration, ridiculously sexy, and I also know not to deny her anything.

My hand fumbles into my pocket to pull out the box, and I quickly hand it to her. She grumbles and pivots so her back is to me.

She isn't fazed by my neighbors and friends since she has met them before. She's even worked for Hudson's sister at her legal firm. "Hi, Spencer. Hi, Hudson. Oh, Gracie is getting so big," she greets them before walking away like everything is dandy.

"Is that a yes?" I call out.

"I'm thinking," she yells back and disappears into the house.

It causes me to smile softly to myself in accomplishment.

"What the fuck? Was that an engagement ring box?" Spencer tries to grasp what just happened.

I bring a hand to the back of my head. "Yeah," I reply in a mesmerized tone.

"Uh, something you want to share?" Hudson asks.

"Nah, just upped the stakes a little. We're seeing Margo tomorrow, and she kind of thinks we're engaged."

"Let me guess, because you told her that," Spencer adds.

Hudson looks at me like I'm crazy. "What kind of neighbors do I live next to?"

"Don't worry, it won't be a fake engagement for long." I can't stop staring at my house where Brielle is inside probably pacing.

"Listen, as the older and wiser one of you two, let me offer some advice. It's only as complicated as you make it. Do yourselves a favor… don't make it complicated," Hudson lectures.

I glance at him as I cross my arms over my chest. "It's not complicated if we were always on a path back to one another."

"You have a kid." His tone is serious.

"And that's not the reason I want her, just a bonus," I admit out loud.

Spencer hisses a breath. "Ford, buddy, I am rooting for you both. I mean, it's obvious that you two are kind of hung up on each other. Just don't… I don't know… ruin an already good thing. You both co-parent so well. Now you're taking risks. You're taking a big chance here; don't pressure her or it could ruin everything."

I rub my face with my hands. "I've been patient long enough, and I finally have her here right here under my roof, alone time, me and her. I don't know how to do anything else right now."

"Yeah, I can tell. You look like a distressed retriever looking for his ball," Spencer informs me.

Hudson wobbles back and forth for the baby who is cooing and staring at me in wonder. "I get it, I really do. We've all been crazed by the women of our lives. There is no backing down, and I think you owe it to yourselves to figure it out."

"Thank you."

Spencer snorts a laugh. "I completely want status updates this week."

"I'm hoping to be too occupied for that."

Hudson chuckles at my reply. "By the looks of it from a few

minutes ago, you may need to work a little extra hard. Brielle is in quite a state."

Rubbing the back of my neck, I smile tightly. "Oh, I know. But it just means she is contemplating." For some reason, I'm at ease; everything feels promising, or maybe I'm just optimistic.

But we are at the edge of our cliff, and I won't let us fall. Well, metaphorically, because figuratively I have every intention that we fall onto my mattress.

"Well, we'll let you head into your house of tension." Spencer waves two fingers in the air and begins to head off.

Hudson takes Gracie's little chubby arm and waves it in the air. "Good luck."

I wave them all off then take a moment to prepare myself. Blowing out a breath, I wonder for a second if I'm being selfish in this scenario.

I'm not. Because I'm only satisfied if Brielle is happy.

That means this plan can only go one way, which is why my feet move in the direction of the back door. I've always been supportive, gentle, and respectful of our dynamic.

But I'm throwing in the towel because persistence is key.

BRIELLE

Back and forth.

That's all I have been doing for the past few minutes, tossing the small black box between my fingers.

Enraged is what I should feel. Ford tricked me and then dropped a bombshell proposition.

But, well, I'm not that furious. Or am I?

I stormed upstairs to one of the spare bedrooms. I'm growing slightly irritated that the designer did a good job, I can't deny that. This room is fresh with white, except for one accent wall of turquoise with matching throw pillows on the white bed.

I flop onto the mattress, blow out a long breath, and am thankful that Ford is outside with Hudson and Spencer, as it buys me time. I drop the ring box onto the mattress so I can pull out my phone which barely fits in my back pocket. Scrolling the screen, I hit Lena's name for a video call.

She picks up after two rings.

"Hey! How's the getaway?" She smiles, and it looks like she's at her desk in her home office, as her hand seems busy with a computer mouse.

"Something has happened. Something bad. Like, *really* bad."

Lena sits up and abandons the mouse. "Is everyone okay? Connor?"

"Connor is fine. Probably having a great time. Long story short, but Connor isn't here."

"What?"

"Ford extended his camp for another week, and he is staying with his aunt. As much as I want to strangle Ford for doing that without consulting me, I know that Connor wanted to. Anyway, that is the least of our worries."

"How so? Ford completely made a parenting decision without you."

I shake off the notion. "It's Ford, he would never do anything he thought wasn't in Connor's interests, and besides, the camp is run by Ford's team, and he helps out, so he can check in on Connor a few times this week."

"You are far more chill than I would be."

"That would be because it's only the icing on the cake." I hold up my finger to pause her while Lena looks at me in anticipation. "Ford wants me to stay here this week… to… *reevaluate* our situation."

Her eyes grow big. "Didn't see that coming." She brings her fingers to her chin in contemplation. "Or did I? Hmmm… yeah, saw it coming." Lena grabs her water bottle for a drink.

"He got me an engagement ring."

She spits out her water. "Huh?"

I have to smile to myself because it's such a Ford thing to do, go a step too far if he knows it will make me smile. "I mean, it's kind of for pretend. He just wants to make Margo happy." Except I saw the conviction in Ford's eyes, and the ring feels like part of his long game.

"Okay, so what are you doing then? I mean, why didn't you get back in your car and drive back to Hollows?"

"I promised I would see Margo tomorrow."

"And tonight you will just…" She draws it out.

I sigh and roll to my back. "That's the problem. I'm under the same roof as Ford, and he threw one hell of an offer at me. I've been programmed to ignore whatever we left behind, but..."

A sly smile forms on Lena's mouth. "Brielle, I don't think you ever left behind the connection between you and Ford."

"Doesn't mean I should jump into bed with him."

"Is that what he's expecting?"

"I mean, he didn't say it as such, but I just kind of—"

Lena interrupts. "Assumed, because your subconscious has a fantasy it wants to play out."

I flop like a pancake to my stomach and attempt to defend my thoughts. "Do not judge me for noticing he has aged well. I mean, he literally has women throwing themselves at him, I would be blind to pretend otherwise."

She chuckles at me. "It's okay."

"No, it's not. What if we crash and burn again? It's taken ten years to get over him."

"You never got over him," she corrects me.

Lena is keeping me in check, damn it.

"This isn't some guy who I lost my virginity to and then see him again at a high school reunion. It's Ford. He's the father of our child, the man I see on a regular basis."

"He could also be the man whom you are missing an opportunity with."

I snort a sound because that's the joke of life on me. "I think that's what scares me the most. What if it's everything I imagined and then some? It'll be a reminder that for the last ten years I didn't have that."

Lena clicks her tongue and smacks her lips out then back. "Good thing we don't go back in time then, we go forward."

I think for a few seconds. "Maybe. Anyhow, I should go. I have to deal with this." I hold up the ring box.

"You're going to wear it?"

"Haven't even opened the box, only stared at it."

"Keep me posted, but I am going to assume if I need to send you a letter that your address is in Lake Spark for the coming week, perhaps eternity." She flashes her eyes at me.

I don't answer, and we say goodbye.

Tossing the box onto the bed, I decide I can't hide in here forever. Walking out of the room and into the hall, the corner of my mouth curls up when I see Connor's room.

Walking to the door of his bedroom, I stand in awe. It's not over the top, nor too childish. There is a double bed with a navy-blue duvet, hockey sticks are hanging on the wall, and there is a desk with a globe and shelf of books. I know there isn't a game system here, partly because Ford and I agreed on no games or computers in Connor's bedroom, and also, I *know* Ford wants the game console in the living room because he loves to play just as much as Connor.

Most of all, I notice that this room is perfect because Connor is no longer a little child. Soon he will be heading into pre-teen life, then worse, the teenage years. It also means he is more aware, and we can talk in a more transparent way with our son. Ah hell, Connor would be on to Ford and me in a heartbeat, even if he doesn't tell us.

And I can't figure out if that's a positive or negative. Better yet, why am I contemplating Ford's offer?

"You approve?" Ford's voice startles me. His hands settle on my shoulders to assure me that all is okay, or at least in this room. Everything else is still a toss-up. "Sorry, didn't mean to scare you."

I slowly turn and come face to face with Ford. "It's okay, just admiring the room. You really made it a home."

"Thanks. Ten is a hard age to decorate for. I'm lucky I hired a designer."

I nod once, unsure why I'm now calm when not long ago my body was riled. Now I'm just warm and overwhelmed because his eyes are on me, dipping down to stare at my mouth. I step back into the hall to get us out of Connor's room; I don't want to taint his space with the discussion that's about to happen.

But no words come out of my mouth. Instead, I stand there with my hands in my back pockets, and I try to avoid staring into Ford's eyes.

"Have you thought about it?"

Quickly, I glance up and then back down. "There is nothing to think about. It's ridiculous."

I do my best to escape, and I head straight for the stairs, but Ford grabs my arm so I don't get far. In fact, I'm now closer.

To him.

His breath.

His scent.

Those eyes that hold me every single time.

"It's not. Elle, we've been doing a damn good job with keeping our promise, but only on the surface."

My eyes shoot up to lock with his because he pretty much nailed down my theory too.

"It doesn't mean that we should have a week of fun to bury our curiosity."

Ford is quick to step forward. Our mouths are now inches apart, and he hasn't let my arm go. "I'm not talking about fun. This is a little more. We have some truths to tell and lost time to make up for. Fun is what you do when there's no history, no future. You and I already have half of that."

"We also have parenting together."

"And we're more than just parents. We deserve more," he is quick to counter. I shake my head gently, and Ford hooks his finger under my chin, guiding my gaze to him. "Let me prove to you that we can have it all. It's our time."

"No pressure or anything," I retort.

It earns me a grin from Ford. "I've already taken the step to possibly make this fucking awkward between us because I've made it clear what I want to try. So you might as well make the leap."

"It's a big leap." I stare blankly at him, wondering why my body still feels so incredibly comfortable in this situation.

"I don't do small for *anything*." The innuendo is there, and I snort a laugh.

He nuzzles his nose against mine as he lets my arm go and instead opts to rest his hand on my waist.

"Oh, I know. You got a ring," I reply.

"Which you haven't given back. You're considering this week." His voice goes soft and raspy.

"So many thoughts are floating in my head. How convenient is the timing, huh? Only when we both seem to have gotten what we wanted."

"It's not like I'm bored and thought 'oh let me fuck up my co-parenting arrangement with the only woman I ever want to share kids with.' It's that I know you've almost achieved your goals and my career is over. Everything that caused that promise is no longer a trigger for us to pretend that we were able to move on."

We are one and the same. His words could literally fall off my tongue except I'm not brave enough to speak them. Lucky for us, Ford woke up determined today.

I lean my head to the side, attempting to get an extra inch or two between us, although the damage has already been done. I'm completely affected by this man.

On second thought, I slant my head back to him and bring my palms to his face, as if I'm going to be bold and kiss him.

He's here for it, as his hand on my side yanks me tightly to his body.

My heart races because I've played this scene in my head a million times. I've imagined what it would be like, I've secretly hoped for it.

I trace his stubbled jawline with my lips, merely a touch but enough to get the oxytocin from this man that I think my body may need to survive. It's why I always allow the gentle touch here or there from Ford.

Closer.

So close.

Nearly the end.

But the moment our lips brush, the feeling is too intense.

I step back, aware that crossing the line with Ford will be a flame that was dimmed but now will be rekindled.

"I think tonight I'm going to take it easy. Study a bit for the Bar."

Even avoiding looking at him, I know he's disappointed. "I can throw some steaks on the grill or order a pizza."

I swallow the chance that I let slip away. "I'm not that hungry."

"Okay. Well..."

"I'll see you in the morning for Margo's."

"Will you play along for Margo?"

I touch my hair nervously. "I'll sleep on it."

Ford throws his hands up in surrender. "That's all I can ask. If you need anything, then just find me. My bedroom door will be open."

My eyes gawk at him in a double take.

He quickly pinches my cheek on the way by. "Take that how you want. All options are on the table, but just remember, I don't sleep with a shirt on," he calls out in passing.

———

AFTER ATTEMPTING TO STUDY, exchanging some texts with my son, and changing into pajamas before braiding my hair, I tried to sleep. An epic fail, as I tossed and turned for a good hour.

It's the middle of the night when I venture downstairs for a drink. The kitchen is big and should be filled with family meals and kids. I shake my head when I catch myself daydreaming. I'm relieved to find myself alone in the kitchen.

Yet disappointed at the same time.

By the time I'm back upstairs, I slow my steps in the hallway, well aware that Ford's bedroom is a magnetic pull, and he wasn't lying about keeping the door open.

I can't help myself, and I stop to check out the view of Ford sleeping. He's a stomach sleeper, so I only see his bare back under the stream of light from the hallway. He looks peaceful. At least one of us can sleep tonight.

God, I could watch him like this for hours. After I had Connor, I did a few times. Sometimes when Connor was a baby and would sleep on Ford's chest, and another time quite recently. Except, I don't think Ford knows. He was resting in the hospital after a game where he yet again got hit too hard.

I won't go down memory lane, I repeat to myself.

I step to the side but don't get far.

"You know you can come under my covers, and I promise to be a gentleman," Ford speaks in a drowsy tone.

I roll my eyes, amused, and walk into his room. "Pretending to sleep?" I plant my hands on my hips.

Ford rolls to his back and slides up the bed against the backboard.

Holy hell, this view is weakening any shred of resolve between my legs.

His biceps are just ridiculously toned but not too bulky, and bare-chest Ford is always a winner too.

He holds open his duvet. "Come on, it's cold."

"It's summer."

"And you're cold." His eyes drop down to my chest, and I look to realize my nipples are hard underneath my tank top. I bring my arms up to cover myself. "I promise," he insists.

I step forward, hesitate, then take another step before easily walking to his bed and sliding under the covers. I don't recognize my willingness right now, but I don't question it either.

We lie on our sides and face one another, oddly aware that this isn't sexual but is by no means platonic either.

"I couldn't sleep," I confess.

His face softens. "You still braid your hair at night."

I look at him peculiarly. "You remember?"

"Every detail. Why were you watching me?"

"I don't know. I was remembering when you were in the hospital a year ago."

Ford slides my braid over my shoulder. "I'm beginning to think watching me when I sleep is a habit for you."

"Ah, so you knew I was there?"

"The hospital? Yeah, a nurse told me."

"How come you never let me know?" I snuggle into the mattress, apparently feeling like I'm going to stay here.

Ford takes it as his cue to also get more comfortable in bed. "Because I wouldn't have let it go, so I kept my mouth shut."

"Until now." My voice sounds delicate.

"There are many times we could have openly questioned ourselves, but we didn't. Here we are now, tired, in my bed and with opportunity."

I playfully swat his shoulder.

"I meant this week, not in this moment. Although, I do have you in a prime location right now." Ford pretends to consider.

"Go to sleep."

"You're staying here?"

I shrug a shoulder. "I'm cold," I remind him.

"Then come here."

He brings an arm around me, encircling us together. When he kisses the top of my head, I can't help but feel like we never missed a page, because lying with him in bed feels as natural as the air I breathe.

"You have good arms," I comment.

"I'm not even going to give a comeback because you know you just gave away that you've been checking me out."

"You're the father of our child, I'm always checking you out," I declare matter-of-factly.

He squeezes me tighter. "I'm more than that and you know it."

I don't answer, instead opting for us to lie with each other, occasionally glancing and touching one another's face or an arm or tracing a vein from the top of a hand up.

Staying in his bed is a one-way ticket to confusion.

"Night, Ford," I whisper.

He sighs as I begin to wiggle out of his bed. "Your loss."

"I'm sure," I retort.

Walking out of his room, I know that the last few hours are enough to encourage me to jump over the cliff.

Because the next morning when I wake, I pick up the ring box.

Staring into my mug of coffee as I lean against the open sliding door to outside, I might appear calm, but I'd be lying if I said that I wasn't nervous. Throwing my shirt on hasn't been a priority this morning either.

I haven't seen Brielle since last night when she walked out of my bedroom after giving me a tease of getting her warm in my bed. She doesn't even know that's what she was doing, or if she did, then she played it steady. Needless to say, I didn't get back to sleep easily, especially as the smell of her hair remained on the pillow.

Damn papaya.

It's almost nine. We are due to see Margo in an hour. It won't take long to drive to her home. Margo runs a routine, and by ten she wants morning tea in her garden, or the conservatory when the weather is too cold.

I tap my finger on the mug handle, and I decide that I'm not in much of a mood for caffeine. I walk out onto the patio and set the cup on a table, heading straight for the edge of the tiles to look out and study the middle of the lake. Old man Pete is swimming. He does it without fail as long as there's no ice. Geez, I hope I'm capable of that when I'm his age.

The pattering of heels grabs my attention, and I twist my body to glance over my shoulder.

Fuck me, Brielle is stunning. Her hair is down in waves framing her face, and her shoes are open-toed to show the pale blue polish that matches her fingernails. She had to choose a baby-pink near-white dress? It's exquisite, with short sleeves, yet it flows out at the waist to above her knees. I never had a fifties-housewife fantasy in my head, but my mind is spinning.

The sunlight shines on her as she stands still by the sliding door. "Really? No shirt? I should have known. Anyway, we should be going soon; I want to stop and pick up some fresh flowers for Margo."

I smirk, kind of proud of my unintentional shirt move, before I scrub a hand across my jawline, taking a breath to prepare myself for the obstacle of the next few hours—keeping my body in check.

I slide my hand into my dark jeans pocket. I'll throw on a white buttoned-down t-shirt. Margo likes effort.

"Yeah, sure. Don't you want some breakfast?"

Elle giggles. "You know she is going to have an array of tea sandwiches and cake that we can't say no to, right?"

I grin to myself. "That she will." I walk in Brielle's direction, and when I notice her adjust her earring, I'm blinded by the light of a diamond on her finger.

A victorious smirk comes over me, and I clear my throat to play this cool. "Nice ring."

She holds her hand up to examine it. "Not bad. Some guy lost his mind and decided to spend God knows what on this so I can wear it for a few hours." She gives me a pointed look. "Only a few hours," she warns.

I chuckle under my breath as I slowly stride to her. "Whatever you say."

She points her finger at me. "No tricks, Ford."

"I wouldn't dare," I lie.

Brielle pouts a sound before pivoting to head in the direction of the garage.

Step by step.

That's how I will get her.

————

AFTER DRIVING into town in silence, I parked on Main Street so we could run into the florist. An overpriced bouquet of purple blooms later, we are walking down the sidewalk, and I'm carrying the flowers that I'm sure will soon make me sneeze.

Brielle touches my elbow to grab my attention. "There's Piper."

My eyes follow her line of sight, and I indeed see Piper holding baby Gracie as she closes the car door. Piper is married to Hudson, so she's my neighbor too.

"Hey, Piper," I call out.

She immediately looks up and smiles. "Hey, Ford." She looks confused when she notices who is at my side. "Hey, Brielle, I didn't know you would be here in Lake Spark this week, with Connor still at camp."

Brielle gives me the side-eye. "Well, it seems everyone knew Connor would still be at camp except me."

I can only give my temporary fake fiancée an innocent look.

"Oh." Piper looks between us. "Will you two stop at April and Spencer's later? He popped the big question last night, so we all, of course, need the play-by-play."

"We'll try," I say.

Gracie fusses, and Piper bounces the near toddler against her hip. "This one has been keeping us busy. No rest for the wicked, right? I'm hoping the drugstore has something for her skin."

"What's wrong?" Brielle asks, concerned, and reaches out for Gracie's little finger.

"She has a little eczema, and nothing seems to work."

"Try pure chamomile oil. There is also this oat oil for the bath. It's supposed to be for Chickenpox, but it works wonders in general. Connor had the same problem at Gracie's age, kept me up for hours some nights because he was itchy," Brielle explains as Gracie grips her fingers.

Piper seems grateful for the advice. "I will go grab those items right now."

They're both chatting about something, but I zone out. Mostly because guilt hits me. I missed a lot when Connor was a baby, and Brielle took the brunt of it all. The sleepless nights, teething, every fever and cold. Her mom helped, but I should have been there.

After we say our goodbyes, we walk to my car and get in, the flowers finding a home on the back seat of my Ferrari.

I start the engine but freeze, debating if I should bring this up now, but the thought wrestles in my brain. "You don't resent me, right?" It falls off my tongue. My gaze leads me to Brielle who looks at me, unsure.

"What do you mean?"

"When Connor was a baby, you had it a hell of a lot harder than I did."

"Did I?" I can't read her.

I touch the top of her hands that are folded on her lap. "Don't pretend. We both know you did."

She sighs. "It's all a blur of sleepless nights. It doesn't matter. You are a great dad," she assures me.

"That's not what I'm asking. You can be a great dad but miss moments. I wasn't there enough for you."

Her eyes narrow in on me. "What do you want to hear? Yeah, it was tough. But you had hockey and…"

"It's okay, be honest."

"I don't want to say it's resentment or disappointment. You were building a career that provides for our son. I just… I don't know…" She rolls her shoulder back. "Let's just go to Margo's, we can't be late."

"Don't change the subject." I hear the edge in my voice.

"Okay, yes. Sometimes I look back and hate how the cards fell, but I also don't regret it. We have a great boy, and it all worked out in the end." She avoids my eyes and looks out the window.

I laugh without humor. "I don't think it worked out."

"Stop saying that!" She raises her voice which surprises both of us. "I mean, Ford, I have a whole list of things that I wish were different, things I could be mad at you for, but we have to parent together, so I let it go."

"Tell me the list," I urge, with my eyes never blinking.

She shakes her head. "No."

"Yes."

"Fine. If you want to go down this road, then let me rip the band-aid off." Her voice is pure frustration. "I hate that it's my choice that put us in this situation."

My heart sinks, and I want to immediately comfort her. I urge her to turn her body in my direction by touching her arm. "Don't. I'm promising you that it's not your fault." Her eyes well with water, and now I feel like an ass for getting her into an emotional state. "I need to hear you say it, that you understand that I don't believe it's your fault. Tell me," I plead.

She nods once. "I do believe you."

"Go on. What else is on the list? Every little thing."

Her eyes flutter to keep her tears in. "You weren't there when Connor had Chickenpox, that was hell. Or when I had to cram for a midterm, but Connor wouldn't sleep, and my parents were on vacation. I hate that you got him a game console when he was only four."

"Whoa, it was educational," I say in an attempt to make her smile.

"It was a nuisance."

I touch her cheek and rub my thumb along her cheekbone. "What else?"

"How every time Connor and I would visit you at a hockey game, you made it a grand experience for him that he would talk about for weeks. Which is amazing, but I couldn't escape hearing your name more than usual. And God, that blonde you dated once was a real bitch, way too doll perfect."

"She didn't hold a candle to you, and I hated that nerd from your poli-sci class. Could have throttled him."

"I know. And he didn't even like pizza, what kind of person is that?" Now she is attempting to lighten the mood.

"I hate that I see you all the time. A great mom, so fucking sexy, and I wish every man knew that I have a claim to you."

"Caveman," she one-tones.

I twirl some of her hair around my finger. "I'd commit murder for you."

"Now you just sound like a true crime in the making."

A half-smile creeps on my lips. "My only crime is not confronting us sooner."

"We were occupied."

"Now we're not."

She laughs and licks her lips. "No, now you have me pretending to be your fiancée, and I have a Bar exam to cram for."

"Our parents will love it," I joke because they may all kill me. I think over time, Brielle's parents slowly disliked me more due to my career, and my own father still believes she's the distraction I don't need.

Brielle gives me a doubtful look. "I'm sure my father still has a shotgun somewhere."

We sit in my car in silence, unsure if this is relief or if the pot has been stirred even more.

"Come on, we really can't be late," she insists.

I nod and get to work on pulling us out of the parking spot.

———

WE ARRIVE at Margo's mansion, with her well-manicured plants and long driveway. She has help, but still, this feels a little too much considering she lives here alone.

Getting out of the car, I circle around the front to open the passenger's side. I offer my hand to Brielle, and she shakes her head, amused. I'm going to be over the top.

She's holding the flowers in one arm. "I swear to God, do not make me regret this."

"Come on, it's for a good cause."

Margo is sad to be moving but feels that Florida and assisted living is the right choice, as she has a son down there, plus the warm weather all year round will be beneficial to her.

We walk to the front door, my hand finding a permanent spot on Brielle's lower back. Someone who helps out around the house lets us in and sends us to the backyard.

Walking out and the fountain and plants are the backdrop for Margo, wearing her pearls, sitting at a table decked out in drinks and food.

She claps her hands together and stands. "Wonderful, you two are here."

I smile as we greet her with hugs.

"Of course, someone is getting younger here." Brielle offers Margo the flowers.

"Darling, age is just a number. Thank you, these are beautiful." Margo holds her hand out to the table. "Please sit, I had my chef prepare a few things."

I hold out Margo's chair, and when she's settled, I find my place sitting next to Brielle.

I'm quick to interlace our hands on the table. Brielle stiffens slightly, but I know she's trying to hide her smile because pushing her buttons is something I can't resist.

"I'm so happy to see you both before I move… and together. Miracles do happen," Margo gushes.

I lean in to kiss Brielle's cheek. "They do, don't they?" I lay it on thick.

Brielle tightens her grip on my hand; it's a tad on the tight side, but I'm just going to assume she's been working out.

"Was his proposal something special?" Margo questions.

My fiancée looks at me. "Yes, Ford, do tell."

"I would like to think so. Just us, I took Brielle to this lagoon that's hidden off the lake, and we had a picnic. It's a special place. When we were teenagers, we would go there, and it's also the place that we –"

My girl cuts right in. "Ford, I think that's enough details." She smiles tightly.

"Sounds delightful and look at that ring." Margo reaches onto the table, and Brielle is quick to offer her a view of the ring. "Tasteful. A lot better than the original choice."

"Original choice?" Brielle asks, perplexed.

I have to divert us. "Wow, are those cucumber-and-cream-cheese sandwiches? You know the way to make me happy."

"Yes, dear, I also have those egg-salad-with-pickle sandwiches. I thought maybe Connor would be with you both, so had the chef make peanut butter and jelly too."

"Thoughtful. Connor is at camp this week. His father thought another week of camp would be a real treat for all of us." Brielle is laying it on heavy, while subtly letting me know her dissatisfaction as of late.

Margo indicates for me to pour her some tea. "Little boys have a lot of energy. I'm sure it's exactly what Connor needs."

"Exactly," I say as I fill her cup. "Brielle is about to sit the Bar," I proudly announce.

Margo looks at her with pure elation. "I knew you would get there."

"Well, I still need to pass it."

"You will," I promise her.

"What will you do after?" Margo wonders.

Brielle takes a sip of water. "The law practice where I had an internship and worked in paralegal part-time has a position opening up, so that's a start."

"But where will you two live then once you are married?"

Brielle and I both croak a sound. "It's in discussion. We have school for Connor to think about," Brielle answers. She isn't a great liar, but she's trying.

"There are excellent schools here," I state. "Plus, the house is all ready for Brielle. Her bench swing, favorite-colored pillows, and a home office. Then there is the lake that she loves more than she cares to admit."

Brielle's eyes snap to me because she knows I'm not pretending. The dots connect in her head. She was in my thoughts when I designed the house.

"Is Connor excited that his parents are back together? He must be over the moon." Margo takes a sip from her tea.

"I think he will be ecstatic at the wedding. A simple wedding, just the three of us." I have no idea what I'm spewing or why this comes so easily. Or why I'm speaking in the future tense, other than I'm manifesting some serious plans.

"You must send me a gift idea. Spare no expense."

Brielle laughs nervously. "Don't be silly. We don't need gifts."

"Fine. When the next child comes, then let me buy a gift."

I nearly choke on the coffee that I poured a minute ago.

"That will be a while. I'm still young and need to focus on my career. Have to mentally prepare for the three kids under our roof, probably all boys, and with Ford's personality too, so pure mischief." Brielle speaks without taking notice of me.

But now I'm wondering what her mind is spinning.

"Your parents?" Margo asks.

Brielle and I look at one another before I jump in and answer. "Best not to talk to them about this."

"Hmm, I can only imagine. You know, they will come around. They did last time, when it came to raising Connor. You just need to be firm."

"Were we not firm enough last time?" I'm slightly offended.

Margo looks between us all very seriously. "You were both young, in a delicate situation, and sometimes you need a little extra intervention. Your parents saw you both as their children, children they needed to guide, and they thought one way was the right way. I just stepped in to let them know there had to be a compromise on their path."

Brielle's eyes dip down to look at the patio floor.

I breathe out a breath and bring my arm around Brielle's shoulders. "We are grateful for that. Do you think there was another path that none of us explored?"

Margo seems taken aback. "Adoption, although a gift to many, wasn't what either of you wanted. Or do you mean marriage? Your ring could have been an option, but then I'm not sure either of you would be where you are today. Sometimes we get our true love later. Look at you two now, so many things to be proud of. A great son is one of them, and now you both get to have what you've been waiting for."

I rub warmth into Brielle's shoulder as we listen to Margo, and I'm grateful Brielle didn't question the ring remark more.

The next hour we talk about Lake Spark town gossip and roses. We would love to stay longer, but Margo needs rest.

As we wrap up our time together, Brielle and I stand. This time our hands connect of their own accord, my free hand sliding down her spine as she leans in to hug Margo.

"You look so healthy and happy," Margo notes to us.

"Thank you," Brielle says. "I'm glad to have seen you again."

"Me too, and I know Ford will treat you right, he's been waiting to be your husband for years."

Brielle laughs. "Why do you say that?"

"Before he upgraded your rock, he had a cheap little one when you two were kids, but you know this."

No, she did not.

Brielle freezes for a second or two before giving me a piercing gaze.

I ignore her for a moment. "I'll call you later in the week, Margo," I promise.

"Don't be silly. You two have a week to yourselves without Connor. Go wild and never leave your home." She winks at me.

I keep Brielle close as we walk to the car. I open the door for her, and she slides onto the seat, clearly agitated.

When I make it to the driver's seat, she is quick to slide the ring off her finger and hand it back to me. "Why does Margo think you got me a ring when we were younger?"

Yep, saw this coming about one minute ago.

My lips press together as I tuck the ring into my pocket, unsure what to say, but honesty is the best policy. "Because I did. Before the appointment, I thought it could be an option. But then Margo walked me through the reality of you not having your dreams, and the next day, when we decided to keep Connor, then something inside me thought our choice was right, so I returned the ring. We were young, confused, and none the wiser."

She sits there quietly for a second. "Why didn't you tell me?"

"Because I'm a selfish asshole who realized that you having support would be better, and you already looked like you were breaking." I heave a sigh.

"Drive back to the house, *now*." She's insistent, but I can't figure out if she's more mad or sad.

I know better than to push her to talk. Brielle is more open when you are patient and let her lead. This is why our car ride back is a stiff silence with an old Goo Goo Dolls album playing, but I make no mistake that I hear a sniffle or two as she stares out the window.

My veins are filled with remorse for how today is going.

I'm unraveling us.

Which up to now was hard to do, as we were tightly wound in what we thought was right.

I bite the inside of my cheek, trying to contain myself from saying anything else. The last thing I want is for her to break. Hell, I don't want her shedding any tears.

The road ahead is winding around the lake, it's dangerous if I'm not careful.

Much like us.

But I keep my hands on the steering wheel, in control.

As soon as we are back at the house, I park in the driveway, and she storms out of the car. I follow her at the speed of light. We both stop in the middle of my lawn, clearly about to face off.

"Ford Spears, why are you torturing us?"

BRIELLE

Ford is stirring so many emotions inside of me, more than average.

"I'm torturing you? Because of this morning?" he dares to ask, his hands hanging at his sides.

I throw my hands up in the air, completely helpless. "Tricking me, getting us alone, a ring. A ring, Ford? Who is their right mind does that? Then this morning, and I…" Didn't want to hear what deep down I knew he probably thought long ago.

My head falls in sorrow.

He steps forward, but I'm quick to hold my hands up to stop him. "Do not step closer to me," I warn.

His head dips down, and his sight tips up to grab my attention. "You feel it too."

"I need you to look away with your luscious puppy eyes because they will not make me fall into your arms."

A total lie.

He knows it too because he smirks. "We can't change the past, but we can write the future, and I'll be damned if it's anything except waking up to you."

My brow slides up. "You're so sure of us."

"Tell me I'm wrong. Tell me I'm imagining that you and I can't let go of one another. Just tell me and I'll give this up… but you can't."

"You didn't give me a chance to tell you." I tip my hip out with my hand on my waist.

He grins sheepishly. "Please, go ahead." He doesn't sound convinced.

"I…" Have no clue what I'm doing, that's what. I look up at him and my heart is fully his, and it scares me. Ford has the key, and I know he'll hide it so nobody will ever have it but him. "I'm so angry," I admit softly.

"I gathered." He doesn't seem fazed.

The lids of my eyes slowly close then open but no calm hits me. Instead, a hurricane passes over my heart and moves through my throat on full windspeed because everything rolls off my tongue in a wave.

"I can't tell you that you're wrong. Okay? Happy? Is that what you wanted to hear?" I raise my voice, my chest thumping with emotional fury. "I couldn't sleep last night because I'm stuck in this beautiful house on a lake that has some mystical powers to get me pregnant and engaged in the span of a decade. I laid awake last night on a soft mattress wishing that for one night I had the ability to let go and be in the moment. With you." Ford looks at me, mute, that I'm at last breaking. Our eyes lock in recognition. "Because yeah… you, Ford, I want more than anything, but we share a son who doesn't deserve a clusterfuck of epic proportions if we get this wrong."

We both seem taken aback by my little monologue.

But before either one of us can say something, a spray of hard cold water comes up from the grass. I shriek from the sudden surprise, my mouth gaping open as I try to understand. Instantly I'm getting soaked through, and the shock has me frozen as I take in what is happening.

I don't realize until Ford begins to laugh. It's only then that I connect that it's the sprinkler, and Ford by chance just missed the brunt of the water. I'm standing in front of him wet, and my dress is now a second skin.

"Are you kidding me?"

He tries to hide his laugh. "You're standing on the grass. It's on a timer."

"Is this my luck? What other stunts will happen on this property?" My hair is now soaked, and I wipe away water from eyes that probably have mascara running.

"You're cold."

"It's summer," I reply.

"And you're cold." Ford steps into the stream of water, and I realize he is repeating what we said last night because my nipples are clearly peaked, and his eyes have noticed.

"It's cold because you keep the air-conditioning high and get me trapped in sprinklers," I argue back, one-toned and unsure what is happening.

The sound of the water becomes a backdrop or it's my ears ringing as my heart beats fast. That's the reason the world seems to be going silent around us. Ford is now drenched in water and so very close, his eyes hungry.

"You're in the moment," he highlights. "With me."

A smile tugs on my lips, because this moment feels like relief and perfection rolled into one. The setting for a memory, and I know it will be one that I'll smile about for years to come.

Because before I can say anything, his hand grabs the back of my neck, and he pulls me to his mouth. His lips slam down onto mine, and I'm drowning not in the water but him. My hands are quick to frame his face in hopes of finding balance, and luckily, his arms snake around my middle to yank me tight to him.

Ford swallows my breath as our mouths realign. Kissing him sets off an explosion inside of me, yet I'm struggling to register it, with my body in slight shock because it remembers his lips.

Only when his tongue slips into my mouth do I relax. Even though I knew where he was all along, this kiss is my lost treasure that I finally found.

I moan into his mouth, which only encourages Ford to kiss me harder. I offer more by slanting my chin up. I can't get enough.

He holds me tighter and kisses me softer, then he growls as he brushes his lips along mine. "Finally," he speaks against the corner of my mouth before giving me a quick peck as a parting.

We need to breathe actual air.

Staring at one another, we're both panting and soaked. Ridiculous smiles are displayed on our faces, and I lean my forehead in so he can kiss my temple.

"I'm staying. This week, I mean," I confirm.

Ford blinks at me, with water running down his face. "I wouldn't have let you leave anyway, and you know we are more than a week."

I don't argue. "Kiss me again," I request.

At the speed of light, he fulfills my request, a kiss full of longing and hope. Tender yet firm because we are working against external forces, and water is as powerful as waiting ten years.

We stay this way for what feels like minutes until we break apart, and without warning, he throws me over his shoulder fireman style and walks us out of the sprinklers.

I giggle and admire his flexed muscles beneath wet clothes that can carry me with ease. He twirls me around before he walks to the side yard.

"What are you doing?" I wonder.

"As much as making out with you on my lawn is a dream come true, we need to get out of these wet clothes."

My stomach flips, possibly with nerves, but mostly excitement. Today, nothing else matters except us.

Ford gets us to the back sliding door and walks us in until he plops me down in the hall by the stairs.

Then I'm on him again. This time I kiss him, short, fast, and over and over. He begins to unbutton his shirt, and I'm quick to assist, peeling the shirt off his arms until it's on the floor, our mouths never parting.

I hop onto him and wrap my legs around his waist before he

takes the first step on the stairs. Halfway up, we fall to a step, and I straddle him as our tongues continue to fuse together.

Now that water is no longer working against us, I feel more. My body is more attuned to what is happening. I'm sensitive in all the right places, and Ford has the key to every single spot.

"We need to get you out of this." Ford's voice is a sexy raspy tone as he assesses me from the waist up and back down.

"Likewise," I counter, and my fingers begin to fumble with the belt of his jeans. The sound of the buckle loosening is mixed with our labored breaths as our lips run wild on our mouths and necks.

He uses his weight to lift us up, and we continue our journey upstairs. Ford walks us straight to his bedroom where he lays me down gently on his bed.

I bring my finger to my mouth to nibble as I watch Ford tower over me and step out of his pants.

Ford in dark boxer briefs and nothing else is a view I could stare out for hours, days, and years. I'm not into muscular overload on guys, but Ford is toned. I could take a marker—or my tongue—and trace every line.

A cocky smirk spreads on his mouth. "Better than the Ford in your fantasies?"

"Debating," I quip.

Slowly, he steps forward, his knees hitting the edge of the mattress. My feet plant on the duvet with my knees up. All he would have to do is lift the skirt of my dress and I'm his for the taking.

His eyes shoot me a warning; pure sin is on his mind.

I gasp slightly when he touches my knees, and he glides the pads of his fingers up my thighs. Every inch higher causes the ache between my legs to intensify.

Ford leans down to delicately kiss my inner knee. "So damn beautiful."

The feeling of my cheeks blushing doesn't faze me; I'm far too familiar that this man electrifies my body.

In a swift movement, he hooks his fingers under the waistband of my panties without moving my skirt up, and it wouldn't matter, as his eyes stay fixed on me. Ford yanks the wet material down my legs, and my feet move to slide them off easily. He throws the wet fabric to the side.

My heart races for what comes next.

Ford holds his finger up, indicating for me to wait a second.

"Now you want to wait?" I tease.

He ruefully shakes his head and walks to his closet on the side, leaving me splayed out on his bed. I can't see from my angle, but he disappears into the closet and remerges with clothes.

Coming to the bed, he throws a hoodie and boxers at me.

"We need to get you warm."

My jaw drops, completely shocked by this change. "W-what?" I stutter.

Ford crawls onto the bed and cages me underneath him. I hate when he has a look that informs the world that he won.

"Oh, trust me, I'm ready to break this mattress and rip every sheet in this house for the way we need to seal this reunion."

"Then what's the damn problem?" I'm stunned.

He leans down to breathe near my ear before placing a kiss in that sensitive spot above my neck. "I have to wine and dine you first."

"No. No, you don't," I answer blankly. "I volunteer as tribute. Take me. Now. Here. Any way you want."

Ford blows out a breath, clearly trying to contain himself. "Good to know for future reference." He propels himself off the bed, and he has a glimmer in his eye, that victorious smirk never fading. "Babe, get dressed," he orders before he disappears again into his closet. "I'll meet you downstairs."

I prop myself up on my elbows. "What?"

He ducks out of the door mid shirt coming on. "Trust me."

I fall back on the bed, defeated.

He leaves me there, completely frustrated yet curious and amused as to what the hell wine and dine means.

9

FORD

Glancing up from pouring white wine into a glass that rests on the kitchen counter, I notice Brielle walking into the room in only my hoodie and nothing else. I have to do a double take for many reasons—one, how magnificent she looks in my clothes, especially with a sexy look gracing her face. Mostly, I'm watching her stride into my kitchen because I'm amazed that I kept restraint upstairs, and now too, as the sweater hits her knees but leaves enough for the imagination.

But we are a long game, and I need to take my time with her.

Everything is now happening, one domino after another.

"I've poured you a glass." I slide the drink to the edge of the counter where Brielle parks her cute behind on a stool. She's already curling the fabric over her hands because my hoodie drowns her.

Brielle looks at me skeptically. "Right, wining and dining me, because suddenly you have an inkling to go old-fashioned."

I grin to myself before I lean over to capture her mouth for a kiss, one that she willingly gives.

"Quick, hard, and to the point wouldn't have sufficed, baby. And once we get naked later, then we are not leaving my bed," I warn her.

She takes the glass between her fingers, leans back, and hums a sound. "You mention later. I'm not so sure you should assume," she taunts.

I ignore her attempt to tease me and instead look at my watch. "Listen, you should take this wine, go relax by the pool, and I'll be back soon. I need to run next door to Spencer's, and you look a little too flushed to join. Have to give them a bottle of champagne as a congratulations, since they got engaged last night. I had promised Hudson I would stop by, as they are throwing a little celebration before Spencer goes back on the road for a game."

"Is it a full moon? Engagements seem to be happening a lot lately." She sips from her glass.

"You're saying that like you're still engaged. You should take it easy; you need your rest for later."

Brielle looks up from her wine. "That's very considerate."

Leaning over the counter, I take her hands in mine. "We should take a breather before we cross the line that I have every intention of repeating… a lot… tonight."

"I'm trying not to think," she mentions.

That worries me slightly. We wouldn't be the first people to get caught up in lust. "Elle, I won't be a regret."

She is quick to offer me a gentle assuring smile. "I meant, I want to enjoy our time together here, today, tomorrow. I just know there are more factors to consider." Nothing she's saying is soothing. Her finger escapes my hold to tap the back of my hand. "Factors we will consider because we are…"

"More than a one-night fuck."

Her lips purse out, and she tilts her head at an angle. "I guess that's one way of putting it."

I return to standing, bopping her nose with my finger in the process, but I catch her in a daze as she stares at me. "You okay?"

"Yeah. It's just kind of… surreal… this." She points between us. "Kind of takes getting used to but not in a bad way. Kissing you feels natural, very natural, but this dynamic is a little new, or rather it's been so long where we haven't been together-together." She tips her wine glass back.

"Way too long," I lament. "We can go slow," I offer.

"I don't think my body can cope," she casually mentions, with a trace of a smirk on her lips. "Besides, you have to dine me, so dinner is slow enough."

"But that's all physical. What about all the other stuff?"

Our eyes meet briefly for a check-in.

"You mentioned something on the boat that we can have a few days where we make up for lost time, be in our own little world before we face reality, and I think that's our first step."

And maybe she's right.

"Sure," I answer.

Yet, I could jump right in, but I need to let her lead the way. I've already thrown a lot at her. That doesn't mean I'm not going to pull out all the stops to woo her.

That's what I think it is, I respect her so profoundly that I want to give her romance before we get lost in one another.

She isn't any woman, she's the love of my life.

"I'll be back soon," I promise. "Go get comfortable. If you want to study and need something, just look in my office."

She chortles. "There is no way I can concentrate now." Her nails tap on the counter, and she seems to have a moment of clarification. "Are you nervous? Am I throwing you off your game? Is that why I'm not lying in your bed right now?" She's entertained.

I smile awkwardly as I swipe my thumb across my chin. "Uh," I croak out.

"It is, isn't it?" Brielle now softens her voice when she realizes the answer that I've been internally denying.

"Don't be silly. I remember every little detail of your body and have noticed every change since."

Her eyes grow big. "You should probably get out of here because I could take that the wrong way."

"I just meant that I notice when you add highlights in your hair, or you've slept well, when you're in a good mood or bad."

She blushes, and I take it as my cue to walk to her, step between her legs, and cradle her head in my hands.

"I like that it's you who notices."

"Good," I say before I kiss her once more as a parting gift. "I'm not nervous. You just bring out the best of me." One more kiss because I can't resist, and I'm out of there.

———

I HAND Spencer a bottle of champagne as I step into his kitchen where Hudson and Piper are talking with April. The champagne is kind of pointless, as everyone in this room has a closet full of over-the-top and highly priced bottles, but it's the thought that counts.

"I'm not going to stay long, just dropping by, as good neighbors do," I announce.

Spencer slaps a hand on my shoulder. "That's okay, I have to leave in an hour. I have a game this week."

"We know you're busy too, Ford." Piper smiles.

It's then that I notice everyone is staring at me peculiarly, with fixed grins on their faces like they're waiting for something.

"You all okay?" I ask.

"For sure. Anything you care to share?" April wiggles her brows, her blonde hair not moving an inch as she stretches her smile.

I'm trying to read the room but failing miserably.

"We saw a little scene of you carrying someone over your shoulder," Spencer mumbles.

Ah fuck, there is a spot between our property lines that is cleared. We figured we should have a path to each other's yards and docks, for safety since there are kids around.

"Total *The Notebook* vibes," April adds.

Hudson rolls his eyes. "Your plan working?"

"Shouldn't we be discussing April and Spencer?" I suggest.

Spencer and April look at one another then shrug their shoulders. "Nah," they agree in unison.

"Brielle and I are taking some time… for ourselves."

The ladies in the room clap their hands together in excitement, and I'm beginning to wonder if I walked into a bear's den.

"Calm down, ladies." Hudson grins, slightly scared for me.

"Pulling out all the stops, huh?" Spencer asks.

I muss my hair. "Trying. I need to figure out dinner for tonight. Tomorrow, I have a few ideas."

"I'll make your dinner," April is quick to volunteer. She's a nutritionist and cooks daily.

"You just got engaged," I emphasize the obvious.

She is already heading to the fridge. "Yes, and my fiancé has a game to catch. I have a bunch of meals in the freezer. Meat or no meat? Maybe a lasagna?"

"Are you sure?"

April is already pulling out a container from the freezer drawer. "Totally. Here, this is lasagna with pumpkin and sage, the instructions are on the container, and let me go grab some bread dough that I've had resting for days."

"Aren't I a lucky man?" Spencer fondly admires his fiancée, the homemaker.

Spencer's seven-year-old daughter skips into the kitchen, with her pigtails swaying in the air. "Is Connor here?" Excitement is apparent in her voice.

I lean down to her eye level. "Sorry, he's at hockey camp."

"Oh." Her face falls, and she stomps away.

"Someone has a crush. So adorable," Piper notes, with her hands on her chest in admiration.

Spencer and I look at one another, thankful we are not yet near the teenage years.

"We should keep an eye on that, right?" I question.

Spencer gives me a cartoonish look. "Don't remind me."

April arrives with a cloth bag full of food. Handing it to me, I'm quick to notice she went overboard, including a bag of salad.

"This is way too kind." I take the tote.

"Nah, it's fine. Besides, I expect a full report later in the week or maybe I will have my dog *accidentally* stroll into your yard, and oops, I need to go rescue him. Would seven be an ideal time for that?" she jokes.

I have to smile at her humor, and I'm thankful that I have such great neighbors. We look out for one another.

"Thank you. I don't mean to dash already, but I really just wanted to say congrats in person real quick." I open my arms to hug April, then Spencer gets a side hug.

A quick round of goodbyes, but, of course, Hudson has to be the last to give me the older-and-wiser advice that he loves to dish out.

"Opportunity is what we make of it. Grab it when you can and don't let go." His advice isn't new, but I appreciate him reminding us when he can.

"I have no intention of letting it go," I promise.

———

RETURNING TO MY HOUSE, I put everything away for later then throw on my swim trunks before I head out back to find Brielle lying on a lounger beside the pool in a black bikini and sunhat as she reads a massive book with a highlighter in hand. She is giving studying a whirl, I guess.

I've seen her in a bikini a few times over the years, but now I'm allowed to look and fantasize without guilt, and I love that.

"Ditched the air conditioner and my hoodie?" I say as I whip off my t-shirt.

She glances up from the book and smiles. "Really? Yet again, you feel a shirt isn't necessary?" I have to grin because she's calling me out. "Illinois summer is good to us this year, so I'm going to enjoy this eighty-five-degree no-wind weather. We know winter is coming at some point. I thought I would try to study, but I haven't made a dent."

I sit on the lounger next to her. "Good, you should relax. My sister sent me some photos of Connor today at camp." I pull out my phone and swipe the screen to show Brielle, who instantly smiles wide.

"He's a cutie." Connor is wearing skates and is holding his

hockey stick as he waits for his turn to hit between the orange cones. "Growing so fast."

"Yeah, he is."

We look at one another with affection, as there is never a moment that we don't look elated when discussing our boy.

I decide to put my phone to the side so we can focus on each other. We can be selfish and not focus on gushing the praises of our son for one afternoon. Today is about us.

"So, how about at six we have dinner?" I suggest.

Brielle closes her book. "What's on the menu?"

"It's a surprise."

"You're cooking?"

"Kind of." Half the truth. I'm turning the oven on at least.

She nibbles her bottom lip, trying not to smile, but I can tell that she's happy. "Okay."

"Shall I go grab more wine?"

"No, I'll save my intake for later, plus it's a little too warm out for wine."

"You're warm?" I stand up and offer my hand. "Come on, let's go for a swim."

Brielle's fingers carefully walk into my palm, but I grab hold of her wrist and yank her up, causing her hat to fall. Quickly, I hook my arm under her knees to carry her.

"Don't you dare throw me in," she giggles.

"Wouldn't dream of it." I grin.

She clings to my neck. "Liar."

And she's right, I drop her in the deep end and dive in after.

We both submerge under the water before swimming to each other. With water swooshing around us, I love the way Brielle brings her arms around my neck before wrapping her legs around me. She knows I'm her anchor both in the pool and life.

Our bodies are close, and it feels so damn right, yet tantalizing. This will be a struggle not to play with the tie behind her neck, but it will make tonight even better.

"Hi," she says shyly.

"Hey." I dip my head down to kiss her neck. "Look at us."

"Crazy."

"Nah, crazy is waiting this long."

She gives me knowing eyes. "Maybe."

I can't read what is hinted in that word, but I don't get too worried as she kisses me with intention.

For the next hour, we just wade in the pool, splashing around and chatting about the Bar exam, Lake Spark, and the training facility that I'm running. It's easy and relaxing. In a way, no different from the way we've been the last ten years, except for the fact I get to touch her, hold her, and kiss her. It's a change but welcome.

We were in a good mood when we both went our separate ways to shower and change. I threw on a fresh t-shirt and jeans before I worked my magic in the kitchen and outside. I've dated, sure, but I've never romanced someone the way I am for Brielle.

By the time I have everything set up, Brielle arrives down the stairs barefoot but in a black cotton dress that clings to her and stops mid-thigh.

Her mouth parts open with a gasp when she walks outside to the edge of the patio where I'm lighting a few candles on the table to keep the mosquitos away. This is the perfect spot to overlook the lake and sunset. My Bluetooth plays music; I'm really on a Hovvdy kick lately, and it fits us for this moment.

"You did this?" She walks to the table. "It's beautiful, romantic, and a little surprising. But unexpected is easy to do, as no part of today is how I was planning my week to go." She notices the warm lasagna, salad, and bread. "You cooked?"

"I might have had April's help so I won't poison you." I bring her chair out to help her in.

"I'm slightly relieved with that news," she admits and slides onto the chair. "Thank you."

We have white wine in a bucket. Olive Owl, her favorite, and I get an abundance of wine supply since Hudson's son married into the family that owns the brand. I'm quick to pick up the bottle and get busy with the cork.

"A toast," I suggest.

"Depends on what we're toasting," she playfully challenges as she picks up the wine glasses on the table and holds them out for me.

I think for a second. This isn't a new beginning because I don't want us to erase what was, especially since it includes our son. I pop the cork and begin to pour. "To timing." It's the best I can do.

"Maybe. Or to waiting. Maybe we'll figure out if we're worth it," she counters with hope in her tone.

Optimism is something we share, which is why we clink our glasses to celebrate the night ahead.

10

FORD

Brielle sets her fork down and looks up at me as she finishes her bite. "This was delicious. I wish I had the ability to cook like this."

I throw my napkin to the side. "You're fine. Connor loves your mashed potatoes."

She laughs to herself. "Not exactly earth-shattering to make."

"I don't know. You have to get the ratio of butter and milk right or it doesn't have the right consistency. Or at least that is what Connor tells me when I attempt to make them."

There it is. Sentimental fondness gracing her face.

"I love him so much," she reflects as she takes her wine glass in her hand. Leaning back in the chair, she looks out over the lake which is nearly dark since the sun disappeared over the pines on the horizon. "You won't let him skate on the lake when it freezes, right?"

"Of course not. I'll take him to a pond nearby or the training facility. Where's that coming from?"

"Nothing. It's just a beautiful lake, and for some reason, I thought about winter and how the lake freezes sometimes, plus you play hockey, Connor loves hockey. My mind spins a little."

"Ah yes, mom instinct."

She throws me a playful glare. "It's a superpower."

"I have a few superpowers too."

Brielle folds her arms onto the table. "Oh yeah? Do tell."

"Restraint, endurance, and pleasure," I confidently inform her before throwing back a sip of wine.

I notice she blows out a small breath between her lips and tucks a strand of hair behind her ear, but her smile never wavers. "I'm sure."

Our eyes hold, with the light of the candles offering a dim reflection. "There is too much distance between us," I inform her.

"You mean the table?" She points down to double-check.

"Yeah."

Her fingers trace the top of her wine glass. "I might consider finding a new seat if you tell me the truth about something."

My ears perk up, as I'm not entirely sure what's on her mind. "What would that be?"

"Why did it have to be Lake Spark where you set your roots down?"

I shrug my shoulder. "It's a great little town, a perfect spot to build a house, great for winter and summer… and it reminds me of you."

Her eyes flick up. "You decided to build a house here already a few years ago."

"Exactly," I confess. "Remembering our time together kept me going. Just like a compass, you always go back to the starting point." Her cheeks tighten, and she seems to have gone mute from my revelation. "I think deep down you figured it out too, otherwise you wouldn't have asked me just now."

The lids of her eyes close for a few beats as she collects her thoughts. When her eyes open, I see it all. I know she is affected, because water swells in the bottom of her eyes, but mostly I recognize the agreement hinted in her look.

"Now tell me the truth." It's my turn.

"What?"

"If I didn't make this week happen, would you have ever told me the truth about how you feel?"

Brielle stands up and takes a few steps to look out over the lake. "Truthfully? I don't know. I got little pieces of you, and sometimes I thought that would be enough to keep me from falling apart."

"Little pieces?" I ask as I grab the bottle to pour us more wine.

"You know, seeing you at pick-ups and a few moments that we just… I don't know." She glances back at me. "Like a few months ago when Connor had the flu, and we agreed it wasn't a good idea for him to go to your house, so you came over to see him and then…"

"I slept on the couch until his fever went down," I finish her sentence.

She nods. "I knew you visited for Connor, but you were in my house, sleeping, just there… so close." She covers her face with her hand, as if she could hide. "Fuck, I just admitted that."

I have to smile to myself. "Sorry I didn't take my shirt off," I say in an attempt to make her laugh, but then my face grows stoic because I know what she's saying. "I pretended to sleep."

"What?"

"I pretended to sleep," I repeat. "I couldn't sleep a wink knowing you were in the other room in your bed. I think I stayed more because I knew it would be the next best thing. I got to be near you for a night."

She laughs, swiping away a tear. "Are we horrible parents? We had a hidden agenda while our son had a fever."

"We're allowed to put ourselves first sometimes. Besides, his fever was going down, and we had the situation under control."

Brielle slowly walks to my side of the table. "I think I'm going to move seats now." Her smile is sultry.

"Oh yeah?" I lean back, ready to welcome her.

She sits on my lap and loops her arms around my neck. "Right here, if you don't mind."

I tip my chin up to get a better angle to kiss her lips. "I insist."

Cementing our lips together, it's Brielle this time who kisses with determination, her fingers raking into the hair on the back of my neck. She has me captivated and at her mercy. Yet, I have the courage to sneak my tongue into her mouth to show her that I'll lead us if she lets me.

Our tongues duel before her lips create a trail of hurried kisses down my jaw and neck.

This is it.

We snap.

There is no going back.

"We can skip the brownies, right?" I husk as my hands roam her body.

She pulls away for a second with a serious look. "Wait, there are chocolate brownies?"

"Uhm… yes." I'm concerned that her love for dessert is one step higher on her pedestal for me.

Her look tells me that I'm being brushed to the side, but then her face breaks. "I guess they can wait."

Relief hits me, and I'm quick to usher her up, never letting go of our interlaced fingers. "Let me blow out the candles." I lean over to extinguish the flames.

"Fire safety, so responsible," she chides.

"I'm a dad," I proudly counter.

Brielle yanks my arm to lead us inside.

OUR HANDS DON'T DROP as we slowly walk into my bedroom, and I'm not quite sure who is leading whom. The problem with slow is that it ups the ante and makes the realization of what we are doing more profound. The air is thick with anticipation, and the beating of my heart feels strong.

When we are near my bed, I reel Brielle into me and wrap my arm around her waist. "You okay?" I have to smile.

"Perfect."

"Not nervous?"

Her lips quirk out. "I mean, it's not every day that Ford Spears, star hockey player, takes me to bed, but ya know, there are worse hardships in life."

A laugh escapes me before I remind her of the obvious. "You're the only one that I've ever wanted."

"Okay, now you're setting the bar high. I might be a little nervous now." She wryly smiles and then jabs my chest with her finger. "It's been a while since we did this. Together. I mean, you and me."

"We were teenagers."

"I got pregnant."

"Oh, we're already there? It was three sons, right? I guess if I aim right…" I tease her. I'm following her cues because she seems to be anxious.

She swats me playfully. "We don't need to worry, I have an IUD. Without going into detail, my priorities haven't been on dating lately. So, if we're good on all fronts, then we are set."

With my fingers, I comb her hair away from her face. "We're good. Look at us being responsible adults."

"I'm stalling."

"I noticed."

Her beautiful eyes lock with mine. "Is it crazy that my body feels like it might explode? Because this has only ever been a dream, and now it's a reality."

"This afternoon you didn't want me to stop."

"I know, but every minute more with you and I realize how deep we are."

I tighten my hold with our fingers, bringing her hand up to my lips for a feathery kiss. "Does that scare you?"

"The opposite."

I gently kiss her lips to ground us, but my attempt to do soft is thwarted by Brielle returning my kiss with what I can only describe as passion. It's fervent, electrifying, and when she invites me to follow her as she walks backward, it's a confirmation that I don't need to go slow.

"I want you," she rasps right before she drops to sit on the mattress.

"There hasn't been a day I stopped wanting you." I begin to pull my shirt up at the same time my knee lands on the bed. With my shirt thrown to the floor, I guide Brielle back until she's under me.

Kissing her, my hand skims the fabric of her dress until I find the hem. Dragging the fabric up, her knee moves which means I'm better aligned with her center.

"You drive me crazy." My voice is gruff.

Her body arches up which causes her dress to bunch around her waist, and her panty-covered pussy presses against my hard length. "I bet I can make you go insane."

I pin her wrists to the mattress, which makes Brielle giggle and squirm, especially as I nibble the base of her neck, trailing my lips along her collarbone. "Keep your hands where they are," I warn her.

Making sure she watches me, I begin to unbutton her dress, and the moment all the buttons are free, I hiss a sound of pure admiration that she is lying in my bed with a matching black lace bra and panties. "Gorgeous," I whisper.

"Take more off." Her hands reach for the buckle of my jeans.

Quickly, I push her hands away. "Arms on the bed."

"Ooh, bossy."

I flash her a fake unimpressed look before I step out of my jeans and return to her. I slide down her bra strap and trace her skin until I reach her breast. My tongue darts out to twirl around her lace-covered nipple, and her body curves from enjoyment.

I peer up to see her watching me. I repeat the movement on her other breast before I move both cups down to twist her nipples between my fingers to play with her.

She moans and breathes heavily, which only encourages me to kiss between the valley of her breasts and lower. Giving a few extra popcorn kisses around her belly button and then moving below her navel.

Brielle writhes under me, and her sweet scent of desire hits my nose as I travel over her mound. I nuzzle over her soaked lace. It's intoxicating, and I want more, which is why I lap my tongue up her panties, getting a taste.

Brielle claws the sheets in surprise and moans a breath.

"I need more," I growl. Peeling her panties off, I dive right back to where I was. Spreading her lips, I lick, taking a moment to swirl and explore. I could do this for hours; I only need to feast on her for survival.

"Ford," she cries.

I dip my tongue inside her center, before swiping back up to her clit, but I pause. "You're ready. Are you aching for me?"

"Yes," she responds and brings her hands to my head. "Don't stop."

"We're just getting started," I promise. My tongue flicks her clit, and my finger arrives at her center to explore her wet channel.

I suck and lick her, until she is panting and near her edge.

"I'm almost there."

I work harder, find a rhythm, and keep her begging for more.

Then she's convulsing against my mouth, and I slow down. I take a moment to enjoy her taste of subtle sweetness and inhale her. I keep my tongue flat against her clit until I feel she's steady.

Brielle is trying to capture her breath, but I decide to kiss her anyways. She seems taken aback when she whimpers a sound, but then realizes her taste is on my lips, and she gets greedy.

My hand travels between her legs to feel her open and wet. She joins me in exploration, giving herself a stroke, but only once because she moves my boxer briefs and takes hold of my cock.

"Inside of me, please," she pleads, ensuring our eyes stay connected.

"Get comfortable, baby."

I invite her to scoot back onto my bed until her head rests on my pillow, and she unclasps her bra while I discard my boxer briefs.

Gliding my fingers up her inner thigh, I find my destination. Settling between her legs, the tip of my cock slides between her, taunting her clit and driving me feral.

"I'll start slow," I promise.

I begin to fill her, and she gasps, but our eyes catch and a reassuring smile spreads on her lips.

"You're mine again," I breathe into her neck.

"I was always yours."

Inch by inch, I enter her, waiting for her cues, which are difficult to read, as her eyes remain committed and filled with what I believe is love.

I interweave our hands against the pillow by her ear, dragging myself in and out just enough to drive us wild.

"It's okay, you can go deeper," she encourages.

I stay inside of her but stop moving, and instead, I take the moment to bring my hand to her face to brush my thumb against her lips. Brielle is the one I'll spend my life with, I know it, which is why I deliver her request. We get lost in this moment until we are riding a wave that involves two sweaty bodies, moving together, locked in a gaze, because the future is ours for the taking.

BRIELLE

I wake feeling fulfilled.

Stretching out my arms and stirring in Ford's bed, I make no mistake that I am in his arms, and he has been holding me all night after we went a few rounds.

He smiles down at me. "Hey, beautiful." His voice is hoarse.

"How long have you been awake?" I yawn.

"A little while. I'm still getting used to sleeping in after years of waking early for training."

His hands rub warmth into my arm near my elbow. I inhale his scent of morning musk, and I enjoy it because it means I'm in *his* bed.

I should pinch myself to confirm that this is reality, but I feel his cock wide awake against the back of my thigh, and I know that this isn't a dream.

"After last night, don't you need a little extra sleep?" I wonder.

He smirks at me before he adjusts our bodies so that I can rest my head against his chest. I eagerly draw circles on his pec with my fingers because his toned physique is a masterpiece that I like to touch.

"I'd rather watch you naked in my bed."

"So be it, but I'm not going easy on you this morning," I warn him.

Ford's fingers caress my back as we lie together, perfectly intent.

"I thought we could head into town for some breakfast, then I need to head to Connor's camp."

My head perks up. "You're seeing Connor today?"

Ford squeezes me closer. "You too. You're coming with me if you don't mind watching me teach a group of ten-year-olds."

I smile. "I'd love to."

"Good. Then we'll head to Jolly Joe's and make our way to the training center after."

"Ooh, you sound like you have us on a tight schedule," I note.

Ford snorts a laugh. "No, but we should be out of the house in about an hour."

A mischievous grin overtakes my face, I can feel my lips curl. I walk my fingers up Ford's chest. "If we have an hour, then I think there is something we can work on."

Ford flips me to my back with a satisfied smirk of his own. "What could that be?"

"We have a lot of time to make up for, so I think…" I wiggle and feel between us to grip his cock, and his head falls low as he enjoys my hand wrapped around him to give him a stroke.

"I couldn't agree more." He slithers his body out of my hold and down the mattress, disappearing under the duvet. I grab hold of the duvet to inspect what he's doing, only to find him parting my thighs open and staring at my pussy. "Just checking how swollen you are and ensuring my mark stayed inside of you."

Fire ignites inside of me from his words. My nipples harden, and my body is awakened with extra sensitivity, including the air that hits my nipples.

"And," I breathe. "Do you approve?" My voice is uneven, as I'm so heightened and I need his touch.

Ford swipes my clit with the pad of his thumb. "I want to fill you up again."

"I want that too." I lick my lips.

I can't take it anymore, and I scoot up to sitting and encourage Ford to swap places. I straddle him with my knee on each side of his hips. Taking his cock in my palm, I wrap my fingers around him to give him a few pumps before aligning him with my opening and sliding on top of him. We both moan at the same time.

"Take what you want from me," Ford encourages and squares my hips with his hands.

"Everything feels too good." My lids go heavy, and my back arches, with my hair falling behind me and my breasts on offer.

Ford sits up, brushing his lips along the curve of my breast. "That's because only my cock should be inside of you. I was made for you, and you were made for me. Now be a good girl and tell me that you understand that only I will ever make you come."

I think I might faint. When Ford says these things, he has a determined edge in his tone, a sort of territorial order that he likes to remind me of, and it only turns me on more, especially when I feel him slide in and out of me.

"I understand."

"Say it, Elle."

"Only you will ever make me come," I promise.

He growls before he sucks on a nipple, while his fingers dig into the flesh of my hips.

I continue to move, bouncing on top of him, and Ford meets me on every thrust. I fall back onto my arms, but I can still see him inside of me. Ford brings his finger to my clit as he takes over setting our speed, and I clench around him, with the world blurring around us.

"Let go, and I will fill you up. I want you to feel me inside of you the whole day," he tells me.

I nod as I circle my hips around him, following his demand. "Ford," I call out as I tremble, and he is quick to catch me.

My orgasm comes easy, and that's mostly because this man knows my body. He feels my needs because everything I want leads me back to him.

———

FORD BRINGS a cup of coffee to his lips where he's sitting next to me in our booth at Jolly Joe's. The soda shop-styled cafe always has something for everyone, from milkshakes to a cinnamon roll with coffee. It's quiet this morning, so the subtle sound of doo-wop can be heard while we look out the big windows onto Main Street.

"I don't remember you drinking coffee. Something about caffeine killing your hockey mojo," I remark as I play with the spoon in my coffee mug.

He wraps his arm around my shoulders. "I no longer have to worry about hockey demands. I run my own show. Besides, you know why I really ordered a coffee here."

I smile brightly as I dip my spoon into my coffee and scoop up a red jellybean. "Because of the ridiculous idea that someone had to add jellybeans to coffee?" It's a Jolly Joe's specialty.

"You never know what color you'll get."

Looking down at the food in front of us, I question how we will get through all of this. We have almost every item on the menu; pancakes, eggs, bacon, cinnamon rolls. This entire week has turned into a week of sex and food, which in retrospect is not a bad thing.

"Remember when you used to take me here for ice cream?" I dig into my cinnamon roll with the side of my fork.

Ford sets his coffee down. "Turtle sundae with butterscotch, not caramel, and an extra cherry on top."

"And you were chocolate with marshmallow."

"We didn't spend much time amongst civilization, though."

I give Ford side-eye and raise my brows.

He rumbles a sound under his breath. "I want to take you to our place. We can go tomorrow."

"You mean the lagoon? I'm sure there's a new set of teenagers who made a claim that it's their spot."

Ford chomps on a bacon slice. "I'll pay them to scram and remind them to keep it safe."

I laugh at how ridiculous that sounds, but I know that it's something Ford would do.

"A few days ago, I would have been petrified to go there. It's too overwhelming with memories of you. But now… it sounds perfectly fitting," I announce and take another giant bite from my cinnamon roll.

"Good. So today we will see Connor, take it easy, and you can study if you want, and then tomorrow, we'll make it a day."

"Sounds good." I move my plate to the side and feel I need to address the obvious. "Seeing Connor today, you know that he—"

Ford quickly interjects. "Can't know that we're kind of a thing again?"

"Yeah, exactly that. We shouldn't confuse him."

He looks at me, slightly irritated, his gaze piercing. "I get it. But make no mistake, we are playing the long game."

I roll my eyes. "Okay, but it requires a little more thought than that. You said give this a week. I mean, I don't even live in Lake Spark."

"Yes, but next summer Connor is switching schools anyway for middle school, so you both can come to Lake Spark."

"And what about my career? I mean, I'm not exactly sure there are a lot of job prospects here for me as hopefully a new lawyer," I highlight the apparent, and I feel like I'm tainting our last amazing 24 hours.

Ford angles his body to me and takes my hand. "First off, no hope, you *will* be a new lawyer soon." I appreciate that he has always been my biggest cheerleader. "And job prospects, I don't know. I'm sure my training facility needs more people on our legal staff."

I shake my head. "No, I'm not going down that route."

"This time we won't let anything or anyone get in our way," he promises, and I love the faith in his voice.

I attempt to smile, but deep down I have a fear that something will get in our way.

"Come on, eat a little more. You need your strength." There is pure sexiness in his voice.

We finish up our breakfast and take a little walk on Main Street, as we have time to spare. I see Piper in her boutique, and she waves at me through the window.

"I should go in and say hi."

Ford steps back and holds his hands up. "Go for it. I'll stay out here."

I look at him peculiarly. "Why?"

"She's my neighbor and Hudson's wife, so I need to remain somewhat respectable. I can't go inside her boutique with you and not go crazy."

"It's just a bouti… ahh." My brain catches up, and I roll my lips in as I try not to grin. "A lingerie boutique."

Ford slides his hand into my hair to pull me in for a kiss. "But go in there and have fun. Use the credit card for it."

I burst out with a laugh. "You want me to use the credit card you gave me, which is for Connor and things he needs, to buy lingerie?"

"Why not? I like providing for my family." He can't control his grin.

I wave him off. "I'll be quick."

I don't look back and head straight into Piper's boutique. The bell chimes over my head and the door closes behind me.

Piper is behind the counter, opening a box, with her daughter asleep in her stroller in the corner.

"How is life with our favorite hockey player? You both look cute walking hand in hand down Main. By the way, there is a rumor that Margo wanted to buy out the florist for your upcoming wedding." Piper has a knowing grin as she focuses on her task.

I assess the array of lingerie and pajamas in the store. I'm not sure where to focus, everything is either beautiful, sexy, or cozy.

"Remind me to fix that scenario. And Ford and me? It's… well," I say as I touch the fabric of a red nightie.

"That's a good choice, but if I may be a little bold, then I would suggest the deep purple color."

My hand retreats back like I touched a hot pan. "Oh, I just came in to say hi and check to see how Grace's skin is going."

Piper walks to her daughter and smiles. "She's doing better, thank you. Sleeping like a little angel. Her bath with the oat oil really helped." Piper steps in my direction. "Let me repay you with something."

"Don't be silly. Advice is free," I protest.

Piper holds a finger in the air. "Exactly, advice is free." She walks to the corner and reaches behind a rack of clothes on hangers to pull out an item hanging in the back. When she holds it up, my eyes nearly bug out. It's a bra-and-panty set with stocking suspenders, black with bright pink edging.

"I can't wear that!"

"Of course you can."

I shake my head in astonishment.

"It's always fun to shake things up."

My mouth opens but no words come out. "I guess… well, Ford and I, we're…"

Piper patiently waits for my explanation.

"We were teenagers when we were first together, kind of sweet. Now, we're adults with a kid." I laugh.

"Exactly. Show him you're a woman now. That's my advice. Remind him that everything is different, and that can make things even better." She holds the set out in front of her. "I think I got your sizing right."

Blowing out a breath, I'm not sure what to say. "Why not." I throw my hands up into the air. "But let me at least pay."

"Nonsense." Piper is already pulling out tissue paper and a bag.

"Thank you," I give up and make a mental note to give back to her in some way at a later moment.

"You're very welcome. Happy neighbor, happy life, right?"

"I'm not your neighbor," I remind her with a smile.

"But Ford is, and he has been pining for you for forever." She hands me the bag.

Taking the bag, I can only agree. "Me too, if I'm being honest."

Saying our goodbyes, I make it back to Main Street to find Ford leaning against a tree with his shades on. That is until he sees I have a bag in my hand, then he propels off the tree and tips his sunglasses down to the tip of his nose.

"I'm curious," he firmly states.

"Me too." I laugh nervously.

He pulls me close and tries to steal the bag hanging off my fingertips, but I don't let him succeed.

"Naughty us will have to wait. We need to go see someone important," I remind him with a fake stern look.

Ford growls into my neck before stepping to the side, taking my hand, and walking us in the direction of the car.

"Our son," he confirms.

Letting go of Brielle's hand when we entered the rink was a difficult task, but I get it.

Mixed signals for Connor are something neither of us intend to do.

Walking down the main hall, there are ice rinks on each side. This place also has other sports. Hudson even trains his football team in a field nearby in the summer.

"This place is impressive," Brielle compliments.

I scratch my thumb over my chin which has some stubble since I didn't want to waste any time this morning. Elle is taking a chance on us, admitting truths, and letting me back into her life the way I want to be in hers. So yeah, there was no time for shaving.

"Thanks. After the summer when Connor is back at school, I'll get my head busy with logistics and planning. We have a lot of staff to handle here, so there will be a lot of meetings, I'm sure."

"But here you are now, volunteering to teach a class for the kids." She smiles with the praise.

"I would like to think even if I didn't have a son that I would still have found myself here. And if I don't like it, then maybe I'll coach college hockey. There is something about eager athletes that would keep me on my toes."

"I could see that. The nearest college to Lake Spark is ironically Hollows."

"I may have noticed." We walk side by side, our shoulders occasionally grazing. "Connor will be on a break soon, and then you can see him."

"I guess I need to get used to this. I don't see Connor giving up hockey any time soon."

"You resent hockey?"

She bobs her head side to side. "I could say it took you away from me, but hockey is part of your identity and what you enjoy. I knew as soon as I discovered we were having a boy that he would probably want to follow in your footsteps. Don't get me wrong, I would be thrilled if he said hockey wasn't for him and he would rather try theater or violin. I get scared that as he gets older, the game gets more… intense."

I touch her shoulder to comfort her. "I understand, but right now, he is still a junior and wears lots of padding, and they take it easy. It's no different to any other sport."

"Except he is wearing skates on ice, and hockey moms scare me. I need to go full-on grizzly mama bear around hockey moms," she tells me in a neutral tone.

I laugh at her statement. "You're the hottest hockey mom there is."

Brielle shoots me a warning glare. "No flirting here."

Up ahead I see someone I know and nod my head. "Hey, Declan," I call out.

Declan is my former teammate; he was new to the team this year, and I took him under my wing. He is also worth billions, thanks to his family and investments. He has proven everyone wrong by demonstrating he earned a spot on the team by pure talent, and lucky for them, he still has a few years left to play.

"Hey, Ford." He walks to me and shakes my hand. His eyes are immediately drawn to Brielle at my side.

Clearing my throat, I set my hand on Brielle's lower back. As much as I would consider Declan a friend, I have no problem giving him the stay-the-fuck-away-from-my-woman stare, because his bachelor status doesn't exactly thrill me, especially since I'm about to hit the ice and leave Brielle alone in the stands.

"You just gave an hour to the kids?"

"Yeah." Declan's blue eyes float between us in slight confusion.

I explain, "Brielle is here to check on *our* son."

Brielle smiles tightly.

"It's good to see you again. Connor is a natural talent," Declan compliments.

"I'll never get tired of hearing that," Brielle responds.

"Those kids wore me out. Good luck," he voices.

I fold my arms over my chest, amused. "It's worth it. Thanks again for volunteering."

"Gets me bragging rights on my next date." He is completely joking because, underneath his steely exterior, I'm sure there is a heart of gold.

I look at my watch and internally groan. "Listen, I would love to hear who the woman of the month is, but I need to grab my skates from my office. Don't make me regret this but can you walk Brielle to the rink? My sister Violet will meet her there."

Declan is already offering Brielle his arm. "My pleasure. Happy to volunteer to take care of your precious goods."

"Oh." Brielle seems taken aback by his arm offer. "Thank you." She's unsure yet entertained, and they both look at me, knowing this scene drives me coconuts.

But alas, it doesn't take much for my inner caveman to come out when it involves Elle, and everyone knows it.

HOCKEY WAS MY LIFE. From the moment I tried on my first pair of skates. There is something about gliding along the ice or the sound of the blade that just brings me peace. Hockey itself is a game where every second is different. It's fast-paced and energizing, yet every move feels like a risk because you don't know how the puck will slide.

But this group of ten-year-olds are slightly different. They're learning more about handling a hockey stick, making goals, and the number of orange cones on the ice are enough to make someone go blind. Point is, they're still kids. Brielle is right, though, soon the game will change as Connor gets older.

The group are all sitting on a side bench snacking on oranges and granola bars. It doesn't take long for me to spot Connor at the end hugging his mom. I skate on over to hear their conversation.

"I'm so happy you're enjoying your week here. I've missed you like crazy." Brielle touches Connor's face.

Our son is the perfect mix of Brielle and me. Connor has Brielle's hair and eyes, although Brielle swears Connor has my eyes, but his mouth is for sure mine. His current haircut is a little too short for my liking, but he is only ten. Brielle always says he is as handsome as can be. I like to think that my boy will be breaking and mending hearts for years to come.

He shakes her hand away. "You came all the way to Lake Spark to see me?" Connor asks his mom.

Brielle pauses for a second, quickly catching me in her view. "Something like that. I'm getting ready for our little family week together after camp."

"Did you see my new room?" He seems excited.

"I did. Perfect for my little prince."

Connor groans. "Don't say that."

Brielle plants her hand on her hip. "Getting too big to be my little prince, huh?"

"I was already too big like two years ago."

I laugh and rustle his hair. "Newsflash, kiddo, there is no age limit for your mom to call you whatever she wants."

"Great." He sounds unenthused.

"Where's your Aunt Violet?" I haven't seen her yet.

"Had to run to the office. She said she'll take me to see a PG-13 movie tonight."

Brielle gives me a pointed look.

I tightly smile. "I'm sure she meant *after* checking in with us."

"Are you going to do drills today?"

"Yeah, I am. Remember I'm coach out there on the ice, not Dad."

Connor bites into his granola bar and speaks with a full mouth. "I know. I mean, every kid here knows already, but fine, we can play along."

Brielle laughs and checks Connor's water bottle, her habit from ensuring he has every snack and packed lunch at the ready. "I'll just be watching in the stands."

"Nobody else's family is watching."

"That's because nobody else here has a dad who runs this place."

"Gah, fine. Just don't embarrass me."

I place my hand on Connor's shoulder. "You're truly a delight today. Remember to be kind to everyone, say thank you, be grateful, and never forget that your dad has the ability to take your game system away," I remind him.

Connor's face falls. "I know."

"I promise I'll stay quiet. You won't even know I'm here," Brielle proclaims as she squeezes Connor's arm.

"Thanks. I should go back to the group."

"Of course," Brielle nods.

The moment Connor has his back turned, I skate closer to the wall so only Brielle can hear. "Breathe. He's just being a kid." Brielle does her best to keep her eyes wide open because I can tell she is about to break.

"He's no longer a little boy. When did that happen? I feel like pre-teen hell is hitting us early," she mumbles.

"Trust me, he will still have his moments where he needs you. It'll also be better when he isn't around other kids," I promise.

I see my sister walking down the steps of the rink. She smiles, and I wave back. Nobody ever figures out we're related. She's petite with black hair and looks nothing like me.

"Hey, Violet," I call out.

Brielle looks over her shoulder and turns to offer Violet a hug. "Hey."

"Sorry, I had to run to the office to check that the next snack will arrive at three instead of two." Violet looks between us. "Got to see Connor?"

"Yeah, he hates that I'm here." Brielle pouts for dramatics.

Violet touches her arm. "If it's any consolation, I'm only cool if I supply pizza. I can't even sway him with watching the Mighty Ducks movies anymore. That was a total win for me. Hockey for Connor and Joshua Jackson."

Brielle touches Violet's shoulder in agreement. "Oh yeah, totally forgot he's in that. So, right, Connor is too old for everything now."

Ignoring their nostalgia, I tell my sister, "Thanks again for helping out."

My sister shrugs. "Kind of needed something to do while I figure out my life. Speaking of which, Margo phoned me to ask what kind of flowers you both might like for your wedding?" She gives Brielle and me a confused look.

Brielle croaks out a sound and pretends to cough.

I rub the back of my neck. "What did you say?"

"That I'll get back to her." Violet is waiting for further explanation. "Something you two need to share?"

"Do you think she told Mom and Dad?" I ask awkwardly. As much as we are adults, we all know my dad will have an opinion on any reunion between Brielle and me.

Violet looks at Brielle for a clue then back to me. "No. She barely talks to them, and why aren't you telling me that Margo lost the plot?"

"Yeah, Ford, why aren't you?" Brielle gives me a cheeky smirk.

Looking at my watch, I pretend it's time. "Wow, look at that. Need to start warming up."

Violet looks back and forth between us, tilting her head to study Elle's vacant finger. "Okay, no engagement ring. Why are you two acting so… oh my God, you two are totally hooking up again," she loudly whispers, her face completely entertained.

I hold my hand up to indicate for her to quiet down. "You're my sister. We are not having this conversation."

"This is why I'm babysitting my favorite little devil, isn't it? You were really serious about your get-Brielle-to-Lake-Spark plan."

Brielle swipes a hand through her hair. "Wow, was I really the last one to figure out his agenda?"

My sister gives Brielle raised brows. "Oh please, Connor or no Connor, you really think you both would have lasted more than a day during 'family time at the lake house?'" Violet uses air quotes.

Brielle attempts to say something but fails.

"Don't you have emails to check? Maybe fill a water cooler? What am I paying you for again?"

"Big brother can't handle the hard facts? Fine." Violet takes two steps then pauses and whirls her finger in the air. "I'm not leaving because you told me to. I'm leaving because I have emails to answer and need to show Declan where he can connect his laptop."

"Oh yeah, Declan had to answer his phone. He said he'll call you later," Brielle informs me.

I shake my head. "Violet, just take Declan to an office. Don't try anything, Declan knows you are to be treated like a sister."

"Lucky me. I will show him to your office, but I'm doing it because I have job responsibilities, not because my brother is giving me orders." She tosses her hair behind her shoulders and stomps up the steps.

Brielle bursts out laughing. "The maturity between you two is really next-level."

"It's the fun of having a sibling." Looking down at my skates, I glide back and forth in place, but when I glance up, I notice a funny look on Brielle's face. "You okay?"

"Totally."

"Liar."

She looks around, checking that nobody notices us. "I like your look. Jeans and skates with a sweater on, it's my favorite."

Assessing myself, I'd say that she has good taste. My jaw flexes side to side. "Truth?"

She nods in agreement.

"Have you always been checking me out every time I hit the ice?"

"Maybe," she plays coy, but it's obvious.

I lick my lips and grin to myself. "Thought so." I lean over the wall. "And you are the hot hockey mom I'm always checking out."

"Thought so," she repeats my words.

Skating back, I don't tear my sight away from her until I have to turn to skate forward.

It never gets old, Elle watching me on the ice. In truth, she gave me the drive to play harder and better. Now? She makes me excited for my next chapter on and off the ice.

The kids all pile onto the ice again and skate a few laps. A few times I catch Connor watching his mom sitting in the stands. When the kids come to circle around me, I'm setting down one more cone. We're going to practice passing the puck side to side.

I notice my son staring at me more intently than normal. I give him a wink, but he rolls back his shoulder.

Fuck me, I wish I could freeze time so he can't grow anymore.

Sometimes I wonder when he's older if he will ever puzzle the pieces of Brielle's and my life together, connecting the dots that we sacrificed a lot for him, but he'll appreciate that we love him so much which is why we lost time. Most of all, I wonder if he will look back to now when his parents decided that the puzzle can only be completed if we're together.

Because that's what we're doing.

13

BRIELLE

Holding my sun hat, I breathe in the fresh air and take in the sunlight hitting my face and skin, as I'm only in my bikini with a mesh cover-up. Ford is driving the boat across the lake. Luckily, this time we are on the speedboat and not the rowboat, which I am fairly convinced he used the other day because he knew I wouldn't be able to row us back if I tried to escape.

Staring at Ford, my mouth forms a half-smile. He looks good with his sunglasses on, no shirt, and steering the boat. He's the man I've always wanted, and he is now within my reach.

"Daydreaming?" he asks as he turns the wheel.

"I'm that obvious, huh?"

"Yeah. I hope you're thinking about when I get to see whatever is in that bag from Piper's boutique."

I wave my finger in the air. "Nuh-uh, I haven't decided yet. I'm never going to hear the end of this, am I?"

After seeing Connor at camp yesterday, Ford and I picked up some takeout from Catch 22, the restaurant on the water, then we went home and watched a movie before heading to bed where he most definitely used his hands and fingers in ways that I can't even manage to say out loud.

The lingerie set that Piper gave me is elegant and deserving of a big reveal, not an afterthought between rounds, therefore I'm reserving it for a special occasion.

"Suspense is your play, I respect that. It just means you envision a very long timeline for us; I do hope you realize that." He smirks to himself.

"I might."

This morning, I arrived downstairs, and Ford was closing a cooler, telling me not to worry about packing the picnic. I'd be lying if I said I don't have butterflies in my stomach.

I haven't been back to this lagoon since, well, before Connor.

"How do you know the lagoon isn't covered in garbage or the trees are gone. Maybe we are hyping this up," I think out loud.

"It's there." Ford is sure of himself.

"You've been back?"

"Once or twice. I would drive by with the boat, never went in, though."

God, is this what the past has done to us? We can't let go of places?

I look along the horizon to the right and see the opening to the spot that is responsible for holding our hearts captive. The trees hang over the passage. Willow trees, to be exact; the tree that blows tears in the wind.

Ford slows the boat down as we approach, and I get up off my seat to take a few steps to Ford, standing by his side and holding his arm before we both duck under the weeping tree as we enter.

We found this place one day when we decided to venture off from our group who were partying on the shore nearby. It became our spot, our refuge.

And luckily, now I can witness that it hasn't changed. It's still quiet and beautiful. Calm lake water with a small little beach, perfect for two.

Ford turns the engine off and throws the rope to the sand. He hops over the edge, with the water to his knees. After he ties the rope to a tree trunk, he returns to the boat to offer me his hand.

"Come on."

Our eyes connect, and everything feels slightly overpowering but in the best possible way.

When I'm about to hop into the water, Ford grabs me in a manner that enables him to carry me and ensure I stay dry.

"What service," I joke.

"For you, I'd crawl on my knees."

I laugh before my feet land on dry earth. We take a few moments to lay out a big blanket and set down the cooler. It isn't long until we are both lying down on propped elbows as we stare at the view.

"Here we are," I announce.

Ford interlaces our fingers on the blanket. "It's good to be back."

"It feels kind of coming full circle," I admit.

Glancing to my side, I see that Ford is ignoring the beautiful nature around us, as his focus is on me.

"It was our own little world."

I snort a laugh. "Oh, I know. Nobody ever came here, except that one time when a fisherman stopped, but then he saw us making out and left."

"Yeah, I remember that," he reflects with a grin of fondness.

"I'm confident this is where I got pregnant."

Ford moves to his side, and his fingers begin to play with the tie on my wrap. "Maybe."

"It was my fault."

He wastes no time to set his fingers on my jaw to guide my gaze to him. "No, it's not."

"I missed a pill."

"So? People take all their pills and still get pregnant. Besides, we have a great kid."

"I love him, but it could have been easier for us," I state.

Ford shakes his head. "We'll never know, and it doesn't matter. Here we are."

My lips roll in, and I can't think of how to articulate the array of emotions stirring inside of me. Something about this place, remembering younger me, the times we would lie here staring at the blue sky and talk about our dreams. We had crazy ideas that being together could be so easy. We'd get a place together, and I'd study law wherever Ford went. I wanted that because a textbook can be read anywhere, and Ford was the one and only.

Looking back, I see how he put me first. Letting go of my dreams wasn't an option to him, which is why he didn't fight our parents when we made the decision to keep Connor.

But damn, we were tormenting ourselves for years.

"I don't want my heart to break again," I whisper softly.

Ford leans down to brush the corner of my mouth with his lips. "It can't break." He is adamant and his voice rasps.

"I think it can."

He gently shakes his head no. "It never broke. I've just been holding onto it for a while, waiting for you to come back."

My heart swells at his words, and I tip my chin up to offer my mouth to him for a kiss. His lips press a firm kiss against my mouth, and I want to get lost in him. I slide my leg up his body until I snake around his waist, pulling him to me.

I murmur into his mouth, certain that everything inside of me has surrendered. My mind gave into his idea of having a week to ourselves, a selfish decision, but in truth, my heart already committed to more than a week long ago.

"I'm scared." Our mouths can't part. It's a constant back and forth of our lips sealing together, attempting to get air, only to return like a magnet. "Of this."

"Tell me." Ford showers me with kisses. "What has you scared?"

I manage to escape his hold and scoot up to sitting, well aware my wrap is twisted and halfway off my body. "We're in the grasp of having it all. It's possible, right?"

Ford flashes me a smile of comfort. "I believe so."

"I can't be responsible around you. We are unable to go slow, with our relationship, I mean." I dip my head down and attempt to hide my happiness from that fact.

Ford tucks my braid behind my shoulder. "I think ten years has been slow enough, don't you?"

"Yeah."

"Listen, soon Connor is back home. *Our* home. I know we need to be sensitive around him, but he isn't a small kid anymore."

"Oh, I noticed." I breathe a sigh.

Ford leads me back to lying. "Let's just take it one step at a time… to our final destination."

"Which is?" I squint my eyes at him.

He scoffs a sexy laugh before nuzzling his nose against my hair. "That ring deserves to be around your finger."

I pretend to be shocked. "What intentions."

Ford tickles me in response, and we both get tangled in one another until we realize we are at the moment where real entwines with dreams.

"I never stopped loving you, Elle."

I wrap my arms tighter around his neck. "I love you too, but I guess you knew that since you had my heart this whole time."

"Damn straight."

His hand moves between us to untie my wrap, and my body is already aching. Ford groans as his mouth clasps onto my nipple through my bikini.

I moan and bite my lower lip. "You're trouble. Not even thirty minutes in and we are adding public indecency to our day."

"You didn't seem to mind ten years ago," Ford reminds me before he lowers the fabric.

My nipple is a prisoner between his teeth, and I hiss in pleasure. "Didn't Lake Spark become more of a tourist destination since then? Are we really alone?"

He peers up from his efforts. "It's just you, me, and the sky."

My clit pulses from the need I have for this man to be inside of me. "Then do things to me that will make the sky wish it could hide." I notice my tone is more sultry than normal.

Ford chuckles deep in the back of his throat before he makes a point to ensure I watch him as his fingers disappear under the bottom of my bikini, his touch launching instant fireworks inside of my body.

"My fingers are already soaking." Ford's voice is thick with approval and heat.

Feeling his fingers slide in a line then circle, I hood my lids closed and sink into his connection. "What can I say? I'm craving your touch."

He brings his finger up to my lips, and I open to suck, knowing he likes to watch me taste myself. Needing more, I rub against his body, feeling his solid length against my stomach.

His finger pops out of my mouth and is replaced by Ford's warm hungry kiss that shoots desire down my spine.

"Roll to your side," he whispers his demand into my ear, causing my sensitive parts to tingle.

Obeying, I roll away from him, and I feel his hand lower his swim trunks just enough before he unties half of my bikini bottoms to give room, and his tip swirls along my pussy, dragging my arousal around until he aligns and enters me with ease.

As I look over my shoulder, he meets my mouth to swallow my moans as he moves inside of me while his hand travels from holding my hip in place, along my oblique, before sneaking up to tweak my nipples.

I gasp from the overload of sensations.

"You feel too good," Ford mumbles against my skin.

Deep inside, I feel him reach a part of me that's the button to awakening extreme pleasure that he can deliver on every move.

"Good thing you don't plan on letting me go," I murmur. I reach my arm behind me to hook around his neck, causing my body to elongate and offer a better canvas to Ford.

The sound of our skin slapping is the only sign that we're not going slow. I'm so lost in Ford that our rhythm is irrelevant because every thrust is heavenly.

"I can't get enough of this."

My breath grows heavy. "Me too."

His finger travels down to my clit, and I'm happy we are lying down because my entire body feels like it's floating, only being grounded by Ford's touch.

Kissing him is my secret weapon for stability. He leads us and keeps me from falling, because I'm about to explode, and he knows it too.

"I want you coming around my cock," he demands into my ear while his finger circles my clit.

"Only if you promise to come."

He laughs sinisterly causing a tickle below my ear. "Baby, I'm only satisfied if you come and then I fill you up."

I nod and close my eyes as my senses heighten, and a few more strokes and I'm almost there.

"That's it," he coos.

Ford thrusts harder, and a wave travels below my navel, flowing until I'm pulsing and shaking around him.

My body goes completely spent and into a state of utter bliss as he continues to move.

It's when his head falls against my shoulder and I feel him still that I know Ford joined me on the satisfaction scale.

He stays inside of me, and that's what I love the most about the last few days, just being completely dissolved into one another, truly one.

I hum a sound to express my current state as Ford places a kiss on my shoulder.

"I feel like my thighs might be shaking for days," I tell him.

"Excellent." He tucks his head into the curve at the base of my neck. "One day we'll come back here and we'll make another baby."

Instantly, I stutter out a sound. "You're crazy."

"No, I'm not."

"You make me feel like you're completely enamored with me."

I feel a loss the moment he slides out of me to drag his shorts back up. "Solid observation."

I roll my eyes as I wiggle to retie my bikini. Ford is quick to help me with the strings around my neck.

Now covered, I move to sit between his legs, with my back to his stomach and his arms finding a home around me.

"I hope you put on sunscreen; the sun is strong today."

He kisses the top of my head. "Remember that time we came out here and we forgot? You looked like a lobster for days."

I laugh at the memory. "Yeah, and I was red everywhere, not one inch spared; bikini lines gone, which meant everyone knew I had been naked."

"With me." He grins with pride.

"Exactly."

"Do you know what I think is amazing?"

I kiss his upper arm that rests across my shoulder. "What?"

"Even when we weren't together, I'm the lucky guy who knew you from the beginning. We have a history. I'm your first, and I know every little thing about you. We share a child, connected for life. Nobody could come close to that; I get to be the one who sees you in a different light."

My tongue runs a line inside my mouth. "I know the feeling. You are my rock, even when I chose not to admit it."

"I promise I won't sink you down." He squeezes me tighter.

"Nah, it's okay, you can. Everything inside of me felt weighted down before. Every time I thought any chance of us would go out the window, I couldn't move on. Now, I know I felt that way because you're worth the wait. We were always going to find our way back, I believe that now."

"Is it possible to feel so incredibly happy that you know it makes up for lost time?"

My shoulders come up to my ears in doubt. "I guess we'll find out."

"Yeah, we will."

Over the next hour or two, we swim and have some drinks from the cooler. As I watch Ford load the boat, I can't seem to shake this feeling that, as much as we trust our change in relationship, we are currently in our own world and bubble.

What happens when the outside world sticks a pin in it?

FORD

Connor drops his bag by the door to the garage and starts to run in the direction of the den off the main living room that houses the game system. Today was the end of camp.

"Hey, cutie, how about we pick up the bag you left on the floor?" Brielle suggests with a sweet smile as she walks from the kitchen, drying her hands with a towel.

I was on pick-up duty, as I wanted to check a few things in my office, and Brielle stayed home to study in quiet.

Our son groans and mopes back on the trail he took until he picks up the backpack, then hangs it on the hook. "Happy now?"

"Very," Brielle answers dryly.

Connor starts his trek, but I grab him by the back of his shirt. "Whoa there, cowboy, how about a hug for your mom?"

"Ugh, fine." Connor walks to his mom and gives her a lazy hug.

"How about I get you a snack?" Brielle ignores his behavior and coddles him.

"I'm starving. Can I have popcorn?" he asks.

"Sure."

Then he is off again.

I rub my face, reminding myself that he's a kid who is entering an awkward age because these sure as hell are no longer the days of never leaving our sides because Mom and Dad are the best thing in the whole world. Following Brielle back into the kitchen, she heads straight to the cupboard to collect a popcorn bag.

"He needs to unwind, but after that, it's full-on family time whether he likes it or not." I grab vitamin water from the fridge.

Brielle is busy pressing buttons on the microwave. "You're right." She turns and heads to the sink to clean a mug she must have used while I was away.

Walking straight to her, I stand behind her and allow my hand to sneak underneath her skirt to tease that soft stretch of skin on her inner thigh.

She gasps instantly. "What are you doing?" she mutters, and I can hear her smile.

"It's impossible not to touch you when the opportunity arises."

"Ford, our son is in the other room, and you better get used to behaving because we're not sharing a bed the next few nights."

I sigh at the reminder, but this morning we agreed that it was for the best. Connor is the priority, and we need to be tactful and slowly ease him into the change in his parents' relationship status.

Ignoring the reality of our parameters, I let us have these few minutes while our son is nowhere in sight. I slip my finger between her thighs, riding up but stopping short, but it doesn't mean I don't feel her heat near my finger. I bet if I touched her pussy, she would be soaking, but I'm not that reckless.

My other hand grabs her hair with a little force to bring her neck to my mouth. "All I want to do is watch you touch yourself to show me how much you want me before I bend you over the kitchen counter and defile you until you scream," I growl low against her throat.

"That's quite a picture you paint," she hisses.

"I'm not the teenage boy you lost your virginity to. I'm a man now who has had years to think of all the dirty things I want to do to you, before I kiss you gently because I love you."

I pull her tight to me, only to feel her shudder as she melts against my body.

"Ford," she hums.

"Why don't we take these off?" I begin to tug on the string of her thong.

A scoffed sound escapes her mouth which now hangs open. "No way. You need to back up and find me a bowl for the popcorn." She shimmies against me but rides my finger at the same time as the sound of corn kernels popping fills the room.

"I can get used to you standing in my kitchen." I move my hand away from her middle and follow the curve of her ass that I gently spank before stepping back. "A bowl you said?" I casually inquire, as if nothing just happened.

Brielle grips the edge of the sink as she catches her breath. "Yeah, and some manners!" She twists her body and playfully swats me as I walk away.

Grabbing a ceramic bowl from the shelf, I proceed to open the microwave that beeped.

"Should we do homemade pizzas for dinner? That's easy, right?" She seems to be focused again.

I wash my hands then pour the bag of corn into the bowl. "Sounds good. Tomorrow, we can just chill by the pool, or go on the boat, walk around town. I kind of feel like Pioneer Park is no longer on the list of options."

Our son rejoins the room and is quick to inform us, "No way. I'm way too old for that shit."

"Whoa, language." I'm not impressed and hold the bowl up in the air so he can't reach it. "Maybe we keep that word out of our vocabulary."

"Why? Other kids and Aunt Violet say it all the time." He attempts to reach for the popcorn.

"You are not other kids, and Aunt Violet is in her twenties, trying to figure out her life, and she still considers ice cream its own food group, so she's not exactly the pillar of goals."

I notice Brielle drop her face into her palm. "How about we try a clean slate from your arrival at home."

Connor sits on a stool and slouches against the counter. "Sure, but it's Dad's home, not yours."

Brielle's jaw clenches, and I can tell she is frustrated with the attitude.

I carelessly drop the bowl of popcorn onto the counter, ready to correct him. "It's family week. My home is your home, it's your mother's home, it's our home. Clear? Got it? Great."

His hand claws the snack. "Fine. Is this all because I told my teacher that you two act strange sometimes?"

Brielle steps closer to the counter. "It's because we should do more things as a family. We don't always need to keep everything to your time with Dad or your time with me."

"I get it. You want to do things together outside of special occasions."

"Bingo." Brielle taps her finger into the air.

Our son now has a mouth full of popcorn. "What's for dinner? I'm starving."

"You're eating right now." Brielle looks on in astonishment.

"I know, but I've worked up an appetite. I built muscle the last two weeks." He proudly flexes his arm.

Brielle and I look at one another and smile. "You're a growing boy."

"A little man," I add.

He chomps on more popcorn. "Exactly."

"I guess I will get to work on pizza then." Brielle walks to the fridge, and I continue to lean against the counter, staring at Connor who is oblivious that he has it so lucky; everything we do is for him.

———

APPARENTLY, food is the key to Connor's growing attitude. His mood pepped up after a second slice of pizza. Brielle made everyone their own, which is perfect since we all have different tastes. We're sitting outside on the patio around the pool relaxing and being together, just the three of us.

For the most part, we've always had a reason to be together for dinners. A birthday, a school recital, or a post-game dinner. We never did this just because… and it feels too right.

"The dog is here," Connor points out.

We all skim our gaze in his line of sight and see April and Spencer's beagle, Pickles, padding along into our yard. It happens occasionally. He is harmless and old, except when he sees Spencer or a squirrel, then suddenly, he has puppy energy.

"Ah, we will need to take him back. Most of the time, April doesn't realize he wandered off. I'm pretty certain a raccoon or something will get to him one of these days."

"Ford," Brielle scolds me.

I roll my shoulder back before picking up my beer bottle. "What? It's true. This is Lake Spark."

"Can I have a dog?" Connor asks before taking a bite of his food.

"Since when do you want a dog?" Brielle grabs the salad bowl.

"I'm a kid, shouldn't I have a phase of wanting a dog?"

I chuckle at his reply. "You're a kid now? A few hours ago, you made it clear you're no longer a kid."

"Stop with the psychology," my son retorts.

"A dog is a lot of responsibility," Brielle notes as she watches Pickles walk to me for a pat on his head.

"True, and soon I will have hockey practice like all of the time," he explains.

I rub my chin, as I can only imagine Connor in a few years playing high school hockey. There is a prep school nearby with a great team.

"How about you take Pickles back after dinner? That's the closest you can get to having a dog," Brielle suggests.

"No way. Hadley is there, and she looks at me all funny."

I grin to myself. "Hadley is younger than you, probably with a little crush, and I'm not sure she's there since Spencer has an away game this week, so April was going to take her to watch."

"Exactly, it's yuck that she has a crush on me."

Brielle reaches to her side to touch Connor's arm with affection. "It's not yuck. It just means you are a handsome guy. And get used to it, because as you get older, then, well, I hate to tell ya, but the girls will be lining up."

"Can we end this conversation? Next thing I know, you will be giving me the baby talk and how it has to happen later in life. Aunt Violet says you two are the exception and made me early, and you won't let me forget it so I won't become a dad in a few years."

Brielle gives me wide eyes, with a look that is half-worried and half-entertained.

"Your Aunt Violet, to my surprise, makes a solid point." Huh, my sister kind of nailed it. I tip my beer back for a sip.

"Tomorrow, can we just hang by the pool?" Connor drops his pizza on the plate.

Brielle nods. "Sounds good. I can study."

"That big test," he volleys.

"Exactly," she says. "I have a really big test to take. Two days of tests, which is why you might spend a little extra time with your dad this summer," Brielle explains.

I notice Pickles is resting at my feet. Hopefully, he doesn't get too comfortable. "We'll hold down the fort, and when your mom finishes her test, then we can celebrate."

"Does that mean we are going to the jewelry store?" Connor innocently asks, but Brielle chokes on her drink.

She attempts to clear her throat. "Why do you say that?" Her voice is strained.

Our son looks at her. "Because that's what we always do when it's a special occasion. Geez, Mom, you know nobody at this table believes in Santa, so who do you think helped me pick out your Christmas necklace?"

A wry smile is now permanent on my lips, especially when I notice Brielle look down at the necklace she is playing with, the necklace from Connor.

"I mean, I assumed you had some help," she says in an attempt to defuse this conversation.

I scratch my cheek. "How about you drop Pickles off, Connor? I'll grab the ice cream from the freezer," I suggest.

Connor stands up, and Pickles' head perks up. "Come on, my parents are trying to get rid of me so they can whisper about me because they think I'm clueless."

Hot damn, even I'm stuck on how to respond, and when I look at Brielle still with a frozen smile, then I know that I'm not alone.

Watching Connor walk away with the dog in tow, Brielle and I sigh a heavy breath of relief that we got away without addressing his comment.

"What do you think he meant?" I wonder.

"I don't know, but that was my cue to open the wine." She laughs.

Since I am ever the gentleman, I stand up to lean across the table to grab a bottle of white and pop the cork for her with an opener.

As I twist the top, I glance up to notice that Brielle is staring at me with deep fondness. "Yes?" I draw it out.

She holds up her glass, ready for me to pour the vino. "His remark about Christmas jewelry, it just has me thinking."

"About?"

Probably the way that I used our son to ensure you wear a piece of me.

"He's right. Santa didn't help him buy expensive jewelry, and that if it hadn't been a gift from him then I would have been adamant you returned it. Do you know what I think?"

I tip the bottle over her glass. "Go on."

"We sometimes used our son to be together in some way."

My jaw flexes side to side, as she caught me out. "You know it's true."

"You put in a lot of thought with gifts."

"It was my responsibility to guarantee that he bought you gifts for your birthday, Christmas, and Mother's Day," I say, brushing it off.

She takes a decent sip of wine. "And I'm the one who maybe enjoys the fact that I know you had a hand in picking out this very expensive, beautiful, and perfect necklace with a little boat on it, which I'm certain Connor has no idea what it means."

I don't flinch, instead soaking in the truth of her theory. Walking around the table, I lean down and touch her chin to bring her lips up, and I capture her mouth for a kiss. "You are so incredibly smart. I have no doubt you will pass the Bar. Then maybe I can give you a gift without using Connor as the middleman."

"I don't want gifts. I want you." Her voice is raspy, and her smile never fades.

Recementing our lips, I take more, maybe I'm even greedy, and she murmurs as our breaths mingle.

"I swear, Elle, after he goes to bed, I'm finding a way to make love to you," I speak against her lips.

Brielle giggles and sinks back in her chair. "I think my beautiful glistening pussy needs a rest from your cock."

My mouth drops open in shock. "Your mouth!"

"What?"

"I've never heard you use such language. It's…" I don't know what it is. She is so prim and proper, yet she has just blown my mind. Do I like her like this? It's a surprise. Maybe I get my kicks out of her acting innocent half the time. I think about it for a few seconds. "Fucking hot."

She shoos me away with her hand, but I ignore her and dive in for one more kiss, only to quickly step back when we hear footsteps.

"Nobody is home, so I put Pickles behind the gate."

I swipe my hand through my hair as I see Connor in the corner of my eye. "Hey, kiddo. Sorry, I still need to grab the ice cream."

He walks back to his seat at the table.

"I'm not an idiot, Dad, I know this whole family-time story is so that you can both tell me that you're changing custody or someone is moving to someplace else, something like that."

Oh shit, we need to rectify this.

"Hey, no, wait, why would you think that? If anything, we'll be doing more things together."

Brielle is quick to jump in. "Exactly. Nobody is moving or changing custody, just more together time. That's great, right?"

Connor looks between us, skeptical. "Oh."

I blow out a breath and rest my hands behind my head. "You okay? Is that what you have been thinking this is?"

"I mean, you're both always awkward around one another, but today you both seem extra… I don't know, like you're happy and gearing me up for something."

Brielle taps her wine glass and nods her head in understanding. "You can relax, really," she promises.

"Okay, cool."

"I'll grab the ice cream." I begin to walk in the direction of the house but stall. "Connor, you don't see it as a bad thing that we're all together the next few days, right? I mean, now that you know nothing bad is happening."

He shrugs his shoulder. "I guess, it still sucks being the only child, though."

My eyes grow big. "Just add it to your never-ending wish list, okay, kiddo?"

Brielle snorts a cute little laugh.

And as I walk into the house, I feel like we may just be lucky, and easing him into our new dynamic might be a breeze. But I also wonder why he never asked if we were getting back together. It doesn't even seem to be a thought in his brain.

I realize that not many things in life make me nervous. I do well under pressure; how else was I a star hockey player? Yet telling Connor about his mom and me? It has me anxious.

Maybe I won't get the father-of-the-year award, but I think tomorrow we rip the band-aid off, because I'm sure as hell not sneaking around.

Walking into my home office, I pause when I take in the mass of post-it notes, highlighters, and notebooks splayed across my desk. My head tilts to the side as I wait for Brielle to look up at me, or at least notice that I'm here, as she is immersed in her book.

Clearing my throat, I wiggle my fingers at my side and my eyes circle the room, taking in the morning light.

"Morning," she says as she finishes writing a note before slamming the pen down and offering me a gorgeous smile.

I approach the desk, happy that she is making herself at home. "What time did you get up?"

"I think six." She doesn't seem sure. "Wanted to get a study session in."

I perch on the edge of my desk and dip my head down to kiss her. Would have preferred if I woke to her in my bed, but Connor is back, and clearly, Brielle has a few things on her mind.

She hums as I kiss her deeper, and I wish I didn't have to pull away. "I think you need a break."

"Oh yeah?" she whispers before her tongue delves into my mouth and her fingers curl around the fabric of my shirt.

I touch her wrists to steady us. As much as I have a few scenarios for this room, we need to talk.

Reluctantly pulling away, I give her one more quick chaste kiss before holding her hands on my lap. "How about we do a pool session this morning, then I take Connor into town so you can have a little space to study?" I suggest.

"Sounds good. Is he up already?" she wonders.

"I heard him stirring when I came down the stairs."

"I should go make him some breakfast." Brielle begins to get up, but I'm quick to hold her wrist to prevent her from getting far, and she gives me a bewildered look.

"He knows how to use a bowl and spoon. One morning of Coco Puffs isn't going to kill him. He's fine," I assure her because I know she insists he eats a big healthy breakfast every morning, often including her slaving over the griddle to make him pancakes.

She smirks to herself. "I guess you're right."

"Relax, okay?" She nods in agreement. "So, I was thinking while I'm with Connor that maybe he and I could have a little talk. Man to man, you know?"

"What do you mean?" She seems a little curious and concerned.

I run my hand along her arm to ease her. "I know we have a lot to discuss, but I think he's old enough that we don't need to be so delicate around him. He's smart."

She sighs and sinks back into the chair. "Shouldn't we tell him together? Wait a little, too? I mean, we're so fresh."

"We've been together for ten years, just not in a physical sense. I think you can agree."

Her nose raises slightly. "After I sit for the Bar, then we can tell Connor and drop the bombshell to our parents, figure out how to make this work."

"We'll work." My tone is a little sharp. "We will do all of that, but Connor is different, and I think sneaking around him only elevates stress levels."

"Maybe." She breathes out. I notice she is biting the inside of her cheek. "Don't you want to tell him together?"

"I think it's a talk that he and I need to have. Can you trust me on this?"

Her eyes meet mine and are filled with faith and contentment. "Okay. Tell him."

A soft smile spreads on both our faces. This time when she stands, I follow her lead and wrap my arms around her middle to kiss her one more time.

I mutter against her lips. "It will be fine."

She nuzzles her nose against my cheek, and I can tell that she inhales my scent. "I hope so."

Me too.

———

CONNOR and I walk down Main Street with ice cream cones in hand. We go slow to avoid our cones turning into a mess of melting ice cream. I motion to the bench up ahead that overlooks the park and gazebo by the lake.

"Mom is going to be upset that she missed ice cream from Jolly Joe's," he comments before taking another lick from his chocolate ice cream.

I swallow and take this as my moment. "It's okay, we'll get her a Turtle sundae to-go after we hit up the general store to grab a few things, as I want to BBQ tonight."

"You remember her favorite ice cream?"

I give my son a strange look. "I've known her longer than you have. Of course I know."

"She'll be happy if we bring her back ice cream."

We both sit down.

"Exactly. Your mom really needs us to make her life a little easier the coming weeks," I begin. "Her test is something she has been working for her whole life."

"She would be a lawyer already if it wasn't for me."

I toss the small remnants of my cone into the garbage not far from us and lean against the back of the bench, examining him, trying to figure out if his comment was an observation with thought behind it or not. "It's a bit more complicated than that. She wanted to spend more time with you when you were younger."

My son doesn't look up from his ice cream cone. "Yeah, because you were always away for games and training."

His words hit me hard, and a twinge of pain flutters across my chest. "Is that what you think?" Connor rolls his shoulder back. "We were young, and hockey was a way I could give you a life with anything you could ask for."

"I know, you guys tell me all the time."

My jaw clenches as I debate where to take our conversation. "Connor, I'm not going to talk to you like a little boy because you've made it clear the last few days that you are no longer one. So here we are, father and son, man to man, and I want to be honest with you."

"About what?" he asks, oblivious and focusing on his ice cream.

Bringing my hand to his shoulder, I decide to dive into the deep end. "Your mom. Me. Your mom and I." His eyes instantly blaze with curiosity. "I know we've raised you where your mom and I are friends, nothing more, but the truth is, we don't want that. We're together again."

"What do you mean?" His eyes turn strange.

"That your mom and I are in a relationship together. I'm telling you because we don't want to hide it from you."

"Why isn't she here?"

"Because I felt you and I needed to talk. I've noticed you have more observations and opinions lately, lucky us." I attempt to offer him a soothing smile. "Us together is new, but the feelings we have for each other have always been there. We just focused on other things."

"Like me."

"Yeah, and other goals. Truthfully, I've wanted to be with your mom for a long time, but it took the moment where we seem to have achieved all of those goals for me to go after the one thing that should have been my priority all along."

My son looks up at me with something that I can only pinpoint as a sensitive understanding or attempting to grasp my words. Gone is the child I carried on my shoulders and helped when he fell the first time on the ice. Here is a man in the making.

"Is it why Mom sometimes seemed sad after you would visit?"

I'm cracking inside from the reminders of the facts I already knew. Hearing it from him feels like a heavier punch, one that even reality couldn't throw at me. "Probably. But I have every intention of ensuring she is never sad another moment in her life."

Connor raises his chin slightly, as if he's sizing me up. "Is this really happening? I mean, you're both not going to change your minds, are you?"

I scratch my chin, proud that he is protective of his mother, the way he should be. "I don't think so. In fact, one day I hope to marry your mom. It's like this, Connor, everything was already there, every little amazing part that you need to make a relationship that lasts forever, except there was one missing piece, but now we decided to take that piece and add it to our lives."

"What's the part that was missing?"

I laugh and gently nudge his shoulder. "Well, I think you noticed we weren't romantic with one another. That's no longer the case. I want to kiss your mom all the time."

"TMI, Dad." He looks at me with funny disgust that is all in good fun. "Does this mean we are going to live together?"

"Can you do me one favor?" He nods. "We will talk about where we will live, school, dog or no dog, and what this all means for our family *after* your mom sits her exam in a few weeks. Right now, she needs us as her cheerleaders, and questions come later."

"Right, I can do that."

I smile. "Good. Now, tell me, how do you feel about all of this?"

Connor takes a moment and eats the last of his ice cream, making a point to drag this out because my boy got my streak of humor and games.

"I think…" he begins, "this is the best news." A smile spreads on his face.

Placing my hand on his shoulder, my face is elated. "I was hoping you would say that."

"What if I said I didn't like it?"

"Connor, as much as we do everything for you because you are our number one, sometimes your parents get to put themselves first, and then it would have been our job to prove to you that we are the real thing, and we make one another happy."

"This news is kind of cool."

We look at one another with an understanding that I'm proud to have with him. It's the type of dynamic that I missed with my own folks. Maybe that is why Brielle and I are so damn good at parenting; we learned what we needed to do better. And here I am in an honest and open conversation with my son, listening and being patient.

The thought of my parents brings a near scowl to my face. "Listen, I know you talk to Gramps and your grandparents via text sometimes. But let's wait to tell them the news, okay? We'll save everything for a few weeks from now."

"Uh-huh. Now is stress-free time for Mom, so just the pool, ice cream, and kissing at dinner when you think I'm not looking," he lists.

He grabs my attention as my head perks at his words, and I connect a few dots. He moves to throw away his napkin, but he doesn't get far because I gently take hold of the back of his shirt.

"You saw us last night, didn't you?" I have to grin.

He shrugs his shoulders. "Maybe."

"That's a yes. Were you going to bring it up or…" I wonder.

A cheeky smile spreads on his mouth. "You told me we were going for ice cream, just you and me. Everyone knows that means a talk is coming. It's a classic parent move."

"So, you let me sweat it out for a little?"

"For sure, Aunt Violet said I should too when I texted her."

I laugh because this is an unexpected turn, and I find humor in it. My sister means well, and I like that she is a sounding board for him, so I'm not mad.

"Anything else?"

Connor shakes his head. "Nah, I'll save the sibling talk for later."

"Yeah, you and me both, kid. Come on, we need to go to the store and get home to Mom." I stand and wait until he is off the bench.

We begin to walk back to Main Street, and I'm relieved that we can finally focus on being the family we always wanted.

BRIELLE

Ripping up pieces of lettuce, I occasionally glance at my phone. Lena is on the other end of our video call, soaking in all the details of my whirlwind few days. Her jaw dropped two sentences in, and I think she is still trying to wrap her head around it.

I probably should be too, but it all feels right. "I know it's crazy, but I feel like Ford maybe has a point and this is now our time."

Lena closes her mouth, and her head moves in different angles as she tries to form a sentence. "It's fast. However, I guess… it's no different to before, just now you upgraded to some serious benefits. I mean, you two were always emotionally there for one another, protective of each other, and now you can openly admit what you've been toeing around, plus add the physical aspect. It's not like you two are strangers. You talk on a daily basis… and have been for ten years."

I grab my half-filled wine glass to sip my Chardonnay. "Exactly, right? I'm not being irresponsible, am I?" Should I have more doubts?

Lena shakes her head. "Ford? He would kill for you, so no; he would never hurt you. Maybe being *together* together is different now that you're older?" Her voice grows squeaky, as even Lena isn't sure what to question. "Nah, it goes back to what I just said, you've both kind of been in a relationship, emotionally unavailable to anyone else, so if the physical aspect feels stellar, then I think you're good to go."

"Absolutely no complaints in that department." I try to keep my face serious, but I can't control the satisfied smirk that wants to break out. It causes Lena to clap like a penguin in excitement for me. "Anyhow, I'll be staying here for a few more days, then I need to head back to Hollows. My study group is meeting up again almost every day until the exams."

"I'm sure Ford can destress you a few times." She couldn't help herself and teases me.

I gulp a sip of wine. "Unfortunately, he is staying in Lake Spark and is going to keep Connor here so I can have some quiet."

Her face softens. "He wants this for you as much as you do."

"I think so. I'm curious how the man-to-man talk went. I think Connor wants us together. What kid doesn't want their parents together?"

She shrugs. "You'd be surprised, families come in different shapes. I'm just happy for you."

"Thanks. I should go, they'll be home any minute."

We both say our goodbyes, and I look down at the bowl of salad that is now home to tiny pieces of shredded lettuce because I got carried away daydreaming while prepping the salad.

Ignoring it, I grab the cucumber and begin to cube the vegetable with a knife. Randomly, I begin to wonder if a cucumber is really a fruit. I'm in doubt now and hold the green thing in the air to examine it.

I nearly drop it when I'm startled to feel two hands sneak up and snake around me, squeezing.

"Don't worry, there is no comparison," Ford informs me from behind.

Rolling my eyes, I lean back as he wraps his arms around me, enjoying being this way with him. "Is cucumber a vegetable?"

"I have no clue."

"It's a fruit," our son announces as he walks into the kitchen.

Instantly, from habit, I attempt to get Ford to back up, but he doesn't give in.

Instead, he leans down to whisper in my ear. "He knows."

Turning quickly in Ford's arms, my eyes grow big. "And?" I whisper back.

"Why don't you ask him?" Ford says in a normal tone with a neutral look, yet a hint of joy is there to ease me.

Stepping out of his hold, I walk into the middle of the kitchen with caution. "So, you and your dad talked?"

Our son doesn't look at me, instead putting something in the freezer before he searches the cupboards for what I can assume is food. "Yeah, no big deal."

"No big deal?" I'm slightly disappointed. I thought for sure this would be one of the greatest days of his life.

Connor turns to me with a box of Pop-Tarts in his hand.

I take the box from him because he will ruin his dinner. His glance down informs me he knows my logic. "Don't want to talk about it?"

"It's cool. Now you guys don't have to pretend everything is fine when it really wasn't."

My mouth opens but only a rambled sound escapes me. I feel Ford's presence behind me, and he rests his hands on my shoulders to send comfort through my blood.

"Connor means he is thrilled. If he's trying to make his mom freak out for fun, then he knows he needs to stop." Ford is speaking more to our son than me. "He saw us last night and didn't let me know until *after* our conversation," he grits out to me.

"Oh. You saw your dad and I..."

"Kissing. It's kind of gross but kind of sweet. Can we not make a big deal about it?" Connor pleads as he opens God knows what sports drink he just grabbed from the fridge that is fluorescent blue.

I pretend to zip my lips. "Not a word from me."

Ford clears his throat, and there is an odd tension in the room until Connor walks around the counter and comes to give me a hug. My ten-year-old is willingly giving me a hug, and I'm not going to waste a second questioning this. I bear-hug the heck out of him.

"Dad can really make you happy now."

I look down at my son who has a twinkle in his eye and a soft smile. I brush his hair back with my hand and cradle his head. "He can."

"I will," Ford corrects me.

"Is this all happening too fast?" I ask our son.

He shakes his head. "It makes life a hell of a lot easier."

"Language," Ford warns him, and I'm grateful that he is here to take the authoritative tone because I don't always want to be the rule mom.

"Sorry."

"I'm happy you're happy," I say.

He nods. "We brought you a Turtle sundae."

I smile brightly. "Is that what you placed in the freezer?"

"Yeah."

"The key to my heart," I reply.

Connor scoffs a sound and backs away. "Don't get sappy on us now."

"My mistake," I one-tone.

"I'm going to play a game now, Dad said I could before dinner."

"Thirty minutes, then I want you outside," Ford reminds him, but Connor is already turning the corner down the hallway.

I swivel on my toes to face the man who made this transition somewhat easy for me.

"What did you say?" I'm far too curious and loop my arms around Ford's neck.

He plays it cool. "Not much. Sometimes the obvious doesn't need to be explained."

Ford kisses my cheek, leaving me there to reflect on his comment.

———

A LITTLE WHILE LATER, I'm walking barefoot out onto the patio where Ford is working the grill. I place my ridiculous bowl of chopped salad on the table. I can't help myself, I drink in the view of Ford. Something about late-afternoon sun hits him just right. He's extra sexy as he flips a burger, occasionally drinking from his beer. He has no clue that I'm admiring him, feeling lucky that he is someone that I get to call mine.

Music plays on the Bluetooth, "My Sweet Baby" by Thieving Birds. I like this song.

Ford glances up, catching me in my near-drooling state. He grins, sets the grill tongs down, and walks around the BBQ to me.

"You look relaxed," he comments.

"I am. It should be one of the most stressful times of my life, yet I feel almost Zen," I remark.

Ford steps to me, pulling me around the waist to his body, and he holds my hand in his when he begins to lead us in a sway. "See? I sometimes have good ideas."

"You mean to get me here under false pretenses and get us to admit what we want?"

"Absolute brilliance," he remarks.

He twirls me around with our bodies flush, but it's nothing compared to his eyes that hold me captive as the sun causes a glint in his eyes.

"It's all okay," he assures me.

"I'm beginning to believe that," I say softly. "Connor does seem fine. He is, right?"

"Totally. I did tell him the sibling request needs to be on hold."

I laugh. "Good, we have time."

Ford tilts me back. "Just tell me when we have the green light on that."

I playfully nudge his shoulder before returning to our embrace for a dance on the patio under the summer sky.

"You just focus on that Bar now, okay? Everything else is for later," he promises.

"Sounds good."

Ford's fingers slide along my cheek into my hair, and he gives me a warning glare before his mouth meets mine for a warm kiss that keeps me grounded to the earth because this man is like a foundation of a house, except it's my heart.

"Everything is ours for the taking," he murmurs against the corner of my mouth.

"It is." I kiss him again, and this time I bring my leg up around his waist as we sway in our dance, and my dress hikes slightly.

He growls as we both laugh, completely lost in our moment.

"You know, I think I can get away with sleeping in your room tonight," I inform Ford with a sultry tone.

"Thank fuck for miracles," he nearly groans before kissing me.

"Okay, lovebirds, don't burn my burger," Connor orders as he walks along the pool and straight into a chair.

Ford and I step back and study ourselves. Our clothes are ruffled and our lips swollen. Admittedly, we are proud of ourselves because we're happy.

And a few minutes later, we are all laughing around the table for dinner. It's a perfect setting.

———

SLIDING my phone to the other side of the counter, I decide to ignore it. My father sent a text checking in on my studying. As much as I know he means well, it also feels like pressure. I just quickly texted back that I had a study session this afternoon, which was true.

But now, I'm done for the day, and tomorrow I head back to my house, and because I am still at Ford's, then that means I get to join my guys right after I bring them a fresh bowl of snacks.

Filling a bowl with tortilla chips, I walk into the den off the hall to the laundry room. A complete man cave, and to my surprise, Ford and Connor are not gaming but watching television and laughing.

They ignore me as I wiggle my way between them on the sofa, offering my son the bowl first.

"What on earth are you two watching?" I look up to see dogs running an agility competition.

I feel Ford bring his arm around me on the back of the sofa, but his eyes stay fixed on the flat-screen on the wall.

"It's the national dog competition, they have to beat a certain time," my son explains.

"This is so ridiculous. This is on the sports channel, with the same guy who used to run commentary on my hockey games." Ford shakes his head in disbelief. "He actually looks serious. It's canines jumping over a pole, how is this earth-shattering?"

I listen in, and when the commentator says, *"Look at that border collie in his perfection, running the weevils, perfect form for his category,"* I snort a laugh, because it does sound ridiculous, so damn serious.

"You've been watching this all afternoon?" I wonder.

"Made him read his book first." Ford gives me side-eye with a proud smirk.

I sneak my hand behind Ford to urge him forward slightly and rub a circle on his back in appreciation, as I may have mentioned at breakfast today that we need to push the reading list a bit.

"Oh no." Ford throws his arms up in the air. "Totally a bad ending."

"That Irish setter was so much better," my son adds.

I glance between my guys. "You both are into this, like *really* into this."

"I mean, if you're going to name your dog Bullet, then you better deliver the score." Ford is still focused on the television.

"I hope they go back to dock jumping, that was awesome."

A half-laugh escapes me. "I'm not sure what I walked into, but I *think* you are the same people I saw at breakfast."

Connor glances back at me. "Can I have a drink?"

My eyes go wide. "You may have a drink, and you can get it yourself since you are fully capable."

He whines a sound but reluctantly gets up and heads to the kitchen.

I focus my attention on Ford, slipping my fingers underneath his t-shirt over his lower back, and a second later his gaze is on me.

"How was studying?"

"Okay. My dad texted, by the way."

Ford gives me a strained look. "He's going to be thrilled when he finds out about us."

I tickle his skin. "I think you kind of enjoy that." They've always had a civil enough relationship, the key word being *enough*.

He leans in to plant a kiss on my lips. "I may get a *little* satisfaction if I get to see his face when he finds out."

"Thought so." I grin.

"I'll run into town to pick up takeout from Catch 22. Mozzarella sticks for my lady?" he suggests.

My hands land on my heart. "I'm in love again."

He chuckles faintly, his hands finding my waist to slide me onto his lap. I take in this moment of pure serenity of the last few days.

Days. It causes my brain to run wild.

"Okay there?" Ford notices.

"We're not moving too fast, right? I mean, a few days in your bed and then here we are, already telling Connor that we are back together. We're not being irresponsible? It's just… it feels right."

A gentle smirk appears on his lips, and he tucks my hair behind my ear. "It is happening fast, but we've always been here. We've talked about this."

"I know. I just find myself in disbelief sometimes," I admit.

"Doubt?" I hear a tinge of fear in his voice.

"No way." I kiss his cheek. "Just trying to be a responsible human." I laugh.

"We are, don't worry. Now watch the Yorkie about to hop over a pole, it will be great for your mental health." He indicates with his head to the screen.

Connor groans as he reappears in the room with a bottle of juice. "Seriously, you two."

He flops onto the sofa, and we all evaluate each other. "Get used to it, my little prince," I inform him.

"Yeah, got the memo." There is a subtle smile on our son's face. "Yes, the frisbee competition is next." He seems to be lost again in the television.

"All stakes are on this round. This spaniel is the youngest in the competition, and if he wins, then this underdog will beat the odds," the commentator announces very seriously.

Examining Ford's face, and he can't keep it in. He loses it, laughing in hysterics. Then Connor follows, and the domino hits me.

We're together, hanging out on a normal day, a family.

Completely content.

The way it was meant to be.

Completely unaware that sometimes life decides to throw you something unexpected at the wrong time more than once.

BRIELLE

Walking into my hotel room, I sigh through my frown.

I'm exhausted, disappointed, and my stomach has been turning since late this morning. After weeks of preparation, I feel like it all went out the window.

Dropping my purse on the desk in the room, I attempt to smile at the flowers that Ford had delivered while I was at day one of my Bar exam yesterday. The last few weeks, I've studied my ass off, and I felt ready. I was always going to stay in a hotel near the test location so I wouldn't have to worry about the commute. Of course, Ford took that as his cue to upgrade my room to a suite in a fancy hotel.

The idea was that after I finished my last exam today, Ford would meet me here for a little celebration and an extra night just us in a hotel room. But I'm not in the mood to celebrate.

I've failed. I know I have.

Yesterday, I killed it and felt my answers were on point for every question that I had to write out. Today? It started with my stomach bothering me, before I struggled to focus. In the end, I just filled out the multiple-choice answers not to leave anything blank, but my head was half absent.

I run my fingers along the card tucked between the roses.

You've got this. I'm proud of you.
Love you, Ford.

P.S. Connor loves you too, but the flowers were my idea because I plan on doing a few things to you later ;)

The sound of a keycard swiping on the door alerts me that Ford must have arrived only a minute or so after me.

Looking up, I see him swing the door open, drop his bag, and offer me his arms wide. "There's my lawyer."

Something inside of me cracks, and I run to him as tears fill my eyes. I bury my face into his chest, and Ford freezes for only a second before his arms wrap around me, walking us back into the room. I hear him kick the door closed, and he tucks my head under his chin to instantly soothe me, with his hand stroking my hair, before he plants a soft kiss on the top of my head.

"Shh, what's going on?" His voice is soft as I weep in his arms, with the sound of his heart under my ear.

"I failed," I mumble against his shirt that now has tears making a mess of the fabric.

"No, you didn't."

I pull back and sniffle. "I did, I froze. I mean, I purposely didn't eat anywhere last night to avoid food poisoning, but my stomach started to feel weird, and then my head just went somewhere else."

"Hey." Ford attempts to catch my eyes with his. "Doesn't mean you failed. You had a great day yesterday, and I'm sure it's just stress that has you thinking this way."

I shake my head sadly. "It's not. I didn't test well today, and without the minimum score, I fail."

"Shh." He pulls me back into a tight hug. "Don't think about it now. It's over."

"All of this work for nothing," I vent. "I didn't even get to finish the exam properly. I blanked, and my answers weren't even relevant."

"I'm sorry, I wish you didn't feel this way. Come on, let's lie down for a little bit." Ford takes my hand in his and guides me to the bed. He lies down, and I follow his move, and he invites me to rest my head against his chest. It takes not even a second before his hands coast over my arms to ease me.

I sniffle again and feel dizzy from the array of emotions swirling inside of me.

"There is nothing you can do now except wait for the facts. Try and take your mind off it."

"It's really hard," I say, my voice cracking. "I was so close, and now I'm still not there."

Ford kisses my forehead, and his hand adjusts my hip so I'm hooked over his middle. "You're still close. You can retake the exam."

I scoff. "Yeah, in February."

"Elle, it's going to be okay."

I muffle another cry and give up on talking about it. I don't *want* to talk about it.

"I guess we have nothing to celebrate." I hiccup through my cry.

Ford rolls me to my back, hovering over me with a burning gaze. "Everything will work out the way it needs to. Have faith in that."

I nibble my bottom lip. "Hopefully."

"I can think of other reasons to enjoy tonight together." His long finger sneaks inside the buttons of my dress to caress my skin.

"I'm happy you're here, I am. I had planned to surprise you on the bed with the lingerie from Piper's boutique, but you arrived to a hot mess instead." I must have mascara running, snot dripping from my nose, and my face is puffy for sure.

Ford trails kisses down my throat, taking every drop of sadness with him, his lips purposely following the path of my tears. "You're beautiful as always, and we can just order room service and watch a movie. You feel a little warm, to be honest." His hand starts to pat my forehead, checking for a temperature.

"Great, failed the bar and ruined our planned night of debauchery."

He chuckles under his breath, plants a quick kiss on my lips, and gets up off the bed. "By all means, explicitly tell me every detail of what you had planned, but let me run you a bath first."

"I like that ide—" I'm unable to finish my sentence as I feel the need to gag, and I sit up, only to confirm that I need to throw up.

I run to the bathroom and heave until my insides are emptied into the toilet. I don't even notice my surroundings the next few minutes or that Ford followed and sits on the floor next to me, holding my hair and rubbing my back.

Flushing the toilet, I hang off the seat, slumped on the floor.

"This is the least romantic night we could have planned," I groan.

"Elle, we've been here before. Remember? It was impossible to hide your pregnancy from your parents because of your morning sickness," he remembers with a gentle wry smile, then he studies me for a second. "We're not..."

"No, I'm not pregnant." I had my period last week.

"Okay, how about I get that bath going?"

I nod once, unable to move much more.

Fifteen minutes later, I'm in the tub with Ford. He washes my back with a sponge while I try to relax. The pain in my stomach has returned, but this time it feels stabbing.

"If today wasn't like this, then what would we have done?" I wonder.

Ford leans back in the tub, and I rest between his legs. "We would never leave the room. I would have taken my time with you before we only stopped to have dinner for energy. After I had you in a state where you couldn't move, we would talk about what comes next with us. I might have had a gift for you."

I interlace our fingers and marvel at how perfectly we fit together. "A gift?" I raise my brow.

"You still deserve it; I'll give it to you when we are dry and wrapped together under the blankets."

"Now I'm curious." Although I think it's probably jewelry, that's Ford's thing.

His other hand is underwater, and even feeling sick, the sensitivity of his fingertips gliding up my thigh combined with the water makes me aroused, and he isn't even trying. My legs part open, wanting more of his touch, but a wave of dizziness hits me, and my head falls back onto Ford's shoulder as I close my eyes.

"I hope I don't make you sick with my flu."

"I'd take it ten times over if it meant you feel better."

"So sweet," I tease. "This is kind of a challenge. Being in a bath with you, naked, and I can't do very dirty things to you."

"Dirty, you say?" He groans into my ear just as his hand travels up my thigh, getting dangerously close to my pussy.

"I would have let you *explore* tonight." My tone dances, and I wait for his filthy thoughts to take over.

His fingers dig into my thigh, holding on for dear life. "Fuck," he grits out. "Everywhere, huh?'

"Everywhere," I reiterate. "If you tell me what my gift is, then maybe I will tell you how I would have used my mouth."

"You have tricks, Elle." He's amused. "But I wouldn't have let you lead, and you know that." Ford's lips brush along my cheekbone. "I would let you suck me the way you enjoy but only while you sit on my face because I'm always starving for your pussy."

The bath, this flu, or Ford. One of them is the culprit for the extreme heat wave flowing through my veins.

To make matters worse... "I'd do it while you wear an upgraded ring that's burning a hole in my pocket," he adds.

Bingo. That's my gift.

I glance over my shoulder and see he is satisfied with breaking the news to me. "I haven't bothered you about it since you gave it back, but make no mistake, I haven't forgotten."

"That's a *big* discussion. But by all means, I should consider your proposition and standpoint." I toy with him and even reach up over my head to hang off his neck before he kisses me on the lips. My entire body stretches out, with bubbles failing to cover me.

"I think," he pulls away, "that we should head to bed, rest, or maybe I lay you down and relax you. You can't lift a finger." Ford kisses me once more then encourages me to scoot up so he can stand, and the sound of water moving fills the room.

Ford grabs a towel to wrap around his taut waist and heads into the other room. I step out of the tub, grab the terrycloth robe, wrap it around my body, and then my world alters.

A pain as sharp as the day I labored Connor hits me. Gripping the sink mantel for support is useless because I fall to the floor, and my world goes dark.

18

FORD

I hold Brielle's hand as she lies in the hospital bed, with the sound of monitors beeping in the background. Her eyes slowly begin to flutter open, and I'm quick to swirl my fingers along the back of her hand.

The nurse who was reading her screen gives me a nod.

I've been sitting here for what feels like hours, worried and terrified. I'm not even going to comment on how I must look like shit because it's nothing compared to her ordeal.

"Elle, baby, hey," I attempt to greet her back into the world again. She woke a few times already, but she was out of it, so I bet she doesn't remember.

"Ford." Her voice is dry and groggy. She blinks a few times, and I can tell she is trying to register where she is.

"You're okay."

"Where am I again?" She attempts to move but winces in the process.

The nurse touches her arms to encourage her not to move. "Sweetie, you're in the hospital. I'm going to grab the doctor, okay?" The nurse leaves the room.

"Hospital, oh yeah," Brielle seems confused, as she should be. "Fuck, why does it feel like I just gave birth or something?"

My lips twitch before I bring her hand to my mouth for a kiss. "You gave birth to your appendix, if that counts?" I do my best to keep this situation light.

She groans at the realization. "That's what was happening?"

"Yeah, I'm afraid so. You had emergency surgery."

"I recall something vaguely." She seems to be taking in her surroundings. "Where's Connor?"

"Still with my sister, he knows you're here. Violet will bring him later."

The doctor and the nurse returning to the room bring a sense of reality.

The woman in her fifties with glasses gives us a polite smile. "Brielle, you're awake again. I'm Dr. Thorpe." She comes to stand near Brielle's monitor. "You gave everyone quite a scare, but the good news is appendicitis is quite a common occurrence, and now with your appendix gone, you never have to worry about getting it out again."

"How did this happen?" Brielle asks, a bit weary.

"There are many reasons why this can occur, stress and digestion to name a couple. Luckily, your fiancé called an ambulance and got you here in time so we could do a laparoscopic surgery before the appendix ruptured. That means a quicker recovery time too. Within five days you should probably feel like nothing happened. We gave you antibiotics as a preventive matter because you can be more prone to infection now."

Brielle attempts to move again but whimpers from the pain, which in turn causes me to tense. I fucking hate seeing her this way and wish I could somehow make it better.

The doctor places her hand on Brielle's shoulder. "Rest. You can start to move around later today."

"I'll make sure she rests." I'm firm, and the doctor smiles at me.

"I'm confident you will have a full recovery," the doctor

mentions again. "You can go home tomorrow; I want to monitor you for one more day."

"I can't even move." Brielle seems horrified.

The doctor laughs in a comforting way. "It feels like that, I'm sure, but I promise as soon as you start moving, it will quickly get better."

I notice Brielle's other hand touch her stomach, and she must feel the bandages.

"They say it is minimal scarring," I tell her.

The doctor nods. "The bandage is bigger than the wound. You have a small incision by your belly button and another one on your side; it will look like a mole."

"Oh." Brielle swallows, and I grab the bottle of water on the side table. She must be thirsty. "What does this mean if I ever want to…"

The doctor looks between us and registers the question. "Have a baby, I presume is what you're asking?"

"Yeah," Brielle shyly responds.

"You'll be fine. Some people find removing the appendix actually helps with fertility and others say to monitor for ectopic pregnancy, but in most cases, there are no problems. Speaking of which, we did take out your IUD as a precaution to prevent infections from spreading, so you will need to make an appointment with your gynecologist to get a new one."

"Sure. So, how long after recovery can we…"

My eyes grow impressed that my girl's mind is already there.

The doctor chortles a laugh. "Probably already in a week or two you can resume intercourse. Rest, and I will check on you during my next rounds." The doctor smiles one more time before mumbling something to the nurse about offering pain medication.

It doesn't take long for Brielle and me to be alone again.

"I was so fucking worried. Going out of my mind," I admit.

She squeezes my hand. "Now you know how I felt every time you had a hockey injury."

Hell. That's what I've put her through so many times. Even worse is I kept her as my emergency contact for most of the last ten years, so she couldn't escape it. Then again, I never had anything close to this. My injuries were mostly concussions and the occasional sprains.

"Well, you've paid me back in full. That was fucking scary. I don't ever want to think what life would be like without you in it."

Brielle looks at me strangely. "Now you're freaking me out. The doctor did just say that it was a standard procedure, right?"

"She did. Doesn't mean I didn't go out of my damn mind." I offer her the bottle of water that I forgot was in my hand. I bring the bottle to her lips, and she slowly takes a sip, then I set the drink to the side.

A laugh accompanied by a whimper comes from Brielle. "Wait a second... I don't remember so clearly, but wasn't I in a towel and nothing else?"

I grin to myself, more because I love how she is doing her best to be in positive spirits. "I found you on the bathroom floor, and yes, you had a robe on, nothing else. I was so concerned and in shock that I didn't even think to at least get more coverage, so some paramedic got an eyeful."

"Hope he was hot." She's taunting me.

"You must be feeling better if you can throw that line at me, knowing damn well it makes me insane."

She moves her head against the pillow, looking at me from a different angle. She still looks weak but nothing like last night when we brought her in. I don't even think she realizes that she was in and out of consciousness for a good part of the night; they gave her a lot of painkillers.

"I'm trying to forget that the last few days have been a complete disaster."

My heart aches again. This is a time when she should be celebrating. She has worked so hard, and if I'm honest, made the most sacrifices. This isn't fair in the slightest.

"I'm sorry, Elle."

I can faintly make out that she shrugs a shoulder. "Not your fault."

"Still."

"Fiancé, huh?" She attempts to keep her face neutral, but I see the line of her mouth twitch.

I lean back in my chair, a little bit proud, not of my move but for the fact that, for a little bit anyways, I got to play the part of her future husband again. "You're more than my girlfriend, and it was the easiest explanation."

"You really are getting bold."

"Only when it comes to you." She smiles lazily before she yawns. "Get some rest. I'll go grab you some real food, and I think you deserve some fresh flowers or a teddy bear from the gift shop."

She nods once before her eyes close again. I watch her for a few moments, taking in the view of my sleeping angel before I leave her room.

———

AFTER STOCKING up on food supplies and a few gifts from the hospital shop, I make my way back to Brielle's floor.

Alone in the elevator, I reflect that the last time I saw Brielle in the hospital as a patient was when our son was born.

I wasn't there at the start. I had to drive down from a game that I was supposed to have. Brielle's mom was with her, and although her mother was kind enough to acknowledge that it was a special moment for us, she only let Brielle and I have a few minutes together. Brielle was in pain then, but I dare say nothing compared to last night, which is why I felt like the earth was shattering.

When the doors of the elevator open, I walk out and turn the corner. I feel like I'm stepping out into déjà vu because there by Brielle's door are her parents, and for some godforsaken reason, my own father.

My body instantly tenses, and my face hardens. Why they are all here is a surprise, or maybe it shouldn't be. I called Brielle's parents when she was in surgery because it's the decent thing to do. It's what I would want if Connor was ever in a similar situation, but having everyone here is kind of the last thing Brielle needs.

Throughout the years, we've all kept our distance from one another. Respecting everyone's roles, yet in no way becoming a tight family unit. As much as I hate to admit it, even shitty parents can become amazing grandparents, and that's what they all are to Connor. The only time that we really all come face to face is Connor's birthday once a year or the occasional hockey game that Connor may play.

But here we are now, and I can't read anyone's expression.

Brielle's parents, Kerry and Jim, are the first to step forward. Her mom is soft in features, and her temperament is much like Brielle's, which means she is the least of my concerns.

"We were worried," Kerry mentions.

It's understandable. "I can imagine. Sorry, I was going to call again when Brielle is settled. Have you seen her?"

"Not yet." She holds onto her husband's arm.

"Strange timing, huh?" Jim's face is solidified, and accompanied by his dark polo and peppered hair, then he isn't exactly the picture of peace.

I set the bag of food on a chair nearby. "What does that mean?"

"Jim," Kerry nearly scolds him.

He shakes off Kerry's hold. "No. Just when Brielle finally gets everything she's waited for, he has to come right in and screw it up for her again."

"What the hell? How is appendicitis my fault?" I'm quick to defend.

"Stress. Commotion. You couldn't wait to throw a relationship at her until after the biggest exam of her life? The nurse let it slip that you two are engaged!" Jim is clearly pissed off at me.

My hands form fists at my sides, and I do my best to stay calm. I shake my head, choosing to ignore him, and instead my eyes catch my father giving Jim a stern eye.

"Why are you here?" I ask.

My father, with his blue eyes and near-black hair, quickly

responds, "Violet explained the situation, and I was in the city for a meeting. They just went to the vending machine."

"Probably to escape you all," I mutter to myself. Scratching my cheek, I know I need to go into action mode. "Listen, Brielle needs rest. I'm not sure it's a good idea that everyone is here. She probably wants to see Connor and then focus on getting out of here."

"She must be devasted that she didn't get to give her best shot at the Bar exam," her father points out.

I glance to him, internally agitated. "Of course she is. But we can't change what happened, since appendicitis can happen at any moment due to biology," I grit out. "We can't go back in time."

He scoffs a sound. "Oh, that we know."

"Let it go," my father suggests.

I hold my hand to stop him because I'm capable of doing this on my own. "Go on, Jim, clearly you have a strong opinion on something."

"I do. It's so easy for you to stand there and bring our daughter flowers because everything you wanted career-wise you got, and now with your checklist of career goals all completed, the one moment Brielle may also get that chance, then you selfishly become a distraction, and now look where we all are." Her dad is seething.

He pushes that sore point inside of me. I hate what he is saying because I believe almost all of it. Maybe he is fucking right.

But I won't let him have the upper hand.

I step forward, puffing out my shoulders. "No. We wouldn't be in this position at all if you just let us stay together. We followed your lead because we were young and confused. But the tables have turned, and we don't need any of your support for anything, and I don't have to stand here and listen to why you think I'm still hell-bent on ruining Brielle's life when it's the opposite."

"You should have waited to throw all your intentions at her," he informs me with his voice raised.

I scoff a sound as I slide the back of my finger along my upper lip. "She already knew my intentions; we just never said it out loud." Inside I'm raging. "You know what, *Jim*? Today is about Brielle, but make no mistake that we were both miserable. I gave up the woman and family that I wanted to ensure they both had a good life. Do you have any clue what that does to a man?"

"I think we all need to take a breather," my father recommends.

I side-eye him. "Why are you here? Like really, why are you here? Want to join Jim on the 'I fucked up in some way' train? Or are you here because you want to take the opportunity to point out some ridiculous flaw when Brielle is weak?"

He attempts to place his hand on my shoulder, but I shrug it off. "I'm on your team, I swear."

"A little late. Could have used that ten years ago when you pointed out Brielle was going to ruin my career because we were keeping Connor."

A twinge of pain flashes on my father's face. For a second, I might even think it's regret.

The sound of the door cracking open draws all our attention to Brielle who is standing in her hospital gown holding onto her IV stand, with the nurse behind her. She uses the door for support.

"What's going on out here?" She looks near baffled when she realizes who is in attendance at this gathering.

I step to her, wanting to pretend all is swell, and focus on helping her. "Everyone is just concerned. Look at you, already walking." I attempt to stretch a smile.

"The nurse here." She indicates with her head behind her. "She's a little strict and made me try walking. The yelling was just a coincidental incentive to move." Brielle sounds less than enthused.

"Yeah," I draw it out. "We were just having a *discussion*."

"Liar," she mumbles to me before she attempts to smile at her mom.

Her mom who, like always, stays out of the drama, reaches to touch Brielle's arm. "We're so happy it's just your appendix. You'll be on the mend real quick."

"Why did I hear you all talking about Connor?" Brielle asks.

Crap, she heard, and that means we triggered her mama bear button.

"It doesn't matter." I know that's not true, but I can at least try.

"How about you all move into Brielle's room not to disturb the other patients," the nurse orders more than she suggests.

We all look at one another and seem to agree without words to step into Brielle's room. It takes a minute for her to get settled on her bed again, but already she looks better than even an hour ago. Though, her face has lost any ounce of positive momentum we had when she woke. My eyes circle the room, and I get it. Our parents are here with serious looks and arms crossed.

When the nurse leaves, Brielle opens her mouth immediately. "I guess we are going to do this now?"

Her father pipes up, no surprise. "We're happy you're okay now, sorry this happened."

"But…" Brielle waits.

"It doesn't matter. I was just chatting with your *fiancé* man to man."

I swipe a hand across my jawline. "Something like that."

"We were going to talk to you all soon about our new relationship status, whatever you want to call it." Brielle avoids anyone's eye contact, and I internally feel victorious that she didn't correct her father about the fiancé title. "It can't be surprising."

"Maybe sudden," my father points out.

I shake my head. "You've all watched us punish ourselves for years."

To my surprise, Kerry speaks. "You both needed to find your way back to each other in your own time."

"*After* our daughter got everything she wanted," her father adds.

Brielle throws her arms up, and I can tell she felt something pull. "Yeah, I know, I failed the Bar, so let's add on another eight months to the '*will I ever accomplish what I was supposed to*' speech."

I want to scream at her not to let them get to her, but maybe now the post-surgery adrenaline is wearing off and she recognizes that her father might have a point.

"We can't go in a circle about this," my father volleys.

I blow out a breath, already exhausted from this.

"Easy for you to say, your son got everything. Brielle just sacrifices over and over for Ford and Connor." Her father clearly hates me, that I've long thought but now established.

"You don't think I fucking know that?" I raise my voice. I'm the one who could probably define selfishness in the dictionary.

"What the hell, everyone," my sister loudly whispers and peeks around the corner of the door. "Knock it off, Connor will be here any second, and this is *not* what he can walk into."

We all nod, agreeing on something.

"Can you all go," Brielle requests, and she looks defeated.

It's when I look at her, study her, that I see it. A sadness in her eyes, and in this moment, I hope her father didn't get to her, because I know he was only highlighting the obvious.

And if I were her, then I would probably be the last person she wants to see.

She reaches for my hand. "Can I have a moment alone with Connor?"

Something inside of me sinks, it's near my heart.

Simply responding with a nod, I swallow my pride and fear that she's pushing me away.

● 19

BRIELLE

It's been a few days since I left the hospital. I decided to take Ford up on his offer to stay at his place. With school starting soon, he and Connor can spend time together, not to mention recovery while looking out at Lake Spark seemed idyllic.

For the most part, the pain has worn off. However, the feeling of general mourning and numbness doesn't fade for a near finish that wasn't mine. Resting against the lounge chair, I watch Connor and Ford throw a ball around in the swimming pool. I adjust my sunhat and do my best to enjoy the scene. No bikini today, instead one of Ford's old pairs of shorts and a tank top because it's easier on my bandages.

"Do you want something from inside?" my son asks me tentatively as he uses his strength to pull himself out of the pool.

"It's okay. I'm still on the last water you brought me." I smile weakly.

Ford's been taking care of me, our son dotes on me, and together they are determined to give me the most relaxing recovery period possible. They are a dream team.

Which is why I can't figure out why I'm so down. Well, I know why. I just can't form my thoughts clearly.

Ford walks up the pool steps, and it catches my breath. How could it not? Droplets of water run down his muscles, and when he grabs his towel to dry off, I'm given a complete show. The kind that women pay a lot of money for, and they have when he participated in charity auctions or appeared in some magazine spread. Now he's mine.

He sits down on the chair next to me. "How's the patient?"

"Not complaining about the view, that's for sure."

A proud smirk forms a line on his mouth. "Happy to oblige, but I haven't seen you smile much today."

"Still coming down from the explosion in my life—failing the Bar, appendicitis, and our parents treating us like we're teenagers again. Ford, if I wasn't on antibiotics then I would be insisting on a strong cocktail right now," I inform him.

His eyes lower to my own. "It will be okay. You'll get back up like you always do."

I don't want to be annoyed with Ford, but it's easy for him to say. He has trophies and millions already. I'm not the type to be jealous, but it's a lot easier said when you're in his shoes. I hate that my father's words seeped into my thoughts and won't escape; it's a pesky fly.

"Other than my text check-in with my mom, I haven't spoken to my dad since. You?"

He thins his lips. "No, haven't heard from my dad, but that's not exactly new."

I look over his shoulder to see that Connor is still busy in the kitchen. "He has no clue we're not thrilled with his grandparents, right?"

"Nah, remember they're all good at grandparenting. Connor is only worried about you. He asked me this morning if you really lost your monkey tail, because apparently, the internet is telling him that's what appendices are."

I snort a laugh. "Cute." I hold the back of my sunhat as I feel a breeze. "We will miss being here."

Ford's eyes lock on me, and he cocks his head gently to the side. "You know how to solve that."

I lick my lips, giving myself a moment. "Connor has school, and we agreed he should finish there before he is off to middle school next year."

"I know, and Hollows is 45 minutes away provided there are no run-ins with foxes, ducks, or lost tourists. Just letting you know that if you want, this is all yours when the time comes."

I play with the drawstring of the shorts I'm wearing. "I guess I won't be a lawyer, so my job doesn't really factor into this anymore."

Ford reaches out to gently touch my shoulder. "You'll take the test again in February, it's not over."

I go wide-eyed, as if he's crazy. "Easy for you to say," I nearly bite it out.

A shade of hurt hits his demeanor because I know I've been pushing him away a little while I wallow in my disappointment.

The sound of the sliding door breaks our odd tension.

Our son wobbles as he carries a giant basket filled with food with a purple bow on top. "I think the neighbors left this."

Ford leaps out of his chair to quickly help Connor by taking the basket, and his head dips while he tries to read the card. "'Get well soon so we can ditch the guys and go for a spa day at the Dizzy Duck. Hugs, Piper and April.'"

I smile softly, as that was very sweet of them. I should have made more of an effort to see them while I've been in Lake Spark, but life has been busy.

"Yes! We got April's coconut brownies." Connor is already exploring the care package.

"Back off, those are totally mine," I challenge.

Ford sets the basket down at the bottom of my recliner, and I sneak a peek at the array of snack options.

"Everyone was worried," Ford adds.

I sigh. "I know. I'm just a little lost about what to do next."

"Grandpa says you're going to come to your senses. I don't know what that means," Connor informs us as he chomps on a cookie.

Ford glances at me with a hardened smile, clearly unimpressed with my father's choice of words, and I can only rub my forehead, feeling Ford's sentiment.

"Your grandfather just needs some time to adjust to your father and me changing our relationship," I attempt to explain.

"We're not inviting him to Thanksgiving, huh?" Connor speaks in a sarcastic tone.

It causes me to half-smile and Ford to crack a grin.

For a second, I'm reminded of how happy I was before the explosion of my life.

———

THE THING about having a ten-year-old is once the sneaking around stopped, Ford and I were free to share a room with no fear of Connor interrupting us, as he is past that stage of childhood. It means Ford and I can get lost between the sheets, although on the quiet side.

I slide into bed with Ford who is already lying with the duvet draped around his waist to reveal his shirtless body. His smirk informs me that he approves of my night dress that is cotton, simple yet short, and the straps fall off easily. I'm quick to find myself in his arms with my head resting against his chest.

"I'm worried," he states, meaning about me. He begins to draw lazy circles on the curve of my shoulder.

"I know." I focus on trailing my fingers on the outline of his pecs. "I'm just so disheartened. I know it's just an exam but passing it would be the trophy that confirms I did it all despite getting pregnant at eighteen."

He places a soft kiss on the top of my head, but he doesn't say anything.

"You're lucky, Ford."

I feel him tense slightly. He feels guilty, and I'd be lying if I said a slither of resentment didn't flow through me.

"I'm only lucky because of you." His voice is delicate. "Is it just the exam bothering you? Or is it our parents?"

"I don't like remembering the way it was, and now here we are ten years later, and our parents still manage to make me feel like we are incapable of making decisions for ourselves. It was shitty, that's for sure." And sad and infuriating. I'm twenty-eight, and they make me feel like a child.

"We either confront them or move on. When we were younger, they put pressure on us, but they don't have that power over us anymore. They have no choice but to accept us or let it all go."

A disgusted sound escapes me. "Until they decide they need to speak their mind."

Ford is careful when he slides out from under me to lie on his side against a propped arm. "That's on me. I'm the one telling everyone you're my fiancée, and deep down I wanted them to find out, not from us. How fucked up is that?"

I reach up to cradle his face. "It's called bitterness, and we are allowed to feel it. Ten years, Ford. Ten years that we could've had it all."

"And now when we have the chance for everything, and you miss your opportunity to have something for yourself," he subtly notes.

My head bows. "I'm used to it."

He kisses the palm of my hand that rests on his face. "You'll get everything. I'll wait with you until you do. If I had a way to fix this, you have to know I would."

I nod before he places a kiss on my inner wrist, delicate and sweet.

"You never gave me the gift." He said he had one when we were at the hotel. "I guess I'm not entitled to it anymore."

He lowers his head and peers up at me. "Well, that's just a lie. You can have it. I just thought you might want the clouds to clear first."

"Show me."

Ford kisses my cheek before leaning across the bed to his side drawer, and he pulls out the box he had that day on the boat.

"I upgraded it a bit." He studies the black box before handing it to me.

"There was nothing to upgrade." I open the box, and I can't help but smile. The diamond looks a little bigger.

"Look inside," he urges.

I squint my eyes as I study the inner band. "Worth the wait. F.B.C."

Our family initials and the words that will forever float around us.

"It's perfect. Let's get married. Tomorrow." I string together the sentence that is delicate, yet my certainty is there.

Ford laughs, and his head falls back on the pillow.

"Why is that funny? I'm serious," I protest.

He's on his side again, staring at me with a smirk. "Nothing would make me happier, but baby, you had an eventful week. I won't let you do something while you are in shock and not feeling yourself. You have a lot of emotions right now."

"Ford—"

He shushes my mouth with his finger. "Know it's there. Dream of our day. And I'm ready to confirm our future when you actually don't have a bandage on."

Maybe he has a point. My thoughts are everywhere. Closing the box with the ring inside, I set it to the side.

His thumb smudges my bottom lip. "How about some sleep?"

A sweet Ford who has a wicked look while he is shirtless is like a tornado forming. You're unsure of the strength, but either way, it's dangerous.

"I want you to make me feel good," I request. Sinking into the mattress and melting into his touch is my escape, the best pain reliever.

"Not a good idea. You're still recovering."

I clasp his fingers near my mouth and guide them down to the fabric of my night dress around my breast. "I'm fine, and I *need* you."

His face informs me that he is conflicted because he doesn't want to hurt me, but he wants me. Always a perfect combination for passion.

Ford's jaw flexes to the side; he's contemplating.

Please, I mouth.

"Lie down, head on the pillow."

I adjust myself, breathing out as I get comfortable.

"You're not going to move a damn inch," he orders before he swivels down the bed.

"What are you up to?" I raise a brow.

He doesn't bother replying with words. Instead, he spreads my thighs, groaning when he finds my pussy bare. It's not a surprise, I never sleep with panties.

His eyes are filled with hunger, and his lips dragging up my skin just hits different this time. Everything inside of me is heightened, sensitive, and aching, but one look at him and it's a confirmation that it's the good kind of pain. It's yearning.

He spreads my lips open, sliding a finger along my center, then softly growls as he lowers his mouth to me. I gasp from his wet tongue hitting my clit, especially when he laps up my juices, and I recognize that he is starving for me. It's been days since we've been intimate like this.

My eyelids become heavy as endorphins take over my body. Thankfully, Ford holds me down for stability, keeping my thighs parted.

"I could lick you all night," he whispers, then his tongue circles.

A wave begins to form inside my body. My fingers dig into his hair to usher him away. "More of you." My breath is beginning to run ragged.

His finger dips inside of me, and I clench around him. This isn't enough. I want it all.

I'm allowed to be greedy right now. Everyone is allowed to have a down period and someone who can help them through it.

Ford moans when he inserts another finger. His teeth grab hold of my dress, and he slowly drags it up, pausing when he sees the bandage on my belly.

"I'm fine," I promise. "But I want you inside of me." I breathe, my body arching as his fingers play with me.

"Elle—"

I grab hold of his wrist, drawing his fingers out of me, and I bring them to my lips for a taste. I need his attention, and I make it clear that recovery be damned, I want him inside of me. I suck, making a point for him to watch my mouth take every last drop.

"Please, you make me feel better," I beg again.

He kisses me, delving his tongue between my lips to open my mouth, stroking my tongue with his own, and making me dizzy in the process.

"Let me take you from behind," he whispers.

We get into a spooning position after he plops an extra pillow in front of me for my body to prop against while he wraps his arm around me. When he works his cock inside me, I feel like I can finally breathe in relief.

"We need to be careful." He kisses my shoulder as he begins to find his speed.

"I'm not in pain."

Our fingers link. "I meant you're not on birth control."

Oh yeah, that.

What a turn of events that at the start of the summer Ford was the one not using logic, and here I am now at the mercy of finding relief.

"Then pull out, just don't end this."

Something about my words causes him to spear into me, still careful yet more robust.

"Shh, just let go." He grazes my shoulder with his teeth. "We'll go slow, as long as it takes, but I'm going gentle."

Glancing behind my shoulder, I'm faced with his determined eyes that are set on me. He made his claim on me long ago, and he takes his job to make me happy very seriously, which is why I feel him circling my clit with his finger again as he pumps in and out of me.

"I love you," I say and kiss him. My words seem to send him into his own world as he holds my hip down and dives deeper inside of me.

"We have our whole lives for me to enjoy you like this, but why does it feel like I need to reassure you?" he manages to ask just as I feel him hit that perfect spot between my internal walls.

"I'm not perfect. I'm lost," I admit.

"You're not lost. You just need to remember what you value the most."

I don't have time to answer because his mouth covers mine to capture my moan as I begin to shake around him, not even from an orgasm, he just works my body in the right ways.

His words don't leave me, though. I just need some time to breathe and figure out my thoughts that are all over the place.

Because we can't survive our hearts breaking twice.

20

FORD

As the days go by, Brielle seems to ease more. Well, at least I catch her smiling while she flips pancakes this morning, barefoot in my kitchen.

I head straight for my prize, wrap my arms around her middle, and sway us side to side. "You're spoiling him."

"It's pancakes." She laughs.

"You cook him full breakfasts every morning. Don't even try to hide it, I see your magic witchcraft."

"They're chocolate chips."

"Exactly."

Glancing over her shoulder, she flashes me an odd look. I just shut it down with a kiss.

She shimmies me away and stacks a plate with pancakes. "Come on, Connor will be down in a minute or two. I set the table outside."

"Okay, I'll grab my coffee." I walk to the machine and make my cup while she grabs a few items.

We walk together, and I take a plate from her so she doesn't need to juggle everything. I'm studying the bowl of scrambled eggs and questioning if Connor realizes he is treated like a prince when I nearly run into Brielle.

"No way!" Brielle shrieks and stops in her tracks when we open the sliding door.

I bump into her slightly before I realize she is frozen, and when I look forward, then I know why.

"Is that…" I angle my head to the side to study the pool.

"A raccoon."

We both stay in place because we don't want to scare away the raccoon that is literally swimming in the pool. It's like a little dog, paddling around in laps.

"This is not normal," she says, adamant.

"Just great, now I'm going to have to empty the pool," I whisper, not thrilled.

"Why?"

"He probably has rabies or something. Doesn't even seem fazed by us."

"I think he's just warm." Brielle takes a cautious step forward. "What do we do? Scare him away? Damn, if only we had a dog now."

I hand her the bowl of eggs I was carrying and take matters into my own hands. I pull out my phone, pull up a song, and turn the outside speakers on because clearly this animal finds us too quiet.

With the song now playing, Brielle looks at me and bursts out laughing.

The racoon finally notices that he has an audience and is quick to swim to the steps.

"Are you seriously scaring him away with Taylor Swift?" She's in hysterics now.

I shrug a shoulder. "You're messing with my playlist algorithm."

Her eyes study me. "Or you are just secretly a Swifty fan."

With the racoon running into the woods, Brielle stumbles her way to the table because she is ridiculously happy in this very moment.

I love that.

Joining her at the table, I bring her to my arms because the rumble of her laughter against my skin is therapy.

"Seriously, what the hell was that, right? I mean, it's never happened," I note.

She places her hand on my shoulder. "It's okay. Most guys are into Taylor Swift, you can admit it now. It's cool to like her."

I roll my eyes. "Not that. The raccoon."

"Oh, that. Yeah, I'm positive it's an omen."

"I'm going to be researching this all morning now."

Her laughter subsides, but it's still there.

"Dad, your tablet in the kitchen is going off. It's the front-gate app," Connor calls out from the door.

I wave to him in thanks then check the app on my phone. I see that we have a visitor at the security gate, as the app sends a notification.

I curse under my breath when I see who is on the other side. I show Brielle the screen.

And there goes any morsel of happiness on Brielle's face.

She straightens her posture. "Why is my father here?"

"I don't know." I turn to Connor. "How about you take your pancakes and go watch some TV or read your book."

Connor doesn't protest.

Checking with Brielle, I know our great morning now took a sharp turn. We were not expecting Brielle's dad, that's for sure.

We both give one another a look of recognition and confirmation.

We'll face him.

And a few minutes later, we do just that.

Brielle's father appears from around the corner of the house, since I told him we were out back.

"Was the raccoon an omen for this?" I mumble as Brielle leans into my arm.

Her father slows in his approach, pausing at a distance from us. "I guessed you would be here."

"You could have called and asked if you really wanted to find me," she mentions.

"It's okay, it's just the proof that you haven't been thinking clearly the last few weeks."

I stand tall and my shoulders roll back. "What the hell does that mean?"

"She's so blinded by your charm that she fails to see she is always following your lead." Jim is coming out swinging, clearly.

Brielle waves her hands in the air between us, doing her best to break the tension. "I'm right here, you know. I think I can speak for myself."

Her father turns his attention to her. "You're really going to marry him?"

"Why would it be a bad thing? Whatever you may think, even if you choose to ignore the fact that I love him, Ford is Connor's father, he will always be in our lives."

"Can't you see it? Everything is always on his damn timeline. Every decision has been around him, and you fool yourself by saying every decision is for Connor."

I step forward, ready to defend, because if I believed in fighting then I would strangle him right about now, and the same thought keeps circling back to me, as it has been the last few weeks. I can't decide if it's because he is planting theories in her head or if it's because I believe it.

"What's the point of coming here? We already heard you back at the hospital," I inform him.

"I'm concerned for my daughter. She's been through a lot lately, and your rushed reunion is cause for care."

Brielle sneers and brings her hands to her hips. "Lately? I've been through a lot *lately*? Why don't we rewind to when you told us that you would only support me if we agreed that Ford and I couldn't be together."

"It was for the best. The statistics on young parents staying together are slim."

I swipe my hands through my hair as I blow out a tight breath. "If you care to disrespect us, then please get off my damn property."

"Exactly, *your* property. You dangle a reunion in front of my daughter, after you build a house that she had no say in, in a place where maybe she doesn't even want to live. You set the parameters for all of her decisions going forward."

"What? As opposed to you and the first years of Connor's life? I'd sell it all if she wants, but look around, and then maybe you'll see that I've only ever had her on my mind. This is her house because I built it with her in my thoughts, down to the bench swing that I know she loves."

Jim searches Brielle's face, but he struggles as she lowered her head. "I'm your father. I'll give you advice whether you want it or not, and I'm going to say that I think you need to slow down because you or Connor don't want to get hurt if you realize that the relationship you had in your head isn't what you dreamed about when you were eighteen."

"You need to go," I snipe.

Brielle has gone quiet, and I can tell she wants to burst into tears.

"Is that what you want, sweetie?" he has the audacity to ask her.

"I think it's for the best," she sniffles.

I grab his arm to lead him away, but he yanks it back, ignoring me. "I do love you, Brielle. Remember, your mother and I supported you and Connor, always have and will."

"You may have been there at the start when we were confused," I snap. "The moment I could, I provided for her. Through the years, you and I, we've managed to be respectful. Thanks for ruining that streak," I say, sarcastic.

"We all know that we will do anything for Connor. Make no mistake, Ford, the moment you moved in on Brielle again, I was reminded of what you will always be."

"And what's that?"

"You'll always be the guy who got my barely eighteen-year-old pregnant who then put her life on hold while you got your hockey dreams."

"Enough!" Brielle holds her palm up, and she's now over the edge of calm. "Get out, please," she begs.

A stiff moment of silence overcomes us before Jim gets a clue and nods goodbye to his daughter.

He disappears around the house, and I turn to look at Brielle who has a red face, tears streaming.

Instantly, I pull her into a hug with her face buried into my chest. "I'm so sorry."

She sobs for a good minute or two, until the moment she pulls away and peers up to me. "I don't know what is worse right now. Everyone looking at me with pity or feeling like I should check that I'm not blinded by lust and missing a clue."

"No. Do *not* do that. Don't let him get to you," I urge with extreme worry and fear.

She doesn't answer.

We've had distance between us before, but it's a thousand times worse when I'm literally holding her in my arms. She's the person who made me believe that all the hope we've both carried was for a reason, because us together could finally be within our grasp.

21

FORD

Sitting at a table in Catch 22, I pass a small toy to Hudson's and Piper's daughter. Hudson is busy cutting up pieces of chicken on a plate. He has a daddy afternoon that he managed to fit into his schedule, and we agreed to meet for lunch. It's a cloudy day, as the last days of summer are here.

"You okay with Connor back at school and Brielle in Hollows?" he asks as he slides the plate to Gracie who attempts to pick up a few pieces with her fingers.

"I mean, I would rather they be here, but it's doable. I try to head there once during the week, and they come here on the weekends. Maybe the space is also a good thing." I'm not going to lie, I've felt a little down lately.

Hudson gives me the once-over. "She's still not feeling great, huh?"

"Physically she's fine. I think she has come to terms with the Bar exam and the idea that she has to repeat the test, but it's more our parents being complete idiots that really triggered her."

"Did she even get her test results yet?"

"No, but she said that she blanked out on the last section, so it isn't possible to get the score she needs. Anyway, she isn't sure what to do career-wise. I also don't ask anymore. I recognize that there are maybe more opportunities in Chicago than there are here, and I'd be lying if I said that I didn't wish for certainty that she would end up here. I mean, I'll follow her wherever."

Hudson grabs his iced tea. "Give it time. When the results come in, then maybe more clarity will come."

I scoff a sound and grab a fry. "We have a few weeks still, but I already told Connor to check the mail so he can grab the envelope before Brielle sees it, then I can guarantee I'm there for her when she opens it."

"And your parents?"

Grabbing another fry, I smile bitterly to myself. "Her parents hate me. Or at least her dad. We had a big blowout the other week."

"Have you tried talking to him?"

"Hell no, I'm not going to waste my breath."

Hudson leans back and grins. "Don't do that. You're a man now who has maturity and class. Be the man you would want your own daughter to marry."

"I don't have a daughter," I rebuff.

"But I do, and I'm older and wiser. Trust me, you may never see eye to eye, but at least be able to say you tried."

I groan because he's right. I owe it to Connor and Brielle at least.

"I have my own father to deal with first. Besides, I feel guilty," I admit. "Her father may have a point. I threw a lot at Brielle this summer, for my own advantage."

Hudson checks on Gracie's eating progress before fixing his gaze on me. "Love makes us do crazy things. The last time I checked, the two of you aren't new. I also don't think entering into a relationship that's been years in the making needs a right date. Love is organic, so it works in its own time."

I tip my chin up. "I kind of pushed fate along on this one."

"And she didn't run away."

"I just…" I bite my inner cheek, frustrated. "I hate that her dad is so damn right. She sacrificed more."

"You can't change what was done. You both have to learn to let it go."

"I feel like I can only do that once I know she is at peace with how the cards fell. I feel like she is lost a little right now, and I hate that." I rub my temples with my fingers. I'm stressed to say the least.

Hudson curls a finger to rub his upper lip. "Patience can be the best medicine. I don't particularly have it, but I know that sometimes people need to figure out something on their own before they return to you."

"I wasn't sure if that's the philosophy that I should follow, but grand gestures and ultimatums don't seem fitting right now."

He taps the table with his knuckle. "Then wait."

I nod and turn my attention to Gracie who squeals and has ketchup all over her face, and it's hard not to smile weakly at that.

"By the way, my sister asked about Brielle." As she probably would since Brielle interned for her a while back. "She wants to meet up with her to give career advice but only after Brielle gets her Bar results, because she believes that you shouldn't plan on a maybe. Lawyers like hard facts."

"I appreciate that."

"She also mentioned that there is a small practice in the county over that will have someone retiring in the spring. She could put in a good word."

I hold my hand up. "As much as I would love for Brielle to work in law and be permanently in Lake Spark, it needs to come from her. I'm not going to push it. I've done enough lately to play with fate."

He smiles to himself. "You'll look back at all of this one day and it will make sense, I promise."

I tap my finger in the air to show I hear him and quite frankly believe him too.

———

SITTING ACROSS FROM MARGO, I admire how she always has fresh tea and cakes at the ready in her conservatory. Granted, my sister has already been here for an hour, so my last-minute visit is a coincidence for Margo's social etiquette. I only phoned her this morning.

Violet pours me some tea that I will never drink, but I can't say no in front of Margo. "After graduation, and as soon as I have enough money, I think I need to set my roots somewhere."

"Of course you do, dear. You're beautiful, and a man will want to snap you up. They are more inclined if you show stability." Margo places her teacup back on the saucer.

I have to chortle because I know Margo is only partly joking.

"Flowers. I'm good with flowers." Violet seems to ignore Margo's statement and speak to herself.

Margo turns her attention to me. "I've been waiting for you to come back to me."

I fold my arms over my chest and lean back. "Why is that?" I ask dryly.

"I'm not a fool, I know your engagement story with Brielle had a few holes. But I appreciated the effort and the fun I had phoning the flower shop. Your parents were shocked for sure when they found out at the hospital. I'm not sure why, though, it's a perfect love story that you both finally get your reunion." Margo seems to be reflecting.

Violet raises her brows at me.

Blowing out a long breath, I adjust my posture in the seat, leaning forward with my elbows on my thighs. "I might have embellished a few facts, but it was also the catalyst to, well… a lot."

"I gathered. I heard a few whispers from your sister when I asked where to send flowers to Brielle after the hospital." She looks up when I hear someone enter the room behind me. "There you are," she smiles proudly.

My eyes land on my father.

Violet leans to my side to whisper, "Truthfully, you've been kind of set up."

I roll my eyes.

"Ford." My father's greeting is short.

"Hello." I can't bring myself to look at him.

"How is Brielle?" He attempts to sound concerned.

Now it grabs my attention. "You care?"

"Of course, she is Connor's mother."

Violet taps her fingers on the table. "Look at you two talking," she says in an attempt to make peace.

"I think you two need to talk like men. Neither Violet nor I are in the mood for children at our table," Margo informs us without losing a moment of dropping a sandwich on her plate.

"You planned this?" I ask Margo.

"You know me, breezing in like a southern wind when you need it." A proud smirk is hinted on her lips.

My eyes turn to my father who is staring at me, before my sister pulls on his arm so he sits down next to her.

Violet clears her throat, indicating for my father to speak.

"It's good we're here. Gives us a chance to talk. I didn't want to disturb you the past few weeks, as I know your focus has been on Brielle and her recovery."

"Yes, and?"

"At the hospital, it occurred to me that you might still hold a grudge against me for how things went down back then."

"That's an understatement." I don't even look at him.

My sister kicks me under the table, informing me that I should be more open to this conversation. Looking up, I see that my father hasn't lost his focus on me.

"I can't change the past, but I need to point out that I think you and Brielle together now makes sense."

My head perks up in surprise. "You what?" I need to double-check.

"You have my full support."

"Why now?" I'm wary.

"You're a real adult now, and Connor is older. You should get everything you worked for, including Brielle." An audible breath escapes him, and he seems surprised by his own admission.

My eyes search Margo and Violet, and they both give a reassuring smile.

"Didn't Brielle ruin my life, according to you?"

A sneer plays on his lips. "I did say something like that once, but the reality is that it takes two to create a pregnancy, plus people change, and Brielle has always been a sweet person."

Violet shakes her head at me. "Don't question the why, but he is genuine, we talked about it."

"I think you have enough on your plate, and I don't want you to think I'm an extra block," my father adds.

I rub my forehead with my hand before taking a deep breath, wondering if aliens landed somewhere.

"Sometimes reconciliation is easy and simple," Margo mumbles to me.

Everyone waits for me to say something, and I'm just struggling to digest the last few minutes.

Maybe they're right, sometimes we don't need to question more.

"I appreciate it," I manage to say. My eyes meet my father's. I'm still skeptical yet convinced enough. To be honest, other than the moment when I told him Brielle was pregnant, he's been supportive for almost everything.

Violet claps her hands together. "Hug it out. You know you want to."

Slightly awkward, but what the hell. Margo is right and we should take the wins without question sometimes.

Reluctantly, or rather unsure, I stand at the same time as my father, and we hug it out. In the awkward-as-fuck, half-a-hug kind of way. I'm not sure why some odd dose of chemicals hits me, but I'm slightly affected, not in a bad way.

"See? I needed this before I move. You get the girl, closure with your father, and a fuck-you to Jim. I hope you all visit me down in Florida." Margo drinks from her tea.

We all look to one another and have to smile.

———

LATER, when I'm back home and staring out my living room window with a glass of scotch hanging from my hand, I take the energy of the day and decide to extend an olive branch.

Phoning Brielle's father, I wait for him to pick up. The rim of the glass hits my lips for one last sip.

"Ford," her father greets me.

Blowing out a breath, I rip the band-aid off. "Listen, we both want what is best for Brielle. You have your theories about me, and I'm only going to tell you that you're right. I'm a selfish asshole. But the thing is, I don't care. If it means I get Brielle and can make her happy every day, then fine, call me selfish. I've waited ten fucking years for your daughter. There isn't anything that I wouldn't do for her. You either accept it or move on, because here is another thing, Jim. She's going to be my wife, and I have no problem flaunting that fact in front of you for the years to come, because Brielle and I make one another happy. You don't need to watch out for her, I'm her protector now. Whether you can move on or not, just know that she's in good hands, and ten years can make your love for someone become unbreakable."

Hitting the red button, I toss my phone to the sofa and finish my drink.

Not exactly an olive branch, but that felt damn good.

● **22**

―――――

BRIELLE

―――――

I hand my glass to Lena so she can give me a refill. We're sitting on my sofa discussing life while enjoying wine and snacks.

"I'll miss you if you move to Lake Spark," she tells me for the millionth time.

"It's not the other side of the earth. Besides, I'm not really sure we can make Lake Spark work because of wherever my career heads." I swirl the wine around inside my glass.

"Huh." She seems to be considering my words.

I take a sip of the wine. "What?"

"I know we're mothers, so we tend to put our kids first, and you are allowed to have something for yourself, but the lawyer thing…" My eyes flutter while I wait for her to finish her sentence. "Is it actually what you want? Or is it what you think you want?"

"Of course it's what I want," I protest.

"I'm merely pointing out that sometimes we are so set on an idea that we want to see it through, even when we may have fallen out of love with it. I mean law, not Ford."

Setting my wine glass on the coffee table, I understand where Lena is coming from. "It was a lot of years of studying to just let it all go. I want to see it through. Does it matter if I change paths later? At least it would be on my own terms."

Lena grabs the chocolate. "The lawyer title would be your trophy to show everyone you achieved what you set out to do."

I roll a shoulder to the side. "Maybe. But I also really do want to succeed at it."

"I think Ford may be the reward. You get to enjoy rewards, trophies you just stare at." She smirks.

"That's a solid point. Anyway, I'm happy school has started again, and we can find a routine. This summer was a whirlwind." I exhale loudly.

"Yet despite your hospital visit and crazy parents, you still have a smile that doesn't seem to leave you. That's a great sign."

"It is, isn't it? Wish my mind would catch up," I admit.

"Sometimes I wonder if we really can have it all. If we always need to sacrifice something, you know, juggling motherhood, career, romance. It is possible, as long as you know that if someone were to snap their fingers, you close your eyes, and the first thing that comes to you is what is important. You know that you probably won't see it all, but one thing. Tell me, the last few years, if you closed your eyes, what did you see?"

That's easy, and instantly a soft smile graces my lips. "Ford and Connor."

She splays her hands out to the side. "Voila, you have both of them. Life is pretty amazing right now. You just need to focus on that."

I laugh. "Trust me, I would love to forget that Ford and my father are completely on the outs."

"Does it get to you what your dad said? Do you believe you follow Ford's lead?"

My lips roll in then quirk out as I twist the stem of the wine glass between my fingers. "Doesn't someone always lead in a relationship?"

This time I catch Lena out, as she seems to be contemplating my words. "That normally means someone is waiting. Sounds like you both have been. Besides, Ford threw everything on the table and now he is giving you space and time. Isn't that what he's doing?"

I don't hesitate. "He is."

"Then tell your father to get a grip."

"I should," I admit. "Especially since I think everything is clearer to me. Life is filled with mixed moments. This summer has been amazing when it comes to Ford and me. Meh on the other stuff. But it's okay, the incredible stuff is what matters."

She taps my glass with her own. "Great. Then don't let anything else get you down, and if it does, then know it's most likely fixable."

It is.

————

MY MOTHER BUSIES herself in the kitchen of my childhood home while I sit across from my father in the living room. "I'll be quick. As long as you don't disrespect Ford in front of Connor, you can continue to see Connor. But if you can't support my relationship with Ford, then I think it's best we don't communicate for a while."

My father brings one knee over the other. "He's now come between us."

"You haven't given me much choice. Clearly, you can't see how happy he makes me."

"You've been miserable for years because of him," he points out.

I shake my head once. "I've been miserable because I thought we weren't possible. We are, and I'm not going to keep repeating how the last years have played out. I get my chance at absolute happiness, and I'm not letting it go."

"It may seem that way—"

"Stop." I hold my hand up. "You either support us or not. I won't go in circles. I'm not a girl confused and trying to figure out how to care for a baby. I'm a woman now who will stand up for anything that gets in the way of what will make my life good."

My father leans back and scratches his chin. "He phoned me, you know."

"Ford?"

"Made it clear that I should accept you two. No matter what I think, either way he intends to make you his bride one day and will enjoy flaunting that."

I attempt to smother a smile because that sounds like him. "As much as I love him for doing that, I'm here to tell you that you should accept everything because *I made* the decision that it's what I want."

He seems to be slightly calmer.

"It's kind of a pain in the ass having two men in my life so hot-headed," I add. If there was ever a chance for lightheartedness in this moment, then it's now.

"Ford and I are not the same," he interjects.

Okay, that was a failed attempt to find middle ground.

"We were all fine until Ford and I changed our status. All I'm asking is we get back on the same damn train." I'm now agitated that we're going in a circle.

"You seem miserable," he notes.

"There is plenty that has gone wrong this summer, but Ford Spears is not the reason. The best moments lately have been because of him."

"It's not just this summer."

I swallow, well aware that I'm not going to drag this afternoon on. "What if I told you I heard what you were saying? But I've made peace with how everything played out. I have a future ahead of me, and that's what I will focus on."

"Brielle." His tone is still too stern for me.

I stand up. "Reach out when you're ready, because I am," I add right before I storm out, frustrated yet knowing that I won't let this situation alter my life.

By the time I'm in the car, I managed to get several grumbles out. Now sitting in the car, I reflect on the last few minutes, and surprisingly, I feel... free.

I'm grateful to my parents for their help, but I'm not indebted. I can make my own decisions, like any woman who knows exactly what they want.

Which is why I grab my phone and call Ford.

He answers on the second ring. I don't even let him say anything.

"You know I researched it and apparently raccoons *are* an omen."

"And?" His voice is gruff, full of interest.

"I found it's the sign you should be more aware of what's around you or you should be adaptable. It feels like life right now. Anyway, I think those are good omens." My voice is slightly whimsical, I must admit.

I can hear Ford's breath. "Sounds like good omens to have."

"I believe so."

"Where are you?"

"Outside my dad's house."

I hear him wince. "Yikes."

"It's okay. He's very much looking forward to your chat about making me your future bride," I tease him.

"Elle, you know I like to make a claim." His voice sounds equally cunning and possessive.

"Don't worry, I don't think any conversation will be happening any time soon, and I'm okay with that."

We hold through a brief silence.

"Everything will be all right," he promises.

I tap my steering wheel. "I'm beginning to see that."

23

FORD

---

onnor leans over the side of the ice rink to reach into his bag. He keeps his feet covered in skates crossed at the ankles to avoid hitting anyone as he grabs an envelope from his sports bag before plopping back onto the ice.

It's Friday, which means we're spending the weekend in Lake Spark after Brielle or I pick Connor up from school. Brielle did it this week, as I had meetings today with sponsors.

He offers me the letter. "I did what you asked."

Glimpsing down at the envelope, I can see that he did. I gently hit his head with the thin envelope before holding it up. "Thanks. It might be a rough night for your mom. These are her results."

"Why didn't you want her to open them?"

"Because according to everyone, I'm selfish, and I don't want her to open it alone. I want to be there for her," I explain.

Connor wipes his face with his shirt. "I think that will make her happy. That you're there."

"Hope so." I scoff out a breath. "Thanks for keeping our secret." I indicate with the envelope, and he offers me a soft smile. "Go. You can have ten more minutes on the ice, then we'll grab a pizza and head home." I stuff the envelope in the back of my jeans.

He tips his head up. "Okay, Mom's back."

Connor skates off, and I turn to see Brielle walking down the steps with a filled water bottle.

"There you are," she says softly. "I was looking for you when we arrived, but the front desk said that you were stuck in a meeting."

I walk a few steps to meet her and quickly kiss her before following her to sit down in the stands. Immediately, her eyes search for Connor who is circling the ice. It's easy to notice that there is something on Brielle's mind.

"You okay?"

She glances to me then back to the ice. "The drive here was peaceful. Only had to slow down once because of a family of ducks crossing."

I look at her peculiarly, as I feel like this is the start of a bigger conversation. "What is it, Elle? You seem different."

She swallows and places her hand on my thigh. "So many times, I've sat in a similar spot as now. Either to watch you or watch our son. I can't stop thinking about what it would be like if things were different, our timeline, goals."

I gently tuck a strand of her hair behind her ear. "And?"

She turns her head, with her eyes set on me, and the corner of her mouth twitches. "I would miss it. I've been doing a lot of reflection —and wine drinking, but mostly reflection. During all these years, I've been wishing for a few things, but there was one thing I wanted the most."

"Which is?" I feel like my heart just sank to my belly.

Have I gotten it all wrong? The last month or so, have I been losing her? Is it possible that someone can slip through your fingers twice?

But then a reassuring smirk appears on her lips. "It's you. You, me, and Connor."

Relief hits me, and I take her hand between my palms because I feel she has more to say.

"I get to have that now, and it's enough."

I tip my head to the side. "I love that you say that, but I won't ever let you settle for less. I don't want you to feel like you're settling."

Her hand comes to my jawline, and she plays with the stubble on my chin with her thumb. "You don't seem to get it. I'll try again with the Bar and see what I do career-wise. It's just that you and Connor are by far more important, and I want to grab everything that I've been waiting for. I want to get married, I don't want to wait. We'll have an odd living situation for a bit, but at the end of the school year, Connor and I will move here."

I would protest if I thought she wasn't thinking from a clear place, but her voice and look say it all. She has thought it over, and she's serious.

Letting go of her hand, my fingers move to the back of her neck to pull her into a kiss. Our foreheads touch, and I make a point to keep us close. "If it's what you want then I'll make it happen."

"It is what I want, and I don't care what our parents think. We're putting ourselves first," she tells me softly before kissing my lips.

"Promise me that you don't resent me, promise me that this is truly what you want. Because I promise that I'm never letting you go."

She smirks. "You never did let me go, you were waiting, remember?"

I laugh because she remembers what I said once. "I'd wait longer if you needed me to."

Brielle shakes her head. "I've wanted this all along, it's just lately, I've been a bit down and lost sight of everything that is possible right now. It turns out, despite a minor blip in the summer, I'm one hell of a lucky girl."

"I think so too," I tease as I wrap an arm around her waist and slide her closer to me.

"Things out of our control made me question a few things lately, but I think we passed the challenge, because I'm still certain that you and I are meant to be."

Kissing her forehead, I smile because her words feel warm and right. "You sound very confident with your newfound happiness."

She pinches me in the side. "It's not new. I've been pretty damn happy since you tricked me into the middle of the lake. Only the universe wasn't letting me celebrate it, instead distracting me. I've lost a useless organ, among other not-so-stellar things."

"But you're at peace with everything? I mean, you've accepted that some things can't be changed?" This is me testing the waters.

"Yeah," she sighs.

Slowly, and reluctantly, I pull out the envelope from my back pocket. I look at it for a second. "Your results came in."

Disappointment floods her face. "It is what it is, I knew it would be any day now."

"Want me to open it for you?"

She holds my arms tighter as she leans her head against my shoulder. "Might as well get the confirmation." She sighs and looks out onto the ice.

I rip the seal and pull out the official letter and skim the lines. "It was a 266 that you needed to pass, right?"

"Yeah. I was aiming for 310, though."

"You know, I love the number 69 for many reasons," I comment.

"God, I did that badly?" She seems to accept her remark.

A giant grin spreads on my face. "I would say you have officially gotten everything you've been waiting for." Her eyes snap in my direction, and she studies my face. I hold the letter up. "You got 269, baby."

Her mouth opens, and I can see the utter shock spread through her body. It takes a few beats before happiness hits her cheeks. "What?" She grabs the letter in disbelief.

"You're pretty badass. I mean, you literally passed the Bar while your appendix was about to burst."

"Barely passed." She reads the paper in a hurry.

I scoff. "Babe, you passed, and I'm sure any future employer will accept your battle wounds for the explanation for your score."

It finally seems to hit her when happy tears begin to fall down her cheeks. She throws her arms around my neck, and I hug her until

I think I might be crushing her. Rubbing her back, I soak in her embrace because this is the fucking cherry on top.

We both get everything we wanted. No concessions or almosts.

I swipe her hair and place kisses around her face, with her arms clinging to me.

"Oh my God, I was not expecting this. I guess I got lucky since it was the multiple-choice section where I went haywire."

"Or you are just amazing."

She creates some space between us and wipes away a tear. "This is…" No words come to her. "How did you have this, anyway?"

"Don't hate me, but I made Connor check the mail every day and hide it. It arrived yesterday. Not a fucking chance was I going to let you open it alone."

It earns me a quick kiss. "We have so much to celebrate now."

"You're telling me. In case you forgot, you said we're getting married soon."

"Oh, I didn't forget. I also didn't forget what I already had planned for tonight."

"Tonight? What do you mean?"

Brielle flashes me the sexiest look. "I believe my idea was after you put that ring on my finger that…" She toys with me by playing with my t-shirt, gripping the fabric at my chest. "Finally, I open the bag from a special boutique here in Lake Spark."

I growl at the image in my head.

I STAND OUTSIDE my bedroom door for one final check, examining the engagement ring that I plan on putting around Brielle's finger for the last time. This poor object probably needs clarification, since Brielle and I have been skirting around the lines of officially and unofficially being engaged.

Smiling to myself, I open the door, and my eyes roam from the floor up to my bed where the only woman I need is splayed out in a way I've never seen her before. My dick instantly twitches from the sight.

Her brown locks splayed out on the pillow, a bra with lace and pink edging that only highlights the curves of her breasts. The panties match, but I have no plan on keeping those on. It's the suspenders with stockings that have me torn. The heels are just plain common sense to keep, as I have every intention to fuck her and make love to her tonight. But hot damn, those suspenders. I love Brielle naked, but I think I want to keep those on.

She beckons me over with her finger. "Care to join me?"

A whistle escapes me. "You're... wow."

"It's different."

Very.

Brielle has always been confident on the intimacy front. Yet, this set-up demonstrates a different era. We're experienced, explorative, and exceptional with each other. If this is any indication of married life, then we better speed up that marriage license.

I crawl on the bed, coming to lie on my side next to her, and my eyes dip down to really study her body.

"Can't believe you kept this from me."

"I wanted a special occasion," she whispers the reminder.

That's my clue.

"Finger," I order.

She holds up her left hand, and I slide the ring down her finger. "Promise me two things."

"Anything," she rasps.

"One, you never take this off." I touch the new accessory on her hand.

"I promise."

"And two. If anyone asks, especially our son, we officially became engaged on a rowboat on Lake Spark and not in bed with you completely ready to undo me in sexy-as-fuck lingerie, knowing damn well that I have every intention of spanking you at some point this evening." I'm dead serious.

She laughs and brings her hands to the back of my neck to play with my hair. "Totally promise on that. Now kiss me."

One kiss. Two kiss. A third.

Quickly, I rise onto my knees and peel off my shirt before my jeans go too. My eyes never leave my fiancée who is watching me with a twinkle in her eye, her fingers exploring her own body and driving me wild.

I need to get my lips back on her, she's my lifeline.

Back on my side, I begin to toy with the tiniest of bows between her breasts, and I hiss a breath because she really is a vision.

I rub my thumb across her bottom lip, and she takes my digit into her mouth to suck, making a point to swirl her tongue around.

I take a deep breath to calm myself down. "You have a few ideas in that head of yours, don't you?"

"Uh-huh," she hums before sucking hard.

Her lips pop off my thumb, and she slides down the mattress, eager to pull my length out of my boxers and stroke me first with her hand, and then her mouth is covering me.

"Fuck," I curse as my head falls back onto the pillow. My fingers weave through her hair as she brings me to the back of her throat. Her sound of enjoyment and eyes seeking approval cause something feral inside of me to unleash. I swipe her hair to one side and pull it into a ponytail that I wrap around my hand, guiding her down on me.

I would be concerned by her slight gag if it weren't for the fact that her delicate hand grips tighter around my base and her tongue glides along my length. I don't want to go savage but the idea of a little drool rolling down her chin has me eager to postpone lovemaking until the next round, because first I need her to beg while she's in this little outfit.

Brielle doesn't relent and continues to work me with her mouth, but coming in her mouth just won't do. Pulling her off me, I gently toss her to the side of me on the mattress, and I'm over her in a flash.

Her legs are already twisting around my waist to pull us flush together. My hand moves with speed, coasting down her body, until I find a strap from the suspenders that I snap against her skin.

She squeals and wiggles underneath me. "Uh-oh, have I been bad?" She plays along with a fun smile on her face.

My hand is back by her wrist to pin above her head. "Nah, you're the image of the kind of woman I want to marry."

I can't get enough of her. As if the atmosphere in the room is drowning me, and the only way for survival is to run my lips down her body.

I grab hold of her bra strap between my teeth, dragging it down and causing her nipple to peek out, then I'm on that with my mouth. I'm being pulled in all directions, losing my mind.

Then I feel her hand with the ring on my cheek. She draws my gaze to meet her eyes. "Ford, inside of me now."

Who am I to deny us that?

A few moments later, I'm inside of her with our hips rocking and lips sealed.

Sometimes in life, we get lucky, and it's only better when what you get has been in front of you all this time, taunting you until you have it.

———

WALKING out of the flower shop, I make a mental note to tell my sister that it's for sale, as she mentioned opening a flower shop after she graduates. She suggested I grab begonias for Brielle, and I had no clue what they were, but looking down at the soft, round pink flowers, I see her point. The color matches pretty much anything, including my jeans and white buttoned-down shirt.

Taking a few steps down Main Street, I grin when I see Spencer leaning against his sports car with his hands in his jeans.

"What brings you here?" I wonder.

"Baseball season is over, and I heard I need to run into town to pick up champagne for my neighbor."

I smirk to myself. "Oh yeah? Why would that be?"

"He has something to celebrate because his plan seems to have worked."

"Still pissed you didn't get an invite?"

He waves a hand at me. "Nah, intimate is more your thing. Doesn't mean you won't have cake and champagne waiting for you. Staying at the Dizzy Duck Inn?"

"Yeah, thought it would be good for a night. Violet will take Connor."

Spencer smiles gently with an affirmative look. "Do everything that I would do when I stay there."

I snort a laugh. "Didn't you make a certain kind of video there?"

"Good times," he reflects to himself with his gaze focused in the distance.

"I should go, I can't be late," I mention.

Spencer steps forward and slaps a hand on my arm. "Congratulations."

"Thanks."

A few minutes later, I'm sitting on a bench outside the courthouse.

"Are you sure you're okay with all of this?" I ask my son.

"I get to miss school, so yeah."

I place my hand on his shoulder. "That's not why we are doing this."

He flashes me a cheeky smile. "I know. It's just a bonus."

"A serious moment now. Man to man. All good? Your mom and me are about to become husband and wife."

"Kind of too late for me to say no."

I ruefully shake my head. Connor enjoys messing with me, yet his smile says the truth; all is well.

We both look up when we hear the patter of heels to find Brielle in a knee-length white dress. I notice some lace around the neckline, with her hair down the way that I like it. It's simple, but her.

I stand to hand her the flowers, and she seems appreciative.

"Ready?" She smiles.

I chuckle under my breath as I offer her my arm. "That shouldn't even be a question."

We decided to keep it as simple as possible. Celebrate between the three of us, relying on the courthouse staff to act as witnesses to keep the invite list small. Connor has been waiting for this day too, he was watching us all along.

This was a last-minute wedding, because we wanted to marry quickly, but it's a long-planned intention that's been floating in our minds for years.

Heading into the courthouse, hand in hand, I'm almost certain that as painful as it is, our journey was always going to be our way to this very moment. And perhaps that just makes it all the sweeter.

EPILOGUE: BRIELLE

SIX YEARS LATER

Summer in Lake Spark always causes my heart to beat in a different way. I know it's not physically possible, but it feels like it could be. It's as if memories and hopes dictate the beat of my heart. Or it simply could be that the season tends to put people in better moods, and I'm no exception.

It's the weekend, which means Ford doesn't need to check in at the training center, and I can leave my cases on my desk, as real estate law has statistically been awarded the least stressful of law practices, and that's what I picked.

I bring the tray of burgers and hotdogs to Ford who is manning the grill, with our new yellow Labrador Puck drooling as he sits in attention. I'm surprised he can still sit, as Ford has him playing frisbee constantly. We're throwing a BBQ with Spencer and April while Connor has a pool party with a few friends.

As I set the plate down next to the baby monitor because our three-year-old, Wyatt, is napping, I feel Ford's arm wrap around me from the side so he can keep me close. I watch Ford give a steely stare at the pool of teenagers while his lips wrap around the bottle of beer. It causes me to smirk because I know what he's thinking.

Spencer arrives at the grill station with a chip in his hand, and he too notices Ford's tense study of the pool. "What's up with him?" Spencer bites the chip.

I chortle a laugh. "There are girls here," I note.

My theory about my son has been proven correct. The girls love him, and he's already playing for the varsity hockey team at the local prep school. The odds of popularity are in his favor.

"I thought you two have the whole 'we're cool parents because we're young' philosophy going." Spencer uses air quotes.

April laughs and comes to his side, bouncing their toddler son on her hip. "Don't you dare. You completely freaked out yourself when you heard Hadley talking about which older boys would be here," April warns her husband.

Spencer's face drops and his nostrils flare slightly. "I blame you two if shit goes down." The humor is there which makes us all smile.

Yet Ford hasn't broken his gaze on the hormone-fueled kids in our pool. "Nah, we're relatable. Connor knows he can talk to us about anything." I snort a laugh because as much as you can be close to your child, they will always try something behind your back, it's part of growing up. Ford glances over his shoulder at me. "What? I would rather they all do stuff under our noses instead of God knows where. Besides, we get them used to hanging out with us so they party here and keep it safe. We'll be those parents that even his friends want to talk to." Ford is confident with his approach.

"Smart thinking, actually," Spencer compliments. "Just keep those hockey players from his team away from my daughter." He points at Ford.

"Likewise, keep those ballerinas away from my son," Ford counters.

April and I give one another a knowing look, and we gently shake our heads.

"By the way, where is your sister?" I wonder.

Violet moved permanently to Lake Spark a few years ago and took over the flower shop in town. It's kept her busy, and we love having her around.

"Late as usual, probably." Ford begins to throw the meat on the grill.

I tap his shoulder with my hand. "Come on, why don't you let Spencer take over for a little bit? I'm sure April will keep him in line." I smile at my friend, and she grins in agreement.

Ford blows out a breath and sets the tongs down in defeat.

We walk to the dock to get a moment alone. The afternoon sun always calms us.

"You okay?" I ask and rest my head against his shoulder while we look out over the lake.

"Sure. Completely. Yep." He smacks his lips together.

"So unbelievable," I add on, trying to suppress my grin. Ford is as tense as the times when my father comes over for dinner. Although the relationship between us all has improved, especially when Wyatt came into the picture, there will always be a wound.

He sighs and his arm hangs around my shoulders. "Want the truth?"

"Always."

"I'm fucking terrified that we are at the point where we have to worry about everything that could alter Connor's life from his choices." Ford seems agitated.

I do see the look of fear on his face, but it only makes my mouth stretch. "Trust me, I worry every day. *But* he'll find his way, and we'll be there for him without question. We promised him."

Ford exhales loudly, and I feel him relax slightly. "You're right."

We both sigh. When Connor was twelve, Ford overheard Connor talking with a friend about his first kiss, and then man-to-man, Connor told Ford. I'm not supposed to know. It was a girl from his music class at a party. I can only imagine where we are four years later.

"Life is good, Ford," I remind him.

He moves because a side embrace simply won't do. He needs both of his arms around me, and I won't ever complain about that. He lowers his mouth to capture my lips for a kiss.

"It really is," he confirms with a whisper. "I love you."

"I love you too."

One of his hands sneaks between us and he places the pads of his fingers on my belly. Instantly, I grin in pure bliss.

"We'll be doing all of this again in sixteen years."

My eyes peer down between us where my husband is touching my pregnant belly. "We'll be pros by then." I'm only halfway, and we just found out that another little boy is going to enter our lives, which Connor very much approved of, as he loves being a big brother and can't wait to train his own little team of hockey players.

Everything is different pregnancy-wise these days. Planned pregnancies, for one, but we also have everything we could possibly want or need to make this smooth sailing.

"How are you feeling?" Ford's attentive eyes search my face for a true answer.

"Perfectly okay. I took a nap earlier, and now I'm kind of starving."

He kisses me fast and hard. "We better get you fed then." Taking my hand in his, he tugs me along back to the seating area. "Spence, how are the burgers? My wife needs her protein."

A spray of water comes out of April's mouth, and she dives her head into Spencer's shoulder to maintain herself. "You should totally know by now that Spencer and I take that sentence completely out of context."

Spencer shakes his head.

Ford laughs and continues on with his mission by grabbing a plate. "You two always liven the party, that's for sure."

My attention on my friends is broken when the sight of a puddle appears at my side, I smile when I see Connor standing there and drying off with a towel. "Mom, where's Aunt Violet?"

"Good question," I reply. I'm fairly confident he talks to his aunt about girls, and I'm sure she is more updated than we are. I hum in response. "She'll be here soon."

"Uhm, Brielle, can you help me with the pasta salad that I brought?" April interrupts us.

My eyes draw a line to the table, and I swear I see the pasta salad there and ready. Looking at April, she is giving me wide eyes and the indication that the pasta salad is a cover.

"Right, salad. Kitchen?" I suggest.

She nods. I quickly kiss Ford on the cheek who is now in a deep conversation with Spencer about sports.

A minute later, I find myself in the kitchen where energy springs into April's body, and her face tells me she is excited. "I can solve the mystery of where your sister-in-law is."

I lean against the counter. "Violet?"

April nods. "I was at the grocery store and heard the old lady from the knitting club tell the cashier that she saw the florist canoodling with some new guy in town. Naturally, I turned to Hadley who was at the ballet studio near Violet's flower shop, and she confirmed that she saw a guy talking to Violet."

I'm intrigued. "Okay, and?"

April's face brights up. "It was a guy with a Maserati." My face stays blank.

I scratch the back of my head, because I'm hearing the story, but something still doesn't connect.

"Brielle, figure out who has the Maserati, and we solve the mystery."

"Or I just ask her."

"It's more fun playing detective."

I peer over her shoulder to see that Violet has arrived, and Ford is already getting her a glass of wine.

"Come on, she'll tell us if there is something to tell."

April groans, as if I am ruining her entertainment.

I interlink our arms and yank her with me back outside to join the group.

"Hey, Vi, we have plenty of food, so help yourself," I offer with a smile.

"Thanks. Sorry I'm late, it was a busy day at the shop."

"Normal busy or unusual busy?" April questions.

I give her a death stare.

"Normal busy, I guess." Violet doesn't take notice as she fills her plate with food.

Glancing around our backyard, I see the guys already offered hotdogs to the kids who are now sitting over on the dock with their legs hanging in the water while they chomp on food.

"We're going to need to throw on another round. Those boys are growing," I comment.

Ford leans over to kiss my cheek. "I'm a step ahead of you. Besides, we have more adults joining us."

"I thought Hudson and Piper went to see his son in Bluetop," I say.

Ford grabs the bowl of salad that I still have not perfected cutting. "They are, but I invited Declan. Now that he owns the Spinners and is adamant that they train here in Lake Spark, he'll be around more."

I hear someone nearly spit out their drink, and my head whips in Violet's direction.

"Are you okay?" I ask.

She pats her chest while her hand returns the wine glass to the table. "Yeah, totally, just drank a little too fast." Her attention turns to Ford. "Around more?"

"Declan? He's thinking of moving here," Ford answers.

Her face drops as the sound of a car motor hits my ears. My focus on Violet is broken when one of Connor's friends who is walking into our yard hikes his thumb over his shoulder calls out, "Con, your parties are always unreal. Not only are the adults here like former pro athletes, but now you have a guy show up in the newest Maserati, and I'm pretty sure he looks like Declan Dash." The teenager shakes his head with a grin.

My eyes snap to April who looks thoroughly satisfied, before my sight pins to Violet who is holding onto her wine glass for dear life as she hides behind another sip of the expensive white.

Mystery solved.

The thing about Ford is that he is a caveman when any man comes near me. When someone goes near his sister? He is a bear, and not the cuddly kind.

This isn't going to end well…

9 781959 094500